# THE DMZ

a novel

**Also by Jeanette Windle**

*CrossFire*
*Jana's Journal*
*The Parker Twins Series*

*The ultimate weapon of revenge against the U.S. lurks in the Colombian jungle*

# THE DMZ

a novel

## JEANETTE WINDLE

Kregel
*Publications*

*The DMZ: A Novel*

© 2002 by Jeanette Windle

Published by Kregel Publications, P.O. Box 2607, Grand Rapids, MI 49501.

For more information about Kregel Publications, visit our Web site: www.kregel.com.

The persons and events portrayed in this work are the creations of the author, and any resemblance to persons living or dead is purely coincidental.

All views expressed in this work are solely those of the author and do not represent or reflect the position or endorsement of any governmental agency or department, military or otherwise.

Cover design: John M. Lucas

**Library of Congress Cataloging-in-Publication Data**
Windle, Jeanette.
   The DMZ: a novel / by Jeanette Windle
      p.      cm.
   1. Americans—Colombia—Fiction.  2. Missing persons—Fiction.  3. Colombia—Fiction.  I. Title.

PS3573.I5172 D58   2002
813'.54—dc21                                    2002003591

ISBN   0-8254-4118-8

Printed in the United States of America

02 03 04 05 06 / 3 2 1

# PREFACE

I FINISHED THE ROUGH DRAFT of *DMZ* the morning of September 11, 2001, satisfied that my research had been as meticulous as possible, but comfortably aware that the book was only fiction. Then I turned on the news. A phrase I had recently written into the mouth of my protagonist took on sudden relevance. "Those who do not care enough to bleed and die for what they hold dear will always be held hostage by those who do." Unless we who have inherited the awesome privilege of a free society are willing to sacrifice our very lives in defense of those freedoms, we will lose them—and deservedly so.

But terrorism did not begin on September 11. Long before then, children cowered under covers, afraid that terrorists might blow up their world around them. Long before September 11, parents feared for the future of their children, dreading what fresh catastrophe tomorrow might bring. Long before September 11, fanatics were murdering innocent civilians to make a political statement or because they were of a different creed and ethnic background.

And long before September 11, in every war-torn and dangerous corner of the globe, heroes—missionaries, doctors, aid workers, Peace Corps volunteers, humanitarian NGOs—were quietly combating the effects of terrorism and oppression of fellow human beings. I have had the privilege of crossing paths with hundreds of these heroes over the years, two of whom are my own parents. I have seen some pay the ultimate sacrifice of their own freedom and lives. To these heroes, with heartfelt thanks, love, and admiration, I dedicate this book.

# PROLOGUE

April 1991, the Persian Gulf:

He brooded.

The top floor of the air control tower gave a clear view of war's devastation. Craters pocked the concrete runways. Where buildings once had stood, hills of rubble thrust up surrealistic silhouettes. The burned-out skeletons of troop transports and aircraft lay scattered like scavenger-stripped carcasses. Even at this distance, he could smell the noxious clouds belching upward at a dozen points on the horizon—the burning refineries and factories that once had fueled his war machine.

It was no consolation that other parts of his country—most of it, in fact—still lived untouched to fight another day.

Cold fury etched its acid through his stomach and up his esophagus. What enraged him most was that his one-time allies had done this. The Americans before had been only too happy to help him build the finest offensive force in the Middle East. They had encouraged him to turn that force upon his neighbor to the east. He had done what they asked— neutralized that neighbor who had been such a thorn in the Americans' flesh as well as his own.

So why this?

The answer was simple. The Americans were treacherous, lying, greedy manipulators. A people without honor.

Well . . . they would learn that he was not some dog to be whistled for when they had a task to be done, then quickly kicked away when his objectives no longer matched their own.

The Supreme Ruler of Iraq shifted his brooding eyes. A plane was coming in. In a moment, even in the fading twilight, he identified it as a Gulfstream, a small private jet of the type favored by millionaires and corporations and which once had been bought in wholesale lots by those favored with this region's oil wealth. Touching down, the Gulfstream swerved violently around a crater.

The Iraqi leader descended the tower, then stepped outside and strode out onto the runway.

His visitor's aircraft taxied closer and braked to a stop. The side door opened, and a solitary figure emerged.

*"Allahu akbar.* God is great," the visitor said quietly as he stepped away from the plane. His greeting was in Arabic rather than in his native Farsi.

Unlike the Iraqi leader striding toward him, Akbar Javad Khalkhali considered himself a scholar, speaking five languages, including the English of their peoples' greatest enemy.

The differences between the two men went far beyond their learning. Khalkhali wore the flowing robes and black turban that befitted not only his position as a mullah, an Islamic clergyman, but his faithfulness as a believer clinging seriously to the true teaching of the Koran. In contrast, his apostate host was dressed in the clothing of the infidel West, and not just any clothing, but that of their warriors. True, practicality had forced his own country to adopt such attire for its own soldiers. But this was not a battlefield.

None of these thoughts showed in the schooled impassivity of the mullah's expression as he submitted to a hearty kiss on both cheeks.

"Allah is great," the Iraqi agreed. "Come." He steered his guest toward a small, relatively undamaged hangar a short distance away. Despite cultural dictates, he wasted no time in small talk as they strode side by side.

"It was good of you to grant my request to come," he said. "Our countries have been estranged too long. After all, we are brothers, worshiping the same God. In a world full of infidels who wish to destroy us, we should not allow small differences that have divided us in the past to stand between two peoples bound together by the one true Faith." He and many in his country had in fact paid little more than lip service to that Faith for a good many years, and the religious differences between their two countries had been significant enough to spawn a decade-long war that brought both countries to the brink of financial ruin and caused the deaths of a million and a half of their citizens—but all this was left unmentioned.

"Yes, we are brothers," the mullah agreed cautiously. "And it is time we stood together as brothers."

He glanced ahead to the hangar they were approaching. Though it was less damaged than nearly everything else around him, much of its roof had caved in, and the rear of the building was reduced to rubble. "The Americans," observed the mullah; "they have not been kind to you."

The Supreme Ruler's lips curled back in a snarl of hate and rage. "The

Americans! No, they have not been kind—they with their smiles and hand of friendship, and all the time with a knife poised to stab one in the back. Was it not they who with their lies and provocations first caused the conflict between our countries? Your former master was right when he called them the Great Satan!"

"Ahh!" For the first time, the mullah thought he was understanding his host. Halting his measured stride, he raised a hand in an admonishing gesture. "I must warn you now that however much we share your distaste for those sons of Satan, my country cannot—will not—involve itself in your conflict here."

Khalkhali conveniently neglected to touch on the fact that his countrymen hated the man at his side little less than they did the Americans, shared faith or not, and would gladly have seen the apostates finish the job they'd started. "Perhaps," the mullah continued, "we could assist you toward negotiations . . . ?"

His host shook his head impatiently. "Do you think I am so foolish as to bring you here for talk of negotiations with the Great Satan?"

The mullah wisely made no reply.

"No," the Iraqi continued, "I will never again underestimate the will of the Americans. No, not their will—their toys! *My* armies have great will to fight and to die as the Americans have not. But there is no denying that the technology of the decadent West is beyond anything of which I dreamed. So when you return home"—his voice thickened to bitterness—"you may tell your masters they need not fear. The humbled lion will remain within its borders."

They reached the door of the hangar. A soldier stood at attention beside it.

"That does not mean I am finished," the Iraqi continued. "The Americans have hurt us. They have trampled our pride into the sands of the desert. But they will learn at great cost that a wounded lion may still have claws. And Allah himself has given us the weapon with which to strike back. Come and see!"

At the snap of the Supreme Ruler's fingers, the sentry hurried over to finger a control panel. With a groan, a heavy metal portal slid upward. Inside they walked to where a second soldier tapped another control panel. A smaller door panel slid open, revealing an elevator. Following his host, the mullah stepped inside, and the elevator plunged downward.

Long seconds later, they came to a stop. The door opened on absolute blackness, and they stepped from the dim light of the elevator cage. The door slid shut behind them.

Annoyed, the mullah stood stock-still in the darkness. Beside him, with what Khalkhali considered unnecessary theatrics, his host intoned loudly, "Behold! The lightning bolt of Allah."

Blue-white lighting glimmered overhead. The mullah blinked as the fluorescent tubes brightened suddenly to full power, revealing a vast subterranean cavern. The shape before him swam into focus, and he blinked again. Containing with supreme effort a gasp unseemly to his position, he walked forward. The hand he put out to touch the smooth surface trembled slightly. No, this was not one of the mirages so common to the desert sand overhead.

He took a moment to rearrange his expression before turning slowly. "Is this . . . ?"

Khalkhali knew well that it was his position as head of his country's intelligence service that had prompted today's startling summons. That he knew precisely what he was seeing made it only more unbelievable. "But how . . . ?"

His host made an impatient gesture. "That does not concern you. It is the one piece of this war that went our way. What concerns you is that we now have a weapon that can bring the Great Satan to its knees." He nodded, his own less-than-stoic features mirroring his elation. "The weapon with which the Americans brought my country down. And now it shall be turned back against them."

Khalkhali reached out a hand again before snatching it back, cursing himself for having betrayed his eagerness. He, as much as his host, knew what an incredible opportunity Fate—or Allah—had dropped into his grasp, and behind his outward composure, his mind was racing with the possibilities.

"So what is it that you request of me?" he asked, already knowing the answer.

His host's upper lip curled again. "The Americans have hemmed me in like a caged beast. I cannot move without tripping over their spies. If it were otherwise, do you think I would ask for this alliance?"

The two men locked gazes in a sudden flare of antagonism, the vestige of an ancient enmity that passed through countless generations, all the way back to the days when soldiers of rival Babylonian and Persian empires faced each other across these same lands.

The mullah relaxed first.

"When two men—or two countries—face a common enemy, old misunderstandings must be put aside. In the name of our common Faith, let us forget the past and see how we can use this gift to do the will of Allah." He rubbed a thoughtful hand over his beard. "This will not be easy. You must know that we do not have the means to employ the weapon from this distance. Not without a system of support that neither we nor you possess. If we are to use this gift from Allah to greatest effectiveness, it must be moved closer to the target."

"I am versed in the tactics of war," the Iraqi snapped. "Why do you think I came to you and none else? Do you imagine I am unaware of your little friends in every part of the world?"

The mullah nodded, acknowledging the effectiveness of his host's intelligence service. Although they generally suspected, few governments knew conclusively that his position as minister of intelligence of his country's security forces was a pseudonym for his greater responsibilities. He coordinated a worldwide network of covert-action groups ("terrorist" was a term applied only by their enemies) with the holy purpose of destroying the enemies of the Faith—of whom the Great Satan was chief.

"Yes," Khalkhali replied cautiously, "we have friends who dwell much nearer to the Great Satan—many friends. Infidels and pagans they may be, yet they hate the Americans as much as we do, and they will carry out what they are asked. But their situation is unstable, and this is a project that will require time. Time and much preparation. We cannot afford to move until the moment is propitious."

"Time." The Iraqi snapped his fingers contemptuously. "What matters if it takes time, so long as our ultimate purpose is achieved? At last the enemy of our Faith and of both our peoples will lie humbled in the dust, and the way will again be opened for the banner of Islam to march across the world; may Allah grant victory to his holy jihad."

*"Allahu akbar,"* Khalkhali replied.

Twilight had thickened to full night when the two men reemerged above ground. As they walked together across the runway, they could distinguish flickers of flame on the horizon at the base of lingering towers of smoke. Lights were blinking on in those fortunate areas where electric power had been restored.

The mullah mounted the steps of the Gulfstream without a backward glance. And he was gone.

Moments later, climbing the stairs to the observation window of the abandoned control tower, the Iraqi watched the visitor's plane lift into the air. His gaze followed its lights until they disappeared over the horizon.

Then His Excellency, the Supreme Ruler of Iraq, turned his brooding gaze again to survey the shattered panorama of his once-powerful country. But this time, beneath his mustache was a thin smile of satisfaction.

\* \* \*

A DECADE LATER:

### COLOMBIAN LEADER PULLS BACK TROOPS FROM VAST GUERRILLA-INFESTED REGION

BOGOTA, COLOMBIA (*Reuters*): Paving the way for intended peace negotiations with his nation's largest guerrilla movement—the Fuerzas Armadas Revolucionarias de Colombia—President Andres Pastrana has agreed to withdraw government forces from a Switzerland-sized swathe of jungle in southwestern Colombia. Opponents quickly derided FARC peace intentions, pointing out that guerrilla attacks have actually increased since the latest treaty was signed. Pastrana has assured the Colombian people that the troop withdrawal will last no longer than three months.

### MOROCCO SPEARHEADS COLOMBIAN INVESTMENT

RABAT, MOROCCO (*Reuters*): Moroccan Prime Minister Armal Hussein has agreed with Colombia's new president, Ariel Batallano, to spearhead Batallano's new economic proposal, Plan Colombia. The plan is designed to attract foreign investment into an economic infrastructure plagued by guerrilla warfare and accusations of mismanagement and corruption. The Moroccan prime minister will promote investment opportunities in Colombia among other nations of the Mediterranean basin and Middle East.

### IRAN AND COLOMBIA AGREE TO ECONOMIC COOPERATION

BOGOTA, COLOMBIA (*Reuters*): Iranian President Kamal Azadi and top Colombian officials signed today an agreement of economic cooperation. Iran has pledged to pump more than 100 million dollars into the Colombian economy, including agriculture, commerce, and the petroleum industry.

Colombian President Ariel Batallano lauds the agreement as a sign of the effectiveness of his controversial new economic program, Plan Colombia.

## SYRIA SELLS MISSILES TO COLOMBIAN GUERRILLAS

DAMASCUS, SYRIA (*Reuters*): Reliable sources confirm that Colombian guerrillas recently took delivery of a shipment of RPG-7 surface-to-air missiles from a Syrian arms dealer. The Soviet-manufactured, rocket-propelled grenade launchers were sold to the Fuerzas Armadas Revolucionarias de Colombia apparently with full approval of the Syrian government. Syria remains high on the U.S. State Department list of nations alleged to sponsor terrorism and has long been accused of supplying military training to FARC members. The shoulder-held rocket launcher is capable of bringing down low-flying aircraft—bad news for counter-insurgency and counter-narcotic-interdiction efforts in Colombia.

## IRAN TO FINANCE MEAT-PACKING PLANT IN COLOMBIA'S GUERRILLA-HELD REGION

SAN IGNACIO, COLOMBIA (*Reuters*): The Iranian Bureau of Economic Development signed a $10 million agreement today with top Colombian officials to finance a meat-packing plant in San Ignacio, a small city lying well inside the demilitarized zone ceded to Colombian guerrillas more than two years ago to facilitate peace negotiations with the rebels. The town has since become the ex officio headquarters of guerrilla operations in the region, which is the country's primary coca-growing area. U.S. State Department officials characterized Colombian approval of the investment as "bizarre," citing the fact that Colombia's main cattle-ranching region lies 300 kilometers away on the other side of the Andes Mountains.

# ONE

DEMILITARIZED ZONE, SOUTHERN COLOMBIA:

Like an ungainly dragonfly across a stagnant pond, the shadow of the DeHavilland RC-7B flitted across the restless sea of the jungle canopy. The U.S. Army reconnaissance plane wasn't really there. Not officially, anyway. This particular patch of Amazonic rainforest was off-limits to military flights. But Washington wanted to know what was down there in that tangle of green, and someone up the chain of command had given an order.

So here they were, a few thousand kilometers from home, flying over a land where they did not belong and that did not want them. The ramifications of that presence were undoubtedly giving someone somewhere pause. But the seven-member crew of the reconnaissance plane cared nothing about the politics involved. They'd been given a job to do, and the powers that be could sort out the rest.

Today, at least, they had earned their project funding.

"Another coca field at three o'clock."

The alert brought Major Thomas Sanchez across the cabin of the plane. The DeHavilland RC-7B had started life as a fifty-passenger civilian aircraft before the U.S. Army decided that the rugged performance of its four powerful turbos and its ability to take off and land on the world's most limited airfields were just what was needed for a flying reconnaissance platform. Stripped of its seating, the interior was now an open work area refitted with the most sophisticated intelligence-gathering equipment known to man. Or to Uncle Sam, which was one and the same.

Stopping at the imagery intelligence—or IMINT—workstation, the major looked over the shoulder of the young lieutenant seated there. A large computer monitor in front of the IMINT officer relayed the images gathered by the collection of camera turrets and infrared scanners on the outside of the plane.

"That's a coca field, all right. What's that—number six today? How many hectares would you say we've got there? Ten? Twenty? Enough for a few hundred keys of coke, anyway."

The major leaned forward to study the video image, then tapped a pinpoint blotch that had just edged onto the computer screen. "Check this out, Johnny. Looks like we might have some company. Can you blow that up on the screen?"

Lieutenant Jonathan Hilgeman—a.k.a. Johnny to friends and, it would seem, to superior officers—nodded approvingly. This was the IMINT officer's first day on the RC-7B, and it was a pleasure to fly with a superior who knew his stuff. That wasn't always the case.

Dragging his cursor to enclose the blotch in a box, he enlarged it to fill the screen, a blur of browns and greens until the young soldier tapped a command into his keyboard. Then it sharpened to become the figure of a man stepping out from the shelter of the trees. His head was tilted downward under the floppy hat, but there was no mistaking the jungle combat clothing. Or the AK-47 slung over one shoulder. The automatic weapon rose in what was clearly a gesture of command.

The IMINT officer, his fingers punching hurriedly at the keyboard, backed off on the zoom just in time to catch a dozen other men in peasant clothing emerging from the jungle. At another gesture from the AK-47, the peasants set to work stripping leaves from the bushes.

The image shifted to the jungle canopy as the DeHavilland moved out of camera range. Major Sanchez let out a low whistle. "Well, well! If we ever needed a confirmation that the FARC is up to its collective eyebrows in narco-trafficking instead of being the innocent bystanders they claim to be, we've got it now."

Straightening up from the workstation, he clapped the IMINT officer on the shoulder. "Good work, Johnny. Let's get those images uploaded to Center right away."

"Yes, *sir!*" Lieutenant Hilgeman blinked as he obediently initiated the satellite uplink that permitted him to send intelligence data to base even while in flight. Fresh from the spit-and-polish of SouthCom—the Southern Command base in Miami—he hadn't been prepared for the casual camaraderie that developed, regardless of rank, between a team of highly qualified professionals flying together day after day.

"Okay, crew, let's say we wrap this one up." Major Sanchez slapped an intercom switch on the cabin wall. "Captain O'Neal?"

A crisp feminine voice came back over the PA. "We're switched over to reserve tanks, Major. Are you boys about ready to call it a day?"

"Take her home, Captain. Oh, and with these latest budget cuts, let's not be wasting flight time." The major glanced out the nearest of the round portholes that lined both sides of the former passenger cabin where the swift dusk of the tropics was setting in. "We should have fuel for a loop back into the DMZ. I'd like to make a flyby over that northeastern sector we haven't mapped yet. Johnny?"

"Sir!" Stiffening into what would have been attention if he'd been standing, the IMINT officer saluted smartly.

"It's going to be full dark by the time we're back inside. Is that upgrade on the infrared scanner on line?"

"No, sir. But it can be." Lieutenant Hilgeman's fingers were already racing over the controls. "Did you want to test it?"

"Might as well. That sector's virgin rainforest. Not so much as a coca field, or *finca,* if the sat intel has it right. The techies are telling me the new IR scanner can pick up the heat signature of a *lapi,* or jaguar, right through the canopy. If that's just the usual PR hype, I want to know it now and not when we've got some bad guys running for cover down there. Oh, and Johnny . . ."

The major was striding toward the cockpit even as he glanced back over his shoulder. Lunch had been hours back, and now that things had settled down, it was time to relieve the copilot to rustle up sandwiches and coffee for the crew. That Captain O'Neal was a very attractive redhead of course had nothing to do with that command decision.

"Drop the 'sirs' and loosen up a little, okay? You're going to be graded on how well you do the job, not your salute."

"Yes, *sir!*" Johnny saluted instinctively, then reddened and dropped his hand as a chuckle went around the cabin. "I'll have it on line in five, si—uh, Major."

As the DeHavilland droned southward and dusk deepened to full night outside the portholes, the cabin settled into the relative silence of electronic bleeps and whirs. There was no visible change in the tapestry of scattered villages and *fincas* and tree tops below their wings, but a tangible rise in tension showed itself in the tightened shoulders and sudden attention to instruments as the plane crossed over the invisible boundary of the demilitarized zone. Lieutenant Hilgeman occupied himself plotting the clusters of light that were villages and farms and the yellow blotches that were herds of cattle ambling across the infrared image. Then the last farming community gave way to trackless jungle, and the screen emptied abruptly of life.

*So much for the techies*, Johnny snorted to himself. Maybe that cutesy upgrade worked just great up in the trimmed-back woods of some North American national park. But that was triple-canopy rainforest down there with 150 feet of varying treetop levels. Any denizens of the jungle bedding down for the night below the wings of the RC-7B were perfectly safe from Uncle Sam's spying eye.

That went for human inhabitants too. A whole battalion of FARC could be hiding under that tangle of vegetation, for all his instruments would warn him. The DeHavilland was flying too high for ground fire, but if base scuttlebutt had it right that the FARC was using some of those narco-dollars to relieve the glut on the world market of surface-to-air missiles . . .

Johnny shrugged off the cold spot that had settled unaccountably between his shoulder blades. He was getting his tail in a twist for nothing. It wasn't, after all, the RC-7B's advanced radar warning system or fancy weapons package or even its low operation profile that had earned it the appellation "Ghost Plane." The DeHavilland had started off on the civilian side, and to any casual glance—someone somewhere having wisely decided against splashing it with the usual army paint job—it was still a commercial aircraft, just one of a hundred midsized commuter planes that regularly crisscrossed the roadless interior of Colombia. Not even the FARC was stupid enough to risk taking potshots at a commercial flight.

At least that was the theory.

Lieutenant Hilgeman dismissed that unproductive train of thought as he leaned forward to study the screen.

He frowned. Yes, there it was—the anomaly that had grabbed at the edge of his vision.

He slapped the intercom switch. "Major Sanchez, we've got something a little odd here."

Johnny had returned to his scrutiny of the infrared image when his commanding officer emerged from the cockpit, a mug of coffee in one hand and half-eaten ham sandwich in the other.

"What is it?" His tone made it clear the interruption had better not be a waste of his time.

"Well, it might be nothing."

"But?" The major's glance at the blank screen was not encouraging.

Johnny hesitated. Maybe this camaraderie stuff only worked from the top down, but all his training told him it was better to be chewed out for wasting his superior's time than to risk missing something that might turn out later to be of vital importance.

"Well, sir, you know how infrared works. This here" —Johnny indicated the screen—"is programmed to reflect the normal background temperature of the ground. A little higher than, say, Montana, because we've got jungle down there, and that's steaming hot to start with. Anything warmer—say, a light or a person or an animal—will show up as a bright spot. That's how we map them. Only that upgrade they sent us isn't picking up warm bodies through all those trees down there, so the screen's dark. But right here— well, that's the anomaly, sir. It's *too* dark."

The major looked for a variation in the screen's blackness without finding any.

"It's kind of hard to see if you're not used to it," Johnny went on apologetically. "But the temperature analysis will bear me out, sir. This spot here, instead of being warmer than the jungle around it—well, it's colder. Kind of like finding a patch of snow where you were expecting a campfire, see?"

"So what do you think we've got?" His interest reluctantly engaged, Major Sanchez set his coffee mug down on the edge of the workstation and pulled up a nearby chair. Johnny reached for the mug automatically, handing it back to the major as he sat down. Keeping coffee away from the sensitive equipment under his care was so ingrained as to not require thought.

"I don't know, sir," he admitted. "Like I said, maybe nothing. Maybe we've got a break in the trees here and some underground spring is spilling cold water onto the surface. It's just—well, I've never seen water quite that cold around here. If this wasn't the jungle, I'd swear someone opened the door and let out the air-conditioning."

"Fine, we've got a little time to play with. It won't be much of a detour to check it out." Major Sanchez leaned over to slap the intercom. "Captain O'Neal?"

The plane began a leisurely turn that didn't so much as ripple the surface of the major's coffee. Johnny kept his eyes glued to the blacker-than-black splotch in the center of the infrared image. Major Sanchez drained his cup and headed for the galley in the rear of the cabin for a refill. Then—

"Hey, where'd it go!"

Johnny didn't even have time to register disappointment when a sudden jolt rippled through the plane like a massive shudder. A fraction of a second later, every system and light went dead.

"We're hit! We're hit!" The call came through the open door of the cockpit, not over the intercom. From somewhere in the dark, Johnny heard a voice blank with shock. "We can't be hit! The radar warning system was clear!"

The blackout lasted only a moment. Then the emergency backup power blinked on, offering only scant illumination to the interior of the plane but powering up computer screens and equipment. Halfway back from the galley, Major Sanchez picked himself up, the pieces of his mug shattered at his feet. Every piece of paper and bit of equipment not fastened down was on the floor with him.

"Anyone hurt?" the major called.

Before anyone had a chance to answer, a second shudder rocked the cabin. Pitching forward from his chair, Johnny grabbed at the surface of his workstation. He began to slide as the floor of the cabin tilted to a 45-degree angle. His computer keyboard slipped past his hands, and his desk chair tumbled down the slope ahead of him, throwing him violently sideways, then forward as the plane continued its nose-down plunge.

Scrabbling his boots into the carpet, he managed to hook an ankle around one leg of the fastened-down desk. Twisting his body to latch his arm over the desk leg, he held on grimly. An unsecured file cabinet fell past him, and from somewhere below he heard an agonized scream that died away into a bubbling whimper, then silence.

"We're going down! We're going down!" Captain O'Neal's Mayday screamed over the intercom.

Incredibly, the emergency power was still functioning, but Johnny didn't dare loosen his grip even to glance around.

The plane twisted in a sideways roll, ripping the workstation from his grasp. Thrown across the cabin, he landed painfully against the bank of windows that now were beneath him as the floor of the cabin tilted to become a wall. He slid helplessly downward, past one porthole, then another, scrabbling for a hold, the G-forces pressing his face to the glass and the air from his lungs. Beyond the glass was relentless black, with no hint of stars or moon or the reaching arms of the hardwood giants plunging up now to meet them.

Then, incredibly, Johnny saw something move on the other side of the window, a shape so dark it had to be an illusion. It flickered and vanished. Then it wavered into shadow again. The breath so painfully gained left Johnny in a rush as his eyes widened with unbelieving horror against the glass.

Somehow, he managed to push himself to his hands and knees.

"Major, they—it—Major, that's got to be one of ours!"

He might have been in a dead ship for all the answer he received. The plane yawed again, rolling sharply in the other direction before tilting even more steeply downward. Tossed away from the windows, Johnny clawed at the deck. Grabbing on to something he had no time to inspect, he pulled himself upward. Whatever had happened to the rest of the crew, he had a job to perform.

Inch by inch, as though scaling a cliff, Johnny pulled himself up what had been the floor of the plane, digging fingers and boots into the carpet, hauling himself from one bolted-down piece of furniture to another. He was reaching for the desk leg of what had been another workstation when he saw the body. The vacant gaze and unnatural angle of the neck made it painfully clear he could expect no assistance from Major Sanchez. Blanking the grisly image from his mind, Johnny focused doggedly on his climb, sometimes sliding backward more than he advanced but propelled steadily upward by all the muscle and stubbornness a farm upbringing and two hard years in Uncle Sam's army had instilled.

Endless minutes later—or maybe it was only seconds—his hand clamped down on the leg of his own work station. Hooking one arm to lock himself into place, Johnny fumbled for his computer keyboard, now dangling down over the side but miraculously still attached. Laboriously, he began typing in commands. The cameras—all of them. Daylight. Infrared. Multispectral. Low-light television. He grunted in satisfaction as one by one they came on line. Now the satcom uplink. This had to reach Southern Command even if no one and nothing else did.

Lieutenant Jonathan Hilgeman was just punching at the Enter key when his world disintegrated around him.

* * *

With the jerk of a startled deer, the young soldier lifted his head, his eyes straining at the looming blackness of the jungle beyond the perimeter floodlights. He could see no apparent reason for his uneasiness. The night was quiet, a heavy downpour earlier in the evening having sent the monkeys scampering for cover and dampened even the incessant serenade of the tree frogs. On the far side of the main gate, the relaxed silhouette of his fellow sentry evinced none of his own alarm.

Reassured, the sentry adjusted his rain poncho against the continuing drizzle and turned his head for a slow scan of the base behind him. The *cuartel* was a new one, the cinder block rectangles of barracks and command quarters still gleaming with fresh whitewash, the cleared field that was the parade ground not yet worn down to dusty earth. There were those who said it was foolishness to build a new *cuartel* on the very boundary of the demilitarized zone. Others argued that the cowards in Bogotá had signed away enough of their country's patrimony. Why should the rebels be allowed the satisfaction of driving loyal Colombians from one more meter of their soil?

The hundred-man contingent of the *cuartel* paid little attention to such arguments. Most were teenage conscripts putting in their required two years of military service, and their biggest concern was simply to survive long enough to hand off to others the unpleasant chore of defending their nation from its more rebellious citizens. Whatever the politicians said, the guerrillas had never respected boundaries any more than they did the frequently called cease-fires. Here or a hundred kilometers away, they were still a target. If not today, then tomorrow or next month.

So the young sentry returned to his uneasy study of the night. He stiffened briefly as his flared nostrils caught the sharp tang of smoke. Then he saw the red glow tracing lazy patterns across the way. He frowned. Smoking on duty was an infraction winked at all the way up to the base commander himself. But at night, when every sense needed to be on alert for intruders, it was a foolish distraction.

"*Hola*, Raul," he hissed. "What do you think you're doing, *idiota*? Put that thing out!"

His only answer was a low laugh.

"Hey, Julio, *hombre*, why so serious?" Raul called back, softly raising the cigarette for another lazy drag. "There's nothing out there! Even the frogs think it's too wet to fiesta and have gone to bed. Which is where I belong. You want me to stay awake over here, you leave me my *cigarillos.*"

"Oh, *sí*? Well, don't blame me if some guerrilla uses you for target practice. That *cigarillo* lights you up like a Christmas tree from a kilometer away."

The retort was more bantering than serious. The night's damp tranquility was having its effect on Julio. Tilting his hat to relieve a trickle of water down his neck, he shifted his M-16 to a more comfortable position and returned his scrutiny to the strip of no-man's-land that separated the perimeter wall from the jungle. After all, even if the guerrillas came, how far would they get?

The young sentry risked another glance over his shoulder to where a small galvanized-metal hangar glinted silver under the floodlights at the far end of the parade ground, and he remembered the impressive aircraft inside. He had been watching yesterday when it hovered to a landing. Its Colombian pilot had explained to the *comandante* that the UH-60A Black Hawk combat helicopter was the *americanos'* latest contribution to their two countries' joint efforts against the *narcotráfico*—to be used for combating drug traffickers, not the guerrillas, the *americano* advisor who had accompanied the machine had added sternly. As if there were any distinction!

Julio could still see in his mind's eye the deadly beauty of the aircraft, long and sleek and bristling with armament. What would it be like to sit behind one of those powerful machine guns he'd seen mounted in the open doors? Or even in the pilot's own seat?

"Hey, Raul," he called softly. "You ever thought of putting in for pilot's training?"

There was no answer. An annoyed glance showed his partner standing in the same half-slump he'd maintained the whole watch. Was he asleep? No, there was the lazy spiral of his cigarette still rising and falling against the night.

The young soldier stiffened. No, *wait,* there was the red glow of Raul's cigarette fallen to rest at his side. Then what was that second red dot centering in on . . .

"Raul!"

The sound was no more than a small *pfff,* and Raul's sudden slump might have been a stumble. But Julio knew with sudden horror that it wasn't. He knew also in that instant why the night had seemed so silent. That wasn't the tranquility of slumbering creatures out there. It was the wary stillness due to some intruder violating their territory.

He hit the ground, and a second *pfff* slammed into the gravel beside his head. Rolling over, he got his M-16 off his shoulder and up. A red dot played toward him across the gravel, but Julio ignored it as he raised the automatic rifle to his shoulder. He'd never seen anything like that probing deadly light, but he'd read of such things—a sniper rifle with infrared laser scope and silencer. One more evidence that the guerrillas were vastly better equipped than his country's own forces of law and order. To have cleared the perimeter wall, the angle of fire had to have come from high up in the branches of those mango trees across the no-man's-land. Pressing down on the trigger, Julio let off a burst of fire. The bobbing red light evaporated into a scream of pain.

Raking the mangos with a final spray of bullets, Julio rose to a crouch and sprinted, not toward his friend—whose still form no longer needed him—but where duty and orders demanded. A single wild grapefruit tree had been left uncleared beside the guard box. Grabbing a rope hanging from its branches, he began to pull. A dinner bell was hardly a standard alarm system for a military base, but it had the advantage of being cheap, unaffected by the area's frequent power outages, and audible for a kilometer around. Glancing up to his right, Julio could see a slumped figure hanging limp over the rail of the nearest guard tower. The raider's plan of attack was obvious and brilliant. If they had been able to pick off all the sentries, they could have been inside the base's line of defense before the alarm was ever sounded.

But this time at least they had failed. Already, running feet and urgent shouts were erupting from the barracks. There was only one meaning for that clanging bell at this hour of night, and every soldier there kept his weapons ready for just such an eventuality. On the far side of the base, the distinctive rat-tat-tat of a guard tower's mounted machine gun said that one of their dead comrades had been replaced. A squad reached the front perimeter as Julio sprinted back to his post, fanning out into empty firing slots along the wall. Slamming another banana clip into place, Julio joined his fire to theirs. A line of dark shadows running low across the no-man's-land melted back into the cover of the jungle.

It wasn't over so quickly. Even as Julio relaxed his grip on his weapon, a streak of lightning screamed out of the jungle and slammed into the gate. The heavy metal buckled under the explosion but clung to its reinforced hinges. A second explosion whistled overhead to smash into a tool shed, sending shrapnel ripping through a unit of running soldiers. Rocket launchers were becoming distressingly portable and easy to come by in the present international arms market.

But the *comandante* was now getting his counterattack organized. Bursts of automatic rifle fire announced the driving back of intruders along the other three perimeter walls. An artillery shell whistling down into the mango trees put an end to the missile launches.

Then the throp-throp of helicopter blades added itself to the clatter of gunfire. Cheers rose from the soldiers as the Black Hawk lifted off to swoop in over the no-man's-land, the M-60 machine guns mounted in its open doors hammering at the edge of the jungle.

The raiding party faded into the jungle under the attack, but still they would not admit defeat, darting forward to let off a burst of fire at the Black Hawk or to lob a grenade over the perimeter wall before ducking back into the trees where the chopper's firepower couldn't reach them. One sniper even managed to put a lucky shot through one of the gunners. The enraged Black Hawk crew answered with an air-to-surface missile that stopped the ground fire from that sector at least. But the shooting continued elsewhere.

The raiders' prolonged fighting surprised Julio. The guerrillas had to know that they had lost this round, and they were not partisans of hopeless causes—unless one counted their continued attempt to overthrow his country's government, and that no longer seemed as hopeless as it once had. So why didn't they quit? Retreat deep into the jungle was their usual habit when confronted with uncomfortable odds. They had, after all, inflicted satisfactory damage for one night.

Julio was slamming his last banana clip into his M-16 when he noticed the shadow. It drifted against the background of the jungle like a black cloud, but not like any cloud he'd ever seen before.

As quickly as the image had registered, it was blown away in an explosion of sound and fire. Stunned, Julio turned his gaze upward. Every eye on the base did the same, every mouth opened with identical expressions of shock and horror as the broken, flaming pieces of the Black Hawk began to rain down. A second explosion slammed through the base's fuel storage tank. The resulting fireball rose high above the treetops and raced outward faster than the wind in a furnace of superheated gases. Expressions of dismay dissolved into screams of agony.

* * *

From the safe cover of a huge mahogany tree, the rebel strike leader watched the carnage until the flames started to die down. Then he lifted a handheld radio to his mouth. He spoke one phrase, then melted silently into the jungle. His work was finished for the night.

* * *

It was well past daylight before an army convoy showed up, wondering why the caretakers of the sector's newest multi-million-dollar asset had dropped from radio contact. One of the recruits there might have told them of that eerie, looming shadow, but there were no survivors.

* * *

The old chief could make no sense of what the *riowa* were saying.

There were two of them. Three, including the one who claimed to be of his people and yet was no less a foreigner than the others, and who wore clothing the chief had seen only in *riowa* pictures of their great ones—including a shirt as white as the chief's had been before many washings in the river. Over it was another garment of a heaviness better suited to the high mountain slopes than the heat of the jungle. Sweat steamed from the dark cloth and made river paths down the visitor's fat cheeks, and he tugged endlessly at a thin length of cloth knotted around his neck.

The man's discomfort seemed as senseless as much of what he'd had to say, but perhaps such clothing was meant to make him feel like one of the *riowa* great ones. He certainly strutted in his useless, shiny footwear, as though he himself were the village chief.

The other two *riowa,* a man and a woman, were not so foolish. The man wore a thin cotton shirt like the chief's own, and his pants did not reach his pale knees. Not even in his years in the outside world had the chief seen a *riowa* like this one—a forearm's length taller than any man in the village and thin as famine with eyes the shade of a stagnant pool and hair that curled up like dead leaves in the sun's heat. Clearly his kind was not intended for this climate; already the sun had touched his flesh with the same fire that burned in his hair.

The woman was dressed like him, in pants as a man. She too was taller than any woman should be, and her hair—a yellow as pale as the sun's rays—was chopped short at the neck. She spoke with the authority of a man, so that only the softness of her form under the man's clothing told that she was indeed a female. The woman reminded the chief of his second wife, who had died two decades ago and had taken many beatings to bring into submission. This one undoubtedly would too. It was she who now spoke sharply to the man who claimed to be of his people in a Spanish even poorer than the chief's own.

"Look, Roberto, are you sure he understands what we're asking here? Surely you've explained just what the oil companies will mean to him and his people. This is the closest village to the drilling site. We have to have their support if we're going to claim this region as part of the reserve."

Her interpreter wiped a damp handkerchief across his face. "I have done my best. These people are slow of understanding—the old man above all. But I will try again."

Roberto Quiroga made little effort to hide his disdain as he glanced around the circle of village men, some naked except for a leather G-string, others in the tattered shorts or pants that exposure to the outside world had taught them to wear. His mother had come from just such a village, a scattering of bamboo huts along a jungle river—a fact he had long consigned to oblivion until his native blood suddenly became politically expedient. The tongue she had taught him in childhood had procured his present coveted position with the Bureau for Indigenous Peoples, but this was his first actual venture into the jungle settlements of his mother's people.

The uneasy murmur of the villagers revealed blackened toothless gums, and the eyes of one small girl peering from the dark interior of a bamboo hut were swollen and encrusted with the early stages of glaucoma. Beside the hut, flies rose from a pile of entrails and discarded skins to settle on his sleeve. Thousands more swarmed over the bloody carcasses of two wild pigs hanging in a nearby tree.

And this was the life these gringos were so anxious to preserve! But then the *americanos* were all loco.

Still, they paid well . . .

Drawing himself up under the suit coat that was the badge of his civilized status, Quiroga looked sternly down at the village chief seated royally before him on a mahogany stump. "Listen to me, old man. These people with me have come all the way from *norteamerica* to help us. They have powerful friends and much money, and they wish to use it to fight *el gobierno*"—he used the Spanish phrase as there was no equivalent in the tongue of his childhood—"on our behalf. It is the instruction of the other leaders of our tribe that your people give them whatever they should wish of you."

The chief gave this veiled order no more consideration than it deserved. The remaining settlements of his small Amazonic tribe lay a considerable distance away; in this village at least his own word was law. With a sharp hand gesture, he cut into the lecture. "Why are they here?"

Quiroga broke off, annoyed. "How can you ask why they are here? Have I not explained again and again? They wish to help us stand against the foreigners who would harm our lands."

"No, no!" The chief waved his words away impatiently. "What I ask is why do they wish to help us? One does not give without demanding something in return. We are but a poor people in a poor country and have nothing to offer them. Why should these *riowa* wish to travel all this way from their own country to give us this help of which you speak? What are they seeking from us?"

"They are spies for the guerrillas," one of the village men muttered from behind the chief's shoulder. Glaring at the visitors, he shifted his spear threateningly. "Is it not the guerrillas who wish the foreigners to leave these lands? And we have seen the written paper the FARC has given these *riowa* to cross our territory."

A rumble of assent rose from the other men.

"Hey, just a minute, what are they saying?" the woman demanded. She sighed audibly as Quiroga translated the chief's comments. "The guerrillas have been decent enough to give us safe passage, but we are *not* in league with them. Honestly, I thought you explained all that to them, Roberto! Okay, let's start over, and this time you give it to him exactly as I give it to you, understand?"

Anger flamed in Quiroga's eyes at her curt tone, and only a reminder of that bonus paycheck kept his annoyance from his face as he began translating her stumbling Spanish. Perhaps some of the old ways had merit after all—at least a woman knew her place.

"Look, the guerrillas may have their own reasons for wanting to keep the oil companies out of here, but I promise we have nothing to do with them. As we've already explained, the Coalition for the Preservation of Amazonic Peoples is totally nonprofit. We have no wish to take anything from you or to benefit from you in any way. The reason we're here is that we admire and respect the life you've built for yourselves, and we want to help you preserve it."

The woman stooped a little to bring her earnest gaze level with the old chief's. "Do you know just how much you have to teach the rest of the world? You people were practicing true ecology while the white man was cutting down forests, stripping the earth of its metals and fuels, and exhausting the soil with his crops. Just look at how you live—in such perfect harmony with the needs of the forest around you. You plant your crops under the shelter of the great trees instead of cutting them down. You move your villages and fields every few years so the land can renew itself. And the way you've held back your population growth so the animals can flourish in their own biological niche in the food chain—it's incredible!"

A tinge of contempt edged Quiroga's translation as the woman's voice rose with the enthusiasm of a fanatic. "And you wonder why we want to help you! You and your people are an example to our polluted, overpopulated world of how we should care for and protect our Mother Earth, not exploit and destroy her. That's why we've come to stand with you against those who would destroy your way of life and push their own ideas and culture on you."

Running out of steam, the woman reached for a briefcase sitting at her feet. She looked around for a surface on which to set it before dumping the case into Quiroga's arms and snapping open the latches.

"Here!" She lifted out a laptop computer and balanced it on the briefcase. "Maybe," she told Quiroga, "if we show them the map and explain just what it is we're wanting to do . . ."

A collective gasp rose from the villagers as the computer screen blazed to life. A mosaic of browns and greens replaced the Microsoft logo. Turning the laptop so that the screen faced the chief, she nodded to Quiroga.

"Tell him this is a picture of his land from far above in the sky."

Throwing her a dark glance, Quiroga deliberately bent to place the awkward weight in his arms on the ground before turning to the chief. But before he could translate, the chief announced with quiet dignity, "I know what a map is."

The woman broke off, nonplused. "Oh, so you speak Spanish," she said with mingled annoyance and relief. "Well, why didn't you—?"

"I know the words you say," the chief went on quietly. "But I do not understand what they mean. This word 'ecology'—we do not know of what you speak. We take from the land what we need to survive. If we have planted in the shade of the great trees, it is because we have not had a machete big enough to cut them down. If we must move often to new lands, it is because the soil in which we grow our crops becomes too poor to produce the food we need. If our people have not spread out across the land, it is because the sicknesses of the wet season and the attacks of our enemies have kept our people few. We have never set ourselves to care for the earth as our Mother. We have simply sought to survive."

The woman was speechless. Then she gathered herself together. "Well, maybe you haven't understood all the implications of what you're doing. But I can assure you, your way of life is exactly what this planet needs. And that's why we're going to do all we can to make sure you keep it."

She broke off to look around for her other companion. The man had stepped away and was prowling around the village, ducking his lanky frame to peer into the low doorways of the bamboo huts. She raised her voice. "Hey, John, let's get some pictures taken here. We're going to need them for PR. Maybe start with those kids over there."

John raised a hand in acknowledgment. Removing a camcorder from the handbag over his shoulder, he focused it in on a trio of naked brown toddlers wrestling in the shade of a mango tree. As his lens traveled on to an elderly Indian woman twisting goat hair into thread on a handheld spindle, his companion hunkered down on her heels to tap the computer screen.

"Okay, then," she told the chief, "you understand that this line here represents your country—or rather the country of the *españoles* who took over your land. The green here is the jungle. These blue lines are rivers. Right here is the one on which you live—see the red dot there? That's your village. The brown here is rainforest that was designated as national wildlife reserves by the Colombian government. And over here—this ugly black splotch—that's what the oil companies want to dig up just to keep the world's wheels turning for a few more months."

The woman paused. "Are you following me this far?"

The chief nodded slowly, maintaining the serenity of his expression.

"Good. Now these red dots over here are the villages where the rest of your people live—quite a ways from your own, I'm afraid. This orange line shows the reserve that the Bureau for Indigenous Peoples has set aside for your tribe. But of course that doesn't include your own village, and as you'll see from this new line"—with a touch on the keyboard, a purple line fell into place on the map—"it's only a fraction of the land your people once held before the *españoles* came. So this is what we want to do. Your tribal leadership, that is, with a little logistical help from C-PAP."

A third line—this one turquoise—fell into place on the screen. "We're going to extend your tribe's claim to include all of this. It's still a million hectares or so short of your tribe's original ancestral lands. But we figure it's a reasonable settlement. As you can see here, the oil company's drilling site is outside the original reservation and national wildlife reserves but well inside the land we—that is, your tribal authority—are claiming. If the reservation is approved, the oil drilling will have to stop."

Her passionate gaze turned back to the chief. "But we need your help. You're the only village from your tribe in this part of the jungle. Unless you stand with the rest of your tribe in demanding that the oil drilling stop and the land be returned to your people, the courts won't even consider including this territory."

The chief studied the screen unblinkingly, using bends in the rivers and the brown and white of mountain peaks to mark in his mind distances he had not traveled in many years. For all its strangeness, this was much better than the old paper maps he had once learned to use from the *riowa*. Then he shook his head slowly.

"But this is much land—many, many days' travel. And my people are few—only a few thousand even with those who live in these other villages. I do not understand. What would we want with so much? And what about those others who are not of my people who live on these lands?" The chief pointed to a scattering of other dots marked with the names of towns and villages. "How then would we be different from the *españoles* if we wished to take all this land for only a handful of people?

"And this place for drilling the oil of which you tell us. It is a great distance from here. Two full days in canoe along the river. It is not even good hunting land. So why should we care if the *riowa* wish to put a hole in the ground there to remove the oil for their villages and their houses? We do not need it."

"Why should you care!" the woman gasped. "How can you ask that?

The oil is the life-blood of our Mother Earth. If it's ripped from her veins, it will destroy her. Your tribe has pledged itself to protect our Mother Earth from violation. Isn't that part of the sacred teachings of your people?"

"Who told you this foolishness?" The chief moved his contemplative gaze to Quiroga, who reddened and looked away. "How could this *petroleo* be part of our sacred teachings? Until the *riowa* began digging it from the ground to burn in their machines, we did not even know it was there. My people who have never left this village do not yet understand what is this stuff of which you speak."

The woman cast her own accusing glance at Quiroga. "Look, the briefings we received on your tribal beliefs said the oil was sacred to you. That's the basis of our legal suit. Maybe the translators got a few things wrong. But whatever your beliefs, you must see what the oil companies will mean to you and your people. Just look how many already have come into your lands over the years, thinking they're superior and demanding that you give up your own culture and heritage for theirs. First, the *españoles*, greedy for your land. And in your own lifetime, the missionaries. We know how the missionaries came in and tried to push their white man's religion on you and get you to change from the ways of your ancestors."

The woman leaned forward appealingly. "If the oil companies are allowed free rein, it will be far worse. There will be roads through your hunting grounds. There will be towns and laws and schools in another tongue. But if you'll stand with us to push through this reserve, you'll be able to shut out the outside world forever. Only those your tribe permits will be allowed to live and build in your territory. You can go back to living as your ancestors did, nurturing and protecting the earth that is your Mother. And no one will ever again try to bring change to your people. The Coalition for the Preservation of Amazonic Peoples has sworn to fight—"

"And if we do not wish to live as our ancestors?"

This quiet interjection stopped the woman at full flood. Was this some kind of a jungle joke? But the chief's expression was as stolid as ever.

"You!" the chief went on abruptly. "Tell me! Do you live as your ancestors?"

As the woman bit her lip, he answered, "No, I do not think so, for then you would not be here speaking as a man. You would be in your hut with your babies, where a woman belongs.

"And these machines. The one that takes pictures." His gesture took in the photographer whose camcorder now focused on a young girl pounding corn in a hollowed-out wooden mortar. "And your *com-pu-ta-do-ra,*" he pronounced carefully. "These are not the ways of your ancestors. I know. I have been in the outside world, and I have seen the pictures of long ago and of the things your people have built. So why do you think that my people are so different from yourselves? That we should wish only what belongs to the past? That we do not choose to wonder and question and explore as your people have done?"

The woman paused to study the village chief with a frown. Somehow this wasn't going as she'd hoped. The chief was very old, his brown face creased into a map of wrinkles, his people's black mane of hair reduced to a few white wisps, his once-stocky body wizened to the size of a child and so frail it had taken two of the village women—daughters? wives?—to settle him onto the stump they'd rolled into the dusty clearing that served as village green. She'd been prepared for stubbornness and the querulousness of age, but not for the intelligence that was gazing calmly back at her out of those shrewd black eyes. She opened her mouth defensively, then shut it again as the chief went on mildly.

"I am old, and there are few who remember the old days better. When I was a boy, I wandered through the jungle and watched the night stars, and I too wondered many things. One day I found a new way to make an arrow. It killed the monkey and the jochi from a greater distance than the old way, and I was pleased. But when I showed it to my father, he was angry. Like you, he said that this was the not the way of our ancestors, and he beat me for having different thoughts.

"Then our chief heard of my arrows. He was pleased as my father was not. But he did not use my arrows to hunt the monkey and the *jochi.* He had many of the arrows made, then he beat the drums for war with our enemies. The arrows shot farther than theirs, and their village was destroyed. But the dead had relatives in another village. They came and attacked our village. We fought them off, but my father and all my family were killed. The chief said that my arrows had brought the evil spirits into the village. He had the witch doctor put a curse on me so that I was driven from my people."

The chief looked directly at the woman. "That is the world to which you demand we return. When I left my people, I wandered for many years in the outside world, and I found much of which to wonder and learn. I learned of the oil and the electricity and the machines. And I learned that all things are not good just because they are new. But the *riowa* outside were not my people, so I returned to my home.

"When I returned, I found the missionaries of whom you speak. Yes, perhaps they did change our ways as you say. They did not fear the evil spirits but taught of a God who wished us to love Him and to love each other. Not all followed their ways but enough that the fighting stopped. Not since my son was a child have any of the peoples of these jungles gone on the war path. The missionaries brought their healing ways too, and our children stopped dying. They taught us how to coax more food from the earth. Were these things so wrong just because we had not known them before?

"Now the last of the missionaries are gone—driven away by the guerrillas who also wish these lands. And I—I am old. But I do not forget. When the young men ask questions, I do not tell them, 'No, you must not think new thoughts. You must do only as your ancestors.' I tell them, 'Go! Learn! There is a world to know beyond our village. But of what you learn there, bring back only that which will help your people.' "

The chief's tone grew suddenly stern. "You and your companions—you are not the first to come and speak to us like this about the ways of our ancestors. We have had the *antropologos* here before. You do not do what you demand of us. You allow your own people to learn and question and grow. But my people—you would keep us always the same, never changing. And why? So that you may come and study us and take your pictures and say how interesting are our dances and our festivals and our ways. It is as though to you we are like the animals I saw in the *zoologicos* in the *riowa* cities."

Almost, the woman could imagine a twinkle behind the chief's shrewd gaze as he waved a hand toward the thatched huts behind him. "If you truly believe our ways are the best, then come and live them. Me—my grandson is going to the university."

There was a chuckle behind the woman. She swung around angrily. "What's so funny?" she snapped in English. "You're not being a whole lot of help here, John."

The photographer snapped a shot of her furious face before lowering the camera. "Hey, Winnie, I like this guy. He's made some good points. He's no fool, for all you treat him like one."

"It's nothing to joke about," the woman said stiffly. "We *have* to get these people's cooperation. Just look at the size of those hardwoods. You realize we were flying for hours over all that without seeing so much as a town? And we're supposed to let all that go down the drain because a bunch of greedy Westerners can't control their thirst for oil? They've built a technotrash society on the rape of our planet's remaining resources."

The photographer grinned maliciously as he glanced down at the open laptop. "You mean technotrash like computers and satellite modems back to C-PAP and that nice little airplane that flew us in here so you didn't have to walk? Like the old guy said, I don't see *you* trying to do without or go back to nature. Hey, if you're really serious about your convictions, I'm sure the chief could find you a man who wouldn't mind an extra pair of hands to scrub his clothes and rub his back."

The woman glanced around the circle of Indian men standing impassively with their arms crossed over their bare chests. The closest ones had been hunting that day, and the rank smell of a recently cleaned monkey skin tucked into his G-string warred with his own body odor. She shuddered. "That's not the point! Okay, so our current civilization won't run without oil. But at least they can get it elsewhere. You've seen what's been happening here. Every time they build a pipeline, the guerrillas blow it up. That's millions of gallons of oil spilled into the ecosystem all over Colombia these last few years. And there's no way it isn't going to happen again if they go putting down wells around here. We're right in guerrilla territory."

"Then tell them the truth," John said reasonably. "Come on, Winnie, you know as well as I do you don't care a pile of turtle droppings about these people or their culture—or any other human being on this planet, for that matter. Nor do you really give two hoots about whether the oil companies are exercising proper environmental controls. If they met every demand you're throwing at them, you'd still be hollering to keep them out of here. The truth is, Dr. Winifred Renken just doesn't want *anyone* occupying one more inch of her precious rainforest."

"And what's wrong with that?" Her Ph.D. project had been the study of an obscure Amazonic orchid. The destruction of that rare flower by a careless lumber company before the ink was even dry on her thesis had shifted her focus from botany to environmental activism. Dr. Renken scowled at her companion. "This is one of the last unspoiled stretches of rainforest on the face of the planet. Who knows how many plant and animal species are here that we haven't catalogued yet! Maybe even the cure for cancer. And where do you get off with knocking my convictions? You're supposed to be my backup here. If you don't support our goals, you have no business with C-PAP."

"Hey, C-PAP didn't hire me to hug trees," the photographer retorted. "They hired me to take pictures. Oh, sure, I'm politically correct. C-PAP wouldn't have touched me otherwise. I don't like seeing trees chopped down anymore than the next guy. But I'm not blind. You think I believe those tribal leaders back at base decided on their own to lay claim to a major chunk of this country? C-PAP was behind that from the start. You know it, and I know it! I mean, let's get real; if every ethnic group is going to start claiming the lands their ancestors lived on four hundred years back, we'd have to redraw every atlas in the library! What are a few thousand people supposed to do with that much territory anyway? Nothing! Which is precisely the point, isn't it? You want the rainforest, untouched and undeveloped, and these people are the easiest way to legitimize your claim to it."

The photographer leaned far down from his lanky height to bring his malicious grin closer to his companion's stormy expression. "Come on, Winnie, I just want to hear you admit it. C-PAP isn't about preserving the Amazonic peoples. It's about preserving the Amazonic jungle. Which is fine with me. I'm all for saving the rainforest. But just don't kid yourself as to how or why you're doing it! And don't try to kid that old guy over there. He's smart enough to see through you like a jug of bottled water."

"Oh, shut up, John!" Dr. Renken said wearily. She pushed her damp bangs back off her forehead. "Okay, fine, we'll try it your way. But it better work, because I'm not leaving without a solid verbal commitment on film."

Slamming shut the laptop, she nodded toward his camcorder as she got to her feet. The villagers had been waiting in patient silence during their English exchange. Ignoring Quiroga's swift offer to translate, Dr. Renken faced the chief.

"Please forgive us," she said with a meekness she hadn't used since she was an undergrad student. "We criticize others for coming in here to tell you how you should live, and now we've been doing the same thing. You are right, and we were wrong. It's up to you to decide how you want to live, whether the ways of your ancestors or a new direction for a new world."

Her hands went out appealingly, not just to the chief but to the whole circle of villagers. "But surely, whatever changes you might choose to bring to your people, you can't want to see all this—the trees, the animals that put meat in your cooking pots, the fish in the river—destroyed. That's what will happen if the *extranjeros*—the foreigners, the white men—are allowed to come into these forests. Not just the oil companies, but those who will come afterward to cut the trees to ship lumber overseas, and dig for gold and silver, and drive away the animals to make room for cattle and farms."

She had the chief's attention now, the conviction in her tone carrying the weight her earlier arguments had not. "You say it doesn't matter if the foreigners come, because what they wish to do is far away from your village. But you must believe me that they will not stay far away. When they have finished destroying one part, they will move on and on until one day your grandchildren will find that there is no more jungle left for their own children. We have seen it happen in other places. That's why, if you love these lands, you must stop the foreigners here and now before they begin."

The startled murmurs and sideways glances were all she could hope for. Evidently, the chief wasn't the only village man who had been in the outside world long enough to learn Spanish. She threw a triumphant glance at the photographer. "We've got them, John. Get that camera rolling."

Her pleasurable assurance lasted only until the chief spoke up, his wrinkled old face showing his bewilderment. "But didn't you know? Those *extranjeros*—the white men—they are already here!"

* * *

The photographer followed Dr. Renken closely on their way down to the river. "Come on, Winnie, this is ridiculous! We can't just rush off into the jungle like this! What if those were guerrillas the hunters saw out there? We could be walking right into their hands! That safe passage your ecologically minded FARC commander gave you was for the village, not for wandering around guerrilla territory. At the least, we should call C-PAP and see what they want to do about it."

He knew some of Dr. Renken's colleagues; *they'd probably just cheer her on,* he thought sourly.

Keeping pace with the six village hunters ahead of her, Dr. Renken didn't slow her rapid strides. "No time. Besides, the chief is adamant those weren't guerrillas his men saw out there. And Roberto interviewed the hunting party himself. Whoever they saw, it wasn't just nonindigenous Colombians. They know the difference. It was gringos. White foreigners. And that means the oil companies have decided not to wait for the courts. They're already sinking their exploration wells, figuring we'd never find out. If they can pinpoint exactly where the oil is by the time the courts rule, they'll have a year's head start. They'll be moving in here like a plague of locusts before we can even file an appeal."

Half sliding down the muddy bank, Dr. Renken swung her briefcase into a dugout canoe. Two of the village men were already laying tall spears and bows and arrows in the bottom of the canoe. The others were pushing two more canoes into the water.

Gesturing toward the hunters, Dr. Renken said earnestly, "Can't you see it, John? If these guys really can take us back to where they saw the gringos—if we can actually catch them on film breaking the law—then we can break this case wide open. Think of the PR! Maybe even international TV. Once the whole world sees just how corrupt and underhanded the oil companies are, no court is going to rule for them, no matter how much government pressure they bring down on the locals."

John scrambled down the bank behind her, his arms flailing wildly as he skidded on a slick patch of clay. Grabbing instinctively to protect his camera case, he sat down abruptly in the mud. "That's fine, but can't we just think about this a little? For one thing, is there some reason we're climbing into this canoe instead of taking the plane?"

A stone's throw upstream, the amphibious Cessna 206 that had flown them to the village was floating just offshore, its Colombian pilot lounging in the open door, watching them, his feet propped up on one of the wide floats. The photographer eyed the dugout canoes with disfavor. Their only visible propulsion was the long wooden paddles the hunters were now lifting out. "Let's be practical here, Winnie. Eduardo can fly us out there. We'll pinpoint the drill site. Then we call the authorities. No sweat!"

"Right! Like we have a map with the coordinates marked on it! The hunters couldn't even tell us whether it's east or west—just 'down that river' and 'around that bend' and so on. That's a lot of territory to be flying around blind, even if we could be sure the site is visible through the trees. No, the only way we're going to find the place is to let these guys take us to where they saw the gringos. Besides, we can't wait for the authorities. If the oil companies finish exploration before we get there or even catch a whiff that someone's checking up on them, they'll be out of there in a flash, and we'll never be able to prove what they're up to. We've got to catch them in the act."

The photographer put out a hand to stop Dr. Renken as she started to climb into the canoe. "Fine! But no point risking the two of us like this. You wait here with the plane while I go take the pictures."

With an incredulous laugh, she shook off his hand. "Just what century are you living in? This is my party, and I'm going! And so is Roberto. We'll need him to talk to these guys. Roberto!"

The interpreter was still picking his way down the bank, stepping carefully to avoid unnecessary mud on his vinyl dress shoes. He personally saw no reason to be chasing a hunter's tale into the jungle, and had agreed to go only because the woman had threatened to stop his pay if he did not. If he needed any further proof these gringos were crazy—!

Reluctantly, he quickened his steps as the hunters began to shove the last canoe offshore. Clambering over the gunwale, Dr. Renken glanced back at the photographer. "Of course, there's no reason *you* can't stay with Eduardo," she remarked sarcastically. "As long as I take the camcorder with me."

"Not on your life!" The photographer waited only for Roberto to crawl into the second canoe before clambering into the third one himself. "C-PAP would have my head if I let you off alone," he called out to Dr. Renken, "no matter what century this is. No—you go, I go. Though I still think it's the dumbest thing this job has landed me in yet."

"Your choice," she answered indifferently. Already the lid of her briefcase was open and Dr. Renken was powering up the laptop. "As for the plane, Eduardo can wait here until we get back. I'll just modem headquarters and tell them we're going to be a few hours late. I mean, how far can this place be? They said it was within their hunting territory."

Hours later she was still asking the same question. The flotilla of canoes had long since turned off the river that flowed past the village into a smaller tributary. Since then, they'd made so many turns and crossed so many intersecting waterways that their passengers couldn't guess in which direction the village lay. The stream they were presently floating down was wide and shallow between high banks.

Dr. Renken shuddered as they passed a beach on which a dozen caimans, the Amazonic version of the alligator, lay sunning. Above them on the bank, she spotted the first human habitation they'd seen since leaving the village—a cluster of thatched huts nestled beneath the jungle canopy. Down on the beach, a barricade of stakes walled off a half-dozen canoes from the sleeping reptiles.

The paddlers didn't slow as they approached the village. Instead they picked up their stroke, casting uneasy glances at the village as they slid past. The three canoes stayed close to each other. The village itself was remarkably quiet, without a sound or movement, as though everyone had gone into hiding as soon as the flotilla of canoes had approached.

"Tribal enemies?" Dr. Renken wondered aloud.

In the other canoe, John only shrugged. He had grown increasingly silent and morose as the hours passed, his narrowed eyes concentrating intently on the wall of jungle on either side.

The paddlers showed no effects of their strenuous activity under a blazing sun on the open river, their naked bronze backs bending rhythmically hour after hour in long, powerful strokes. Roberto, meanwhile, had been forced by the heat to abandon coat and tie.

Over her shoulder, Dr. Renken addressed her interpreter. "Roberto, find out how much farther this is going to be. I really don't care to spend the night out here."

Roberto complied sullenly. The front paddler in his canoe turned his head at Roberto's sharp interrogative. His terse two-word response had been repeated often enough by now to need no translation: "Not far."

This time, though, there seemed to be some truth in the assurance. Just a few hundred meters past the village, the paddlers eased the canoes into a narrow, deep channel. A kilometer later, the channel emptied into a wide, algae-choked slough. The hunters paddled toward shore, where another complication arose.

"What?" Dr. Renken demanded, after only she, John, and Roberto stepped out of the canoes. "What do you mean, they won't come with us?"

"They say that if you go that way"—Roberto gestured up the bank where some of the tallest hardwoods they had yet seen soared to form a thick canopy high overhead—"you will come to where they saw the foreigners. But they will not go beyond this *laguna*. They would not have come this far if the Wise One had not ordered them to guide you. They say the white *riowa* are not truly men at all but ghosts. White ghosts who will destroy anyone who enters their territory."

"Well, more proof that it's the oil companies!" Dr. Renken snorted. "Come on, Roberto, that's the oldest trick in the book! Scare off the natives by making them think the area's haunted. Stay away, or the ghosts will get you!"

"It is no tale." Roberto glanced nervously toward the lengthening shadows along the bank. "The village we passed—they say it is empty because the ghosts snatched the people away. And two of their own party disappeared when they were last here."

"Maybe we should reconsider this," John started, but Dr. Renken cut him off. "Not you too, John! So the villagers didn't like the invasion and decided to clear out. Or took a job at the drill site."

The stolid expression of the hunters made it clear nothing would change their minds.

"Fine, then, they can stay here with the canoe. We'll go take our pictures. When we get back, I'm calling in Eduardo. He'll have to find us here and pick us up. There's no way we'll be back now by dark. No, not you, Roberto!" she added sharply as the interpreter started to climb back into the canoe. "We might need you."

"But I know nothing of the jungle," Roberto protested. "I have lived always in the city. This is foolishness. Without a guide, we will all be lost out there."

"Oh, no, we won't. John, you did bring the GPS, didn't you?"

The GPS unit John pulled from his camera bag was the latest Motorola sports edition, little larger than a cell phone. Calling up their present coordinates on the tiny screen, the photographer keyed in the direction the hunters had indicated. Shouldering his camera bag, he reached for Dr. Renken's briefcase.

"Oh, just leave that here," she told him. "They say it's not much farther, and I don't want to be dragging that through the jungle. We won't need it until we call in the plane." She saw one of the hunters eyeing the black vinyl case. "Before we leave," she told Roberto, "just make sure these guys understand they're dead if they touch that."

Roberto gave the warning, then shed the rest of his dress clothes and fashioned a loincloth from a length of cotton he found in the canoe, making him look remarkably like his jungle relations.

As they stepped away from the canoes, the forest canopy closed around them, the tall, straight columns of hardwood and the canopy's green ceiling so unvarying that without the GPS the three would have been lost almost immediately. But passage underfoot was easy, since the thick canopy cast a perpetual gloom on the forest floor that inhibited undergrowth.

Dr. Renken took the lead, the photographer quietly calling occasional corrections when she strayed from the course marked out on the GPS. Roberto brought up the rear, looking incongruous and unhappy with his makeshift loincloth and the dress shoes he'd kept on. Whatever the outward similarities, his city-bred feet lacked the leathery hide that allowed his jungle cousins to roam barefoot over stones and thistles.

Predictably, the trek was much longer than their native guides had indicated.

"At this rate, it's going to be too dark to film!" Dr. Renken fumed, slapping a dangling vine out of her face.

But several more strides brought a satisfied smile. "Well, well! Would you look at that!"

"It's a road!" Roberto exclaimed. "But out here—how can it be?"

"The oil companies!" Dr. Renken informed him. "Big bucks! Concrete, too. I can't imagine how they got that kind of equipment out here. And look how wide it is. What are they planning—a superhighway?"

She strode out of the cover of the trees and down the shallow bank. John grabbed her arm before she reached the concrete. "Are you nuts? You're hoping to blow the whistle on these guys, and you want to march right through their front door? You're the boss, Winnie. But don't you think it'd be a little more discreet to stay out of sight?"

Shooing the other two back into the jungle, John took the lead, steering them through the huge trees with silent purpose and speed on a zigzag course that nevertheless kept them parallel to the concrete road. With surprise, Dr. Renken admired his quick and soundless movements.

"Hey, John," she called. "Where did you learn—"

The photographer stopped so fast she stepped on his heels. Spinning around, he grabbed her by the shoulders.

"Look," he whispered furiously, "maybe you think this is some stroll in the park, but it isn't! It's stupid and dangerous. So if you don't mind, I'd like to get in there, get your pictures, and get out—without being seen or heard. If you would please just *shut up!*"

Dr. Renken's mouth dropped open in shock, then clamped shut. Subdued, she obeyed. Only a few paces later, John waved them to a stop.

"A surveillance camera!" he pointed out grimly. "These people don't want visitors."

His eyes narrowed as he scanned the quiet woods around them. "I have a funny feeling about this. Maybe we should just turn around right now . . ."

"Not without my pictures." Dr. Renken was already striding forward, ignoring the camera. "There's the drill site!" she exclaimed triumphantly. "And—what do you know! There's our missing Indians. So much for ghosts! They're working for the oil companies—the lowlifes! Come on, John, get this on film."

She broke off suddenly as the photographer reached her side, Roberto trailing reluctantly behind. "Oh my! John—is that what I think it is?"

For a long moment, no one moved or spoke. Then the photographer, his hands reaching for his camera bag, put it into words. "This is no drill site!"

Dr. Renken edged backward as dawning fear overtook her stupefaction. "John, we've got to get out of here!"

His agreement never came. Dr. Renken felt the sting on the side of her neck even as she saw the camcorder tumble from her companion's hands. It might have been a particularly aggressive mosquito or even a wasp. But already, as the tiny dart came away in her hand, she could feel its effects racing through her veins, seizing her vocal chords so she couldn't scream, turning her limbs to heavy wooden things that wouldn't hold her up.

Through the deepening twilight—or was it a fog?—a voice rose in the demanding upswing of an interrogative. But the words were garbled and unintelligible, like a cassette tape playing too fast. When hard hands lifted her from the ground, she could sense them only dimly, hardly able any longer to see or feel.

\* \* \*

Juan Quintero was standing on the verandah when he saw the vultures wheeling black against the sunrise. There were too many for them to be scouting for their morning feed. No, death had come to his *rancho* during the night, and he could not hope that it would be only a wild animal or even one of the *rancho*'s more elderly dogs or cats. His luck had been too devastating for that.

"Celia!" The roar brought his wife scurrying from inside the house. Worry clouded her eyes as they looked up at the birds circling purposefully above the eastern horizon. There was no need for words. Shoving his coffee and half-eaten *arepa* into her hands, Juan left the verandah at a run.

The dawn breeze was sweet-smelling and still cool as he hurried down the path. Songbirds and small creatures chittered softly in the tall grasses. A litter of piglets nesting under the mango trees added their own domestic chorus to the morning. It was a beautiful land—his *rancho*. A good land.

Juan's father had brought his family here in the seventies, when Colombia's agrarian reform was still offering free land to any peasant courageous and hungry enough to brave the jungle and its dangers. Over the years, the Quintero family had battled the wild beasts and the heat and the mosquitoes and all the plagues that came with them. Malaria. Typhoid. Yellow fever. As with every homesteading family, the burial ground had seemed to grow faster than the cleared fields.

But now Juan had two hundred hectares that he could call his own. Banana and plantain groves edged the path along which he was now hurrying. Beyond were rice fields, a patch of yucca, coffee bushes heavy with ripe fruit. His cinder block home was small, but it was neatly whitewashed and tight against the monsoons, its tile-roofed verandah wide and shady for hanging the hammocks during the heat of midday.

Yes, it was a good life they had carved from the jungle.

But today there were other enemies than nature to threaten the hard-earned peace of his home. The guerrillas, who labeled as "capitalists" and "oppressors" the men like himself who had paid in sweat and blood for their land. The paramilitaries, self-styled defense squads who claimed to protect the common people against the guerrillas but whose vigilante tactics were often more ruthless than the guerrillas' own. And, no less, the military themselves, who had abandoned to fate the countrymen they were sworn to protect, while they remained behind the safety of their barricades and guard towers.

As Juan left the path, the vultures became a squirming black cluster against the ground. His nostrils pinched shut at the stench of rotting flesh. What blow had an evil fate struck him this time? The mule? One of his remaining pigs? At least his children were safe in their hammocks.

The scavenger birds rose in an angry flutter at his approach, and he saw that his premonition of ill had not been misplaced. The disturbed meal, however, was no animal. There were three of them, spread-eagled face-down in the soft clay of the bank. The vultures had made vicious tears in the clothing and flesh, but the limp and sprawling bodies were intact.

Or almost.

Stripping twigs from a branch to make a pole, Juan used it to roll over the nearest body, this one almost naked in the loin wrap of the poorest peasant or jungle Indian. His stomach heaved at the bloody mess fire ants had made of the dead man's face and chest. Who were these unfortunate souls? Rebels shot down and abandoned by soldiers on patrol? Suspected guerrilla sympathizers murdered by the paramilitaries? Or simply innocent citizens caught in the crossfire between them all? There were no bullet wounds that he could see. Nor any visible sign of what had caused their deaths.

They had not died here—that was certain. All three were muddy, but not with the yellow clay of the stream bank. They were so muddy that the shorts and T-shirts of the other two hardly showed their original color, and their hair was matted and brown with murk as though the bodies had earlier been tossed face up on mucky ground.

Then something new caught Juan's eye, and the cold sweat of his nausea chilled further. The hair of these other two showed lighter roots under-neath the filth. Much lighter. And the skin at the base of the neck, where neither sun nor the vultures had yet touched, was pale as a full moon.

Rolling the two bodies over, Juan swallowed bile as he studied the re-mains of those ruined features. Even through the ravages of insects, there was no doubt. These two were foreigners. Worse, one was a woman.

This would have to be reported; for people like this, someone was sure to come looking.

But reported to whom?

The military base that claimed authority over this zone was a full day's travel by mule. The FARC commander was much closer, and his followers had made clear to the local farmers that anything unusual in the area must be reported to him. But if Juan obeyed, it would only earn the paramilitaries' accusations that he was collaborating with the guerrillas. Whichever way he turned would bring the others down on him.

Juan swore helplessly. That was the injustice of it all! That he should have to choose. The truth was, he did not wish to ally himself with any of them. All he wanted was to be left alone in peace to work his land, battling nothing more than the elements and nature's own bloody teeth and claws. Was that so much to ask?

The peasant farmer calmed himself with several deep breaths. There was another option. To do what had been done to him and simply move the bodies elsewhere. Then, whether they were found or not, they would no longer be his concern.

The vultures fluttered back down as he went for his mule.

When Juan returned, the animal objected to the smelly burden being thrown across its back, but it was old and not easily spooked. Tying down the bodies, Juan shooed the vultures and led the mule down the path. He breathed easier as he crossed the boundary of the *rancho*.

A snort from the mule was his first warning. Then he heard the quick beat of approaching horses. Abandoning the mule, Juan scrambled under cover of the underbrush that bordered the trail. A band of horsemen pounded around a curve just ahead. There were the expected exclamations as the horsemen discovered the mule. They stayed mounted as they made a half-hearted search through the brush for its owner.

Juan did not move. Which authority they represented, he couldn't guess. Military, FARC, vigilante squads—all wore the same uniform of battle fatigues and lethal-looking weapons.

The peasant farmer didn't emerge until several minutes after the horsemen had gathered up the mule's reins and disappeared down the trail. Then he started home at a run. They were gone, but sooner or later they would take the time to discover the owner of their confiscated beast of burden. Then they would be back. And he could be sure the blame for the three deaths would end up on his own shoulders.

An hour later, Juan Quintero paused on the verandah steps for a final survey of the little *rancho* that a generation of hard work and sacrifice and love had carved from inhospitable surroundings. The rising sun had burned off the coolness of dawn, but still the birds twittered their morning songs and the piglets made happy grunts under the mango trees. The vultures had dispersed, and the pastures lay lush and peaceful beyond the banana and coffee groves.

Tearing his eyes away, Juan shouldered his pack and took his youngest by the hand. Then, nodding for the other children and Celia to fall in behind, he led them down the path from their home to join the sea of refugees set awash by Colombia's civil war.

# TWO

THIS OFFICE DIDN'T CARRY QUITE the clout of the oval one down the hall. Still, its occupant was accustomed to a certain deference, consideration, and above all, recognition of just how valuable his time was. James Whitfield, the president's national security advisor, had zero tolerance for those who interrupted his busy schedule for trivialities.

Even when those trivialities included the deaths of American citizens abroad.

Slamming the stack of files down on the huge mahogany desk that was a measure of his importance to this establishment, he glared at the three visitors relaxing in leather chairs on the other side.

"I have here another bomb blast in Jerusalem. A demand that we extend our security forces to stop the latest tribal conflict in southern Afghanistan. A fresh threat against our embassies in northern Africa. Pakistan and India are rattling nuclear sabers once more. China is playing war games again on the border of Siberia, only this time they've invited North Korea to play along."

With each statement, he'd picked up a file and dropped it with marked emphasis onto a new pile.

"I've been in meetings all morning with three of those ambassadors, not to mention the UN Secretary-General, who like a typical woman figures it's her job to single-handedly clean up the mess the world's in. With the U.S. footing the bill, of course! I've got two more ambassadors on their way in right this minute, then I face a defense committee screaming over the sell-off of Russian military hardware to every Third World terrorist who can scrape up the bucks.

"So maybe you'd like to tell me why I'm giving up the fifteen minutes I've managed to grab onto for lunch just because some idiot American tourists chose to disregard every embassy warning we've issued and get themselves killed by Colombian guerrillas? I do catch CNN. *And* read your intel briefings. Neither of which links the incident to imminent war. Or international upheaval. Or even so much as a policy shift with the Colombian government. In other words, not a single good reason this couldn't have been filed on my desk with the rest of these reports!"

Whitfield was as massive as his desk and of much the same rich hue, a giant of a man often assumed to be a former NFL player, though the closest he'd ever come was the Naval Academy football team. The ferocity of his scowl had made steel-tough Marines tremble in their size-twelve boots. But his three visitors evinced only mild interest in the bulging veins at his temples and other symptoms of rising blood pressure.

Charles Wilson, director of the Office of National Drug Control Policy, exchanged a wry glance with his two companions before rejoining mildly, "We wouldn't be wasting our own lunch hour if it wasn't urgent, and you know it, Jim. So just take your mind off your turkey-on-rye for a few minutes and listen."

"What we need to discuss," the man on Wilson's right added quietly, "you won't hear on CNN." Martin Sawatsky, director of the Central Intelligence Agency, was a slight, unobtrusive man of medium height. He looked more like a law firm accountant than the head of the world's most powerful intelligence network, and there were those who complained bitterly at how misleading that impression had been.

"Those dead tourists who turned up yesterday—well, the fact is, they weren't tourists. Nor were they—exactly—environmentalists, which was the ostensible reason for their presence down there. At least, not all of them. One of them was ours."

"What do you mean—*ours?* Yours?" Whitfield demanded. "Or *yours?*" His choleric gaze moved to the third man before him, General Brad Johnson of SouthCom, the American military's Southern Command. Then on to Wilson, the drug czar. "Or *yours?* Are we talking spooks or Special Ops? And who knew about this? Let's have some specifics here!"

"Well—" Charles Wilson was drawling when General Johnson cut in abruptly. "What we're seeing here is a pattern, Jim. That's why I flew up from Miami as soon I got the news. This is the third incident in the last three months where we've lost American assets in Colombia. The problem is, we have no idea why. I think we may have a serious situation on our hands."

Whitfield's gaze didn't mellow. "What kind of a serious situation? Internal? External? Nuclear? And when? Today? Tomorrow? Next year?" he added pointedly, glancing at his watch. "And what does this have to do with your dead tourists, or environmentalists, or whoever they happen to be? One of whom turns out to be 'ours.' "

"Whoa!" The general raised a hand to stem the flow. "Look, Jim, it'll be a whole lot easier if we can just brief you from the beginning," he said firmly. Johnson was as small and wiry as Whitfield was massive, proof that bulk wasn't the top criteria for the Marine Corps in which they both had served. But he had known the other man for too long to be overawed by his volume or size. "We're going to need more than those fifteen minutes you allow yourself for lunch, though."

Whitfield glanced from one dead-serious expression to another. He hadn't risen through the minefields of both military bureaucracy and politics without learning to smell trouble.

Slapping his intercom switch, he bellowed, "Susan, tell the Pakistanis we're bumping them to Friday. And don't take any guff from Ambassador Oman about India getting preferred treatment."

He kicked back in his customized, reinforced armchair. "I'm all ears, Brad. Shoot."

"You know of course," Johnson launched in, "that Southern Command is responsible for all American military activities south of the Mexican border. At the moment, between the counter-narcotics war and the escalating guerrilla situation, Colombia is our main headache." The general hesitated, faced with the dilemma of quickly summarizing an expert's mountain of information. "I don't know how extensively you've been briefed on the situation in Colombia."

"I know it's tense," Whitfield said bluntly. "I know they've got drugs and guerrillas—lots of both. From there you'd better figure on starting at the beginning."

"Good. For starters, Colombia doesn't deserve the bad press it gets. Granted, they've always been a little rocky as far as internal stability. But on the whole, they've been one of our more stable and democratic allies in the hemisphere, clear back to Simon Bolívar himself. In fact, during the Pan-American boom in the sixties and seventies, they were one of the showpieces of the region. Per capita income climbing. The economy booming with dozens of new industries added to the traditional coffee and emeralds. Health and educational systems that were a model for a developing nation."

The general had fallen unconsciously into the pedantic tone of the political science instructor he'd once been at Quantico. He broke off with a slight smile. "You can read the encyclopedia as well as I can, Jim. Point is, the place was doing fine. Oh, sure, there were guerrillas. The Russians and Castro had been hawking their brand of Marxist revolution in Latin America for the last forty years, but in Colombia at least, the peasants said no. They had more to gain by homesteading land distributed by the agrarian reform or by simply sending their kids to school and working their way up the economic ladder as we Americans did a century back.

"Then came the cocaine boom and the drug war."

"Something we can't blame entirely on the Colombians," Charles Wilson interjected as Johnson paused. There was fire in the drug czar's eyes. "American money and the American propensity for self-destruction are what's fueling this situation, and we'd better not forget it. That isn't to downplay the viciousness of the Colombian drug cartels and the undeniable corruption narco-dollars have spread through every legal and political institution they have. That much easy money would tempt a saint, which none of us are.

"But the Colombian people have fought a bloody—and losing—battle against the narco-traffickers. The narcos have targeted judges, journalists, government officials—anyone who takes a stand against them. We have to ask ourselves how many Americans would be willing to run for office or speak out against drug dealing if the reward was almost certain assassination—for one's family as well as oneself more often than not."

Brad Johnson cut back in. "Then on top of the drug violence, we've got the civil war that's ripping Colombia apart. On one side are the leftist guerrillas, who have grown in the last two decades from a few scattered bands skulking around the jungle to some twenty thousand members between the different factions. On the other side we've got the right-wing paramilitaries. They may claim to be simple self-defense units banded together to protect their farms and homes against the guerrillas. But they've massacred thousands of civilians whom they allege to be guerrilla sympathizers.

"And then there's the government forces, police and military, who haven't been totally blameless either of spilling innocent blood. Granted, we've got to remember that the Colombian military and police forces have been badly hurt by the guerrillas, who have the advantage of being able to hit and run back into their jungle while the military are sitting ducks spread out across a hopelessly large territory. Because of this, the military have tended to look the other way for anyone who will whittle down the odds for them. At least the paramilitaries aren't trying to blow them up or their country."

Wilson broke in again. "And fueling all the conflict is the drug trafficking. We no longer have any doubts that both the guerrillas and the paramilitaries are financing their operations and arms purchases with narco-dollars. Estimates are that the FARC alone pull in more than half a billion dollars a year between the drug traffic and their kidnapping for ransom and extortion. With that money, they've been buying up SAM missiles, grenade-launchers, and who knows what else, to the point where they're now better armed than the Colombian army itself."

"In the meantime," Brad Johnson put in, "the civilian population is caught in the middle. More than a million Colombians have been dislodged from their homes in the last few years. But since they've crossed no borders, they get little sympathy or aid from the international scene."

Martin Sawatsky had been listening quietly while the other two talked. The CIA director caught a certain glazed impatience in James Whitfield's eyes and raised a hand to interrupt. "Let's not wander off the subject here, men. However we may feel for these people, it isn't really our business to resolve other countries' internal problems. The issue here today is our own national security. And not just in relationship to the drugs pouring across our borders. The American government has long recognized the threat drug trafficking poses to our citizens and has spent a fortune down there fighting it. But Jim, it's our contention"—he nodded toward his companions—"that the armed conflict in Colombia poses more of a threat than the cartels. If the guerrillas continue making their present inroads into Colombian territory as well as expanding their connections with the drug traffic, we may soon be looking at the first literal narco-republic. On top of that, we have reliable reports that the guerrillas are beginning to cross all of Colombia's borders—into Panama, Venezuela, Ecuador, Peru, Brazil. If this situation is left unchecked, we face the possibility of half of Latin America going up in flames. And this is no Kosovo, halfway around the world. It's on our own back doorstep."

James Whitfield looked less than impressed. Despite his disclaimer of ignorance, he had yet to hear anything new, and only the rank of his visitors kept him from summarily dismissing the session as he'd done often enough with subordinates who were less than concise and to the point. He leaned forward abruptly with a force that crashed his front chair-legs onto the polished floor. "Hold on just one second. There's no point in starving while we do this."

Slapping the intercom, he bellowed, "Susan, have the cafeteria send up sandwiches all around. And coffee. Lots of it. Black."

Swinging back to his guests, he grunted, "Okay, let's get on with it. I don't have all afternoon. There's one thing you can explain to me. Just what is it these guerrillas want? I'd understood that most of those Marxist revolutionary movements down there had faded into the woodwork once the end of the Cold War dried up their outside support. Surely after what happened in Russia and Eastern Europe, these people can't still believe the workers of the world want their brand of socialist paradise."

Sawatsky leaned forward to answer. "We don't understand their motivation either," the CIA director admitted. "That's partly why we're here today. Our own analysts predicted the Marxist movements would dry up in Colombia just as they have elsewhere. The guerrillas certainly can't claim the support of the Colombian people. According to a recent poll down there, three-fourths of the Colombians feel that the guerrillas *have* no political ideology beyond drug trafficking and kidnapping. So why don't they just give up? Lay down their arms, cash in their bank accounts, and settle down to live on the proceeds as leftist rebels have done from El Salvador all the way down to Chile?"

James Whitfield had never appreciated being handed questions rather than answers. "Okay, I give up—*why?*" he said bluntly. "I'm assuming yours was a rhetorical question."

"That's what we'd like to know," General Johnson said. "At SouthCom, we've been watching this pot boiling higher for years, and we can't help wondering if there isn't something—or someone—more behind the continuing mayhem down there than the general cantankerousness of the guerrillas and paramilitaries."

"You mean, outside manipulation—like Castro sending Che Guevara into Bolivia?" Catching his visitors exchanging a glance of surprise, Whitfield added dryly, "I do catch an occasional movie outside my own field."

"Well, yes, that's exactly what we suspect," the general agreed. "We've been receiving reports for years of foreign terrorists working with Colombian rebel groups. Of course, the Cubans and Russians have been supplying military advisors and aid to leftist rebel groups all over the globe for decades. Che Guevara was one of theirs. But that aid dried up along with everything else in the Soviet Union, and as for Castro, he's far too busy trying to keep his internal problems under control to be wasting money down south.

"Still, we have intel on Chilean and Argentine Marxists down there as well as Peru's *Sendero Luminoso*—the Shining Path movement. We know FARC members have received pilot and weapons training in Syria and Libya. Irish IRA operatives were caught down there not long ago, and members of both the Japanese Red Army and the Iranian Hezbollah have been seen among the guerrillas. Add to that confirmed contacts with al-Qaida as well as the Egyptian Islamic Jihad and possibly the PLO, and it's enough to make our people down there start getting antsy."

"We can't rule out that these may be simply mercenaries," Sawatsky cautioned. "A lot of terrorists were left out of a job when the Cold War ended. A lot more were scattered when al-Qaida operations were ended in Afghanistan. Some may simply be hiring out their services as consultants. The guerrillas certainly have the cash flow to do so these days. However, we must consider the possibility that these reports represent a concerted effort by outside interests to destabilize the zone."

A knock on the door heralded the sandwiches.

"So why would any outside interest want to screw up Colombia?" James Whitfield mumbled around his turkey-on-rye. "The place is a mess. It isn't strategically valuable territory to anyone but the Colombians. What would they have to gain?"

Sawatsky set his sandwich down on the bone-china plate that was one of the perks of government dining. "Nothing—directly. Until you look at the long-term results of that destabilization. Look what's happened even now with the guerrilla advances over the last couple of years. Narco-traffickers operating with complete impunity within the DMZ. Coca and heroin crops proliferating everywhere. Drug labs and flights under the direct protection of the guerrillas.

"Who does it hurt? The major recipient of those illegal drugs—the United States. And that goes for armed conflict down there too. It's the same trick the Soviets pulled back in the seventies with the Contras and Sandinistas. They couldn't hit us directly, but they could sure light a few fires on our borders. Whether we go into Colombia and end up with another Vietnam on our hands or stay back and watch the entire hemisphere south of our borders go up in flames, the mess is going to be ours to clean up."

Washing down the last of his sandwich with a gulp of black coffee, James Whitfield set down his mug with an audible thud. "Gentlemen, I'm sorry, but I do have engagements I can't cancel this afternoon. Would you mind skipping all the intel line and just tell me who your money is on?"

Martin Sawatsky opened a folder on his lap. Taking out a handful of newspaper clippings, he tossed them onto the desk. "Let's just ask ourselves who has the most cause to hate the United States."

Whitfield picked up the clippings, frowning as he read the headlines aloud. "Morocco spearheads Colombian investment. Iran and Colombia agree to economic cooperation. Syria sells missiles to Colombian guerrillas. Iran to finance meat-packing plant in Colombia's guerrilla-held region.

"What's all this mean?" he asked.

"What it means," Sawatsky answered, "is that we're seeing the same pattern down there as in every other corner of the world. Socialists are out. Islamic fundamentalists are in. Just take a look at the evidence. First we've got Islamic terrorists buddying up to Colombian guerrillas. Why? We know Muslim fundamentalists have nothing but horror for Marxist ideals. Now we have Middle Eastern neighbors tumbling all over each other to develop economic ties with Colombia. Again, why? As you said, it's hard to find a less stable investment right now than Colombia. That Iranian meat-packing plant is one good example. The proposed site is smack in the middle of FARC-controlled territory. There are no major roads or river traffic in and out of the area. On top of that, it's nowhere near Colombia's cattle-ranching zone.

"Add to that the reality that no one—not even Russia at its worst—hates us as much as the Islamic fundamentalists do. And not just a few rogue extremist organizations, either. Plenty of their governments do too. Partly because they see us as the staunch ally of their sworn enemy, Israel. But they have other reasons. Iran has hated us since we supported the Shah and did our best to overthrow the man who dethroned him, the Ayatollah Khomeini. Let's not forget that we actually supported Saddam Hussein in his war of aggression against Iran. Then there is Iraq itself, only nominally Islamic at the level of the ruling class, but with their own reasons for hating the U.S."

James Whitfield couldn't argue with that. In the wake of the Persian Gulf War, it was a little-remembered fact that the United States had been Iraq's major ally during the decade-long conflict with Iran that preceded their invasion of Kuwait. The reasons were clear enough for any student of that political arena. It had always been in the interests of the United States—

and of Britain before her—to keep the oil-rich region of the Persian Gulf splintered into states small and weak enough to need the West to help defend its wealth. This was possible only as long as the region's two major powers, Iran and Iraq, were kept too busy to turn their ambitions on their smaller neighbors.

Fortunately for Western peace of mind, those two nations had been enemies since the fabulous Babylonian Empire—present-day Iraq—had been invaded and assimilated by its mortal enemies the Persians—present-day Iran. During the reign of Iran's dictator, Shah Mohammed Reza Pahlavi, the United States had encouraged Iranian ambitions against Iraq. That happy alliance ended abruptly when Khomeini blew in from exile to depose the shah and return a cheering population to the tenets of their Shiite branch of Islam. Any U.S. hopes for cooperation soon evaporated as the ayatollah instituted his own reign of terror, branding the decadent West, especially the shah's former ally, the United States, the Great Satan, and harshly punishing anyone suspected of harboring favorable sentiments toward the infidels. When Khomeini compounded that expression of contempt by taking fifty-two American citizens hostage in the U.S. embassy in Tehran, the United States promptly shifted allegiance to Iraq.

Saddam Hussein's invasion of Iran in September 1980 kept both countries nicely occupied for almost a decade, along with providing the United States a market for war materials, which the Americans, regardless of supposed alliances, sold profitably to both sides. It was an unpleasant surprise when, more than a million casualties later, Saddam Hussein actually managed to force Iran into a stalemate.

The Iraqi leader had been naive enough to assume that its Western ally both understood and supported his next goal—the annexation of Kuwait, which Iraq had long considered a rebel province. He had actually called up the U.S. ambassador to Baghdad and informed her of the impending invasion before going ahead with his plans. To Saddam Hussein and others, Kuwait was the expected reward for Iraq's support of American policy in the region.

But the United States had never had any intentions of allowing Saddam Hussein's imperial ambitions to go beyond his advantageous quarrel with Iran. It was simply too dangerous to have one man—and such a man—controlling the bulk of the region's oil supply. When Iraq struck, so did the United States.

The rest was history.

"Then we've got Syria," Sawatsky continued. "And Libya. And Sudan. All Islamic nations where terrorism has been as much a part of their foreign policy as economic development. To these countries, we're still the Great Satan, and for all their current rhetoric supporting the war on terrorism, we'd better not kid ourselves that their two chief goals have changed—the destruction of Israel and the downfall of the United States."

Whitfield was no longer glancing at his watch. "So which is it?" he demanded. "Which nation is stoking Colombia's war? Or is it the whole bunch? Do you have any hard evidence? Or is this more speculation?"

"That's the problem," General Johnson answered, with an edge of bitterness to his tone. "We have no hard evidence. And not a whole lot of prospects right now of getting any. You know the state of our operations down there since SouthCom relocated to Miami. I'm not going to discuss the pros and cons of returning the canal to the locals. But walking away from our air bases down there—at the least, we've placed ourselves out of easy range for radar coverage of the Andean region. And with the refocusing of the bulk of our armed forces on the counter-terrorist operations in the Middle East and Asia—I'm not questioning the urgency of that mission, but it's left SouthCom gutted to the bone in both resources and personnel. Surveillance flights alone have declined by two-thirds down there, and the narcos know it—and so do the guerrillas. The biggest problem is right here."

Out of his seat now, Johnson strode over to where a huge global map covered one whole wall of Whitfield's office. "Some forty-two thousand square kilometers of territory that former Colombian president Andres Pastrana turned over to their largest guerrilla group, the FARC—excuse me, that's the Revolutionary Armed Forces of Colombia—over the heads of the Colombian congress, the military, and the Colombian people as well. The original idea was a short-term demilitarized zone to pave the way for peace negotiations. But the original ninety-day negotiation period has already extended to more than three years, and the FARC show no intentions of giving that territory back. Nor the Colombian government of demanding it.

"Nor, for all the compromises the Colombian government has made in ceding the DMZ, have the guerrillas shown any sign of taking the peace negotiations seriously. On the contrary, they've stepped up operations against both military and civilian targets everywhere in the country, and they've been using the DMZ as a launching pad—just as we predicted."

James Whitfield cleared his throat. "Brad, I appreciate the geopolitical lesson, and I agree we have a situation on our hands. But we're straying from the point. What does any of this have to do with our dead Americans down there?"

Johnson spun quickly away from the map. "That *is* the point, Jim! We've had three major incidents involving the loss of American military personnel in the last month—all in and around the DMZ. Including the loss of our foremost intelligence asset down there."

Whitfield nodded. "The surveillance plane that went down."

"That's right. The DeHavilland RC-7B. We may not be allowed—or even want—to flex our muscles against the guerrillas, but that doesn't mean we can't keep an eye on what's going on. We've been watching the DMZ since the beginning. Worthless jungle it may be, but don't forget the only war we ever lost was fought in jungle, and we've never had much faith in the sincerity of the FARC's protestations of peace. No one—not even the Colombian president—really believes the guerrillas have any intention of relinquishing their control on the region as part of the peace process. Not without a fight. Why do you think he keeps extending their deadline? It's easier than admitting to himself or the Colombian public that he couldn't take back the zone if he tried."

"The RC-7B's purpose," Martin Sawatsky explained, "was collecting intel on new coca and poppy plantations and monitoring radio and cell phone communications in territories occupied by either guerrilla or paramilitary forces. But the crew was also making a systematic mapping of the demilitarized zone with every tool we've got—sonar, radar, infrared, low-light television—looking for anything out of the ordinary that might shed some light on what exactly the FARC is up to."

"The DeHavilland had earlier turned up some valuable intel," Brad Johnson continued, "and it allowed the Colombian military to foil a major FARC raid. On the night it went down, the crew radioed that the plane would be making a swing down through the DMZ before heading back to base—to test some new night-flying infrared and heat-sensor technology. That was the last we heard from them. Our sat link data indicates there was some attempt at communication just as they went down. But whatever they were trying to tell us never made it through. We wouldn't have known how or when they went down except that one of our surveillance satellites caught an explosion over the DMZ at the same instant as that aborted communication."

"I remember that," Whitfield said. "The assumption was that the guerrillas got lucky with a SAM."

"The media's assumption," Sawatsky said. "And we haven't bothered to set them straight. But there's major problems with that scenario. The DeHavilland was flying well out of reach of any surface-to-air missile the guerrillas have presented us with so far, even the new RPG-7s they got from Syria. And the plane was equipped with a state-of-the-art missile defense system. Besides, how did they even know we were up there? The plane had the markings of a commercial aircraft. And it was nighttime.

"As for the other scenarios being tossed around—equipment failure or pilot error or even a bomb—again, no way. That plane was carefully maintained and continually checked over. And the pilot was one of our best. Whatever took that plane out, the fault wasn't on our end."

"We might know more," Brad Johnson added, again with some bitterness, "except that we haven't been able to get into the zone. The Colombians say the area is off limits, and they won't risk jeopardizing what little progress the peace talks have made by violating the DMZ's sanctity. They say we had no business flying over it in the first place—as though their government hasn't been falling over backward for any intel we can get them. Not that there would be much to find even if we could get in there. The satellite image pinpoints the DeHavilland's last position to within a fairly close radius, but with the force of that explosion, there won't be much left of the plane, and what there is will be scattered across who knows how much roadless, townless, triple-canopy jungle."

"Which is one reason," Sawatsky said, "that we didn't push it with the Colombians. But only a week later we lost our second asset in the area. Part of the White House's new counter-narcotics package"—he nodded toward Charles Wilson—"was a consignment of Black Hawk combat helicopters. The first one went to a brand-new military base just north of the DMZ. In fact, the brigade stationed there was one that had been run out of the DMZ itself. The Black Hawk was designated for counter-narcotics operations only—though the FARC may not have known that or cared. In any case, the very next night after the delivery of the Black Hawk, the FARC hit the base, wiping it out without a single survivor."

"Which should have been impossible!" the general interjected forcefully. "That's what doesn't make sense. One of our guys was there at the time. He'd gone along to help break in the local pilots. The only communication we got was that the base was under attack and that the Black Hawk was going up after them. No suggestion of panic or a situation they couldn't handle. Then—just like the plane—*nothing!* When the area commander sent in a convoy the next day to see what was up, they found pieces of that Black Hawk everywhere and the base looking like it had been hit by World War Three.

"It's crazy! The guerrillas have never been able to take on a full-fledged military base, however much they might like to hit and run. They just don't have that kind of firepower. Not even with these new RPG-7s. Those'll hurt bad enough. But to wipe out a whole base with the kind of destruction we saw there? No way! And the Black Hawk was no Vietnam-era Huey. It was a state-of-the-art, all-options-included combat helicopter that should have been able to take out those guerrillas in two minutes flat."

Charles Wilson had been listening with only an occasional assenting nod as the others talked. Now the drug czar spoke up slowly. "None of it makes sense. Whatever mayhem the FARC has been up to in the rest of the country, it's to their advantage to maintain a certain level of stability in and around the DMZ. This is the guerrillas' first serious social experiment. They want to show the world they can bring at least some semblance of order and peace to the zone in order to give legitimacy to their political aspirations. What they *don't* want is to provoke action from the Colombian military, which is already upset over what they see as an unconscionable pandering to criminal elements by a weak government. Or to provoke the U.S. into stepping outside their present 'counter-narcotics only' policy and taking a direct hand against the guerrillas ourselves. So why—and how— these two vicious attacks on American military assets both in and around the DMZ itself? Three, including yesterday's outrage."

"Your American tourists," John Whitfield said with some satisfaction. At last his visitors were getting to the point.

"Not tourists. Environmentalists," Sawatsky reminded. "And only one was ours."

"When the DeHavilland went down," Johnson explained, "we took flak from Colombia's media once it was made public that an American spy plane, as they termed it, was invading their sovereignty. It was suggested— clearly by some desk jockey who's never left the padded seat of his executive armchair—that we shift to covert ground surveillance of the DMZ. We're talking a jungle here the size of a European country with hardly a road or a town, overrun by hostile forces, infested with who knows what-all wildlife—and we're supposed to mount a meter-by-meter ground search?"

Sawatsky spoke again. "But if we can't scope out the whole place, at least it makes sense to nose around a bit. This environmentalist bunch made the perfect cover. Save the Amazon, or something like that. They've been facing off with one of the big multinationals for a couple years now over drilling rights in one of the last true virgin rainforests on the planet—which just happens to overlap a good part of the DMZ. If nothing else, the guerrillas have done wonders for conservation in scaring settlers and development out of the jungle.

"Anyway, the Amazon Protection Society, or whatever it's called, roped one of the local indigenous tribes into backing their campaign to save the rainforest. And since keeping American business interests out of the area is right in line with what the guerrillas want, the local FARC commander gave the group a safe-passage through their territory. It seemed the perfect opportunity to get into the DMZ. And these indigenous people move freely in the jungle. Not even the guerrillas bother them. Who better to notice if something funny is going on out there? So we got one of our people attached to the group as photographer. John Goodson. Special Forces training. Photography was his hobby."

General Johnson took up the narrative as Sawatsky reached for his cooling coffee. "Three weeks ago, John Goodson flew in with a conservationist named Dr. Winifred Renken, plus a national interpreter, to an indigenous village in the DMZ. They had already notified the proper rebel authorities, so they shouldn't have had any problems. They arrived at the village and talked to the chief. That much we know from the pilot. Then, according to the pilot, they left the village by dugout canoe downstream toward the DMZ itself. He wasn't informed why—just that they'd be back by dark. The pilot wasn't overly concerned. The party had a GPS locator and a laptop computer with sat-phone modem. They could holler if they ran into any trouble.

"But they never came back—and they never called, either. The pilot waited all night, trying to raise the party by sat-phone. When they didn't respond by daybreak, he began a pattern search of the jungle, checking rivers and lakes for any sign of the canoe. He found nothing. Finally, low fuel forced him back to base. By the time he returned to the village with some of Dr. Renken's colleagues, he found the place abandoned. But sitting on a stump in the middle of the village was Dr. Renken's laptop.

"They ran another air search until they ran low on fuel again, but they found no sign of the American party or the villagers. At least one of the local guides who were paddling the canoes must have made it back, because Dr. Renken had the computer with her when she left. But how or why they got separated from our people or why the tribal group abandoned the village, we have no idea. My guess is they got spooked after whatever went wrong with John and his party. Three weeks later—yesterday—the bodies of all three were found dumped on a *rancho* outside the DMZ. They hadn't been dead more than twenty-four hours, so the question is—where were they those three weeks they were missing?"

There was a moment of silence in the office. Then Whitfield asked, "Have they determined the cause of death?"

Sawatsky shook his head. "If so, they haven't told us. It's bizarre. The local FARC front where John and the others were found have the bodies in their custody. They claim they were discovered dumped in a pasture. They also claim that the FARC is not responsible for the deaths. The rebels are demanding a public autopsy in their presence before they'll release the bodies—presumably, to demonstrate their innocence in the matter. They've called for a press conference and are offering safe passage to a neutral location in their zone for a limited group of press, international observers, and medical examiners. They'll turn over the bodies only in the presence of foreign observers and examiners. They say if they turn the bodies over to the Colombian authorities, evidence will be manufactured to put the blame on them. They seem a little paranoid."

*And with reason.* The thought went around the room without being voiced aloud.

"Anyway, there'll be embassy personnel in that group flying down tomorrow. All we know for now is that they were *not* shot—the usual rebel method of execution."

"Then why are you so sure the FARC is responsible?" Whitfield asked. "After all, you said the guerrillas themselves had granted these people safe passage and that they approved of what they were trying to do. So why turn around and murder them?"

"Who else would be operating in there?" Charles Wilson responded reasonably. "Even the paramilitaries limit themselves to settled areas. Besides, let's not forget those two earlier attacks. There's no way that's a coincidence. As to why three separate attacks on American citizens and assets—well, there are several options. First, that the FARC leadership is stupid and bent on cutting its own throat. Of which, whatever their faults, they've given no indication. Or maybe the attacks were carried out by rogue elements without the knowledge or approval of their commanders. Though the sheer magnitude and sophistication of the attacks makes that unlikely. Or . . ."

His pause was fractional and not intended for dramatic effect, but the words seemed to hang in the air.

"Or?" Whitfield prompted.

"Or there's something there the FARC doesn't want us getting wind of," Charles Wilson said slowly. "Something John Goodson stumbled over, and that's why they killed him and his companions. Something vital enough to their interests to risk the backlash of shooting down a U.S. plane and taking out a combat helicopter they may have thought to have surveillance capabilities. They may not even be expecting a backlash," he admitted. "They're arrogant enough, they may figure there's nothing we can do about it. Given the present political situation, they may be right."

"So what is it? What do you think is out there?" Whitfield demanded.

Charles Wilson shrugged. "I have no idea. Maybe there's a whole lot more rebels in there than they want us to know about. Maybe they've got some kind of permanent training base these foreign terrorists have set up. Maybe they're building the biggest cocaine lab in the world so they can *buy* Colombia. Or all three. I don't know. But whatever it is, we need to make it a priority to find out."

James Whitfield let his full weight sag back against the protesting frame of his armchair. He now knew where this was going and why an incident that—for all its admitted implications—could still have been easily reported in writing had instead brought these three today in person. And he didn't like it one bit.

"So just what is it you're wanting from me?"

General Johnson hardly needed to consult the list in his hand. "We want the DMZ made a Priority One intelligence objective. We want another RC-7B immediately to renew surveillance flights over the area. And to service it and our other operations in northern South America, we want the reestablishment of a land base in the region pushed to Priority One as well. The best option would be renegotiating our former headquarters at Howard Air Force Base in the Canal Zone. I know the

Panamanians would fall over themselves to hand it back over to us. They've already had several guerrilla attacks across their borders, the last reaching within spitting distance of the canal, and they're as panicky over the situation as we are.

"Also, we want more land-based radar sites within Colombia to cover those gaps I mentioned. And finally, we want an immediate full-scale U.S. military investigation of the deaths of American citizens in the DMZ. Including a ground insertion large enough that the guerrillas won't dare harass our forces. Searching for the wreckage and bodies of our downed plane should give us the political justification to nose around, both with the American public and down there. We won't present it as a counter-insurgency operation, but as a routine crash investigation. Given enough resources and time, if there's anything out there, we'll find it."

Whitfield was shaking his head even before the general finished. "Brad, you know you're asking for the impossible. We only had a half-dozen RC-7Bs altogether before you crashed one, and they're tied up in places a lot more urgent than Colombia. That goes for the radar too." Remember, you aren't the only command stretched to capacity right now. Sure, you've made a decent case. But . . ."

He picked up the stack of files on his desk. "I've got reports here of a full-scale uprising of Islamic separatists in the Philippines. North Korea is moving into biological warfare research. We know Iraq still has weapons of mass destruction. And Iran may be buying nukes from the former Soviet republics. Even with the recent increases in defense appropriations, we just don't have the assets to keep an eye on everything that's happening out there. Much as we'd like to be, we're *not* Big Brother.

"And you, Martin . . ." He looked accusingly across at the CIA director. "You especially know just how stretched our intelligence capabilities are right now. I'm sorry, gentlemen. You may be absolutely right. Maybe I'm making the wrong decision here. But so far, all I've had from you is speculation. Possibilities. Maybe even nothing but coincidences. Certainly nothing that warrants going to the mat with the Pentagon to have our limited surveillance assets reassigned to a place most of them refuse to even acknowledge as a problem."

Whitfield's exasperation whistled out through his teeth as he dropped the folders back onto his blotter. "Tell me, do you still have other human intelligence assets on the ground?"

As the other three exchanged a quick glance, he went on, "Of course you do. Then I'll tell you what I can do, since you have them—"

"Not them—*him!*" Johnson interrupted bitterly. "One person! Those limited assets, remember?"

"Them, him, whatever. You get me something—anything—I can take to the Joint Chiefs of Staff to prove that this Colombian insurgency presents a clear and present threat to our national security, and I'll get you what you want. Until then—well, I'm sorry, but I just can't justify any alteration in our government policy in the country of Colombia."

As the storm of protest broke out, he reached out a long arm to buzz his secretary, a clear signal that the session was over. "I really am sorry, gentlemen. But until you have something more, that's just the way it has to be."

\* \* \*

TEHRAN, IRAN:

Across the world, the occupants of another conference room were also discussing Colombia and the latest deaths of American citizens there. Here there was no desk or customized armchairs, but cushions and gorgeous hand-woven rugs scattered across a vast mosaic floor. A low, ornate table held a silver coffee service. The coffee, served in tiny cups of almost translucent porcelain, was thick and black and of a syrupy sweetness. Unlike his counterpart in Washington, D.C., the discussion leader knew precisely what was going on in the DMZ. And he was furious.

"They shot down an American spy plane?"

The last twelve years had brought little change in the appearance of Akbar Javad Khalkhali. Though he was now entering his eighth decade, he was still spare and lean with the disciplined carriage of the soldier of the Revolution he had been. His gaze was still the flat, cold look of a man who had lost little sleep over the countless death sentences for which he had been responsible since assuming the mantle of ayatollah, supreme spiritual leader of his people. The absolute power and authority that came with that mantle was something no Western member of the clergy could imagine having.

The icy incredulity of his tone was like the crack of a whip in the room as he demanded, "And you allowed this to happen? Are you insane?"

The man seated cross-legged on the other side of the coffee table was

Taqi Nouri, Khalkhali's successor as head of VEVAK, the Iranian intelligence service responsible for maintaining the purity and internal security of the Islamic Revolution.

"They say they had no choice," Taqi Nouri replied. Like his master, he was a mullah, educated to holiness and orthodoxy in the holy city of Qum. Also like his master, he had long lost track of the deaths over which it had been his duty to preside.

Nouri was not a man accustomed to feelings of discomfort. But his hard gaze slid away from his master's relentless glare as he went on to explain. "The plane was directly above them. Their instruments detected a full radar and sonar probe. They *did* have orders to do anything necessary to prevent discovery or attack."

"And?" Khalkhali responded coldly. "The Americans would have found nothing. The base is not visible even to their satellites. Our own experts have tested this often enough. But this attack is another matter. Do you think the Americans will not ask questions? Even if there have been no signs left of how it was destroyed, do you think they will not ask how the guerrillas can have such a long arm that they can snatch a spy plane from the sky? And then this attack on the military base—again there will be questions. This is madness!"

"They thought it probable that the helicopter had been sent to take the place of the spy plane."

The explanation sounded lame even to its giver. The ayatollah's snort ratified that assessment. "They thought it probable! Even I across the world can go to the Internet and see just what an aircraft is this Black Hawk helicopter. It is not a spy craft. It is a combat aircraft, one of many given openly by the Americans to their Colombian confederates. A nuisance, yes, for our allies there. But it is not our mission to fight their small battles for them. Not now."

Taqi Nouri gave a nod that could have been a gesture of helplessness or apology. He could have made the excuse that he had not been informed of the attacks until they were over or that he had been as furious as his master when he'd found out. But it was not an excuse his master would have accepted, except as proof that their dubious allies were not as strictly under their control as Nouri had boasted.

The ayatollah didn't allow his glare to soften, though he understood well the other's frustration and fury at seeing a faultless plan sabotaged by incompetence. Akbar Khalkhali himself, in the wake of the 1979 Islamic Revolution, had helped the former Ayatollah Ruhollah Khomeini build VEVAK from the ruins of the infamous SAVAK, the Shah's own secret police. He had been personally responsible for the assassination teams that had taken out dozens of the Revolution's most outspoken enemies, both in the homeland and overseas. He had also been responsible for teams that had failed, from which he had learned that the price of command was to shoulder the blame for the errors of one's subordinates.

"Perhaps it is not so bad." For the first time, the conference room's third occupant spoke up. "At least these attacks will discourage the Americans from any more of their insolent interference in Colombian affairs—and in ours. It is well known they are cowards. They will pull out before they risk more of their people."

"You think so?"

The ayatollah shifted his gaze to the foot of the coffee table. His expression did not change, but the speaker shrank back on his heels. Like the other two, Minister of Transport Parviz Gangi was also a mullah, as were, in fact, most of Iran's present leadership. But even under the loose robes that billowed up around him where he sat, it was evident that his short, heavy frame knew nothing of his companions' ascetic discipline of the flesh. A plodder of no more than average intelligence, only Gangi's blood ties as the son of Khalkhali's youngest sister had facilitated his present government post or his inclusion in this restricted circle. Even at that, he had only the haziest idea of what was really going on.

Still, his very self-indulgence and lack of curiosity made him a useful tool for carrying out administrative tasks that were best not examined too closely. With the patient tone of a teacher with a dense student, the ayatollah asked, "And what, then, do you think is the significance of the three spies we have now caught? Is it a coincidence that they come stumbling into our camp on the very heels of these attacks?"

"Only one was a spy, and they came upon it by accident," Gangi muttered sullenly. "The interrogation showed that. And the spy did not have opportunity to pass on what he found. The interrogation showed that, too. The bodies were taken far away. No one will ever know where or by whose hand they died. The danger is over."

"The danger is not over," the ayatollah contradicted flatly. "It has aroused American interest in the zone. You do not know the Americans as I do.

That they are weak in will and decadent in morality does not signify that they are also incompetent. They are not. And when they sink their teeth into something, they do not easily let go. Our neighbor to the west found that to his cost."

Taqi Nouri nodded. That was his assessment as well. There was so much to despise about the Americans. They lacked political will. With the power they wielded, they could make the world whatever they chose. Yet the weakest opponent could defy them—as their neighbor across the border had also proved—and they would do little more than bluster and plead for good behavior like a parent pleading with a defiant child rather than applying discipline. The Americans had somehow never comprehended the reality that men were by nature self-seeking and prone always to violence, and that law and order needed to be just that, and not the matter of personal choice that the Americans had made it. As a result, the richest and most powerful nation on earth was besieged with violence and crime, its citizens disrespectful and foul-mouthed even to their own leaders, their children vicious and undisciplined, roving the streets unchecked like packs of wild dogs with no fear that the harsh hand of the law would ever descend upon them.

Yet they had the arrogance to dictate to the world how a nation and a government should conduct its affairs!

Still, when the Americans did choose to act, they did so with astonishing competence. Granted, this was due largely to the superior technology their great wealth had permitted them to develop, technology that itself was suspect as a tool of the devil. Yet there was no denying that it made of the Americans a formidable opponent.

"You are right," Nouri said aloud. "I too know the Americans. The killing of their people was a mistake. They will now be angry and curious, and they will not let this go until they find the answers they seek. It may not be soon or easy. They do not yet know who they are truly fighting or why. But in time they will find us out. They always do."

Khalkhali swore forcefully, spitting out the colorful Farsi phrases with such venom that moisture flecked his beard. "Curse him!" the ayatollah said. "We should never have allowed him to bring his people into this."

No one had to ask who "him" was. It had been far longer than Akbar Khalkhali had anticipated since that astonishing meeting with Iraq's supreme ruler on a black night in the rubble of an unnecessary war. For many years, the political climate had not been favorable—either the forces of law and order were too strong or the turmoil of combat too great to risk the establishment of a permanent outpost so near their enemy's borders. Colombia had always been a strong possibility. The country had vast expanses of uninhabited territory and an already well-established revolutionary movement. As one after another of the surrounding political conflicts sputtered out, Khalkhali and the task force he had handpicked for the mission had shifted patiently to the Colombian insurgency, courting all factions even-handedly with weapons and military advice and contacts to the outside world. Nouri's whispering in the ears of the FARC leadership had led to their demand for a demilitarized zone. Other quiet maneuverings in Bogotá had led to its approval. Only then had the audacious plan dreamed up by the Iraqi madman and tempered by Khalkhali's own wise planning and counsel been able to move ahead.

"We had little choice," Nouri reminded his master. "He has never quite trusted that we would not turn the weapon against him. And so he would not release it until all was ready. Even now he will allow only his men to handle it. And perhaps he is right," he conceded. "Our people are not as expert in these areas." As the ayatollah's burning glare flashed to him, he added quickly, "Though our own could soon be trained to replace them, given the need."

"He is a madman—and not even of the true Faith!" the ayatollah snapped. The Iraqi leader and his people followed the Sunni branch of Islam, to which the majority of the world's Muslims belonged, while the Iranian fundamentalists clung to the Shiite interpretation of the Koran. The differences seemed minute to outsiders, involving chiefly the proper choosing of Mohammed's successor as spiritual leader of Islam. But then, factions within the Christian camp had fought and died for centuries over little more.

"But"—the ayatollah graciously made his own concession—"it would seem that Allah himself has a purpose for the apostate and has made him a part of this. *Insha Allah*. It is the will of God. But the man must not be allowed to interfere further with the carrying out of the mission."

Parviz Gangi shifted nervously, drawing his feet up under his robe. His plump face had been growing steadily less happy as the conversation wore on. "Uncle Akbar—Ayatollah, I do not like this. Perhaps if there is truly such danger of discovery, we should think further. Is it not possible that this is a sign from Allah? After all, the world has changed since we began this mission. Is not our government even now reconsidering our relationship with the Americans? And it is clear that the infidels are weakening toward us. In my own ministry, they have made many concessions of foods and products that may now move between our two countries. May it not be that our president is right? That the Americans can be made of more benefit to us as allies? If we do not rush to destroy our boats behind us too soon."

The venom of Nouri's spat-out curse matched his mentor's. "Allies! Benefit! Parviz, you are as always a fool! And you forget who it is that rules in this country. Not the president nor the parliament, for all the rumblings of elections and reforms. It is the Guardians of the Faith who determine the course of our nation. And that course will never lie with the Americans. To use them, yes! But never forget that this is not the first time they have come with soft speeches because they coveted our oil and our support against enemies they hoped would be our enemies too. They betrayed us then. They will betray us again. The servants of Allah do not treat with traitors. They destroy them as the infidels and sons of Satan they are. No! No matter what lies and manipulations the Americans may come with to deceive us, we will not swerve from our just and holy path."

"But . . . I was just thinking, have you considered the consequences to us, to our people, if we are discovered? If the mission fails? Or even if it succeeds, the effect on the economy and our exports, the retaliation if they ever find out . . . "

Gangi's stammering appeal trailed away under Nouri's withering glare. Khalkhali did not even deign to consider his nephew's nervous pleas. He had been only an adolescent in 1953 when the Americans' Central Intelligence Agency had staged the coup that brought down Iran's prime minister, Mohammed Mossadegh, freely elected by the Americans' own democratic rules. They had forced back onto the Iranian people that corrupt and venal ruler, Shah Mohammed Reza Pahlavi, a man his own CIA puppet masters despised as a coward and a fool, yet supported simply to ensure their own masters' control over Iran's oil.

The Iranian people had suffered another quarter century under the godless oppression of the shah until the Ayatollah Ruhollah Khomeini returned from exile to lead the nation to Allah and freedom in the Islamic Revolution of 1979. Khalkhali had spent much of that intervening quarter-century in the shah's rat-infested detention cells for his own role in Khomeini's crusade to turn his nation's course from the greed and decadence of the West to the unswerving allegiance Allah demanded of his children. The sessions in the SAVAK's interrogation chambers, as much as the teachings of his spiritual leaders, had burned into both flesh and soul just who was the true enemy of his people, and though he was now an old man, the steel forged by decades of hate still blazed unabated from his eyes and stiffened his backbone with the carriage of a man far younger.

This new generation of gutless leaders who thought only of their stomachs and the comforts of life might talk of making peace with the infidels Khomeini himself had correctly labeled the Great Satan. But Khalkhali never would, and if he accomplished nothing further in his long life than to strike a blow—with Allah's blessing, a mortal one, though even a serious wound would eliminate their interference in Iranian affairs—then he would leave this life content.

And now they were so close. The signatures were barely dry on the Colombian peace initiative when they had made their move. They had chosen a site deep into rainforest so heavy and wet and tall that it had perhaps never known human footfall except from the primitive aborigines whose few remaining descendants still roamed its depths. Impenetrable, people called the place, and they believed it. But where there were rivers for transport and a limitless budget, anything was possible. They had worked slowly and cautiously, under the protection of the guerrillas themselves—though even their leaders did not know exactly where or what they were protecting. Nor would they necessarily approve if they did know. After all, they too were godless infidels.

And now it was done. A local village of aborigines had been conscripted for the heavy labor. The new airstrip in San Ignacio, ostensibly built to facilitate the meat-packing plant, had provided a runway heavy enough for cargo planes. From the runway's edge, the Ipa River fed into the jungle's own maze of streams and lakes and swamps. Only when the site was complete had the Iraqi madman whom Allah, in some dark twist of humor, made their unlikely ally—only then had he consented to release the weapon. The involvement of his own followers was the unpleasant condition he had set for his prize. The blunders of these last weeks should not, perhaps, have been such a surprise. Their neighbor, after all, had a history of rushing across bridges without considering the consequences.

Still, however annoying these recent incidents with the Americans, they did not really change things so much. Only a few steps remained to be taken before their enemies' own tool of destruction would be turned back on them. Then the United States would cease to exist—or at least be crippled enough to remove it forever from the center arena of world affairs.

Raising a hand, Khalkhali made a sharp negative gesture. "No! No, Parviz, we cannot allow fear and doubt to delay our holy mission. On the contrary, we will advance its day of unleashing so that even if the Americans do uncover what is hidden, they will come too late. Taqi, you will go personally to see that this is done and that neither of our allies interferes further with the successful accomplishment of Allah's judgment."

He rose to his feet with a movement surprisingly swift and smooth for his years, indicating the conference was over. His companions scrambled up to join him.

"I will fly out tonight," Taqi Nouri informed his master. "But there is one other matter. Our Colombian allies are not happy about the deaths of the three Americans. They object to being blamed for acts of terror they have not themselves committed. So they have invited outsiders to where the bodies were found to see for themselves that this was not their doing. There is little we can do to stop this since we have not considered it prudent to inform their leaders of the true purpose behind the eliminations. But the Americans will use the opportunity to send in another spy. I know. It is what I myself would do."

The ayatollah looked thoughtfully at the minister of intelligence. "They will find nothing there. So what is it you suggest?"

"It is not that I am concerned," Nouri answered carefully. "It is not possible that the Americans will uncover the truth before it is too late. Still, it would be useful to have someone of our own to observe this gathering. If possible, even to determine who their spy is that we may establish our own watch upon him. Then we need have no fear of the eyes and ears of their satellites and radar and other technology."

Khalkhali nodded agreement. "Your caution is right, Taqi. When the stakes are as high as this, even the smallest risk must be smoothed away. But whom do you think to send? We cannot openly send an observer of our own people. The Americans are looking now at the guerrillas, but they are not such fools that we dare dangle a puzzle piece under their very noses."

Nouri smiled faintly. "I have already considered this, and I have just the person. One of the finest we have. Not once has this operative shrunk from any mission no matter how difficult or . . ." he hesitated over the word—"unpleasant. Already I have made the arrangements, and even now the operative is en route to Colombia. And this I promise you. Not in all the thousand and one nights of Sheherazade herself will the Americans ever conceive that this one is ours."

The ayatollah's grunt of approval dismissed the two men. But as Parviz Gangi plodded off with an ungraceful flopping of robes across the vast mosaic floor, Khalkhali stopped his second-in-command. Quietly and without inflection, he remarked to Nouri, "My nephew's heart is no longer entirely with us."

The head of the Iranian secret service didn't even blink.

With the same, even inflection, the ayatollah went on, "Allah has given us an opportunity never before envisioned by man. It is not his will that anything be allowed to interfere with its completion."

The two men's eyes met in perfect understanding. Then Taqi Nouri followed his fellow minister out of the conference room, his own strides swift and silent.

\* \* \*

The headquarters in Washington, D.C., of the Wildlife Conservation Institute were a restful enough sight, its abstract angles and the blues and greens of its glass shell designed to blend gently into the ecological balance of its ten acres of botanical gardens. Pastel walls, country scents vented through the air-conditioning, "nature" music playing softly in the background—all were carefully calibrated for a maximum soothing effect on visitors and ecologically conscious sponsors.

But the soothing effect ended abruptly at the door of the office of Norm Hutchens. Inside, the walls were bare, the filing cabinets cold metal. From behind a desk scarred with cigarette burns and piled high with stacks of paper and files, the editor of WCI's quarterly magazine, *Our Earth*, glowered at his youngest staff writer.

"Blast it, Julie! When are you going to be reasonable?"

Norm "Bulldog" Hutchens had earned his sobriquet as much for the tenacity associated with that canine breed as for his squat body and drooping jowls. That tenacity had never been so evident as when a doctor's orders forced his retirement from the rat race of the *Washington Post* for the less stressful life of overseeing WCI's printing needs. Channeling his resentment into the institute's money-losing periodical—at the time little more than an in-house information newsletter—he had in short time transformed *Our Earth* into America's most widely read environmental magazine.

He hadn't done it by being nice. The acidity of his tongue had prompted more than one sloppy staff writer to tear up his journalism degree for a less dangerous profession, and his glower above the heavy jowls that really did bear an uncanny resemblance to the canine species was enough to set assistants, staff writers, and even lowly graphic artists and typesetters caught in its path scrambling to look efficient.

The "bulldog look," as his underlings irreverently termed it, had never been more pronounced than at the present, his small eyes narrowed to an intimidating slit above the fat cheeks, every one of his multiple chins thrust forward pugnaciously. But the young woman facing him across the untidy surface of his desk showed little sign of wilting under the heat of his gaze. A cloud of cigar ash rose with a puff as she slapped a crumpled green memo slip down onto the pile of newspaper clippings in front of him.

"Don't you talk to me about reasonable, Norm Hutchens! You're not going to get away with this. Did you really think I wouldn't find out? Well, for your information, I *do* watch the news, and the murder of those activists has been all over it. With the environmental angle, I knew you'd be angling for a place on that team. So there I was, rooting around for my passport, and I find out that even the cleaning staff knows you've assigned Bob Ryder to the story, while I get a memo shipping me off to British Columbia! Are you trying to tell me *Our Earth* is wasting space on some stupid beetle with an extra stripe turning up in logging country? Or is this your sneaky Machiavellian method of getting me out of the way?"

Julie was a third the age of Hutchens and barely more than a third his weight. But it was the editor who shifted his gaze first. "Now, you see here, Julie Baker!"

"No, *you* see here! You're cheating, Norm Hutchens. Just like you've been cheating since the day you hired me. You promised me the Latin America beat. *I'm* the one with the background and culture. *I'm* the one with the language. And what have I gotten so far? Puerto Rico protesting New York's garbage being dumped in their territorial waters. Interviewing

Florida orange growers as to their opinions on the spread of citrus canker. Meanwhile, Bob Ryder gets Peru. And Ecuador. And Venezuela. This is a guy who thinks 'native' is some sort of obscene linguistic terminology and whose Spanish would make a high school language teacher cringe!"

The old newspaperman glanced around for an ashtray, failed to locate it under the heap, and stubbed out his cigar on the edge of the desk, adding another scar to its wood finish. "Now, wait a minute! Those hurricanes in Ecuador and Venezuela were rough business. The relief teams were working in water and mud up to their waists. The press had to travel rough. As for Peru, have you forgotten that the coca growers were rioting? All those road blocks and clashes with the army? Not to mention terrorists? It could have gotten ugly."

"It did get ugly," came the implacable retort. "When Bob Ryder tried to interview the *cocalero* leader and—accidentally or not, I've never been too sure—ended up calling the man's mother a—"

"Language!" Hutchens remonstrated mildly.

"The point is, the police had to intervene to pull the guy off Bob, and you had him shipped home the next day. You ended up having to send out Chris Walter to finish the job. *With* an interpreter. As for traveling rough, I'm not the one who turns in written complaints over hiking a mile in the mud. Or gets sick eating refugee camp food.

"Besides, the man can't write, no matter how many years he spent typing up corporate brochures and yearly reports. You tell me how much of that last article you had *me* rewrite for him. I could have done a better job with my hands tied behind my back, and you know it. I heard you tell Ken Jackson so yourself, when he came up to review the magazine's finances."

Hutchens chose to ignore that. Ken Jackson was his own boss, president of the Wildlife Conservation Institute.

"And now we finally have a story worth sinking our teeth into! I mean, how often do we get a story that combines politics and some genuine suspense with environmental issues? And world attention too—the team's going in with a UN contingent. Even better, the press slots are limited. Not even your pull would have gotten us a seat if it hadn't been for C-PAP's connection with the institute." An accurate evaluation the editor again chose to ignore. "Which means the story could be picked up by other magazines, maybe even the big news weeklies. Who knows, maybe even *National Geographic*. And in Colombia, of all—"

"Oh, no!" The old newspaperman raised an imperious hand, the ponderous shake of his head setting his jowls to waggling. "Let's not get started on that. You want to argue Peru and the others, fine. Maybe I should have sent you instead of Bob. You certainly couldn't have done worse. But you're not going to Colombia, and that's that! The situation there is just too volatile. Have you forgotten these people were murdered? They're flying right into the heart of guerrilla territory. Who knows what the security setup is going to be like? No, you can give me that puppy-dog look of yours all you want, but there's no way I'm going to be sending a green reporter with the ink still wet on her diploma into a war zone. I've got to think of the safety of my staff, and for that I have to choose the most qualified and experienced man for the job."

"But I *am* the qualified man . . . woman! Bob doesn't know the culture. Or the political situation. He's never even *been* to Colombia! I know those people. I know that area. If anyone would be safe there, I would. More to the point, I'm not a six-foot towhead who screams 'gringo' from a mile away and shoves his foot down his throat every time he opens his mouth. Unless I choose to broadcast it, no one, guerrilla or otherwise, will ever know I'm not a local."

Hutchens made no attempt to argue the point. Sinking his jowls into his neckline in a manner that shifted his animal kingdom equivalent from a bulldog to a squatting toad, he studied his youngest staff member with an eye no less observant for the gold-rimmed trifocals advancing years had forced him to adopt.

What he saw was a slim girl somewhere in her early twenties and of average height. A mass of curls dark enough almost to be black tumbled to her shoulders where it had escaped the hair clip in which she had confined it that morning, and her long-lashed eyes were almost as dark, when not blazing molten copper with anger. Allied to an olive complexion that owed itself more to a healthy tan than her natural skin tone, Julie Baker could pass for a good percentage of the world's ethnic groups from her actual Irish/Welsh/French roots to Mediterranean or Hispanic. Norm Hutchens was already acquainted with her language proficiency, of an idiomatic perfection attainable only in childhood.

But the wholesome directness and honesty in her face was to his thinking a drawback in today's cutthroat field of communications. Her empathy and just plain *niceness* might be responsible for Julie's success at personal interviews, but it clashed badly with the hard-boiled reporter image she tried to project. And her defiantly tilted chin did little to conceal a vulnerability that would rouse the protective instincts of any decent male—a fact that would have horrified this independent young woman, if she'd had any inkling.

Julie Baker was, even to her editor's cynical old eyes, a very attractive young woman. And so he told her.

"You think the guerrillas are going to care if you're an American or a local? All they're going to see is a pretty girl. And down in those macho parts, pretty girls don't go wandering the outback on their own. Not unless they're asking for trouble. Besides, you always said you never wanted to go back to Colombia. I thought you hated the place. After what happened to your parents, you vowed you'd never set foot there again. I took you at your word."

Julie lifted her shoulders impatiently. "I was sixteen. Things change. Little girls grow up. I'm not making any plans to retire there, but that doesn't mean I'd turn down a story that could put my career on the map just because of a few less-than-pleasant memories. This is the biggest story our magazine has ever had. Maybe even a prize winner. And I'm the best person you have to write it. I've earned this assignment, and I want it!"

Her employer was still shaking his head implacably. "No, I'm sorry, Julie. You're a good writer, and I really would like to give you a break. Maybe next time. But for now, you're just going to have to face the reality that some jobs just aren't appropriate for a young girl."

The horror of her gasp might have been more convincing were it not for the gleam of triumph in Julie's eyes. "Norm Hutchens, I can't believe I just heard you say that! You are actually admitting that you're denying me an assignment for which I am the most eminently qualified on the basis that I'm a *woman*? What century are you in? Do you know what your lawyer would be advising you right now if he could hear this conversation?"

"Well, he can't hear it," Hutchens retorted. Picking up the green memo slip, he smoothed its crumpled folds and handed it back to her. "Now that we've got that settled, you'd better get home and packing, young lady. The team for British Columbia is scheduled to be at the airport in two hours. If you value your position around here, you'd better be there."

There was an elongated moment of silence. Then Julie placed her hands flat down on the desk and leaned over until less than twelve inches separated her own slim features from her employer's multiple chins. "No!"

"No?" Eyebrows rose incredulously above the heavy jowls. "Are you defying me, young lady?"

"And don't call me young lady! You wouldn't dare call another member of this staff 'young lady'! I am not going to British Columbia. This story is rightfully mine, and you know it! If you won't let me go, so help me, I'll sue you for sexual discrimination, just see if I don't! And I'll win, too!"

The two glares clashed, and there was something surprisingly similar in the two expressions. Then, abruptly, the one-time terror of the Washington newspaper world threw his hands in the air, sending another shower of cigar ash across the papers on his desk.

"Okay, Julie, you want Colombia that bad, you've got it. But it's on your head. Get down to T & E and pick up your tickets and travel vouchers. Pick up a camera too. You'll have to take your own pictures—we've only got one seat on the plane. You'll meet up with the rest of the team in Bogotá. I'll let Bob know he's going to BC."

The defiance eased from her taut muscles. Rounding the desk, Julie leaned down to kiss her employer on one sagging cheek. "Thanks, Uncle Norm. You're a sweetie. I won't let you down, I promise."

"Some sweetie!" he grumbled. "A chip off the old block you are. Get your own way, and butter won't melt in your mouth."

"Yeah, well, I had a good teacher." Julie tossed the words over her shoulder, already heading for the door.

"You just come back in one piece," the old newspaperman called after her. He watched his goddaughter's long legs lengthen almost to a run. As the door slammed behind her, he muttered to himself, "Because if I have to sit through your memorial service too, it's going to break my heart."

# THREE

JULIE BAKER WAS SMILING as she bounced—there was no better word to describe that exuberant spring in her step—down a flight of stairs to the lower level of the World Conservation Institute's publishing division. Getting your own way wasn't so difficult! It just took determination, plenty of hard work, and an absolute conviction that you were in the right.

Julie would have been astonished had she seen either the worry or the pride that followed her out of the old newspaperman's office. She'd been managing her own affairs—and quite competently, thank you—since her teen years, and neither asked nor needed others to concern themselves with her activities.

As for the gruff old newspaperman who had signed her boarding school bills since her parents' death seven years earlier and who had—with all apparent reluctance—permitted her an entry-level position with *Our Earth* once she'd waved her magna cum laude journalism degree in his face, it had never entered her head that she was more than a pain in his side, an unwelcome responsibility thrust upon him because of a casual commitment made twenty-three years earlier. Certainly, her godfather had given Julie no breaks on the job because of their ambiguous relationship.

*I've worked my tail off to please the old coot!* Julie defended her recent unladylike behavior as she threaded her way through the maze of cubicles where the lower ranks of the magazine worked, remembering her godfather's constant admonitions: *"Rewrite, Julie! You can do better, Julie! Maybe next time!"* Meanwhile, incompetents like Bob Ryder got by with butchering every journalism rule in the book—just because he'd been working for the magazine since Noah's Ark outsailed the world's first ecological disaster. For just an instant, Julie entertained a possible correlation between her godfather's unrelenting demands and the very competent journalist she'd become, but that outrageous suggestion was immediately dismissed. *Julie, my girl, it's time to shed the cocoon and spread those wings!*

Speaking of which . . .

Thrusting her head around a divider whose tacked-up lettering announced simply "Travel & Equipment," she said sweetly, "Hey, Kenny. Got a ticket to Bogotá for me?"

A lanky young man with a shock of fire-engine-red hair glanced up from the file drawer through which he was rooting. "Oh, hi, Julie!"

He broke off as the import of her question sank in. Slamming the metal drawer shut, he let out a low whistle. "You didn't! And I had a bet with accounting you'd never pull it off."

Perching herself on the edge of his desk, Julie hunched her shoulders in a no-big-deal shrug. "Oh, he screamed and fumed and breathed fire—and a whole lot of cigar smoke. But he finally saw reason. Now where's that ticket?"

Unearthing a folder from the chaos on his desk, Kenny handed it over with new respect in his tone. "You've got it. Round-trip ticket. Hotel reservation. Both in the name of the institute, since I wasn't sure who was going. Just flash your WCI badge. You'll need that to get on the UN flight too. The rest of what's in there is background data—not that you'll need it. But what about Bob?"

"Going to BC," Julie informed him carelessly, picking up the packet. "Where maybe he'll take a few lessons from the purple-striped Pacific rainforest beetle—or whatever it is—on the survival of the fittest."

Kenny shook his head in mock amazement. "Hey, keep it up and you'll be as hard-boiled as the old man."

Julie assumed a wounded expression. "That's not fair! I don't kick dogs. I pat little kids on the head. And I help old ladies across the street. Besides, a journalist is supposed to be hard-boiled. You know what the boss always says." Her voice dropped an octave in a wickedly accurate imitation of her guardian's gruff tones. "A journalist is an invisible bystander on life's stage. He doesn't get personally involved. He doesn't influence events. He simply—"

"Records them," Kenny chimed in. "Yeah, we've heard it before. So tell me, my hard-boiled friend who doesn't get personally involved, what's this about you organizing a neighborhood clothing drive for those earthquake victims in El Salvador?"

Julie went pink under her tan. "How did you hear about that?"

"This *is* a news office," Kenny reminded her dryly. "Anyway, just so you know, we're all rooting for you. You think everyone doesn't know who's been pulling most of the weight around here these last few months? Or who rewrote those last three articles of Ryder's? But better you than me! Colombia isn't exactly on the State Department's recommended vacation list right now."

Julie sobered instantly. "No, it isn't, is it?"

Rushing through an assortment of good wishes and congratulations from other cubicles, Julie quickened her long-legged stride as she crossed the parking lot to her elderly Plymouth Neon. The flight to Bogotá didn't leave till late afternoon, but check-in was in an hour, and she still had to stop by her apartment to pack.

Sprinting up the five flights of stairs that were her chief source of physical conditioning, she threw a few changes of clothes into a knapsack. Two pairs of khaki pants. Four accompanying shirts. Four sets of underclothing. Toiletries. A single long skirt and blouse of some uncrushable synthetic material in case a formal engagement presented itself. Sandals to match. And mosquito repellent—two bottles. Travel papers. Oh, and better throw in a jacket. Bogotá would be cool, however tropical the jungle might be.

She added the pocket-sized digital camera that had been a Christmas present from her godfather—unused till now. Photography was not one of her strong points. It distracted her from the research angle of the assignment. She found herself either too busy taking pictures to track down the people involved, or so caught up in the story that she simply forgot the pictures. On other assignments she'd traveled with a staff photographer; this time she'd just have to do her best or barter with one of the other news teams for pictures.

The last item to go in was her laptop computer. Packing fast and light was one carryover from Julie's childhood that had come in handy in her present occupation. It was so much easier to clear customs or walk away from a broken-down bus if you were carrying all your belongings over your shoulder.

The flight was issuing its final boarding call by the time Julie cleared security and found the right gate. The door clanged shut behind her as she entered the cabin. "Just take a seat anywhere," a flight attendant told her hurriedly over the rising pitch of the jet engines.

The aircraft was a Boeing 727, with rows three seats across on each side of the aisle, and reasonably filled. Julie passed up with a shudder an empty seat next to a whining toddler and his harried-looking young mother. Not on a working flight. Halfway down the aisle, she stopped. Row 24 on her left had only one occupant, a woman seated next to the aisle, though her belongings spilled out across the other two seats. She was tall, brunette, and elegant, carefully made up, with huge, dark eyes and perfect, sculpted features. She looked vaguely familiar.

Julie gave an introductory cough. "Excuse me . . . ?"

The woman raised a disinterested gaze. Crossing nyloned legs so that her tailored business suit slid dangerously high, she conducted a leisurely survey of Julie's own khaki slacks and knit top that left Julie feeling underdressed as she hadn't since she'd inadvertently worn jeans to a Capitol Hill fund-raiser designated "casual."

"The flight attendant informed me these seats were unassigned," the passenger said coldly.

"Yes, well, I got here late."

With an audible sigh, the woman shifted her high heels so Julie could squeeze past, but made no attempt to remove her belongings from the other seats. After moving a makeup bag and two books into the middle seat, Julie dropped down next to the window and tucked her own knapsack beside her feet.

Unbuckling her seatbelt, the woman beside the aisle stood with a graceful motion and opened the overhead bin. Lifting down a laptop computer, she powered it up and busily began typing. From the corner of her eye, Julie caught a few words of the e-mail she was writing. *Dear James: Concerning the Frankfurt convention this weekend, the NBC executives were happy to agree to your TV contract terms. . . .*

So much for polite conversation! The woman was the stereotype of the YFP—young female professional—who seemed to equate her generation's career success with the right to feel superior to the rest of mankind. Or rather, womankind.

*Okay, two can play at that game.* Extracting her knapsack, Julie opened up the data packet Kenny had included with her ticket. She smothered a smile when the flight attendant told her neighbor to shut down her computer for takeoff, but as Julie scanned through the computer printouts a staffer had included to mitigate Bob Ryder's abysmal ignorance, her pretended concentration on her work became real.

Colombia.

The northernmost country in South America, this republic covered three times the area of Montana. Forty million inhabitants, the majority living in the cool plateaus and valleys alongside the Andes Mountains. The land was 4 percent farmable, 48 percent forest and woodlands—interpret that "jungle." Capital: Bogotá. Elevation: 8,500 feet.

Julie flicked through the pages impatiently. There was nothing here she didn't already know. It was a beautiful country. Majestic mountains whose slopes produced the best coffee in the world. Sandy beaches washed by surf warm enough for a bathtub. Jungles, lush and mysterious. A land rich in petroleum, gold, emeralds, and the exotic flowers that had become one of the country's major exports. Soil that produced so lavishly, a peasant farmer could practically feed his family from the fruit trees growing in his backyard: papaya, avocado, banana, mango, citrus, and the less-known guanábana, lulo, curuba, maracuya.

And the cities. Crowded, busy, with an increasingly sophisticated industrial infrastructure. A country famed for its cultural wealth. Literature. Art. Music. Dance. Theaters. Bookstores. Museums.

A people with a reputation for warmth and generosity. Hardworking. Passionate.

Her birthplace.

And a country at war.

Abandoning the country profile, Julie pulled out the latest State Department human rights report and began thumbing through its pages. The question wasn't who are the combatants; it was who *isn't* fighting. There were dozens of guerrilla groups alone.

Julie skimmed through the background data on the guerrillas. The largest number of pages dealt with the FARC, the Revolutionary Armed Forces of Colombia. It was by far the largest guerrilla faction, with more than fifteen thousand armed fighters. Established in the 1960s as the fighting arm of Colombia's communist party, the FARC had been hard-hit in the seventies by the government's counter-insurgency operations. Somehow they had survived, and by the late 1980s, they had made a remarkable comeback under the leadership of their redoubtable commander, Manuel Marulanda, known as "Tiro Fijo" ("Sure Shot"). Though the demilitarized zone was their official base, their tentacles of power now extended to every region of the country.

The FARC's chief rivals among the guerrillas was the *Ejercito de Liberación Nacional*, or National Liberation Army, boasting some five thousand combatants. Furious at the preoccupation by both the Colombian and American governments with the larger FARC, they had resorted to bank robbery, sabotaging the country's energy infrastructure—especially the oil pipelines—along with the usual civilian massacres and kidnappings.

There was also the Maoist Popular Liberation Army, and the M19, notorious for taking hostage the entire Palace of Justice in November 1985. The resulting shoot-out with the military had ended in the deaths of eleven justices, countless civilians, and all the hostage-takers themselves.

*Nice people,* Julie thought sardonically, shuffling quickly through the remaining printouts. Each of the guerrilla factions offered a different political perspective and plan for bringing peace and prosperity to the country should the Colombian people have the wisdom and foresight to turn the reins of government over to them. Fortunately, the conviction that their way and only theirs was right kept the factions at each other's throats as much as at everyone else's. But Julie could see no significant distinction between them. Each group claimed to be fighting for justice and equality on behalf of the hapless *campesinos*—peasants—who had assuredly received the short end of the economic stick in Colombia. Perhaps initially each group's motives had been as pure as they claimed, but they all resorted equally to robbery, kidnapping, intimidation, and murder to achieve their ends. And their victims were often the very poor for whom they had pledged to fight.

Then there was the drug dealing. It had long been common knowledge that the guerrillas levied a "war tax" on *cocaleros* and narco-traffickers in their zones in return for protection against government interference. Now rumor had it that they were moving into a more active role in the narcotics trade, relocating landless *campesinos* into their jungle strongholds and setting them to work to clear the land and plant coca. It was also rumored that peasants who refused to cooperate found themselves staring down the barrel of an AK-47.

Which might be one reason why the *campesinos* for whom the guerrillas claimed to be fighting showed so little enthusiasm for them. For all their boasting of popular support, it wasn't devotion that bred loyalty to whatever faction claimed local jurisdiction of a zone. Or kept lips tight-sealed when government forces made their rare incursions into the countryside.

No, it was fear.

Julie's hands stilled on the file in her lap. Funny how after all these years she could still remember the very scent of that fear. A scent that was dust and heat and the sour body odor that came from tension and too much adrenaline rather than honest perspiration.

"A Bloody Mary. And go easy on that Worcestershire sauce."

Her neighbor's curt order was followed by a tinkle of ice as the flight attendant placed the drink on her tray, but Julie didn't notice. She was sixteen again, just back from boarding school, back to the riverbank town in the Colombian lowlands that was the only home she'd ever known.

Spending much of the year away from home did not make for close relationships, but there were a few childhood playmates who still bothered to drop by when word got out of Julie's infrequent visits. Evenings in a jungle town were for outdoors, there being little room or fresh air inside the small cinder-block houses for entertaining, and Julie had taken refuge with a handful of other teens in a small plaza across the cobblestone street from her home, not doing anything constructive, just enjoying the cooler breeze that came with twilight, the young men strumming guitars idly to a Ricky Martin hit playing on a transistor radio they'd propped up against a potted palm.

It was the silence that first alerted Julie to the horsemen, the sudden stilling of guitar strings, the hushing of music and laughter and chattering voices along the length of the street. The tinny sentimentality of the transistor radio crooned on alone as the riders made their way toward the plaza, hoofs echoing against the cobblestones and splashing through mud puddles. Behind them, children were snatched into doorways, and verandahs emptied of inhabitants.

Julie hadn't understood the tension vibrating from her companions. These riders seemed no different from any band of cowboys riding into town for an evening at the cantinas, a few in the combat fatigues that were a common leftover of every Colombian male's stint in the *cuartel*, the others in civilian shirts and baggy pants. Even the weapons thrown casually across the saddles were not abnormal. On more than one holiday, Julie had watched the gauchos galloping into town, shooting their guns into the air in sheer exuberance.

Nor was she surprised when the horsemen drew up outside her front door. Everyone knew the region's only resident gringos, and the Baker house was always the first stop if there was a problem. When her father emerged for a low-voiced conversation with the leader, nothing in the calmness of his expression gave her cause for alarm.

Until the riders turned their heads in her direction.

They made no threatening moves, but just sat there looking at her, a band of grim men, some as young as herself, with unsmiling faces and unreadable eyes. She still didn't know who they were, but she recognized the smell of fear around her. Tasted it in her own mouth. The choking dryness of dust kicked up by impatient hooves. The hot musk of the horses. The strong ammonia smell of underarm perspiration that was not only from her companions.

The leader snapped his fingers. Wheeling their horses, the band thundered back down the street. By the time the darkness swallowed them up, her friends were gone, melted away into the night. They didn't come around again. The next day she was on a plane back to boarding school. "Leftist rebels are moving into the area"—that was her father's only explanation. It was better that Julie stay where it was safe until this blew over. Maybe next vacation, things would be better.

But by her next vacation, her parents were gone.

\* \* \*

"Miss? Are you sure I can't offer you something to drink?"

Julie glanced up as the flight attendant's patient repetition registered. "Oh, I'm sorry! I was just . . . " Following the attendant's inquiring glance, she saw that the printout in her hands was crumpled beyond readability. Thrusting it back inside the data packet, she hastily unlatched the tray from the back of the seat in front of her. "Uh . . . just some water, thanks."

Julie waited until the flight attendant deposited cold water and a bag of pretzels before picking up the last report. It was on the largest paramilitary group, the *Autodefensas Unidas de Colombia* or United Self-Defense Forces of Colombia. At least with the paramilitaries, Julie could understand their motives and objective. Government presence and protection had always been minimal in Colombia outside the major population centers. Even she could remember that. It had been the recommendation of America's CIA back in the sixties that Colombia's counter-insurgency operation include the arming of the peasants to defend their lands against guerrilla incursions. The American pioneers had once done the same, banding together to fight off the attacks of Indian tribes.

But if, like the guerrillas, the paramilitaries had started with noble goals, then by the statistics she was reading, those had quickly disintegrated. The Colombian government might have approved the self-defense strategy, but they'd had no funding to make it a reality. The only ones with money to equip a peasant defense force were the large landowners and the narcos.

Over the decades, the self-defense units had degenerated largely into the personal armies of the wealthy and of the drug cartels, and in their fight against the guerrillas, they stooped to even worse atrocities than the guerrillas themselves, routinely entering villages and towns to round up and execute locals suspected of sympathizing with the guerrillas.

Julie sighed as she replaced the report in the file and shoved the whole folder under the seat into her knapsack. For decades now, senseless violence seemed to be the pattern of Colombian society.

If a country could be said to have a temperament, Colombia's had to be that of the artist—passionate and excitable. It was this passion that gave richness and depth to Colombian music, art, literature, and to the close interweaving of personal relationships that was the heart of Colombian society. But that passion was also the curse of Colombia. The same fervor that made them so generous in friendships was as easily roused against an enemy. And since Colombians were as passionate in their politics as in their friendships, a political opponent *was* an enemy. Put two Colombians together, the saying went, and you had a political debate. Three and you had a multi-party system.

Julie could still remember the stories told by village old-timers of *la violencia,* a virtual civil war between the two main political parties, Liberals and Conservatives, that spanned almost two decades and left three hundred thousand Colombians dead. A coalition government dividing power between Liberals and Conservatives brought an official end to *la violencia* in 1958, but the political passions and anger lingered on to become the roots of today's guerrillas and paramilitaries.

Still, the present climate of violence in Colombia could not all be conveniently blamed on the warring political factions. It was something Colombians didn't like to talk about—that Colombia was not only the homicide capital of the world with a per-capita equivalent of a quarter-million Americans being murdered each year, but that, according to the human rights report Julie had just read, less than 8 percent of those deaths had any political motivation. Had the decades of violence loosened the restraints that kept most people from giving rein to the inner rage and hatreds that would take another's life? Or was there something fundamentally wrong with Colombian society?

It was impossible for an outsider to judge. But the reality was that a Colombian was more likely to be shot by a jealous neighbor or knifed by a

drunken cantina companion or gunned down by a fan for poor performance, as more than one Colombian athlete had died in the last years, than
kidnapped by the guerrillas or butchered by the paramilitaries. In Bogotá
or Medellín or Cali, a mere one hundred dollars slipped to a *sicario*, or
professional assassin, would take care of a business or social rival.

And why not, when 99.5 percent of all crimes in Colombia went
unpunished?

The question was why. And how. Surely the country had a police force.
And what of the other factors? How did the drug trafficking that every
American citizen thought of first when "Colombia" flashed onto their TV
screen figure into this mix?

And what of Julie's own country? Not her birthplace, but the country of
her citizenship. What was the United States doing to stop this pot boiling
over only too close to its own borders?

For all her claims when fighting for this assignment, Julie was only now
realizing how much she *didn't* know about Colombia. Sure, she'd been
born there. But a child's view of a jungle village was as little a reflection of
an entire country as growing up in rural Montana made one an expert on
the complexities of American politics, and consciously or unconsciously,
she'd given little more than cursory attention to news that crossed her path
on Colombia since she'd left it seven years earlier.

*And I was slamming Bob Ryder for poor preparation.*

"I ordered a vegan meal when I booked my ticket!"

The dinner cart had now reached their row, the flight attendant looking
flustered and apologetic under the angry barrage from the woman beside
Julie. "I'm sorry, miss, but pasta is our only meatless choice."

"It still has animal products. No, take it away. Just give me another
Bloody Mary. What kind of airline doesn't offer vegan in this day and age?"

For a moment, Julie thought her seatmate was actually speaking to her,
but a glance showed that the complaint was being addressed to the ceiling.
Settling for the beef, Julie ate half of what was purported to be filet mignon before shoving her own food onto the middle tray and setting up her
laptop. Not waiting for this morning's confrontation with Norm Hutchens,
she'd spent several hours last night on-line running key words through her
search engine. Colombia. Drugs. Guerrillas. FARC. Demilitarized zone.
San Ignacio. The resulting data had been far too vast to more than skim
through, but she'd stored the downloaded files on her laptop to study

during the flight. Julie pulled up the first file: "U.S. Targets Colombian Cocaine Crop."

"We are now making our final approach to the International Airport in Bogotá. If you will please store your belongings and return your seats to their upright position."

The announcement brought Julie abruptly back to her surroundings. Twilight closed in early on the equator, and it was now full night outside the portholes of the plane. Beyond the wingtip, Julie could make out a hazy glow—the city lights of Bogotá. Perhaps because of air traffic, the plane had banked in a circling pattern over the city, and as it dropped in elevation for the final descent, the haze of light separated into the twinkling box forms of skyscrapers, a fiery circle that was the coliseum, the glittering spires of the central cathedral. Crisscrossing it all were the rivers of light formed by boulevards and overpasses alive with rush-hour traffic.

Bogotá was nestled on a wide mountain plateau more than eight thousand feet up into the Andes. The floor of the valley was dark beyond the glitter of the city, but Julie didn't need daylight to know what lay below the outstretched wings of the plane. Dairy farms with their fat Jersey and Holstein cattle. Strawberry fields and greenhouses filled with roses and orchids. Forests of pine and juniper sweeping up the mountain flanks to snowy peaks. Lush vegetation patchworked with coffee and banana plantations tumbling down from the plateau to lower elevations.

It really was a beautiful country, her birthplace.

If only its people hadn't spoiled it!

Julie slammed the laptop shut. That was what it all boiled down to, wasn't it? These people just couldn't seem to solve their own problems. So was it really fair to expect others to do it for them—all these environmental groups and human rights organizations and government aid programs?

And of course, the missionaries.

Why *should* other people sacrifice their time and energy and very lives to help people who quite evidently didn't want to be helped?

Julie found that her hands were trembling slightly as she shoved the laptop into her knapsack. This was crazy! Uncle Norm was right. She should never have come. When she'd said goodbye to those mountain peaks down there, it had been with relief and for good. *What was she doing here?*

If it hadn't been for these last two years of running senseless errands, writing reports on garbage dumps and squirrel populations! But she needed this story if she were ever to get out of the basement of a small-time environmental quarterly. The opportunity was too good to pass up.

*A journalist doesn't get personally involved,* she reminded herself fiercely. *None of this has anything to do with me! Not anymore! This isn't my country. These aren't my people. I'll get in, get my story, and get out.*

The landing wheels touched down with a thump. Julie checked the instructions Kenny had drawn up for Bob Ryder. For the night, she was booked into the local Holiday Inn. For the next leg of the trip, she was to meet the rest of the press corps and the UN mission at 10:00 A.M. tomorrow at a military airfield that the American embassy used for its chartered flights.

Her seatmate had disappeared without a backward glance. With no luggage to collect, passing customs was a brief affair. The airport was as modern and clean, its personnel as smiling and polite, as any American airport. By night, the skyline from the taxi might have been any North American city, the hotel room a clone to the one Julie had stayed in last week in Miami. Flipping through the cable channels to the English-language CNN, Julie called room service to order a filet mignon that was a world apart from that served on the plane.

She did not open her notes or her laptop. For this night at least, the confusion and complexity that was her birthplace could remain outside the walls of her hotel room.

\* \* \*

A good night's sleep did much to restore Julie's enthusiasm for the assignment. Polishing off an *arepa,* the toasted corn cake that was a Colombian breakfast tradition, she sipped a steaming cup of mountain-grown coffee as she shook out the morning paper the hotel had included with the meal. A news item bordered in black on the back page caught her eye.

*DIED: Iranian Minister of Transport Parviz Gangi, age 42, in a car bombing outside his residence in Tehran. Parviz Gangi administrated Iran's involvement in Plan Colombia, President Batallano's international investment program.*

The last sentence explained the item's inclusion in a Colombian paper, but it meant nothing otherwise to Julie. Of more interest was the front page headline: FARC KIDNAPS PROMINENT CONGRESSMAN.

*Same-ol', same-ol'!* Julie grimaced. Checking out of the hotel, she flagged down a taxi. She gave directions to the driver, then turned her attention to the streets passing outside the cab window. What changes would daylight reveal in the Bogotá she remembered?

Whatever she had expected, it was not what she saw. This Bogotá looked even more modern and prosperous than the one she had left seven years ago. She noticed new skyscrapers, expressways to alleviate the traffic congestion she remembered, a new stadium. A huge new shopping mall flashed by on the right.

Everywhere there were people, thronging the sidewalk, honking their way through the snarls of traffic, all in a hurry. It wasn't a hurry born of anxiety or fear, or a need to get off the streets before something unexpected occurred. They were simply busy, intent on their own affairs.

Street venders were doing a brisk business hawking the country's most widely read dailies, *El Tiempo* and *La Republica*. Tables in front of a bakery were crowded with men grabbing a cup of coffee and pastry and a glance at the headlines on their way to work. Only last week, CNN had carried the story of a grenade exploding in just such a sidewalk café. Didn't these people worry that disaster might strike them as well?

And where were the depredations of conflict Julie had read about? She'd expected at least some shattered windows or bullet-pocked walls, if not an actual bomb crater or two. Some sign of the human misery decades of violence had spawned.

But in this part of the city, at least, the buildings were freshly painted. The metal shutters rolling upward with a clang revealed shop windows filled with luxury items. Even the beggars squatting on street corners looked well-fed.

*This* was a country at war?

A scrawl of graffiti spray-painted above an overpass seemed to echo her incredulity. *El pais se derrumba y nosotros de rumba.* Rumba was a dance. The graffiti was a sarcastic play on the verb *derrumba*—to tumble down, to cave in.

We rumba as the nation tumbles.

The taxi driver was whistling a popular salsa tune as he maneuvered in and out of traffic. Leaning forward, Julie asked, "And how is Bogotá these days?"

In Colombia, even a cab driver counted himself a political analyst, and

Julie was not disappointed. "Good, good!" The driver glanced at her in the rearview mirror before cutting across two lanes of traffic to zip onto an exit ramp. "Business is good. The city is growing. Bogotá does well for herself, and so do her citizens."

"But what about the guerrillas?" Julie asked. "I've heard there is much violence these days. Three bomb attacks in the last week. And just two days ago, three foreigners were killed. Three Americans."

"Were they?" the taxi driver answered indifferently. He speeded up as the traffic light ahead turned yellow, just clearing the intersection as the opposing lane of traffic began to move. "I did hear of a bomb last week, but not in this neighborhood."

"Oh, this was down south in the lowlands. Near a town called San Ignacio."

"Ahh!" The taxi driver's exclamation was dismissive. "Down south. But of course, that is another world out there."

His glance was shrewd in the rearview mirror. "Me, I think *la guerrilla* is convenient for *los políticos*. If they can point to the guerrillas and say, 'Look, these rebels are destroying our country,' then they do not have to answer for all else that is wrong. The poverty. The children on the streets. The crime that goes unpunished. The *campesinos* with no home and no land. The *ricos* who own this country while the rest go without. If they can blame the guerrillas, then they do not have to answer for their own broken promises."

"But . . . don't you think the government has a responsibility to fight the guerrillas?" Julie asked. "All the kidnappings and murders . . . you can hardly travel in Colombia anymore. At least that's what I'm told. Don't you worry for your own family?"

The taxi driver gave a comfortable chuckle, visibly calming down a nervous tourist. "Oh no, señorita, it is not as bad as they say. *La guerrilla*—it is a long ways from here. Out in the jungle, you know. But here in Bogotá you are safe. *Aquí no pasa nada.*"

*Aquí no pasa nada.*

"Nothing happens here."

Julie had first heard that popular Colombian phrase repeated wryly by a Colombian environmentalist, now safely removed to OAS headquarters in Washington, D.C. The guerrillas might be blowing up the oil pipeline. The paramilitaries might be massacring villagers. But as long as my city, my neighborhood is quiet, *aquí no pasa nada*.

Julie had never understood that attitude. In the United States, if an attack was made on any part of society—whether the bombing of government buildings or the gunning down of school children—the American public rose up like an infuriated elephant, trumpeting rage, pointing fingers of blame, and demanding that the government do something . . . anything! To ignore pain and death as long as it didn't touch one personally was inconceivable to the American mind.

But now, little though she could agree, Julie was beginning to understand something of where these people were coming from.

"It's a long way from here," the taxi driver had said as if that dismissed it all.

It was true that the very geography of Colombia contributed to such a mind-set. In most countries, cities and towns sprang up on the waterways and coastal ports that facilitated trade. Not so in Colombia. Here civilization had emerged in the mountains. The Andes mountain chain that formed a backbone ridge along the west coast of South America split when it arrived in Colombia into three *cordilleras,* or ranges, that intersected Colombia from southwest to northeast, neatly dividing the northern coastal region from the southern jungles. Nestled within its mountain valleys were every major Colombian city. Bogotá. Medellín. Cali. Bucaramanga. There also lived the overwhelming bulk of the Colombian population. Industry. Education. Wealth. Political and economic infrastructure.

The reason was simple. In Colombia's position on the equator, where summer and winter cancelled each other out, climate was determined not by season but by elevation. The coastal areas and the southern jungles were steamy, hot, and abounding in tropical diseases and fevers like malaria, typhoid, and yellow fever. The mountain valleys were cool, healthy, and fertile enough to feed an increasing population. To the average Colombian, the *cordillera* region with its large and modern cities and busy industrial areas *was* Colombia. The steamy coast and the southern jungles were "a long way out there." So might a New Yorker dismiss the permafrosted tundra of Alaska.

And if what happened out there in those sparsely populated wilds could not be fixed, they—and their few inhabitants—were no big loss.

*Aquí no pasa nada.*

The words rang in Julie's ears as the cab turned off the highway at a sign reading, *Fuerza Aerea Colombiana*—Colombian Air Force. At the gate, a sentry checked her WCI pass against a clipboard in his hand before waving them through.

Out on the airfield Julie counted at least a dozen fighter planes and combat helicopters, but she also noticed a scattering of civilian single-engine planes as well, and even a Fairchild prop jet. Like many other military airbases around Colombia and all Latin America, this one made up its budget deficit by servicing private air flights.

As the cab pulled up outside the terminal building, Julie spotted a two-engine plane drawn up on a runway to her left. She recognized the brand—a forty-four-passenger Douglas DC4. Clustered in front of it was a crowd that screamed gringo.

After paying the cab driver, Julie shouldered her knapsack, then grimaced as a gust of wind blew her dark hair into a tangle of curls around her face. She checked her watch: 9:50. Time enough to make herself presentable before beginning introductions. Besides, if that DC4 out there was her ride, Julie knew from unpleasant experience that it was unlikely to have lavatory facilities.

Two more sentries checked her press badge, then shifted their machine guns to allow Julie into the terminal, which looked to have been converted at some distant period in the past from an aircraft hangar. More recruits wandered the vast concrete floor, some pushing baggage carts or carting boxes, others simply on patrol with their M-16s hanging down their backs. A knot of women were clustered around one baggage cart. Ranchers' wives, Julie gathered from their shrill chatter, waiting for the weekly supply run into their rural community. Spotting the word *Damas* on a nearby door, she headed toward it.

The bathroom was as utilitarian as the terminal, the stalls of rough plywood, the sinks clean but rusted over with mineral deposits. Julie had just entered the farthest stall when the bathroom door slammed open, followed by a babble of feminine voices and the tramping of feet. The ranchers' wives.

"The guerrillas are worse all the time!" a voice asserted, separating itself from the rest. "My husband called to say they took ten cows last night as their *vacuna*"—a "vaccination" against trouble. "Hah! When the only trouble we see comes with them. They are bleeding us to death. Last week the *paramilitares* came to the *rancho*. They say we must all come together. We must fight. We cannot allow *la guerrilla* to drive us from our land. Where would we go? For two cows, they say they will bring men to our *rancho* to fight on our behalf."

There was a snort from one of the other women. "Two cows! That is what they told us too! They brought their men. Fifty of them. They stayed a month, eating and drinking like pigs! They went out. They came back. The guerrillas are taken care of, they told us. They took twenty cows. Because we have given you much time, they said. My husband could say nothing. And then we went out . . ."

The woman's voice suddenly dropped. Julie had to strain to hear. "We found them. They were not *la guerrilla*. There was the schoolteacher from the village. And others we knew . . ."

A sudden and absolute silence followed. Julie was ready to emerge from the stall, but the feeling that she was eavesdropping on a very private conversation kept her where she was. Then the first voice said soberly, unhappily, "But what are we to do, then? Give our land away? Leave our children with nothing? At least the *paramilitares* promise peace. To whom else are we to turn? My husband went to the *comandante* of the *cuartel*. My neighbors and I are being robbed, he told the *comandante*. The *comandante* told us there was nothing he could do. His men were not authorized to leave the base. It would seem the *militares* have nothing more to do than to eat and drink our taxes."

"The blame cannot be placed on the *militares*." It was a new voice, angry, bitter. "It is not their fault that they cannot leave the *cuartel*. The *políticos* do not give them the money, the arms, to fight the guerrillas. I know. My sister's son, only seventeen years old, was cut down with all his class of cadets and all in the *cuartel* only last month, down south near San Ignacio. Should the *comandantes* continue to send our boys out to be butchered by the guerrillas? That is not the answer!"

"There *is* no answer," the second voice said somberly. "There is no right or wrong. Only killing and death. So who do we follow? We wish only to stay alive."

A murmur of assent answered her; then Julie heard the door open. She waited until their retreating footsteps had died away into silence before emerging from the stall. Digging a scrunchy out of her backpack, she pulled her curls back into a ponytail, then shook her head at her reflection in the mirror. What she'd heard was in a nutshell Colombia's response to the chaos that was this country: Keep your head down. Mind your own business. Survive.

But then, who was she to criticize? Wasn't that, after all, what she had chosen to do? Maybe personal survival *was* the only option. Certainly many of those in this country who had been noble or foolish enough to make a public stand against the guerrillas, the narcos, the paramilitaries—even the government, many whispered—now lay in their graves, gunned down on their doorsteps, shot in the back emerging from church, victims of a car bomb or a tossed grenade or a passing motorcyclist with an AK-47 or Uzi machine pistol blazing.

Snatching up her knapsack, Julie pushed the bathroom door open with more force than necessary. Wasn't it enough to live a decent life that didn't hurt anyone else, to aim for the top in your own profession, and maybe even in the process make some small contribution to society? After all, if the world wasn't willing to be saved, why break your heart trying?

# FOUR

WHEN JULIE EMERGED FROM the terminal, the ranchers' wives were leaving, trailing behind their baggage cart toward the Fairchild, now taxiing out onto the runway. Julie headed toward the DC4, matching the registration number on the tail with Kenny's instructions in her hand.

Not that there was any doubt this was her party. Her professional colleagues were unmistakable. They milled around with the slightly hungry expression of a reporter after a story, loudly asking questions of each other since there was no one else available. Off to one side, Julie recognized the familiar features of a CNN anchorman talking earnestly into a TV camera, the DC4 carefully positioned beyond his shoulder. Their departure would be on the midday news.

Other well-known faces in the media world were there as well. Reuters. Associated Press. And not just North Americans. Julie picked out German and French from the babble as well as Spanish, and even what must be Japanese or Mandarin from a pair of Asian reporters. It drove home more than ever just how extensive were the connections that Norm Hutchens still wielded in the world of journalism—and just how fortunate she was to be on this flight.

Especially since it would seem that other editors thought like her godfather. She couldn't see a single other woman represented among that swarm of press members.

No, that wasn't true.

Julie turned her head at the click of high heels on the concrete runway, her eyes narrowing as she recognized the latecomer hurrying up to the group, an enormous handbag over her shoulder, a wheeled travel bag in tow. She had changed her tailored business suit for a long, flowing skirt, but the stiletto heels were just as high, her bored expression just as haughty. Behind her, a burly black man balanced a video camera on one shoulder, his own travel bag over the other.

The woman checked as her line of vision crossed Julie. She swept an impatient glance over the crowd of reporters, then walked over to Julie, offering her a curt nod as she approached.

"You were on the flight last night, weren't you? I didn't realize you were part of this mission. You know how it is . . . you let people find out who you are, you never get a moment's peace."

It was the closest she'd get to an apology, Julie recognized. "No problem, I understand." She held out her right hand. "I guess if we're going to be together on this mission, introductions are in order. Julie Baker. *Our Earth*, if you know the magazine. We're with the World Conservation Institute."

The other woman barely touched Julie's fingertips. "Sondra Kharrazi. NBC." She clearly considered any further identification unnecessary. Maybe she was right. Now that she'd been given the woman's name, Julie immediately realized why she'd looked so familiar. Julie didn't normally waste time watching live coverage, preferring to download the news on-line. But she had seen those haughty features on an occasional morning newscast.

The tall brunette cast an irritated glance at her watch. "Aren't we supposed to be boarding? They told us ten o'clock, and it's 10:05. And where is the UN team? All I see is the press."

"I haven't seen anyone but us," Julie told her. "Except for the military." She gestured to a detail of soldiers standing guard around the plane, a precaution in this country that Julie appreciated.

"Well, at least we can catch the arrival on tape. William, get the camera ready." As the black cameraman removed the lens cap from his camera, Sondra glanced around, her long-lashed eyes narrowing as she surveyed the rest of the press corps. "I see CNN sent Tom Chaney. Hogging the limelight, as usual. And there's Andy Rodriguez from the *Miami Herald*. They say he's single again. Hey!"

The beautiful features suddenly lost their peevish expression. "Now there's someone worth checking out. No, at three o'clock. Who do you think he's representing—the Moral Majority?"

Julie didn't need Sondra's sharp elbow in the ribs to pick out the object of the reporter's interest. By anyone's standards, the man merited a second glance. He was big, especially next to the Asian reporter with whom he was carrying on an animated conversation. Not overweight, but solid, like one of those Olympic skiers or an ex-football player who hadn't yet lost his conditioning, and well over six feet tall. He might have been anywhere from Sondra's own thirtyish to forty-plus, but he was so blond, it was impossible to detect any silver strands blending with the flaxen paleness of his trim cut. Nice tan, though, without the pinkish overtones that so often went with that kind of fairness.

But it wasn't the man's Nordic good looks that had caught Sondra's attention and now drew Julie's fascinated gaze. It was the book he carried cradled under one arm, a massive thing with three-inch gold lettering that screamed "Holy Scriptures" clear across the runway.

"Moral Majority or not, he's cute!" Sondra went on. "I could die for that smile."

It was quite a smile. The man practically sparkled good humor, his blue eyes twinkling merrily as he bent his head to something his shorter companion was saying, his show of perfect teeth one that invited the rest of the world to share his enjoyment. At any moment, Julie expected him to throw back his head and let out a hearty "Ho! ho! ho!"

"I've never seen him," Julie admitted. "He's certainly not from one of the major networks."

"So do you think he speaks English? He looks Dutch or German."

"Well, 'Holy Scriptures' is certainly English."

As though he'd caught their remarks, the man lifted his head from his companion and looked straight at Sondra and Julie. His smile broadened into a grin so infectious that Julie found her lips twitching to meet it. Evidently taking her response as an invitation, the man murmured something to his companion and took a step in their direction.

Whatever his intentions, they were distracted by a sudden surge forward from the press corps. Alerted by the shifting of cameras, Julie swung around in time to catch a cavalcade sweeping through the gates of the base. There were three limousines, each flanked by an escort of military police on motorcycles. A pair of troop transports brought up the rear. The entire parade swept onto the runway, coming to a screeching halt only meters from where Julie was standing.

"Hail the conquering chiefs," Julie heard a press member comment behind her.

She swallowed a laugh. The better known members of the press corps might dispute the assessment, but it was clear the real VIPs of this expedition had now arrived. The security alone was impressive. A detachment of what looked to be Colombian Special Forces in green berets and BDUs—battle dress uniforms—jumped down from the army trucks and fanned out around the cavalcade. The contrast with her own arrival was striking. *In other words, no big deal if the guerrillas pick off a few news reporters!*

Soldiers hurried to the doors of the limousines. A pair of Colombian military officers stepped down from the first, their uniforms displaying an impressive amount of gold braid. They were followed by a handful of civilians, including two who wore pilots' uniforms. A party of three—two men and a woman—emerged from the second limousine, all wearing the white coats of a doctor or lab technician. They circled immediately to the rear of the vehicle where a detail of soldiers was already unloading boxes.

The third limousine drew a gasp from Sondra Kharrazi at Julie's side. "I don't believe it! William, get that on tape!"

The two men climbing out of the third vehicle also wore military dress, though their fatigues and combat caps were the mottled green and brown of camouflage rather than the plain khaki of the others. Unlike the rest of the Colombian military personnel, neither was armed, though they both carried empty pistol holsters at their belts. Nor did they display any of the gold braid or insignia that adorned the officers in the first limousine. Still, their sole occupancy of the limo, and the detail of soldiers who rushed in to flank them, certainly signaled some kind of VIP.

Sondra grabbed at Julie's arm, her long nails digging into Julie's skin as she whispered excitedly, "Do you know who those two men are? They're FARC leaders—guerrillas!"

"Are you kidding?" Julie demanded incredulously. She was already taking mental notes.

"No, I'm not! See the shorter one there, the older one? I did an interview with him a few months back down in the demilitarized zone. He's their PR guy. Manuel Flores, he calls himself."

Flores was no taller than Julie, with the barrel-chested frame of a heavily Indian *mestizo* mix. He was stoop-shouldered and no longer young, though the sleek blackness of his hair showed none of the telltale gray that plagued those of Caucasian descent. He looked more like a rural schoolteacher or someone's favorite grandpa than a terrorist or even the soldier he claimed to be. But there was something about him, a smugness, that roused Julie's immediate aversion. He was practically strutting as he paraded from the limousine toward the plane, raising his hand with a benevolent smile to the cameras flashing all around, as though he and all his comrades were some kind of heroes instead of killers and criminals.

"They love getting themselves on the news." Sondra dug a cordless microphone from her handbag. "Though I've never seen the younger one, I'd love to have him on the other end of a mike!"

Julie followed her nod, and her caustic thoughts caught in her throat. Unlike his older companion, Flores, this man fit all her preconceived stereotypes of a guerrilla. He looked to be somewhere in his upper twenties, and stood head and shoulders above his companion, though that still made him only medium height by American standards. His coloring was much lighter as well, closer to Julie's own olive complexion. His hair was dark brown rather than black, worn shoulder-length in a tangle of curls that might have looked effeminate were it not for the hard, definitely masculine planes of his face and at least a week of unshaven stubble.

But those weren't the differences that drew Julie's attention. It was the ease with which he wore his military gear, like a second skin rather than the dress-up costume it seemed on his companion. The baggy combat fatigues did little to disguise his superb physical conditioning. And his peculiar, stiff-backed, ball-of-the-foot stride was something even Julie's inexperienced eye recognized for what it was. Despite the nonregulation hairstyle and half-grown beard, he was no *campesino* dressed up in a stolen army uniform. He'd had military training—and lots of it.

The two guerrillas were heading toward the DC4. Julie lost her companion as the NBC correspondent pushed in front of her cameraman, mike in hand.

Tom Chaney, the CNN correspondent, was as usual out ahead of the pack, his mike thrust into the path of the FARC leaders, his cameraman nearby jostling a heavy camcorder over his shoulder. "Excuse me! I'm told you are representatives of the Revolutionary Armed Forces of Colombia. Do you speak English? Do you have a message you would like to share with our viewers this morning?"

For once, it did him no good. A soldier placed a hand over the lens of the camera, and another elbowed the correspondent from his path with only minimal civility. The two guerrillas didn't miss a stride, Manuel Flores still waving and smiling, his younger companion running an indifferent, almost bored gaze across the pack of shoving, jostling foreigners.

No, not indifferent.

As the guerrilla's slow scan crossed her own curious gaze, Julie felt the shock all the way down into her toes. That was anger blazing behind those narrowed eyes—though the hard planes of his face showed no expression at all. The party had just drawn abreast of her when Julie saw him bend his head to mutter something inaudible to his shorter, older companion. His companion was not so discreet.

"You are being concerned for nothing," came his audible reply as the two guerrillas strode past. "After all, what safer place is there for us than before the cameras of the world. The *militares* will not dare to try anything with such eyes on them. Besides, should we not take advantage of any opportunity to shout our cause to the world? The media are our friends even if their governments are not."

The younger guerrilla was clearly unhappy about this mission, did not want to be here, and—unlike his companion—did not appreciate the cameras that were recording his every step for the world to see. *Probably got his face on a wanted poster somewhere!*

The occupants of the other two limousines were making their way toward the plane now, the soldiers holding back the press corps so they could get through. The two groups converged at the foot of the roll-away stairs that led up to the open door of the DC4. A slightly built man in the international business uniform of suit and tie separated himself from the second group, the two Colombian officers at his heels. As he climbed the roll-away stairs to the platform at the top, the TV crews pressed forward with a babble of shouted questions. Ignoring them, the young man paused to adjust a clip-on microphone before turning to address his audience.

"Ladies and gentlemen, if you'd give me your attention for the next few minutes, my name is Bill Shidler. I'm the political/economic officer for the American embassy here in Bogotá. It's our pleasure to be of service to you this morning."

He didn't look as though it were a pleasure. He seemed harried and tired, with the beginning lines of worry across his forehead and down both sides of his mouth.

"I know we're running a little late, but we'll be boarding in the next few minutes. However, I've been instructed first to make a few announcements on behalf of the embassy. To begin with, if you want to save your film, we will *not* be making any further press statements than we've already made. At this point, we know no more than you do."

When this statement was greeted with a skeptical silence, he cleared his throat. "Okay, then. First of all, we would like to express our appreciation to the representatives of the *Fuerzas Armadas Revolucionarias de Colombia* who have traveled here to escort us into their territory."

The two guerrillas might not have understood the English, but the name of their movement elicited another beaming smile and wave for the cameras from Manuel Flores and impassive silence from his younger companion.

"We would like to extend our appreciation and welcome as well to the United Nations forensic unit who have consented to be part of this operation—uh, humanitarian mission"—he nodded toward the party in white coats—"along with our own State Department team who will be assisting in this investigation into the deaths of our citizens." A briefcase-toting pair from the first limo raised their hands in unsmiling acknowledgment.

"Also to the Colombian government, which has graciously undertaken your travel arrangements into the demilitarized zone." This time his nod included both the pilots and the Colombian military officers who had accompanied him.

"And of course those of you of the press who have traveled here today to chronicle the events of the following hours for the citizens of your respective countries. However . . ."

He cleared his throat again, this time louder. "However, I've been asked to make it very clear that neither the presence of the media nor that of any other civilians on this mission is sponsored by the U.S. State Department nor supported by this embassy. The United States government does not maintain diplomatic relations with any guerrilla movement. This means we aren't in any position to guarantee the safety of private citizens who choose to participate. Our State Department has, in fact, issued an advisory warning against the travel of American citizens anywhere in Colombia. In view of this, I have here a waiver"—he held up a pale-blue form—"that each of you will be asked to sign before boarding, releasing both governments from any responsibility for your decision to ignore that warning. If anyone should wish now to reconsider their participation . . ."

*And blah, blah, blah!* Julie's own restless shifting echoed the impatience around her. They'd all been through this routine before. The idea, as any reporter knew, wasn't to discourage anyone from the trip, but to cover the State Department's posterior. If the media allowed themselves to be spooked by every embassy advisory warning, not much news around the world would ever be reported. But then, the media had always been out on the front line of war and disaster where the State Department feared to tread.

"I also have here a preliminary press release from the State Department and what background data I'm authorized to release to you at this time. The flight will last approximately ninety minutes. The plane will remain on the ground in San Ignacio until the United Nations forensic unit is satisfied. We expect that to be sometime this evening.

"Okay, then, we're now ready to board. Of course, the use of electronic devices will not be allowed on this flight, so if you have last-minute press releases to file"—for the first time there was a glint of humor in his gloomy expression—"I would do so at this time."

AP and Reuters were the first to slap their cell phones open. Babble erupted again as reporters speaking a half-dozen languages scrambled frantically to slant the zero they had just received into a news item. Beyond the circle of soldiers, Julie spotted Sondra talking into the camera balanced on William's shoulder. Julie, responsible for a magazine article rather than the evening's news, didn't bother to unearth her phone. Instead, she chose to beat the rush, filing forward to scribble her name across the blue waiver form and receive her briefing file, then strolling leisurely up the stairs and onto the plane.

The two guerrilla leaders had already boarded, and so had the State Department representatives who had accompanied Bill Shidler. They were clustered together in the front row of the plane, though neither side gave any sign of noticing the other's existence. The UN team was still filing to the rear of the plane. Through the open door to the cockpit, Julie could see the two pilots.

Julie selected a window seat just in front of the wing. The plane filled up quickly behind her, others abandoning last-minute communication with their news bureaus in a rush for good seats. The CNN crew grabbed two full rows across from Julie, their correspondent Tom Chaney staking out one window seat while the cameraman took the other.

It suddenly occurred to Julie that she hadn't seen any locals among the media teams. But then, the Colombians weren't foolish enough to put their heads into a noose, and their journalists had been a prime guerrilla target for years.

Not that in this case there was any danger. The FARC had personally guaranteed their safe passage—an assurance that was less of a comfort to Julie than it might be to others on board.

Her eyes strayed to the mottled green of two combat caps visible over the seat backs only two rows ahead. She tried to forget the anger she'd sensed in the younger guerrilla's eyes.

"This seat taken?"

Julie glanced up at the terse question to see her last night's seatmate, Sondra Kharrazi. Without waiting for an answer, the NBC correspondent gestured for her burly cameraman to lift her carry-on into the overhead compartment. She glanced around fretfully as Julie snatched the folder Bill Shidler had given her out of the other seat.

"What I wanted was a window seat. Look at Tom Chaney over there. Two of them. Like they need more than one camera!"

Sondra threw a pointed glance at Julie's window, but when Julie didn't rise to the hint, she sank reluctantly into the aisle seat, dug a paperback from her handbag, and buried her nose in it without another word. Julie caught a glimpse of the cover. A romance novel. So her seatmate no longer felt a need to impress Julie with her intellectual qualifications. But maybe that wasn't being fair. Maybe Sondra had already done her homework.

Speaking of which . . .

Julie dutifully opened the State Department folder, but once they were in the air, she couldn't keep her eyes on the page before her. By daylight, the view of Bogotá was much as Julie had visualized it the night before, the urban sprawl maybe a little bigger, but the surrounding patchwork of dairy farms and wheat fields and the pine forests sweeping up to snowcapped peaks were as beautiful as she remembered.

Julie swallowed repeatedly as the plane rose higher, the drop in cabin pressure pushing against her eardrums. Below, a glacier glittered blinding white under the morning sun. Then the DC4 skimmed through a pass and they were dropping down the other side, the green flanks of the Andes tumbling away beneath them to open grasslands spotted with wandering herds of Brahmin cattle. The DC4 was flying low enough for Julie to make out the tiled roofs of farmhouses perched above fields and coffee planta-tions set so steeply on the mountainsides that a favorite Colombian folktale was of the family cow falling out of the pasture.

Tucked into mountain canyons where no fumigation plane or helicopter could reach were signs of a less innocuous crop—bright red fields of pop-pies, whose byproduct, heroin, was beginning to rival cocaine as Colombia's most profitable export.

A thin silver line snaked along a ridge below—the pipeline built by multinational oil companies to carry oil from the petroleum-rich lowlands north to Bogotá. Julie grimaced at this reminder of why she was on this plane.

Then the plane banked away from the mountain range. Here the grassy plains with its cattle ranches intermingled with patches of uncleared scrub jungle. The ranches grew more scattered and the patches of scrub jungle larger and taller until at some undistinguishable point, they were flying over an unbroken sea of rainforest.

This was country Julie knew well. The planet's most majestic hardwoods towering high above the rest of the jungle canopy. Lazy, wandering rivers that connected the scattered villages far more efficiently than any dirt track. Dugout canoes and flat-bottomed barges and, along the riverbanks, bamboo shacks built on ungainly stilts far out over the water.

Julie swallowed hard again, though her eardrums had long since adjusted to the change in altitude. The countryside down there meant nothing to her now, of course. But it was more unsettling than she'd expected to see childhood memories unrolling under the wings of the plane.

Tearing her eyes from the window, she fastened them on the first page of Bill Shidler's briefing. *A jungle is a jungle is a jungle. You've seen plenty of them in other countries, so what's the big deal?*

The first article in the folder was a field report from C-PAP. Julie skimmed through it quickly. She was already well acquainted with the project that had ended in the death of three of its members. The Coalition for the Preservation of Amazonic Peoples was actually a conglomerate of several of the more extreme environmentalist groups, their mission statement, according to this report, being the preservation of the Amazon Basin's remaining ethnic groups from the contamination of outside cultures.

Julie grinned as she read that piece of creative writing. Anyone who'd ever had anything to do with the Coalition knew that C-PAP's real passion was the planet's untouched expanses of rainforest, not the scattered handfuls of human beings living within their margins. The advantage of championing the Amazonic tribes, rather than the thousands of other ethnic groups living in equal misery around the planet, was that the jungle tribes were both few in numbers and could invariably lay claim at some point in their uncharted history to vast tracts of virgin countryside, the competition having either died off or long since melted into the *mestizo* gene pool.

Julie had enjoyed the C-PAP personnel she'd interviewed from time to time. But they made no secret of the fact that they were a lot more interested in the four-legged creatures running around their precious rainforests than in any two-legged ones.

"There's plenty of humans," one C-PAP activist had told Julie acidly last year when she'd been covering their demonstration outside Triton headquarters. "You don't see them in any danger of extinction."

The World Conservation Institute was much more balanced—at least in the estimation of its members. However much it might wish matters to be otherwise, WCI recognized that the conservation of the earth's remaining resources had to be balanced with the needs of the human beings who shared the planet. You just couldn't ask Third World populations living in grinding poverty to selflessly starve to death so the environmentalists could have another unspoiled habitat to study. Especially when those same environmentalists drove new cars, lived in houses replete with modern conveniences, and rejoiced in the benefits of a top-notch education—all products of a society that had grown rich through the rape of its own resources and those of other nations.

WCI didn't waste time demonstrating outside petroleum headquarters and logging sites. It chose to concentrate its efforts on what it *could* do rather than on what it couldn't, negotiating with local governments to create national parks and wildlife reserves while at the same time working together with other aid organizations to teach the locals how to increase productivity on their present land and how to develop their remaining resources in a way that would minimize negative impact on the environment. They had done so competently enough that any recommendation from WCI was taken seriously by both the U.S. Congress and the United Nations.

Colombia, though, was one place where WCI was in accord with the more extreme activists groups. Hence their present alliance with C-PAP. The Amazon Basin of southern Colombia and northern Brazil contained the largest remaining primeval rainforest on the planet. It was home not only to a host of unique plant and animal species, but to some of the oldest remaining hardwoods in the world.

And there was no reason for the rainforest's destruction. Colombia had plenty of undeveloped territory that could be ceded to colonists. WCI had been working with the Colombian government for the past two years to have most of the remaining rainforest declared a natural reserve (it was no coincidence that C-PAP's claim on behalf of their present protégés, the I'paa tribe, covered exactly that same territory).

Then Triton Petroleum had discovered oil on the very edge of the proposed reserve. Lots of oil. Enough to keep the whole of North America on the road for a year, if you believed Triton's estimates. The Colombian government was naturally interested in the proposed financial bonanza. They immediately rescinded the Ministry of Environment's tentative approval of the nature reserve and issued a permit to Triton to conduct seismic operations to determine the extent of the oil reserves. WCI's warnings that the environmental costs would more than offset the projected profits had fallen on deliberately deaf ears.

Julie knew plenty about those costs since she'd done the research for an editorial Norm Hutchens had written about the reversal. Triton claimed—with some justification—that the environmental impact of drilling operations was minimal beyond the boundaries of the drilling sites themselves. And they were perfectly willing to sign any kind of settlement to restore such sites to their original state.

But it wasn't the drilling sites themselves that had the most negative impact on the environment. It was getting that oil to market. Triton's projected pipeline ran smack through the middle of the proposed nature reserve. Regardless of the oil company's assurances, environmentalists had planet-wide experience with what happened when a pipeline ran through a fragile ecosystem. Constructing a pipeline meant clearing the land and building roads and maintenance camps. Villages would spring up along the new roads as colonists moved in to take advantage of opened-up land. Uncontrolled development would spread from either side of the pipeline like a canker until the nibbled-away edges met the rotted-out center, and the ecosystem was no more.

There was also the political unrest to add to the scenario. Blowing up pipelines was a favorite pastime of the guerrillas, an environmental disaster that had already cost the Colombians more than Triton's ambitious proposal could ever earn them. Beyond costly damages to the pipeline itself, millions of barrels of oil had been dumped onto the ground and waterways, poisoning the soil and animal life. To make matters worse, Triton's proposed drilling sites were not only within the threatened rainforest but perilously close to the demilitarized zone. The guerrillas weren't going to take the intrusion of multinationals lying down. Which meant not only the inevitable spills and environmental contamination, but a greater military presence moving into the area to protect the pipeline—a further erosion of the fragile balance of the ecosystem.

Julie shuffled through the rest of the folder. There was a history of the I'paa people, written by the murdered anthropologist Dr. Winifred Renken, a press release detailing what little was known on the deaths of the three activists, and a State Department warning on travel in Colombia. Nothing of interest.

Tucking the file into her knapsack, Julie straightened up to find Sondra Kharrazi's eyes on her, plucked brows arched high.

"You actually read all that stuff? Why bother? I haven't read a briefing myself in years. That's what researchers and staff writers are for."

Julie didn't bother enlightening the NBC correspondent as to the gap in their respective professional positions.

"Though I'm going to have to do some work on this one," the other woman went on fretfully. "No matter how much I screamed, they wouldn't give me more than two seats on the flight. One of the top news teams in the world, and they barely get my cameraman on board. Forget a script writer or even a hairdresser!"

Her morose gaze roved across the cabin. "I see Tom Chaney over there has that fabulous make-up artist of his along. *And* his full camera crew. What does CNN have that the rest of us don't?"

Another question best left unexplored.

Pulling out a powder compact from her purse, the NBC correspondent carried out a meticulous inspection in its tiny mirror. "I wonder if he'd make a deal. I can't go on the air like this, can I?" she demanded, shaping her full mouth into a pout as she outlined it with blood-red lipstick.

Julie made a noncommittal sound she hoped could be interpreted as sympathetic, a feeling she was having a hard time conjuring up. She could just hear some of Norm Hutchens' more caustic observations on the types who figured all there was to journalism was smiling into the camera and reading a teleprompter. Why had this woman bothered to come? With a story like this, there must have been dozens of NBC reporters who would have jumped at the chance.

The answer came almost immediately.

"So!" Sondra cut short an inspection of her nails—long, sharp, and the same blood-red as her lipstick—to slant Julie another condescending glance. "Did someone send you down here—or were you dumb enough to volunteer?" She swept on before Julie could answer. "You wouldn't have caught me dead on this trip if it wasn't for all this C-PAP stuff."

Sondra gave her face a dissatisfied glance in her compact.

Julie's eyebrows went up. "C-PAP? That's right—you told me you'd been in this area before. I didn't realize you were involved with the environmental movement."

Sondra hardly looked the sort to be involved in environmental activism—or any other outdoor activity.

"Well, you have to have a cause in this business." She snapped her compact shut. "And rainforests are in. C-PAP once asked me to do some interviews with that tribe of theirs. It sounded good on my résumé—save the planet and all that." She gave a theatrical shudder. "Though I'd have never taken them up on it if I'd known how dirty the place was going to be. And those Indians!"

She lowered her voice. "Do you know what's weird? I was supposed to be on that trip with Dr. Renken. She wanted me to do an interview with that tribal chief she went to see. Only I came down with Montezuma's revenge the night before."

Her shudder this time wasn't feigned. "And now they're wanting me to ID the bodies. Can you believe it? They said it would save a seat on the flight. And my producer agreed! Just because I spent a week with them down in that filthy little base camp of theirs! All I can say is, I'd better get that triple hazard pay I put in for. And they'd better be right that this is no big deal with the guerrillas. Surely that embassy geek wasn't serious about just dumping us down there if something goes wrong!"

Julie eyed her seatmate. For all her posturing, for once the NBC correspondent seemed sincere in her concern, if only for her own skin.

"Oh, he was serious, all right," she assured her, not without some malice. "But I wouldn't worry too much. The whole point of this mission is for the FARC to convince the world—on international TV—that they're fine, upstanding citizens who wouldn't dream of killing three foreign environmentalists."

Julie's glance went again to those two olive green caps. "Whatever they might be capable of, they're not going to want to spoil their little PR exercise by letting anything happen to the very people they're hoping will persuade the world that they're really pretty nice guys after all. Not, at any rate, while those cameras are pointed in their direction."

Julie broke off as she caught the NBC correspondent staring at her with unexpected shrewdness.

"Well, that's more than I know, and I spent a week down there! Where did you learn so much about what makes these people tick?"

"I know the area," Julie answered briefly. She was spared any further explanation as Bill Shidler entered the cabin from the cockpit.

Fiddling with his lapel mike, he announced, "Ladies and gentlemen, we're about a half-hour from San Ignacio. And we're now flying over an area you might find of interest in relation to our present oper—uh, mission. Directly below us is the town of San José. This is one of Colombia's key outposts in the war against drugs, as well as headquarters to the United States government's counter-narcotics programs in this region."

Sondra Kharrazi looked eager for more information; whatever journalistic instincts she possessed were clearly aroused. But as the political officer droned on, she tuned him out and craned over Julie's shoulder to look out the window.

Julie herself studied the landscape below with interest. She'd already taken note of San José in the research files she'd downloaded the night before, recognizing the name as a sleepy jungle village she'd visited with her parents as a child. But she saw nothing familiar in the sprawling military base that lay below the plane's wings. The gravel airstrip where her father had once landed his Cessna was now a modern asphalt runway capable of landing a fair-sized jet. Huge barracks, a fleet of army vehicles, and a scattering of aircraft and helicopters were visible as well.

But that wasn't the biggest change. In Julie's childhood, the rainforest had stretched in an unbroken green carpet all the way from San José to San Ignacio. Now, as they left the military base behind, Julie could see that the jungle canopy was pocked with holes, as though war or some bizarre disease had attacked it.

Most prominent were the cleared patches where nothing grew but a low shrub. Other clearings were brown and parched, with nothing growing at all. Blackened char marked more recent slash-and-burn operations that had left centuries-old hardwoods tumbled on top of each other like so many toothpicks.

What on earth has happened here?

She soon found out. Bill Shidler continued his lecture. "Down there in San José, members of our 7th Special Operations Group out of Fort Bragg, North Carolina—known as Green Berets to the general public"—he actually permitted himself a slight smile—"have carried out an outstanding training program for Colombia's new counter-narcotics battalion. The spray planes you might have noticed parked at the base are part of a secondary U.S. aid program that eliminates illegal coca and poppy fields with a gentle, biodegradable herbicide."

As though on cue, Julie caught a flash of motion out the window to her left. It was another plane, a small fixed-wing like the crop dusters still used in rural America, flying well below the flight pattern of the DC4. The plane dropped low over an open field of bushes. In its trail, a mist caught the morning sun, its droplets glinting diamond-bright before drifting down over the foliage. Farther off over the jungle, another spray plane dropped down below the tree line. Hovering far above both, Julie spotted the dull green of a Huey combat helicopter—their watchdog.

*Gentle, right!* Julie swallowed back nausea. She'd read the reports about what was happening to the rainforest in this area. But seeing was vastly different from reading. As an American citizen who hated drug abuse as much as anyone, she could appreciate the need to do just what was being done down there. As an environmentalist, she felt sick.

And for every coca field out there scorched brown with herbicide, the *cocaleros* would simply retreat further into the jungle to slash and burn a few more hectares of rainforest and plant more coca. Maybe these programs were necessary. She was no political expert to know. But the result was a destruction of the region's fragile ecosystem that not even the oil companies could match.

Boom!

The explosion of sound rocked Julie back into her seat.

IT WASN'T UNTIL BILL SHIDLER grabbed at the nearest seat that Julie realized the blast had rocked the plane as well. A shudder went through the aircraft, and the engines perceptibly slowed. Bill Shidler dove into the cockpit. Pandemonium erupted in the cabin.

"We're hit!"

"What's going on?"

Already the DC4 was recovering its equilibrium. With a quiver like a dog shaking off an unexpected ice-bath, the plane settled back into its flight path, the powerful prop engines returning to their normal purr. Spinning around back to the window, Julie spotted the aftermath of the explosion—a plume of smoke hanging above a clearing. Beyond the dispersing cloud, she could see a crop duster spiraling skyward.

Bill Shidler emerged from the cockpit, looking flushed and annoyed. Holding up his hand for silence, he announced, "There's nothing to be concerned about. It would seem the coca growers have launched a SAM attack on one of the spray planes. This does happen on occasion. However, our own flight path lies well above range—"

Bang!

This new explosion didn't rock the plane, but it effectively interrupted Shidler's reassurance. Half the passengers were now out of their seats, craning to get a sight—and video shot—of the air battle. Julie traced the blast by its smoke cloud, much higher this time and close enough to the crop duster to throw the little plane sideways.

The spray plane fell in an out-of-control spin toward the jungle canopy. Julie's feet were pressed against the cabin floor as she mentally urged that nose to pull up. It was brushing the upper levels of the jungle canopy when at last it leveled out and began an agonizingly slow ascent. Julie let out a breath she hadn't known she'd been holding. This was war! Where was that watchdog Huey?

Finally it appeared, coming in high over the edge of the clearing, close enough for Julie to see the open door, the cylinder shape of its enormous field gun spraying a rain of bullets below.

Another explosion erupted directly beneath the helicopter. The gun fell silent, and the Huey banked away, leaving the crop duster weaving a zigzag circuit like a lost sheep.

But more help was on the way. Another helicopter, no Vietnam-era Huey this time, but long and sleek and gray. Julie recognized it from her research. A Black Hawk, an integral part of the U.S. government's newest counter-narcotics aid package. The cabin of the DC4 broke into cheers as it came in low and fast over the treetops. Julie's glance was drawn to the two FARC representatives at the front of the plane. The younger guerrilla was raised half out of his seat, his body lines tense as he bent to observe the action below.

*What is he thinking?* Julie wondered. After all, those had to be his people down there firing at the planes and being shot at in return. But his un-shaven profile revealed no expression, and Julie couldn't see his eyes.

She glanced around the plane's interior. Sondra was out of her seat barking orders to her cameraman, who had managed to squeeze in next to a window. Julie's eye fell on a blond head just a few rows behind. Sondra's Bible-toting hunk. He hadn't bothered to join in the jostling but was watch-ing his fellow passengers as though fascinated by their frenetic activity.

His glance crossed Julie's, and his handsome features relaxed into a broad smile, as though they were long acquaintances instead of strangers. Julie's lips twitched in automatic response, and she wiggled her fingers in ac-knowledgment of the eye contact before turning her gaze back to the Black Hawk.

The battle outside drove the man instantly from her mind. The DC4 should have been beyond the range of the fire fight by now, but instead it seemed to be making a lazy curve around the clearing. Two more smoke plumes in the direction they had been heading gave a possible explanation.

The Black Hawk was coming in low across the clearing, but no gunfire issued from its open doorway. Julie thought she saw why—an odd down-ward tilt in the nose of the chopper that kept it from leveling off to shoot. Its nose still dangling, the combat helicopter rose out of range. The crop duster, still unable to gain height, seemed to flutter over the clearing. The Huey dropped again to offer cover, its own machine gun blazing.

Then it happened.

The blast was close enough to the DC4 to set it rocking. With horror, Julie watched the Huey disintegrate before her eyes, the pieces raining down to the fields below. Even in her shock, she saw the younger guerrilla's fist clench shut two rows ahead. *Triumph?*

The cabin fell silent. Bill Shidler emerged again from the cockpit, this time looking pale and grim.

"Please don't be alarmed; there's no danger," he reiterated. "We're well out of range of any ground armaments the rebel forces in the region are known to possess. However, in light of a continuing air battle that seems to be going on at several points in this zone, we've deemed it prudent not to proceed further until an all-clear is given. We'll be setting down at the base in San José. We don't expect the delay to be long."

There were a few grumbles as the DC4 turned back but not many. A story was a story, wherever it came from, and across the aisle Julie could hear the CNN crew already discussing how to turn to the best advantage the last quarter-hour's video footage.

Moments later, buildings flashed by as the plane's wheels touched down and the hydraulic brakes came on. As the DC4 slowed, the parked aircraft Julie had seen from the air came into view. Behind them rose two enormous steel tanks.

Army trucks and soldiers were boiling onto the runway, but not to welcome their surprise guests. As the DC4 taxied around to draw up beside the other aircraft, Julie spotted a crop duster coming in over the other end of the runway. A fire truck raced past the DC4, its siren wailing.

Sounds could be heard outside the door of the plane. Bill Shidler twisted the wheel that held the door shut. As it swung open, a man dressed in combat fatigues ducked his head to step inside. He gave Bill Shidler a curt nod, then strode to the front of the cabin. He wasn't young, his crew cut iron-gray, the grooves around mouth and eyes cut deep. But his body under the battle uniform was as lean and fit as any recruit fresh out of boot camp. He surveyed his visitors before speaking, his gaze lingering unsmilingly on the cameras the CNN cameramen already had to their shoulders, his narrow mouth tightening as he took in the FARC representatives in the front row.

"Welcome to San José. I'm Colonel Jeff Thornton, Joint Task Force commander for U.S. operations in this region. Sorry for the trouble, but we're calling in our aircraft right now. Things will calm down as soon as they're out of the air. So if you'll just sit tight, you'll be on your way in about half an hour."

The American officer turned to duck back out the plane door, but Bill Shidler put out a hand to stop him. "Uh, Jeff." Shidler cast a quick glance around the cabin, then murmured too low for Julie to hear anything but the phrases, ". . . passengers . . . amenities not in service . . ."

Colonel Thornton let out an exasperated snort. "So your bathroom isn't working! Okay, I guess we can handle that."

He swung around to face the cabin. "Ladies and gentlemen, if any of you need to . . . uh, stretch your legs, you'll find restrooms and some refreshment in the first building to your left. My men will direct you there as you disembark. Just be on the alert for our call to re-board. We'd hate to have to leave any of you behind." There was no relaxation in the uncompromising line of his mouth to indicate this was a joke.

*And if that isn't an enthusiastic welcome!* Julie thought with amusement, abandoning her knapsack in her seat and filing down the aisle after Sondra Kharrazi. The two guerrilla representatives hadn't moved from their seats, nor the State Department team that had stationed itself beside them.

None of the news crews had remained on board. What reporter could resist the chance to poke around a restricted military base? Julie was as interested in the place as any of them. San José—a name familiar to her—had cropped up repeatedly in the Internet files she'd downloaded the night before, and she'd done a little digging.

Out on the runway, a squad of soldiers was directing the passengers across the runway toward a whitewashed cinder-block building, but Julie didn't follow. Instead, she lingered in the shade of the DC4. Off to her left, the crop duster she'd seen coming in had taxied to a stop near the two steel tanks. The fire engine was drawn up beside it and soldiers swarmed around, but the little plane showed no visible damage. Another spray plane was just coming in for a landing at the far end of the runway.

The view to her right held more interest. Behind a chain-link fence, a series of metallic rectangular screens were tilted at a slightly upward slant. An interesting array of protrusions and metal tubing performed functions Julie could only guess at, and the whole thing looked like a futuristic version of the old drive-in movie theaters that she knew only from TV reruns from her parents' generation. But Julie knew what it was. A radar installation.

"Just what do you think you're doing here, Shidler?"

Julie started as the angry words sounded directly above her head. Glancing up, she spotted two men at the top of the movable stairway next to the plane. The last of the news crews were now trickling across the runway, and neither the political officer nor Colonel Thornton seemed to be aware of the eavesdropper to their conversation.

"I figured communications was pulling my leg when they said you were landing here with a planeload of civilians. And in the middle of the mess going on right now! Just who in tarnation made that harebrained call?"

"I did, as it happens." Shidler sounded less sure of himself than he did in front of the reporters. "What else was I supposed to do? They were shooting out there, and I've got a whole planeload of VIPs on my hands. If something happened to them, it'd be my neck."

"Yeah, well, you know what I think of that too. You guys are crazy bringing civilians into the zone right now, and I told your boss so yesterday when he called. Why you State Department johnnies even bother asking my opinion, I don't know, when you never pay any attention!"

"Your superiors happen to disagree with you," Shidler said stiffly. "This is a vital mission, and they judged the risks to be minimal."

"Minimal! Is that what they call a bunch of SAMs in your face these days? For that matter, what were you doing overflying the eradication project anyway? Didn't you know that's just asking for trouble?"

"We judged it safest to stay in San José air space as long as possible. After all, you're the closest American presence in the zone. And we made it here all right, as it turned out. Look, Jeff, I don't know why you're getting so hot under the collar." Shidler was beginning to sound heated himself. "We ran our flight plan by SouthCom. And you authorized this landing yourself!"

"Sure, what else was I supposed to do with your wheels practically on the runway? You'd have been a whole lot safer to keep as far out of our space as possible, as I'd have told either SouthCom or your people if anyone had bothered running that flight plan by me. And I can tell you, the Colombians aren't happy about it either! Colonel Serano is breathing fire. This place is supposed to be his show, not ours, and he doesn't appreciate a flat order from the American State Department to extend his base facilities to a planeload of foreigners, or risk losing his share of the latest aid package. Was that your doing as well, Shidler? Real diplomatic! Serano's on the phone to Bogotá right now, complaining about the *americanos* strong-arming the local authorities."

Shidler protested even more stiffly. "I simply made it clear that we expected some reciprocal courtesy for all we've done down here. He wasn't being very cooperative."

"Right! And that isn't strong-arming? I can't blame Serano for being upset. This *is* a restricted military installation—and you're bringing in *guerrillas?* And *reporters?*"

By the disgust in his tone, he might have been talking about tapeworms. "If that isn't all we need! As it is, Serano's already issued orders to keep this crowd out of his end of the base. Maybe that's nothing to you, Shidler, but we've got a job to do here, and we can't do it without cooperation from these guys."

From Julie's position in the shelter of the stairway, she saw the colonel turn to descend the steps and the political officer following. "Okay," Shidler said in a placating tone, "so the San José flyby wasn't the greatest idea. And maybe we could have flown on to San Ignacio instead of turning back. I panicked. I've never had anyone shooting missiles at me before. Come on, Jeff, lighten up! We're going to be out of your hair in half an hour. How much trouble can they get into in that much time?"

"With these media pukes, any time is too long!"

The two men were heading across the runway. Julie watched their receding backs with mingled indignation and amusement. It wasn't the first time she'd come across the colonel's attitude. All these military types seemed to have made up their minds that reporters were enemy agents bent on spying out all their activities and broadcasting them to where it could do the most harm. A premise, Julie thought, not totally without foundation.

Colonel Thornton suddenly called out, "Hey! You over there! No cameras!"

His harsh shout was directed at a TV crew setting up its equipment in front of the radar installation. Julie recognized Tom Chaney—his makeup artist even now was adding the last touches to his face. Colonel Thornton strode purposefully toward them. "I don't give a rip who you are!" Julie heard a moment later.

Collecting their gear, the news crew moved reluctantly toward the building where the rest of the passengers had disappeared, prompted along by an escort of Colombian soldiers who had appeared out of nowhere at the JTF colonel's shout.

Julie, her conscience clear since she'd left her camera on board with her knapsack, strolled over to the fence the others had just vacated. A sentry moved in her direction, but upon taking in her empty hands, he drifted away. Peering through the diamond links, Julie heard a whirring noise from the nearest radar, and the screen suddenly shifted position by several inches. What was it tracking up there in the sky?

"Young lady, we'd appreciate it if you'd join the rest of your party inside. This area is off limits to civilians."

Recognizing the stern voice, Julie turned around to find her eyes level with Colonel Thornton's lapel pocket. His expression was scarcely encouraging, but Julie had been on the news beat too long to be cowed by him.

"I'm not taking any pictures," she said quietly. With a smile that usually worked wonders on overbearing bureaucrats, she nodded toward the radar screens. "I was just wondering about your radar. Those are the TPS70s, right?"

"Maybe." Colonel Thornton showed no softening of expression, only a quick sharpening of his gaze. "Excuse me, young lady, but who did you say you were?"

"I didn't. Sorry!" Digging out her press badge, Julie showed it to the colonel. "Julie Baker. World Conservation Institute. I'm a staff writer with their magazine, *Our Earth.*"

Lifting the badge from her fingers, Colonel Thornton studied both sides as though it might be a forgery. "And just what do you know about the TPS70, young lady?"

Julie gritted her teeth, both at his tone and his form of address. *How'd you like it if I started calling you "old chap"!* In the higher interests of her profession, she kept her thoughts to herself.

As another whir preceded a new shift in the direction of the radar screen, Julie turned her attention back to the fence.

"Well, I know the TPS70s have a range of—what is it, two hundred nautical miles? They were very effective in operations Laser Strike and Green Clover, your counter-narcotics operations down here awhile back. But back then they were supplemented by air surveillance from Panama. Most of that evaporated when SouthCom relocated to Miami. And now with budget cuts, you're down to just the three radar bases here in southern Colombia—this one and the ones over in Leticia and Vichada, right? And they're a whole lot more than two hundred miles apart. So what I was wondering—what's to keep drug smugglers from plotting your radar parameters and just flying right down the air corridors in between?"

The silence that followed her last question was not friendly. Julie turned her head from the radar screens. There had been no shift in the colonel's expression. It was how a law enforcement officer might look at a prisoner before reading his Miranda rights.

"Young lady," Colonel Thornton said grimly, "the information you have just given me is classified. May I ask where you got it?"

"I—"

"No, just one moment. If you would accompany me, please."

She had little choice without making a scene—as by some mysterious signal, another military escort materialized around them. She was led to the same building the other passengers had entered, but toward a different door. Outside it, another recruit jumped to attention, hastily pushing it open for them.

The room inside was high-ceilinged with whitewashed walls and cement floor, but the equipment was that of any office. Seating herself in the chair to which Colonel Thornton waved her, Julie took in an enormous map of Colombia covering most of one wall. Red pins and miniature figures of airplanes dotted an area she recognized as the region around San José.

The colonel followed the direction of her eyes with a grim expression. Taking his own seat behind a desk that occupied the center of the room, he said curtly, "Now, maybe you'd like to explain to me how a reporter from some"—he glanced again at Julie's badge, which he still hadn't returned—"two-cent tree-hugger periodical manages to get her hands on classified information concerning our operations in this region."

He looked dead serious and not at all friendly, and Julie, who at first had felt an impulse to laugh, for the first time appreciated how a suspect must feel sitting on the opposite side of an interrogation table. Only her own clear conscience allowed her to meet that gimlet gaze squarely.

"I got it off the Internet. I was researching the region for this trip, and San José came up in some of the articles. I recognized the name, so I started digging a little further."

"You recognized the name," Colonel Thornton cut in expressionlessly. "You want to tell me why? San José isn't exactly a standard social studies project for your average American citizen."

"I grew up around here," Julie explained simply. "Well, actually, over in San Ignacio. My parents were missionaries there, and we visited San José when I was a kid. It was just a gravel airstrip back then for the local military police outpost, but the commander used to let my father land his Cessna. That was before they started growing coca around here, but even then, I remember the stories of how they'd take marijuana through here on river boats."

When the colonel didn't interrupt, she went on. "Anyway, when I started cross-referencing San José, the counter-narcotics operations came up. Then I came across an article—I think it was from the *Miami Herald*—that mentioned the three radar bases and the problems with air surveillance since SouthCom moved to Miami. I got the specs on the radar from the Department of Defense Web site. It wasn't hard. Just standard research techniques. If I can do it, so can anyone else."

The colonel was swearing steadily by the time she finished, but his fury no longer appeared to be directed at Julie.

"Internet! You got it off the Internet! We run a highly sensitive military operation here, we do our best to keep a low profile, watch every communication, warn our people to keep their mouths shut. And some wet-behind-the-ears reporter waltzes in with our weakest points pieced together off the Internet!"

Pushing back his chair with a force that slammed it into the wall, Colonel Thornton strode over to the wall map. "You see this! These pins . . . these planes. They're real people, real problems. In case you didn't notice, some of them died out there today—maybe not Americans, but men we know. Colonel Serano's people are out there picking up the pieces right now. We've been sent down here to do a job. No, not a job—to fight a war. And it's not a war we're winning right now. This mission is hard enough without waking up to find everything we're doing splashed across the front pages of the morning newspaper."

"Look, I'm sorry," Julie apologized, even as she wondered why she should. "I didn't mean to cause any trouble. If it makes you feel any better, I wasn't planning on writing anything about your operation here. It has nothing to do with the story we're covering anyway. I was just curious—"

"Curious! Well, that does describe you media types. Like a bunch of weasels sniffing through the trash, looking for what garbage they can dig up. And not one of you gives a rip about the consequences of what you write."

He dropped back into his desk chair. "Excuse me, that was way out of line."

"No, that's okay. I know what you mean," Julie said in earnest. "Only, my godfather calls them polecats. I don't practice that kind of journalism, really! Only, I was just wondering . . ."

She caught the look in his eye and couldn't help laughing. After a moment, the grim line of the colonel's mouth relaxed into the barest hint of an answering smile. "Okay, young lady—excuse me, Julie Baker—just what is it you're wondering?"

"Well, if you say you're losing the battle—and it does look like it from what I saw out there—why do you keep on? A lot of people are saying it's the U.S. presence here in Colombia—not to mention all the military aid we're giving these people—that's keeping the whole thing stirred up. Not just the drugs, but the guerrillas too. Wouldn't it be easier—and maybe better for both sides—if we just walked away? You know, concentrate on the drug war on our own side of the border?"

The colonel's brief affability evaporated instantly. "I couldn't agree with you less! You're right, a lot of people are saying just that. But you might as well ask why fight a forest fire when it just keeps blazing bigger. Of course you have to keep fighting it, or you'll never get it under control.

"And that goes for Colombia. The guerrillas and narcos aren't going to just trot along home and be good little boys if we drop out of the picture. We've already seen what happened when Colombia's military pulled out of the demilitarized zone. The FARC just stepped up their attacks and started clearing the jungle for coca. They're not looking for peace, no matter what they claim. If for nothing else, we owe it to the people of this country who really want peace to win this fight!"

"But there's a lot of people who say the guerrillas will win," Julie argued. "They compare Colombia to Vietnam. A lot of Americans are afraid that if we keep getting more involved down here, pretty soon we're going to have a lot of American soldiers losing their lives here too. And for a war they can't win."

The colonel snorted. "That, young lady, is what you get for listening to the press, if you don't mind my saying so. The guerrillas are *not* winning. They're just not losing—and that's a big difference. It's simple mathematics. Out of forty million Colombians, the guerrillas have maybe twenty thousand altogether—and that's splintered between dozens of factions. Nor do the guerrillas have a popular base among the people, like the Vietcong did back in 'Nam. The Colombian people have already seen what the guerrillas have to offer, and they've just plain said no!

"Oh, sure, it's easy to keep the advantage when you're attacking small, isolated police posts or unarmed villagers. But if the guerrillas actually seized any seat of government, they'd be as vulnerable as the Colombian government is now. You have to stay in one place to run a country, and then their numbers would tell against them."

Colonel Thornton tilted back in his desk chair. "No, their winning is an illusion, and the guerrillas know it, if no one else does. They control huge chunks of countryside only because there's no local population or police force to stand against them. But they can't touch the cities, and that's where the government is. The only reason they haven't lost already is that the rest of the Colombians won't unite against them. They don't have the will to get tough. Like you media types, they bleat that someone will get hurt if they actually go after these guys, and ignore the fact that hundreds of thousands of people are getting hurt because they don't!"

"So why do the guerrillas keep fighting," Julie asked, "if they know they can't win?"

"I'm danged if I know! They're idealists, heavily indoctrinated in Marxist socialism. Or maybe, for all their talk of peace and political convictions, they simply don't want to give up the power they enjoy right now. It has to be a heady feeling to be *ipso facto* rulers of almost half their national territory, uninhabited jungle though most of it is. Personally, I think there's more to it than meets the . . ."

He broke off. "Of course, everything I've said is strictly off the record," he informed Julie severely.

Julie kept her smile inside as she murmured agreement. Colonel Thornton knew, and he must know she knew, that it's too late to say "off the record" after the fact. But he need not worry; she would be discreet—not because of any legal obligation, but because as a patriotic American who cared as deeply about this country as her own, she would do nothing to cause trouble for those striving to bring about a fragile chance of peace.

"No problem. Like I said, San José isn't part of my story." Julie glanced at her watch. "Oh, no! Has it been that long? I'd better get back to the plane, or they're going to take off without me."

"Hey, no hurry, you've still got a few minutes." Colonel Thornton's swift strides beat Julie to the door. "I'm waiting for the last two planes and their escorts to touch down just about now." To Julie's surprise, he offered her a wry smile as he pushed open the door ahead of her. "And that you can print! Goodbye, Julie Baker."

"Goodbye, Colonel Thornton. And I really will keep what you've said off the record. All of it."

* * *

Julie sprinted out onto the airstrip. But as Colonel Thornton had said, the DC4 showed no signs of readying for takeoff. There was, in fact, a new group standing in the shade of its fuselage. Julie picked out the green-and-brown fatigues of the two guerrillas. The shorter FARC spokesman was gesturing enthusiastically as he addressed two men in white coats. The heat must have driven them out of the plane.

Julie felt her own curls tighten with perspiration as the reflection of the sun's rays from the asphalt hit her in sweltering, almost visible waves. She slowed to a trudge. The military contingent of the base didn't appear too enthusiastic about having a pair of their traditional enemies standing free on their territory, UN mission or not. An added detail of soldiers had closed in unobtrusively around the two FARC representatives and the rest of the UN team.

Others of the news crews were trickling back to the DC4 as well. At the far end of the runway, another crop duster was coming in, one of the planes for which Colonel Thornton had been waiting.

Julie stopped short in the middle of the airstrip, staring at a dark smudge against the blue sky above the crop duster. It was smoke, ominous black billows of it boiling up around the fuselage.

She wasn't the only one to notice. The fire truck was already moving out, and soldiers boiled onto the runway as the plane dropped down above the asphalt. Julie watched, transfixed. The plane was coming in too fast, too low.

Then, miraculously, it was down, the fixed wings tilting wildly from side to side; the pilot seemed unable to touch both wheels to the pavement at the same time. The fire truck sped forward. Julie let out her breath in relief—only to catch it again. Why wasn't the pilot braking? The fire truck swerved out of the way as the crop duster raced full speed down the airstrip. On its present course, it would plow right into the DC4.

The pilot clearly recognized his danger, altering his course to a zigzag pattern that seemed to slow the plane down only fractionally. The fixed wings wobbled more wildly than before.

Julie could see the stitching of bullet holes along the plane's side. Flames were licking through the smoke on one wing. Now it was tilting over so far onto one wheel, it seemed sure to keel over.

The left wing touched the asphalt, and Julie heard the screech of tortured metal. Pieces of fiberglass and metal cartwheeled across the runway as the wing shredded away from the body of the plane. Then, somehow, the plane had righted itself, slamming down hard onto both wheels.

Not until the shouts began behind her did Julie realize her danger. Her eyes widened unbelievingly as she saw the triangle of ripped fiberglass cartwheeling toward her, black smoke and flames still streaming from its jagged edges. *Move!* her mind screamed, but her breath was still caught in her throat, and her feet felt glued to the asphalt. Like some giant boomerang intent on cutting her down, the broken wingtip swelled to fill her plane of vision. There was no way she could escape its path in time.

Then arms closed around her, and Julie felt a hard body cushion the concrete that slammed up to meet her. Winded, she lay unmoving for a moment, thankful just to be alive and still in one piece as far as she could tell. Her rescuer was masculine—the strong arms around her told her that, as did the solid muscle under the rough cloth beneath her cheek.

*One of the soldiers,* she thought, and as she rolled loose and scrambled to her feet, she turned to thank him. But the words froze on her tongue as her eyes fell on the sleeved arms that were helping her up. They weren't khaki, but the green and brown of camouflage material. Julie raised her head slowly.

She'd never stood in the embrace of a self-confessed terrorist before, nor had she ever expected to. The younger guerrilla was bigger than she'd calculated, her own medium height reaching only to his shoulder and making little impact against the muscled bulk of his chest and wide shoulders. The longish hair and unshaven beard gave him the raffish look of a pirate or maybe a bandit in an old western, and even without the combat fatigues, Julie would have known him immediately for a dangerous man. His eyes met hers. Brown eyes, like his hair, not black, and the smoldering fire in them warned her that the anger she'd perceived earlier was still simmering.

*The eyes of a killer*, Julie thought confusedly. Yet he had just saved her from certain injury, if not death.

As quickly as he'd snatched her aside, he released her and strode away.

Around her, soldiers and some of the other passengers had hurried near to see if she was hurt. It had all happened so fast, Julie was almost shocked to see that the crop duster was no longer barreling down the runway. Some quick-thinking soldier had steered an army truck into its path, bringing it to a halt only meters from the DC4. The nose of the crop duster was crumpled, and so was the side of the truck. But like herself, both were in one piece, and the fire truck was already alongside, white foam spuming from a hose to smother the flames. To her right, the broken wingtip now lay harmless on the asphalt.

Brushing the dust from her clothes, Julie started back toward the DC4, assuring the other passengers and soldiers that she was fine.

Ahead of her, the State Department team closed in around her rescuer. Julie felt their eyes on her as well as she passed them. The CNN crew rushed by her, cameras rolling. Julie passed Sondra Kharrazi, snapping orders to her cameraman. At the base of the roll-away stairs, she stumbled, unnecessarily. A hand reached out to steady her. "Hey, are you all right there?"

It was Sondra's blond hunk, though with a video camera this time instead of that enormous Bible. Julie offered him a vague smile of thanks as he released her, and she trotted up the metal steps.

\* \* \*

Eyes watched Julie climb the steps to the DC4. Those same eyes had been watching with undiminished interest since Colonel Thornton had first approached her and led her off. Why would this young reporter with less than impressive credentials—a young woman listed on the passenger manifest as Julie Baker—trigger so much attention from the U.S. commander of this military operation, a card-bearing officer of the American Special Forces? What did she have to say to him? More important, what did he have to say to her? And this last incident—could it be as coincidental as it appeared?

As the eyes watched Julie disappear into the plane, their vigilance did not diminish.

# The DMZ

*  *  *

From beyond the soldiers swarming over the airstrip, other eyes watched Julie trot up the stairs as well. So the daughter was returning to her birth-place. The years had been long, and it had taken sharp eyes to recognize the girl in the young woman who had descended from the metal bird with the other foreigners. Was she as changed inside as well? Perhaps it would be an act of wisdom to find out.

WELL, IF THIS WASN'T THE biggest screw-up in a duty tour of screw-ups!

The door hadn't even closed behind the *Our Earth* reporter before Colonel Thornton had crossed his office and grabbed the phone on his desk. It was a sat-phone, a connection by satellite relay that could tap Colonel Thornton into the Department of Defense communication network at any point of the globe.

With more force than necessary, he punched Memory 1 on the keypad. A satellite dish behind the headquarters building caught the signal and bounced it skyward to an orbiting satellite—hopefully, one that was still on the classified list—and from there down to a geographic point in southern Miami.

"Yes?" The voice did not identify itself. If you didn't know who you were talking to on this line, you had no business calling.

"That you, Keith?" Colonel Thornton demanded curtly. "Jeff Thornton here in San José. Get me the boss, would you?"

"I'm sorry, sir, but he's out of town right now. Up in Washington."

This was no big surprise. General Brad Johnson, commander of Southern Command, was not a man for hanging around the office.

"Fine, then get me Crawford."

Colonel Thornton drummed his fingers impatiently through an instrumental rendition of the Stars and Stripes. Colonel Winston Crawford the Third, of the original Charleston Crawfords and inordinately proud of it, was new as the general's executive officer.

A supercilious drawl came on the line. "Jeff, what can I do for you? I'm sitting here watching CNN. Looks like you're building up to quite a party down in your area."

"A party is right! Crawford, are you aware of who just blew in here? I'd like to know who the idiot was who gave Bill Shidler the heads-up on that one." At least Colonel Thornton could speak his mind with Crawford in a manner that would have been injudicious to a superior officer. "You *are* aware," he continued, "that this is a restricted fly zone? And a Colombian military facility, not one of ours. Colonel Serano is still screaming up the lines to headquarters. To add fat to the fire, neither he nor I got word this crowd was coming through until they were already in the air. You just tell whatever moron handled this up there that next time they want to run a mission through my base of operations, I'd appreciate being asked."

"Well, actually, I was the moron." The rejoinder was cool and totally unapologetic. "Shidler called up this morning and asked if they should route their flight plan over San José. Perhaps we might have run it by you, but this whole mission has been a last-minute scramble, and I had no reason to think you'd have any objections. After all, we've got UN and State Department personnel on that mission, as well as a good number of American citizens, which means we've all got an obligation to do anything in our power to ensure its success. Anyway, I don't know why you're getting so hot under the collar. You've had visitors down there before."

Thornton gritted his teeth. "Sure, embassy personnel. Special Forces TDYs down here on a duty tour. Congressmen wanting to see where their dollars are going. People with security clearances. But not reporters! These guys carry cameras, for crying out loud! I've just spent the last half-hour chasing them away from our gear. They were all over the TPS70, and some of them had their research done. That stuff *is* supposed to be classified. Maybe it has escaped your notice that we're running a counter-narcotics operation here, not a State Department tour!"

Crawford's condescending chuckle did nothing for Thornton's rising blood pressure. "Haven't you got it, Jeff? Nothing's classified anymore. At least not much. Thanks to something called the Internet, for those who've entered the twenty-first century. If people want to know what's going on, they will. And why shouldn't they? The public has a right to know what we're getting our boys into. Besides, there's nothing less than aboveboard in the aid we're offering the Colombians down there. Or is there something you've left out of your reports, Jeff?"

"Of course not!" Thornton's tightened jaw was beginning to ache. "But does your 'right to know' include offering a guided tour for the bad guys? Narcos watch the news too, you know! For that matter, this whole operation is a crazy idea to start with, as I informed you in the very lengthy report I sent you yesterday. Did you even bother reading it? We're not talking a neutral zone down here. We've got a shooting war going on! What if those wackos in the DMZ change their minds and decide your planeload of VIPs is a whole lot more valuable bunch of playing chips than this PR stunt of theirs? Are you guys going to gamble those people's safety on the goodwill of a bunch of terrorists?"

The shrug on the other end was almost audible. "Our intel analysts don't foresee any problems. The guerrillas need our cooperation a lot more than we need theirs right now, and we have no reason to question their sincerity. This might even be a breakthrough in the peace negotiations— something I'd think you'd be happy for, Jeff. Unless you want to spend the rest of your life spreading poison on other people's crops. Either way, the call's been made. You were informed through the proper channels, however belatedly, and there's nothing I can do about it. Except pass your complaint along to General Johnson—something I wouldn't advise. He hasn't been in the best of moods lately."

*However belatedly!* The man talked like a lawyer's manual. Or maybe it was that Southern blue blood of which he was so proud. "Yeah, well, that's your assessment, not mine. And I'm the one sitting down here with my rear on the line. So next time you decide to include my zone in an operation, you talk to me first. This happens again, and I *will* take it up with General Johnson."

"You do that, then." Crawford didn't sound at all intimidated. "Because I've just talked to Bill Shidler and suggested he stop through there for refueling on their return flight this evening. We don't want our people depending on those guerrillas down there in San Ignacio for a fill-up. We're not totally insensible of the security risks."

The force with which Jeff Thornton hung up the sat-phone couldn't have been good for that piece of sensitive equipment. All that from a guy whose aristocratic rear had been parked in an office chair since boot camp!

Unfortunately, however, the man had a point. What good did it do to try to keep anything confidential these days when the average citizen could find out more in an hour's research than the colonel usually managed to squeeze out of intel? Blame the Internet for that—something he did know how to use, despite Crawford's derision. Thanks to the Freedom of Information Act, there'd always been a lot more data floating around out there than those responsible for his country's defense found comfortable. But the very difficulty of gathering and piecing together that data had been its own safety valve.

Not anymore. Not when the click of a mouse could search out and correlate more data than the CIA once had available at their fingertips.

One thing was for sure: if a female reporter still wet behind the ears could figure out the holes in his defense, the narcos wouldn't be far behind.

The girl was right on the money, Colonel Thornton told himself moodily. Only three years ago, U.S. radar coverage of the Caribbean and Andean areas had been so tight it had virtually destroyed the air bridge bringing in coca and coca paste from Bolivia and Peru to Colombia and processed cocaine from there on to the United States This, of course, had simply forced the narcos to stay on the ground, using alternative routes by water and land. But for a little while, at least, there was a check on the flow of cocaine and heroin flowing north.

Then came the turning over of the Panama Canal along with the closing of the American military bases there. Colonel Thornton had been on TDY—temporary duty—in Panama during the handover. "A showpiece of international relationships," the politicians had bleated.

What wasn't mentioned was that the Panamanian authorities had begged the Americans to remain, and that Colombian guerrillas had promptly capitalized on the withdrawal of American troops by crossing the border into Panama.

At the same time, radar coverage dropped by two-thirds after Southern Command relocated its headquarters from Panama to Miami. The distance from Colombia was now too great for quick response. The drug smugglers were taking to the air again.

And if this Julie Baker could plot a ground radar detection range, so could they!

"*Coronel* Thornton?" At the door connecting his office with the communications station in the next room, a soldier had rapped a polite knock. He was one of the Colombian Air Force pilots in the coca eradication program. "The other planes and the Hueys are ready for lift off," he reported. "What is it you have chosen to do?"

The colonel glanced out the window that overlooked the airstrip. The base's remaining contingent of aircraft had been gearing up for their own morning run when word came of the SAM ambush. There were three of them, elderly Turbo Thrush spray planes. Their escorts—two combat helicopters—were warming up their engines, and the ground crews were pulling the hoses that snaked from the Turbo's wing tanks to the two huge metal tanks containing herbicide.

The herbicide they were using was glyphosate, a common weed killer in the United States It was nontoxic and left no permanent damage to the soil, for all the squeals of the environmentalists, but it killed any vegetation that came under its acid blast.

The Colombian pilot addressing Thornton reeked of the stuff. It was a smell the colonel had come to hate. Despite the insinuations of that reporter, he didn't enjoy seeing the rainforest stripped away or the patches of parched earth where herbicide had withered the vegetation.

Still, he wasn't the one ripping out the forest to plant a crop designed only to bring misery to millions and immeasurable wealth to the few. The problem was, you don't always get to choose between best and worst. Sometimes your only choice is between bad and badder. And as far as he was concerned, the guerrillas and their narco protection racket were the badder. Drive them out, and maybe the land would have a chance to heal.

But not today. A few more hectares of destroyed coca wasn't worth the lives of his men or the lost aircraft that too many of his superiors would consider more urgent. For today, the narcos—and the guerrillas—had won another reprieve.

"No, too much risk," he answered. "Tell them everything's grounded until we get some backup and find out just what's going on out there."

"Colonel Thornton!" The urgency in the call from the next room had the colonel out of his seat and through the door into the communications office.

"One of the Turbos is in, but it's taken a hit. They're saying it's pretty bad. I'm not sure about casualties. Can't get any sense out of . . . "

Colonel Thornton was already out the door. One swift glance at the runway showed him the crumpled crop duster and the battered army truck.

Breaking into a sprint, he snatched a hand radio from his belt. But it wasn't necessary, he saw immediately. His emergency response force was proving worthy of their training. He nodded approval at the blanket of foam, the ambulance racing toward the spray plane.

Then he took in the news crews swarming over the scene, and his jaw tightened. Spotting Bill Shidler on the runway, he ran to him, gripped him by the shoulder, and spun him around.

"I don't have time for this!" he gritted through his teeth. "You get your people on that plane and in the air, okay? You're cleared to leave!"

The colonel pounded up to the crop duster just as the medics were helping the pilot out of his seat. He was American and a seasoned veteran of Third World projects—one of the civilians contracted by the U.S. government, along with the whole Turbo Thrush fleet, to carry out the coca fumigation project.

He was pale with shock as he climbed down from the cockpit but seemed otherwise unhurt. His Colombian copilot was less fortunate. The medic unit was already lifting him onto a stretcher. Blood had turned one leg of his khaki slacks to muddy purple.

Color flooded back into the pilot's face when he saw the colonel. "I'm out of here," he announced with an overloudness triggered by the temporary deafness of being exposed to too many decibels. "I didn't bargain for a shooting war out there! You said we'd have protection."

"What happened?" Colonel Thornton demanded urgently. "Where's the other Turbo? And where are your escorts? There were two more Hueys, blast it!"

The pilot swallowed visibly and hard. "The Hueys . . . they just blew up! Both of them! Some kind of rocket. They just—blew up! All those men. I saw one fall . . ."

Colonel Thornton cursed silently as he gripped the man's shoulder. In actuality, the pilot had more protection than anyone else flying from here. His half of the cockpit had been reinforced with armor shielding, but it proved too heavy to add to the copilot's side as well. The Hueys had no armor at all.

Still, they'd been more than a match for the AK-47 assault rifles that until now had been the guerrillas' only defense of their crops. This morning's attack was unexpected. Sure, there'd been rumors that the FARC was now sporting portable surface-to-air missiles. But those babies were costly, and no one would have anticipated the guerrillas would waste them on routine crop protection.

"But what about the Black Hawk?" the colonel asked. "We dispatched it your way. Where was it?" He had deployed their newly arrived Black Hawk combat helicopter for the first time that morning.

The pilot spat angrily, the moisture making a sizzle on the hot asphalt. As a civilian, and one whose salary was several times Colonel Thornton's own hazard pay, he had no obligation to show respect to the head of operations—one more thing the colonel disliked about Capitol Hill's policy of hiring outsiders to do what he considered a soldier's job.

"That Black Hawk isn't worth the spit holding it together! The guns jammed on the first run. They just sat there and watched that Huey go down! I called it quits for the other Turbo myself. There it comes now."

A drone that had been at the edge of Colonel Thornton's hearing grew into the roar of approaching aircraft. Colonel Thornton swung around. Yes, it was coming in—and hovering above the crop duster, like a mother eagle anxiously guiding her eaglet to its first landing, was its remaining escort, the sleek, gray shape of the Black Hawk. From the ominous forward tilt in the helicopter's nose, Colonel Thornton pinpointed its problem immediately.

The Black Hawk circled overhead until the spray plane touched down, then settled slowly to the runway beside it. The Black Hawk's flight crew was from Colonel Serano's battalion—part of the U.S. government's compromise with its own citizens that it would not send American soldiers into this combat—but a U.S. training officer was on board. As the soldiers jumped down, he came to the open side door. Hunching his shoulders in apology, he made a helpless gesture toward the cylinder shape of the huge machine gun that thrust its deadly muzzle through the door. Walking over, Colonel Thornton saw that part of the mountings had ripped loose from the floor, causing the entire weapon to slide forward toward the nose of the helicopter.

He cursed aloud. He'd warned those idiots in Washington that this would happen. The GAU19 Gatling mini-gun was a good piece of equipment, powerful enough to penetrate the jungle and reach anything—or anyone—taking shelter under cover of its canopy. That was why it had been proposed for this job. But it was too heavy for the Black Hawk and too temperamental for an inexperienced crew—which Colonel Serano's men certainly were. Colonel Thornton hadn't been the only one to warn that replacing the smaller M-60s was a recipe for disaster. But the congressmen pushing the deal and certain Colombian Air Force officials shared a predilection for the bigger-and-better syndrome. It was nice to be able to say "I told you so," but the deaths of a lot of good men wasn't the way Colonel Thornton liked to be proved right.

Bill Shidler had his people on board the DC4. Colonel Thornton could see the political officer standing in the open doorway as the portable stairway was pulled away. The colonel made no effort to see off his unwelcome guests. He'd be meeting them again soon enough. He snapped a few orders into his hand radio, and after a moment saw the DC4 begin taxiing down the runway. The rest of their trip should be uneventful.

He would have to make an immediate report on today's fiasco, but Colonel Thornton didn't head directly back to his office. Walking across to where a neat lawn swept down to the perimeter fence (there were advantages to having an entire base of young, strong arms to keep occupied), the JTF commander studied with narrowed eyes the tangle of trees and vines not far beyond that marked the edge of the jungle.

They were out there—his enemies. Laughing up their camouflaged sleeves, no doubt. *Farclandia.* That's what the locals called it. Forty-two thousand square kilometers of jungle and rivers and plains where the guerrillas reigned supreme—though their territorial kingdom was actually many times that, since the FARC's long arm of terror, kidnapping, and murder reached far beyond the borders of the demilitarized zone. Colonel Thornton had been only one of many American and Colombian advisors who protested bitterly against former President Pastrana's decision to hand over a major chunk of Colombian territory without so much as a fight.

*Give the guerrillas an inch,* he'd written in an angry memo, *and they'll never hand it meekly back—or sue for peace. They will push and push and push until that inch stretches to a mile.*

And he, like others, had been right. Pastrana had sworn that his initial troop withdrawal would not extend beyond a three-month trial period. Three years later, the FARC was firmly entrenched in what they clearly considered a permanent territorial concession. Nor had they returned that concession with the slightest serious peace gesture. The *zona de despeje,* the DMZ was referred to in Spanish. It was an aviation term, meaning the "takeoff zone." And that's exactly what it had become for the FARC—a launching pad for their attacks on unarmed civilians and scattered, undermanned military outposts.

Colonel Thornton turned his morose gaze from the jungle to the base itself. It looked neat and trim, with gleaming asphalt, freshly painted buildings, and whitewashed stones that bordered every path, all clean and bright under the noon sun. Beyond his own command post were the headquarters and barracks of the Colombian counter-narcotics police who shared this end of the base with the Americans. At the far end of the base, in front of their own barracks, a squadron of Colonel Serano's latest recruits were wheeling in smart formation.

It was a far cry from the dusty airstrip that he had first seen here in San José, and he could claim credit for the changes as much as anyone. He had been one of the first American training instructors, one of the principal voices who'd lobbied for a radar station in the zone and for increased U.S. aid to combat what was, after all, primarily an American problem. He'd returned to San José time and again on TDY, each time at a higher rank, and just last year had been appointed Joint Task Force commander of U.S. operations here.

Theoretically, of course, he was under the jurisdiction of the Colombian base commander, Colonel Serano, and after him, the head of the Colombian counter-narcotics police, Colonel Atiencia. But President Batallano listened to Washington, and so Serano and Atiencia listened to him. Under his charge were dozens of American advisors, technicians, and pilots, as well as the usual DEA and CIA task forces, who weren't strictly under his command but shared the facilities.

At the moment, he also had a full TDY contingent of Special Forces. All were members of the Special Operations 7th Group based out of Fort Bragg—known to popular fiction as the Green Berets, though that was not their official title. They had been handpicked for their Spanish language proficiency and trained in a wide variety of special skills needed for jungle warfare instruction.

And an occasional other task as well.

The Colombian soldiers they were training had few of their own combat skills or training. But they were proving eager to learn—spurred on, perhaps, even more than their North American counterparts by the brutal reality of warfare in which they and their families lived. If they did not yet measure up to their instructors, they were now more than ready, in Colonel Thornton's expert opinion, to kick some respect into their adversaries lurking in the jungle.

Still, against that enormous swathe of territory out there, all of San José was but a dot on a satellite map. As that reporter woman Julie Baker had pointed out, they hadn't yet managed to even dent the spread of coca into the rainforest, much less patrol that huge territory for drug traffic.

If the colonel didn't sigh as he started back toward headquarters, it was only because he considered that pessimistic gesture unseemly for a soldier. Colonel Jeff T. Thornton, scion of three generations of U.S. Army officers who had fought in every American conflict from World War I to the present, believed in his mission. The coca out there in those fields and the cocaine that was its final product were poisoning millions of young people around the world. The people taking up arms to defend that crop were criminals and the aggressors in this war, and if they wandered into the path of return fire while attempting to shoot down those unarmed crop dusters, he wouldn't lose any sleep over it.

But that wasn't the only reason he believed in this mission. He liked the Colombian people, liked their grit and resilience and even the independence that made so many of them squawk at his government's interference in their problems. He didn't blame them. No one liked a handout, even when they needed one. Colonel Thornton had the deepest admiration for the Colombians at all levels of society who had made a stand against corruption and narco-dealing, often at the cost of their own lives.

These people deserved better. The *campesinos* out there. The political and civic leaders—and there were plenty of them—who really wanted the best for their country. The war-weary ordinary citizens. Even the guerrillas, whose tactics he certainly couldn't condone, but who had a legitimate gripe as to the disparity between the handful of oligarchs and wealthy landowners who controlled the country's treasure-house of resources and the masses who went without. All of them deserved better than year after year after year of futile and unending conflict.

Or even worse, an expansion of Farclandia, with its totalitarian, repressive regime, to the rest of the country. The United States was supposed to be in the business of supporting democracy, and Colombia, whatever its problems, was a democracy and a loyal ally of the United States for decades.

Yes, Colonel Jeff Thornton believed in his mission. But he wasn't as confident as he'd tried to sound while talking to that reporter in his office. Theoretically, the whole thing was simple: Destroy the coca crops that were the power base not only for the guerrillas but also for the paramilitaries and the narcos. Give the *campesinos* a fair shake with land reform. Then everyone could shake hands, go home, and take up farming or whatever they chose.

But the United States had made that mistake in both Somalia and Yugoslavia—the naive assumption that if you poured in aid, patted the quarreling factions on the head, and begged everyone to shake hands and get along, the fighting and hating and killing would stop. Unfortunately, that wasn't the way it worked. Not in Somalia, where he had been one of those trying to shepherd Red Cross convoys through the clashing warlords. Not in Yugoslavia.

And not, it would seem, in Colombia.

The problem was that it had gone on too long. Many sociologists blamed the continued conflict on *la violencia*, the civil war decades ago that had killed so many Colombians, largely *campesinos*. But it had begun long before that, as Colonel Thornton had found out when researching for his master's degree in Latin American studies. It had, in fact, been going on almost since Simon Bolívar led the country to independence from Spain, from the inauguration of the two great Colombian parties, the Liberals and the Conservatives.

The lines were firmly drawn from the beginning. The Liberals stood for federalization—absolute freedom at the local level from interference from a central government, free trade, and religious freedom from a state designated church. The Conservatives believed in a strong central government and protectionism, as well as absolute control by the state-sponsored Catholic church over education, marriage, and virtually every other aspect of national life.

Even back then, Colombians had been passionate about their politics, and then as now, the leaders set the policies while their peasant followers were used as shock troops. The two parties had fought one bitter, bloody civil war after another, the worst being the War of a Thousand Days a century ago, leaving the country in economic and social ruin. Over the generations, every family had horror stories of fathers and brothers and cousins butchered by the other side, until political affiliation became less about ideology than loyalty to family and clan and to the "martyrs" who had died for the cause. It was popularly said that Colombians were born with party identifications attached to their umbilical cords.

And now their descendants fought on in the paramilitaries and guerrillas. Again, it was the leaders who made the decisions while their *campesino* followers paid the cost. And if Batallano and the politicians of Colombia or the United States really believed the warring factions would so easily lay down their arms and go home, they had forgotten their history. Perhaps in the melting pots of the cities, the wounds of the past were easily dismissed, but in the countryside old loyalties ran deep and cruel memories were not forgotten. There was just too much history of hurt and hatred for easy forgiveness.

Though the colonel had been long inured to the jungle's heat, he found himself unpleasantly damp in the armpits by the time he reached his office.

Stepping with relief into the cool hiss of the air-conditioning, he shut away the heated subject of Colombian politics as deliberately as he had the humid furnace of outdoors. It wasn't his position to debate policy on American involvement in this country's dirty little war. He'd been given a job to do. If all his side did was stamp out the drug trade that was pouring billions into the pockets of those whose interest lay in keeping this conflict alive, then maybe it would give the rest of the Colombians enough of an edge to have a chance at overcoming this thing.

He grabbed a towel from the coffee cart, using it to mop his damp face while he poured a cup of coffee.

In the meantime, what if it were true that there were outside interests who had a stake in keeping this conflict stirred up? If so, all the aid America could pour in might not be enough to make a difference.

If only they knew just what the guerrillas were up to out there under cover of the DMZ. Well, it was his job to find out. But this had to be the worst possible time to drop a whole new batch of bargaining chips into the guerrillas' hands. It was craziness, no matter what the State Department or his own superiors back in Miami had to say.

The colonel's thoughts returned to the gang of reporters that had intruded into his world today and would soon be back again. Along with being a persistent security threat, the media were a real pain—always wanting to talk to and "understand" the bad guys. Aiding and abetting, that's what he called it. Only last week he'd read a sympathetic AP article based on interviews with a group of female guerrillas, as though their Marxist revolution was just some new version of women's lib. If they ever gave the forces of law and order the kind of good press they gave the bad guys . . .

Still, there were government employees on that plane as well. And even among the media pukes, there probably existed a few real human beings. The image of an eager young face swam reluctantly to the surface of the colonel's mind—suddenly he swore long and loud. Throwing the towel aside, he slammed his coffee cup down on his desk and strode over to the sat-phone. The satellite dish caught the signal, but this time it didn't bounce it northward to Florida. Nor was its reception at the other end an audible one.

"I know you're out there," he said curtly. "In case you haven't noticed, you've got trouble coming your way. Get in touch with me as soon as you can."

* * *

He already knew trouble was coming. He could see it out the porthole of the DC4. He watched as the ambulance transporting casualties shrank to the size of a Matchbox toy. There might be men he knew among them, and in the downed combat helicopter as well. It hadn't been easy to project the indifference he was far from feeling, but then a talent for dissimulation had been a part of his qualifications for this assignment.

Call it what it is. Lying!

Had he been recognized? Not that it mattered now. Those few who knew his identity would keep their mouths shut, and this new mission had already compromised the usefulness of his cover. Worse, it was jeopardizing hard, patient months of labor. And he was so close! He could feel it. When he was out there, he could taste it on the jungle breeze—an unease that diffused through the villages, the jungle camps, the very branches of the trees, so that even the wildlife seemed spooked.

The next step was to track it back.

If there was time.

And time was something this latest development had snatched from his grasp.

* * *

Julie tightened her seatbelt as the DC4 left the military base behind and banked left over the coca fields. She had both seats to herself, her former seatmate having shifted across the aisle, hands gesturing rapidly as she murmured to a sleek, bent head. Who had Sondra booted out to squeeze in with the CNN correspondent? *Talking Tom Chaney out of his makeup artist, I'll lay a bet!*

Well, more power to her! Julie wasn't going to complain about the extra leg space. Her eyes strayed again to the back of a green-and-brown cap two rows ahead, worn by a man who had saved her life.

What a strange incident!

What a strange man!

She dismissed him from her thoughts because the DC4 was once again leaving the cleared cropland and villages and winging out over the unbroken expanse of rainforest. Like a magnet too powerful to resist, Julie's eyes were drawn to that tossing green sea. *A jungle is a jungle is a jungle.* So why did every square meter seem suddenly familiar, every towering hardwood thrusting its crown above the other trees seem to be one that Julie knew, the curves of each muddy stream seem recognizable?

The tension that had been there since Julie's first glimpse of Colombia was building again in her stomach. In another half-hour—no, less now—she would no longer be able to dodge her past. But not yet! Forcing her eyes from the window, she snatched up an unread printout from the embassy folder.

The file was Dr. Winifred Renken's history of the I'paa tribe. Julie had recognized the name while doing her earlier research. A small clan of the tribe lived downstream from San Ignacio, and in fact the Ipa River flowing past the town had been named after them. Their village was an easy Cessna flight from San Ignacio, and Julie had often visited there with her parents as a child. An organized history of the tribe should prove interesting. Burying her nose in the report, Julie began to read.

As a distraction, it proved more than adequate. Julie hadn't finished the first page before a rising indignation drove away all thoughts of her approaching destination. This wasn't history; it was sheer fictional propaganda! If you believed what Dr. Renken had to say, the I'paa—in fact, all the jungle Indians—were a bunch of saints, living for thousands of years in perfect harmony with both a benevolent Mother Earth and their neighboring tribal groups, never stooping like other peoples to the use of weapons or war.

*Yeah, right!*

Julie knew and appreciated the I'paa more than this anthropologist ever could. But if the I'paa had been so peace loving, they'd have been wiped out long ago by their more aggressive neighbors. That was just the way human history went. Tribal culture with its warring nomadic lifestyle had varied little over the centuries from the North American Indians clear back through Europe's own Celts and Britons and Gauls all the way to the dawn of recorded history. You either fought or were absorbed by your enemies until one group grew large and powerful enough to move to the next inevitable social experiment—a peace imposed at the end of a sword that allowed for the beginnings of settled towns and organized agriculture.

The Aztecs and Mayans and Incas had reached that point before the arrival of the Spanish, hence the remnants of their great civilizations. The scattered jungle tribes, isolated from mainstream society as many still were today, had not. And since the I'paa had no written language, and survivors tended to edit history to their own liking, who was to say now what the past history of the I'paa really was—except those present-day tribal liaisons whose cultural dictates entailed telling their foreign benefactors exactly what they wanted to hear. Their very continued existence argued that they'd been no less aggressive than their jungle neighbors.

As for this so-called symbiotic relationship with Mother Earth that Dr. Renken described as some sort of amiable communion between the I'paa and benevolent spirit guides who steered the tribe into ecological practices and sent the occasional challenge to their bravery and manhood—where had this woman been? Certainly not with the same tribal people Julie had known.

The relationship the jungle tribes had maintained with nature had never been one of love. Always, it had been a relationship of fear. Fear of famine and disease and flood and enemy attack and countless other disasters that could—and frequently did—wipe out their fragile grip on existence. Fear of the spirit beings they believed responsible for every aspect of their world and who must be kept constantly placated if disaster were to be averted. Fear of the witch doctor who claimed to stand between them and the spirit world and who in turn controlled their lives with his threats of cursing and death for anyone who crossed him.

The world of a jungle tribe was harsh, full of treachery and attack, dominated by taboos that were their way of trying to control a nature whose forces they did not understand and at whose constant mercy they lived. Julie had seen firsthand how quickly fear could turn to viciousness against anyone accused of breaking those taboos. If bad times came, it was safest to point a finger before fingers could be pointed in return.

And so to other fears was added the fear and distrust of each other.

As for the devil masks and amulets with their bizarre ingredients, the witch doctor's ceremonies and spirit dances that anthropologists like Dr. Renken interpreted as folk art and attractive cultural rituals—could they not see the desperation behind them, the terror of invisible forces they were designed to drive away?

"Hey, what are you reading now?"

It was her seatmate, back from across the aisle. From Sondra's satisfied expression, her mission had been successful. She glanced over Julie's shoulder. "I've read that one—used it in one of my specials. Those poor Indians—they sure did get the short end of the stick. All those conquistadors. And then the missionaries coming in to finish where the Spanish left off."

Julie's grip tightened on the edge of the pages in her hands, but she kept her voice even. "What do you mean by that?"

"Oh, you know, Julie—destroying the local culture. Forcing their own morality on them." Sondra's expression suddenly grew quizzical, and she nodded toward the report. *"Baker*—that name's in there. Those missionaries who screwed up the I'paa. They're no relation to you, are they? You said you'd been in the area."

Julie didn't answer, but something in her face must have pierced the correspondent's self-absorption because she got up hastily. "You know, speaking of religious types, Moral Majority back there has a seat open. I think I'll check him out."

As Sondra disappeared up the aisle, Julie looked down to find the edges of the page crumpled in her grip. She scanned through the rest of the report. Yes, there were the names—Richard and Elizabeth Baker.

Dr. Renken's terse phrases jumped out: "*Western missionaries' invasion of indigenous settlements . . . corruption of native cultures . . . interference with indigenous healing practices . . . contamination with the outside world . . . lack of respect for native spirituality . . . imported religious practices . . . narrow-minded . . . intolerant . . .*"

Julie's eyes burned hot as she wadded up the report and stuffed it into the seat pocket in front of her. What did Sondra Kharrazi or this Dr. Renken, who spoke of change as though it were some terminal disease rather than a normal part of any viable culture, know of people like her parents? How dare she judge them?

To the anthropologists and environmentalists, the I'paa were some kind of living museum exhibit they wanted to freeze in time for their own study purposes.

To Richard and Elizabeth Baker, they were individuals with dreams and hopes and ideas of their own, whose needs and problems were no ongoing anthropological study but something the Bakers had the knowledge to immediately ease. A mother whose dying child had not been healed by all the chants and rattle-shaking of the witch doctor—did she cry "contamination" when a shot of antibiotics restored her baby to her arms? Was it "corruption" to teach nutrition and more efficient agricultural practices so

I'paa children could grow up strong and healthy instead of dying in infancy? Was it "interference" to broker peace with a neighboring tribe and put an end to the continuous bloodshed or to intervene with state authorities when settlers began encroaching on I'paa land?

Was it "narrow-minded" and "intolerant" to offer these people the love of a Creator-God in place of fear and bondage?

That was the element these anthropologists didn't seem to grasp—the love that had led Richard and Elizabeth Baker and tens of thousands of other missionaries over the years to leave comfortable homes to toil for people who more often than not neither accepted them nor appreciated them.

Perhaps they had made mistakes. It was always easy to pick out flaws from hindsight, especially for those who had never left the comfort of their own easy chairs, and missionaries were as human and as bound by their own cultural baggage as anyone else. But they did not exploit these people as had the conquistadors and the multinationals, the mestizo settlers and the guerrillas and paramilitaries—or even the environmentalists and anthropologists with their own agendas in tow.

They had simply loved them and given their lives to them.

So who was this Winifred Renken and others like her to accuse and criticize? What had they done for these people but study them and walk away? It had been the missionaries, in fact, who had preserved hundreds of tribal languages by reducing them to writing, an accomplishment whose cultural value was not lessened by the fact that the missionaries' purpose had been the translation of the Bible into those dialects. Many developing nations had acknowledged the missionaries' role in preserving their tribal groups, even if the anthropologists refused to do so.

Ultimately, however, maybe the anthropologists hadn't been so far off. Because in the end, Julie thought, it had all proved for nothing—both for her parents and for the people to whom they had gone.

Julie felt her hands trembling again. No, she did not want to go where those memories led!

But she could hold it off no longer. Not when below the plane's wing she could see the wide, muddy river on which she had learned to paddle her first canoe. Around that bend was the sleepy riverside town where she'd taken her first breath twenty-three years ago.

*A jungle is a jungle is a jungle*, Julie repeated like a litany. But it wasn't true. This was *her* jungle, and like a dam bursting, the memories she'd kept firmly bottled up since she'd stepped onto the plane in Washington, D.C., swept over her.

* * *

It was almost forty years now since Richard and Elizabeth Baker had arrived in San Ignacio. He was an army doctor whose enlistment had expired just in time to miss Vietnam; she was a beautiful young conservatory grad who had given up a concert career to follow her husband to the jungles of Colombia. Elizabeth Baker's beauty had faded by the time Julie knew her, but there had been a picture kept on the battered piano some American church group had shipped in that showed a radiant young bride in white lace beside a tall, handsome officer in dress uniform.

That picture and a few snapshots of Julie herself were all she had salvaged from San Ignacio.

The Ipa River was the only access into the region in those years, and the day Richard Baker's Cessna, equipped with removable pontoons for either land or river travel, touched down on its mud-colored surface was still a red-letter date in San Ignacio history. Had her parents been dismayed by the bamboo huts and dirt streets and total lack of conveniences? If they had, Julie had never heard it. They set to work building the area's first clinic. The generator Julie's father brought in by river launch to power his medical equipment provided the region's first electricity.

A measles epidemic triggered by injudicious contact with *mestizo* colonists brought the Bakers' first contact with the I'paa. Both Richard and Elizabeth had set themselves to learn the I'paa language, and Julie herself had grown up chattering it as easily as English or Spanish. It was Julie's mother who began the arduous task of reducing the dialect to grammatical structure and written word. The Gospel of John had been the I'paa's first printed book—no easy task when much of the vocabulary did not even exist in the I'paa's simpler language. Elizabeth Baker had continued by translating other parts of the New Testament. What had ever happened to that manuscript?

Julie herself had been a joyous surprise to the Bakers after more than a decade of childlessness. Dr. Baker performed the delivery, an unseasonable monsoon having interrupted plans to airlift his wife to the city. Her mother had told Julie the story of her birth, the water flooding across the cement floor of their bedroom, the rain rattling on the tiles loud enough to drown out her screams. There had been no further children, and if Julie would have enjoyed siblings, being a long-awaited and cherished only daughter had its pluses, and she had a whole village of other children with whom to play and squabble.

For the first eight years of her life, San Ignacio and the I'paa village had been the natural boundaries of Julie's world. Then it was time to join the other missionary kids at the mission boarding school across the border in Venezuela.

"It isn't that you're better or more deserving of privilege than your friends," her mother had explained carefully. "But you *are* different, and we want you to have the advantages of a better education and at least some acquaintance with your own culture, more than we can give you here. Besides, it's safer there—not so much sickness."

Had she been lonely at boarding school? Not really—at least not after the first months when she'd cried herself to sleep aching for her parents' good-night hug. Independent, yes. Boarding school did that to you. You got up, got yourself dressed and ready, and as long as you did your chores and homework and didn't get into any trouble, no one bothered you. There were compensations in the outstanding education her mother had promised and in plenty of social activities with other kids in the same boat, and if your friends were always coming and going as missionary families arrived and departed from the field, you learned not to depend too much on any particular others in your life.

It had certainly made possible the years that came after.

No, Julie hadn't resented the unusual circumstances of her life.

At least not for herself!

When had been the first time she'd returned home from boarding school to notice how old and haggard her parents looked? She'd never known them young. By the time she went off to boarding school, her father was graying, his tall frame stooped with overwork and his constant bending to a shorter people. The radiant bride in the wedding portrait was thin, the fresh young complexion yellowed with quinine and etched deep by bouts of malaria and typhoid and other tropical fevers that seemed to be the indigenous people's revenge for the measles and chicken pox and other deadly European diseases colonization had unleashed on them.

But the twinkle in her parents' eyes was still youthful, and no amount of hard times could squelch it. Years of patient service had written wisdom and kindness and tolerance into every line and wrinkle of their faces, making them far more beautiful to Julie than the movie-star pose of their wedding day portrait. She had adored them with the fierceness of a child having only one point of family reference in her life.

It wasn't until she went away to boarding school that Julie realized just how primitive were her parents' circumstances. The cinder-block house with cement floor and a tiled roof that sprang new leaks at every storm. The hand-built furniture that seemed shabbier every time Julie came home. The water tank in the back patio where clothes were washed by hand. The Coleman lanterns that only in the last year had been replaced by a single electric light dangling on its cord from the rafters. The constant battle against dirt and the cockroaches, tarantulas, and other creepy-crawlies that came like an inexorable tide under doors and over walls.

And always, the people.

Pounding on the door in the middle of the night for a medical emergency. Standing patiently in never-ending lines for the daily clinic. Demanding an airlift out of the jungle for reasons that might be urgent or not. Pleading for someone with knowledge of the law to intervene on their behalf with the local authorities. Requesting Don Ricardo's aging Toyota pickup to haul something too big to carry on mule back. A tribal messenger conveying the chief's request for a lift to the larger I'paa settlement a Cessna flight away.

If her parents complained, it was not in Julie's hearing, though she sometimes heard low, troubled murmurs behind their closed door at night. Nor had she ever seen them cry, not even when they left her at boarding school with a fierce hug that reassured her she'd be missed. During Christmas vacation of Julie's freshman year, a fresh leak in the living-room roof had damaged the battered upright piano out of which her mother coaxed such beautiful melodies. Some days later, Julie had walked in to find her mother seated at the piano bench, head bowed on the worn ivory keys. At Julie's footsteps, she'd sat up and slammed down the lid, wiping her eyes quickly before swinging around to greet her daughter with a semblance of her usual serenity. When Julie tried the piano later, she discovered that the water had rusted the strings into uselessness. Julie had never again seen the lid raised on the keys, and her mother never mentioned her loss.

No, it was not her parents but Julie who with each visit home resented their poverty more and more. The knock at the door that interrupted every vacation plan. The way these people intruded on her parents, not even seeming to notice or care what their demands were costing. The way every extra penny that came in went to medical supplies or teaching materials rather than the smallest comfort for themselves.

Dr. Richard Baker was a brilliant pathologist. An award from the American Medical Association, mounted in a dusty frame on his clinic wall, for having identified and developed a vaccine for a new strain of tropical fever, said so. So did a letter offering him a research position in a prestigious medical university in North America. Her father should have been in suit and tie on a conference platform, not bandaging machete wounds from a drunken bar brawl or taking the temperature of naked I'paa children.

And her mother, who had once played Rubinstein's *Komenoi Ostrow* on a Chicago concert stage. She belonged at a grand piano, receiving the applause of the crowd, not bent over a sickbed in a bamboo hut whose occupants couldn't even be bothered to sweep the food scraps from the dirt floor. Her long, graceful fingers that had once spanned an octave and a half became roughened and chapped.

Perhaps Julie would have felt differently if Richard and Elizabeth Baker's sacrifice had been for anything in the end.

But it hadn't.

The arrival of the guerrillas had revealed how much the Bakers' love and giving meant to the people of San Ignacio. The little brick church they'd built next to the clinic had emptied out, the vacant benches showing just how shallow was the villagers' commitment to the God of whom the Bakers taught. Her parents were shunned, the knocks coming no longer on the door except in the dead of night and under dire necessity. Julie's own friends—or the town youth she'd liked to consider her friends during vacations from boarding school—had evaporated with the coming of the horsemen. Not one had come around to say goodbye.

Right on the heels of Julie's precipitate return to boarding school had come the cholera epidemic, a particularly virulent strain. The guerrillas refused to allow government or international aid into the area. Her parents worked alone to stem the tide, expending the last of their medical supplies, even traveling by dugout canoe to the I'paa settlements when the guerrillas impounded the Cessna.

*They saved those people's lives!* Julie reminded herself now with anguish. And in return, what villager had dared approach their house when the Bakers, exhausted, contracted the disease themselves? How many of the people they'd birthed and doctored and taught over the years had stood up to the guerrillas to demand that they be airlifted out for medical attention?

Julie began worrying when her parents' weekly letters quit coming, but a well-regulated postal service had never been one of Colombia's strong points, and the ham radio with which the Bakers maintained contact with their mission base was one of the first things the guerrillas had confiscated.

Ironically, Norm Hutchens, an intimidating figure Julie remembered only vaguely from the Bakers' infrequent visits stateside, had proved better informed. His own news sources had alerted him to the cholera epidemic and the guerrilla blockade. It was his furious badgering of the embassy, of the Colombian government, of the local officials, and even of the guerrillas themselves that finally won safe passage for a Red Cross team into the area—too late.

With the deaths of Richard and Elizabeth Baker, the last of their labor crumbled into sand. The I'paa, whose language her parents had so painstakingly learned and reduced to writing, drifted away into the jungle. Who knew if they remembered or even cared about any of the things the Bakers had taught them? The two Colombian pastors in the region, whom her father had trained and ordained, had been found murdered not long after her parents' deaths. As the guerrillas' reign of terror tightened, church doors slammed shut all over the jungle region. A lifetime of selfless ministry had been stamped out as though it had never been.

*So what was the point, God? Why did You bother sending them in the first place—for nothing? How could You ask them to sacrifice everything—even their lives—if it was all going to be one big waste in the end?*

*Or was it all some big mistake?*

*Theirs—or Yours?*

The guerrillas had not yielded to the request from Norm Hutchens to remove his friends for burial in their homeland, so Richard and Elizabeth Baker were buried in San Ignacio where they had lived and served.

Or so Julie had been informed. None of it seemed real to her. For years, in fact, it had felt like just one more boarding school separation, as though if she could only make her way home, she might still find her parents tending their patients in the clinic dispensary or puttering around the patio of their small, cinder-block home.

Julie herself was too numb to protest the strange old man who appeared at boarding school with guardianship papers and the explanation that he was a longtime friend of her parents. Meekly, she had followed Norm Hutchens aboard the American Airlines flight to Washington, D.C., walking away from the country of her birth without a backward glance.

Nor had she ever wanted to. The leftist guerrillas hadn't killed her parents. Colombia had!

Colombia had used them up, sucked them dry, and spit them out.

The elite New England boarding school in which Norm Hutchens had deposited Julie—with relief, Julie was sure, though to give him credit, a teary teenage girl must have been a daunting charge for a bachelor—was a world apart from the austere mission school she'd attended till then. Julie had never really fit into the American teen culture with its giggling cliques and obsession with hair, nails, clothes, and rock stars. Didn't these spoiled rich kids realize there was a real world out there where people got hurt and went hungry and died?

Still, she'd managed to cut her prison sentence short by condensing her last two years of high school into one, and at least in college she was not the only new kid. Her grades were high enough that she could have followed her father into the medical field, but she steered deliberately away from that path. If she'd learned anything from the tragedy of her parents' lives, it was that it didn't pay to pour yourself out for people who didn't appreciate it.

Julie had followed instead in the footsteps of her guardian, graduating magna cum laude with a degree in journalism, and if she'd spent the last two years doing more grunt labor than she cared to remember, she was at last on the path to making a serious mark in her profession. A mark that—if she was successful—would bring Julie far more public acclaim than her parents had ever received.

But who would have ever believed this path would bend to force her back to the last place on earth she wanted to see again? It was just too wildly improbable to be coincidental.

*God, is this Your quirky idea of a sense of humor? Are You still messing around with my life?*

# SEVEN

THE DC4 WAS DROPPING IN ALTITUDE. The bend in the river was just ahead, and they were low enough to make out the water traffic. It was busier than Julie remembered, the wide-beamed shape of shipping barges having been added to the river launches and dugout canoes. The sleepy town of San Ignacio had evidently prospered during the seven years she'd been gone.

She didn't have to look far to see the reason. When she'd left, the first slash-and-burn clearings of colonists had been cutting into the jungle along the banks of the Ipa River, creating scattered *fincas* for several hours up and down the stream. Now, vast expanses on either side of the river revealed no jungle at all. The tall trees had been replaced by hectare after hectare of gray-green bushes. And unlike the area around San José, these coca fields were glisteningly healthy, untouched by the wilt of herbicide.

How dare they?

"Are you all right here, Miss—?"

Julie felt the sag of a heavyweight dropping into the next seat. She spun around in her seatbelt.

The eyes only inches away from her own were a far cry from the last pair she had stared into. They weren't brown and angry, but blue and smiling and warm with concern. Sondra's hunk. Julie glanced back to see Sondra looking displeased three rows back. What had she told him?

Julie flushed at the realization of the picture that must have drawn the man over. Clenched fists. Nose practically glued to the window. Nothing like the cool professional image she'd worked so hard to perfect.

"Everything's just fine," she answered firmly. "I was just—"

"Nervous?"

"Interested in our destination," Julie corrected flatly. She was not going to get bogged down again in her past connection to San Ignacio.

The concern in the blue eyes grew to a twinkle that was as sympathetic as it was disbelieving. Either the man was born with the most perfect smile ever created, or somewhere along the line he'd invested in a very expensive set of dentures. At this close range, Julie could understand Sondra's interest. He was *so* big and blond and good-looking. As to his nationality, Julie was no longer in any doubt. With that drawl and extroverted friendliness, he could only be American.

"Look, being a little nervous is a natural reaction for this kind of scenario," he said gently. "Terrorists . . . murder . . . guerrilla strongholds—that's not exactly your everyday news story. And I did notice you're traveling alone. It doesn't seem quite the situation into which most editors would choose to send a young woman on her own. That's assuming you *are* a journalist, Miss . . . ?" His pause made the question a double interrogative.

"Well, yes, as a matter of fact, I am." Did all men think alike? Or was worrying about her well-being some innovative new pickup line? After two years in professional journalism, Julie had stopped keeping track of the countless ways in which men chose to introduce themselves. At least Sondra hadn't wasted time gossiping about the other woman on the press team.

"I'm Julie Baker. Staff writer with *Our Earth* magazine. And my editor didn't *choose* to send me on this trip. I volunteered. And I wouldn't characterize being with a group this size as traveling alone. So how about you? Doesn't what's down there bother you—guerrilla strongholds . . . murder?" Julie tossed back his own phrases dryly. "Or maybe these kinds of assignments are old hat to you."

"Not old hat. But this isn't the first time I've been down here," he admitted with another flash of teeth. "Nothing like this, of course. Though I've learned to deal with the locals."

"Really?" Julie couldn't keep a skeptical note out of her voice as her gaze swept down his enormous, patently gringo frame. "And you haven't had any problem with the guerrillas? Or the paramilitaries? They just let you wander around free? No questions asked?"

Limpid blue eyes met hers. "If God calls you to go somewhere, it doesn't matter who else is out there. Not guerrillas. Not paramilitaries." He made a solid thump against his chest, and Julie realized he was still cradling that absurd museum Bible. "I'm sure you know the stories. David and Goliath. Daniel and the lions' den. Nothing can touch you if you're where God wants you—even if it's in the middle of a guerrilla camp."

*Yeah, right! Tell that to my parents! Who was this guy?*

"Excuse me—uh, who did you say you were? I didn't catch your name. Are you with the embassy—some kind of chaplain?" Julie glanced dubiously at the Bible. "Or a missionary?"

The missionaries she'd known weren't so . . . so—well, so in your face.

Julie tried to imagine her father parading a Gutenberg-sized specimen of the Holy Scriptures through an airport and failed.

Her new seatmate caught her glance and offered a wry grin that had Julie liking him more than she had. "It *is* pretty big, isn't it? A friend pushed it off on me when he knew I was coming on this mission. His idea of a joke! He figured it would make a good conversation starter. I brought it over—well, you looked in need of some cheering up. Habit, I guess!"

Dropping the huge volume into his lap, he thrust out a large hand so that Julie had to twist in her seat to shake it. "Tim McAdams, at your service. And actually, yes, you could call me a missionary. A missionary journalist, to be precise. I'm in the area to cover Colombia's war from the religious angle. I don't know if you're aware that a lot of churches and pastors have been wiped out by the guerrillas these last few years."

"Actually, yes, I did know that." For the first time Julie looked at her seatmate with genuine interest. "So what news service are you working with? And how in the world did you ever wangle a seat on this plane?"

She must have imagined the check of his body movement, because the geniality of his expression didn't change. "What do you mean?"

Julie had meant that last remark only as a casual exclamation, but since the missionary journalist was clearly waiting for an answer, she shrugged. "Well, just take a look around you. Except for the embassy and UN team, they're all pretty public figures—by name and reputation if not face. See the guy over there?"

She nodded across the aisle to where a slim young man with dark hair and olive complexion was scribbling furiously in a notebook.

"That's Andy Rodriguez. *Miami Herald* correspondent. Does a lot of articles on Colombia—which is why he got a seat. Sondra Kharrazi covered the environmentalists down here for NBC. Tom Chaney is the Latin American correspondent for CNN. The *Chicago Tribune* didn't make it. No room. Nor did the *LA Times*. Or the *Boston Globe*. And I happen to know they put their names in. Now you . . ."

Her apologetic glance was meant to take any sting out of her words. "I don't recognize your name—and I would have remembered. I have a photographic memory, and I do know most of the bigger-name journalists who deal with Latin America. I don't know what Christian magazines or radio networks you write for, but—"

The white teeth were no longer showing. "But they're probably a lot smaller than the *Tribune* or the *Times*. Well, I'm sure you're right—though there are more religious news services out there than you might think. Maybe the powers-that-be felt as I do that the church-going segment of our population should be represented on this mission. A lot of the evangelists and pastors killed by the guerrillas have been from this area. For that matter, I've never heard of you either. This magazine you mentioned . . . *Our Earth?* Is that some kind of science digest?"

"Well, no, actually it happens to be the largest environmental magazine in North America."

"And what would you say your circulation was—say, compared to the *Chicago Tribune?*"

Julie laughed and lifted her shoulders in retreat. "Okay, you've made your point. I guess the powers-that-be felt the ecological viewpoint should be represented. Remember, the three victims *were* environmentalists. Look, uh . . . Mr. McAdams, I'm sorry. I didn't mean to pry or insinuate you don't belong here. Being nosy is an occupational hazard for a journalist, I'm afraid. It's just that I have a personal interest in your field. My parents . . ."

The thump of landing wheels hitting asphalt cut off her explanation. Glancing out the window, Julie saw with some surprise the palm trees and fields rushing by. At least her new acquaintance had proved a distraction from their arrival. As the hydraulic brakes went on, Bill Shidler emerged from the cockpit.

"Ladies and gentlemen. We've now landed in San Ignacio. If you'll keep your seatbelts fastened until the plane has stopped moving, I'd like to use this time to cover a few last-minute items. Ground radio has just informed us of a slight disturbance . . ."

But he'd lost his audience. The press members were out of their seats, shoulders jostling for a view, TV cameras pressed against windows. The DC4 shook as the brakes slowed their rush down the runway, but experienced hands held lenses steady. Bill Shidler's angry voice rose futilely above the din. Showtime was here, and no one was going to be accused of missing the first shots.

"Excuse me, Miss . . ." Blocked on his own side of the aisle by the CNN crew, Andy Rodriguez leaned over Julie and her companion, a digital camera in his hands. "Would you mind if I squeeze in here for a few shots?"

"Can I get copies?" Julie demanded shrewdly, quick to see a solution to her own problem.

"What mag are you with?" The reporter's thin body was practically vibrating with impatience.

"*Our Earth*. World Conservation Institute. Norm Hutchens, editor."

The *Miami Herald* correspondent wasted no time debating. The next issue of the environmentalist magazine wouldn't be out until long after his own release. "You've got it. Now if you'll excuse me."

Squeezing past Tim McAdam's knees, Andy leaned across Julie to get his camera to the window. Not that there was much to see yet, as he'd quickly find out, since this side of the plane gave a view only of fields and the muddy expanse of the Ipa River in the distance.

As another reporter crowded in behind to lean over Rodriguez's shoulder, Julie found herself crawling over the seats to get away from their armpits. The missionary journalist, Tim McAdams, had already rescued his own large frame from the crush and was working his way back down the aisle to his original seat. She caught his eye as he glanced back, and he paused to lift his hand in a genial wave. At least he didn't seem the type to hold a grudge.

The babble rose to new heights as the DC4 slowed to a complete stop.

"Hey, what's going on out there?"

"You see that crowd? What the dickens?"

"Ladies and gentlemen! If you'll kindly return to your places, I can assure you this door will not be opened until everyone is in their seat and quiet!"

This time the political officer's angry roar had an effect. The camera kept rolling from the CNN crew's porthole, but the other news people began filtering back to their own seats like unruly children chastened by their schoolteacher. Andy Rodriguez dropped into the window seat that had been Julie's, leaving her on the aisle.

At the front of the plane, Bill Shidler was looking absolutely furious. "Ladies and gentlemen. Members of the press." That last sarcastic phrase differentiated the former from the later. The political officer struggled visibly between his training in diplomacy and what he really wanted to say. Diplomacy won.

"This is a historic moment for the United States and the other countries represented here. We deplore the tragic events that have necessitated this mission. But we also recognize that these events offer us an unprecedented opportunity, and it's our sincere hope that along with the investigation at hand, the United Nations team will also be able to address the peace process with the guerrillas. You, the press"—his voice grew drier as a sardonic gaze swept the first two-thirds of the plane—"are not here because we consider you necessary to that process. You are here because—and only because—the guerrillas wish to present their story to an international audience. Just what they want, we're still not sure. But we are now in their territory, and here they make the rules. Once we disembark, the UN team will be making the first contact. You will *not* shove your cameras into their faces. You will *not* yell and shout and ask questions. You will simply listen and observe. No matter who you are or what kind of audience you may have, if you do anything—*anything*—to jeopardize these proceedings, by the authority vested in me as head of this mission I will have your press credentials confiscated and have you confined to the interior of this plane until the time of our departure. Any questions?"

There were none, despite plenty of grumbles. Aggressive might be one of the kinder adjectives applied to the news media, but stupid they weren't, and they were capable of recognizing a nonnegotiable boundary line when they saw one.

Julie made no effort to join the peering out of portholes as she filed down the aisle between the CNN crew and Andy Rodriguez. Tension again knotted her stomach. If the emotional impact upon her of the jungle canopy and the familiar curve of a river had been enough to attract the attention of this Tim McAdams, what kind of a spectacle would she make when she actually set foot in the place she'd considered home for most of her life?

But as she stepped out onto the landing stairs, nothing in the scene that lay before her evoked unwanted memories. In her time, the only airfield in San Ignacio had been a grassy strip that her father had talked the town council into clearing. The only terminal had been a storage shed for off-loading cargo. What greeted her eyes now was a modern, if modest, airport with an asphalt runway nearly as long as San José's. Beside the runway was an honest-to-goodness air control tower with a galvanized-metal aircraft hangar next to it. The DC4 had taxied in close to the hangar before stopping, and through its open doors, Julie identified a smaller version of their own plane—a DC3—and beside it a Fairchild two-engine.

The smells carried to her nostrils by a hot, dusty breeze were wrong too—not the fresh sweet scents of the jungle that had bordered the grass strip of her memory, but petroleum fuel and the hot tar of the runway and other strong chemical smells Julie couldn't identify.

"*Coca o muerte! Coca o muerte!*"

The furious chanting drew Julie's eyes past the control tower. So this was the disturbance that had drawn her colleagues' attention—and cameras—during the landing. When Julie had lived in San Ignacio, the airfield had been open to fields and jungle. Now a chain-link fence bordered the runway, topped with nasty-looking coils of concertina wire. Behind that fence was what could only be described as a mob, their angry roar rising even above the babble of the disembarking news crews. They swarmed over the bed and cab of several cattle trucks parked close to the fence, and many held placards and banners above their heads. Even at this distance, Julie could make out some of the slogans.

"NO to Plan Colombia."

"*Yanquis* Go Home!"

"Make Peace, Not War."

And of course, *Coca o Muerte*—"Coca or Death!"

Julie studied the angry mob with disbelief. There were more people in it than had comprised the entire population of the sleepy riverbank town she'd known. Was it possible the guerrillas had diverted their flight, and this wasn't San Ignacio after all?

"Hey, you're kind of blocking things!"

So she was! Julie threw an apologetic smile over her shoulder and clattered down the rest of the steps—only to find her view abruptly cut off by the press of reporters who had descended before her. As the plane continued to empty behind her, Julie gave up trying to thread through the pack. She wasn't going to see a thing while trying to crane over the shoulders of this predominantly male crowd.

Dodging a camera tripod that a German crew was setting up, she ducked instead under the wing of the plane and made her way forward to the nose, slipping under it to the other side. The news crews hadn't made it this far, and Julie, leaning against the base of the nearest landing wheel, had a clear view of the runway and the river beyond.

No, this was San Ignacio, however changed. There were the docks where her father had preferred to tether his Cessna with its pontoons attached for easier flying up and down the river. Beside the docks was the blackened shell of the building that had served as both customs office and police station. It had been San Ignacio's sole law enforcement, its only task enforcing the excise taxes collected from passing cargo boats. Its destruction was surely the handiwork of the guerrillas.

"*Alto!*"

An armed man silhouetted against the bright sunlight suddenly materialized to block her path. Instinctively raising her hands, Julie took a step back under the nose of the DC4.

"*Alto!*" The man followed her, and as he stepped from the sunshine into the shade, Julie blinked with astonishment, her hands dropping forgotten to her side. This soldier in the mottled greens and browns of combat fatigues, holding her at gunpoint with a deadly looking assault rifle, was no man. He was a boy!

Barely taller than Julie herself, he had the gangly awkwardness of a teenager who hadn't yet reached full height, and his brave attempt at trimming the few straggling dark hairs on his upper lip only made him look younger. His battle uniform was too big, hanging loosely from the shoulders and cinched in tight around the waist. But there was nothing childish in the practiced ease with which he swung his weapon around to follow Julie's hasty retreat, nor in the implacable black chips of ice that were his eyes.

"*Vaya!* Go! You are not allowed here."

The gesture of the barrel was as unmistakable as the words. Julie backed quickly away, and as she did so, she saw what the press of disembarking passengers had hidden. Other guards fanned out to form a loose circle around the plane, each cradling an assault rifle across his chest, eyes alert and wary under the shade of a camouflage cap.

Julie blinked again with fresh shock and outrage. That these were the guerrillas they had come to interview was clear. But they were all so young. None, surely, out of their teens, and several barely into them.

Nor were they all male. The soldier's clothing did little to disguise a scattering of softer figures and an occasional ponytail hanging down from under the green-and-brown caps. The shadowed eyes of male and female alike displayed cool vigilance, and the casual handling of their weapons left no doubt that they could—and would—be instantly deployed.

A chill gripped Julie's stomach. What—or who—had done this to children, that they should look so hard and cold and . . . and *old*?

"I want a shot of the river." The authoritative voice belonged to Tom

Chaney. "And that burned-out building there too." Julie scooted backward as his camera crew followed him under the nose of the plane.

"*Alto!* You cannot come here!"

"Now, wait a minute! We just want a few background shots. You tell him, Ron."

Seeing the young guerrilla sentry start forward, Julie melted back into the welcome anonymity of the other news crews. They had scattered out, allowing for easier passage. Technicians were setting up sound equipment and testing mikes and satellite feeds.

Their focus was on a makeshift stage that had been set up beside the air-control tower. Made up of nothing more than planks thrown across a collection of fuel drums, the stage had a clean tarp tossed across it to dress it up. Julie threaded her way toward it.

She paused beside Andy Rodriguez, who had put away his digital camera and was fiddling with the telephoto lens of a much larger Minolta 35 mm. "Are we still on for pictures?" she asked.

"You pay usual rates and give me credit, and you've got them!"

Julie nodded, pleased. That worry off her hands, she'd be free to concentrate on her story. Turning away, she caught a wave and beaming smile from Tim McAdams, who was setting up not only the biggest camcorder Julie had seen yet but two still cameras as well. He looked to be thoroughly enjoying himself, and as Julie lifted a hand to acknowledge his wave, he called, "Piece of cake so far, eh? This is really something!"

His enthusiasm was catching, and Julie found her own step lightening as she made her way closer to the makeshift platform. Beside it, the white-coated UN forensic unit—two men and a woman—were riffling through boxes, lifting out pieces of equipment and sorting through them. Bill Shidler and his State Department team stood around aimlessly, looking less happy. Their guerrilla charges had disappeared.

Glancing at his watch, Bill Shidler turned to throw an annoyed glance behind him at the platform. Two youths in combat fatigues were there setting up their own sound system—a mike stand and two enormous loudspeakers—while a third youth prowled nearby with his assault rifle in hand. A bright orange extension cord trailed off the stage and into the control tower. The contrast with the news crews' battery-powered, wireless technology was striking.

"Julie!"

Julie didn't need to turn around to identify those imperious tones. There was only one other female voice on the press team. "Yes, Sondra?"

The NBC correspondent hurried up, her burly cameraman at her heels, already red and sweaty under the weight of the heavy camcorder on his shoulder. A Japanese newsman hissed angrily as they blocked his lens angle, but Sondra ignored him, waving for William to take up a position in the front row. She grimaced as she shifted on her stiletto heels, and seeing the expression increased Julie's appreciation for her own sensible walking shoes.

"Where are the FARC leaders?" Sondra demanded tensely as though Julie might have access to information she didn't. "All we've seen are these—these kids! If they think we're going to stand around in the sun all day!" Digging into her handbag, she pulled out a lace handkerchief and dabbed at the perspiration that was marring her makeup. "I want to get this over with and get out of here! If this is some kind of scam!"

Julie was surprised to see Sondra's hand trembling as she shoved the handkerchief back into her purse. She felt a twinge of compunction and touched Sondra's arm gently. "Hey, it's going to be all right!"

A roar of cheers and whistles from beyond the fence drowned out her reassurance. Julie and Sondra spun around. On the stage, the three guerrilla youth sprang to attention. An excited buzz rippled across the runway. Julie felt her own breath quicken.

Five men strode across the runway from the control tower. One walked a step ahead—he looked to be in his forties or perhaps older but had the carriage and fitness of a man decades younger. The other four were fanned out behind the frontrunner like some kind of ceremonial guard detail—or perhaps not so ceremonial, by the constant roving of their eyes.

Of these four, two were the FARC representatives who had been on the DC4. Manuel Flores and the younger guerrilla were no longer unarmed. Their pistol holsters bulged with weapons, and like their companions they had donned some sort of multi-pocketed ammunition vest over their combat fatigues. Assault rifles fit in their hands as though they'd been a missing piece of clothing. The two men surveyed their former fellow passengers with a newly arrogant lift of the head.

They drew near the stage. The frontrunner stopped before the steps leading up to the platform, and the other four came to a halt a precise pace behind him.

Bill Shidler hurried forward to greet them. *"Guillermo Shidler, a su servicio.*

*Embajada de Estados Unidos."* His Spanish, credibly pronounced, was carried by his clip-on mike across the airstrip. "We wish to express our appreciation for your hospi—"

Another roar—this time jeers and catcalls—from beyond the chain-link fence drowned him out. A handful of demonstrators on the cab of a truck lifted up an American flag. It had been scorched at the edges and torn, and a swastika splashed in red paint across the Stars and Stripes.

Ignoring Shidler, the FARC leader lifted a hand, and the commotion immediately died away. Then he snapped his fingers. The young man who had rescued Julie stepped up beside him, slinging his assault rifle over his shoulder. His fluent and only slightly accented English explained why he had been chosen as interpreter. *"El comandante* Raul Aguilera demands to know where are the United Nations doctors he requested."

The three persons in white coats abandoned their equipment and took a step forward. The guerrilla interpreter gave a curt nod. "Which of you is the leader?"

The three hesitated, murmuring among themselves. Then one stepped forward. He was small and meek-looking with the dark, fine features of southern India.

"I am Dr. Ravi Gupta, the senior member of this team." He indicated the other two in white coats. "These are my colleagues, Dr. Kristin Gustofferson of Sweden and Dr. Roger Elliot of Scotland."

The interpreter murmured to the FARC leader, whose barely perceptible nod seemed to indicate satisfaction. "It is well. Then may I introduce you to *Comandante* Raul Aguilera, commander of the Eighth Front of the Revolutionary Armed Forces of Colombia." The interpreter then gave a slight nod toward the older guerrilla who had been with him on the plane. "You are already acquainted with his second-in-command, the honorable Manuel Flores, a brave spokesman whose voice on behalf of our cause has been heard in many parts of the world. In the name of freedom and justice, they bid you welcome to San Ignacio. Is there any among your group who speaks Spanish?"

Bill Shidler stepped forward, displaying annoyance at being ignored. "Most of the news crews have been chosen with an eye to language proficiency," he said. "There will be no need to translate speeches. Any dubbing can be done at the newsroom end."

The guerrilla interpreter made no response to the political officer's attempt to regain control of the situation. The doctor from Scotland, Roger Elliot, spoke up. "I speak reasonable Spanish."

"*Bien!* Then you will serve as communicator for your team during the investigation to come."

"Now, wait a minute," Bill Shidler interrupted heatedly. "These are American citizens we are talking about here. The agreement was that we would have our own people involved in this investigation. If you need an interpreter, we've got them here." His angry wave indicated the State Department team.

Commander Aguilera's murmur to his interpreter made Julie wonder if perhaps he knew more English than he was letting on. The interpreter turned for the first time to speak directly to Shidler, and the arrogance in his tone was a reminder of how their positions had reversed. "You will listen and observe, no more! We will not allow the *americanos* to obstruct the fair and open execution of this inquiry."

Bill Shidler's mouth dropped open slightly at this twist on his own lecture to the news crews, then shut to form a thin line. Lifting his hands in admission of defeat, he gave a curt nod to his associates, who faded back behind the UN team. As they did so, the woman from the forensic team stepped forward in their place.

"If you don't mind, we would really like to get started," she said quietly, her own English revealing not a hint of her Swedish background. "Every hour counts in these situations, and we've already lost a lot of time. As you can see, we've brought our own equipment with us, so if you will take us to see the victims, we can begin immediately."

Aguilera murmured again to his companion, and the interpreter said stiffly, "You need not be so concerned. We are not savages here. We have taken the necessary steps to preserve the bodies. You will be escorted to them shortly. But first, the *comandante* will address your company and the world."

Raul Aguilera spun sharply on his heel and strode up the steps to the platform. The interpreter slapped his assault rifle back into his hands with military precision, then fell back beside his fellows, and the four of them stepped briskly onto the stage behind their leader. Despite the tenseness of the situation, Julie had to admire the dramatic skill of the guerrillas' theatrics. These people knew how to put on a show.

The cheers of the mob outside the fence swelled anew as the FARC commander stood unmoving at the mike. Then he raised both hands in the air, palms outward. Instant silence fell. *Like one of those audience prompt cards that read "Applause" and "Silence,"* Julie thought irreverently. All around her, TV cameras shifted their focus from their correspondents to the man on the stage. Reaching into her backpack, Julie pulled out her hand recorder and switched it on.

"Distinguished guests," the *comandante* began, "my fellow Colombians, listening citizens of the world, we welcome you here today. Envoys of that great body of freedom and brotherhood, the United Nations, we bid you to witness for yourselves our innocence of the accusations fabricated against us. Journalists of many nations who have traveled here today, we thank you for this forum to present our struggle for freedom and justice to the world. Representatives of the environmental organizations, we praise you for the commitment you share with us to protect this land from the rapacious greed of capitalists and imperialists." He pointedly left out any reference to the State Department team.

There was no attempt to provide a translation into English, but that didn't seem to faze any of the news crews. Even Sondra Kharrazi was making a low-voiced translation into her lapel mike, an indication that she had a lot more qualifications for this job than Julie would have guessed.

Aguilera continued. "A crime has brought us all together to this place—to this time. But it is not the crime of three brave men and women who have lost their lives in the struggle for the rights of our indigenous brothers. No, today's investigation will show that it was no crime but Mother Nature herself who brought about their deaths.

"The real crime that brings us here today is far greater. It is the crime of a political oligarchy steeped in greed, rapaciousness, and violence. An oligarchy that through an oppressive capitalism concentrates the land and wealth of our nation in the hands of the privileged, leaving hunger, unemployment, and death for the masses who do not take part in their corrupt machinations."

The guerrilla leader's tones were soft, almost conversational, more like a lecturing professor than a leader of armed insurgents. "Yet the crime here is not only that of an oppressive and corrupt government that dares to call itself a democracy while grinding under its foot all free expression of protests against its oppression. Simon Bolívar, the great Liberator of Latin America, himself once declared, 'The United States appears destined by Providence to plague the Americas with miseries in the name of freedom.'"

A murmur and an exchange of glances rippled through the press corps. A few feet away, Julie saw Bill Shidler's mouth press into a thin line.

"We generations who have followed after have found the Liberator to be a true prophet. Latin America has long suffered under the heavy hand of the various imperialistic policies of the White House and its occupants. In the past they came in the name of freedom and democracy but with the corrupt capitalism of their multinationals to rape our land of its wealth and add it to their own."

"Got a point there!" Andy Rodriguez murmured beside Julie.

"But today," the *comandante* continued, "it is not in business suits, but with guns and war planes and soldiers that they come. 'You have a drug problem,' the gringos tell us, while they, the principal consumer of narcotics in the world, do little to combat or imprison the great drug mafias that exist within their own country. And in the name of this counter-narcotics conflict that they have forced upon the sovereign states of this region, they place weapons of war into the hands of the very forces dedicated to oppression and violence."

A fresh round of applause followed from beyond the fence, and Aguilera's passionate voice rose above it.

"Is the United States of America so naive that it does not know with what it has allied itself? Americans, you who call yourselves friends of freedom, listen to me! It takes no university education to see that the present political order of Colombia is a vicious regime that has imprisoned millions of workers while at the same time criminalizing every form of social protest, so that everyone is indiscriminately labeled as subversive when he protests because of hunger, because of thirst, because of a desire for education, because of wanting to work when no one will give him employment, or because of wanting just wages if he is fortunate enough to have employment.

"It is not we who fight for the disenfranchised people of this country who are criminal. It is those who label us subversives! And what are their crimes? Their continued refusal to institute any true agrarian reform, to give the land to those who would work it. The absence of health care, housing, education, jobs. And to this we must add the institutionalized violence of the state, exercised through their repressive organs—the military and the police and the paramilitary butchers who are their allies. All to maintain unchanging the established social order for the benefit of the ruling class."

Despite the storm of cheers from beyond the fence, Julie caught a low chuckle behind her. She turned her head to meet Andy Rodriguez's ironic gaze as he lowered the Minolta. "That bit about 'butchers'—he's kind of forgetting their own share in all this, isn't he?"

Aguilera lifted his hand again for silence.

"He's good," Julie said, "I'll say that. If I didn't know better, I'd fall for it myself."

"Yeah, well, an even balance of truth and fiction makes the best deception, they say. One thing's for sure, with a vocabulary like that, he's no illiterate *campesino!* Or even just a soldier. If it wasn't for that military getup, I'd swear he was one of my old sociology profs—leftist speeches and all." He shifted the camera to snap a shot of the nearest sentry. "Do you think Mr. FARC Commander and those kid followers of his really believe what they're saying?"

Julie glanced over at the guard whose picture he had just snapped. A girl in her early teens, she wore blazoned across the upper arm of her uniform the emblem of Che Guevara, the Cuban freedom fighter martyred in the sixties. Julie's throat ached as she caught her expression—open adoration for Aguilera.

She turned her attention back to the *comandante*. What was there about him that attracted such fanatic devotion? He wasn't a big man, less than average height and slightly built—or underfed. His features, the warm brown of *café con leche* under the graying beard, showed a very Colombian mix of African, Indian, and European, the ethnic groups that had happily intermingled here for generations. But life—or his present fugitive circumstances— had honed his features so that the bones pressed against the skin, leaving his cheekbones a visible line and his eyes deeply sunk into their sockets.

No, Andy was right. Take away the combat fatigues, and even that air of command could belong to some inoffensive middle-aged professor. A very effective one, to be sure. There was something almost hypnotic about the rise and fall of his speech, from calm, almost dispassionate persuasion, crescendoing to fury and passion, then dropping down again almost to a whisper. It was a gift every TV evangelist and the best car salesmen possessed—the ability to hold and play an audience like a musical instrument.

Still, there had to be more to it than simple charisma—something every TV evangelist and car salesman knew as well. Nothing compelled more than a genuine belief in your product, and even a skeptical Julie could feel the conviction that breathed in every phrase of the guerrilla leader's speech and burned in those deep-sunk dark eyes.

"Oh, yes, they believe it all right!" she said soberly. "That's the scary part. There's nothing more frightening than a revolutionary truly committed to his cause."

"Hey, that's really good!"

Julie turned, startled by the tap on her shoulder. She had to look up to meet Tim McAdam's cheerful blue gaze. The missionary journalist had his camera hoisted on his shoulder. "I was chased out of my other spot," he hissed in a very audible whisper. "CNN. I wasn't trying to eavesdrop on you, but that was really good. Mind if I quote it?"

A nearby *shh!* hushed him up. Julie shrugged an indifferent assent. "Just keep my name out of it," she mouthed before focusing again on the FARC commander's speech.

"If the United States would truly help the people of Colombia, then let them invest in health care and education. Let them invest in agricultural development so our people will have an alternative to planting coca in order to survive. Let them build roads to take our crops to market and send seeds to plant in our fields.

"But instead, they send us guns! They rain down poison to destroy the food that feeds our families! They say it is to fight the narco-traffickers. Yet it is not the drug dealers who are their target. It is the *campesinos,* the poor, those who have no other option. This is not a plan for peace. It is a plan for war!"

To Julie's left, Bill Shidler and his embassy team stood tight-lipped under the growing acidity of Aguilera's language. Listening unmoved through anti-American rhetoric was a necessary discipline for State Department personnel. Beyond the fence, while Aguilera paused, the crowd took up a low chant of "Coca or death!" As the angry chorus rolled on, Julie found her own attention wandering across the stage.

The *comandante's* four aides had taken up position in a neat row across the center of the stage. Manuel Flores stood directly behind Aguilera, and the interpreter was at the far end. Julie's rescuer seemed to have gotten over his camera shyness, and he looked almost relaxed as he swept the audience with that same slow scan Julie had encountered at the Bogotá airport. Did he even recognize her as the woman he had snatched to safety?

Julie didn't realize how long she'd been watching him until the corner of his mouth curved unpleasantly, and he looked deliberately away. He'd recognized her, all right. Julie shifted her own gaze hastily, her cheeks hot with sudden anger. What was he thinking—that she was trying to flirt like those adoring teenagers out there hanging on his boss's every word?

Her eyes landed on one of the other guerrillas on the platform, a young man who had been patrolling the stage during the setup of the sound equipment. He now stood at attention in the back corner behind Aguilera's aides. Julie gave him a cursory glance and was already dismissing him from her thoughts when she took a startled second look.

She knew that face! No, there had to be millions of Colombian youths with that same riot of curls the blue-black of a crow's back and that exact shade of coffee-brown skin. But surely—she knew that face when it was younger, a little rounder, the wide lips curved in mischief, those somber black eyes twinkling irrepressibly.

Julie's stomach went cold. How had it not occurred to her that there could be children she knew among these adolescent warriors? Children she'd played with in the streets of San Ignacio or supervised at the swimming hole or even taught in her Sunday school class.

*Carlos.* That was his name. He'd been an imp of a boy. He was six years her junior, the younger sibling of one of her girlfriends, and he'd tagged along after the older crowd during her visits home on vacation from school. He had been in the plaza that night . . .

From beside her, Julie heard the irritated mutter of Andy Rodriguez. "Does this guy really think we're going to broadcast all this? If he does, he's got way too big an idea of his own importance!"

But Aguilera was finally winding down. He held up his hands again for silence, then spoke again quietly. "It is because of these crimes that the people's army, the Revolutionary Armed Forces of Colombia, wearied with pleading for political equality, have chosen to take up arms in the fight for a free Colombia. In the mountains and in the jungle, we will stand with arms at hand, inspired by the scientific principles of Marx and Lenin and the philosophies of freedom of Simon Bolívar himself, until we reach our goal—a free and equal socialist republic under our rule."

In a sudden move that transformed him from orator into soldier again, Aguilera thrust out his right arm in front of him and shouted into the mike, *"Contra el imperialismo!"*

With a clatter of arms, the other guerrillas followed suit. *"Por la Patria!"*

*"Contra la oligarquia!"*

*"Por el pueblo!"* rang out in a single note across the airstrip.

*"Hasta la victoria final!"*

*"Somos FARC-EP, Ejercito del Pueblo!"*

This was clearly a regular ritual. Julie translated the responding couplets in her mind.

"Against imperialism"—"For our native land."

"Against the oligarchy"—"For the people."

"To the final victory!"—"We are FARC-EP, the Army of the People."

Fine-sounding phrases, as long as you weren't too picky over how you reached that final victory and who you chose to classify as an enemy. Still, the fervor on those young faces made a stirring picture, and Julie noted with approval that Andy Rodriguez was taking plenty of them. Slipping out her digital to add a few snaps of her own, she heard a pleased comment behind her. "Well, if that won't boost the ratings!"

As Aguilera stepped back from the mike, the interpreter stepped up to take his place and said, "We will now allow some questions. I will translate for *Comandante* Aguilera if you do not speak the language."

An annoyed rustle rose from the forensic team, but the press corps immediately broke into a confusion of shouts. Ignoring them, the interpreter gestured toward the front row, signaling for one person to step forward with a question. Julie, who had chosen not to contribute to the chaos, didn't catch the signal until Sondra Kharrazi jabbed her in the ribs. "Get out there, girl! He's calling you!"

Julie hung back. She really had no questions, and now that she had spotted at least one person who might recognize her, she hesitated to draw more attention to herself. Then she glanced back at the hard young face of Carlos—a face she once knew as mischievous and alive with happiness—and her own expression hardened. She spoke up coolly.

"One of the criticisms commonly heard against the FARC is the recruiting of children for warfare. What is your response to this, and why do you allow minors into the ranks of a fighting organization?"

Her rescuer's cool glance met hers. Then he turned to the FARC commander. Aguilera stepped up to the mike.

"We do not recruit children. In fact, there are many children who, because they see what we do as exciting, come to us and beg to join. We tell them to go home to their parents. But there are many who have nowhere to go. Their families have been killed by the military or the paramilitaries. There are others who are very poor and who are being exploited by employers. If they come to us, we do not turn them away. If we did, we would be no better than their oppressors. At least with us they have respect, a uniform, an education, and food in their bellies."

He made it seem so reasonable. And he didn't mention that these kids were being taught to kill and that there *were* other alternatives. Julie gritted her teeth at the murmur of approval that rippled through the press corps.

As the questioning continued, Julie shifted restlessly. If only she'd had the foresight to bring an umbrella! Maybe these guerrillas were inured to the heat enough to stand in the blinding sun all day . . .

She heard shouts. "Hey, get your hands off me! No, no, keep it rolling! Let them see what's going on!"

The press conference broke up with a buzz. Not even Aguilera's angry shout returned their attention to him. There was something more exciting on which to focus their cameras.

Julie saw at a glance what had happened. Hot and bored, CNN's Tom Chaney had decided to combine a search for shade with what had become his trademark as a correspondent—personal interviews with the locals. He'd no sooner slung a microphone through the chain links of the fence when the guards had descended on him.

"Keep it rolling, keep it rolling!" he called over his shoulder as the young sentries herded him toward the platform. But already the guerrillas were confiscating the camera equipment from the rest of his crew.

On the platform, Aguilera slapped the mike, making painful claps of sound that had the same effect as a judge pounding his gavel. His gaunt features darkened ominously. As the uproar quieted, he called over his interpreter, and after a low exchange of words, he spun on his heel and strode from the platform.

The interpreter took his place at the mike. "This press conference is at an end," he announced curtly in his accented English. "You will now advance toward the hangar to your left. But the *comandante* first requires me to convey to you the following instructions, which will continue in effect for the remainder of these negotiations. You may broadcast to your news agencies any communication granted by the *Comandante* Raul Aguilera. You may take any pictures required of the glorious experiment of peace we are conducting here. But no one—*no one*—is authorized to approach or converse with any resident of this zone or any member of the *Fuerzas Armadas Revolucionarias de Colombia*. This is for your own protection. The inhabitants of this region are hostile to foreign intrusion, and we wish to prevent any incidents. You will be under surveillance at all times. Any infractions of these instructions, and you will be detained and your equipment confiscated. That is all."

# EIGHT

A UNIT OF ADOLESCENT SENTRIES escorted the press corps toward the hangar. Julie, hanging back, looked among them for Carlos—if that was really who the young man was. But the delegation on the platform had disappeared, and she saw no one else who looked familiar.

The hangar wasn't much cooler inside than the airstrip, the aluminum roof radiating heat downward like an oven. Trouble began almost immediately.

"What is this?" a plump German reporter yelled. "They're going to pen us up like animals? We're journalists, not prisoners! We've got some rights here!"

The enclosure toward which the guards were herding them did bear an unfortunate resemblance to an animal pen. It was literally a corral constructed out of shoulder-high sections of plywood in an open area of the hangar behind the aircraft. An actual farm gate, rather rusted, reinforced the image.

The German reporter planted his feet in the gateway like a balky mule. "You aren't going to get me in there!"

A rumble of agreement spread across the press corps. Their escorts made no attempt to argue. The assault rifles went up, and the distinct click of magazine slides being drawn back cut through the grumbling. Silence fell instantly, and the German reporter hurried through the gate, followed by the rest of the group.

Inside, it wasn't as bad as that first impression. The guerrillas had scattered folding chairs around the enclosure, and extension cords ran under the plywood to a floor fan in each corner. Just inside the gate, a card table held bottled water and plates piled high with *empanadas,* a meat-filled pastry.

Julie hadn't realized how thirsty she was until she saw the water. Making a beeline for the table, she picked up a bottle and unscrewed the top. Behind her, the gate clanged shut as the last news crew filed in. The guerrillas, remaining on the outside, spread out to take up guard positions around the perimeter of the enclosure. A few of the press corps dropped resignedly into folding chairs, but most rushed immediately to the barriers. Julie spilled water down her khaki shirt as bodies surged against her, literally pinning her against the plywood walls. The nearest was the plump German.

"Hey, you!" he called over the barrier—and her head—in passable Spanish. "You can't do this! We want to speak to someone in charge."

A guerrilla boy peered over the gate, but he made no answer. Clearly they were taking seriously *Comandante* Aguilera's prohibition against conversing with the visitors. The German tried again.

"This isn't fair! There are international conventions that govern the treatment of the press. We have a right to free and unrestricted investigation of the news. I will lodge a protest if you do not release us immediately!"

A babble of agreement arose. Julie tried in vain to wriggle free from the crush of bodies. It didn't help that her slim build brought her right about to armpit level on most of these men, and an hour in the sun had done nothing to improve the efficacy of their deodorant. Her irritation boiled up. The whole bunch were acting like toddlers throwing a tantrum because their toys had been taken away. Where was their professionalism?

Shifting her backpack so it offered some protection against the shoving, she raised her voice tartly. "Look, you guys want what's fair—this is Farclandia, remember? The only 'fair' here is what that guerrilla commander says it is, and somehow I don't think lodging a protest will ever change his mind. Now, if you will please excuse me!"

Rather to her surprise, her acid comment had immediate effect. The press of bodies eased, and the overweight European stepped back sheepishly. "Yes, well, I will certainly make mention of their lack of consideration in my coverage of this event. And what about the autopsy? Should we not at least be free to film that? I told my editor there would be shots for the evening news. A terrorist on a platform is news, but it doesn't bring ratings the way a body does."

Julie wriggled past him. Come to think about it, the other journalist had a point. Where was the UN team? Or even Bill Shidler and his State Department bunch? Only the press corps had ended up here.

The German reporter dropped into a nearby seat. "I don't like this!" he complained, wiping his sweaty face with a large white handkerchief. "We've been on the ground less than an hour, and already they're placing us in jail! How do we know this isn't a trap? Maybe capturing us was their plan all along."

Andy Rodriguez strolled up to grab one of the pastries.

"More likely, they've stashed us here until the forensic team can make its report," he said dryly. "Which is understandable. Can you imagine conducting any kind of exam with this whole bunch crowded in to watch? Let's not get too wild with our imaginations here."

"Yes, and you heard what they said about protection."

This time it was Tom Chaney who strolled up. The refreshment table was becoming a gathering point.

"If they're concerned about that mob out there, this is the best way to keep them—and us—out of trouble. They went to a lot of work here to make us comfortable. Maybe it isn't much, but these people don't have a lot. I think we should be appreciative of their hospitality."

His comment earned a dirty look from the German. Ignoring it, Chaney reached for a bottle of water. Taking a long swig, he went on thoughtfully, "In fact, it might be of interest to explore the issue of that mob out there. If the FARC has to go to these lengths to protect us from those people, then maybe this iron-fisted control the guerrillas are supposed to exercise over the locals has been exaggerated. And who knows what else about these guys has been exaggerated as well? Including all these stories of massacres and drug dealing. Their commander certainly addressed some valid social issues."

Julie looked at him in disbelief. Was she the only one who had done her homework for this assignment? And this was what made it to the evening news!

"I'm sorry to disagree," she spoke up firmly, "but if you think that was a spontaneous demonstration out there—or that *Comandante* Aguilera was trying to protect us—I don't think you understand how things work around here. There isn't a person out there who would dare wiggle if the FARC didn't give them permission. They've seen too many people die who rubbed the FARC the wrong way, and they're scared to death. And they're just as scared *not* to demonstrate if Aguilera orders them out. That's not a mob out there. It's a carefully arranged PR exhibit for your cameras, designed to impress upon the world how much support the guerrillas have from the local population. The size of that crowd alone is a dead giveaway. There's more people out there than live in the entire San Ignacio area, even counting all those new coca farms out there. Aguilera must have trucked them in from kilometers around."

The respectful silence that followed extended well beyond the refreshment table. Julie, glancing around at the battery of eyes on her, dropped hastily into a nearby chair.

"A very possible interpretation," Tom Chaney admitted smoothly. His gaze touched Julie briefly as though trying to figure out who she was. Then he returned to his audience. "Which makes you wonder who's running their PR program. Pretty professional for a bunch of backwoods revolutionaries."

"I thought it was interesting how much of the guerrillas' rhetoric was directed against America," Andy Rodriguez put in. "Granted, the counter-narcotics fight has put a crimp in their operations. But you'd think from the way he talks that the United States was their enemy rather than the Colombian government. . . ."

"Well! You really did do your homework!"

The bored drawl was Sondra Kharrazi's. Julie turned her head to see the NBC correspondent pull up a chair, placing it—coincidentally or not—where it received the most benefit from the nearest fan. She had the laptop Julie had seen on the plane. Opening it on her lap, she began running a modem from it to the smallest sat-phone Julie had ever seen. Behind her, William lowered the equipment bag to the floor.

"So," she asked Julie, "you never did tell me. How did you get to be such an expert?"

Uncomfortable at the attention, Julie chose to take the question as rhetorical. "You've done your homework too. I didn't realize you spoke Spanish until I saw you out there."

The other woman's penciled brows lifted. "I speak a lot of languages. That's why I have this job."

Julie accepted the rebuke meekly. Maybe the woman *did* deserve that cameraman. And the research crews.

"Mind if I join you two?" Tim McAdams hauled up another chair beside the two women, its metal frame creaking as he settled into it. For all his fair coloring, the missionary journalist showed little effects of the last hour in the sun, and neither his affable grin nor the twinkle in his blue eyes had diminished.

Opening a briefcase on his lap, he told Julie earnestly, "I heard what you had to say. I'm impressed! You really do know your stuff—more than anyone else I've talked to around here. I'd kind of like to pick your brains myself. Got a few minutes?"

He looked at Julie hopefully as he extracted a micro-recorder from the briefcase. His good humor was irresistible, and Julie found her lips twitching in response. "Sure, pick away! Just leave me a few for myself. I don't have a lot to spare."

Her eyes widened with appreciation as he opened the briefcase further to add a micro-cassette to the recorder. Julie was far from up-to-date on high-tech equipment, Norm Hutchens having barely moved himself—and his magazine—into the computer age. But Tim's laptop and sat-phone equipment were at least the equal of Sondra Kharrazi's or even Tom Chaney's. "Nice tools! Now *that's* what I call impressive."

The lid of the briefcase snapped shut. "Yes, it is, isn't it?" Tim agreed, his blue eyes limpid as they smiled down into hers. "A donation from a Christian organization interested in improving the quality of religious news."

A Christian organization with some funds. Julie's own parents had never moved beyond an outdated VHS camcorder that someone had donated to film footage of their medical ministry. *Oh really? Which one?* was on her lips before Julie remembered his earlier reaction and bit it back. Just because she had been raised in missionary circles and knew a lot of these groups gave her no right to be nosy.

"Look, I'm really no big expert on Colombian affairs," she said instead. "But I do know the area a bit. What is it you would like to know?"

"Señorita?"

Julie glanced up, startled at the interruption. A young guerrilla girl was peering down over the top of the enclosure. The black ponytail hanging down under the army cap was the same as every other female guerrilla Julie had seen, but the Che Guevara insignia on the upper sleeve identified her as the same girl whose picture Andy Rodriguez had snapped earlier. The tip of her assault rifle was thrust up over the plywood with a carelessness that made Julie hope the safety was on.

The girl looked from one woman to the other. "Are you the señorita Sondra Kharrazi? They are in need of your presence."

Julie saw the self-complacency visibly drain from Sondra's beautiful features. "Great!" she muttered. "I'd forgotten about the ID."

Stuffing the sat-phone into her purse, she shoved the laptop and other equipment at William. She glanced down at Julie as she rose gracefully to her stiletto heels, and Julie was surprised to see appeal there.

"Julie—?"

Julie knew what the NBC correspondent was too proud to ask outright. Julie was, after all, the only other woman here and not entirely a stranger. She jumped to her feet.

"Would you like me to go with you? Hey, no problem! I'd be glad to!"

* * *

Despite the tense occasion, Julie felt a sense of release as the young guerrilla girl led them out of the enclosure. They were led around the DC3 to a door set into the side wall. This opened into a hall with smooth cement floors and whitewashed walls, which Julie surmised was the control tower.

Her guess was confirmed when their guide led them through a second door into a large tiled room. A scattering of wicker couches offered seating for passengers, and at the far end a plate-glass window looked out over the airstrip. Beside it was a boarding gate.

Two armed guards prowled the lounge, and another stood at attention in front of a door across the room. There was no sign of the forensic team, but Julie immediately spotted Bill Shidler and his State Department associates standing in a stiff group over by the plate-glass window. Her mind raced as she followed the guerrilla girl across the tiled floor.

*Talk about a press scoop! An exclusive look inside the guerrilla stronghold. And the autopsy too!* This would put the final laurels on her article, if nothing else did. Maybe even open the doors for some extra pieces. AP and Reuters, for sure. Now if she could discreetly manage a few snapshots on that digital camera . . .

Julie caught the rigidity of Sondra's expression and with shame remembered she was here to offer support to a friend—well, acquaintance, at least—not to further her own career.

Still, even as she offered Sondra a reassuring pat on the arm, her mind was cataloging every detail. It was cool in here, despite the sun streaming in through that plate-glass window, almost chilly after the sweltering furnace of the hangar.

And the smell.

It caught at her throat, dampening Julie's enthusiasm. Not that it was, objectively, so unpleasant—a cloying sweetness oddly reminiscent of a hospital with its masking deodorizers and a high-school biology experiment she preferred to forget. And something more. Sondra stumbled on her high heels, clutching at Julie's arm, and Julie felt her own steps falter as she recognized it for what it was.

The smell of death.

Both the smell and the chill grew stronger as their guide led the two women across the lounge to the door with the armed guard outside. Julie's steps faltered further as she recognized the guerrilla on duty there. The young man who had been on the platform. *Carlos.*

But there was no recognition in the black eyes as the guard reached behind him to knock on the closed door. Either Julie was mistaken, or the passing years had blurred any resemblance of her adult person to a small boy's memories.

"Hey! Excuse me." Bill Shidler hurried across the lounge. "Excuse me, but if these women are to identify the victims, then I must insist that you allow me to accompany them. These people are American citizens, and my embassy *must* have visual confirmation that there has been a positive identification."

His response was an assault rifle blocking his passage.

"I'm sorry, sir," Carlos returned stiffly. "I have not been given such orders."

"I am not interested in the orders you were given. A personal identification by a member of the U.S. State Department was one of the conditions agreed upon by your own superiors when this mission was arranged."

His protest broke off as the door swung open. The interpreter, Julie's rescuer, stepped out into the lounge. He took in the altercation with an indifferent glance, then gave the sentry a curt nod. "Let them in."

Bill Shidler was first into the room. Sondra's nails dug painfully into Julie's arm as the two women followed. The cold hit like an icy blast as soon as they were inside, refreshing at first to Julie's heated cheeks, then biting into her exposed skin. One shivering glance explained the temperature and the guerrillas' assurances to the forensic team. Lacking a proper morgue to preserve the bodies for autopsy, they had with the ingenuity born of small resources constructed their own.

It was a baggage storage room, with wide shelves and a pair of luggage carts pushed up against one wall. The guerrillas had brought in one of the huge walk-in refrigeration units used to hang beef quarters in the meat markets that had access to electricity—another sign of progress for San Ignacio. When Julie's was a child, livestock were butchered fresh each dawn and sold before the sun was high enough to spoil the meat.

The bodies were laid out on three wooden tables, set directly in front of the open doors of the refrigerator unit so the stream of cold air played over them. Around the tables, the forensic team bustled in their white coats while an assortment of guerrillas in their battle fatigues stood back out of their way watching. They were the same group, Julie recognized, who had accompanied the FARC commander on the platform.

*Comandante* Aguilera himself stood at one end of the tables, forcing the medical examiners to walk around him as he scrutinized every move the forensic team made. Neither the UN team nor the guerrillas seemed bothered in the least by the cold or the bodies in front of them.

Or the smell, which was unbearably strong now that the door was shut, its sickly sweetness separating itself to Julie's senses into some powerful commercial disinfectant, formaldehyde, a jumble of other chemicals, and carrion scent underlying it all, a smell that reminded Julie horribly of those same meat stalls in the market when the sun was high and all that remained were the pools of spilled blood and fly-infested scraps.

The interpreter led Bill Shidler and the two women across the room. "Well, one thing is for sure," the woman examiner—Dr. Kristin Gustofferson from Sweden, if Julie remembered correctly—was saying to her colleagues, "this was no crime of violence. No knife wounds. No gunshots. No blood. We're going to have to move to pathological analysis. Tissue samples. Cultures. Drug tests. And that's going to mean taking specimens back to New York."

"Maybe they drowned." The East Indian head of the forensic team, Dr. Ravi Gupta, was carefully setting out what looked suspiciously like the tools of a butcher shop. Long carving knives. Smaller short ones. Even a saw with serrated edges. "Maybe their canoe overturned. Their Indian guides panicked when they drowned and just dragged the bodies ashore and dumped them."

"With that three-week gap? Impossible. Don't forget, Dr. Renken's effects turned up at that village long before the time of death. Though it's possible we're looking at some tropical fever." The Swedish medical examiner straightened and looked impatiently around. "Blast it, where's that tree-hugger! We can't get started until the ID is done." Her choleric eye fell on Julie and Sondra. "Oh, there you are! Well, let's get on with it. We don't have all day!"

That not everyone might share her own cavalier approach to death didn't seem to occur to the medical examiner. Julie yielded reluctantly as Sondra's tight grip on her arm practically dragged her toward the tables. She had never seen a dead body except as a child at the occasional village funeral, which in this climate was held within hours of death.

This was vastly different. Despite the present refrigeration, time and the elements had not treated the three victims well. Their clothing was fairly intact, though ripped and stained with a dried muck that must have been rinsed off the bodies themselves. The rest was intact as well, but the exposed limbs were faintly bloated so that they strained at the cloth that covered them like human-shaped balloons that had been blown up too full. Julie could see muscle-deep tears in the pale flesh of the nearest body—a woman's—that were made more grotesque by having been rinsed clean of blood and mud.

As for the faces . . .

Julie's stomach heaved. How could anyone make a positive ID through that ruin? Then she caught a gagging sound beside her, and a glance at Sondra's pale face reminded her that this was a whole lot worse for the NBC correspondent than for her. After all, these were people Sondra had known and worked with, however briefly. Gently loosening her arm from Sondra's clutching fingers, Julie put it instead around Sondra's shoulders. Her hands under Julie's were cold and clammy as she spun away from the tables.

"It's them. Those are the clothes they were wearing when they left. And their watches. The size . . . the hair . . . John Goodson had red hair like that. And that scar on the left arm . . . Dr. Renken was bit by a monkey the first day I was there. The native—I don't know. He wasn't dressed like that, but those are his shoes. He was so proud of them he had to wear them everywhere. . . ."

"That will be adequate," the Swedish doctor said. "Now if you will please clear the area." Bill Shidler shrugged his acquiescence, and *Comandante* Aguilera clapped his hands together sharply. At the sound, the door flew open and the young guard stepped inside to escort Shidler and the two women out. Julie kept her eyes down as she stepped past Carlos. She was fairly certain by now that he hadn't recognized her. Still, why chance any jogging of his memory?

Instant relief swept over Julie as the door closed, shutting away that scene of death. Even the air smelled fresh in comparison. The rest of the

State Department team was no longer standing at the plate-glass window but were seated on one of the wicker couches around a coffee table and were eating. She was reminded that it was long past lunchtime.

"Señor? Señoritas? *Su almuerzo.*" The young guerrilla girl who had guided them from the hangar called out to them. She carried a tray with three enamel bowls filled to overflowing with some thick stew. Their contents were redolent of beef and fat and garlic, at any other time an appetizing combination. But with the stench of death still in her nostrils, Julie felt her stomach heave. Beside her, Sondra clapped her hand to her mouth.

"Get me out of here!" she said through gritted teeth.

Julie spotted the familiar sign across the lounge and steered Sondra toward the door at a run. She breathed deeply, forcing her own stomach under control as Sondra dove into the nearest stall. The NBC correspondent emerged some time later, her beautiful features pallid and a decade older.

"Boy, I don't know what's gotten into me!" she admitted shamefacedly. "Nothing's ever gotten under my skin like that. It's just . . . I've just never been that close to a dead body . . . people I know!" A deep shudder went through her. "That could have been *me* there. . . . It could have been me!"

"Hey, it's okay!" Julie had seldom felt so inadequate as she again put her arms around Sondra. Her parents would have surely known what to say. Or even Tim McAdams, who had demonstrated his glibness in her own distress.

God is in control; He will bring good out of this.

They died for a good cause.

Unless a kernel of wheat falls to the ground and dies, it remains only a single seed. But if it dies, it produces many seeds.

The Bible verse was one of many she'd been assigned to memorize at that missionary boarding school. Why had it come so clearly to mind now?

*Real comforting! How about, they were stupid enough to go wandering around the jungle where they didn't belong and got what was to be expected. You stick your neck on the line, you get it chopped off.*

But Sondra was already pulling away. Drawing her slim figure to its full elegant height, she sauntered over to the sink and began repairing her ravaged makeup.

"Interesting that they haven't found any cause of death," she commented as she outlined her lips in bright red. "I wonder if I could get that out on the sat-link before CNN has a chance. Maybe live on the six o'clock news. I need a scoop on Tom Chaney."

Sondra was fast returning to normal, Julie saw wryly. She glanced around as they emerged from the bathroom. But the guerrilla girl wasn't there, and the meal she had served had been cleared away. The coolness of the air felt wonderfully refreshing compared to the steam bath that would be awaiting them back in the hangar, and after that autopsy room, even the hospital odor wasn't so bad.

"So what do we do now?" Julie wondered aloud. "Ask one of those guards to check us back into jail?"

Sondra snorted. "Are you kidding? We've got air-conditioning here, decent seats, *quiet!*" Dropping her handbag onto the nearest couch, she pulled out her sat-phone and began punching in numbers. "They're going to have to drag me kicking and screaming to get me back out there."

Sinking down onto the end of the couch, Julie tucked her feet beneath her. Draining the rest of her water bottle, she dug into her knapsack for some granola bars she'd picked up in the Washington airport. They were a much more appetizing proposition right now than stew. Julie offered a bar to Sondra, who took it without dropping a beat of her animated phone conversation.

Bill Shidler and his State Department team hardly acknowledged the two women's presence in the lounge. They were huddled in a meeting of their own, their heads close together in earnest discussion. Julie was struck by the air of quiet competence that characterized the two men with Bill Shidler, their heads coming up constantly to scan the lounge with much the same wary vigilance she'd seen on the faces of the guerrilla sentries. State Department—or military intelligence? She'd bet her press tag those two weren't civilians.

Her eye fell on Sondra, talking earnestly into her sat-phone, her hands moving rapidly in heated argument.

*I am the most frivolous person in this room,* she thought suddenly. *All these people are at least passionately dedicated to a cause they care about, however misplaced that dedication might be. Even Sondra with her rainforest. So what am I after? A story that's going to be back-page news in a week and forgotten in a month.*

*No, not just a story,* Julie reassured herself. *Fame. Glory. A future. And really, that's what they're after too. Sondra, Shidler, even the guerrillas. They're no different underneath.*

Sondra put away her sat-phone, then stretched out to nap, tucking a cushion under her neck so her hairdo would not be disturbed. Julie, driven away to another couch, pulled out her laptop and worked desultorily on some notes. At some point she must have dozed off, because she jerked upright to find that her screen had gone dead, as it did when inactive to conserve battery power, and the sky outside the plate-glass windows was fading to dusk.

Beside her, Sondra was still asleep. Bill and his team too were scattered around the remaining seats, not asleep but stretched out resting. Like her, Bill Shidler had his laptop out, and he'd seated himself where he could watch the storeroom door. A swift glance told Julie that Carlos was no longer on guard. Nor did the other sentries look familiar. At some point there'd been a guard change.

Shutting down her laptop, Julie shoved it back in her knapsack and rose restlessly to her feet. Shouldering her knapsack automatically, she walked over to the window and looked out. The DC4 stood abandoned on the runway, the stairs pulled away from its door, even the guerrilla sentries no longer in sight around it.

Past the plane, another chain-link fence marked the far side of the airstrip. Beyond the fence Julie could see the burnt-out shell of the old customs station and beyond it a glimpse of moving, rippling gold—the setting sun reflecting off the muddy waters of the Ipa River. The far side of the river hadn't yet been cleared for cropland, and in the fading light the uneven skyline of the scrub jungle rose in stark silhouette to the fantastic play of pinks and flames and pale greens that were the leading edge of twilight.

Here at last was something familiar—a thousand such perfect sunsets over just that patch of jungle.

Julie spun away from the window. She had to get out of here—even if it was back inside that stuffy enclosure with the other journalists. Walking over to Bill Shidler, she waited until he glanced up from his laptop, then asked abruptly, "Are we allowed to leave here? Walk around—or go back into the hangar?"

He looked surprised and faintly annoyed. "Of course! Just tell the guard where you want to go." With a glance to the baggage-room door, he added quickly, "Stay out of the storeroom, of course. Security's important in a situation like this. But we're not prisoners here, you know. We're guests! I'm sure you're welcome to stretch your legs. Their hospitality and the accommodations supplied for us are for our comfort."

*Sure, and you haven't seen where the rest of the press corps are stashed!*

Julie kept that thought to herself. Thanking Shidler, she headed toward the door by which she and Sondra had entered. She was still several strides away when, behind her, the storeroom door opened. She turned to see the figures in combat fatigues and white coats emerge from the autopsy room. With her journalistic instincts quickened, she abandoned any idea of leaving.

The Swedish doctor was again in the lead; even Aguilera trailed her rapid stride. As Bill Shidler sprang to his feet, she broke into urgent English.

"This is ridiculous! We have nothing. No results. These people were not assassinated. They did not drown. As near as we can tell, they died of disease. But how? What? And was it natural or induced? What do we tell the world? That they have simply died, and we have no idea how?"

Julie was mentally scribbling notes even as she rummaged through her knapsack for her recorder. What an irony it would be if the three activists' deaths did turn out to be from natural causes. It would certainly put a dent in her own story—though she might be able to salvage the environmental angle. Still, no one else would fare any better. A final blip on the evening news. A work-up on "mystery death in the jungle," if she knew Tom Chaney and others. And that would be it.

"We can't go any further without proper cultures and tissue analysis!" Dr. Gustofferson stormed on. "And those we cannot do in an afternoon. Nor without a proper lab and data banks. But these . . . these . . ."—the Swedish doctor paused, visibly exchanging terms in her mind—"these freedom fighters won't let us take samples out of here. Or airlift the bodies for further study. And now they say they're not letting us leave. This is in direct violation of UN conventions. If they think the world will stand by while they hold us hostage—even Saddam Hussein wasn't that foolish!"

*Comandante* Aguilera made an impatient gesture to his interpreter, and the younger guerrilla stepped forward.

"We are not holding anyone hostage," he translated curtly. "Just look out the window. It is already growing dark. The regulations of this airport do not allow *despeje*—takeoff—after sunset. We made arrangements for such a possibility. Even now, we are bringing in supplies from the town to provide a comfortable stay for your people.

"As for your tests, it does not interest us which disease was responsible for these deaths. You have seen for yourselves that no violence was involved.

That is all that matters. They became lost. They wandered in the jungle. They died. Their families are welcome to come here for their burial. But we will not allow them to be removed where evidence can be manufactured against us. No, we know the lies of those in power too well. All that we require of you is that you report the truth of what you have found—nothing! Then in the morning you will be free to leave."

"Fine!" Dr. Gustofferson responded. "Just make sure it's early. My colleagues and I have a conference in New York tomorrow evening. And don't think you've heard the end of this!"

Julie had remained motionless and silent, but the Swedish doctor's eye suddenly fell on her. Swinging around on Bill Shidler, she demanded, "Who is that, and why is she still here?"

At the political officer's murmur, she exclaimed louder, "A journalist? Then what is she doing here? Get her out of here. She can get her briefing when everyone else does."

Aguilera made another brief gesture, and the interpreter started in Julie's direction. Julie didn't wait to be ejected—nor even to remind Bill that Sondra, still asleep despite the racket, was being allowed to remain. With a shrug, she headed for the door. She had information no one else had, and it wouldn't hurt to jot down a few notes while it was fresh in her mind.

The interpreter caught up to her as she reached the door, but instead of hurrying her away, he strode out ahead of her and jerked his head for her to follow him. Julie eyed him warily as she stepped into the hall behind him. He had pushed back his assault rifle casually across his shoulder, but its gray metallic length and the shapes of banana clips and a grenade under the cloth of his ammo vest only reinforced her first impression of a very dangerous individual.

Still, there was something she'd been wanting to say.

Halfway down the hall they came to the door leading to the hangar, but the interpreter strode past it. He nodded toward the far end of the hall where a sign above a larger metal door announced *Salida*. Exit.

"This way, señorita."

Julie followed obediently, lengthening her stride to walk beside him instead of on his heels. "Please, I wanted to thank you for what you did back there in San José. I . . . I think you probably saved my life!"

She had shifted without thought into Spanish, and it was in Spanish that he answered, his glance down at her as sardonic as the curve of his mouth.

"You need not be so surprised. We're not all barbarians."

It was the same crack he'd made to Bill Shidler earlier. Julie flushed. A flicker of his eyes took in her discomfort, and he spoke again with a shrug that lifted his assault rifle up and then down again. "You were in danger. I saw it first. I acted. Any man would have done the same."

*"Any man" isn't a terrorist who goes around shooting people!*

Julie lagged back a step. She'd been handed an incredible opportunity here—a personal interview with one of the guerrilla leaders himself—while no one else on the press corps was being allowed anywhere near their hosts. And here she was blowing it! Norm Hutchens would rant and rave. That, or fire her if she let this one slip through her fingers: *My Chat with a FARC Commando.*

Tacking the headline prominently in her mind, Julie took a long step forward. The worst he could do was to tell her to shut up, and even that could be turned into a nice little news clip.

"You speak very good English," she began conversationally. "And *Comandante* Aguilera—he's an incredibly knowledgeable man. Are all of your people so well educated? Where do you manage to study? Or do you maintain schools out here? And—could you please tell me your name? You saved my life, and I would like to know a little about you. If that's okay."

Julie didn't quite hold her breath as she finished that artless bit of dialogue. Getting someone talking was the tricky part of an interview, but hard experience had taught her that younger males like this responded better to the airhead blonde—or rather brunette—routine than the intelligent and well-informed reporter who coaxed answers out of people like Colonel Thornton. She didn't quite turn on the "oh, you're such a big, handsome man; tell me about yourself" eyebatting that she'd seen colleagues like Sondra Kharrazi utilize, but her gaze as she waited for his response was guileless and innocent.

His own eyes, as they held hers, were unreadable. For one nasty moment she had the sensation that he knew exactly what she was doing. But as he paused in front of the exit door to lift a heavy key ring from his belt, he shrugged and said brusquely, "Enrique. Enrique Martinez. And if you are wanting a story for your news service, you may report that I was a university student in Bogotá when I chose to use my education to fight against the political and social injustices of this country. As for education— no, there are very few of our people who have access to education or any of the other services they need. Something *Comandante* Aguilera is determined to change."

Sorting through the dozens of keys on the key ring, he chose one. "So—is there anything else you wish to know for your story?"

There were countless things she wished to know, countless lines of inquiry she could have followed. But it was the question that had burned on her lips since he'd snatched her from harm's way back in San José that spilled out before she could stop it. After all, for all his weapons and intimidating appearance, he wouldn't touch her in this time and place, and she might never have another opportunity to ask.

"Yes! If . . . if you can risk your own life to save someone you don't even know, then . . . then *how* can you kill innocent people? Burn down villages? Bomb people's houses and businesses? *Shoot* people in cold blood? Doesn't it bother you that a lot of the people being killed are the very ones you're supposed to be fighting for?"

There was no answer except the jangling of the key ring. Julie caught a bleakness in his expression that made her wonder with a tightening of her stomach if perhaps she had gone too far after all.

Indifference slid over his face like a mask. With measured coldness, he said, "There is a saying: 'The blood of the martyrs is the seed of the church.' The priests like to quote it, and like all such sayings it has its grain of truth. This is a war! And in a war people die. Men, women—yes, and even innocent children." He might almost have been trying to convince himself. "It's regrettable, certainly. But no nation has ever gained its freedom except through the sacrifice of its citizens who are willing to shed their own blood on behalf of their country. And Colombia will never have peace or freedom until its people are willing to stand up and fight—yes, and die—for them."

The intensity in his tone reminded Julie of *Comandante* Aguilera. Julie, staring up at this man Enrique Martinez, thought with the same chill she had felt earlier, *He really believes it!*

Inserting the key in the lock, he pushed the door open and motioned for her to step through.

The door opened onto the airstrip in front of the control tower. The earlier color show above the horizon was fading to twilight, but there was still enough light to make out the DC4 off to her left, wings outspread like a giant insect settling down for the night. To her right was the hangar. Out on the runway, knots of people were wandering around, some with the bulky outline that could be nothing but a camcorder on their shoulders. Neatly situated under a portable spotlight, Tom Chaney was addressing his camera crew. CNN viewers around the globe were getting their evening update.

Enrique nodded toward the news crew. "Now that the day is cooling, your colleagues have emerged to refresh themselves. You are free to join them. In a brief while, there will be a statement to the press. Your colleagues have already been informed. In the meantime, the people of the town will shortly be providing you food and bedding to make your overnight stay comfortable. We apologize for the inconvenience this may be causing any of your people."

His words were as short and succinct as a prepared press release, and with them given, he stepped back inside. Julie caught the door as it was swinging shut. Dropping the airhead pose, she said quietly to Enrique, "But these people aren't giving their lives for their country. They are having them ripped away. They never asked to be part of this crusade of yours. All they've ever asked is to be left in peace."

With a sharp tug, the door came loose from her fingers, clicking shut with an audible squeak of its springs. Julie stared at its metal exterior. *Boy, did I blow that one!*

Still, for all the terse remarks Norm Hutchens might be addressing her way right now, she'd managed to get some usable quotes from this Enrique Martinez. And it would seem that Bill Shidler was right—they weren't prisoners here, but guests.

Dropping her knapsack to the ground, Julie dug out a notepad and began jotting down every word and impression of the last half-hour, squinting against the failing light as her fist raced across the page. Others preferred to dictate into a recorder, but Julie thought better with pen in hand. Only when she could think of nothing else to write did she wander out onto the runway.

As she strolled over toward the hangar, Julie saw a truck pulled up inside the cavernous entrance. Several men in the cotton shirt and pants of *campesinos* were unloading baskets of potatoes and rice under the watchful eye of an adolescent guard. Others were lifting down rolled-up *esteras*, sleeping mats woven of bamboo stalks and leaves.

Beyond the control tower, the demonstrators had finally abandoned their post, and the only noise was the cheerful chatter of the news crews. Sentries still stood at attention along the length of the airstrip, but they were no longer making any attempt to curb their visitors' explorations. Dodging a stalk of plantains—the enormous cooking banana that was a staple here— as it was lowered from the truck, Julie strolled on past the hangar.

She came to a service gate set in the chain-link fence. Outside the fence, an ancient Volkswagen pickup had pulled up to the gate. A guard strode around the truck bed, inspecting its contents. In the fading twilight, Julie could make out only vague shapes, but she could both hear and smell. Chickens and at least one pig—still living. Their dinner was going to be very late, but it would include fresh meat.

As the guard carried out his leisurely inspection, Julie wandered over to the fence. It was indeed much cooler out here, the evening breeze across the airstrip blowing away the heat of the asphalt. The pinks and oranges of sunset had faded to pale green, and above the remnants of scrub jungle that separated the airport from San Ignacio itself, the first stars were twinkling. A flock of parrots swooped down to roost with a raucous caw.

Outside the fence, a gravel track ran from the service gate parallel to the airstrip until it intersected with the main entrance on the far side of the control tower. There it turned at a right angle to make its way into town. Seven years ago, only that main road had been there, and the airstrip was unfenced and graveled like the road. Julie knew now exactly where she was.

Straight across from where she stood—give or take a few meters—had once been a footpath, a shortcut through the jungle that petered out just a few blocks from the little plaza on which the Bakers' house was situated. Behind Julie, the footpath had crossed the runway, continuing on down to the docks where her father's Cessna had floated on its pontoons. She'd traced that path so often, she could probably follow it in the dark even now.

"Uh . . . excuse me—Julie . . . Julie Baker, right?"

The laughing drawl drew Julie's gaze behind her and up—a long way up—into twinkling eyes that were no longer blue in this light but dark. Tim McAdams stood, briefcase in one hand and the other fiddling with that digital camcorder of his. Julie frowned when she saw that the lens was focused on her.

"You did say I could pick your brains," he said cheerfully. "Is this a good time?"

Julie reached over and deliberately took the camcorder from his hands.

Shutting it off, she handed it back to him. "Just what is it you want to know?"

The big American showed no irritation at her action. He grinned down at her, relaxed and confident as he looked her over with candid interest. Twilight had paled the flaxen blond of his hair to silver, and his teeth flashed white against the fading light in that heart-stopping smile of his. Julie thought with renewed incredulity, *This guy is really a missionary?*

"Everything," he said, stuffing the camcorder into a pants pocket that on most men wouldn't be capacious enough to hold it. From another, he removed the recorder she'd seen earlier. Clicking it to record, he grinned again. "Just tell me about yourself. You're quite an expert on the politics of these people for someone who writes for an environmental magazine. Any personal interests in the region? Or are you this well-versed on every country you travel to?"

Julie stifled a sigh. Tim McAdams was good-looking, reasonably intelligent by all signs, and certainly not lacking in charm. And though she had reached her twenty-third year untangled of heart, Julie wasn't unaware of his attraction. But not tonight! Not now with a torrent of unwanted memories facing her just across through those trees.

"Look, I'm sorry!" she said apologetically. "I'm just not in a very good mood right now. I'd really like to be alone for a bit. Maybe over supper?"

Whether he was disappointed or indifferent to her answer, it was too dark to tell. "Sure, no problem," he answered cheerfully. "I'll catch you then."

He strolled back toward the air control tower, recovering his camcorder from his pocket. As he did so, Julie saw that he'd already focused on his next target—Sondra Kharrazi, tripping out onto the runway in her stiletto heels. So she too had been run out of the inner sanctuary. Sondra paused to scan the runway, and Julie spun quickly around. She didn't want any more company.

Quickly, Tim and Sondra were dismissed from her thoughts. In that swift transition to nightfall distinct to the equator, it seemed that a moment ago there had still been remnants of dusk and now it was full night. A floodlight blinked on above the service gate, and on the far side of the fence, Julie could see a firefly glitter of lights flickering through the tossing branches of the scrub jungle. The evening ration of electricity had been turned on in San Ignacio.

The pickup truck rolled through the gate, its animal cargo noisy in the back. As the floodlight fell on the truck bed, Julie saw that the animals were not its only cargo. Half a dozen women were sitting back with the pigs and chickens, with huge aluminum pots at their feet. The cooks for tonight's meal. Julie found herself straining to see their faces as the truck moved slowly out of range of the floodlight.

That bent old lady hardly bigger than the pot at her feet. Allowing for passing years and fuzzy memories, she could be Doña Nina, one of her parents' most faithful parishioners who had cooked for dozens of church events. And the bigger, plumper one beside her. Her back was to Julie, but her build could easily be Doña Carmen, their next-door neighbor. Or had either of those women survived the madness that had hit San Ignacio?

A gust of wind blew suddenly across the airstrip, its force whooshing through the treetops like surf on a beach, sweeping away the acrid odor of petroleum and chemicals and hot tarmac, and carrying in their place the sweet perfume of night-blooming jasmine—and another scent, moist and green, that was an indescribable fusion of flowering trees and sun-warmed grasses and an underlying citric tang that told of lemon and orange groves nearby.

The scent was achingly familiar, and as it filled her lungs and caught at the back of her nostrils, Julie found her heart racing unaccountably, her breath whistling through her teeth in short, sharp gasps, her hands cold and clammy as they tightened on the steel links under her fingers.

Her more rational side told her sternly, *You're crazy! You can't go out there! You don't even want to go out there!*

But she had no choice. For better or worse, the first sixteen years of her life lay out there beyond that patch of scrub jungle, no more than a ten-minute walk away. If she turned away now, the lost opportunity would never cease to haunt her.

*I'll just go look and come back.*

And why not? As Bill Shidler had said, they weren't prisoners. The FARC commander had made a big deal about warning the press away from his followers. Fine, she had no intention of making contact with a living soul. It was dark enough now that she shouldn't have to. She could easily slip over, have a leisurely stroll around her old home and town, and be back in plenty of time for that dinner engagement with Tim McAdams.

*After all, what's the worst that could happen? Say I get caught or the gate's closed when I get back. What are they going to do? Exile me for the rest of the mission? Dump me in the plane and keep me locked up till morning? I've already got my story. And Andy Rodriguez has my pictures. One way or another, I'm out of here tomorrow—with a prize-winning piece to show for it too.*

Nor would getting out be difficult. For all their weapons, these teenage guerrillas showed little experience in keeping tabs on a group this size. Even now, one of the supply trucks was returning from the hangar. Stepping away from the gate, the guard held up a hand to flag it down. With a squeal of brakes, it ground to a halt. The guard strode around to the driver's window. All Julie had to do was slip up along the other side and—walk out the gate.

The thought was mother to action.

Stepping away from the fence, Julie walked quickly back toward the hangar as though she were following Tim McAdams, but as she rounded the tailgate of the truck, she halted beside the rear right tire. She couldn't see the guard or anything but the wheel and the high side of the truck. But after a moment the wheel shifted into movement, and she simply walked alongside it as it rolled toward the gate. The truck slowed to ease over a speed bump, then picked up speed so that she was forced to break into a trot.

And then she was through.

The guard would have seen her lonely stance at the fence—and earlier, her conversation nearby with Tim McAdams. But if her sudden disappearance roused concern, Julie heard no raised voice of alarm behind her. The truck picked up speed again as soon as it pulled out onto the gravel track so that Julie was soon running beside it. This was the tricky part. Could she get across the road unseen once the truck pulled away?

It didn't prove so difficult after all. The guerrillas hadn't been overly generous with electrical power at the airport complex, and once beyond range of the floodlight above the service gate, the blackness of night closed in over the gravel track. Julie smothered a cough as the dust stirred up by the truck's passage swirled over her. Then she slipped through its concealing billows and into the cover of the scrub jungle on the other side of the road.

\* \* \*

Narrowed eyes watched Julie's exit, and a cold smile curved with a satisfaction that could not be seen in the shadows that nightfall had laid across the airstrip. *So soon, confirmation!*

Swift fingers tapped in a number on the sat-phone dial. The signal went to a communications satellite hovering over the equator, then bounced to a GPS position that should have been trackless, uninhabited jungle.

Taqi Nouri left the unloading job he was overseeing to take the phone a subordinate hurried to bring him. He nodded with equal satisfaction as he listened to the low Farsi.

"How can you be so sure she is the one?"

The question had been anticipated. "Elimination. I have verified every member of the mission. The UN doctors are who they say they are, and they are too publicly known to be otherwise. The non-American reporters were a gambit I considered, but they have proved to be faces well-known on camera. The State Department team were a logical consideration, but they are too conspicuous—clearly Special Forces dressed as civilians, and they must know they are under close surveillance. This eliminates all but the American news crews, an obvious choice. But most have worked long in their present positions, and I have visually confirmed their identities with the computer files. I seek a person who is new to the scene and not what they appear to be."

Taqi Nouri stroked his black beard thoughtfully before replying. "And you—are you not who you appear to be? A good agent supplies himself with good cover."

"True. But there is a balance that leave signs to the experienced eye. This woman's cover is classic—a journalist from a magazine too obscure to be readily investigated, yet with a readership broad enough to justify wide travel. I could not have chosen better myself. But in that lies their error. I ran her too through the computer. She is an underling at this magazine with but a few trivial published credits—too unknown to be selected for this assignment. And there are other factors. Too many for coincidence."

"What factors?"

Taqi Nouri listened with an occasional nod. He had told the ayatollah that this agent was his best, and if the facts were as he was being told—and there was no reason to think otherwise—then his own assessment agreed with the agent's. The Americans had again proved themselves predictable. It would one day be their undoing.

"It is well then. You have your orders. We must know how much the Americans know and what are their suspicions. And it must be done swiftly. The time is growing short. Even as we speak, the final pieces are moving into place."

"It will be done."

The connection was severed. Taqi Nouri returned to the growing stack of crates. A man in a technician's white coat walked over to hand him a sheet of paper. "The manifest of today's shipment. Our friend across the border came through as promised."

Nouri glanced through the handwritten list. "The lightning bolt of Allah," he mimicked softly, and there was no mockery in his imitation.

* * *

Colonel Thornton picked up the sat-phone on the first ring. This voice too was low, almost a whisper, but the words were English. "I saw you from the plane today."

"I saw you too," retorted Colonel Thornton. "Just about freaked me out. What are you doing mixed up in this mess?"

A muted chuckle. "Last-minute orders. Did I make it onto the evening news?"

"Haven't had time to watch it. We're having our own troubles here, remember?"

"Yeah, well, I don't like this. It's gone way too public. Cameras all over the place."

"Hey, your cover's good. Don't sweat it! What about the op?"

"There's something out there, I can feel it. But whoever knows what's going down, it isn't Raul Aguilera and his bunch. They think they're telling the truth, whether they are or not. I can't buy that 'natural death' verdict the *comandante* is handing out. John was too good for that. No, they ran into something out there, I'd swear it. But what? I'm running out of options, sir."

"Give it more time. Something might break yet."

"Time." The voice on the other end was suddenly somber. "Sir, I have a feeling we're running out of time."

The same urgency for haste was dogging at Colonel Thornton's heels. But he chose not to discuss it. "What about the mission?" he asked. "Any trouble there?"

"They're fine. Both sides wallowing in the PR. There's a reporter, though—she's better informed than I like."

"Ms. Julie Baker." This time the chuckle was on the San José end. "She checks out okay," Thornton said. "Just one smart cookie, from what I can see."

"Yeah, well, let's just hope Aguilera doesn't decide to have a few of these cookies for dinner! They have to look pretty tempting from where he's standing."

"HQ claims there's no risk of that. And they're probably right. Still, if something does blow, don't go breaking cover to bail them out. There's a lot more at stake here than a few politicians and reporters, and Shidler has a whole lot more resources than you do. You just keep your eyes open and let me know if something goes down."

"Hey, no worries, I've got more invested here than you do. I'll keep an eye on your reporter friend and her pals. But that's it. And another thing. Don't ask me to check in again unless it's urgent. There's too many eyes and ears around me right now. This has been too long already. You hear from me again, it's going to be calling for the cavalry."

"Roger. Just watch your back, man."

The answer was muffled, but distinctly dry. "I always do."

*　*　*

So the report that had come was true. The daughter had returned to San Ignacio. And just in the needed time. The shadows of evil were growing dark across the jungle. Too dark to ignore any longer. But was the daughter like the parents? Would she listen—and help?

And if she did not, what to do then?

Perhaps the course of wisdom would be to watch and to see.

# NINE

A TANGLE OF BRANCHES AND VINES hung low over the road on the opposite side. Underneath was the blackness of midnight—the perfect cover as Julie slipped back toward the footpath.

Ouch! Not so perfect when you couldn't see where you were going!

Pushing aside the branch that had raked through her hair, Julie slowed to a more cautious progress. Maybe the footpath didn't exist anymore. Seven years was plenty of time for it to grow over—especially as it no longer provided a swift passage down to the docks.

But it was there. Julie's feet fell onto the path and she felt relief. The packed earth under her sneakers allowed her to feel her way, and as she left the road behind, the trees were sparse and even cleared back in spots so that the starlight shone through, offering a dim illumination to the trail. This was clearly still in frequent use—something that puzzled Julie until her foot connected with a round object. A soccer ball, her hands informed her as she picked it up. Children, slipping down the trail to spy through the chain-link fence of the new airport.

And perhaps not just children.

The footpath petered out sooner than Julie had expected. The trail ended in a banana grove. Stacked to one side were branches and limbs from the trees that had been cleared to plant the bananas. Through the banana fronds, Julie spotted a bamboo hut, its thatched roof extending well beyond the cane walls to shelter at least one strung hammock. The smell of smoke signaled a cooking area on the far side of the hut.

Stooping to dodge a stalk of bananas, Julie threaded her way through the grove. A rooster, settled in a nearby orange tree for the night, set up a noisy crowing as she passed. Julie quickened her pace before someone came out to see what had caused the disturbance.

Julie slipped past several other farmyards. Then she came to the first town street. Here the houses were adobe, or cinder block for those more prosperous, their whitewashed fronts forming one solid wall along the street.

The lane itself remained unpaved and ungraveled. There were still no streetlights, though the gleam of electric lights spilled through several open shutters.

Cooking areas were indoors or in a back patio, and Julie caught an occasional uplifted voice behind those walls. But something troubled her, and she wasn't sure what it was until she realized that the streets themselves were empty. Dark as it was, this was still early evening here on the equator, where nightfall fell like clockwork at 6:00 P.M. the year around. She should have seen men and women enjoying the evening breeze on their front steps, young people strolling through the streets or playing their guitars, children kicking a soccer ball like the one she'd found.

Was this what the guerrillas had done—driven all joy and life and merriment from the town?

Julie passed the closed-up stalls of the open-air market, and with that orientation, made an immediate right. She began to hurry, anxious to have this over.

And then—there it was. The little plaza lay empty and silent under the stars. It had once possessed a single streetlight, product of the generator Dr. Baker had installed for the clinic. The light was now broken or shot out, its lamp case a mess of shattered glass. The building fronts around the plaza were mainly shops, their heavy wooden portals and shutters fastened tight.

The promise of moonlight, not yet risen over the town but reflecting a dim luminosity from whitewashed walls, allowed Julie to make out the shapes of ornamental shrubs here and there. The light gleamed softly from large triangular flower planters, also painted white.

Julie walked slowly to one of the planters and sank down onto its concrete border. This was where she had sat that night as the music and laughter had fallen into silence, when the young people she'd called "friends" had dissolved into the darkness and out of her life. That rutted lane, empty now along its length as far as she could see, was the street down which the horsemen had clopped their way. And over there . . .

She turned her head, almost reluctantly. It hadn't changed—her home. Its street frontage was longer than that of its neighbors, due to the clinic, whose large wooden portal was just beyond the smaller door that had opened into the Bakers' living room. Otherwise it was just like the rest of the buildings surrounding the plaza—the same square, flat facade, the same peeling whitewash. Behind those cinder-block walls, Richard and Elizabeth Baker had lived and worked, pouring out their lives and their selves.

And there in the end they had died—alone. Julie didn't even know where they were buried, or if their bodies had been left for the birds and creatures of the jungle, as the guerrillas had been known to do often enough.

*Okay, you've seen it. Time to go.*

But Julie didn't move.

Like its neighbors, the windows of her old home were shuttered—heavy wooden shutters that her father had barred from the inside only at bedtime. Time and weather had warped the wood so that a yellow sliver of light showed around the edges. The jasmine and bougainvillea that Elizabeth Baker had planted and trained still curved up around the doorway, and the sweetness of their scent drifted across the plaza.

A macaw, protesting raucously from the patio out back, might have been the same that resided there in her childhood. An aroma of cooking in the air reminded Julie of just how scantily she had eaten so far that day.

For all the somberness the guerrillas had brought to San Ignacio, beauty remained, Julie recognized with surprise. A beauty that came from the tranquility of the night and the heady perfume of the flowers that was released by the cooling dew of nightfall and the gentle evening chorus of bird life and frogs and even the scampering monkeys restlessly choosing a place to sleep. Almost, Julie could see the ghost of a small girl perched on those concrete steps across the way, knees drawn up to her chin as she waited for a call to supper, her wondering eyes on the stars that were so much more glorious here above that tossing sea of jungle than at boarding school where the city lights competed with their splendor.

Across the plaza, a murmur of voices rose suddenly from beyond those closed shutters, and an indignant squawk from the macaw signaled that someone had thrown water—or worse—to silence it. For one agonizing moment Julie *knew* she had only to cross those paving stones and knock on that wooden portal for her father and mother to step out into the doorway and pull her laughingly inside.

The compulsion was so strong that Julie's fingers dug into the concrete rim of the planter to keep her where she was. She hadn't known what reaction to expect upon seeing her old home. Bitterness. Anger. Pain. She'd been prepared for all of those.

But love?

That was the emotion ripping her apart.

*I . . . I loved this place,* she thought dazedly. *I loved these people. I . . . I was happy here! How could I have forgotten?*

The sudden release of memories flooded her in a torrent that threatened to sweep away the image of the cool, well-adjusted, highly professional young woman she had constructed so carefully after the emotional turbulence of her teen years.

She remembered playing in the streets with the other town children, a knot of rags as their ball, two pairs of rocks their goal posts. Floating downriver in a dugout canoe, eyes wide with shivering delight at the toothy grin of the piranha the fishermen pulled in. Sitting at the feet of an I'paa storyteller, spellbound by his tales of hunts and battles. The I'paa in turn squatting around the village green while Dr. Baker told the stories of how the universe began.

Were the I'paa still in their village downriver, or had they vanished with the coming of the guerrillas?

In that house over there, she had shrieked with laughter at the antics of her neighbor's pet monkey. No, she couldn't have one, her mother had regretfully told her demanding daughter, not with Julie gone so much of the year. And Doña Carmen had assured the downcast little girl that she could consider their pet as her own when she was home. That monkey had been part of the excitement of boarding school vacations, stepping off the plane into her parents' welcoming arms and the hugs of her village friends, and knowing that for a few joyous weeks at least, her world had been returned to her.

There was Christmas Day with fireworks and a midnight feast at the church that stood just around the corner, but which was now undoubtedly a burnt-out shell like the customs station. Scampering through the rutted lanes of the town with absolute assurance that she would find a smiling welcome through any doorway into which she cared to poke her curly head.

And coming home at night to crawl under the voluminous mosquito net that had made her narrow cot her own little fairy tent. Falling to sleep with her father's deep voice reading a bedtime story, her mother's soft lullabies. . . .

How many other memories had she shut away and forgotten in the anger and pain of those last disagreeable visits home and the death and separation that followed?

Yes, she had been happy.

*Then why? Why after all their sacrifice did You have to take it all away? Why did You have to make it for nothing? You let the guerrillas win! You let them wipe out my parents—my life!—as though they were nothing.*

"Unless a kernel of wheat falls to the ground and dies . . ."

The guerrilla leader Enrique Martinez had said something similar in defense of his murderous activities. *The blood of the martyrs is the seed of the church.*

*Yeah, right! And what is that supposed to mean? They fell—they died—and everything they ever did, everything they ever* were . . . *where is it now? Gone! Gone just as they are!*

"Señorita? Julia, *hija?*"

Her name emerged from the night—with the "h" sound of the Spanish "j"—and for a moment Julie thought that the soft whisper too was a ghost of her past. Then she felt a tentative, hesitant touch on her shoulder. Springing to her feet, she whirled around, her hand to her throat.

It wasn't the guerrilla sentry she'd half expected. This was a woman, dressed in the shapeless black dress and head scarf of the older generation of *campesino* women, and so bent with age or arthritis that her covered head barely topped Julie's shoulder. The moon was rising over the plaza now, and its soft light illumined small black eyes that were no less sharp for the maze of wrinkles in which they were set. It was the elderly lady Julie had glimpsed earlier this evening, clutching a pig in the back of the pickup, a cooking pot at her feet.

"Doña . . . Doña Nina?"

"Then it is you, Julia!" The old woman threw her arms around Julie in a fierce hug. "We knew you would come back one day . . . we hoped . . . all of San Ignacio has been waiting. But why did you wait so long? Why did you not come before?"

Julie felt as though she had somehow slipped over into a twilight zone. They had *hoped* for her to come back—these people who had done nothing when her world had come apart, who in their not-doing had driven her away from her birthplace?

But the old woman was still talking in the same soft, urgent whisper. "You were spotted from the demonstration . . . the *comandante* ordered out all of San Ignacio to greet the Americans. You have not changed so much, little one. When I saw you beside the gate, I knew what you would do . . . that you would come here. And so I left the others and returned here to find you. We know why you have come, and I will take you myself. But first, we must leave this place—so open. There are new dwellers in this town who do not know you and would not hesitate to inform the *comandante*. Let us go quickly, and then you must go back where it is safe, little daughter."

*Go where?* Julie thought dazedly as she obeyed the old woman's urgent tug on her arm. How could her father's elderly parishioner know why she had come when she didn't even know herself? A few quick steps took them across the plaza into the shadow of the tiled roofs that overhung the closed-up shops, Doña Nina scuttling along in an odd, crablike gait that came from her deformity, but moving so fast Julie was hard-pressed to keep up. By the time they rounded the corner, Julie knew just where they were going.

She stared with astonishment at the high, plastered wall. Its pale blue color looked gray in the moonlight. The building was half again as tall as its neighbors, its apex an inverted V rather than the more typical flat roof. The front entrance featured a double door, its tall, curved portals standing wide open.

Julie stepped inside, dazed with shock. "I . . . I was sure this was all gone. I thought the guerrillas destroyed it. They've destroyed so many."

A dim glow sprang up in the darkness. Doña Nina handed Julie a cheap wax candle and turned to tug shut the heavy doors before lighting another for herself. "It is the largest gathering place in San Ignacio except the cathedral. It would have been foolishness to burn it down. And so we informed the guerrillas. There are no more services held here, but the *comandante* uses it when he wishes to speak to the people of the town."

Shielding her candle against the breeze of her movement, Julie walked slowly down the aisle of the church Dr. Richard Baker had built for the people of San Ignacio. The benches were rough wood and backless. The walls were plaster over cinder block, painted the same pale blue as the outside. High above the pale circle of candlelight, the ceiling was galvanized aluminum stretched across rafters made from the stripped-clean trunks of hardwood saplings.

The platform at the end of the aisle was of the same smooth concrete as the floor. The wooden lectern her father had built to hold his sermon notes still stood forlornly in the center. Here her father had preached to a faithful but small congregation, the majority of the town's inhabitants preferring to accept the aid of Dr. Richard and Elizabeth Baker without the inconvenience of worshiping their God.

Julie had reached the platform before she realized that she and Doña Nina weren't alone in the church sanctuary. Faces peered through an open door beside the dais. Julie knew where it led. The courtyard where in good weather she and her mother had taught the children while Dr. Baker taught the adults indoors.

Julie lifted her candle, the dim light bringing into sharp relief the faces in the doorway. The nearest was a tall, powerfully built woman with the chocolate skin and broad features of a strongly African-Indian mix. Her face brought back uncertain memories of a dusty patio where Julie had learned to wrap pork tamales for the steaming kettle, and a small, vociferous monkey she had cried over when she left.

"*Tía* Carmen?"

A swift movement brought warm, plump arms around her. Then the others surrounded her, hugging, touching, patting her as though to judge if she were real, their low murmurs excited, even joyous. "Julia, *hija. Qué bella!* You are looking so well! So beautiful!"

Half a dozen villagers pressed in on her—all vaguely recognizable, if older and more careworn than her memories. It took a moment to process that there were no men among them nor even the younger girls with whom Julie had once played. These were the older women of her father's congregation, the *tías* or honorary "aunts" who had played their role in the proper upbringing of the little foreigner who had made their village her home.

Then Doña Nina was upon them, urging them toward the side door. "Come, friends, we have no time for this," she whispered authoritatively. "She cannot stay long—it is dangerous. Let us show her what she has come to see."

The wind blew out the candles as soon as they stepped into the open courtyard. But the moon and stars were bright, and Julie stepped confidently away from the cinder-block wall of the church sanctuary. Branches waved like dark arms above her, and the tangy scent of lemon and orange was sharp in her nostrils. She knew where she was. Under this citrus grove she had once gathered the youngest toddlers for Bible stories and songs. But why had she been brought here now?

The hiss of a match being struck and the acrid whoosh of fuel catching fire banished the darkness. The baker's wife—what was her name?—held up the lantern she had just lit, its bright light sufficiently discreet behind the high walls of the church courtyard. Stooping beneath the branches of the citrus grove, she hurried forward. The other women surrounded Julie, guiding her onward with soft murmurs and urgent hands. Julie followed the bobbing light of the lantern, the feeling of being in a twilight zone growing stronger.

The church courtyard was far larger than the sanctuary itself, a good-sized piece of property where her father had hoped someday to build Sunday school classrooms and even a school. Beyond the citrus trees was another open bare area where the church youth had kicked around a soccer ball. Finally they reached a pair of enormous mango trees through whose huge overhanging branches Julie could see the back wall of the lot. Bewildered and impatient, she halted.

Then—even before the baker's wife set the lantern on the ground—she saw it. A mound, too even to be natural. The women held back as Julie walked forward, slowly, hesitantly. At the far end of the mound, almost hidden by the drooping branches of the mangos, she noticed an upright, curved shape.

A tombstone.

This was a grave.

The baker's wife adjusted the Coleman lamp so that its soft gleam fell directly on the stone, bringing its chiseled inscription into sharp relief. Two names, one above the other.

Dr. Ricardo Baker.

Sra. Elizabet Dorsey de Baker.

Whatever Julie had imagined, it hadn't been this, and the impact of it cast her to her knees. "I never knew . . ." she managed to say dazedly. "I thought . . . I had no idea."

"The guerrillas would not allow us in to see them," her former neighbor Doña Carmen said quietly. "They kept all houses with the cholera quarantined to keep the disease from spreading. But afterward—we brought them here. We thought you had heard. We sent a letter with the Red Cross team and wondered that we did not hear. Perhaps the *comandante* took it from them as he took so much else. Things have been—difficult in these years."

Julie reached out to touch the cold, smooth face of the tombstone. Other words were inscribed below the names. In the pale beam of the Coleman lamp she saw, not the usual *QEPD*, the Spanish acronym for *Que*

*En Paz Descanza*, "May You Rest in Peace," but other letters and numbers. MT. 10:39. JN. 12:24. They were Scripture references, she realized, and translated them mentally into the Bible passages she had memorized as a child.

Matthew 10:39. *"Whoever finds his life will lose it, and whoever loses his life for my sake will find it."*

John 12:24. *"I tell you the truth, unless a kernel of wheat falls to the ground and dies, it remains only a single seed. But if it dies, it produces many seeds."*

That verse again! Julie's hand dropped to the mound. It was covered with grass, a thick, lush carpet of it. To keep it trimmed and weedless and green would take constant effort in this jungle climate.

A labor of love.

The realization shook her. She touched a bouquet of flowers at the base of the stone. They were fresh—orchids and jasmine tied together with vines of deep purple bougainvillea. The baker's wife picked up the bouquet and pressed it into her hands. "We thought you would wish to have them tonight."

Julie had not cried when the news had reached her of her parents' illness and death. There had been too much stony unbelief for that. She hadn't allowed herself to shed tears in front of the tough old man who had become her guardian, nor later at that New England boarding school in the room she had shared with three other giggling, careless teenagers. Indeed, she had prided herself on having quickly and sensibly set aside her grief.

But now, as she lifted her eyes from that simply tied bundle of flowers to the anxious faces that were all that remained of the lively congregation that once had filled this church property, something gave way inside her, rising hot and scalding into her throat, and for all her efforts, she felt the tears spilling down over her cheeks and onto the flowers in her hands.

Above her, the women murmured softly, making clucking noises of sympathy, but with the innate dignity of the *campesino*, they did not intrude on her grief.

*"Mommy! Daddy!"* The silent cry was wrenched out of her in the childish names Julie had never had the chance to grow out of.

"Julie?"

The startled rustle of the women warned Julie only an instant before a familiar American drawl shattered the silence. Julie sprang to her feet, furious at the adrenaline jolt his voice had given her. If one more person sneaked up on her—!

Snatching up the Coleman lamp, she raised it high as Tim McAdams stepped into its circle of light. The soft gleam of the lantern caught his eyebrows arched high in astonishment as he glanced around at the women who were with her, then at the grave at her feet. Then his face smoothed into gentle concern. "Julie, what are you doing here?"

"What am *I* doing here? What are *you* doing here?" Julie hissed, angrily mopping at her damp cheeks with the bouquet in her hand. "How did you get here, anyway?"

"I followed you. I saw you leave. Not that I was spying on you, believe me. But—well, I know you said you wanted to be alone, but I couldn't let you, seeing you were kind of upset. So I hung around, hoping I might be able to be of some assistance. When you did that Houdini act with the truck—well, I just did the same when the next one came through."

Julie should have been grateful, but she felt only irritation. He was speaking in English much too loud for the quiet night. "Shh! You want to bring in the whole town? Are you crazy? Don't you know how dangerous it is to be wandering around in guerrilla territory?"

"That didn't seem to stop you!" He stepped farther into the circle of light. The soft gleam of the lantern's flame shone golden from the tall crown of his hair and gleamed from his teeth. "I figured if you thought it was safe to come here, there shouldn't be a problem."

"You *figured*." Julie struggled to keep her own voice down. Unfortunately, this was definitely in part her fault! If she'd dreamed someone was watching . . .

"There *is* a problem!" she said severely. "I know this area. And I don't stand out like a sore thumb—or some glow-in-the-dark torch! I can't imagine how many people must have seen you come in here."

She sighed. "Come on! We'd better get you back before we're both in trouble."

But Tim made no move to go. "So—what are you doing here, Julie? What do you mean, you know the area? And who are these women—your contacts? You might want to reassure them that I don't bite!"

Julie caught his quick glance around the silent circle of women, then saw for herself the frozen fear on their faces.

"It's okay," she reassured them. "He's only one of the reporters from the airport. But I must return with him immediately before we bring trouble to you."

The news didn't change their frightened expressions, and Julie felt their tension in her own stomach. She handed the lantern back to the baker's wife, wishing she could remember the woman's name, then hugged each of the women in turn. "Thank you! Thank you so much! What you have done—I don't have words to tell you what it has meant to me."

Spinning around on her heel, she pushed ahead of the missionary journalist. "Come on! I want to get out of here before we bring anymore trouble to these people."

This time Tim followed her rapid strides. "What did you mean back there?" he reiterated. "You said you knew the area. Well, that's obvious, but how? And whose grave was that?"

"My parents," Julie said shortly. Stooping under a low-lying lemon branch, she saw the dark mouth of the sanctuary door across the courtyard and hurried toward it. Tim McAdams caught up to her just as she stepped inside.

"Your parents!" he demanded. "Then . . . you *lived* here? You were serious about . . . those people? They really weren't your contacts?"

"My contacts?" Julie answered blankly.

"For your research. I assumed you were out here in search of a story."

Julie stopped dead in her tracks. "Look!" she said fiercely. "Not all of us will do anything for a piece. You think I'd jeopardize these people just for some added column space? They're simply villagers who knew me as a child."

"But—" Tim stopped as well, his large frame only a wavering shadow in the unlit sanctuary. "What in heaven's name were you doing here as a child? I thought you were an American."

"My parents were missionaries." Julie started off again down the dark aisle, her feet tracing the path by memory. "Like you."

Tim's only response was the creak of a bench as he bumped into it, followed by a low mutter that could have been swearing were it not for who he was. There was no sign of the women who had accompanied her to the grave. Once again, they had vanished into the night, but this time Julie took no offense. She didn't blame them for being afraid. She only wished them safely home.

Feeling in the dark for the two-by-four that kept the heavy front doors of the church blocked shut from the inside, she lifted it from the metal hooks that held it in place. Leaning the beam against the wall, she pushed the doors open.

"Come on," she said impatiently, turning swiftly as Tim emerged to shove the doors shut behind them. "Let's get you back before someone squeals to the guerrillas that their corralled sheep are going astray."

Her answer came as the soft clop of a hoof on the cobblestones. Then— from a different angle—she heard the gentle whoosh of a horse's breath being released. Slowly, reluctantly, Julie turned around. The circle of riders, their faces hard, shadowed silhouettes under the moon, carried her horribly, terrifyingly back seven years.

"I think it's a little late for that," came Tim McAdam's American drawl from beside her, and for once there was no joviality in his tone.

# TEN

THERE MUST HAVE BEEN A DOZEN of them—dark equine shapes differentiated only by the toss of a head or the glimmer of moonlight in a liquid eye, the dappled pattern of battle fatigues rendering the riders almost invisible against the night. Julie had just noted the empty saddles among them when wails broke out behind her, along with the guttural shouts of men.

With despair, Julie turned to see the women stumble out the front door of the church, prodded forward by the deadly shape of assault rifles, then glanced over at Tim McAdams. He was so big, so blond, so . . . so gringo, standing there with the moonlight shining bright on his flaxen head! It seemed clear that what she'd feared had come to pass. Someone had spotted his tall, fair frame in the streets and reported him to the guerrillas who now passed as town authorities.

*Or was it me they saw?* she wondered. *If only I hadn't come!*

Even if it was Tim the guerrillas had spotted, that too was her fault. *If I hadn't practically given him a green light to follow me!* Still, how could she have known her impulsive act would endanger these old friends?

Yes, friends. Julie could say that now. The realization sent a tendril of warmth through the chill in her veins, giving her courage to step forward toward the nearest horseman. "Look, I'm really sorry about this, but there's been a mix-up. My friend and I are members of the United Nations mission over at the airport. I know we shouldn't have been wandering around, but—we just wanted to see the town. We didn't mean to cause any problems. If . . . if you will just take us back to the airport. Or we can make our own way. . . ."

The man on the horse ignored her. His fingers snapped loud in the night as he ordered, "Search them."

Two riders swung down from their mounts. Both were armed with assault rifles. Julie stood stiff with outrage as the nearest man confiscated her backpack, then proceeded to run his hands over her. The town women were being searched as well, and Julie forced herself to imitate their stoic posture, though her fingers curled angrily when the man's hands lingered longer than necessary.

As he finally stood back, Julie risked a glance sideways at Tim. He was taking this surprisingly well, she admitted grudgingly, not ranting or demanding his rights like a typical gringo but standing quietly, keeping his arms calmly in the air while the other horseman searched him even more thoroughly than Julie had been.

Satisfied, the other horseman stepped back and shook his head. The men who had rounded up the town women signaled that they too had found nothing. "Bring them," the speaker ordered curtly.

As he started to wheel his horse around, Julie tried again. "Look, I'm sorry, but there really has been a mistake. My companion and I are reporters with the United Nations mission—I'm sure you've heard about it. We are here at the request of your own *Comandante* Raul Aguilera. If you don't believe us, please just contact the airport. The *comandante* will confirm that we have been given safe passage. Or—or . . ."—Julie groped for other names—"or you may speak to Manuel Flores. Or Enrique Martinez."

Her only answer was a sudden stab of pain in the base of her spine. Whirling around, she realized that the horseman who had searched her had just jabbed her with the barrel of his assault rifle. Another sharp prod sent her stumbling into the street. To her right, Doña Nina and the other women were being herded forward as well. They made no resistance. Experience had taught them the futility of that. But the hopeless slump of their shoulders twisted at Julie's heart.

"Please—at least let the women go!" she called to the hindquarters of the horse, now moving away from her at a slow clop-clop. "They have nothing to do with us. They're just townspeople we met!"

*I might as well be talking to a brick wall,* Julie thought despairingly as two of the armed men started the group of women down the street on foot while the others swung back into their saddles. Were these guerrillas also under orders not to speak to their hostages?

Or was it possible they weren't guerrillas after all? Paramilitaries, maybe, sweeping through the town on a raid to round up suspected guerrilla sympathizers. Maybe this had nothing to do with Julie and Tim, and they had just been in the wrong place at the wrong time. But paramilitaries, though they committed even more massacres than the guerrillas, didn't generally practice the kidnapping of foreigners. They were too busy presenting themselves as the allies of law and order.

Julie shook her head as one of the other horsemen led up a riderless horse.

"No, thanks," she said. "If you're going to take us, I'd rather walk with my friends."

The upraised gun barrel was so unexpected, Julie didn't even have time to flinch. But before it could come down, a large hand reached out past Julie to block it.

"There's no need for violence," Tim McAdams told her guard mildly in Spanish that was reasonably fluent if strongly accented. "We'll cooperate."

To Julie's astonishment, the man made no retaliation but simply motioned with his gun barrel toward the horse. With an effortless motion that made nothing of her 120 pounds, Tim boosted Julie to its broad back.

"Look, I know you're concerned about your friends," he told Julie in a low voice as he swung himself into another empty saddle. "But you're not doing them any favor advertising your relationship there. These guys are just following standard procedure—separate you from your local contacts before you can compare stories or pass on a message or something."

"But they're not my contacts!" Julie wailed softly. "They're just people I ran into. I didn't even know they'd be there." It was useless. If a fellow journalist like Tim had jumped to the conclusion that she was out here rooting around for a story, how much less would the guerrillas—or whoever they were—accept the truth!

At a gesture from her guard, Julie nudged her horse into a slow trot down the street. Tim brought his mount up alongside hers with an ease that showed he was no novice on horseback.

"Anyway, thank you for back there," she whispered, nodding toward the horseman who had struck at her, now trotting along on her other side. "I didn't know you spoke Spanish."

Julie caught Tim's raised eyebrow in the moonlight. "I told you I've been knocking around these parts for a while. I'll never pass myself as a native, but I've learned enough to get by."

Julie eyed him with new appreciation and some envy. He was riding easy and relaxed in the saddle, his handsome features as calm and untroubled as though the two of them were embarking on a moonlit outing instead of possibly being kidnapped and taken into captivity. Despite what Tim's intrusion into her evening had likely precipitated, Julie had to admit that his large presence beside her was comforting.

"So what does it take to shake you up—an earthquake?" she asked, trying to infuse some humor into her tone. "I . . . I was terrified back there, and you—I didn't see you so much as blink an eye! Or maybe run-ins with Marxist guerrillas are all in a day's work for you. Or . . ."—Julie's whisper turned suddenly sober, and her eyebrows drew together in the middle of her forehead. "Or you just have more faith than I do that we're going to walk away from this."

Tim reached forward to adjust his reins before he answered, the corner of his mouth curving wryly.

"I hadn't realized I was giving such an impression of having it all together. An erroneous one, I'm afraid. But yes, I suppose I do have the confidence that everything will work out, however bleak our present circumstances. After all, the Scriptures tell us that God is more than powerful enough to keep His children from harm. If an Almighty God can open wide the waters of the Red Sea or muzzle the mouths of lions, He can certainly handle our present situation."

*His voice actually changes when he talks like that,* Julie noted, bemused. Deeper, graver, beautifully sonorous with that warm, velvet tone. *A preacher's voice.* His eyes, dark in the moonlight, held Julie's as he spoke, gentle, compelling. Julie had to swallow hard before she could comment dryly, "Yes, and sometimes God allows bad things to happen to good people, remember?"

"Ssst!"

The menacing hiss cut short their whispered exchange. The dusty lane was silent and dark as they passed through it, even the glimmer of lit windows gone as shutters had been hastily bolted at the first sound of hoofbeats. Their progress was slow, dictated by the pace of the other captives, and it infuriated Julie to see Doña Nina and the other women scuttling ahead on foot while their captors kept the horses breathing down their necks and hemming them in so close that they stumbled repeatedly.

This was not about having enough mounts for all the prisoners. This was about power and humiliation and the intimidation of guards and weapons looming above and all around, so that by the time they reached their destination, the prisoners would be too cowed to offer resistance.

*The creeps are enjoying this!*

The trek wasn't long. Once beyond the outskirts of San Ignacio, the whole party turned onto a wide dirt track with deep ruts that showed the passage of motorized vehicles as well as horses and carts. They followed this only a few hundred meters before they came to the river. A long wooden dock extended out over the water. Rocking lazily beside it was a riverboat with its flat, barge-like bottom and a canvas awning that made an open cabin in the center of the deck.

The horsemen were already swinging to the ground. Dismounting, Julie found herself separated from Tim as a gun barrel in the small of her back prodded her forward onto the dock. Nor far upriver, she could see a twinkle of lights that had to be the San Ignacio airport, but the only light here was a flashlight with which the original spokesman of the horse party was motioning the prisoners onto the boat. Herded momentarily together with the other women, Julie snatched the opportunity to whisper, "Oh, Doña Nina, *Tía* Carmen, I'm so sorry!"

Doña Nina fumbled to squeeze Julie's hand in the dark, her fingers dry and bony and incredibly frail under Julie's own. *"Hija*—daughter—do not blame yourself. That which happens is God's will. He is with us, do not ever let yourself doubt." The old woman's soft murmur cracked treacherously on the last words, and yet somehow Julie found them more reassuring than all of Tim's velvet-toned homilies. *O God, please, just let them go! You have me, just let them go!*

Then the guards were between them, roughly shoving Julie away from the others. "You—back there!" the man with the flashlight instructed harshly, and with that order, two of the guards began prodding the other women forward toward the stern.

"And you—over here!" The man flashed his light on a pile of burlap bags to the left of the enormous spoked wheel that navigated the riverboat. His curt orders identified him as the leader of this raiding party, and as Julie obediently moved where he directed, she tried once more.

"Look, I think there really has been a mistake. If you will just take us to the airport there"—she gestured toward the twinkle of lights upriver, a beacon of warmth and welcome in the darkness—"you will see. *Comandante* Raul Aguilera—"

The flashlight beam shifted abruptly, illuminating his dark, broad features. "There is no mistake," he said coldly. "You are an American spy, and for that crime, under the direct mandate of the command council of the Revolutionary Armed Forces of Colombia, you have been placed under arrest!"

Then they *were* guerrillas! And FARC at that. But what in the—?

Stunned, Julie made no further attempt to argue. As the raid leader strode over to the wheel, she sank down onto the pile of sacking. The other women huddled together at the far end of the riverboat. Looking around for Tim, Julie found him sprawled comfortably against a mound of sacked rice on the opposite side of the deck, a guard crouched down on either side of him, the outlines of their assault rifles barely visible against the dark night. Only half of the raiding party had boarded with the prisoners. The others, taking up the reins of the extra mounts, wheeled away from the dock as the riverboat's engine sputtered to life. From across the deck, Tim caught Julie's eyes on him and gave her a thumbs-up. Julie forced an uncertain smile in response.

*It's got to be a mistake!* she reassured herself.

She and Tim had been caught stupidly wandering out of bounds, and they were now paying the penalty. But the guerrillas undoubtedly operated on preset orders for these situations, she reasoned, and sooner or later these men would have to report the detention of two gringos to their own superiors, and then it would all be straightened out soon enough. As Julie had explained to Sondra Kharrazi and the others, *Comandante* Raul Aguilera and the FARC leadership had too much at stake with this mission to risk its success by indulging in random kidnapping.

In the meantime, it would be best—both for herself and Tim and for the women she'd inadvertently pulled into this mess—not to make anymore waves. Julie settled herself among the scratchy, fish-smelling burlap sacks and set herself to wait. Her belongings hadn't been returned to her, but she could see her knapsack tossed next to the wheel along with the rectangular shape of Tim's briefcase. At least her notes were safe.

Once away from the dock, the raid leader extinguished his flashlight. After that, the only light came from moon and stars, the river a ribbon of black sliding past the side of the boat, broken only by the occasional splash of a fish.

\* \* \*

Julie had long since lost track of time and was dozing off, her head bumping against the hard wood of the gunwale, when the engine died. A cold muzzle against the hollow of her throat prodded her awake. Stumbling to her feet, she saw blearily that they were no longer on the Ipa River but on a much smaller stream. Here there was no dock, just a muddy bank and a narrow trail leading from the river edge into the jungle. Again, the guerrilla band divided. Two of the men started up the engine and steered the boat away from shore once the others had herded the prisoners up the bank.

Julie's heart sank as the raid leader's sharp orders moved them out single file onto the jungle trail. The farther they went, the more difficult it would be to get back to San Ignacio, and they had a flight leaving in just a few hours!

Julie was slogging along between two of the guerrillas. The stars and moon had disappeared, and though the leader of the column had his flashlight on, Julie was far back where no glimmer of light could reach, and she stumbled constantly over unseen roots and stones. How was poor old Doña Nina possibly handling this?

To make things worse, it began to rain. The thick canopy provided a partial shield against the downpour, but Julie was soaked through by the time they stumbled into the open.

A campfire burned in front of them, and lanterns hung from tree branches. The yellow glow revealed that underbrush and smaller saplings had been hacked back from the base of a grove of the biggest mango trees Julie had ever seen. Spreading branches closed in high above them to hide the encampment from any curious eyes, human or electronic, that might pass overhead.

Nearby were four makeshift huts constructed by thrusting stripped saplings into the ground to mark four corners, then wrapping heavy plastic around three sides as walls. The plastic was a light blue of the type sold in huge rolls for awnings or tarps or even an improvised rain poncho. Palm and elephant leaves piled across a latticework of branches made a thatched roof.

Through the open side of the nearest hut, she saw cots of the fold-up, army type. In another, she spotted a UHF radio perched on a wooden table. So there was communication to the outside world.

The huts were arranged around an open center. Here, along with the campfire, a rusty metal drum had been fashioned into a crude stove. A tarp stretched across several branches overhead kept rain from putting out the fire beneath the makeshift burners. Another tarp sheltered a table laden with cooking supplies. Bags of rice. Beans. A five-gallon container of oil. Scattered around the campfire were aluminum pots and tin plates and cups.

Behind the nearest hut was another structure, this one with solid walls, though it was no larger than a telephone booth. *An outhouse?* One thing was certain: This was no temporary campsite. The guerrillas had held kidnap victims here before.

As the raiding party leader herded his captives into the encampment, other guerrillas stood up from around the campfire or slipped out of hammocks strung between branches. They retrieved their weapons as they got to their feet, the low murmur of their Spanish a soft music as they mingled with their arriving companions. They weren't all male. Julie spotted several slighter figures and pulled-back ponytails under the camouflage fatigues and combat hats.

Julie was too tired to protest when she was again cut out of the knot of prisoners. The townswomen were herded inside one of the plastic-sided enclosures while she was led to another. She was exhausted enough to feel only gratitude when, in response to her awkward question, her guide, one of the female guerrillas, silently led her to the telephone-booth structure. An outhouse, as Julie had hoped, though inside the walls there was nothing more than a few planks balanced over a pit in the ground.

As they returned, she passed Tim on the same errand. He smiled and gave her a thumbs-up. Back at the sleeping hut, a Coleman lantern had been shifted to a branch just above the open end of the sleeping hut, and a hard-backed wooden chair placed directly outside. As Julie stepped into the shelter, the guerrilla woman placed herself in the chair, with her back to the camp and her eyes on Julie, her assault rifle laid across her lap.

Doing her best to ignore that implacable stare, Julie walked over to the nearest army cot, covered neatly with clean bedding. She grimaced to see the mud and damp that stained her khaki shirt and slacks, thinking of how it would soil the bedding as well. Julie solved this by pushing aside the thin mattress and seating herself gingerly on the bare metal springs. Across the camp, she could see the shapes of the other women moving around behind the translucent blue walls of another sleeping hut. Wearily, she dropped her head into her hands. She didn't realize she had company until the springs beside her groaned under a heavy weight.

"What are you thinking about, Julie?" Tim asked quietly. "I don't expect they'll hurt us. The guerrillas have a reputation for treating their captives well."

Julie lifted her head, pushing back her curls to look at her companion. The missionary journalist certainly made a better picture than herself. He was damp, of course. But he had missed the grime that bespattered her own clothing—and face, no doubt, as well—and he'd even managed to comb his hair since his arrival in the encampment. Julie managed a faint smile, feeling the crackle of drying mud around her mouth as she did so.

"Oh, I'm not worried about that. I'm sure this is all a mistake. Once they find out we really are with the UN mission, *Comandante* Aguilera will order us back. I just hope we don't miss our flight." Julie glanced over at the other sleeping hut. "And that these people don't get in trouble for our stupidity."

Brushing at her face in a vain attempt to dislodge the drying grime, Julie wrinkled her nose in a rueful grimace. "No, actually, I was thinking what a great story this is going to be when we get out of here."

"A story?" Tim's eyebrows shot up unbelievingly "You *are* kidding!"

"I know. Crazy, isn't it, at a time like this? But after this morning . . . add on a genuine kidnapping experience, an inside look at a guerrilla camp—we're talking Pulitzer Prize material! Now if we could just come up with the pictures." Julie's lips twitched at the expression on his face. "An obsessed journalist, right?"

Tim studied her, and she had the sensation that for some reason beyond her understanding, she had astonished him. But if he was going to say so, he had no opportunity; the female guard who had been sitting outside was entering the sleeping hut.

She carried Julie's knapsack, and Julie took it from her with relief, cheered by the very thought of clean clothing. Tim's briefcase didn't correspondingly appear. No surprise, since it hardly contained personal belongings, and though it would have been nice, Julie couldn't imagine the guerrillas being stupid enough to let them get their hands on that sat-phone and modem. But the guerrilla woman laid out a selection of articles on the nearest cot. Toothbrush. Toothpaste. Bar of soap. Roll of toilet paper. One very worn towel.

She handed Julie a duplicate of the last three items—proof that she, or someone, had been through Julie's belongings—then left without having addressed a word to either prisoner. Julie dug eagerly into her knapsack. Almost immediately, she discovered that her own belongings hadn't been left untouched either.

"Hey, my computer!" she called after the guard.

But the woman had returned to her position outside the shelter, weapon across her lap. Julie checked hurriedly through the knapsack. Gone were her camera, cell-phone, even the notes she'd scribbled after the autopsy.

The notes were the worst loss—everything else was replaceable. Julie blinked back her disappointment. She'd been foolish to expect any less, and maybe when this whole crazy mess was straightened out, she could get them back.

She dropped the knapsack as another guerrilla—another woman, though it wasn't always easy to tell with their loose military clothing—ducked into the shelter. She carried a basin, and Julie took it from her gratefully. Water to wash up, and another well-worn piece of terrycloth for a washcloth.

It felt so good to have clean face and hands that Julie attacked the enamel bowl of rice and beans that followed with a better appetite than she would have expected. At least it seemed the guerrilla's reputation for treatment of prisoners wasn't unmerited.

Though to Julie it was more a depressing indication of just how much experience these people had with taking hostages. *I just hope they're treating Doña Nina and the others this decently.*

"So why did they put you in here?" she asked Tim as they ate. "Didn't you say it was protocol to separate everyone so they can't compare notes?"

Tim's spoon scraped the bottom of his plate with a metallic clink. "Who knows how these people think! They said something about gringos together. Maybe they figure we know each other better than we do—that we've got no secrets left to share."

He accompanied that last remark with a grin, and Julie did her best to respond in kind. The truth was, she wasn't happy about the idea of sharing sleeping quarters with a man, however unavoidable. And a virtual stranger at that.

Still, what difference did it make when she had to sleep in full sight of the entire guerrilla camp? Not to mention that guard with her eyes glued on them. She had to admit there was some comfort in having her fellow American hostage close enough to talk to. *He's big and strong and some protection, anyway. And maybe even cute. I could have been stuck here with Bob Ryder.* There was a horrifying thought.

*Now if I can just figure out how to get out of these filthy clothes and into clean ones without every eye in camp on me.*

In the end Julie waited until the Coleman lanterns were turned out for the night. It didn't take long. From the foot of her army cot, Julie watched two of the guerrilla women—it would seem this army was sexist in labor division—wash the dishes with water dipped from a barrel set beside the supply table. The rest of the group, except for the guards on duty, gathered around the campfire, some playing cards, others—much to Julie's astonishment—clustered around an old black-and-white, battery-operated TV set. A Colombian soap, from the dramatic Spanish.

The leader alone did not socialize, disappearing instead into the hut where Julie had seen the UHF radio. When he reappeared, the lanterns were turned off. Their female guard was replaced by a hard-faced young male, but not before she showed them how to unhook mosquito nets from the thatched roof. This was no new experience to Julie, who found the knack of shooing out the bug-life while simultaneously tucking the netting under her pallet, coming back as naturally as riding a bicycle.

And none too soon, as once Julie was no longer moving, the mosquitoes, previously only a minor nuisance, began to congregate around the net with a high buzzing whine piercing enough to drive all sleep away.

Slipping under the thin blanket that was all the bedding provided, Julie maneuvered a clothing change, doing her best to ignore her roommate, lying close enough to hear every rustle she made, and the guard, who at frequent intervals ducked his head into the sleeping hut to shine a flashlight over the cots until Julie wanted to scream with annoyance. How was she ever supposed to sleep with a light in her face all night?

In the end, though, she slept better than she'd expected, blocking out the shrill whine of the mosquitoes, as she had also learned in her childhood, and sliding gradually into an exhausted slumber that even the brilliant flash of the guard's inspections couldn't disturb.

\* \* \*

Oddly, Julie awoke to a sensation of peace and well-being that she hadn't known in years. She lay for a moment with her eyes still closed, just listening and breathing. There was the soft sigh of wind through treetops. A twitter of birds. Not just any birds, but a jungle chorus she had once known intimately. The raucous morning demands of macaws, and from somewhere overhead the angry hiss and scamper of monkeys quarreling. A lingering perfume of flowers just closing up their petals against the coming day's heat and the pungent minty fragrance a certain grass released when trampled underfoot. The smell of green things and warm earth and the last cool whisper of the dawn breeze across her cheek.

It all felt—so right!

Then last night's events flooded into her consciousness, and Julie's eyes jerked open. She wasn't back in her childhood home but in a jungle camp, a hostage of human beings who had no reason to wish her well. The guard —a new one, Julie thought, though all those young faces under the billed caps blurred together—was sitting stiff-backed in his chair as though he hadn't shifted all night, his black eyes fixed on her and one hand on the weapon across his knees.

Julie turned her head on the jacket she had rolled up as a pillow. Tim McAdams was awake, sitting on the edge of the next cot. His gaze was on her, and when he saw that she was awake, his good-looking features beamed with pleasure.

"So you're up, are you!" he commented affably.

Rolling to a sitting position, Julie eyed her fellow hostage with scant appreciation. He had been up for some time, for he was washed and shaved and combed, and even his clothes had stood up to sleeping in them better than her own. Julie knew what she herself must look like, and she flushed with embarrassment and annoyance as she pushed back the rat's nest that sleep always made of her curls. The public was meant to be faced only after a decent interval and an encounter with a bathroom, and as for that much cheerfulness at this hour of the morning . . .

Ignoring Tim's remark, Julie snatched up her knapsack and strode to the front of the hut. The two guerrilla women from the night before were standing at the cook table, slapping white dough between their hands into the round, flat shapes of *arepas*.

*"Baño, por favor?"* Julie called hopefully.

One of the women—a girl, really, still in her teens—rinsed her hands in a basin and hurried over to escort Julie to the outhouse. By the time she'd washed up in a basin set for her under a tree and tugged a comb through the tangle of her curls, Julie was feeling more able to cope with the day— and that barrage of eyes.

Then she checked her watch and groaned. It had taken them hours to reach this remote jungle camp, and the morning was already well-advanced. Surely the DC4 would be readying for takeoff by now, and Bill Shidler would be fuming over his missing press team members.

*Uncle Norm is going to kill me!*

For all his severity, the old editor would worry if she didn't return on that plane, and Julie felt remorse at the trouble her impulsive excursion had to be causing not only herself but others. Yet she couldn't be sorry about taking those rash steps beside the truck and out the gate. She had accomplished what she came for, after all. And to see her parents' grave—more, to see the love and attention the townspeople had lavished on that tiny cemetery—was worth all the inconvenience of her present predicament.

They really did care! At least some of them.

The other women were being led out to the outhouse and wash basin now, and Julie managed a small wave to Doña Nina before her guard's frown warned her to be more circumspect.

Back in their own shelter, the guard served Julie and Tim a breakfast of *arepas* and coffee. Tim kept up a light, cheerful conversation throughout, trading anecdotes of journalism assignments in odd corners of the world with a self-deprecating humor that slid Julie's estimation of him up another few notches.

"So . . . back to you," Tim said finally as their tin plates and cups were being collected. "Come on, I've been dying of curiosity. What were you *really* doing out there last night?"

Julie glanced up in surprise. "I told you. I grew up here—in San Ignacio, I mean. I just wanted to see it again. I know it was stupid, but I just couldn't pass it by after all these years. And after all"—she waved a hand that took in the row of army cots and the blue plastic walls and the guard sitting right outside—"I wasn't figuring on something like this."

"You grew up here? Then your parents were Colombian?" Tim ran an eye over Julie's dark curls and the tan she never quite lost even during Washington winters. "Yes, I can see where they would be. Your English is so good I just assumed you were American—though of course, your Spanish is just as good."

Julie brushed *arepa* crumbs from her hands and wished she had the wash basin back. She settled for her towel, still damp from her earlier wash-up. "But I *am* an American! With a name like Baker? What else would I be?"

Tim's eyebrows shot up. "Julie, your story has more twists than a New York pretzel. If your parents were American, then how did you end up in San Ignacio? What in the world were you doing in the middle of a Colombian jungle?"

Julie looked at him oddly. "Isn't it obvious? I thought I told you last night. My parents were missionaries—like you."

Tim looked momentarily taken back, then smiled ruefully. "Of course, what was I thinking? You did say something about that last night—right before our friends out there crashed the party and drove everything else out of my limited brain. Missionaries. That explains a lot. Then—that grave . . . you were serious? That was your parents? I'm sorry about that."

He studied Julie, his blue eyes thoughtful on her face before he went on. "So you haven't been in these parts for a while. Then how in the world did you connect with those women out there? I didn't think the guerrillas were allowing a lot of open communication in and out of the zone."

"I *didn't* connect with them. I told you that too, remember? They just recognized me and followed me. They've known me all my life. I guess I hadn't changed as much as I thought." Julie shook her head, half annoyed, half rueful as she eyed him, bent slightly forward on the edge of the cot, his hands in his lap as though itching for a notepad, his good-looking face settled into that bland expression of the experienced interviewer, belied by the sharp interest in his eyes. "You really *are* a journalist, aren't you? That instinct to start grilling as soon as someone gets across the table . . . or in this case, the army cot!"

"Am I grilling? Sorry about that!" Tim's return survey was appreciative. "It's just that I find you a very interesting young lady. You have an unusual grasp of the situation down here. And of course, one doesn't run into a whole lot of Americans born in a guerrilla hot zone."

Julie hunched her shoulders dismissively. "Well, of course it wasn't a guerrilla hot zone then."

"No? Is that why you left, then—because the guerrillas arrived? And— pardon me if I ask . . ." His deep voice gentled. "I don't mean to intrude, but I can't help wondering . . . just how did your parents die?"

Julie's face hardened. "Talk to the guerrillas!"

Springing to her feet, she paced over to the open front of the enclosure where she could see the guard, a cup of coffee in the hand that wasn't on his weapon. Beyond him, the rest of the guerrillas were gathered around the campfire, eating their own breakfast, a transistor radio blasting out salsa on the supply table. She swung away. "Let's just say these . . . these *terrorists* are responsible for a lot more deaths than the people they murder."

"Sounds like you hold quite a grudge against the guerrillas. I guess that's to be expected. This place must hold a lot of bad memories. In fact, I'm surprised your boss would put you of all people in the position of having to come back here. Surely your magazine could have sent someone else."

Julie sighed. "Look—I really don't like to talk about it, okay?"

She swung around again to the opening, then stiffened with an excitement that dismissed their discussion from her mind. "Hey, look, they're coming! It's about time. I just hope that plane hasn't left yet."

There were four of them, on horseback. They rode in single file with the relaxed effortlessness of country folk who spent as much time on horseback as in a motorized vehicle, and Julie recognized them all. *Comandante* Aguilera himself was in the lead, and right behind him was the guerrilla spokesman, Manuel Flores. Their English interpreter, Enrique Martinez, followed, and trailing in the rear was the young guerrilla boy who looked so familiar. "Carlos."

As the men pulled up near the cooking pit and swung down from their mounts, Julia's eyes were drawn to Enrique. What looked so different about him?

Then she realized that he had shaved off his unkempt start at a beard, leaving only a thin line of moustache above what was now revealed to be a very firm mouth. Without the stubble, his features looked at once younger and harder, the set of his jaw that had been masked before uncompromising, even obstinate.

*I'd sure hate to try to take one of his toys away!*

Enrique dropped his reins and stepped away from his mount. Then his eyes, sweeping around the camp, alighted on Julie, and she quailed under the smoldering fury in them. This wasn't going to be pleasant.

# ELEVEN

THE RAID LEADER CAME FOR Tim and Julie. Two armed guards ensured their cooperation, but Julie had no intentions of protesting. She was eager to speak to the new arrivals.

*Comandante* Aguilera and his men had commandeered the communications hut. The UHF radio had been set to one side, and the FARC commander now sat behind the table where it had been. No other seats had been provided, and Manuel Flores and Enrique Martinez were standing at attention on either side of the commander, their assault rifles slung over their shoulders.

Carlos met them at the entrance of the hut. With a jerk of his head toward Julie, he announced, "The *comandante* says the man may stay here. The girl will come with me."

Julie was less frightened than surprised. This was a *machista* culture where women were still considered little more than an extension of their men folk—as evidenced in those female freedom fighters out there, still doing all the cooking, washing, and cleaning up just as they might at home. So why were they picking on her rather than Tim?

Carlos avoided her eyes as she obeyed his gesture to precede him, and once again, she couldn't tell from his expression whether he recognized her. Not that it mattered now. He motioned her to a stop in front of the table, taking up guard position behind her. Julie was left standing like a defendant before a tribunal. She glanced back over her shoulder to see the guard detail leading Tim over to one side. Another guerrilla had unrolled a length of the plastic used for the walls and was sealing off the open end so that no one in the camp could see inside.

A sudden shiver of apprehension went up Julie's spine, but she straightened her shoulders and lifted her chin as she turned to face the three men before her. Aguilera had watched her approach with hooded eyes, his narrow features as impassive as a bronze sculpture from some long-gone Andean civilization. She could pick up nothing of what was going through his mind.

Manuel Flores too had showed only mild interest in her progress across the dirt floor. But Julie felt another chill at the grim line of Enrique's mouth and the fury she could still feel behind his current stony expression. She hurried into speech, putting all the sincerity she could muster into her apology.

"Look, I'm so sorry about all of this. I know we've caused you a lot of trouble, and I really do apologize. I guess we shouldn't have been wandering around, but we never expected these . . . these people of yours to—to grab us like this. It's all been a big mistake."

Her apology brought no change to the hard, unrelenting expressions in front of her, and when Julie's pleading gaze reached her former rescuer, those long dark lashes so at odds with the almost harshly masculine planes of his face dropped to hood his gaze. Julie faltered, uncertain for the first time. But she continued speaking, directing her plea at Aguilera.

"You . . . you do remember me . . . from the airport? I am one of the journalists from the mission. Julie Baker from *Our Earth* magazine. I'm on the list—just check. I asked one of the questions you answered . . . and I saw you in the autopsy room—remember?"

"There has been no mistake." Aguilera's tone was flat and chilling. "You are no reporter, Julie Baker. You are a spy for the *americanos,* and for that crime we place you under arrest by the authority of the Eighth Brigade of the Revolutionary Armed Forces of Colombia. Are you prepared to answer for your crimes?"

"A . . . a *spy!*" Julie's mouth literally gaped open. Had she wandered back into that twilight zone? Sure, the raid leader had accused her of the same, but she hadn't taken that seriously for a moment.

"What are you talking about?" she stammered. "I'm not a spy! Okay, so I shouldn't have left the gate. It was stupid! I just wanted to look around. And Tim, the . . . the blond man over there—he's no spy either, I promise. None of this is his fault. He just followed me out."

Her voice had risen higher than prudent, and she took a deep breath to calm down. "Look, why would I want to spy? Why would *anyone* want to spy on you? There are no spies here, okay? We're just on a humanitarian mission. Please . . . just let us go!"

*Comandante* Aguilera might have been watching an insect battering its wings against a collector's pin. "There is no mistake," he repeated coldly. "We have been informed that there is a spy on this mission. We know this to be true. And we know that you must be that spy. The evidence is indisputable."

"Evidence?" Julie searched her memory frantically. What action of hers could they possibly have misinterpreted? "What evidence?"

"Do you think we are fools, Julie Baker? You are an unknown in the field of journalism—we have checked. Yet you have no difficulty attaining a place for which many have competed. You speak with an intimacy of our cause and our people and our town that is not of an outsider. You meet secretly and alone with the American commander who leads forces against us. You cannot deny this; you were seen. You escape the vigilance of my guards with the ease of a professional. You make contact with my people, corrupting them to turn against their comrades."

*Comandante* Aguilera ticked off his points as though reciting a shopping list. "These things are enough in themselves. But there is also this!" He snapped his fingers, and Enrique stepped forward to lift an object to the table. Julie looked at it blankly. Her laptop.

"The files on this computer—they are yours, are they not? Many, many files with information about our cause and about the workings of the American government as well. Files that no civilian would possess. And yet you say you are not a spy?"

Julie felt dizzy with bewilderment. How had this man known all this—her professional standing, even her chance meeting with Colonel Thornton? Someone on that plane had to have been watching her all along, listening.

That was what shook Julie the most. There had been a spy on that plane, all right. Their spy! But who? Someone who had been close to her, talking to her. Sondra Kharrazi? She had admitted that she'd spent time with the guerrillas, even interviewing their PR man, standing there with that smug expression. Had there been other motives for her social overtures than a desire for female companionship?

Or had there been someone else listening? Someone who had never stepped out of the shadows around her.

Her glance stole from Manuel Flores to Enrique's stony expression. Of course! *Comandante* Aguilera's two sidekicks had been on the plane. They must have overheard more than she would have thought possible.

Aguilera slammed the laptop shut. Rising with a fluid motion, he strode around the table. "So—you will now tell us for which American agency you are working and who is supplying your information." He spoke in the same dispassionate tone Julie had heard in his speech, not angry, but like a professor asking a question on an exam. "You will tell us what you have learned here and what you are looking for. And these women—you will tell us who they are and just how many others in San Ignacio have betrayed us as well."

Julie took an instinctive step back, but the hard, cold circle of a gun barrel in the small of her back stopped her retreat. She licked lips that were suddenly dry.

"Look, this is crazy!" she said desperately. "Please believe me, this has all been a misunderstanding. I am *not* a spy! No one gave me those files. I dug it all out myself. I'm a reporter—that's what I do! I always research a story before I get there. Check it out for yourself—all that information is out there in the public domain."

Despite her resolution, Julie's voice had risen again, and she bit it off, frustrated. How did you explain the Internet to someone who lived and fought in the jungle?

"As for the rest," she went on more calmly, "yes, I do know a lot about this area. But that's no big mystery. I was born here—I grew up here. Really . . . there's a very simple explanation for all of this. I told you I was sorry for leaving the airport. But . . . well, I was curious to see what it looked like after all these years, that's all."

Julie didn't add that in fact it had taken no professional training to slip past his guards.

"The women—they are just old neighbors. When they recognized me, they came to greet me. That's all, I swear!"

"Liar!" The crack of *Comandante* Aguilera's voice was almost as much a shock as the blow across her face. Tears of pain sprang to Julie's eyes. She raised a trembling hand to her mouth. It came away red. The guerrilla commander slapped her hand down. Seizing Julie's chin in a grip that further bruised her stinging lips, he forced her eyes up to meet his.

"Do you think us so stupid? You are not of San Ignacio. Your citizenship is American, not Colombian—do you think us foolish enough not to check? Your name, your speech . . . the very arrogance of your walk is of the Americans! So—you will begin to tell us the truth."

The pinch of his fingers kept Julie from shifting her eyes from his. They were only inches above her own as the guerrilla commander wasn't much taller than Julie, nor with his honed-down, almost emaciated frame, much heavier. After that first furious crack of sound, his tone had become again flat and unemotional, the almond-shaped black eyes that told of ancestors on this soil long before the coming of the Spaniards revealing no anger. But Julie found this no comfort.

It wasn't that his cool, dispassionate gaze boring into hers was what Julie would ever have thought to be that of a killer. There was none of the rage and battle lust she'd seen in some of those other young eyes, or even the anger she could still feel almost physically radiating from Enrique Martinez. They were, rather, the eyes of someone to whom the killing—or not killing—of another living, breathing human being had become a matter of complete indifference. As though somewhere in *Comandante* Aguilera's crusade of liberation and vengeance, of considering other persons as mere pawns to be moved around and even sacrificed as need be, he had lost his own humanity.

Until now, Julie had not been truly frightened. Bewildered, indignant, annoyed, even outraged, yes. But she'd had full confidence that this was all a misunderstanding and would sort itself out. Now as she stared helplessly into that flat, cold, *inhuman* gaze, terror swept over her in sickening, dizzying waves that left her skin chill and damp. This was no story, no adventure from which she could count on walking away to book rights and a Pulitzer Prize. This was real. She, Julie Baker, could die here. And so could the others who had been dragged into this mess with her.

"Who do you work for?" Aguilera demanded. Julie could feel the garlic and onion of his last meal hot on her face. "How have you made contact with your accomplices in the zone? How far does your spy net go?"

Julie shook her head hopelessly, a futile gesture against the steel grip of his hand. Here was when every American hero showed his—her—mettle, defying the foe with backbone and courage. But if there was a shred of courage inside her, she couldn't find it. A hard, almost painful sensation pressed somewhere in her bladder area, and all the jokes of being scared enough to wet your pants were no longer funny.

"I . . . I *told* you the truth. I don't work for anyone but my magazine. And the women—they're just old friends of my parents. *Please!*" She was pleading now. "They had nothing to do with all this. Please don't hurt them. Please—just let them go!"

Slap!

A sob broke from Julie before she could suppress it. Her hand rose to her jaw as the commander released her. From a corner of her eye, she saw Enrique Martinez take a quick stride forward, his brown eyes blazing copper with fury. Was he going to strike her too? Instinctively, she cowered, even as she hated herself for displaying her fear to the whole world. Where was her big, blond knight-protector in all of this? Couldn't he at least be raising an objection here?

A frantic glance showed her there was little Tim McAdams could do to help her. Not backed into a corner with two muzzles thrust into his stomach. Julie cringed as Aguilera raised his hand again, and she was horrified to hear an actual whimper escape her throat.

"Señor! What the woman is saying, it is true!"

The *comandante* stopped in mid-blow, hand upraised. Julie felt the gun muzzle leave her back. Stepping forward, her young guard snapped to attention.

"Señor, this woman—Julia Baker." He gave her name its Spanish pronunciation as had Doña Nina. "It is true as she said that she lived in San Ignacio. It was many years ago. Before your time. I myself was just a boy when she left, but I too recognized her, though I could not be sure until she spoke now. Her father was the gringo doctor who built the clinic and the church. They died in the cholera epidemic, and the daughter never returned to San Ignacio. And the women . . ."

The boy hesitated as though he himself felt trepidation. "Señor, it is true too that these women were friends of her parents. They are not spies—I know them well. They are only *campesinos* without education or cleverness for American plots."

"Do not underestimate the *campesino* mind," *Comandante* Aguilera answered coldly. "It is on the shoulders of the rural peasant that our revolution has risen." His hand dropped to his side, and he stepped back from Julie.

Julie was almost sobbing with relief. Then this really *was* Gabriela's little brother, Carlos, who had tagged at the older teens' heels during her vacations from boarding school. Now surely these men would believe her and release them.

But when the guerrilla commander spoke, it wasn't the release she had hoped.

"Because the woman lived in San Ignacio does not mean she is not an American spy. On the contrary, who better to choose?" Aguilera's black gaze contemplated Julie for a moment. "Still, we have heard enough until we have spoken with the other women. Now I will interrogate the man."

Striding back to the table, he reached underneath to lift out what Julie recognized to be Tim McAdams's briefcase. As he snapped open its latches, the three men guarding Tim prodded him forward. He threw Julie a sympathetic glance as he reached her side but had the good sense not to try to speak.

Seating himself again, *Comandante* Aguilera waved a hand toward Julie. "Carlos, Enrique, you will take this Julie Baker and watch her closely until I summon her again. Victor . . ."—he shifted his gaze to the raid leader who had captured Tim and Julie—"you and your men will go and bring to me the women of San Ignacio."

Tim's guards immediately dropped their weapons and turned to go. Stepping forward to Julie's side, Carlos beckoned for her to accompany him.

Enrique didn't move immediately. "But *Comandante,*" he said, "we know nothing of who this man is or even if he speaks our language enough to understand you." He swept a measuring eye over Tim's large frame. "He is big enough to be dangerous. Do you not wish me to stay—to interpret, if it is necessary?"

The glare *Comandante* Aguilera turned on his interpreter was as icy as the one Julie had received. "You rise above yourself, Enrique. Do you think that Manuel and myself are incapable of handling one gringo without you? We were fighting men like this one before you had yet crawled to your mother's arms!"

In agreement, Manuel Flores unslung his assault rifle. Cradling it in his gnarled hands with the ease of long practice, he stepped with a smug smile to Tim's side.

"Actually, I do speak your language," Tim put in peaceably. "What would you like to know?"

Julie stared at Tim in disbelief. He sounded as calm and unruffled as always, and towering as he did over the seated commander and the short, stocky guerrilla PR man, who was now his only guard, he gave no impression of being on trial. Julie, only too conscious of the tears and terror that had been shaken out of her, felt almost angry. *Doesn't he even realize how much trouble we're in?*

"Then it is settled!" The *comandante* snapped his fingers again, and Enrique and Carlos closed in on Julie to escort her out, the glare Enrique turned on Julie making it clear he blamed her for his eviction from his superior's side.

Back in the sleeping hut, Julie flung herself down on her cot, ignoring the two men as they took up guard position in the entrance. If she could just talk to Carlos, ask him some questions. How had the merry little boy she'd known ended up here?

But she didn't dare ask under Enrique's unrelenting glare. *If a plane wing came at me now, he'd probably let it slice me to bits,* Julie thought.

She rolled over, burying her head in her arms. Now that the terror of the interrogation was receding, Julie felt like writhing with shame. Like most people, she'd always imagined that, handed a life-and-death situation, she would rise to the occasion and acquit herself well. Yet how quickly *Comandante* Aguilera had reduced her to a whimpering, cringing, broken creature.

*Some spy you'd have made! The first slap in the face, and you'd have been spilling your guts.* Julie felt hot tears wet her arms.

*O God! What are You doing to me? I thought it had to be some real sick humor of Yours to bring me back to San Ignacio. But this?*

Whether her prayers were doing any good, Julie had no idea. She'd lost too many people in her life to believe God handed out happy endings for the asking. A lot of decent people had lost their lives in guerrilla captivity— even other missionaries like her parents—many at the hands of these very terrorists. Why should she expect any less?

*O God, at least let the women go! Doña Nina, Doña Carmen—and Tim McAdams too. I couldn't bear it if my stupidity got someone else hurt. Please, God!*

"Hey, Julie?"

Julie recognized the heavy sag in the springs even before the deep, melodious question.

"Still thinking on that story?"

Tim scooted out of the way as Julie rolled over. The narrow bed threatened to tip over, so he hastily removed himself to the next cot. His blue eyes were bright as he looked down at her, and he looked as little touched by the interrogation that had shaken her to the core as he had been by their jungle march. But then, that guerrilla commander would never dare slap this large man as he had Julie. It wasn't fair.

"No!" she said flatly. "I wasn't thinking about my story. Actually, I was thinking more along your lines. You're the missionary. So maybe you can tell me what divine purpose there's supposed to be in all of this." Her gesture took in the sleeping hut and the camp beyond. "Or maybe there is no purpose. Maybe God is just letting the two of us reap the natural consequences of our own stupidity in stepping out of bounds. After all, you've got to admit, a good part of the mess we see in this world is just people reaping the consequences of their own stupid actions—not some lighting bolt from God."

Tim's blue eyes darkened immediately into grave sympathy. "I really don't know just what to say to that, Julie. I'm sure God has His reasons for all of this. We just need to trust Him and be patient. Everything will work itself out, you'll see."

"Patient!" Julie rolled abruptly to a sitting position. "That's easy for you to say. I don't see you being smacked around or . . . or being accused of being a spy!"

She broke off to look him over consideringly. "For that matter, why aren't you? Why are they so sure *I* am this big spy they're looking for, and they don't even look at you?"

"Are you kidding?" Tim's eyebrows shot up, giving him a look of comic disbelief. "Hey, I'm not the one who can pass as a native! And sound like one too. I'm no big expert on this zone, either, and I sure don't go around meeting locals in dark churches—or U.S. colonels in military bases."

Tim reached over and touched a gentle finger to her bruised cheek. "I'm really sorry about that, Julie—and even more that there was nothing I could do to stop it. Still, I have to say I can see where it would all look pretty suspicious to someone like Aguilera. Me—well, you said it. I stand out like a glow-in-the-dark torch, and all I have to do is open my mouth to announce that I'm an American. No one is going to take me for an undercover agent. Not unless these guys think the CIA—or whoever is supposed to be running some operation down here—are stupid enough to practically advertise they've got a spy around."

*Yes, and maybe the CIA, or whoever, is smart enough to know that's what they'd think.*

Julie didn't push the argument. Tim was right. She could see, unfortunately, where her innocent actions could have been misread, and it wasn't going to help anything to try to spread the blame around.

Mollified, she asked, "So what did they ask you about?"

Tim's broad shoulders lifted in a shrug. "Oh, the usual. Who are you? What are your credentials? How can you prove you are who you say you are? Do you work for a government agency? What is your acquaintance with *la señorita* Julie Baker? And of course, are you a spy of the *americanos?*"

"Right, the usual," Julie said dryly. "Like being accused of being a spy is your average, everyday occurrence." Her mouth curved in sudden irony. "Actually, that's not so far off. When I was a kid, the missionaries were always being accused of being CIA. The leftist leaders never could figure out why Americans would be out in the jungle otherwise. The number of times I had to help scrub '*Yanqui* Go Home' off the walls of our house! I remember one student union organizer who had come through town asking if *I* was CIA. I was fifteen! I told him I was just waiting until I reached recruitment age."

"And were you?"

The question came so lightly, it didn't register at first. Then Julie asked slowly. "What is that supposed to mean?"

Tim threw a glance at the guards, then lowered his voice. "Okay, look! Maybe it's that journalistic nosiness you mentioned, and you have every right to tell me to take that nose elsewhere. But, well, I guess the puzzle pieces have just been clicking together in my head. If some government agency *did* want to investigate these murders—on the quiet, outside of Bill Shidler's 'official' inquiry—then what better way than to slip someone of their own on that plane? Someone less conspicuous than those State Department types, someone who could do a little hands-on research of his— or her—own. Someone who maybe has his—or her—own grudge against these guerrillas."

He lifted his hands. "If it's true, you've got no problem here. I'm in full agreement with what our government's doing down here, and I can keep my mouth shut in the service of my country. I might even be of some assistance if you need it. But if we're going to be in this together, it would be nice to know what's going on."

Julie stared at him, both astounded and outraged.

"Well, it's *not* true!" she hissed when she could speak again. "Are you crazy? How could you think such a thing? For the last time, I am *not* a spy!"

She bit her tongue as Enrique's head shot up. Better keep in mind that he understood English. Dropping her voice to a whisper, Julie added forcibly, "I am *not* a government agent, I promise! Do you think I would lie about it?" Her voice quavered suddenly. "Do you think I'd really go to pieces like that if I was some trained government agent? I feel like such an idiot. I was so afraid . . . I felt like I would have done anything just to get them to leave me alone."

"Hey!" Tim put out a hand again, patting her on the shoulder, the sympathy deepening in the blue eyes. "You did just fine. Look, of course you were afraid. You would have been some kind of super-being if you weren't. These guys are experts, remember? They know how to twist a hostage's mind, get them to where they're groveling with fear and will do anything to cooperate. You reacted like a normal human being, and that doesn't make you a failure. In fact, I thought you kept your head admirably. They certainly didn't get anything out of you that you didn't want to give away."

"That's because there wasn't anything to give away!" Julie retorted. "And I sure didn't notice you doing any groveling."

His words, true or not, eased her humiliation a little. "Anyway, I told you—and them—what happened and how I got here. If you don't believe me, that's your problem. As for the State Department or CIA or whoever, if they have some undercover guy sneaking around, he's probably still at the airport doing his job. At least maybe we're doing some good by taking some of the heat off his back. If there really is such a person."

"Señorita Baker? Señor McAdams? You will come with me." Enrique's tone was formal and courteous and gave no indication of having been eavesdropping on their conversation, but the tension that had been slowly seeping from Julie's muscles tightened again as she stumbled obediently to her feet.

"Wh—what do you want?" she asked apprehensively.

Motioning with his assault rifle barrel for them to move, Enrique answered brusquely, "The *comandante* wishes to question the two of you again. Come quickly. He does not like to be kept waiting."

Julie felt the sickness return to the pit of her stomach as they crossed the camp. The side of her face was throbbing painfully, and she wished she'd taken time for the outhouse—to throw up, if nothing else. *Please, not again! I don't think I can even pretend to be brave if they hit me again.*

As the two guerrillas ushered their charges into the communications hut, Julie immediately spotted the group of women huddled against the far wall. Doña Nina looked exhausted, even older and more frail than Julie remembered, her dark eyes sunk deep into their sockets, and the baker's wife's face was swollen with crying. Hadn't she had small children when Julie was last in San Ignacio? If so, she must be frantic with worry. But the whole group stood quietly and unresisting, their eyes lowered to the ground with the stoicism of the Colombian *campesinos* who have long experience in bracing themselves against the fresh disaster any day might bring.

Julie tried to emulate their submission as Enrique and Carlos herded their two prisoners forward into the center of the hut, her eyelids lowered to hide her fear. *Comandante* Aguilera stood behind the table. Her laptop and Tim's briefcase were still sitting on the table itself, the latter standing open. Julie eyed with longing the sat-phone equipment inside. At the end of that signal was help—no farther away than San José, in fact. Would Colonel Thornton come for them if they could somehow get a message out?

Or would he consider the disappearance of two reporters a small loss? Neither the American nor Colombian governments had a track record, after all, of coming to the rescue of Colombia's thousands of kidnap victims, American or otherwise.

*Comandante* Aguilera snapped the briefcase shut. Again he ignored Tim, addressing himself to Julie. "I have interrogated these women and spoken by radio with San Ignacio. Their story agrees with you. It seems you are indeed the daughter of the *americano* foreigners who lived many years in San Ignacio, now deceased these seven years."

The guerrilla commander's glance was indifferent, and with it, Julie's shoulders slumped with relief. Then this nightmare was all over, and they were all about to be released. But with his next words, his tone chilled to solid ice, and Julie's stomach with it.

"That does not alter the other charges against you, Julie Baker. You have little reason to love our cause or our people, is this not true? Why should we believe that you would return here unless it was to spy? And your parents, this Dr. Ricardo and his woman, Elizabet? Is it not true that they too were spies? That they came into our lands under the pretext of bringing aid only to spread the imperialistic empire of the *americanos* and to deceive our people with their fascist schemes? Is it not true that they were agents of the *se—eee—ahh?*" The Spanish pronunciation of the U.S. intelligence agency practically spat itself from the guerrilla leader. So this man too had heard that old accusation. And it was clear he believed it.

Julie had to swallow hard before she could speak through lips that were as stiff with sudden panic and resentment. "My parents were *not* spies! They were missionaries—doctors, health workers. They . . . they did a lot for the people of San Ignacio, as your . . . your communications must have told you. And they never worked for any American agency except their mission organization."

Julie made a hopeless gesture with her hand as she tried to keep her voice from quavering. "Please, can't you see? All . . . all they ever did—all they ever wanted to do—was to help and . . . and to love the Colombian people."

"You lie!" The fury of the words was like a blow. Startled into raising her eyes, Julie saw with another sickening jolt of her stomach that the guerrilla commander's cool demeanor had cracked. His black eyes burned with the same fanaticism she'd seen during his ranting on the platform back at the San Ignacio airport, and the narrow, sculpted features were flushed even darker than their normal deep bronze with the rage that twisted the thin line of his mouth.

*He hates us!* Julie realized with what should not have been shock. *He really hates us—the Americans. He hates me!*

Striding out from behind the desk, Aguilera walked up to Julie until his face was only inches from hers, the taste of his breath in her mouth as overpowering as his hate.

"The American imperialists do not come here without ulterior motives!" he hissed. "No, they come to steal our resources for themselves. To impose their capitalistic ways on us for the benefit of their own markets. To poison our crops with their pesticides and brainwash our children with their foreign ways of thinking. Your parents and you—you were never asked to come to Colombia—to San Ignacio! What business was it of yours to thrust your ways . . . your religion on us here? Are we so incompetent that we cannot help our own people, teach our own people, without your intervention?"

Julie stood literally frozen with terror, her gaze trapped in the fury of his so that she couldn't pull it away. The FARC commander was so angry that she could feel the vibration of his body, the heat of his rage in the words he spat into her face.

*But you haven't helped your people!* she wanted to cry out. *None of you have! You don't care about these people—not unless someone else comes along and tries to care about them. If it wasn't for my parents, no one would have helped them at all!*

"You will admit this now!" the guerrilla leader hissed again, his face coming so close, Julie couldn't help flinching under the moisture of his saliva. "You had no business coming here. Not you . . . not your parents . . . not any of you imperialist capitalist American pigs who arrogantly assume you know more of what is best for the Colombian people than we, their brothers and comrades!"

There had to be something pacifying she could say, but her mind was blank of all but that torrent of anger and hate boring down on her. "I . . . I," she stammered.

With one furious movement, the guerrilla leader flung himself away from her. Before Julie could even breathe out her sobbing relief, it turned to horror as *Comandante* Aguilera's quick strides carried him over to the huddled party of women. He hesitated only long enough to run a cold eye over the group. Then he grabbed Doña Nina by the arm and jerked her forward. Julie froze in fresh terror as he slid his pistol from his belt. It was a long-barreled weapon, shiny and gray and deadly looking, and the metallic click as he cocked it hung loud in the air.

"You will admit this, or I will shoot this traitor who calls herself your friend."

The silence that followed his ultimatum was so complete that Julie could hear the rattle of tin dishes somewhere outside the plastic walls. Every eye was fixed on her, she saw with despair—the frightened, desperate ones of the women, the furious glare of the *comandante,* the impassive gaze of Enrique and Victor and the other guerrillas within her range of vision. She didn't dare glance across at Tim.

*So what am I supposed to say? No, they didn't have any business here? They had no business trying to make a difference in one podunk little town in a Third World banana republic? They had no business wasting their careers for a bunch of peasants who had no real desire to change themselves or their country? They had no business pouring out their lives for people who didn't want them or appreciate their sacrifice?*

Julie's heart turned over inside her chest as her eyes met Doña Nina's and she read in those sunken sockets an outpouring of love and concern and forgiveness along with the fear that all the old woman's quiet dignity couldn't totally disguise.

Yes, there had been some who cared. The evidence was in these very hostages. That carefully, lovingly tended grave.

Though what difference did even that revelation make in the end? It was still all for nothing, a futile investment of two lives with the good guys losing, leaving nothing but a grassy mound and the fond memories of a few old friends.

Dropping her head, Julie let out a sob that was no longer relief. "Yes, you're right," she said dully. "My parents had no business coming here. They had no business in Colombia. They had no business in San Ignacio. None of us did."

It was like watching a mask slide over the guerrilla leader's face. The controlled, indifferent mask of a professional soldier. But Julie had now glimpsed the passion and hate that seethed underneath that impassive expression and no longer wondered that an obviously educated, civilized man could join a crusade of murder and destruction. What terrible story lay buried there?

Abruptly, *Comandante* Aguilera released Doña Nina to scurry back to the other women. Reholstering his pistol, he strode back to Julie.

"So! You will lie even to your own cost. The mark of a good agent. But you will not lie to the expense of others. That has always been a weakness of the Americans, not a strength, Señorita Baker, as you will learn. But we have no more time for this. There are faster ways to find out who you are and what it is that you have been doing over these past seven years."

Snapping his fingers at the guerrillas who were guarding the group of townswomen, he ordered curtly, "Take the women out of here. Victor, bring the chairs."

The wooden chair *Comandante* Aguilera had been using was still behind the table. The raid leader brought over another chair that hadn't been there earlier. Julie was exhausted enough to obey without protest when he ordered her to sit.

Enrique brought the other chair, and Tim lowered his large frame carefully into it. It creaked ominously under his weight, and as the back legs began to sink into the soft dirt of the floor, the guerrillas and even Julie herself paused to watch. But the slow tilt leveled off before it had sunk more than half an inch, and when the chair looked to be holding up to Tim's bulk, *Comandante* Aguilera gave another signal.

Pulling Julie's arms roughly behind the back of the chair, Victor began to wrap a cord around them. Like Enrique, he seemed to be a fairly senior officer in whatever hierarchy these guerrillas had. Tears of pain sprang again to Julie's eyes as the man tugged at the cords until they bit viciously into her wrists.

Of anger as well. No one was shoving Tim around like this! Even the guerrilla who was tying his hands behind his back was doing so gingerly and under cover of a gun barrel thrust right in his face, as though they were all afraid to venture within arm's reach.

Tim caught her eyes on him and gave a short nod, an encouraging smile touching his lips before he turned his face straight ahead, his eyes closing under the tug of the ropes as though in thought—or prayer. *Is his faith really so much stronger than mine?* Julie wondered disbelievingly.

*God, I believe in You! I believe You know I'm here and even that You know what You're doing! I've prayed! But I'm still scared to death, God! So how can Tim sit there as calm as if he were in his own living room? And I— I'm completely losing it.*

The not knowing was the worst. Julie had seen movies, read books, even news releases, of the tortures and brutal interrogations other hostages had endured at the hands of terrorist organizations. Possessing none of the information they wanted only worsened her situation. Julie felt the bile rise into her throat as *Comandante* Aguilera picked up an instrument—a knife? a scalpel?—from the table and strode toward her.

Stopping in front of her chair, *Comandante* Aguilera held up the object in his hand. It was a syringe. Julie watched with unwilling interest as the guerrilla leader depressed the plunger until a single droplet of liquid quivered at the end of the needle.

"What . . . what's in it?" she heard herself say, and the absurdity of the question at a time like this actually lightened some of her fear. *You just can't stop being a journalist, can you?*

To her surprise, Aguilera took her question seriously. "I do not know what is in it, only what it does. A gift from our *musulmanes* allies."

The guerrilla leader stepped behind Julie as he spoke. The prick in her forearm was no worse than the sting of a bee. "Perhaps it is not as effective as those drugs the Americans are said to have. But it will serve. You will tell the truth, whether you want to or not."

Some kind of truth drug, then.

*Musulmanes.* That was a Spanish term with which Julie wasn't familiar. "Muslim," she translated in her mind. Unusual friends for Marxist guerrillas to be having. To the Islamic fanatics, the tenets of communism and Marxism were as much a heresy as capitalism and independent thought. Still, hadn't there been something in all that Internet material about Islamic terrorist groups hiring out as consultants to South American guerrillas? Something Middle Eastern—Islamic Jihad . . . and the Hishbo . . . Hezbo . . .

The slow heat radiating up her arm was interfering with her thinking. Her limbs grew so heavy, she couldn't have moved them if she'd been free. Letting her head flop against the back of the chair, Julie closed her eyes against a rush of dizziness, then opened them again. The guerrilla leader was bending over her, but it was as though his sculpted features were receding away from her down a dark tunnel. Enrique Martinez was there too, hovering in the background, clear but distant, the line of his mouth grim under his moustache. Why was he still so angry? Wasn't she cooperating?

Then the flames were licking through her whole body, a curious mixture of nausea and euphoria that wasn't unpleasant, though they set the plastic walls revolving around her in a dizzying carousel of blue. From a distance she heard *Comandante* Aguilera say with satisfaction, "Now . . . you will tell us for which *americano* agency you work."

In some corner of her mind that could still register astonishment, she was surprised to hear herself answer back. But what she was saying, she had no idea. She was falling down a well that was a swirl of the blue of the plastic and the brown of the dirt floor and the green of the uniforms. And then there was only black.

# TWELVE

"AND THEN I SAW THAT THE guard wasn't paying any attention, so I just slipped out alongside that truck. . . . Doña Nina was a real surprise and so was the church. I thought it had been burned down . . . and then Tim McAdams showed up. I could have killed him for following me. . . ."

Julie had listened to the inane female prattle for some time before her clouded brain registered vaguely that it was her own voice. Like a tape, the stream of chatter kept running until she discovered she had control over it. The silence that followed was a relief, and she let it carry her back down into the dark sea from which she had emerged. It was so much more comfortable there.

When she surfaced again, Julie frowned mentally to hear that the talking had started again. Her head hurt as she tried to focus. No, this was a man's voice. More than one, and she felt that she should know them, but her mind was too fogged to place their voices or even to recognize in which language she was listening.

"She is very good. I would have sworn not even a trained agent could withstand those drugs."

"And maybe she really is who she says—a stupid novice reporter nosing around in the wrong place! Maybe the *musulmanes* were wrong, and there never was a spy. After all, the girl is right. Why should the Americans waste a spy down here? Their news teams are nosing around often enough. What is it that your friends are hiding out there, that they are so afraid the Americans will come snooping?"

"That is none of your concern. You will know soon enough. In any case, it doesn't matter. The rest of the foreigners are on their way back to civilization, and we have this one—whoever she is! The Americans have not found what they were looking for, and before long it will no longer matter."

Julie stirred. She was no longer sitting up, she recognized gradually, but lying on her side, and the surface under her cheek wasn't the hard wood of the chair she had last been in, but yielding and reasonably comfortable. Her arms were still tied behind her back, but they were no longer painful. In fact, she couldn't feel them at all.

"Ssst! The girl is coming around." The voices went silent at her move-ment. Julie raised her eyelids slowly, because they were weighted with lead. The surface under her proved to be an army cot. Beside her was another cot, and on it lay Tim McAdams, hands pulled behind his back, his eyes shut. So they had drugged him too.

Julie turned her head, an excruciating process that shot pain through her temples and left her vision whirling. The hut seemed empty, the guards and the women all gone, the plastic drawn across the entrance to seal her into a square, blue box. So who had been speaking?

She heard a rustle above her head, and two blotches of green and brown shifted into her line of vision. She blinked, and they coalesced into battle fatigues with faces under the army caps that she knew well by now. *Comandante* Aguilera and Manuel Flores. The two guerrilla leaders looked down at her without speaking, and Julie closed her eyes against the un-pleasant whirl of their outlines. What were they thinking? Were they going to let her go now?

Julie felt hard hands jerk her upright, her legs pushed roughly over the side of the cot so that she was in a sitting position. The movement sent the beginnings of life back into her numbed arms, and she almost blacked out again at the pain of it. A hand slapped her across the face, lightly this time. "Señorita Baker, you will look at me."

Reluctantly, Julie opened her eyes again. *Comandante* Aguilera's narrow features made another slow revolution above her, then finally stood still.

"So, Señorita Baker, it appears that you may be who you say you are."

There was no anger now nor accusation in his tone, only a statement of fact, and Julie felt her hopes begin to rise. "Then . . . ," she managed to get out through throat and lips that had become so dry she could feel her tongue sticking to the roof of her mouth. "You're going to let us go? It . . . it really was all a big mistake, right?"

When the guerrilla leader made no immediate answer, she pressed on, the urgency of her pleading making her head throb again. "You can't keep us, you know! We came here under safe passage, under your own protec-tion. The whole world knows that! They've been watching it on every news channel. Our kidnapping—it's got to be all over TV and radio and even the newspapers by now. All those news crews will make sure of that. What do you think that is going to do to your press conference and world opinion of your cause?"

She leaned forward beseechingly, the movement sending another stab of pain through her arms. "Look, this doesn't have to be a problem. We wandered out of bounds . . . okay, fine. You found us and brought us back. But if you don't let us go—if you keep us hostage like this—the whole world's going to know you can't be trusted. If you can kidnap press team members right out of your own peace conference, there's no way you can convince anyone you have a legitimate cause—"

Julie broke off as Aguilera suddenly straightened, and she braced herself for anger, irritation. Maybe even, by some miracle, agreement.

She wasn't prepared for the glance of amusement that flickered between the two guerrilla leaders. Turning to look back down at Julie, the *comandante* spoke smoothly, a thin-lipped smile like a gash below his hollow cheeks. "On the contrary, the foreign news crews have made themselves very useful in documenting the search we have ordered for two foolish journalists who wandered away from the protection we had arranged for them, allowing themselves thus to be kidnapped by paramilitaries seeking to destroy the peace process."

"Paramilitaries!" Julie gasped.

Already, as Aguilera went on, Julie was seeing how this story would work, and the sickness of despair rose up from her stomach into her throat.

"You see, while you were discreet enough to leave the grounds undetected, your very large, blond friend here was not. It would seem that he is well-liked by women, because there was at least one watching him closely enough to notice when he disappeared through the gate. A Sondra Kharrazi with whom we are already acquainted because she has been granted our safe passage before. She said nothing at first, as she didn't wish to make trouble for this Tim McAdams. But when the two of you were declared missing, she came forward with the information. She was kind enough not to wish accusations to be made that we, your hosts, had snatched you from the premises."

Sondra again! Had she really just been keeping a casual eye on a blond hunk who had attracted her interest? Or was she the very contact who, it would seem, had fingered Julie to the guerrillas as a spy? Her role in this was just a little too convenient for coincidence.

Leaving Julie, Aguilera strode to the front of the hut and barked an order through the plastic sealing the entrance. When he came back, he nodded toward the UHF radio, now returned to its table. "Your colleagues did not wish to leave without you. But they understood the necessity of removing further valuable targets from a zone of war. We confirmed the arrival of their plane in Bogotá an hour ago. Already, they are organizing a—what do you people always call it?" He snapped his fingers impatiently. "A crisis team to work for your release.

"And these news teams of which you speak—they have called publicly on the paramilitaries to surrender their hostages. We have already seen their broadcast on our *tele*. Manuel and I are on that broadcast, pledging our men and resources to search for the missing journalists. Though we have made it clear that the paramilitaries would have swiftly removed you from this zone for fear of our interference. Your people will not be looking for you here."

The *comandante* broke off as the plastic that sealed the entrance folded back. Enrique Martinez stepped inside, his glance flashing to Julie before he gave a nod to his superior officers. The sunlight, filtered first through the thick leaf cover of the jungle canopy, then through the blue plastic of the makeshift walls, gave a gloomy, almost underwater feel to the interior of the hut, making it impossible to judge the passage of time without the watch tied down behind Julie's back. But the length of Enrique's shadow was that of late afternoon. She'd been out for hours.

"The orders have been given." It was a statement, not a question. *Comandante* Aguilera jerked his head toward Julie. "Take the girl and clean her up. We will convene the unit in fifteen minutes to issue my instructions."

The two guerrilla leaders strode from the hut. As they disappeared from view, Julie twisted hurriedly around. Tim was still lying unmoving on the other cot, his eyes closed and his breathing so quiet that Julie was alarmed. Then she saw his massive chest rise slowly and fall. He was only unconscious, not dead.

"Señorita Baker."

The touch on her shoulder brought Julie back around with a convulsive jerk. Enrique was looming over her, his assault rifle thrust back out of the way and a large knife gripped in his hand. It was the biggest knife Julie had ever seen, smaller than a machete, but heavy and sharp enough to cut through a small sapling with one blow. A combat knife. Julie's eyes widened with fresh panic until she realized with some chagrin that the man was only trying to cut her bonds.

"If you will please refrain from movement."

Julie felt the pressure of the knife on the cords. Then her wrists were free. As the blood returned with a rush to her arms, she choked back a cry of pure agony. Her arms and hands felt like dead things, and she couldn't draw them forward. Enrique had to do it for her, and he let out a sharp hiss when he saw the mottled purple and blue of her hands and the bracelets of bloodied flesh the cords had etched around her wrists.

Rising with a fluid motion to his feet, he strode to the entrance, and even through her pain, Julie was struck again by the lithe, almost catlike power of his walk with that forward-tilted, ball-of-the-foot stride that was a dead giveaway of the combat trained soldier. A pounding of running feet answered his shrill whistle. A guerrilla male young enough to be suffering from a severe case of teenage acne rushed into the hut.

"The first-aid kit," Enrique ordered curtly. "Quickly!"

The young guerrilla disappeared, returning almost immediately with a standard Red Cross first-aid box. Enrique took the box and returned to Julie. Hunkering down on his haunches, he extracted a bottle of hydrogen peroxide and poured a generous portion of it over her wrists.

"I am sorry about this," he said quietly as the stuff fizzed and bubbled. "Unfortunately, in times of war, certain inconveniences must be endured. But this—this was not necessary."

Julie stared in amazement at his bent head. So yesterday's rescue act hadn't been the only decent impulse in this man! Was it possible after all that some humanity remained in these guerrillas? Or in this one at least?

She glanced at the entrance, where the adolescent who had brought the first-aid box still lingered. Keeping her voice low, she switched abruptly to English. "Enrique, what is going to happen to me—to Tim? If . . . if you aren't going to let us go, what are you going to do with us?"

Daubing her wrists dry with a wad of cotton, Enrique began spreading some kind of anesthetic ointment on them. The sting of Julie's cuts dulled immediately to a bearable throb. The guerrilla interpreter wound a length of gauze around her wrists before responding, and when he did, it was in the same low-voiced English as Julie, his accent no longer as noticeable as the first time Julie had heard him.

"Look, Señorita Baker. I know you are afraid. But please believe me that your detention is only temporary. You will be released. Not now, perhaps. But when the situation has changed, when your ransom is paid—I cannot say what the *comandante* has in mind. But there is no need for fear. The guerrillas do not kill hostages, nor do they mistreat them."

*Right! That's why I'm black and blue and bleeding!* Still, if Julie had heard too many stories of guerrilla kidnappings gone bad to take Enrique's assurances at face value, the sincerity in his low voice was some comfort. Maybe there was at least no immediate threat to her life.

"Enrique, the *comandante* wishes you to bring out the girl!"

This time it was Carlos who thrust his head into the hut. Julie didn't wait for Enrique's order but rose wearily to her feet. The lingering effect of whatever drug they had fed her sent a fresh wave of dizziness over her, and she couldn't suppress a cry of pain as the blood surged through her swollen hands. They looked terrible, her fingers appearing like huge, purple sausages thrusting out past the bandages Enrique had put on. Without their use, Julie found that she couldn't keep her balance.

Enrique caught her as she stumbled. Enemy or not, she leaned gratefully into the support his solid frame offered, the tang of his cologne, a musk of the overpowering potency that Colombian men seemed to favor, intermingling in her nostrils with a sharper, acrid smell of burnt gunpowder coming from his ammo vest, which pressed into her cheek.

"Here." One strong hand supporting her shoulder, Enrique dug into the first-aid kit with the other and brought out two white capsules. "These will kill the pain."

Even then he had to help her, since her hands were useless at raising the pills to her mouth. Julie, swallowing them with a glass of water Carlos hurried off to bring, showed her gratitude with a faint smile as she thanked him. The guerrilla interpreter didn't return the civility, but the expression in his eyes wasn't unkind as he released her to try walking on her own again, and the grim set of his jaw relaxed.

It still seemed odd to find decency—much less, kindness—in any of these men. Could it be that not all of the guerrillas were in total agreement with the brutality their leaders were using? If she could cultivate an ally like this man . . .

Whatever goodwill she had gained with Enrique evaporated as soon as they emerged from the hut.

"You wish me to accompany the girl?" Enrique's mouth tightened ominously, and the glance he threw in Julie's direction was far from friendly.

Aguilera had called together the entire contingent of the camp to receive his orders, with Julie hemmed in between Enrique and Carlos so that she couldn't make the smallest move without their being aware of it. The other hostages were nowhere in sight, and a glance into the hut where Doña Nina and the others had been held revealed that this was now empty. Something cold squeezed at Julie's stomach as she saw that even the army cots and mosquito netting had been removed. Where—and for what—had they been taken?

*O God, please!* she pleaded silently. *Oh, please, no!*

Julie had already concluded that a trip was imminent. The horses that *Comandante* Aguilera and his company had ridden into camp were saddled and stamping their hoofs restlessly on the other side of the campfire. From the saddle of one horse, the commander was finishing his terse instructions.

"Yes, that is correct," he answered Enrique now. "And Victor too. He will be in command, with you second after him. You will take as well . . ." —he glanced around consideringly—"Carlos and these two, and you three over there. Victor, you know the camp to which you will take her. You will leave immediately so that you may reach your next position before it is dark. The rest will finish tearing this camp down, then return with me."

Enrique made no further public objections, but Julie couldn't avoid hearing his terse argument with Aguilera as the guerrillas returned to dismantling the camp and the raid leader, Victor, began organizing the party's departure. Though Enrique's tone was respectful, Julie was learning to recognize the signs of anger in the rigid set of his shoulders and the bunching of muscles along his jawline.

"Señor, I do not wish to question your orders. But I am a trained fighter. You know my skills. When my own faction offered my services to your cause, it was to train your men—to fight at your side. Not to be a *niñera!*" The word meant "nanny" or "nursemaid," and wasn't in the context meant to be complimentary to those of his comrades who served on guard detail. "Surely Victor and Carlos are capable of overseeing the watch of one single woman without my presence. They have done so often enough before."

"Enough!" The *comandante* cut him off with a sharp gesture. "You are a valuable fighter, Enrique, that is true. One of the best that the Central Command has ever assigned to me. But I do not permit the dispute of my orders," he added coldly. "Not though it were Tiro Fijo himself, commander of all the FARC battalions, who sent you to us. You will obey me and go with the woman."

Aguilera immediately moderated the sharpness of his response, in itself an indication of how high Enrique stood in the hierarchy of these guerrillas. "Our allies have demanded extra care for this one. Whether it is truly necessary does not matter. We need their cooperation—and their weapons—so we will do as they request. You . . . you speak the woman's language. This could prove useful if the woman should let something slip. For this you will stay near her even in her sleep.

"And then there is Carlos. I cannot entirely trust him in this. I send him because he once knew the woman, and perhaps she will speak to him as she has not to us. Still, past acquaintances can be dangerous—you and I both know this. Carlos has become a good soldier, and he has his own reasons for loyalty to our cause. But it is only prudent that a watch be kept on his sympathies. I am trusting you to be my eyes and ears in the camp."

"And the man? This Señor McAdams?"

"He will stay with me. He has his own uses." Aguilera leaned down from his horse to clap a hand on the younger guerrilla's shoulder before gathering up the reins of his horse. "You are a good soldier, Enrique, and a loyal one. Rest assured that when the hour comes to fight, your skills will not be wasted on the sidelines. And it will not be long, that I promise you."

His superior's assurance did little to improve Enrique's mood. He nodded a curt agreement, but the black look was back on his face as *Comandante* Aguilera trotted away. The younger guerilla's mouth thinned to a straight, angry line as he shouted for one of the women to bring Julie's pack. Julie, who had dropped wearily onto a sawed-off stump during the frenzy of departure arrangements, wondered that they would speak so freely in her hearing until she realized the picture she must present, slumped down with her back to the two men, giving no indication that she was even aware of what was going on around her. *These guys don't watch enough TV. They should know someone's always listening.*

All around Julie, the camp was coming down with astonishing speed. The plastic was coming off the walls of the huts, and as it was rolled up and stuffed into packs, the thatched roofs and trimmed-off limbs that supported them were pulled apart and scattered around the clearing. *Comandante* Aguilera, over by the supply table, was directing the loading of food sacks onto the horses' backs.

Julie's pack appeared, and with it came Victor and Carlos and the other five guerrillas chosen for her guard detail. Two were women. One of these accompanied Julie to the outhouse, then pressed a bowl of rice and beans into her hands and watched her eat it, her hands still stiff and awkward as she handled the aluminum spoon.

Each of her guard detail hoisted a pack on their backs and adjusted their arsenal of weapons. Assault rifles slung over one shoulder. Ammunition and grenades tucked into some ammo vests. Artillery belts jangling. A pistol holster at Victor's hip and two others of the new men.

Julie, who still found the world revolving around her if she moved too quickly, was relieved to see Enrique lead up a horse. His order to mount was curt, and he didn't glance in her direction. But he wasn't ungentle as he gave her a boost into the saddle and passed up her knapsack, and Julie was encouraged to ask a question that had been burning in her since she'd recovered consciousness.

"Enrique, what about Tim? Why isn't he coming with us? What . . . what are they going to do with him?"

Julie was well aware they couldn't afford to release him. Not if the guerrillas were to maintain their charade of paramilitary involvement in the two journalists' disappearance. The other possibilities didn't bear thinking about.

It was the leader of the party, Victor, who, overhearing, answered brusquely. "He will be held as insurance for your behavior, and you for his. If you try to escape, we will shoot him. If he tries to escape, we will shoot you. He will be informed of this. Is this clear?"

Julie nodded, wishing she hadn't asked. No, it was better to know! At least that meant there were no immediate plans against Tim's life either, and with that knowledge she could relax a fraction.

The guerrillas began moving out, single file. Enrique gave Julie's horse a slap on its hindquarters, and the animal joined the progression. Enrique closed in behind to take up the rear.

Julie glanced back as the jungle trail swallowed up the guerrillas ahead of her. The plastic walls were being stripped from the radio hut, exposing the two army cots in the center of the dirt floor. Julie had just registered that they were both empty when she caught a glimpse of a tall form standing beside one of the posts, his broad frame hidden by the shadows, but the late afternoon sun glinting unmistakably off his blond hair.

So Tim was alive and conscious. The sting of her eyes was a revelation of just how worried she had been.

The vegetation closed around Julie, and the camp vanished from sight. Reluctantly turning her face forward, she settled herself more comfortably in the saddle. The trek was far different by daylight than it had been the night before, and under other circumstances, Julie would have enjoyed it. The broad fronds of palm trees closed in above the trail, their shade offering an illusion of coolness despite the actual steamy heat of the jungle day. Orchids in a myriad colors and shapes climbed tree trunks and dropped down vines into her face. Monkeys scampered overhead, and the jeweled plumage of macaws and toucans flitted among the green leaves. Heavy on the air was that unique rainforest scent of damp, musty decay and ancient vegetation that dinosaur exhibits the world over had sought in vain to duplicate.

Only the mosquitoes spoiled the tranquility of the jungle afternoon. Julie, slapping at a fresh welt on her bare arms, finally dug her repellant from her knapsack. As she slathered it on, she caught one of the guerrilla women, striding just ahead of her horse's front hooves, watching the process over her shoulder. She had brought Julie's pack and food, and Julie, wanting to return the courtesy, held out the bottle to her. But at her action, hostility slammed down instantly over the interest Julie had glimpsed in the woman's eyes. Whirling around, she turned her attention back to the trail in front of her.

Without the other prisoners or the obstacles of night and rain, the party reached the river in far less time than the trek had taken the day before. This time no riverboat waited; instead, Julie saw one of the long dugout canoes that were still the most common transportation in the jungle. Two guerrillas were waiting in it when they arrived. One came up the bank to take Julie's horse, swinging into the saddle as she dismounted and heading back down the trail toward camp. The other started an outboard motor attached to the stern of the canoe.

The two women took over as guards as the men loaded the packs into the canoe. Julie had learned their names as they spoke back and forth. The older woman—if twenty or so could be termed "older"—was Linda. The other, no more than thirteen or fourteen years old, was Marcela. Linda ordered Julie to climb in and lie down, throwing a burlap sack over her as they pushed off from the bank.

Some time later, Julie heard Victor's warning call, then the rumble of another motor. The guerrillas didn't want any local fishermen spotting their hostage. But it was sweltering hot and airless under the sacking, and by the time the canoe bumped against solid ground and the sacking was pulled back, Julie was drenched with sweat, her hair plastered to her head.

Clambering out, she found that they had docked at another isolated river landing. Up the bank lay another jungle trail. Already the guerrillas were hauling their packs from the canoe and putting them on. Once they were all on the bank, the man who had navigated the canoe pushed off, and at an order from Victor, the party started out again.

This time the trek wasn't so pleasant. The afternoon had been well advanced when they left the first camp, and twilight was now setting in, leaving the trail under the dense jungle canopy little less dark than at full night. Julie, still suffering under the lingering effects of the truth drug, couldn't keep up with the trail-hardened pace of the guerrillas, which earned her a steady stream of caustic comments from her personal guard until Victor finally swung around and shouted, "Shut up, Linda! If the *gringa* can't keep up, take her pack and carry it yourself! We do not have all night!"

Linda—an ironic name, as it meant "beautiful" in Spanish—shot Julie a dirty look as she added Julie's knapsack to her own load, but she did keep quiet. Happily, only a few minutes later they stumbled into another clearing. Julie was allowed to sink wearily to the ground, her knapsack tossed into her lap, while the guerrillas set to work building a campfire and preparing places to sleep.

These were not the bigger huts of the last camp; instead, they were little more than individual sleeping pallets built up off the ground by piling branches and twigs about a foot high, then covering them with a bed of palm leaves. Mattress pads even thinner than a sleeping bag came out of the packs and went on top. An individual frame was built above each bed, and mosquito netting was suspended over it. A plastic tarp thrown over the whole thing kept out the rain, theoretically.

The clearing must have been used before as a camp. There were plenty of machete-trimmed lengths of wood scattered around on the ground that were snatched up and put to use. Enrique and Carlos were already hammering together a rough table. Victor sent two of the guerrillas to dig a latrine. The two girls started a campfire and pulled aluminum pots from the packs to boil coffee, rice, and lentils. A Coleman lamp hissed into yellow flame and was suspended from a tree branch above the cook area.

Julie, hugging her knapsack on her lap as she watched, was astonished at the speed and efficiency with which they all moved, like a well-rehearsed military operation. By the time supper was ready, so was the camp.

This time there was no radio or chatting around the fire after supper. Linda, still sulky from Victor's scolding, brought Julie a basin of water to wash up with, then sullenly produced a flashlight for a trip through the underbrush to the latrine—no walls this time, Julie discovered with a grimace, but a pit with a board for each foot propped across it and a roll of green toilet paper threaded onto a small branch.

Julie crawled into the bed to which the woman led her and tucked in the mosquito netting. It was beginning to drizzle, and the male guerrillas retired almost immediately to the shelter of their own pallets, leaving the two women to clear away the meal. Enrique had taken the shelter next to Julie's. Through the mosquito netting, she could see the long silhouette of his body, stretched out with his arms folded behind his head in a way that should have looked relaxed but didn't. *Hoping I'll talk in my sleep!*

Still, better Enrique next-door than some of the others. Perhaps because he had already twice shown her a quixotic chivalry, Julie felt fractionally safer with his dour presence stretched out between her and some of those other men.

Kitchen duties finished, the women—or rather, girls—crawled into their pallets, and the Coleman lantern winked out. Only Carlos, who was taking the first watch, remained outside. The camp had no chair, so he was forced to stay on his feet, pacing slowly back and forth in front of her shelter. The young guerrilla had hauled a piece of the same plastic used as tarps over his shoulders, and he had his assault rifle underneath its folds to keep it dry.

Julie, tugging on a thin blanket in a fruitless attempt to cover her shoulders and feet at the same time, listened to the thud of Carlos's boots as they marched back and forth. It still seemed incredible that this tough-looking young man with the hard, sullen expression could be the merry little boy who had once tagged at her heels. Ever since she'd first recognized Carlos, she'd wanted to speak to him, ask him how he'd ended up here, where his family was. Maybe now was her chance.

She sat up on her pallet. As last night's experience had taught her, the movement immediately drew the beam of a flashlight. As it rested on her face, Julie whispered, "Carlos."

The frame of the shelter was high enough that he didn't have to stoop far to look inside. Above the light, Julie caught the glimmer of her reflection in his dark eyes.

"Carlos, you really do remember me?"

His nod was barely perceptible. Julie drew in a deep breath, then whispered her most pressing question. "Doña Nina, Doña Carmen, the others—what have they done with them?"

The beam of light held steady on her face. "You do not need to be afraid on their behalf," Carlos said softly. "They have been released. That is why we broke camp—so they might be set free to return to San Ignacio. And also because no camp is used for long. The women will not speak of what they have seen. They know too well the consequences to their families. But *Comandante* Aguilera is not a butcher. He would not hurt without need those who have given him faithful service."

Julie's relief came out in an exhaled sob. "Thank you, Carlos! And—what about you? Your family? Gabriela? Where are they?"

There was a hesitation, the beam of light wavering on her face. Then his toneless reply. "They are dead."

"Carlos, you will not speak to the prisoner!"

The harsh order was Victor's. Carlos straightened up hastily. Switching off the flashlight, he resumed his tedious march. Lying back down, Julie rolled over and buried her face in her arms. The tears of relief she had refused to release under that searching beam now stung her eyes. They were safe—Doña Nina and *Tía* Carmen and the others. At least they wouldn't suffer further for her stupidity and Tim's. If Carlos was telling the truth.

But then, why would he lie? The women came from families well-known in San Ignacio. Between them all, they were probably blood relatives to half the town. It made sense that *Comandante* Aguilera wouldn't stir up his own nest any more than he had to. No, she would choose to believe that Carlos was right and that these women who had touched both her past and her present were on their way back to home and safety.

And herself?

Julie stirred to slap at a whining mosquito that had slipped inside the netting and was feasting on her cheek. High above in the canopy, the breeze had dropped, stilling the restless sighing of the trees. The parrots and other feathered life had fallen silent. Julie knew, though she couldn't see them, that their heads were tucked under their wings for the night. The monkeys had found a tree fork in which to curl up, for they too were silent.

But the night was not quiet, for now the amphibian choir had begun its evening concert. The piping soprano of the sticky, bright-green tree frogs. The croaking baritone of the toads that grew in these parts to the size of a dinner plate. And a booming rhythmic bass that sounded as though its proprietor must be platter-sized but which came, in actuality, from a tiny frog whose throat swelled up to a bladder as large as itself. Above their chorus whined the shrill violin of the cicadas and the sharp piccolo of the mosquitoes.

As a child, Julie had been able to shut out the jungle's nightly serenade as a city child blocks out the roar of traffic. But now it seemed unbearably loud. Never in her life—not after her parents' death, not in the long years of boarding school and college—had she ever felt so alone. Until now, the very shock of what had happened, the adrenaline of fear and anger, the worry about her fellow hostages—the certainty that it was all some kind of mistake!—had carried her along, given her strength of will to show some measure of courage in front of these people, however little she felt it.

That courage was fast ebbing into the solitude of the night, the knowledge that not a single other human being who was not an enemy or a guard lay between her and the vastness of the wilderness into which she had been dropped like one small and inconsequential seed.

*"Unless a kernel of wheat falls . . . whoever loses his life . . ."*

The verse had been referenced on her parents' tombstone. But now it was she who was fallen, lost, alone. And for all Carlos's assurances and Enrique's before him, there was no guarantee she wouldn't lose her life as well. There had been too many hostages far better than herself—missionaries, pastors—who had been taken by the guerrillas and the paramilitaries and never seen again. Why not her? Why not Tim?

*God, are You out there?*

It was a stupid question, all her theology told her. Of course God was out there, running the universe, weaving together His ultimate plan despite the stubbornness and stupidity of the creatures with whom He had to work.

Did He notice her enough to intervene on her behalf? Enough to make her prayers a worthwhile investment of either God's time or hers? Was there any good—any "fruit," as the Scripture inscribed on her parents' grave affirmed—that could possibly come out of this bizarre situation? Or would she, like her parents, be left trampled into the ground as a horse's hoof might carelessly trample a flower that dared lift its head from the earth in which it sprouted? Would anyone back home ever even find out what had become of her? Of Tim, lying right now, if the guerrillas were telling the truth, in another such shelter in another jungle camp?

Would anyone care?

A sob rose unbidden to Julie's throat. Oddly, it wasn't of herself she was thinking. It was of a gruff old man, sitting in a grimy, smoke-choked office, waiting for her to return home. Yes, Uncle Norm would care—how much she was only now beginning to admit! He had stormed down to Colombia when her parents had found themselves in trouble, and though she had allowed his sternness and crusty exterior to blind her all these years, Julie knew with sudden conviction that he would storm Washington itself when he discovered she was gone.

Worse, he would blame himself for having let her go. And so was added another person to the list of those her stubborn self-will had hurt.

Tears fell hot and heavy, but Julie stifled them against her thin mattress so her captors would not hear.

* * *

They watched.

These intruders thought themselves alone, hidden, not perceiving that in the jungle one is never alone. Always, by day and even more so by night, there are eyes and ears—soaring overhead on the wing. Hunters marking the intrusion of another predator into their territory but not showing themselves, in turn, unless threatened. The small creatures and insects underfoot to whom the intruders were but the thunder of a giant passing overhead.

And other dwellers of the forest whose danger-sharpened senses made it easy to spy unseen on these noisy, clumsy trespassers.

The watchers heard the sounds of the girl's tears.

* * *

The three members of the UN forensic team chose to share a cab from New York's La Guardia airport. They would normally have headed in opposite directions to their homes, but their flight from Bogotá had run an hour late, and the pathology conference they were scheduled to attend that evening was due to start in less than an hour, so Dr. Kristin Gustofferson curtly ordered the driver to take all three of them directly to the conference location. She was still fuming as the cab left the airport behind.

"If this was not a total waste of time and resources! I would never have agreed to this had I known we would receive so little cooperation." Dr. Gustofferson shook her head angrily. "To be sent away with our investigation incomplete!"

Dr. Roger Elliot yawned. It had been a long and stressful couple of days, and he was looking forward to dozing through the opening session of the conference, then ducking out early to his Jacuzzi and bed. "We did what we went for," he said. "There was no sign of murder. I see no reason not to accept Aguilera's hypothesis. The Americans got separated from their Indian guides. They wandered around in the jungle for a couple of weeks, in the process picking up some tropical bug. The pathology was consistent with flu or even pneumonia. Certainly some kind of virus. They finally stumbled out to civilization. And when they died, the locals got scared and dumped them somewhere the bodies would be found. Nothing mysterious, really."

Dr. Gustofferson, seated between the two men in the back seat of the cab, turned a disapproving eye on her Scottish colleague. "Well, we would know more if we'd been allowed to take proper specimens, do a proper analysis. They set no prior restrictions. They allowed us to take our own equipment, then they tell us we cannot take the time for the proper tests. And we cannot remove the bodies nor even appropriate specimens to run cultures and tests through our own lab and data banks. These are not the actions of innocent men. To say they do not trust our analysis is outrageous. Why should we lie?"

She shook her head emphatically. "No, it is more as though they received new orders after they agreed to our team. I think they are hiding something. And now two more are missing. Will they too show up somewhere dead, without a mark on them?"

Dr. Elliot rubbed a weary hand over his face. What he needed right now was a strong dose of espresso—and a less zealous colleague. "Yeah, well, maybe you're right. But it doesn't make much difference now, does it? We *don't* have the bodies or the specimens. I for one feel we did everything we could. Either way, it's pointless to keep stewing about it now."

"Actually," Dr. Ravi Gupta began after clearing his throat, "that is not precisely the case."

The diminutive Indian doctor so seldom intruded into their debates that his two colleagues immediately broke off to stare at him. "What do you mean?" Dr. Gustofferson demanded.

"We may not have the bodies, but we do have specimens." Reaching into his shirt pocket, Dr. Gupta extracted the glasses case he always carried and flipped it open, revealing a cloth-lined interior, presently empty. Taking off his glasses, he inserted the end of one of the ear-pieces into what appeared to be a screw hole at one end of the case. With a faint click, the bottom lining snapped upward. Inside, to his colleagues' incredulous eyes, were slides and tiny vials.

"But how—?"

Dr. Gupta closed the glasses case carefully. "I have spent my life in countries less . . . *safe*, one might say, than you two. One learns talents."

Leaning forward, Dr. Gustofferson tapped the cab driver on the shoulder. "Excuse me, but we've had a change of plans. If you will take us to . . ."

At the name of the research lab, Dr. Elliot sat up straight in protest. "But what about the conference?"

"Forget the conference, Roger!" the Swedish doctor snapped as Dr. Elliot groaned. "And that Jacuzzi of yours too. We're going to nail these people if it takes all night!"

\* \* \*

It didn't—quite. Neither businesses nor government offices would be open for hours yet when James Whitfield picked up the phone. It was one of the few people who possessed his home number, Martin Sawatsky, CIA director.

"Did you get that report I faxed over?" he demanded.

The national security advisor swallowed half a pint of coffee to clear his mouth of the Danish he was eating. "I sure did. I'm trying to make sense of it now. So they found traces of an obscure South American poison? Only known use by Amazon natives to tip their hunting arrows and blow gun darts. What does that mean—that our personnel were kidnapped by some jungle tribe, not the guerrillas? Is it possible we had this all wrong?"

"Just finish the report," the CIA director said somberly. "They didn't die from arrow poison."

"So what did kill them?" As he continued skimming the fax, Whitfield reached for another Danish. It stopped partway to his mouth. Carefully, he returned the pastry to the plate. "Does this mean what I think it does?"

"The implications are certainly there."

James Whitfield's prodigious morning appetite was gone. "We'd better call the president."

\* \* \*

He shifted on his pallet, listening with resignation to the steady plop-plop of dripping water hitting the dirt not far from his head. What was keeping him awake was not the maddening monotony of the rain dripping through a leak in the roof nor the hardness of the bed beneath him. He'd slept on far worse.

It was the girl.

Yes, this Julie Baker was who she said—he knew the voice of truth when he heard it. Though he'd wondered at first. Wondered which agency had set up such an inept competition to his own operation. Wondered even if HQ had sent in new assets over his head and Thornton's. But the girl had given nothing away, had by all appearances accepted his own cover at face value.

He stirred again, restively. This girl was who she claimed—and that said much. She had, in fact, done far better than he'd expected, facing what had been a brutal interrogation without whining or hysterics, with a quiet dignity and uplifted chin. The girl had courage.

And yet she hadn't been able to hide her terror, her fear of her captors and worry for her friends, and he couldn't avoid a twinge of conscience. How easy it would be for him to end all this. Walk away from here—he was trained to do so easily enough. Activate his GPS locator. Call in the cavalry. Then go back for the girl.

But then all the effort it had taken to get here would be for nothing. No, his orders were clear. The girl was safe enough, whether she recognized it or not. Little though he liked it, there was far more at stake here than the feelings or comfort of one admittedly attractive young woman.

Or his own.

The drizzle lifted. Gradually, the incessant dripping slowed, then ceased. But just as sleep finally closed in, a stirring of voices told him that night had ended and it was time to face another day.

* * *

Taqi Nouri raised his eyes from the packing crate whose contents he was inventorying to study his companion coolly. "So—it would seem the Americans are not so predictable after all."

"Perhaps. It may be they did not choose to send a spy as we expected. It was not a certain thing, after all. Or perhaps the spy never left the airport. Perhaps our demonstration of innocence was sufficient to allay any remaining suspicions."

Nouri's companion paused before going on. "There is another possibility. The girl may be programmed to give the story she told. The Americans have long experimented with such things for their agents—a cover story triggered to come out under drugs or hypnosis. Our intelligence was that their success had been minimal, but that data may be inaccurate. Though Aguilera is satisfied that she is who she says. He regrets that he cannot ask for ransom."

The Iranian minister of intelligence gave his companion a hard look. "And the man. What does Aguilera say of him?"

"That his computer check shows him to be what he related under the truth drug—a harmless religious reporter who has been in this country several times before. Too big and too gringo to be a spy. Besides, he was seen following the girl out of the gate . . . it seems he found her attractive. A plausible story. The girl has been told that her friend is being held hostage for her good behavior."

"Much effort for small results. But no matter. Either the girl is not a spy, in which case the Americans are more shortsighted than we believed, or if she is a spy, she is in our custody, in which case she is no longer a danger. Which means that we can now proceed to the final test." Taqi Nouri returned to his inspection of the open crate, feeling both triumph and revulsion as he peered inside. If these weapons had ever been turned against his own countrymen . . .

Nouri made a brusque signal that brought over the senior officer of the Iraqi security force, and he ignored the barely veiled insolence of the Iraqi's salute. It was unfortunate that their dubious ally had insisted on his own forces to guard this treasure. But at least the Iraqi commander in chief had made clear to his subordinates who was the supreme authority here.

Switching from Farsi to Arabic, Nouri ordered, "Bring the natives."

The Amazonic tribal group was an unprepossessing sight to the fastidiously clean Muslim cleric. Half-naked men, and worse, women, children clinging to a parent's leg, babies tied to a mother's back—they were all filthy, diseased, and foul of odor.

But none of his revulsion showed on Nouri's impassive features as he addressed the group.

"You have done what we asked of you. Now you are free to go. All except for you." He had the Iraqi guards separate out a half-dozen able-bodied adults. "You will be needed a short time longer. The rest may return to your village. You will find waiting there the goods you were promised for your labor. My men will take them ahead of you by river."

The tribal group had brought little with them when conscripted to labor for the foreigners, so it took little time to take leave of family members remaining behind and set out on the long trek home. Dusk was beginning to fall by the time the excited call of an advance scout announced the first glimpse of the thatched huts that were the village they had left so many months before. The tribe began to hurry.

The village was untouched except for the inevitable depredations of animals that had scattered belongings and food supplies. And for once the foreigners had kept their word. A mound of goods lay dumped onto the village green in the center of the thatched huts. The tribal group crowded around the heap excitedly. Sacks of rice. Cloth. Metal knives to replace those of bone. And a priceless treasure—salt—that would make jerky keep much longer. This year would be a good one.

It was a small girl who found the canister. It was not big, but it glinted silver in the last rays of the setting sun that slanted down through the gap the village had made in the jungle canopy. Pushing aside a bolt of cloth, she picked up the shiny object. She blinked as the action triggered the release of a cool mist in her face. It felt good after the heat of the day's march. When an older child snatched the object from her hand, she began to cry.

Then she began to cough.

# THIRTEEN

THE NEXT DAY WASN'T AS BAD.

Perhaps it was only that nothing could be. Or maybe it was because the drizzle had stopped and the seamless blue of a perfect day was already burning away the last pinks and oranges of sunrise when Julie tugged the mosquito netting loose from her pallet and crawled to the edge of her shelter to look out over the encampment.

This turned out to be a more open site than the last camp. The shelters themselves were tucked back under cover of the trees. But just beyond the campfire that Linda and Marcela had thrown together for cooking the night before was a sandy beach, and beyond that, a wide stream, too shallow for navigation but invitingly clear where it burbled over a bed of rocks. Julie eyed it longingly, the freshness of the jungle morning making her only more conscious of her grime.

Her guard seemed to be enjoying the morning's beauty as well. A young man in his early twenties with loose, dark curls and the light skin and tall, lanky frame of predominantly European descent, he was whistling a pop song under his breath. He broke off his whistling as he caught Julie's movement and hunkered down to peer in at her.

"*Buenos días,* señorita," he greeted cheerfully, hazel eyes twinkling down at Julie. An attractive young man, and well he knew it!

A loud whistle from him brought Marcela scurrying over from the campfire to lead Julie to the latrine. By the time they returned, the whole camp was awake and bustling, and the appetizing odors of coffee and frying *arepas* were chasing away the last fresh scent of the jungle dawn.

The coffee was very black and sweet, the jolt of caffeine improving Julie's outlook still further, and when Marcela approached to retrieve Julie's breakfast dishes, she lingered to say shyly, "If there is anything you need, señorita, you have only to ask me. Perhaps there are foods you do not care for, or a request you would like to make for dinner? Or if you have any questions, *el Comandante* Victor says that you have only to ask. We wish you to be comfortable here."

So she was not to be ostracized forever.

Julie was dismayed to find tears springing to her eyes at the girl's words. *You're losing it, when you can get that excited about having a terrorist stop and talk to you.*

Not that Julie was under any illusion as to Victor's sudden willingness to allow her contact with his troops. She'd been on her way back from the latrine when she'd seen the camp leader bent over the radio and had heard *Comandante* Aguilera's furious words coming through the explosion of static.

"What is this, Victor, that you do not allow the woman to mix with the others?"

"But, *Comandante*, the orders have always been—"

*"Idiota!"*

Another flurry of static, and Julie, herded back to her shelter, heard no more. Yesterday's eavesdropping allowed her to piece together the rest. If normal hostages were kept isolated from their guerrilla guards—to keep sympathies from forming if nothing else—the FARC commander wanted Julie talking. *As though a real spy would let something slip that easily.*

Still, anything was better than being treated as though she were invisible.

Not that there was much chance during the rest of the day for social interchange. After breakfast the shift changed again, and her new guard was a taciturn man of almost pure African stock. Too tall to hunker down comfortably, he dragged over a sawed-off piece of log he'd unearthed from among the previous camp's discards and seated himself on it, his eyes fastened unblinkingly on Julie.

Under Victor's orders, the rest of the guerrillas set to work. A deeper cooking pit was lined with stones from the river and the grass cleared away around it. A thatched shelter rose above the supply table, and Enrique hammered together another rude table for the radio. A second pit was dug for garbage, and stones were laid down to the river edge to keep feet out of the water when it rained.

Julie's new guard responded with no more than a surly grunt to her tentative questions. So Julie, without a book or even paper and pen for distraction, spent the day cross-legged at the edge of her pallet, watching and listening and making mental notes on the activity around her. If it was whistling in the dark to pretend this was a research expedition, at least it helped keep her anxieties at bay.

After lunch—more beans and rice—the guerrillas set to work on a swim hole, laboriously rolling the boulders out of one of the deeper spots along the streambed until they had a shallow pool big enough for bathing. This they took in turns to do, by pairs, the two women in their bras and panties, the men stripped to their undershorts.

Julie was led out last, the older guerrilla girl, Linda, keeping guard from the bank as Julie bathed. The water was wonderfully refreshing in the sultry heat, but Julie, conscious of more than just Linda's eyes on her, didn't linger. Nor did she strip to her underwear like the others. She tucked the worn terrycloth towel she'd been given around her, preferring to scramble wet into her clothes than expose herself to the whole camp.

She scrubbed the clothes she'd been wearing as best she could, using the same sliver of soap Linda had provided for bathing. But she wasn't going to need them again, Julie found when she emerged from the water. Waiting for her on the bank was a set of the same army fatigues the guerrillas wore. They weren't a bad fit, and from the size might even have been Linda's, though worn with Julie's tennis shoes rather than the boots the guerrillas used, they were on the baggy side around the ankles.

Linda watched with clear amusement as Julie maneuvered to pull on the new clothing under the wet towel. "You *gringas* must find it difficult to get a man when you are so skinny," she commented, a supercilious tilt to her mouth. "Though I have heard the *americanos* think it beautiful to be thin. The *Colombianos* prefer flesh on their women." And she glanced down at her own ample bosom.

*Yeah, well, standards differ,* Julie felt like retorting. Instead, she picked up her wet towel and clothing and silently preceded the guerrilla girl back to camp. Spreading her bundle of laundry on the thatched roof of her shelter to dry, she returned to her cross-legged position, this time watching the guerrillas take apart and clean their weapons.

Once night fell and the Coleman lantern was lit and hung from a branch, the mood of the camp changed. While Linda and Marcela were clearing away the *sancocho*, a traditional Colombian stew thick with rice and plantains and manioc root and potatoes, the other guerrillas had rolled several logs up to the cooking pit. Then they sprawled around the fire, some sitting on the logs, others leaning up against them. A transistor radio played softly, and Julie's early-dawn guard crooned along in a remarkably good tenor to a Ricky Martin love song.

The guards had changed three more times during the day—a four-hour shift, Julie had timed with her watch—with everyone taking a turn except Victor and Enrique, who evidently considered themselves above such duties. Carlos had been sent over to replace Marcela while she worked on supper, and he was slumped down on the stump with his eyes drifting as much to the campfire as to Julie when Victor called out, "Hey, Carlos, fiesta time! Bring the woman out to join us!"

Julie heard the order with mixed feelings. If sitting in her shelter with one terrorist only a few feet away was bad, socializing around a campfire with eight of them was a daunting proposition. Still, if she had to sit here alone one more minute, she was going to go crazy.

Following Carlos over to the campfire, Julie took the seat he indicated on one of the logs. Lowering himself onto the log beside her, Carlos glanced over at Victor for approval before unslinging his assault rifle and laying it on the ground in front of him. On Julie's other side, Enrique lay slouched up against the log, whittling idly at a chunk of wood. Beyond him, Marcela sat with her knees drawn up to her chin, her eyes following his movements wistfully, though Enrique showed no signs of noticing the teenager's devotion.

Across the fire, Linda was cuddled up against Julie's stolid guard from that morning. The tall black man frowned as the guerrilla girl leaned across him to call out a laughing remark to the singer. His name was Jaime, Julie had learned over the hours of listening. The singer was Alberto, and the last man in the group was Rafael, a young man about Alberto's age, but sullen instead of laughing, with the stocky build and oriental features of the *mestizo*.

All in all, they might have been a student group on a hiking trip, Julie thought bemused, were it not for the uniforms and the weapons that lay within easy grasp of each guerrilla.

Alberto broke off his song as Julie settled herself onto the log, the smile he flashed her direction as winning and confident as too much female attention had made it. *"Bienvenida,* Señorita Julia! Welcome! Come, please tell us about yourself. They say that you once lived in this area. Is this true?"

His interest seemed genuine enough, and Julie saw no reason to discourage his friendliness, so in a few short sentences she explained how she had been raised in San Ignacio until her parents' death seven years earlier. As she finished, Linda threw her a scornful look. "But that is silly. No one dies of the cholera anymore. You tell us they were doctors, yet they couldn't heal even themselves? I say you are lying!"

Her hostility was patent, and while Julie knew the guerrilla girl wouldn't dare touch her without permission from the camp leader, her muscles tightened instinctively. She kept her voice even as she answered, "You're right—no one dies of cholera anymore. That is, unless they can't get medical supplies or care. Unfortunately, there were no more medical supplies and care in San Ignacio when my parents died. The FARC wouldn't permit the Red Cross to send in supplies or bring them medical help. So,"—she swallowed to cover a catch in her voice—"they died. Just ask Carlos here if it isn't true."

Beside her, Carlos shrugged. "She is telling the truth, as I have already told *Comandante* Aguilera. I was only a child when the cholera came to San Ignacio, but I remember it well. Others in the town died besides Don Ricardo and his wife, but not many. My father was one to whom the gringo doctor brought medicine so that he recovered. There were many with the disease, so when the gringos became sick themselves, there was no medicine left. But it was not *Comandante* Aguilera who kept the *medicos* from the outside from coming to save them. It was *Comandante* Orellana, who died in the attack on Los Pozos last year."

A brief silence followed his statement, and when Alberto spoke, it was with sympathy. "That is too bad, Señorita Julia. You must know, however, that the FARC is not really like that. We take good care of our hostages and the people for whom we fight as well. We have doctors in our cause, and we have brought much medical care to villages to which the government gave nothing. Still, sometimes there are commanders who do not follow the principles by which we are pledged to live."

"So!" The spite in Linda's tone was in direct contrast to the singer's amiability. "Is this why you chose to become a spy? Because you blame this *comandante* for the death of your parents? You came here for revenge?"

The accusation was like a blow. Even the rank and file had heard that ridiculous story! Julie wanted to scream with frustration.

"I am not a spy," she said firmly. "Look, you have to believe me." She felt Enrique's gaze lift from his wood carving to give her a measuring look, his eyes hooded and dark in the flickering flames, and put all the sincerity she could into her tone. "Please believe me that there is no reason for

America to spy on you. Why would we? This is not our fight. I'm just a reporter, I swear! In fact," she added in a lighter tone, "if any of you are interested in a news interview, I'll be happy to make sure your picture makes the front page. If you will let me go so I can get it into print, of course."

That brought a patter of laughter and an appreciative murmur, and Julie began to relax again.

Suddenly Rafael leaned forward. "I remember you—I know now who you are!" he announced abruptly, and his sneer was patent even in the flickering firelight. "And this *misionero* Ricardo Baker. He came to our village too, one day many years ago. Oh, yes, we did not live so far from San Ignacio. He came in his rich, capitalist plane to tell the elders of the village that they must allow him to give his shots to the children. Because my sister had the tuberculosis, the *misionero* insisted she must have more medicine than the others. To pay for it, my father took our cows into the big town and sold them." The guerrilla's mouth curled disagreeably as he added, "We went hungry many times afterward because of your father. And then the girl died anyway when we could no longer pay for her treatment."

Every eye now swiveled to Julie. Glancing around at their unforgiving faces, she protested, "But—that doesn't make sense. My father gave medicine away to just about anyone who asked him."

"And we should stay in debt to a gringo?" Rafael retorted with total illogic. "Even then my father belonged to the Party—he knew who our true enemies were! The *americanos* as much as the fat *politicos* in Bogotá. The *Comandante* Orellana made no mistake in keeping the *medicos* from coming in to help the *misioneros*. If anything, he was too merciful! Are these *misioneros* any less dangerous because they invade our land with soft words of God and bribes of aid instead of helicopters and oil rigs? On the contrary, they are worse because they confuse the people with their opiate of religion so that they do not see the true revolution that alone can save us."

Rafael alone of the guerrillas still held a weapon—not his machine-gun, but a long-barreled pistol that he had been polishing with a piece of terrycloth toweling. Now he lifted it to eye level and sighted carefully along it.

"No, if it were up to me, I would execute every gringo on Colombian soil, if only to teach the *americanos* that we will not tolerate their interference in our affairs any longer, telling us how we should live by their decadent philosophies of capitalism and democracy, as though their own society were without sin or injustice."

Giving the chamber a spin, ostensibly to check the bullets, he added insolently, "So, Señorita Baker, it would seem that the death of your parents has taught you this lesson at least. You do not come here like these others to feed our hungry and cure our sick as though we cannot handle our affairs without your help."

Rafael continued to sight along the pistol as he spoke, shifting his aim until the gun was lined up right on Julie's head, and for one horrible moment, she thought he was planning to use it.

"Enough!" Victor said sharply.

With a sardonic bark of laughter, Rafael lowered the gun. Julie was at once so frightened and so furious she was actually shaking in the dark. To think she'd almost begun to see these guerrillas as . . . as *people*. Her jaw clenched with the effort not to respond when she saw that every head had again turned expectantly in her direction.

*They're waiting for me to answer,* she realized incredulously. *They're . . . they're enjoying this—like some high school debate.*

The realization gave her the courage—or the recklessness—to clasp her hands tightly in her lap, straighten her back, and answer in a voice as tight and cold as though there were not a dozen loaded weapons only feet away.

"Yes, you're right, Rafael! I *have* learned my lesson. Americans don't belong here. My parents didn't belong here. They had no business building clinics and schools, or giving kids vaccinations so they would grow up and add to Colombia's overpopulation. My parents' interference, as you put it, in San Ignacio did no good either to this country or themselves. In fact, if they had stayed in their own country where they belonged, they would probably still be alive and certainly have a whole lot more of that capitalist wealth you keep talking about. So, yes, I agree! Colombia should be left to the Colombians. In fact, if you will just let me out of here, I will be happy to go back to my country and do just that."

Julie stood up abruptly, not caring whether they had grasped her sarcasm or were actually taking her "confession" at face value. "Now if you will excuse me, I am tired."

There were shrugs and exchanged glances, but no objections. With a wave of his hand, Victor ordered, "Carlos, go with her."

Carlos followed silently at Julie's heels as she walked rapidly back to her sleeping shelter. She wasn't at all sleepy—too much adrenaline was pumping through her veins for that—and once she had crawled under the mosquito net and tucked it in, she sat up on her pallet, drawing her knees up to her chin. Carlos took up his guard position outside, but instead of pacing as he usually did or even making himself comfortable on the upturned stump, he hunkered down on his heels just outside the shelter, his machine gun balanced across his thighs. He glanced at the campfire as Alberto burst out into another ballad, then turned his head to look at Julie.

"Señorita Julia," he said softly. "Please, you must not give attention to what Rafael says nor *Comandante* Aguilera. They do not know Don Ricardo and Doña Elizabet as I did, and so they do not understand. Please do not think that your parents should not have come to San Ignacio. They were good people, and they taught good things and helped many people. We were all very happy that they were there. You know that. Surely . . . surely you cannot truly wish that you had never come!"

His young voice sounded almost pleading in the dark, and Julie's heart lost a little of its soreness even as she answered, "But it didn't do any good, Carlos, that's the point! Look at San Ignacio. The church and clinic shut down. The pastors all gone. The guerrillas running everything. We might as well never have been there for all the lasting good we did."

Carlos shook his head vehemently, his boyish features earnest in the scant light that reached them from the campfire and Coleman lantern, and Julie was reminded again of how young he was, though he stood a head taller than her and was sturdy and muscled from the outdoor life he led.

"The people who live today because of the medicine of your parents would not agree with you. Without Don Ricardo, how many children in San Ignacio would have died as they do in so many other places? And the things that your family taught us—about God, about *Jesucristo* His Son. Can you not see, Señorita Julia? Perhaps the churches are gone and the people scattered far away. But the teachings still go with us in our hearts. You must not think that they have been forgotten only because you cannot see them on the outside."

Julie looked with despair at the boy squatted down outside her shelter. It was as though his hard young face—his defection to a cause, a way of life she found despicable—summed up all the waste that had been the lives of Richard and Elizabeth Baker. "How can you say that, Carlos? Look at you!

You were in my Sunday school class. Your sister was one of my best friends. And now—you're a terrorist, a guerrilla, a *murderer!* What would your family say if they could see you now with an assault rifle in your hand, holding *me* a prisoner?"

The look on his face cut through her outburst like a knife.

"What is it, Carlos?" she said sharply. More quietly, she added, "You said last night they were dead. What happened?"

Carlos dropped his eyes to the weapon across his thighs, struggling to compose his features into an expression that was as adult and indifferent as that of Victor or Jaime or Enrique but failing miserably, and the desolation that won out hurt Julie unbearably. "It was the *paramilitares,*" he muttered. He swallowed convulsively before raising his head to look at Julie.

"Señorita Julia, I am truly sorry about your parents. I grieved when they died. All of San Ignacio did. But . . . but you must understand how it was afterward. Don Ricardo was not there anymore, and . . . with the guerrillas it was not all bad. If they were harsh, they brought law as the government had not cared to do so. As even Don Ricardo was not able to do. You remember Don Martin?"

The old fisherman had been a notorious town drunkard and thief.

"The guerrillas caught him robbing my *tio* Simon's catch. They took away his boat and put him to cleaning the marketplace. And if they confiscated the church because it was tainted with *americano* money, they did not prohibit those who wished from coming together to pray and worship God. Not then. Not . . . not until the *paramilitares* came."

His young voice thickened, and tears stung suddenly at the back of Julie's nostrils as though she already knew what was coming. "It was never found out who called the *paramilitares*. Perhaps Don Martin because he was angry at the guerrillas and at the town, and after that day he was never seen again. They came when the guerrillas had left San Ignacio to fight. The mayor—he . . . he called the *militares* when it was seen that they were coming. On your father's radio. He begged for their help. But the *militares* never came, though we waited and hoped. And the *paramilitares*—there were many of them. Hundreds. They gathered everyone in the town and lined them up in the plaza. They asked who had invited *la guerrilla* to San Ignacio, and they said that the penalty for sympathizing with the guerrillas was death. Then they . . . they butchered every man of age to fight.

"It took a long time. There were many in the fields, on the roads, who escaped. But . . . my father, my older brother—they were spared by the cholera but not by the *paramilitares*. My mother—she tried to save them, and they shot her too. They . . . they were laughing!"

His low-voiced recital was a flat monotone, but the anguish of his memories was in his face, his eyes wide open and blank like a child still caught in the horror of a nightmare. "There were other women who tried to intervene. They shot them too, and the young women—they took them away. My sister Gabriela—I learned that she died before the *paramilitares* were done with her. I . . . I was but twelve and poorly grown. They came to me and put a gun to my head. But one laughed and said I was but a child—to let the chick grow into a rooster first."

Tears poured down Julie's cheeks, and she found that her fingernails were digging into the palms of her hands. No wonder there had been no men that she recognized among the villagers. Those she knew were probably all dead. The laborers at the airport were from new families the guerrillas had moved into San Ignació.

"The guerrillas returned when we were burying the dead. I had no place to go, but *Comandante* Aguilera—he had come to replace Orellana—he gave me a place with his battalion, a chance to fight those who killed my family. I . . . Señorita Julia, you must understand! I let my family die because I was too afraid that day to fight. But someday—someday I will see those who killed my family, who took away my sister, down the barrel of my AK-47, and then you will see what I am brave enough to do."

The hatred was back in his voice, the fury and bitterness too. Some of it welled up inside Julie as well, for a people she had loved and a young life shattered in an instant. For the first time she understood the impulse to take up arms and lash back out of rage and despair and hate. If she'd had those men within reach right then and a gun in her hands, she wasn't sure what she herself would have done. She couldn't imagine the trauma of such an experience to a boy of twelve.

She had to swallow hard to speak. "Carlos, you can't blame yourself for your family. If you had fought, they would have just killed you too."

At some distant edge of her consciousness, Julie registered that the campfire sing was breaking up, Alberto's voice falling quiet so that only the radio continued its crooning. The guerrillas were scattering to the latrine, the river, their shelters. All except for Enrique and Victor, who were striding in their direction. Grabbing her blanket to wipe the tell-tale moisture from her face, Julie whispered urgently, "Carlos, you won't get in trouble for telling me all this, will you?"

Carlos looked surprised. "Oh, no! The *comandante* likes us to tell our stories. It brings sympathy to our cause. More martyrs to the cause. I have even been chosen to tell my story for a reporter. They have told me it was put in the newspapers in another country."

Julie stifled a sigh. What could she say? It was that age-old cry—why did bad things happen to good people? And she had no answers for it. *What words of wisdom am I supposed to give him, God? I . . . I don't even have answers to my own questions!* But she couldn't just turn away from the chilly resolve that had replaced desolation in the boy's black eyes, the hardened, cynical lines that had settled again over his young face.

"Carlos, I . . . I can't blame you for losing your faith in God. I don't understand why He let the paramilitaries butcher your family anymore than I understand my own parents' death or all the other bad things we see happen in this world. And if the other guerrillas have gone through experiences like that, I can understand why they'd choose to turn their backs on God and pretend He doesn't exist. But you must believe, Carlos, that God—"

"Oh, but I believe in God, Señorita Julia."

The simple statement startled Julie, and she broke off to blink at Carlos in astonishment. "But I thought—"

"We with *la guerrilla* are not all godless men, Señorita Julia. Oh yes, Alberto and Rafael, they are followers of Karl Marx. They believe in nothing that they cannot see. They believe that religion is but an 'opiate for the masses' and that religious teachers like your parents should be destroyed. We too are communists. We believe that the land, the wealth of our country, should be returned to its people. But that there is a God—yes, I believe and so do many others. It is not He who is evil. No, it is the government, the *paramilitares* . . ." Carlos raised his head as Victor and Enrique strode by the shelter.

"Is that not so, *Comandante?*"

Victor mumbled something Julie didn't catch, crossing himself quickly as he did so, before hurrying on toward the latrine. To Julie's surprise, Enrique paused to hunker down beside Carlos, balancing himself easily on the hard heels of his army boots.

"Yes, to be sure, I believe in God," Enrique said quietly, and his hand went to the open neck of his fatigues. Like so many Latin men, he wore a gold chain around his neck, and as his hand closed around it, Julie could see the soft glimmer of a small cross dangling from the end of it.

Julie looked at the guerrilla leader with exasperation. Enrique had taken time to shave as well as bathe that afternoon—it would seem that he reserved the unkempt look for international press conferences when he had his terrorist reputation to maintain. His longish curls had been ruthlessly combed back, and as the flickering light of the Coleman lamp wavered across the hard, clean planes of his face, Julie realized for the first time, and with something of a shock, that—given other circumstances—Enrique Martinez might be considered a very presentable, if not even handsome, man.

Which, illogically, made his hypocrisy even worse.

"How can you say that, Enrique?" she protested impatiently. "I don't understand you people! How can you say you believe in God and . . . and be what you are—do what you do? You . . . you're an educated person, that's easy to see. You have to know communism has failed—even in Cuba. Your cause is lost. You'll never win. And if you believe in God, you have to believe in right and wrong too. How can you justify war and fighting and killing and . . . and murder?"

She'd gone too far, Julie recognized immediately. Enrique's expression hardened, and the firm line of his mouth curved in that unpleasant tilt she'd seen before as he answered deliberately, "You talk like a civilian. It is not murder for a soldier to fight—and even at times to be forced to kill—for his country and people. You civilians are always the same! If there is fighting, you are quick to call for those with guns to stand between you and your enemy. As soon as the fighting is over, you begin to point your fingers and call those who risked their lives in your defense 'killers' and 'murderers.' I became a soldier . . ." He stopped. "I became a guerrilla, because I believe in what I do. I believe that what I am doing is the best—maybe the only—chance this country has to find peace and justice. And as for believing in God, the very pages of the Scriptures are full of soldiers who fought for their country and their God."

Enrique broke off abruptly, as though he'd said more than he'd intended. Rising in one fluid motion to his feet, he walked away with long, rapid strides. Julie watched his departure with unwilling interest as he disappeared down the path toward the river. However mistaken the man might be, there had been real feeling, even passion, in his answer.

"What is Enrique's story?" she asked curiously. "What brought him to join the guerrillas? Was his family killed by paramilitaries too?"

Carlos shook his head. "I don't know. He was transferred here not long ago from another front. Up north."

"And *Comandante* Aguilera?" Enrique was out of sight now, and Julie turned her head to look at Carlos. "Why does he hate us so much? The Americans, I mean. And some of the others hate us too—like Rafael. I don't understand it. If their families and villages are being massacred by other Colombians, why should they turn around and hate us? We haven't done anything to hurt them."

Julie could see the boy's hesitation. He shrugged. "I have heard it said that *Comandante* Aguilera's father was one of the leftist leaders when the *americanos* . . . the *see* . . . *eee* . . . *ah*"—he gave the abbreviation for the Central Intelligence Agency its Spanish pronunciation, as Aguilera had—"first began to train the *paramilitares* to fight the guerrillas. Have you heard of this?"

Julie nodded. The CIA's involvement with the self-defense groups had been short-lived, and the agency certainly had never endorsed the groups' degeneration into random violence, but the guerrillas were hardly likely to appreciate that distinction, and she already had an unpleasant feeling where this was going.

Carlos went on, "I have heard that he was but a child when they gunned his father down in front of him. They say *Comandante* Aguilera has never forgiven the *americanos.*"

Julie let out a tired sigh. So many sad stories. So much hatred. No wonder it was so hard to break the cycle of violence! How could people be expected to forgive such atrocities against the people they loved? And yet they would have to if this was ever to end.

"And what about you, Carlos?" she asked quietly. "Do you think Enrique is right—that God approves of all this killing and murder? On all sides? Do you really think your family—Gabriela—would want you to avenge them by killing other innocent people who just got in the way of your war?

"Can't you see?" she pleaded. "Someone has to be willing to just let it go!"

"I . . ." The young face was suddenly troubled. His eyes slid sideways to Julie, then dropped. "I have not yet killed anyone," he mumbled to his assault rifle, and there was both defense and shame in the admission.

"Carlos! Enough! She is not your *compañera.*" The camp leader had returned from the latrine and was standing over the young guerrilla. Flushing at the caustic comment, Carlos stumbled to his feet. Victor paused only to turn off the Coleman lamp before striding toward his shelter with a curt command over his shoulder. "Rafael, your shift."

Rafael, like Jaime, showed no inclination to talk on duty, which suited Julie fine. Tugging her thin blanket over her shoulders, she buried her head in her arms to get away from that baleful glare.

She couldn't as easily shut out the images evoked by Carlos's story. How was it she had never wondered what had happened to San Ignacio after she left? She could probably have found out over these last years if she'd made any effort. Other journalists had interviewed the guerrillas in this zone. Groups like C-PAP had been in and out. Julie had been too wrapped up in her misfortune to even consider that the people from whom she'd walked away without a backward glance might be undergoing tragedies of their own. It had hurt to believe what she had thought to be their betrayal. The reality of pain and anguish and senseless violence, the images of which she could picture only too well in her mind's eye, hurt far more.

*As senseless as lying in a guerrilla camp with a guard at the foot of my bed.* Feeling Rafael's flashlight play over her in response to her shuddering breath, Julie forced back fresh tears, turning her thoughts into a new channel. No matter how she wracked her brain, she still could make no sense out of any of this. No, by all rules of logic, her first assessment should have been correct. Whatever infractions she and Tim had committed, it had been in the best interests of the guerrillas to treat them as guests, not enemies. The only reasonable reaction to their offense would have been to return them with a reprimand to the airport.

Except for this spy thing.

And that was what it all came down to. Why were the guerrillas so sure she was a spy? Why would anyone want to spy on these people anyway? The life and activities of the guerillas were well-documented, after all, by reporters if not government sources. What did they think she could learn down here that could possibly hurt their cause?

And who had fingered Julie to the guerrillas? The question replayed itself endlessly in Julie's mind. The two guerrillas on the plane—or someone else? Who were these *musulmanes* she'd heard *Comandante* Aguilera refer to through her drugged stupor? Come to think of it, wasn't Kharrazi a Middle Eastern name?

But no. Sondra had been genuinely affected by her encounter with the dead environmentalists. Julie herself was witness of that. The woman's pallor and her icy hands could not have been faked.

So why can't both be true? Even a spy might be unnerved by the sight—and smell—of decomposing human bodies. The NBC correspondent had hung around Julie from the beginning, and there was that Middle Eastern name. Maybe, for all that outward frivolity, Sondra Kharrazi had another cause besides the rainforest.

Julie stiffened so suddenly that Rafael's flashlight clicked on again, the light playing over that part of her face not buried in her arms. Was it possible she'd just stumbled over the key to this puzzle? Not the guerrillas, but these Muslim friends of *Comandante* Aguilera, whoever they were? Hadn't she overheard something in that haziness of the truth drug wearing off about being afraid the Americans would find out what was going on out here? So why the Americans and not the Colombians? Unless . . .

Unless it's something that affects Americans.

Sudden excitement gripped Julie, driving away personal fears and sorrow. That was it—it had to be! These Middle Eastern terrorist allies of the guerrillas were planning some big attack involving American presence in the country. Something so big even *Comandante* Aguilera had not been trusted with the details. Maybe San José and Colonel Thornton's operation there? Or somewhere else. Whatever their plan, it was something they were afraid the Americans could—and would—stop if they found it out.

*I've got to get out of here and warn them!*

Julie raised her head cautiously in the dark. The shelter was built like a tent, open at both ends. With the jungle canopy overhead blocking out even the dim light of moon and stars, she couldn't see, but she knew that the endless cover of underbrush and trees lay only a few meters away. If she could escape into that . . .

Rafael's flashlight probed her shelter again, and the excitement abruptly ebbed. *Who am I kidding?* These people were experts at kidnapping—the best in the world by many assessments. If she couldn't even twitch in her bed without drawing attention, how was she to slip unnoticed from her shelter and into the jungle? Nor could Julie hope that those weapons out there were just for show. If she failed in her bid for escape, she had no doubt that Rafael at least would positively enjoy using that assault rifle or the pistol he fondled with such affection, to gun her down.

And even if she didn't fail—what about Tim? Victor had made it clear that he would be shot if she escaped. Was she to risk his life, wherever he might be right now, to pass on—what? Some vague reference to Muslim allies? The U.S. government had to be as well aware as she that the guerrillas had contacts with Islamic terrorist groups. Her own unclassified research, which had brought her so much trouble with Aguilera, had given her that much. And surely Colonel Thornton and the rest of the American military leadership were aware that they were a target of the guerrillas.

Besides, even if she made it out of the camp, how would she ever find her way out of the jungle itself? She hadn't the slightest idea where she was. The rainforest was vast, and Julie knew better than most that the only predators to face out there would not be the two-legged kind.

*No!* Julie let the rigidity ebb from her body. She would not compound one stupid blunder with another. If some miracle opened a reasonable opportunity for escape, she'd take it in a flash. In the meantime, she'd do what countless other guerrilla hostages had been forced to do. Wait.

At some endless point later, Julie slept.

# FOURTEEN

THE BOREDOM WAS THE WORST, Julie had decided by the second week. Every day began the same. A pleasurable wakening to the freshness of the jungle dawn, the odor of wood smoke and brewing coffee, the morning chorus of birds and monkeys. Familiar scents and sounds, even loved. Then a glimpse of mottled green and brown and the metallic gray of an assault-rifle barrel, and the feeling of well-being would evaporate like the lingering coolness that burned off as soon as the sun rose.

Breakfast was invariably coffee and *arepas*. The rest of the day stretched endlessly ahead, with nothing to mark the long hours but dinner and supper. Julie found herself anticipating these as she had never looked forward to meals before, just to break up the day, though again the food rarely varied from rice and beans or *sancocho*, with an occasional piece of meat added to the pot if one of the guerrillas had gone out hunting.

Victor did not again prohibit the guerrillas from talking to Julie. But besides Carlos himself, only Alberto and Marcela showed any inclination to friendliness, and even these three grew visibly uneasy if Julie dragged them into too long a conversation. Since she didn't want to focus unwelcome attention on them, Julie soon learned to limit her communication to a minimum. After that first night, she wasn't invited again to join the guerrillas' evening activities.

Nor was she allowed to help around camp, though by the second day she had begged Marcela to let her assist with the kitchen chores. It was Victor who vetoed her offer, shouting at the young girl that the prisoner was not permitted to move around the encampment. The camp leader seemed to have his eye on Julie at all times, and even an overly long trip to the latrine could trigger an eruption of anger.

Julie spent most of her day sitting cross-legged on the pallet in her shelter, fanning herself with a palm leaf against the humid heat. When her muscles protested that position, she stretched out on the thin mattress, pretending to be asleep. For a person who had always taken pride in filling her days with productive output, the idleness was a worse torture than the mosquitoes.

These continued to plague Julie and everyone else in the camp. Her capture had occurred at the tail end of the wet season, and in a few weeks the rains would be gone and with them the mosquitoes. In the meantime, there continued to be at least one good downpour almost every day, and if the rain itself washed away the mosquitoes and brought momentary relief to the heat, it was always followed by an increased insect population, as though the puddles left standing after the rain were breeding tanks for them.

Julie's bottle of repellant ran out after the first few days, and after a day without, she was desperate enough to submit to what the others were doing. They had brought along one of those flit gun sprayers filled with Baygon and at intervals sprayed it over their clothing, rubbing the residue into hands and face. What toxins could be seeping through her skin from the stuff, Julie chose not to think about, and at least it brought some temporary relief.

The guerrillas were no less bored than Julie herself. In the mornings they kept busy with chores and added camp improvements, digging a new latrine and garbage pit every two days, taking turns at hunting details that brought in lapa, a rodentlike animal that made delicious stew, and on one occasion a wild pig which Linda and Marcela roasted over the fire. That night they'd had a feast.

In the afternoons when the sun turned the lingering dampness into a sauna, the guerrillas just lay around the camp. A few hammocks had been strung under the trees, and the guerrillas napped, rocking themselves lazily by pulling at a rope hung from a nearby branch. They read magazines and books as well, somewhat to Julie's surprise. Picking a pamphlet off the ground on her way back from the latrine, Julie discovered it to be a discussion of Karl Marx and his theories on world economics.

The guerrillas spent considerable time cleaning their weapons, breaking them down, oiling and buffing the pieces, and putting them back together again. These were not all the uniform assault rifles as Julie had thought, and with time she learned their names. The AK-47s were the most common. These were Russian-built assault rifles of a quality that seldom broke down, Carlos explained to her, donated in the earlier days of their struggle by like-minded comrades from Cuba. There were a few Israeli Galils as well, automatic rifles that to Julie differed little from an assault rifle. Victor himself carried an M1 assault rifle, American made, that he bragged he'd taken from the wreckage of a military helicopter he'd shot down.

They had hand grenades, too, and Semtex, a plastic explosive from which Victor and Jaime were training the younger guerrillas to fashion home-made bombs. It made Julie nervous to be even meters away while they fiddled around with detonators and lengths of fuse.

Julie was learning other new vocabulary as well. The little shelters in which they slept were called *caletas*. The larger huts with plastic for walls were *cambuches*. One of these had been erected to shelter the radio and to store supplies out of the rain, and on wet evenings, the guerrillas—all but the one on current guard duty—gathered there to listen to their transistor radio and Victor's political lectures.

These were like a well-worn record of *Comandante* Aguilera's speech. The rich oppressing the poor. The guerrillas as champions and saviors of the people. The perfidy of the Colombian government, along with a hodge-podge of Marxist philosophies and communist political propaganda. Julie was frightened by the intensity and the hate in the camp leader's tone.

There was anti-American rhetoric as well, as though every problem Colombia faced was somehow a product of U.S. government policy, and when the weather was good enough for the lectures to be held around the camp-fire, Julie could feel all eyes turn accusingly in her direction.

Victor also held lectures on hygiene and first aid. These guerrillas were fanatics when it came to their rules of cleanliness—the only way to keep their combatants healthy in these jungle conditions—and Julie had seen Victor actually pull a gun on Rafael when the garbage wasn't buried properly, and reduce Linda and Marcela to tears when the drinking water had not been boiled the requisite twenty minutes.

The lack of privacy was almost as bad as the boredom. The thatched roof and open sides of the *caleta* were high enough to keep Julie in plain view at all times, and the guards never took their eyes off her, even if they were in conversation with another guerrilla who had stopped by their post to chat. When Julie had to go to the latrine, either Linda or Marcela, the younger guerrilla girl, stood over her, weapon leveled down at her, until she was finished. It was horribly humiliating, especially when one of the men was on duty and she had to ask permission for one of the women to take her.

After the first day, Julie complained to Carlos that she was going to get sick if she didn't get some exercise. He must have repeated it to Victor. The next morning the camp leader decreed that she was to have a daily exercise period. For a half-hour each afternoon, she trudged around the perimeter of the camp in a large circle, her guard at her heels. *Like a dog on a leash.* She ignored the glances, both amused and hostile, that followed her circuit. It was keeping her muscles in usable condition, and that was all that mattered.

Her workout was always followed by a trip to the river, and here again she was forced to bathe in full view of Linda or Marcela, who were always assigned this guard duty, as well as any other guerrillas who might saunter along the bank. Julie no longer bothered to hurry. To be stared at in the river or her *caleta* was all one. She kicked lazily in the cool water, making the most of the opportunity for further exercise, until her guard shouted at her to get out. To the guerrilla women's derision, she continued to cover herself up as she bathed, trading her towel for the thin blanket she'd been provided, which she wrapped around her as a sari, then spread out on the roof of her *caleta*, where the heat would dry it by bedtime.

Julie found Linda's contemptuous scrutiny even more humiliating than that of the men. Still hostile, the guerrilla girl never seemed to lose a chance for a derisive remark, until Julie wished Victor had continued to prohibit conversation with the prisoner. One afternoon two weeks into her captivity, Linda yanked Julie's blanket away as she emerged from the water, so that Julie had to scramble for her clothes.

"Why you should worry so to hide yourself, I do not understand," Linda sneered. "Even a gringo would not wish a woman as thin as you have become."

Julie bit back the sharp retort that rose to her tongue. An AK-47 was a great advantage in a cat fight. But it was true that she'd lost weight, a surprise since even with her walks and evening swim she was getting far less exercise than usual. But then, between the heat and her captivity, she'd had no appetite for the starchy, monotonous meals she was being served. She would give much for a piece of fruit or a green salad.

Nights were the best, when the Coleman lamp was blown out and Julie could stretch out in the dark with the illusion of being alone, though eight other people breathed the night air around her and she could hear the quiet thud of the guard's boots. Even that illusion of privacy, and her rest as well, were interrupted by the flashlight beam probing her shelter at regular intervals all night long.

Still, the guerrillas weren't unkind to her. Julie ate as well as the guerrillas themselves, and when Linda took her to the latrine each morning, she would return to find that Marcela had straightened and swept her *caleta,* even gathering up any belongings Julie had left strewn outside her knapsack until Julie, out of boredom as well as a wish to appease her captors, began doing it herself as soon as she got up.

Marcela insisted on washing Julie's uniform, presenting her with a clean one every third day, and if any dainty was prepared from the few supplies they had—*tortas,* a doughnutlike pastry, or Kool-Aid mixed up from a package—Julie was the first to be served. If companionship was lacking, at least her guards hadn't raised a hand against her since that first horrible interrogation. As Enrique Martinez had said, and *Comandante* Aguilera after him, and even Carlos—these people weren't butchers or savages. They were— what were they?

With nothing else to do, Julie began spending more of her time watching and listening to the guerrillas. After that first day, they had separated themselves out into individuals, and with time began taking on personalities and backgrounds as distinct as their appearance.

Jaime and Victor were both long-term, hard-boiled guerrilla fighters who had been with the cause since their teens. But where the camp leader was harsh and stern, easily exploding into anger even with his followers, Jaime was a stolid man who went about his responsibilities silently and buried his face in his pamphlets and books the rest of the time.

Julie never found out where Linda had come from, nor did she dare ask. But Marcela answered her questions readily, if without detail. Like Carlos, she had been left without a family or home when a paramilitary attack wiped out her village. She had been with the guerrillas for two years, but this was her first assignment to active duty, she told Julie with pride before a glare from Linda shut her up.

Alberto, in contrast, had been a university student in Bogotá before joining the guerrillas, and he never stopped lording his superior education over the others, especially Rafael, who with his peasant upbringing could hardly read and consequently never said much when Alberto and the others argued Marxist philosophy or politics over the campfire at night.

Still, if there was anyone of whom Julie was afraid besides Victor himself, it was Rafael. Unlike Alberto, who would laugh and sing and flirt not just with his female comrades but also with Julie, Rafael never lost his sullen expression, and where Alberto bragged of his education and city contacts,

Rafael would boast of the soldiers he had shot and the raids in which he'd participated. One night around the campfire, when Linda asked Rafael what he thought about the breakdown of the Soviet revolution, he answered simply, "I do not think. I just kill."

The cruel straight line of his mouth supported that claim, and his black eyes, narrowed always as though on the lookout for an enemy, had a flat, almost dead look that gave Julie the shivers. Especially as she began to find those eyes on her every time she turned around. The beam of his flashlight in her *caleta* when he was on night guard wasn't merely checking that the prisoner was still there, but became a leisurely study of her body under the thin blanket. And several times as she was led back and forth from the latrine or river, he managed to come close enough to brush up against her. The insolence of his stare as he did so added a new fear to Julie's life.

Until Enrique caught him at it.

Julie was returning from her afternoon swim, Linda at her heels, when Rafael stepped onto the path to block her way. Under Linda's smirk, he ran a suggestive hand over Julie's wet hair and down the side of her face and neck. Disgusted and furious as she was, Julie didn't dare move, not with Linda's assault rifle blocking her retreat and the look of sly amusement on the guerrilla woman's face. Before his exploration could descend any farther, a hand shot out and grabbed Rafael by the arm. Twisting the offending limb behind Rafael's back, Enrique spun the other guerrilla out of Julie's way and off the path, his eyes blazing with such anger that even Julie shrank back.

"You touch the prisoner again," he told Rafael in low, furious tones, "and I will personally break both your arms!" With a final glare that took in Linda and unaccountably Julie herself, he released Rafael and strode away. Without a backward glance, Rafael stalked off in the other direction.

Whether Enrique told Victor or the camp leader saw the scene for himself, Julie never knew. That evening around the campfire, Victor announced that any man caught molesting the prisoner would be taken out and shot. He spoke matter-of-factly and didn't even glance at Rafael, but the guerrillas clearly knew their leader well enough to believe he meant it. Neither Rafael nor any of the others bothered Julie again.

The imbalance of women was a source of discontent in the camp. Linda, the older guerrilla girl, was Jaime's girlfriend—though what she saw in that withdrawn individual, Julie couldn't imagine—and she shared his *caleta* at night. After the first night, Marcela joined Victor in his shelter—a fact that bothered Julie as much because of the guerilla girl's tender age as because of the moral ramifications. Julie had overhead Victor mention to one of the other men that he had a wife and family "out there," as they termed it.

Though Alberto and Rafael in particular groused that this left them without a *compañera,* or companion, they all acted as though this were the normal privilege of a camp leader. Marcela herself seemed quite pleased at the arrangement and even found the courage to defy Linda when the older guerrilla girl kept pushing her to do the lion's share of the camp chores. Hers was a plump prettiness that owed itself to the freshness of youth and wouldn't last many years in this environment.

Carlos too had that freshness of youth, and here in the camp where he was no longer a soldier on duty, that hardened look that had shocked Julie relaxed into the eager young lines of the boy he should have been. This reminder of the child she'd once known infuriated Julie, the more so as she saw his hero worship of the older guerrillas, especially when he hung on Rafael's tales of the people he had killed and the villages and police outposts he had burned, pillaged, or in other graphic details obliterated.

*Can't you see what they're doing to your life?* she wanted to cry out to her childhood friend.

Then there was Enrique. The guerrilla interpreter was the only one of the unit who showed no signs of relaxing as the days went by. Once his responsibilities were completed, he prowled—that was the only word for it—pacing restlessly around the camp as though he could hardly contain himself within its boundaries, stalking to the edge of the jungle and peering into it or standing on the bank, watching downstream. When he wasn't prowling around, he was sprawled out next to the transistor radio, listening to news bulletins until someone yelled at him to turn it to a music station.

*Is he in such a hurry to get back out and start killing people again?* Julie thought bitterly. Yet once again, he had taken the trouble to intervene on her behalf. And there had been that astonishing declaration of faith in God. What a strange, complex, and yet not totally heartless man! Would he one day, with enough killing, be as single-mindedly cruel and hard as Rafael or Victor?

Except for his intervention with Rafael, Enrique rarely glanced in Julie's direction, at least not that she could see, and since as second-in-command, he didn't share in the guard shifts, there was little occasion for them to come in contact. Though Julie had hoped to turn their earlier, more friendly contact to her benefit, she was quickly disillusioned.

From their exchange back at the airport, Julie knew Enrique had also been a university student. But he never paraded his superior education as Alberto did, and while he would join the others around the campfire at night or in the *cambuche* when it rained, he took little part in their heated discussions. It surprised Julie that Rafael and the others showed him such careful respect until one day, when the encampment was as finished as it was going to get, Victor ordered out the men of the unit for a session in unarmed combat.

Enrique taught the session down on the open, sandy stretch of beach. From her *caleta,* Julie watched in astonishment as he laid each of the guerrilla men in turn, even Victor, on their backs in quick succession before demonstrating the move he was teaching in slow, deliberate steps. To Julie, who had begun to think of Enrique as one of the less dangerous of her captors, the display served as a fresh reminder that this man was a highly proficient killer. Any fantasies of attempted escape dwindled still further, and with it her frustration grew.

Could she stand to live this way indefinitely? For years, maybe? Other hostages had done so, Julie knew. Still others had never been seen again—those the FARC considered political prisoners more often than kidnap victims. Soldiers and police officers captured in battle. As an alleged spy, Julie had to put herself into that camp, and despite the assurances of Enrique and Carlos, she could see no real reason why they should ever let her go. What happened to those people in the long run? Surely the guerrillas couldn't be bothered to feed and house them forever.

*If you don't find something to do besides think, you're going to go stark raving mad,* Julie told herself desperately. She began her thirty-seventh count of the mesh holes in her mosquito net—she had yet to tally the same number twice. When that failed as a distraction, she switched to tracing pictures in the patterns the dried palm fronds made on the ceiling of her *caleta.* Those two frond ends there with the fat-bodied stem in the middle could be her father's Cessna lifting off. That banana-leaf curve looked like one of the fishermen's canoes pulling out into the Ipa River.

*No, let's not go there.* Julie blinked away a sudden mist that blurred the palm-leaf ceiling. She would not think of the past, would not let the memories pressing in on her break through the careful barrier she had erected.

Not with a camp full of eyes on her, watching eagerly for any hint of weakness. The mesh holes were safer. *One. Two. Three.*

But by the next evening, Julie would have welcomed a return to her boredom.

# FIFTEEN

Marcela was just delivering her breakfast when Julie heard the distant drone of an aircraft. After the last seven years in the city, where the rush of man-made machines was constant background noise, Julie didn't at first register how out-of-place the sound was.

The guerrillas were not so complacent. Julie snatched her coffee cup from Marcela's hand just before the guerrilla girl let it fall. All activity in the camp ceased, and every eye turned upward, though there was little to see through the thick shield of the jungle canopy. Carlos was down by the river, filling an aluminum pot for washing dishes. At Victor's shrill whistle, he snatched up the pot and sprinted back toward camp, water sloshing over his boots as he ran.

The drone grew into a roar, then separated into the distinct throp-throp of propeller blades. Helicopters, and more than one. They were heading straight toward the camp.

"*Los militares!*" Victor barked. "Break the camp—now!"

The frozen stance of the guerrillas dissolved into frenzied activity. The shelters were kicked apart, the sticks and palm leaves of which they were made tossed back into the underbrush at the edge of the clearing. Julie snatched up her backpack as her *caleta* went down. Bedrolls, the *cambuche's* plastic walls, and remaining supplies were bundled into packs at lightning speed. The rocks lining the fire pit were kicked away and dirt dumped over the smoldering coals. Within minutes, the clearing gave little sign that nine people had lived there for more than two weeks.

And none too soon. The helicopters were coming in now, fast and loud.

"The prisoner!" Victor barked.

Rafael, who had been on guard duty when the aircraft were heard, grabbed Julie by the arm and yanked her back into the underbrush. A growth of elephant ears closed in overhead as he shoved her down flat to the ground, then squeezed in beside her.

"Keep your head down and don't make a sound!" he hissed. "If they see us, you die first!"

The other guerrillas had melted into the underbrush as well, so silently that Julie could spot only Enrique, lying under the same patch of elephant ears a few feet to her other side. He met her gaze briefly, his own unreadable, then turned his attention back to the clearing, his eyes narrowed speculatively as he watched for the approaching aircraft.

Two olive-green army helicopters came into sight, roaring down the stream bed.

One raced on past the clearing. The other slowed to a hover, the wind of the blades stirring up a dust storm on the beach. It was so close Julie could see the huge gun mounted in the doorway, the soldiers in khaki crouched behind it. Was this just some routine counter-narcotics or anti-insurgency operation, or could it be they were looking for her? Had they noticed the signs of recent occupancy in the clearing? The stepping stones and swimming hole?

Or could they even see through that sandstorm they were kicking up?

An overwhelming impulse swept over Julie to jump to her feet and dash out there. *If I could just make it to the beach, that gun would cover me.*

She caught Rafael's black eyes on her, implacable and cold, his AK-47 braced and cocked against his shoulder. That he would kill her as he'd said, Julie didn't doubt for an instant. Besides, in these camouflage fatigues, how would the soldiers know she was a hostage instead of one of the guerrillas? With the Colombian military's well-known propensity for shooting first and asking questions later, it would be suicide to rush out there. It occurred to Julie that this was precisely the reason the guerrillas had supplied her with this clothing.

Then her opportunity was gone. Rising from its hover so that the sandstorm began to subside, the helicopter continued on down the stream bed, picking up speed as it left the clearing. The guerrillas didn't move until the drone of the aircraft had completely faded from hearing. Then they emerged from their hiding places. Sick with disappointment, Julie made no resistance as Rafael prodded her to her feet. Shouldering her knapsack, she obeyed Victor's terse order to move out, taking her now customary position in the center of the single file.

This time there was no boat waiting when they reached the river. Victor led them upstream, not along the river edge where walking was easy but back under cover of the jungle canopy. The underbrush along the bank where the sun could reach was thick enough that the guerrillas had to resort to machetes to chop their way through. Even with this cover, the guerrillas were visibly on edge, starting at every rustle in the bush and stopping frequently to listen for aircraft. Once Julie heard the drone of the helicopters heading back in their direction. But it was at a distance and did not come closer.

After the first hour, they left the river, following one game trail after another for the rest of the day, resting only once briefly to gobble down the *arepas,* cold now and hard as rocks, that Linda and Marcela had prepared for breakfast. Victor used the stop to set up the radio and call *Comandante* Aguilera about the change in their situation.

It started raining shortly after they headed out again, adding mud and slippery footing and even an occasional rush of water across the trail, to their misery. Julie, who had spent much of the last two weeks sitting, wasn't sure she could slog forward one more step when Victor finally called a halt.

This wasn't a campsite, just a knoll high enough above the surrounding terrain to keep the rainwater from collecting. After a scanty supper of boiled rice—beans took too long to cook—the band huddled together under the plastic salvaged from the *cambuche* and settled down to wait out the night. Julie, shivering in her wet clothes, was for once happy to have her captors close by, accepting with gratitude the body heat from Marcela on one side of her and Carlos on the other.

The following day was a repeat of the last, though by the end of the morning, the rain had stopped. The rainforest into which they were now moving was much denser and taller than around their last camp, the trees massive, soaring hardwoods whose spreading branches kept any sunlight from filtering down to the forest floor so that the ground underfoot was at once spongy with decaying plant matter and at the same time almost bare of underbrush. This allowed Victor to pick up the pace, and by midafternoon, they had reached their next camp.

Like the first camp, this was not a clearing but a spot in the jungle where the size of the hardwoods allowed ample open area around their base to set up shelters. There was no stream nearby, but the water table was so close to the surface that past campers had simply dug a hole deep enough to hold an oil drum with the bottom knocked out. Seepage kept the drum filled to the brim, and the water was surprisingly clear, whatever microscopic creepy-crawlies might be swimming around in it.

Julie now knew the routine of setting up camp, and as soon as her *caleta* was ready, she crawled into it, awakening only briefly when Marcela carried over a soup of rice, lentils, and a *lapa* that Jaime had shot along the trail. She was asleep again before Marcela removed the bowl, and didn't awake until morning.

* * *

The watchers had followed along to the new site as well. This was easy, for the outsiders continued to be too noisy to pay attention to the small sounds and drifting shadows of the forest.

As the watchers trailed behind, their unease grew. Each new camp of the outsiders was moving them closer to the great evil in the forest. Was this deliberate? By now they had realized the girl was not free in this camp as she had been at the airport. There was some debate as to what they should do. But while their woodcraft was much greater than that of these intruders, their weapons were far less powerful.

Uneasy and afraid, they settled down again to wait and watch.

* * *

Colonel Jeff Thornton eyed the sat-phone, willing it to ring as he dropped his final report into his outbox. *Drat it! Where is the guy?*

Finally acknowledging that willpower alone would not be enough, he slammed his desk drawer shut and strode for the door. The eradication personnel were throwing a barbecue tonight in celebration of a sizable reduction in the zone's coca acreage, the technical difficulties with the Black Hawk's GAU19 Gatling mini-gun having finally been ironed out. With that powerful combat machine riding shotgun, the Turbo Thrushes hadn't been targeted by enemy fire in more than a week. As commander of the U.S. contingent, Colonel Thornton would be expected to make an appearance.

He nodded to the soldier on duty outside his office. "I'll be locking up now."

His hand was still on his keys when he heard the phone ring. With two strides he was back across the office, snatching up the receiver.

"Thornton?" The supercilious drawl wasn't the one he'd hoped for.

"Crawford," he acknowledged curtly. "What gives?"

"That's precisely what I was about to inquire of you," the SouthCom commander's executive officer returned. "Do you realize it's going on three weeks now since the San Ignacio report, and we don't know a thing more than we did then? The president is demanding answers. And what he demands, he expects to get!"

Colonel Thornton felt his jaw tightening at the patronizing tone. "He can't get what doesn't exist. Do you think if we had hard data—or anything at all—we'd just be sitting around here? We've called in every intel chip we have, every informer, every connection. No one has heard the smallest rumor of trouble. You tell General Johnson—and the president—that we need some serious resources down here if we're supposed to come up with the kind of answers they want."

"What about your asset in the zone? Surely by now he must have something! What's he been doing in there all this time?"

"Good question!" Colonel Thornton glanced over to make sure the office door had swung shut behind him. However close the working relationship between the U.S. force and their Colombian colleagues, this kind of intel wasn't something they shared. "I haven't heard a peep from our operative in the DMZ in over two weeks. Granted, in this kind of operation, regular communication isn't always possible."

The door had appeared shut. But from Colonel Thornton's angle, there was no way to see that the sentry's combat knife had caught it before it clicked into its frame, leaving a crack just big enough for the guard to overhear the San José end of the conversation. Nor would the commander have been overly concerned, despite his careful adherence to procedure. Of all segments of Colombian society, the military were the most ardent supporters of U.S. objectives because in spite of American assertions of noninvolvement, they were helping to whittle down the Colombian military's enemies. Besides, those Colombian recruits out there didn't speak English.

Colonel Thornton would have been less complacent had he seen the sentry's ear pressed close to the crack in the door. Jaime Ramirez was not part of the first Colombian family to be divided by politics, with one son in the armed forces and another with the guerrillas or the paramilitaries. When he had finished his mandatory service, an older brother, a brigade commander with the FARC, had suggested he could be of use if he remained in the military. Even more so, if he could get close to the Americans who had invaded their country.

To that end, Jaime had not only studied English, but he'd been one of the first to volunteer for the new counter-narcotics battalion. This wasn't the first time he had stood with his ear to a crack, listening to the *americanos*. But the gringos were careful, and he had learned little worth passing on to his brother beyond the vague rumor that the Americans had human assets in the zone.

Until now.

"In one of the guerrilla camps, that was my last report. . . . Yes, with the plane that went to San Ignacio. . . . This operative is the best we have. . . . No, we haven't heard a word since the UN mission returned." The American officer was pacing back and forth behind his desk, and Ramirez couldn't catch all he said. Nor did he understand all he heard, but he had caught enough.

Striding around to the front of his desk, Colonel Thornton noticed that the door was still slightly ajar and kicked it into its frame. "Yes, Crawford, of course we've tried to make contact. But in a covert op like this, it's 'don't call me, I'll call you'—as you'd know if you spent a little more time away from your desk. Our man is under strict orders not to compromise his cover for anything less than critical. . . . Yes, we know where he is, and we're assuming he's alive and kicking until we hear otherwise. Either way, it's time we stopped betting our entire hand on one card. If the president's concerns are justified—and we would be fools to ignore the slightest chance that they are—we need to rethink our whole strategy in here. . . . No, I want to speak to General Johnson myself. . . . Just give him my message and let him make that call."

The sentry watched the American commander leave his office, his narrow mouth grim with anger or concern as he strode away, though it was hard to read these gringos' expressions.

The American's departure was his release from duty, and minutes later Jaime was back at his barracks. The palm-sized phone he unearthed from a slit in his mattress was enough to earn him a court martial if it were discovered. A toilet stall gave him privacy.

"The *americanos* have a spy in the zone. . . . Yes, I heard it myself. . . . With the plane that went to San Ignacio. . . . They have not heard from the spy in two weeks. . . . They think perhaps in one of the jungle camps."

The guerrillas were efficient, though they lacked the technology of the Americans. Within the hour, Taqi Nouri was listening with mouth thinned in anger to a recap of the sentry's message. Severing the connection, he turned a cold eye on his companion.

"So—a new delay presents itself. It would seem we were once again mistaken about the American spy."

His companion glanced up from the lunar calendar spread out on a table. A symbol circled there matched the moon that couldn't be seen through the jungle canopy overhead. "We have little time for delay. In less than a week, conditions will at last be ripe to strike."

"Then it must be resolved with dispatch." Taqi Nouri permitted himself a relaxing of the lips that few would have termed a smile. "Though I do not foresee any difficulty. There is nothing this spy can do to impede us now."

*   *   *

It was the third afternoon in the new camp, now a virtual replica of the old except for the lack of bathing, which had been reduced to sponging off with a gourd of water. Julie was stretched out on her stomach, outlining an article she'd probably never write on the social predilections of the Colombian guerrilla, when she saw Alberto head over toward her *caleta* from the radio hut. Hastily, she sat up.

Alberto squatted down outside the *caleta*. "We have just heard on the radio why the *militares* came the other day. They were looking for you. It seems that a very big, fat gringo has come to Bogotá from the United States to organize a search. He must have great influence and money, because the *militares* are looking as they do for few others. He has even hired civilian planes with . . . with . . ." He snapped his fingers. "I do not know the names, but they have equipment to listen for radio talk and search for camps in the jungle. *Comandante* Aguilera says we may have to move you again. And we may not speak on the radio anymore."

Getting back to his feet, Alberto gave Julie an odd look. "I had come to believe your story, Señorita Julia. But there are those who now say you must be a spy if this man, who is not even a relation, should spend so much money and effort to find you. For we have learned it is true that you are not rich."

*Uncle Norm,* Julie thought with despair as he walked away. As she had feared, he had left his job and home and, as he had done for her parents, come storming down to Bogotá and the American embassy to mount a rescue attempt. She might have known he would be one to reject at face value that paramilitary story. Julie could see him clearly in her mind's eye, bellowing his demands to the top level of the State Department, his bull dog jowls set obstinately, small eyes squinting in a glare calculated to cow even the ambassador himself.

But for all his force of will, Norm Hutchens was a sick man, and this was just the kind of thing that could trigger the heart attack of which his doctor had warned. And now he was spending his own savings hiring private planes and surveillance equipment and bribing—though he wouldn't put it that way—the Colombian military to search for Julie. They did not send out search helicopters for the average kidnap victim, not unless someone paid the expense.

*Oh, Uncle Norm, don't you know it's a waste of money? Like looking for a needle in a haystack.* Her guardian wasn't a poor man, but neither could he afford this kind of financial outlay. Still, it was just like Norm Hutchens to insist on doing something, however futile, instead of sitting around and waiting for events to take their course. *If something happens to him, I'll never forgive myself.*

A wave of helpless fury swept over Julie then caught up Carlos, on duty again and openly watching her reaction, his young face so placid and unconcerned that Julie wanted to shake him. Rounding on him, she demanded angrily, "How can you do this, Carlos? How can you . . . just *torture* people like this—kidnapping them and holding them until their families are crazy with worry? Making them spend every centavo they own just in the hope they might someday get their loved ones back!"

Carlos looked totally uncomprehending. "But how can you say that, Señorita Julia? We don't torture people. You have seen that. And the kidnapping—it is not like that at all."

He hunkered down on his heels to face her directly, his newly adult voice taking on an earnestness that only emphasized how young he was. "You must understand that it is not really even kidnapping. We call it a *retencion* . . . a temporary retaining for the purpose of benefiting society. We do not target the poor—only the rich who have built their wealth on the suffering of the Colombian *campesino*. Is it not only just, if they have so much and others have so little, that they should give up part of it to those in need? And if they must also give up some time out of their lives, is this not a reasonable price?"

He sounded as though he were reciting a well-rehearsed school lesson, and Julie asked skeptically, "Are those your own ideas, Carlos, or someone else's?"

Carlos shrugged, then grabbed at his AK-47 as it threatened to slide from his lap. "They come from our leaders. See, here is what one of them has written. I have been studying it."

Hauling out a handful of the pamphlets Julie had seen the guerrillas reading around camp, he selected one and spread it out. "See? Right there he says it."

Julie read the paragraph he indicated halfway down the column of print.

> We utilize the term "retention" to refer more precisely to the content of our actions. We differentiate them from kidnappings because that is the term used to refer to the actions of delinquents whose only objective is personal enrichment. In our case, we temporarily deprive people of their freedom for political reasons in the context of a revolutionary war and class conflict. . . .

"You see?" Carlos said as she read. "It is only justice. It is these people who oppress the poor. Should they not pay? After all, they are treated well, and as soon as they pay, they are released to their families. You are a foreigner, Señorita Julia, though you grew up in our country, and so you do not understand. But the people of Colombia—they understand."

*Yeah, and a rose by any other name. . .*

Julie couldn't deny Carlos was telling the truth as far as he understood it. Kidnapping was a way of life in Colombia in a way no one else in the world could understand. People here paid for kidnapping insurance the way those in other countries paid for health insurance. And if you did get kidnapped, the whole process was bound by rules that both sides knew well. The guerrillas treated their captives with relative decency—Julie herself could testify to that. They took only those they considered wealthy. Even the kidnapped missionaries were understandable, as the rural Colombian considered all Americans to be rolling in cash.

And once the ransom was paid, the hostages were quickly released, not only to demonstrate good will, but to encourage prompt payment of ransom by their next victims. The guerrillas were even good about leaving the family alone in the future, considering they'd paid their debt to society—

though that didn't guarantee protection from the next guerrilla faction to come along.

So if you played by the rules, you went home—and promptly moved to Miami if you could afford it.

It had become so commonplace that it was even a point of pride in some circles to have gone through the process somewhere in the extended family and survived. And only too many, even among the social classes most often targeted, seemed to accept their country's bizarre cultural anomaly as somehow inevitable and even, to some extent, deserved.

Until something went wrong. The blowing up of a ranch-owner's wife whose ransom didn't arrive before the time bomb wired to her chest detonated. The death of a kidnapped child too frail for the rigors of extended captivity. It took such an atrocity, it seemed, to shake the Colombian people from their apathy to public outrage.

"What about the ones who don't pay up—or can't? What about the ones who never do go home? Who . . . who die—or disappear forever?" Looking the young guerrilla directly in the eye, Julie added, "What about me, Carlos? We were friends—your sister was one of the best friends I ever had. Could you really shoot me in the back if I made a run for it right now? Could you really shoot *anyone* down in cold blood?"

She had shaken him, Julie saw. The troubled look was back on his young face, dissolving its hard lines into confusion and distress. His eyes dropped to his hands, clasped tightly around the stock of his AK-47, and he rubbed a thumb over the polished barrel before he admitted in a low voice. "I . . . I do not know, Señorita Julia. You must not even think of trying because I . . . I do not wish to make that choice. I . . . I think about it often. I even dream about it—and sometimes I am afraid I would not be brave enough to shoot. When I think of the men who destroyed my family—how they died . . . the blood . . . their faces—then I think it would be easy to pull the trigger. I want to kill. I *thirst* to kill!"

His eyes rose to Julie's, and they were the eyes of a child, hurt and bewildered. "But other times I remember the things Don Ricardo taught us—of a God who loves us and who calls us to forgive, not to kill. And . . . and my own father, who was a man of God like Don Ricardo—he did not even curse the *paramilitares* when they shot him. I know he would not wish that I avenge his death in this way. And I wish there could be an end to this—to the killing. But it is not so easy to walk away from the guerrillas."

Carlos's head shot up as heavy footsteps approached the *caleta*. It was Victor, just passing by from the radio hut toward the water barrel, but he paused to look thoughtfully from Carlos to Julie, and under his expressionless gaze, the boy's face flushed, then hardened. As he strode on, Carlos snatched the pamphlet from Julie's hands.

"Enough! You are confusing me. I have made my choice. The guerrillas will bring peace to our country as the government never has. And if there must be some injustice as a price, then so it must be. There is no other way."

He sprang to his feet. Julie didn't try to pursue the conversation. Crawling back into her *caleta,* she stretched out on her thin mattress. She could understand where Victor and Jaime and even Rafael were coming from. She'd grown up, as they had, with a firsthand view of the inequalities of Colombian society, the poverty and misery of the rural *campesino,* the wealth sewed up into the hands of the few. If a small segment of society kept all its resources locked up in their greedy clutches, wasn't there justice in taking some of it and giving it to those in need?

And if the ransom money actually went to the guerrillas' cause rather than to the suffering masses, didn't they consider themselves to be fighting on behalf of those poor? How did you explain to these people whose lives and families were so fractured that kidnapping—what it did to a person, a family, the pain and anguish of lives ripped apart from each other, the loss of personal freedom, the uncertainty and worry and fear by those waiting on the outside—was far more wrong than a simple redistribution of wealth?

From somewhere outside the *caleta,* a new sound that didn't come from the rattles and clanks and people noises of the camp impinged on the edge of Julie's consciousness. But it wasn't loud enough to distract her deliberations.

*I should hate these people. I did hate them all these long years.*

But not anymore. She couldn't. Their lives were too sad, more deserving of pity than anger. And if Julie could not condone their actions, she could at least understand the torturous paths and lines of thinking that had led them to this isolated spot in the jungle.

Oddly enough, in fact, Julie was finding that there were even things to admire in these people. After less than three weeks, she herself was sick of the inactivity, the rain and mosquitoes, the primitive living quarters, not to mention bathroom facilities, even the food that rarely varied from rice and beans and *arepas.*

These men and women put up with such conditions for years at a time—and by choice. They lived on the run, often one step ahead of the military and paramilitary, hiding out in these jungles, slogging through the mud, building and rebuilding their camps, battling mosquitoes and loneliness as often as they did their enemies. If they were being paid or were profiting personally from the millions the guerrillas were said to acquire from their kidnapping and the drug traffic, they showed no signs of it in their personal belongings or lifestyle.

Nor did they allow their vagabond lifestyle to degenerate into the slovenliness Julie had seen so often in the poorer huts in San Ignacio or among the Indian tribes. Julie couldn't help being impressed at their discipline. Under Victor's sharp eye, they practiced a rigorous hygiene, brushing teeth and bathing daily, washing clothes, re-digging the latrine every few days, keeping garbage and food strictly covered against flies.

They were not allowed to forget why they had joined the guerrillas. Despite the heat that made the outdoors—and their heavy uniforms—a misery once the sun had burned off the last coolness of the dew, they held daily exercise and military drills and target practice as well. And if Julie had overheard plenty of grumbles at both the constant drills and the rigorous camp discipline, they were not loud.

Propped up on one elbow, Julie surveyed the encampment. Linda and Marcela were starting supper. Jaime and Rafael had a book spread open on the supply table, and Jaime was explaining something in its pages with uncharacteristic animation. Alberto and Enrique were bent over an automatic rifle Enrique had been breaking down.

No, her captors might be terrorists and kidnappers—even killers. But they were not the run-of-the-mill criminals she had once written them off to be. They were soldiers, and dedicated ones.

So what prompted these men and women to give up families, wives, friends, the comforts of even a simple home, to swelter and train and fight out here in the middle of this wilderness? Food and clothing? A place to lay their heads? Maybe for the most destitute. But that wasn't enough. Certainly not for someone like Alberto, who had come from a comfortable middle-class home.

No, they were out here in this awful place for the most dangerous of reasons: they had a cause in which they believed, to which they were passionately committed. A good cause too, even noble—bringing the benefits of their country's great resources to the oppressed and hungry masses of their society. It was beside the point that their cause was hopeless, that the means to which they resorted in carrying it out had alienated their would-be supporters and forever destroyed any chance they'd had for building their new society (for how could a people who resorted to kidnapping and murder be trusted to supply a fair and just government?), that their actions were transfiguring them into the very cruel and deadly oppressors against whom they had pledged to fight. These guerrillas believed in their cause, and to bring it about they had chosen to sacrifice their comfort, their families, their very lives.

And that, Julie admitted grudgingly, was something to be admired.

Sacrifice. There it was again.

Julie rolled over, burying her face in her arms.

*Except a kernel of wheat fall into the ground and die . . . whoever loses his life . . .*

It was odd to think that her parents had anything in common with these guerrillas—and yet the comparisons were glaring. They too had turned their backs on family and friends, given up the comforts of an easier—even luxurious—lifestyle. Maybe they'd gone about it in a better way, building instead of destroying, their motives less vengeful and self-serving. But the passionate commitment to improve the lot of a hungry and desperate people was disturbingly similar.

And so was the hopelessness of their cause.

No, that wasn't entirely true. Carlos was right. Richard and Elizabeth Baker *had* made a difference. Maybe not a big one or a lasting one. But not only had they healed bodies; they had touched lives. Those women, that lonely grave, were proof of that.

*And me?*

The futility of the guerrilla's struggle, the scattered remnants of her parents' life work, only underscored the logic of Julie's choice of path. It was, after all, the choice most people made—to mind your own business, live your own life, dream your own dreams. After all, did people have a responsibility, or even a right, to throw away their lives on senseless, altruistic causes?

And yet . . .

*I'm putting up with this because I have no choice. Maybe I'd even volunteer for this kind of adventure for a good enough story—if I knew I was going to get out safe in the end. But could I ever sacrifice my whole life or even my future for a cause or people who mean nothing to me personally?*

*Would I?*

Julie rolled over onto her back, suddenly weary from more than inaction. *I don't think so,* she admitted and found that she was ashamed to do so.

The thought lasted only an instant. Her movement brought into sharp focus the sound that had been slowly growing on the edge of her consciousness. The quiet thud of hooves on the soft ground of a dirt trail.

Julie sat up with a jerk, pushing her curls hastily away from her face for a better view. Horsemen were riding into camp. Half a dozen of them. And one, Julie saw with a sudden leap of her heart, was tall and broad with pale hair glinting in the afternoon sunlight.

Tim McAdams.

# SIXTEEN

CARLOS MADE NO ATTEMPT TO stop Julie as she scrambled out of her *caleta*. He was watching the horsemen with the same startled interest. At the head of the party rode *Comandante* Aguilera, and behind him was the guerrilla PR man, Manuel Flores. But Julie had eyes only for Tim.

Tim's clothing, like Julie's, had been exchanged for combat fatigues. Unlike hers, his uniform fit like a glove and didn't look at all out of place on his tall, powerful frame. He looked tired, Julie thought, though that might only have been the dust and stiff muscles of a long ride, and a jagged scar ran up one cheekbone into his hairline as though someone had struck him viciously.

His strong, handsome features showed none of the strain of captivity Julie could feel in her own face muscles. Though he sat unarmed in the middle of a band of armed guards, he might have been the one in charge instead of a prisoner, by the self-assured lift of his blond head and the cool, unconcerned survey he was making of his new surroundings.

Not until that calm, blue gaze met and held hers did it hit Julie just how much worry and guilt and *aloneness* she'd been pushing to the back of her mind these last weeks.

*He's alive! He's okay! I didn't get him killed.* The relief took the stiffening out of Julie's legs. She sank down quickly onto a length of log that had been rolled up as a seat for her current guard.

The horsemen dismounted. Letting his reins fall to the ground, Tim strode directly over to Julie. Two of the other horsemen followed hastily at his heels, unslinging their AK-47s as they did so, but they made no attempt to stop him. Julie jumped to her feet again as he approached her *caleta*, resisting a sudden impulse to throw her arms around him, she was so relieved to see him alive and in one piece.

Her expression must have given her impulse away. As he reached her, Tim said cordially, "Well, if this isn't a nice welcome! Am I wrong, or are you actually happy to see me?"

A smile tugged at the corner of his mouth as he looked down at her, and Julie could feel the heat rise into her neck.

"If you knew how worried I've been!" she retorted. "I wasn't even sure you were still alive. If something had happened to you because of me, I'd never have forgiven myself."

She glanced past Tim. Her first hopeful thought when the horsemen had ridden into the camp was that they'd come to take her away, even—however optimistic she knew the prospect to be—to end her captivity. Now she saw with a fading of hope that the newcomers were unloading bags of rice, potatoes, and other provisions from the horses. The FARC commander hadn't come to set her free but to supply the new camp for an extended stay.

Pulling her eyes away, she turned back to Tim. "What are you doing here?" she asked with determined cheerfulness. "Are . . . are they going to let us stay together now?"

Tim McAdams had followed her troubled glance. His smile faded into seriousness as he answered. "I wish I could say, Julie. All I know is that Aguilera got off the radio this morning in a real flap. The next thing I know, he's giving orders that we're to ride out with the supplies he's sending over to your camp."

He shot a quick glance at his guards, then lowered his voice several decibels. "I have to tell you, Julie, that whatever it was, it didn't sound too good. Aguilera and Flores were both furious, and I heard your name come up."

Julie glanced over at Aguilera, who was now deep in speech with the camp leader, Victor, his hands punctuating the discussion with rapid gestures. At the same instant, the two men turned around to look across at the two prisoners. Julie's stomach gave a sickening lurch at the cold glare she read in the *comandante*'s black eyes. Tim was right. Whatever was on the guerrilla leader's mind, it boded no good for Julie Baker.

Wheeling around on his heel, Aguilera called sharply, "Enrique!"

Enrique finished hefting a sack of flour onto the supply table before striding quickly over to the commander. "*Sí*, Señor?"

"Enrique, when I leave here, you will be ready to accompany me."

"*Sí*, Señor!" Julie caught the guerrilla interpreter's quick glance in her direction, and though she couldn't hear what he added next, she knew what the question had been by Aguilera's sharp reply: "The girl is no longer of any concern to you."

So Enrique would get his wish to return to the fighting.

Julie was startled by the pang of disappointment the thought caused her. Though he had largely ignored her, Enrique had twice intervened on her behalf, and Julie had come to count on him as a protector against Rafael and the others. With him gone, what would happen to her?

And *Comandante* Aguilera—why was he looking at her like that? What did he mean—that she, Julie, was no longer of concern? *Why did he come here? What does he want from me? Oh, please, not another interrogation!*

Her legs went suddenly weak, and Julie found herself fumbling for the support of the log behind her. She sat down hard, unable to ward off the wave of terror sweeping over her.

"Hey!" Tim McAdams dropped down beside her, his large frame filling the remainder of the length of log. Julie could feel the warmth of his body close beside her. Turning at a sideways angle, he reached over to take her hands in his own, his blue eyes darkening with concern.

"Your hands are ice cold!" he said remorsefully. "Look, I'm sorry. I didn't mean to scare you. Ten to one, that call had nothing to do with you—or either of us. Maybe Aguilera's just ticked off because they've lost a battle or something. Either way, it's not the end of the world. We're both alive, aren't we? And together again. I can tell you I'm as happy to see you alive and in one piece as you looked to see me. I've been worried sick about you, girl."

Under the comforting flow of his voice and the warmth of his fingers on hers, Julie gradually stopped shivering. Withdrawing her hands unobtrusively from his, she glanced again at Aguilera. Maybe Tim was right. Far from making any threatening moves, *Comandante* Aguilera was no longer even paying attention to the prisoners. He had called together the more senior members of the guerrilla unit—Victor, Enrique, and Jaime, along with himself and Manuel Flores—and they had retired to the *cambuche,* where through the unenclosed end she could see them clustered around the radio table, heads close together in conversation. If Tim could be this cheerful and optimistic, maybe she was just overreacting.

Forcing a smile to her lips, she apologized. "I'm sorry. I don't know what came over me. This place is just . . . is just getting to me, I guess."

"Hey, that's nothing to be ashamed of. It's only natural to feel fear at a time like this."

*So you keep telling me. Except that you aren't afraid,* Julie thought wryly. She lifted her chin and did her best to infuse some of his cheerfulness into her speech.

"Okay, if you're trying to make me feel better it's working. So tell me what's happened since I saw you last. Have you been with *Comandante* Aguilera all this time? How far did you travel to get here? Have they . . ." Her voice wavered as her glance went to the wicked slash along his cheek. "Have they been mistreating you or . . . or beating you?"

Tim fingered the scar with a rueful grin. "Are you talking about this? No, I'm afraid I can't blame that on the guerrillas. Just a little fight with a thorn bush across the trail. Actually, the guerrillas have treated me pretty fair. The food gets a little monotonous." He raised an inquiring eyebrow. "How about you?"

"They haven't mistreated me," Julie admitted. "But where have you been all this time? I saw you on your feet just before they took me away, so at least I knew you were alive and had come out of that drug they gave us." She shuddered at the memory. "I still have nightmares about that."

"Yes, I know what you mean. Though I really don't remember too much after they shot me full of that stuff. I must have been coming out of it about the time they were taking you away because I do remember your voice floating around whatever cloud my mind was on. By the time I managed to pull myself off that bed, the shelter was coming down around me. I did see you riding away, but you were gone before I could even register a protest. As to where I've been . . ."

Tim glanced around the encampment. "Basically, it's been a lot like this. We moved two or three times, but I couldn't tell you where or even what direction. One jungle clearing looks like another as far as I'm concerned."

"And what about *Comandante* Aguilera?" Julie asked anxiously. "Has he been with you all this time? Have you been able to find out anything about what he's been doing?" She lowered her voice. "Or overhear anything he might be planning?"

Tim's blond eyebrow shot up. "If I'd known you were expecting a full report, I'd have kept better notes." More seriously, he added, "Actually, no, Aguilera's been kind of coming and going—sometimes with us, sometimes not. Come to think of it, probably more not. When he turned up yesterday, I hadn't seen him around in almost a week. And no, he hasn't advertised his plans a whole lot. At least not in my hearing."

He turned a quizzical eye on Julie. "Any particular reason for asking, or just that general journalistic nosiness?"

Julie looked over at Tim's two guards, squatted down near Carlos, one with his eyes fixed on the two Americans, the other with his attention wandering visibly toward the two female guerrillas working on supper around the campfire. Catching her anxious glance, Tim dropped his voice another decibel. "They don't speak any English, if that's what you're worried about. So shoot!"

"Well, it's just that . . ." Julie forced herself not to glance at the guards again, keeping her voice on a normal conversational level. "I think I might have an idea of why they grabbed us, why they were so sure there was a spy down here to start with, why the Americans would even *want* to have a spy down here. Do you remember when they drugged us—how *Comandante* Aguilera mentioned his *musulmanes* friends who gave them the stuff they used to interrogate us? Well, *musulmanes* means Muslims. The research I did for this trip had some stuff about Islamic terrorist groups being involved with the Colombian guerrillas. It sounds to me as though *Comandante* Aguilera is one of them. Anyway, when I was waking up from that drug, I heard the *musulmanes* mentioned again. I don't know who was talking, but there was something about the Americans not finding what they were looking for until it was too late."

Julie had to take a deep breath to keep excitement from creeping into her tone. "So what do they think the Americans are looking for? And why is it soon going to be too late? Whatever it is, it has to be big enough that they're worried we might find out about it and stop it. Worried enough that they had their own spy on the job—I mean, someone had to finger me to the guerrillas."

She was about to mention her suspicions of Sondra Kharrazi, then remembered the attractive brunette's determined play for Tim. He had certainly made no objection. Better not get into that now.

"I know it sounds crazy. But I've been going over and over this since the day we were captured. And it keeps adding up to the same thing. They are planning something down here, and it's going to happen soon. Either these Muslim friends of Aguilera's, whoever they are, or the guerrillas—or maybe both of them together. And it isn't just another of their raids on some village or police outpost. They wouldn't be worried about an American spy for that. It has to be something that concerns us—the U.S. Maybe an attack on the base at San José or one of the other places where we have our people. Maybe they have some new weapon they're afraid we'll find out about. They'd almost have to if they're thinking of taking on American forces."

This time Julie couldn't resist a glance at the guards. The newcomers were tossing a pair of dice in the dust, and Carlos was engrossed in the rapid patter of their betting. "Anyway, I was just hoping maybe you'd heard or seen something more. I . . . I just have this horrible feeling that we need to get a warning out—and soon. I've gone over and over in my mind, trying to think of some way to escape or even to get out a message. But they've been watching me too closely. And of course, there was you. They said they'd kill you if I tried to escape. I couldn't take that chance. But now that we're together . . . Oh, I know it seems pretty hopeless with all these guards, but I just can't help feeling that together we could do something."

Someone over by the campfire was lighting the Coleman lamp. There was a strong smell of lantern fuel, then a yellow gleam lit up the growing twilight. In its dim glimmer, Tim's eyes on Julie's were bright and still.

"Then you *are* a U.S. government agent," he said slowly.

*"What?"* Julie turned her exclamation into a cough as all three guards swiveled their heads around. Moderating her voice, she said indignantly, "Please, not that again! Of course I'm not—"

"No, wait! Hear me out!" Tim's large hand rose to cut her off. "Look, I'm sorry to bring it up again. It's just . . . well, I did overhear one thing when *Comandante* Aguilera was organizing this sudden expedition. You're right—they do have someone on the inside. A report came in for Aguilera that there's an American operative out here in the DMZ. Someone who was in that airport with the UN mission and who is presently out somewhere with the guerrillas. And that someone," he added deliberately, "has been missing for the last two weeks or more."

"But—" Julie broke off as the significance of his last statement sank in, staring at Tim with disbelief. "And they think it's me!" she said when she could speak. *"You* think it's me! Well, I don't know what to say except that it isn't! Maybe their source just plain got it wrong. But even if they didn't, I'm not the only possibility out here. How do they know it was one of our UN mission at all? How do they know it isn't one of their own guerrillas? There were plenty of them at the airport—including Aguilera and Manuel Flores and Enrique and Carlos and that whole bunch. Or it could be you!" she challenged. "I still say you're as good a candidate as I am."

Julie broke off again as she felt the sudden rigidity of his body. "What did I say?"

"Nothing. I was just thinking." Tim cleared his throat. "Look, Julie, I don't care who you are or what you're doing here. All I'm saying is, if you have information you feel is so urgent to get out, or if you have a link to someone out there who could help us, I'd appreciate it if you'd share it with me. Maybe two heads aren't always better than one. But at least if I know what you do, it doubles our chances of one of us getting the news out . . . especially if they split us up again."

His voice grew suddenly stern. "More urgently, if you're even *thinking* of pulling some risky escape attempt, don't! I've been watching these people too. They know what they're doing. You wouldn't have a chance of getting away with it. No, I hate just sitting here as much as you do, but we've got to be patient, to wait for a realistic opportunity. However urgent you may feel this warning of yours is, it isn't worth sacrificing your safety—"

"Sacrificing!" Julie turned a choke into another cough. "Tim, if you only know what a joke that is. No," she said ruefully, "you don't have to worry I'm going to do anything stupid and risk my life. I'm afraid I'm not the stuff of which martyrs are made."

She pressed the back of her hands to her eyes in sudden weariness. "And if I do think of something, I promise I'll tell you. I wouldn't leave you here to take the fall. Besides, it's all speculation anyway. It isn't as though I have anything really concrete. Just those fuzzy references to *musulmanes* I mentioned. I'm not really sure how much of that was the drug. It's just . . . maybe it's silly and I'm overreacting, but I wish I could at least tell Colonel Thornton to keep an extra-careful eye out."

Julie's eyes went to the *cambuche* where *Comandante* Aguilera's meeting seemed to be breaking up. Marcela and Linda were dishing up supper, carrying the enamel bowls into the radio shelter. Her own meal would be coming soon, but Julie felt no appetite for it. She let out a small sigh.

"You know, it's funny you should mention sacrifice. I've been doing a lot of thinking on the subject these last couple weeks—maybe because it's something I know so little about. Watching these guerrillas—the way they've given up their whole lives to fight for their cause. I mean, it's sheer foolishness. They can't win. They've been fighting for decades without getting anywhere. And yet they'll give up everything—families, homes, a normal life—to a fight for a hopeless cause. Talk about sacrifice! However much you might hate what these people are doing, you've got to admire them for that."

Julie slid a sideways glance at Tim. The rigidity had gone out of him, and if he still had the ridiculous idea that she was a government agent, at least he was no longer pursuing the subject. "I know it sounds like a crazy comparison—guerrillas and missionaries—but they remind me a little of my parents. They gave up their careers, families, culture—everything—without batting an eye. Well, maybe not without batting an eye. I wasn't born then, so I wouldn't know. It wasn't easy, that I'm sure of. And yet they did it, spent an entire life out here for—what? A handful of churches—now mostly burned to the ground. A few villages with longer life expectancies. A few congregations scattered over half of Colombia by the guerrillas. Oh, maybe their cause wasn't quite as hopeless as the guerrillas'—though I've sure thought so all these years since they died. But these last couple of weeks—seeing San Ignacio again, those women . . ."

Julie cleared the roughness from her throat. "Either way, they sacrificed their whole lives out here without ever asking for anything in return. At least not for themselves. And me?"

Her gaze went blindly to the darkness of the jungle beyond the pale bubble of light cast by the Coleman lantern. "You know, I always thought I was the smart one. I was going to avoid my parents' errors, build something really constructive with my life instead of throwing it down the drain, wasting it on people who don't really want to change, anyway. But now I can't help wondering. At least they cared about something beyond themselves. And so do these guerrillas. I just wish—"

Julie broke off, flushing suddenly. Tim was listening courteously, she found as she glanced up, his head bent slightly down toward her. Whether he was genuinely interested or just being polite, she couldn't tell.

"I'm rambling, aren't I?" she said apologetically. "Too much time, I guess, with no one to talk to. And *way* too much time to think. I'm afraid it's caught up with me."

Tim shook his head, his eyes not leaving her face. "No, please go on. I want you to, really. I'm . . . interested in how you think."

Julie's mouth curved wryly. "Actually, it's your thinking I'm interested in. You're a missionary like my parents were. Maybe a little different. You aren't permanently stuck out in the middle of the jungle, though I'm sure you've probably made your own sacrifices. So tell me, do you think God gives people lives and homes and family and careers—and then just asks them to throw them all away? My parents really believed God called them to go to San Ignacio. And I have to say there's been a lot of times these last years when I've wondered if maybe they just heard Him wrong. And yet . . ."

Julie paused, giving Tim an opportunity for input, but he said nothing. After a moment she went on pensively, "Maybe they weren't completely off—I just don't know. I guess, after all, when you think about it, God did something like that Himself. Leaving all the glory of heaven to come down here to the jungle we've made of our world. And giving His life for a whole world of people who didn't appreciate Him. And not because we did anything to deserve Him, but just because He loved us. John 3:16 says it pretty plain."

"John 3:16?" The question was asked lightly. Julie glanced up, thinking she'd misheard. "You know, 'God so loved the world that He gave His one and only Son, that whoever believes in Him shall not perish but have eternal life.'"

"Oh yes, of course." Tim's response was smooth, deepening to that velvet, melodious tone Julie had come to associate with his "preacher's" voice. "The gospel of John, chapter three, verse sixteen. God sending His Son to earth to die for man's sins. A favorite passage of sacrifice and belief in God. And of course, you're right that God Himself is the supreme example of sacrifice. The giving up of His Son to die on the cross."

Julie didn't move as Tim ran down to a stop. He had recovered well, his blue eyes holding hers bright and guileless in the pale glimmer of the Coleman lantern, the curve of his mouth tilted upward in a smile that was at once sympathetic and companionable. He was an extraordinarily handsome man and even more charming in personality, and Julie, who would never deny she was as susceptible to an attractive member of the opposite sex as any single adult, had wondered at times why, for all her worry and concern for his safety, his blue eyes smiling down into hers had tugged so little at her heartstrings.

But now it was as though those handsome features were suddenly no more than the rubber mask with which a stunt double duplicates a real-life counterpart, with a stranger who could be anyone peering out at her from behind it, and the words falling from those smiling lips were just as meaningless. Even Enrique's statement of faith had sounded more sincere. Pulling her eyes away from his, Julie let out a small sigh.

"You aren't really a missionary, are you?" she said quietly.

This time she wasn't imagining his sudden rigidity. For one full measure of the pop song Alberto was whistling beyond the campfire, Tim didn't answer, and when Julie looked up, she saw that while his smile was still fixed on his lips, it had faded from his eyes. As Alberto switched abruptly to another tune, Tim relaxed, one eyebrow going up and a corner of his mouth tilting in a rueful grin. "Well, thanks a lot! What did I do to bring that on?"

*You smile too much,* Julie thought. *The missionaries I've known aren't always smiling and cheerful. And they don't have the perfect little religious speeches to offer at a moment's notice. They stammer and stumble and wonder if they're saying the right thing. They aren't impeccably groomed even in the middle of the jungle or perfectly calm and fearless in a crisis situation. Missionaries get worried and tired and afraid just like other people, and even cranky and out of sorts sometimes when they've had a rough day. They're human, not Superman. They . . . they just have a lot bigger hand to hold when they're scared—and only that keeps them going.*

Aloud, Julie said, "John 3:16. There isn't a missionary alive who doesn't know that verse. Or a Sunday school student either. It's just about the first thing out of the Bible you ever memorize when you're a kid. But you didn't recognize what I was talking about, did you?"

There wasn't the smallest shift in Tim's smile or the eyes twinkling down into hers. "You're mistaken, Julie. I'm sorry to spoil your mystery scenario here, but I do know the verse. 'For God so loved the world . . .'"

He repeated it flawlessly to the end, his eyebrow raised humorously high. "See? Just a slip of the tongue—or brain, you might say."

"Or a photographic memory," Julie said quietly. "Look, you don't need to worry. You're good. Anyone who doesn't know missionaries as I do— well, to be honest, you fooled me too. If it hadn't been for that slip—" She hurried on before he could make the denial she could see trembling on his lips. "So—who are you, really? CIA?" Her breath caught in her throat, and her eyes widened. "You're the American they're looking for, aren't you? You're the spy they think I am!"

Julie glanced quickly at the three guards, making sure they'd returned to their dice before going on, "You *are* good! You had me convinced you really thought I was the spy. If that was to keep me from suspecting you, it worked!" Tim was looking at the guards as well, and when he didn't answer, she went on, her voice dropping instinctively, "What I told you—is that why you're here? To investigate what *Comandante* Aguilera's doing out here? Is that why you left the airport . . . to let yourself get caught—to get into the guerrilla camp? And then I . . ." Her breath caught again. "I wasn't supposed to be out there, was I? I . . . I messed everything up, didn't I?"

"Shh!" The quiet scrape of a footstep jerked Julie's head around even before Tim put out his warning hand. Her stomach tightened with dismay. The roller coaster that had been her emotions these last hours was sinking this time all the way down into her toes. *Comandante* Aguilera and Enrique had come up around the back of the *caleta* from the direction of the water drum, and they stood only a few feet away. The FARC commander's dark features were unreadable, but Enrique's narrowed gaze was bright and watchful in the light of the Coleman lamp as it rested on the prisoners. How much of her careless English had he overheard?

Then Julie saw it wasn't she who had drawn Enrique's attention, but Tim.

Tim turned his head to meet that watchful gaze from Enrique, and as the two men stared at each other, Julie suddenly saw something very similar in the cool, wary intentness of their silent scrutiny. At the same instant, the two men turned to look at Julie, and somewhere in that three-way glance, Julie felt a chill go through her that was as cold and deadly as the passing of a sentence of execution.

# SEVENTEEN

LIGHT INTRUDED ON HER DREAM.

It was a bizarre jumble of Julie and Victor and Enrique and a vague blur of other guerrillas riding horseback through the jungle. Julie was arguing hotly with Enrique about the best kind of camera to pack on a jungle trip, when the horsemen drew up in a circle around her. Julie's horse had vanished, and she suddenly found herself on the ground under their accusing eyes.

They were unslinging their weapons when the light began to nibble at the edges of the dream. Julie had learned to sleep through the guards' flashlight probes, or at least force them to the edge of her consciousness. But this time the light wouldn't go away. It grew into a dazzling ball that swallowed up the guard and the camp and the guns. To get away from it, Julie opened her eyes.

"Shh!" The sound was a bare whistle through teeth and caught Julie's annoyed stirring before it began. As the flashlight beam dropped away from Julie's eyes, Julie could see above it the dark outline of Carlos's face. His expression would have bound her to silence even without the finger at his lips.

The light blinked out as Julie eased noiselessly to a sitting position. The night was very dark with no glimmer of moon or stars filtering through the jungle canopy. But it wasn't the absolute blackness of an underground cavern. Julie could see the movement of her hand in front of her face and a dark shape that was Carlos hunkered down outside her *caleta*, the outline of his head raised high and alert like a deer listening for the footstep of a hunter. Julie found herself holding her breath as she listened for any sign that someone else was awake. She heard only Alberto's soft snoring in a hammock under one of the trees, and at last Carlos turned his head to whisper in the barest breath of sound, "Señorita Julia, you must leave here! They are going to kill you!"

The words drove the air from her lungs. Yet Julie found herself accepting them immediately as truth. They were, after all, the summation of everything she had been bracing herself for—far more than the actual pacific occasion the evening had turned out to be.

* * *

Julie wasn't sure what she'd expected after the episode with Enrique and
*Comandante* Aguilera. The two men strode on without missing a pace, but
Julie had seen them in close conversation afterward, a sight that destroyed
her appetite for the meat stew Linda and Marcela had made in honor of
Aguilera's visit. Had her careless conversation put Tim in danger? And
when was the *comandante* going to get around to the purpose of his visit
here? Surely he hadn't come just to talk to the camp leaders—something he
could have done by radio.

Her stomach tightened further when Aguilera called for Tim's guards to
escort him to the radio hut. To Julie, this was an ominous sign. The FARC
commander could so easily have interrogated Tim at their own camp. Were
they even now grilling Tim as to who he really was?

Admittedly the interrogation looked peaceable enough from what Julie
could see through the open end of the *cambuche*. It was being carried out
by *Comandante* Aguilera and his PR man, Manuel Flores, his guards withdrawing to a less menacing stance at the edge of the radio hut, and they
had even rolled in for Tim one of the logs her keepers had sawed off to use
as seats. Maybe Enrique had overheard fewer of her low words than she'd
feared. Certainly Tim himself evidenced no concern—not that he ever did.

Tim's interrogation hadn't lasted long. As he was led away, Aguilera had
called for the senior members of the camp—Victor, Jaime, and Enrique.
The open end of the *cambuche* had been closed off during their meeting,
and Julie had watched Tim instead. She'd wanted to ask him what had
happened, but his guards had taken him back to the horses, and while she
might have asked Carlos if she could join him, Rafael was now on guard,
and his dark glance as he took up position outside the *caleta* had only
increased her unease.

Still, when Julie was summoned to join him, *Comandante* Aguilera greeted
her arrival with an almost benign nod, waving her to the same log where
Tim had sat.

"Señorita Julia," the commander announced affably, "you will be pleased
to know that we are now convinced you are indeed who you say you are.
We regret that it has been necessary to hold you in this fashion, and we
would beg your understanding of the urgencies of our struggle that have
compelled our actions. We are honorable men and do not hold prisoners

when it is possible to release them. And so tomorrow you will be returned to your people. Victor, Enrique . . ." The rest of the camp contingent had filed in as well to hear the commander's announcement, and he nodded to the two men mentioned. "You two, and Jaime as well, will accompany the woman to San Ignacio, where her people will be contacted to retrieve her."

Julie should have been overjoyed, but she felt stunned. Was it really going to be this easy? And what about Tim? Had she with her careless words traded her own release for his?

Aguilera's next words didn't allay this concern. "The rest of you will tear down the camp, then return to San Ignacio as well to await my next orders. The man will return with me. It will not be necessary to stay the night after all, so I will be leaving camp shortly. But first—Victor, I will use your radio."

And that had been it. As she was led back to her *caleta*, Julie looked around for Tim. His guards had permitted him to swing up onto his horse rather than stand, and he was sitting there easily while the guards checked over harness and saddles on the other horses.

"I have to say goodbye to my friend," Julie informed Rafael, and without waiting for permission, she walked quickly across the camp. After all, he could hardly shoot her now.

Tim swung down from the horse's back as Julie approached. Without glancing at his guards, Julie demanded tensely, "Tim, why are they keeping you? Is it . . . ?" Her voice dropped. "Do you think it's what I said? If . . . if they think you're the spy, they may kill you!"

Dropping his reins, Tim turned to look down at Julie. His blue eyes holding hers were uncharacteristically grave in the light of campfire and lantern, but there was a half smile on his firm mouth as he shook his head. "Julie, you're worrying for nothing. I'm sorry to disillusion you, but you're wrong on all accounts. I'm not what you think, and I've got plenty of published articles on these parts to prove it. Don't you worry about me. Just go on home—get out that warning of yours, if you feel it's urgent. Me—I'll be fine, believe me! Besides, I've got God on my side, remember?"

The quiet assurance in his voice was convincing. Julie studied his face, her head tilted far back against the height of his tall frame. Had she misread him? Whoever lived behind those handsome, confident features, Tim McAdams wasn't a person to dismiss lightly. If he was who—or rather, what—Julie suspected, maybe he really would be fine. In fact, he might be a lot better off with Julie out of the way. Without her, maybe he'd even be able to complete whatever he'd come here to do.

And if she was wrong?

*Then maybe God really will protect him. Either way, there's nothing I can do. And if Comandante Aguilera is really decent enough to send me home, maybe I've been worrying about Tim and everything else for nothing.*

The radio session in the *cambuche* had broken up, and *Comandante* Aguilera and the rest of his party were striding toward them. Victor was with them, listening with grim expression to the *comandante's* low, rapid speech. He shot Julie a black glance as they approached. So someone at least wasn't happy about her release. The camp leader brought up Aguilera's horse for him, then stalked away.

Swinging back to his saddle, Tim looked down at Julie, the half smile still on his lips. "Goodbye, Julie Baker," he'd said softly. "And don't you worry. This will all be over before you know it, I promise."

Julie stood watching until the night swallowed up the riders, then allowed Rafael to lead her back to her *caleta*. She still felt stunned and disbelieving. Was it really possible that this time tomorrow she might be on her way home?

The guerrillas themselves were in a mood of jubilation, laughing and singing around the campfire. They too were looking forward to freedom from this jungle confinement. All except Carlos, who had seemed morose, not joining the others but retiring early to his *caleta*.

*Is he still worrying about having to fight?* Julie wondered. It had been late before she herself fell asleep. Perhaps that was why it had taken so much to wake her up.

\* \* \*

Now, though, she was wide awake.

"When?" she got out in the same breath of a whisper. "How?"

The "why" she didn't ask. Her release had seemed too good to be true, and so it had been. They couldn't afford to release her—not because of any vague warning she might give about some unknown plan, but because she could give the lie to all their stories and witness to Tim's continued captivity. How had she ever entertained for a second the hope that they might free her?

"Today when they take you away," he answered. "I heard them talking—Victor, Enrique, and the *comandante*. They do not plan to take you to San Ignacio but into the jungle, where you will be shot and left."

So that chill of a death sentence she had felt last night under Enrique's narrowed gaze had been real—and addressed at her. A surge of fear and panic drove the breath from Julie's lungs. With it came an unexpected pang of hurt and disappointment. Had she forgotten that Enrique Martinez was a killer, passionately dedicated to a cause that held human life cheap?

Yet the hurt was uppermost in Julie's mind, more than the mortal danger she faced. However quixotic his reasons, Enrique had twice intervened on her behalf and had treated her with humanity and even kindness. She had hoped . . . what had she hoped?

*Okay, so you hoped he'd get soft just because he could show some decency to a prisoner. Like he said, he's not a barbarian. Just a soldier who takes orders, whether it's to keep the prisoner safe one day or to kill her the next.*

To think she'd thought Enrique less calloused than Victor and Rafael and the others! But he could plan a cold-blooded execution while allowing her to hope she was actually going home.

All that was irrelevant now, and Julie thrust away both hurt and panic to breathe out the most important question. "What do I do?"

Surely Carlos hadn't awakened her in the middle of the night just to provide her with this information. Though it was no longer full night, Julie discovered, catching a glimpse of the phosphorescent numbers on her watch face. It was past 4:00 A.M., and in another hour or so, the camp would begin to stir. An hour after that, she and Victor and Enrique and Rafael would be embarking on that final—very final—jungle trek. The panic rose up again into her throat.

"We go—as though to the latrine. Now!"

Carlos rose noiselessly from his squatting position. Julie reached over to snag her belongings, an easy matter since she'd kept her knapsack packed and ready ever since that last horrid dash into the jungle, and crawled out after him, wincing as the palm leaves under her mattress rustled. Rising stealthily to her feet, she froze, listening.

There was no answering stir among the sleepers. Obeying Carlos's tap on her shoulder, she stepped silently in front of him onto the path feet had worn to the edge of the encampment. She had immediately grasped his plan. If anyone challenged them, the prisoner had suffered a nighttime call of nature. The knapsack she'd have to explain by her needing some kind of toiletry or change of clothing, because she wasn't about to leave it behind.

And if no one stopped them, then when they arrived at the latrine, Julie could just keep on going. She had an hour before the camp stirred. She could be far away from this place by then. She wouldn't even think about the other dangers that lay beyond.

A surge of gratitude warmed Julie's heart as she glanced back at the dark shape of the young guerrilla fighter behind her. Carlos, unlike Enrique, had in the end shown too much conscience to shut his eyes to her murder. Would he have made the same choice if Julie were not a girl he'd known since childhood? Maybe not, but at least he *had* chosen. If only her escape didn't get him into too much trouble!

Out here in the open, the red glow of the few remaining coals in the campfire made the darkness less complete, and the black shapes of the *caletas* and the packed dirt of the path under their feet were enough to guide Carlos and Julie to the edge of the encampment. Julie's heart almost stopped as they passed the strung hammocks and Alberto stopped snoring to turn noisily over in his sleep. But the snoring resumed at once, and no one raised a voice to stop them.

The latrine was newly dug, the path hardly yet worn through the brush, and Carlos had to turn his flashlight on to find their way. He pushed his way ahead of Julie, keeping his hand over the glass so the light filtering through his fingers was too dim to be seen from behind. Julie herself had to keep a hand on his ammunition belt to keep from stumbling.

The crude box shape of the latrine loomed before them. Beyond the glimmer of the flashlight dancing on its bamboo walls, Julie could sense more than see the black tangle of trees and vines and underbrush that was rainforest so dense and primeval it had rarely known human footfall, much less machete or axe. Once swallowed up in that vast wilderness, people disappeared forever, even when they wanted to be found. With any luck at all, Julie could be well beyond the reach of her pursuers long before dawn. But even as she took a step toward its welcome cover, she hesitated.

"Are you sure about this, Carlos? If you let me go—won't you get in trouble when they find out I'm gone?"

The flashlight beam was still dimmed by his hand over the glass, but above the pale light filtering through his fingers, Julie caught the drawn lines of fear and strain even before his harsh whisper. "They will shoot me.

I have seen it happen before when a prisoner escaped. I cannot go back. Besides . . ."—Carlos patted the gun barrel of his AK-47 with his free hand, and the bravado in his young voice wrenched at Julie's heart even more than the fear in his face—"it would not be right to leave a woman to travel this jungle alone. You will need me to protect you. Come."

Pushing the assault rifle back over his shoulder, he reached for Julie's knapsack, adding it to his load with a gallantry that touched Julie anew. But as he did so, his fingers slipped from the face of the flashlight, leaving the electric beam to flare up with a brilliance that brought a gasp from both of them. Carlos fumbled for the switch, and the light blinked out. The darkness closed in like a heavy black blanket as they stood again, frozen, listening.

Once again it seemed they'd been fortunate. That flash of brilliance must have been visible in the camp only twenty meters away through the maze of hardwood trees, but they heard no stir to indicate that anyone had been awake to see it.

"We will have to move without a light," Carlos whispered, and the despair in his words echoed Julie's.

"How far will that get us?" she whispered back with vivid memories of her stumbling, groping trek from the airport to San Ignacio. There at least she'd had a path and some glimmer of moon and stars. "We won't make it a kilometer if we have to feel our way through that!" And how soon before someone awakened to discover their missing guard and prisoner? They would be after them with lights that would not have to be shielded from searching eyes.

Shielded.

"Here, let me have that flashlight!" Julie fumbled in the darkness to remove the flashlight from Carlos's hand, then slid her knapsack from his shoulder. "If we're here to use the latrine, let me use it."

Pulling the rickety door shut after her, Julie switched on the flashlight, setting it face down to the ground to limit even the smallest seepage of light through the cracks in the bamboo walls. Hurriedly under its faint illumination, she rummaged through her knapsack. To do so, she had to shove together the two boards propped over the open hole and kneel on them, but she ignored both her precarious perch and the stench of the sewage below as she pulled out what Julie called her "survival kit"—a tight little package that stayed in her knapsack from one trip to the next and hadn't been removed with notepad and computer. Extra pens. Super Glue. Scissors. Batteries for the recorder that had also been confiscated. A tiny sewing kit and some basic over-the-counter medications. And a roll of masking tape.

Triumphantly, Julie snatched up the tape. Switching off the flashlight again, she propped it between her knees face up and hastily began ripping off lengths of tape, crisscrossing the glass lens with them until, at one too hasty movement, she lost her grip on the tape. A thick splash told her where it had landed. But it had served its purpose, and when Julie switched on the flashlight, only a faint glow made it through the thick layers of tape. Little more, in fact, than the luminescence of a clock face at night. It would be enough.

Carlos was nervously pacing back and forth in front of the latrine as she emerged. His eyes widened with relieved approval when he saw what Julie had done. Reaching again for her knapsack, he nodded for Julie to go ahead with the flashlight, his AK-47 unslung and cradled across his chest as he followed hard on her heels, his nervous glance going continually back over his shoulder.

The sounds of pursuit for which they braced themselves never came, and though the dim glow through the masking tape wasn't enough to really illuminate their way, it allowed them to make out the next massive hardwood trunk and then the next. Their pace quickened as they grew accustomed to the faint glow marking the next step ahead of them, and with each added meter between them and the camp, the knot in Julie's stomach eased and Carlos looked less frequently over his shoulder.

Dawn came not with the pinks and oranges of open sky but as a gradual lightening to gray, almost imperceptible at first, until Julie realized suddenly her light was no longer leaving any impression on the tree trunk in front of her. When they could see each other clearly, Carlos stored the flashlight away in Julie's knapsack, and they quickened their pace until they were moving almost at a trot.

"They will be awake now," Carlos told Julie, and he no longer bothered to whisper. "But I do not think they will be able to overtake us. Even if they can follow our tracks—and Jaime at least knows the ways of the woods— it will take them much time to trace the way we have gone."

Not long afterward, it began to rain.

Though it didn't last long, it was a thorough downpour, one of the last torrential gasps of the rainy season, thundering like a percussion band on the jungle canopy overhead and dumping rivulets of water down palm fronds and tangles of vines. Soon they were both soaked through. But for once Julie minded neither the wet nor the mud, for the same thought was in her mind that Carlos voiced as he surveyed the rushing streams the rain had left across their back trail.

"They will never catch us now. Our tracks will be washed away so that not even Jaime can find them again."

The utter relief in his voice and the sudden relaxing of the drawn lines of his face told Julie he'd been less confident of their escape than he'd given her to believe. Julie herself felt almost giddy with the release of fear. After all the weeks of captivity, the gradual acceptance that she might never be released, the shock of that death sentence, and these last hours of forced march with every sense straining back over her shoulder for the pursuit that was certain to come, it didn't seem possible she was really free. She wanted to shatter the jungle's quiet with her jubilation or let loose a torrent of pent-up tears. Instead, she leaned against a tree trunk and said dazedly, "I . . . I just can't believe it. We really did it!"

Her head turned sideways to where Carlos was already using the halt to check his weapon for water damage. "No, you did it," she said quietly. "Carlos, I . . . there just aren't words enough for what you've done."

A dark flush rose up to stain his cheekbones, and as he shook his head in mute denial, she had mercy on his discomfiture and added matter-of-factly, "So what do we do now? Do you have any idea where we are, Carlos? Or how we're going to find our way out of here?"

The relief fled from his face. His eyes dropped to the ground, and Julie saw the budding Adam's apple on his throat move before he raised his eyes to admit resolutely, "Señorita Julia, I . . . I was not giving any thought to where we were going. I thought only of escape. I . . . I am afraid we are lost."

His dejection was clear, and Julie hastened to reassure him. "It's okay, Carlos. You've done well—incredibly well! Think of it this way. If we don't know where we are, they won't either."

Pushing up the sleeve of her fatigues, Julie checked her watch. Seven-thirty. They'd been pushing through the jungle for almost three hours. No wonder she was tired.

"Do you think it's safe to take a break?"

Wiping the AK-47 with his shirt, Carlos restored the weapon to his shoulder. "Perhaps it would be best. While we decide what to do."

For a spot to break their trek, it wasn't a bad choice. The umbrella canopy of the hardwoods through which they had come had kept the underbrush scarce and allowed them to see back through the trees the way they had come. Directly ahead not twenty meters away, Julie could see blue sky between two tall trunks and with it a resultant explosion of plant life. Ferns and elephant ears—not the dainty versions sold back home as house plants but towering higher than a man. And beyond them, a glimpse of reeds and tall grasses.

That much vegetation could only mean a slough. The jungle swamps, choked with grass and floating hummocks of vegetation and infested with water snakes and crocodiles, could extend for kilometers. Carlos and Julie would have to turn to the right or to the left to circumvent it.

In the meantime, the simple dance of sunlight on leaves and tree trunks did much to lift Julie's spirits. Nearby to her right, an enormous tropical cedar that had stood at the edge of the slough lay toppled to the ground, felled either by storm or disease. The opening its fall had left in the canopy had allowed the tangle of ferns and elephant ears to proliferate along its rotting length, promising cover if they should need it.

*Now why am I thinking of that? We've lost them.*

But the thought dimmed some of Julie's lifted spirits. Sinking down onto the ground, she leaned wearily against a protruding root. Carlos stood beside her, the AK-47 cradled in his hands as though he were still on guard. This time his surveillance was directed outward instead of at Julie, his eyes roving constantly from side to side, an indication that he too felt a lingering unease.

Julie's stomach cramped from hunger as well as tension, reminding her of other problems they had as well. To quiet her fears, she said quickly, "Tell me, Carlos, now that we have a minute. How did you find out? That they were going to kill me, I mean—Enrique and the others."

Carlos made one last scan of their back trail before dropping down to the root beside her, lowering the AK-47 to rest across his knees. "I heard them. In the *cambuche*. After Rafael replaced me as guard. I . . . I have never disobeyed the *comandante* before. But I could not believe he would come only to bring supplies or to order your release when any of his men could have done so. When he did not even ask to interrogate you, I . . . I grew afraid. And so when I was released from duty, I did what is forbidden and slipped up in the dark behind the *cambuche* to listen. That is how I found that I was right to be afraid. *El comandante* told the others—Victor and Enrique and Jaime—that it had been determined you were indeed not the spy they had thought and that he could no longer waste fighters to guard you. He said you could not be released because he had told your government the *paramilitares* had you, so you would have to be disposed of. It was Enrique who said they should take you away from the camp and dispose of you there."

Enrique! So much for any illusions that he'd harbored any friendly thoughts toward her.

"Enrique said it might be troubling for some of the guards to see you killed. That sometimes the guards grew attached to their captives and that it would be better to take you away before disposing of you." Carlos slid his glance away from Julie. "I . . . I think he meant me because I once knew you. And perhaps some of the others. In any case, the *comandante* said this was what he also had in mind. He said it would be announced that you were to be released, so you would go quietly when the time came."

*That rat!* Julie thought bitterly, and whether she was thinking of the FARC commander or Enrique, she wasn't sure. "And what about Tim?"

She hadn't had time during the terror of their escape and their mad dash through the jungle to give more than a fleeting thought to her fellow prisoner. Now she had the leisure to wonder—and worry—about his welfare. He'd practically ordered Julie not to try to escape. But that was before the alternative had been death. Would they still punish him? Or had he too, unknowingly, already been condemned to death?

Carlos was shaking his head. "I heard a noise then and was afraid of being seen, so I slipped away. But though nothing was said, I think some of the others knew the truth. I heard Linda laughing with Rafael, and it was your name they spoke. Nor do I think they cared about your death. I wanted to warn you then, but it was not my turn to guard. Then Marcela asked that I take the early morning watch for her because she wished to stay with Victor before he left the camp, and I knew then what I would do. But I still had to wait until Rafael, who was on guard before me, was deep asleep before I could awaken you."

Julie swallowed. So modestly he'd dismissed his own courage. Not to mention the agonizing choice it had to have been between the comrades who had become his new family and a condemned prisoner to whom he owed nothing but a childhood acquaintance. How much easier—and certainly safer—it would have been just to shut eyes and ears and let her disappear out of his life.

"You saved my life," she said again. "I can never thank you enough. But what are you going to do now? Do you still believe in what *Comandante* Aguilera is doing? Are . . . are you going to go back to fighting?"

He looked away, and his adolescent Adam's apple rose and fell before he said softly, *"Comandante* Aguilera has been kind to me—like a father in the time after the *paramilitares* butchered my family. He gave me food and shelter and a new life, and I will always be grateful to him for that. But in this he is wrong. I still believe in what the revolution teaches. I believe the social wrongs and the injustice that plague our country must be addressed if there is ever to be peace. But not like this—I see that now. If the *comandante* will have an innocent woman killed just because you are not convenient to his plans, then he will do other things that are unjust as well. And so will the other guerrillas. How can they bring peace to Colombia any more than those who already practice corruption and injustice in high places?"

He swallowed again. "No, I will not go back to the revolution. I . . . I miss my family, but I do not want anymore to kill. You were right. It will not bring them back. And it is not how my family would wish me to avenge their deaths." His young face looked suddenly forlorn, like a lost child. "I do not know what I will do. It has been so long—I can hardly remember a life without fighting and training and running. Perhaps . . . what I would truly wish to do is to return to school. To become the professional my father hoped I would be someday. But . . ."—he lifted his shoulders in what was meant to be indifference but failed—"what future is there in this world for one who has been a guerrilla? The authorities would never permit it."

Julie's throat tightened as she looked up at the young man sitting on the root just above her. Carlos had seen his family murdered, had spent the years that should have been his youth fighting a bloody war for a losing cause, had learned to face up unflinchingly to hardship and hunger and pain, and had developed a multitude of other skills that were valueless in the more civilized world in which Julie had spent the last seven years.

Yet despite the camouflage fatigues and the combat cap and the almost frightening air of competence with which he handled that AK-47, he was only seventeen years old. A child still with a whole life stretching before him. A life that would hold more than rage and bitterness and painful memories if she, Julie Baker, had anything to do with it.

"You will," she told him softly. "You will go to school and to university, and you will have a future in this country or any other you choose if I have to turn two state departments on end to make it happen."

A sudden light flared in Carlos's eyes, and for a moment his young face was alive with warring hope and disbelief. "You can really do that, Señorita Julia?"

The jerk of his body came simultaneously with the clap of gunfire.

It was so unexpected that Julie's mind at first refused to process it. Then another fury of thunder stitched a row of bullet wounds across the tree trunk above her head. Scrambling to her feet, Julie rolled rather than dove after Carlos over the root where they had been sitting. As she hit the ground, she caught a glimpse of dappled green and olive detaching itself from a tree to their left. Above it Linda's face twisted in malevolent triumph. Julie froze behind the inadequate cover of the root system as Linda raised her Galil automatic rifle again.

Then Carlos's AK-47 came up beside her, and his answering blast almost deafened Julie's ears. A scream rose from the trees to their left, and Linda ducked under cover. But the scream had been of rage, not pain, so Julie didn't think Carlos had hit anything. Obeying his frantic gesture, Julie rose and sprinted toward the nearest cover—the fallen cedar with its explosion of vegetation overgrowing it. Carlos was right behind her, running awkwardly backward so that he was facing the attack. As Julie scrambled under a tangle of ferns, he let loose another long burst of gunfire before diving in beside her, and this time the *rat-tat-tat* that responded came not from Linda's Galil, but another AK-47 or an M-16.

*Where had they come from?* Julie wondered, twisting around to look back. Even if the guerrillas had been hard on their heels from the beginning—and surely she and Carlos would have seen some glimmer of searchlights if that were the case—they should have had more of a respite than this. It was simply impossible. And yet there they were!

As Carlos dropped to his belly and slammed another clip into his assault rifle, Julie saw them, pushing through the belt of reeds and grass and elephant ears that marked the edge of the swamp. Rafael had a machete and was chopping a path with one hand while the AK-47 in his other sprayed an indiscriminate volley of gunfire into the air. Stepping out from behind him, Victor and Jaime sprinted for cover behind the nearest tree trunk, their weapons up and blazing. Farther in, where Julie had seen Linda, she spotted Alberto and Enrique racing forward in a zigzag pattern through the trees.

No wonder they had so quickly overtaken the fugitives. The guerrilla band hadn't followed Carlos and Julie's trail at all. Instead, they had evidently taken the much faster route of the waterways, following the rivers up into the swamp either by boat or dugout canoe. They had radios to whistle up men and equipment. But how in all the universe had they known where to intercept their escaped prisoners when even Julie and Carlos hadn't known where they were running?

The two fugitives were hidden from view, the ferns overhead swallowing them up in a lacy green arch. But their pursuers knew where they had gone to ground. Julie heard Victor's shout. Then a line of camouflage fatigues, hardly visible against the vegetation, began to flit forward among the tall columns of the trees.

Carlos let loose another spray of bullets. He was deliberately aiming high, Julie realized as she saw the bits of bark fly well above the heads of the oncoming guerrillas. But the blast had the effect of freezing their advance. As the running figures dove for cover, Julie heard Victor's harsh order. "Enrique—go left! Rafael—to the right!"

"They are afraid to come in after us now," Carlos whispered urgently. "They will circle to cut us off instead. We must reach the other side first. Now, go! We do not have long!"

Motioning frantically for her to move, Carlos raised his AK-47 to his shoulder again. As Julie scrambled deeper into the underbrush, he let loose a final round before crawling after her. It wasn't easy to move fast, Julie found. The very explosion of life that curved fern fronds and elephant ears above their heads had left a tangle of other growth to choke their path— vines and other thorny plants that snatched at Julie's feet and tore at her clothes, pressing in around her. Sometimes she was running forward at a half crouch while other times she was forced to her hands and knees or even to her belly as she wormed her way under a tangle of vines.

Julie could hear Carlos at her heels, his breathing loud and raspy as though the pace of their escape had taken more out of him than she had realized, but she dared not pause even to glance over her shoulder. She weighed their options as she pushed onward. The fallen cedar was far big-

ger in circumference than a man was tall, and they would have to abandon
their cover to climb over it. They had entered the underbrush where the
crown of the huge tree had hit the ground, and while its branches were
choked and tangled with the plant life that had grown up through them,
the branches themselves were no thicker here than a normal tree trunk.
Julie was able to scramble alternatively over and under them. If they could
get through this labyrinth to the other side . . .

What then?

Pushing aside a riot of orchids that would have brought a fortune in a
florist shop, Julie stepped across a limb to find herself in an open space
created by the fork of two large branches. Breaking with relief into a run,
she was halfway across the V-shaped break in the maze when she realized
Carlos was no longer at her heels. She glanced back to see him lift his leg
with an audible grunt to clear the log she had crossed, his shoulders bowed
under the weight of her knapsack and his assault rifle and the heavy ammo
vest he was wearing. Julie was reminded with sudden guilt that he had been
carrying the full weight of their possessions. No wonder he was tired!

She caught sight of his face and saw with a shock that his grunt was not
from exhaustion but pain. She saw the dark stain soaking through the
camouflage material of his pant leg.

"Carlos, you're hurt!" Racing back to his side, Julie helped him ease his
leg over the log, then caught him as he slumped to the ground on the
other side. "You're bleeding! Why didn't you tell me you'd been hit?"

"It was when we ran for cover. It . . . it is nothing—just a scratch."
Carlos struggled to his feet, and Julie saw with alarm the drops of fresh
scarlet on the ground where he was standing and another trail of red marking the branch he had just crossed as well as the broken twigs and leaves he
had cut across before it.

"Carlos, you can't go on like this. You're losing blood badly!"

Already Julie was pushing him back to the ground, and it was a sign of his
weakness that he didn't resist but slumped with a groan of pain to the tangle
of orchids and moss that carpeted the open V between the forked branches.
Easing her knapsack from his shoulder, Julie rooted frantically inside until
she found what she was looking for—the silk slip she had tucked in along
with her one dress for that possible special occasion that had never arisen.

Ripping the slip right up to its elastic band to double its length, she
slipped it under his pant leg above where the blood stained the cloth and

yanked it tight. She was probably doing it all wrong, but the rapidity with which the stain was spreading and the bloodless pallor of his face terrified her. Rooting again in her knapsack, Julie found the scissors from her survival kit and slit open his pant leg just below the tourniquet. Carlos bit into his lip hard enough to bring back the color as she ripped away the material, but he made no other sound.

What lay underneath was even worse than Julie had anticipated. Yanking out the dress that was to have gone with the slip, she pressed it to the wound. The dress had been a dainty cream affair, and Julie had to bite back her despair while the tourniquet above the wound immediately turned crimson. She was reaching for another article of clothing when Carlos stopped her with a hand on hers.

"There is no time for this. Listen! We have been still too long, and I . . . I am afraid they have been following my trail. They know where we are, and they are coming in after us."

He was right. Julie could hear it too as she lifted her head to listen. A rustle that was not the wind sounded from a patch of elephant ears beyond the labyrinth of branches. Then the sharp snap of a twig under someone's boot. Emboldened by their long silence, the guerrillas were closing in on them. Struggling to a sitting position, Carlos rested his AK-47 on the log and fired off a burst. A loud curse followed, then silence. Carlos slumped back with a groan. "That will not hold them long. You must go before they try again."

"I . . . I don't think we can, Carlos!" Her makeshift pressure bandage had finally stemmed the flow of blood, but Julie didn't dare lift her hands from it lest it start again. "There is no way you can walk on this."

"I know I can't." His voice was suddenly wooden, his face without expression as Julie glanced in surprise. "Even if I could walk, I would only hold you back. That is why you must go on without me."

"But . . ." Julie stared at him in dismay. "How can I? They'll take you prisoner!"

"They'll take us both prisoner if you don't!"

Julie shook her head in disbelief. How could he be so calm about this—as though he were the adult instead of her? "But Carlos, you said they'd shoot you! There's no way I'm going to leave you to them! Not even if they catch both of us again."

"But you must!" The adult reasonableness of his tone dissolved into urgency. "If they catch you, they will kill you for sure! And me—I exaggerated. Remember that the *comandante* has been as a father to me. They will take me prisoner, to be sure. Punish me perhaps. But shoot me—no, that would be too much. Now, please . . ." His young face twisted suddenly with an anguish that was not just the pain of his injury. "Go, Señorita Julia! Do not make all of this for nothing. You cannot help me by staying. At least let me know my help has not been in vain."

He was right, and Julie knew she should go, if only to get out that warning and the news that Tim was in captivity, and because there was an old man whose heart was breaking over her loss. She could do nothing by being caught again, but she could accomplish much with her freedom. That didn't make the doing of it easier.

Julie bent her head over the bloody cloth beneath her hands, and with tears burning in her eyes she whispered desolately, "Oh, Carlos, this is all my fault! If only I hadn't come here! I was so determined to get my big story—and I didn't really think about anything else or anyone. And now I've hurt so many people by coming here. I . . . I just can't bear it if something happens to you too!"

Carlos dropped a hand from the barrel of the AK-47 to cover hers, and though it was sticky with blood, its grip was surprisingly strong. "No, don't say that. Don't ever say that. You, Señorita Julia, you cannot know what it has meant to me that you came. All these years, so many long years since . . . since my family, it seemed to me as though God had left me too, as though He were so far away that I would never find Him again. And I have been so afraid! Afraid of killing. Afraid I would not have the courage to kill when I had to. Afraid that one day I would look down the barrel of my gun and find someone that I knew in its sights. And then—you walked down from that plane."

The wonder in his voice drew Julie's head up, startled. "When you came, it was as though God Himself leaned down from heaven to say, 'See, Carlos, I haven't forgotten you.' You gave me hope that there was another way, another life than killing. Señorita Julia, you are here because God sent you to me. I know this as surely as I know that I live."

Julie shook her head, the tears streaming down her cheeks and splashing hot onto both of their hands. "But . . . but I couldn't save you! Just like I couldn't save my parents! You saved my life, and now you're hurt, and they're going to catch you . . . and maybe punish you, and it's because of me!"

Carlos moved his head in a negating gesture. The wonder was still in his eyes, along with the fear. "Don't you see? You have already saved me, Señorita Julia. Whatever happens, it does not really matter. I will not go to my family, to my God, with blood on my hands. Besides . . ."

A brief smile twisted at the pain lines around his mouth, and the bravery of it wrenched Julie's heart. ". . . I will be all right. I will be a prisoner, but I will be alive, and perhaps when you are free, you may send to ransom me. They will not ask too much for one such as I. Now, you must go quickly. No, do not forget your bag. You may need it. Hurry, before it is too late! This is my last ammunition clip."

Another rustle sounded in the elephant ears, this one closer, and Carlos fired off another burst of the AK-47. An answering burst came from somewhere on the other side of the forked branches. None of the shots came anywhere close, and as soon as they stopped, Julie obeyed Carlos's urgent gesture and got reluctantly to her feet. At least this way he would get medical attention. Snatching up her knapsack, she sprinted across the open V. As she scrambled over the other branch of the tree fork, Carlos let loose another burst, this one shorter. Then she heard behind her the audible click of an empty gun.

The guerrillas had heard it too. This time there was no answering gunfire but a shout, then the crackle of pursuers who were no longer trying to be stealthy. Julie knew she should keep going, that it was foolishness to waste precious seconds. But she couldn't go without knowing. She crouched on the other side of the fork, hidden by a drooping frond of a dwarf palm, and looked back.

She saw Victor step over the log and wrest the AK-47 from Carlos's grasp. And she saw his next action, so quick and without hesitation she would not have had time to scream her protest even if it hadn't caught in her throat. There were no words, no recrimination, not even anger on his impassive dark features as Victor slid the pistol from his belt, put it to Carlos's temple and pulled the trigger.

Julie gagged as Carlos twitched once, then slumped sideways. Linda stepped over the log behind Victor, and the spiteful pleasure with which she glanced down at the dead boy, then turned to search the open space, galvanized Julie into movement. Dropping to her hands and knees, she scrambled into the underbrush, worming her way into a dense tangle of vines and orchids. Behind her she heard Linda's angry shout. "Where is the girl?" Then Alberto calling, "Which way now, Victor?"

Julie wanted to stop and cry—or at least throw up. But she threw herself frantically forward even as the horror of what she'd just seen replayed itself in vivid technicolor over and over in her mind. Had Carlos known what would happen? Julie was certain he had, despite his assurances to her. He had deliberately sacrificed himself to let her get away.

With that conviction, Julie's horror and the terror that propelled her onward gave way to a terrible anger and a steely determination. She was not going to let these men—and women—waste that sacrifice. As Carlos had said, she could not allow this to be for nothing. She would get away, and she would be free, and if she couldn't bring Carlos back, she would at least bring retribution on these people if . . .

*If it's the last thing I do.*

A sob caught in Julie's throat, but she pressed forward, crawling under branches, rising to a hunch-backed scuttle when the tangle around her lifted a little, pushing herself always to greater speed until she was gasping for breath and she didn't know whether the salt trickling into her mouth was tears or sweat.

The resistance to her groping hands gave way so suddenly that Julie sprawled forward onto the ground. She was out of the underbrush, and ahead of her lay only the tall columns of the hardwoods and the open forest floor between them. Pushing herself to her feet, Julie broke into a staggering run. If she could put enough of those massive tree trunks behind her before her hunters burst out of the underbrush . . .

That was when she saw him.

He was standing in a direct line between Julie and the beckoning freedom of the forest trees, tense and motionless and almost invisible in his battle fatigues against the dappled backdrop of a moss-draped tree trunk, his head raised high as it turned in a slow, deliberate survey, his AK-47 unslung and cradled in a rock-steady grip. Enrique Martinez had obeyed Victor's orders to circle around, and he was waiting for her.

Julie checked in momentary panic. She saw to her left the belt of grasses and reeds and other tall plants that marked the edge of the swamp through which the guerrillas had come. It was a dangerous place with the possibility of snakes and alligators and other things she didn't even want to think about. But its cover was her only chance. Julie veered in that direction.

She was too late. Her movement had caught Enrique's peripheral vision.

He spun around, the AK-47 coming up as he did. Julie braced herself for the impact of the bullets. But they didn't come, and for a measureless instant his eyes held hers, the guerrilla killer who had once saved her life and now had planned her death, and Julie saw blazing fury there and a determination as steely as her own. As Julie whirled around and began to run, he broke into an easy lope in her direction.

He didn't shout for his companions, but ran as silently as she, shoving his assault rifle back over his shoulder for easier movement as he did so, racing through the zigzag pattern of the trees at a tangent calculated to cut Julie off before she reached the cover of the swamp.

Julie ran with a speed born of despair, forcing her laboring lungs to find fresh reserves from somewhere. But he was fast and strong, and he wasn't exhausted by hours of marching or that last desperate scramble through the brush. When she glanced sideways, he had gained on her visibly, and though Julie wouldn't let herself look again, the heavy pounding of his boots grew ever louder and closer in her ears. Her outstretched hands were brushing the first green fronds of the swamp when she felt a hand come down hard on her shoulder, spinning her around to meet the molten copper blaze of his glare.

She had lost, Julie knew with despair. He had caught her, and he would kill her as his companions had killed Carlos. But she wouldn't give him the satisfaction of making this easy for him. If she had to go down, she would go down fighting, as Carlos had.

As he shifted his grip to her arms, Julie fought back, lashing out with feet and hands, twisting and turning in his grip, and more than once she almost broke free. The fury of her resistance carried them deeper into the vegetation that edged the swamp. Fronds closed in above them and mud oozed over her shoes. He grunted as her teeth sank into the heavy material of his sleeve, and for one hopeful moment his grip slackened.

But he was vastly stronger than she, and the adrenaline that had carried her this far was ebbing fast. Though it seemed she had fought him for an eternity, it was probably only seconds before he caught her hands behind her back and kicked her feet out from under her. Julie lay face down with mud in her mouth and the heavy length of his body pressing her down so she couldn't breathe, and she could feel the shudder of his quickened breathing against her back and smell the sharp tang of his sweat and the faintest lingering musk of his cologne.

Then she felt his diaphragm tighten for speech, and his breath came hot and close against her ear. When he spoke, it was nothing her wildest imagination could have expected.

"Would you shut up and keep still before you get us both killed?"

His low furious order had been in English, not Spanish, and Julie grew instantly still under the weight of his body as it registered that he hadn't spoken in the stilted accent she'd heard the guerrilla fighter use until now, but with the idiomatic fluency of a native-born American.

As though he sensed her capitulation, her captor slackened his grip and rolled off her so she could breathe. Rolling over, Julie stared up at him, stunned, taking in—as though she had never seen him before—the hard, clean planes of his face, shadowed now by the lack of a shave that morning, the unyielding lines of jaw and mouth only inches above her, and the narrowed gaze that was not looking down at her but was already busy searching their surroundings with the professional vigilance of a soldier.

"You're not a guerrilla!" she whispered with sudden incredulous certainty. "You're not even Colombian, are you? But if . . . if you aren't Enrique Martinez, who are you?"

His glance flickered briefly to her face before he rolled with one smooth movement to his feet and reached down to pull her up. "Captain Rick Martini," he answered curtly, "7th Special Operations Group, Fort Bragg, North Carolina."

# EIGHTEEN

"NOW, GET THAT UNIFORM OFF!" Enrique—no, Rick—yanked at her knapsack, pulling it loose from her shoulder, where it had somehow managed to stay during all her frantic scramble. Julie stared at him in bewildered outrage. Had he lost his mind—or had she?

He was already rifling through the bag, yanking out a pair of the khaki pants and shirts she'd packed for the trip and hadn't touched in these last weeks. Shoving them into her arms, he snapped impatiently, "They've got a tracker device on you. How do you think we found you? We've got maybe two minutes until they're on us, so stop wasting time."

Julie went cold as his meaning sunk in. She scrambled to unbutton the shirt of her camouflage fatigues and tug off her shoes to pull off the heavy pants. Rick turned his back on her and stepped away. Pulling a two-way radio from his belt, he barked into it in the flawless Colombian Spanish that turned him suddenly back into Enrique, the guerrilla. "Go right! Go right! She's out there and headed away from the swamp!"

The reeds and swamp grasses closed around Julie so that she couldn't see, but she could hear the thrashing and snap of broken branches as her pursuers burst out of the underbrush. A blast of gunfire followed, directed toward the woods rather than the swamp, a total waste of ammunition since the guerrillas rather obviously had no target in sight. She heard Victor echo Rick's order. "Go right! Go right! She's in the woods!"

Julie was buttoning up the khaki shirt with fingers trembling from haste as Rick spun around on his heel. "That will give us maybe five minutes—until Rafael over on the other side lets them know you didn't come that direction. You're lucky I found you and not him or you'd be dead right now," he informed her curtly, as though she needed that information. "Now where's the boy?"

Julie swallowed hard against a fresh stinging in her eyes. "He . . . he's dead! Victor shot him."

Rick's mouth set grimly, but he wasted no time asking for further details. As Julie tugged her sneakers on over the soggy mess her quick change had made of her socks, he scooped up her muddy fatigues from the ground.

Running his fingers along the bottom edge of the shirt, he stopped as he came to a small protuberance under the hem. "There it is." Taking a banana clip out of one of the pockets of the ammo vest he was wearing, he swiftly wrapped the uniform around it. "It's a waste of ammo we might need later, but I don't see any rocks out here."

Leaving her side, he pushed through the reeds until he was out of sight. Julie heard a splash. Then he was back. "Let's go! Their tracker is an old Russian-bought one—nothing like ours. American, I mean. It'll give a GPS coordinate, but their grid is so small, all they can do is pinpoint a general location and rely on a visual to ID the suspect. With that bug buried in a couple meters of swamp water, they'll have to check every bush before they can be certain you're no longer in the area."

His explanation had lost Julie. But it didn't matter. She'd caught the pertinent points. The guerrillas had not just depended on their guards but had planted some kind of tracking device in the clothing Linda had given her. One more indication of her importance to the guerrillas—or rather, the spy they'd thought her to be—since they surely didn't waste such expensive and hard-to-get technology on their typical kidnap victim. Another gift from Aguilera's *musulmanes* allies?

And Enrique—or rather Rick Martini. Julie's mind was still reeling with the effort to process this new development. First Sondra, then Tim, and now Enrique. Was anyone who they appeared to be? The hand radio at the guerrilla fighter's belt sputtered static. No, she couldn't call him a guerrilla anymore. What was he? She'd just have to call him Rick.

"Enrique! Where are you?" The angry voice through the static belonged to Victor. "We don't see the girl anywhere!"

Rick snatched the radio again from his belt. "Keep heading straight. I'm going after her. You'll catch up with me if you stay on her trail."

He hit a button, and the radio went dead. "We're going to have to keep this off. Which is too bad, as we won't be able to track what they're up to. With any luck they won't realize I've gone AWOL for some time yet. Now, let's get out of here. You step where I step. And keep up!"

Unlike Carlos, Rick made no gallant offer to add her load to his own but stepped out immediately, AK-47 in hand, barrel pointed upward, leaving Julie to snatch up her knapsack and scurry after him. He led her not up onto firm ground but through the tall reeds that bordered the swamp, and he was not moving as Julie had, in a headlong scramble that strove for as much speed as possible, but carefully, almost slowly, sliding between the reeds and the occasional patches of ferns and elephants ears so noiselessly, their tops didn't sway. Julie, stretching her legs to match his longer stride, wanted to scream to him to hurry, to run. And why was he dragging her through this mud and water and who knew what else when dry land lay only meters away?

Glancing back, Julie saw that swamp water was filling their tracks almost as fast as they abandoned them, and that the reeds closing behind them gave no sign of the trampled trail she'd left behind in her own scramble. He knew what he was doing, she admitted grudgingly. Who—or what—was this man? Seventh Special Operations Group . . . where had she heard that before?

Of course! The Green Berets Bill Shidler had mentioned when they were flying over San José. What had he said—that there were Green Berets training Colombian counter-narcotics forces there? Was this Captain Rick Martini one of them? Did he know Colonel Thornton?

Keeping her eyes on the green and brown of Rick's back, Julie concentrated on setting her feet precisely in his steps. Rick had shoved his assault rifle back up on his shoulder where it couldn't bump into anything, but Julie could see his hand hovering near a sheathed knife on his belt, and as he slipped silently forward through the reeds, he was constantly swiveling his head from side to side. Every few meters he turned to glance back, not at Julie but over her head to study their back trail. He might almost have forgotten that Julie herself was at his heels except for her clear impression that nothing went on around him that those narrowed eyes did not note.

Their leisurely pace lasted only until they stumbled upon a stream draining into the swamp. At first it was just a muddy, meandering delta where it trickled through the reeds and grass. But once Rick swerved their path into it, a few paces brought them into the open where a narrow brook burbled between shallow banks that led at a right angle from the swamp edge deep into the tall marching columns of the rainforest. There was nothing to be gained now by stealth, and Rick immediately lengthened his stride to a trot, splashing up the middle of the stream as easily as though he were on dry land.

This time Julie instantly grasped the reason for his action. Like the swamp edge, the brook would hide their passage from anyone still following their trail. She didn't like the feeling of exposure the open forest gave her so she willingly quickened her pace as well.

But she couldn't keep it up for long. The rushing water that Rick was splashing through as though it were not there came almost to Julie's knees, and the stones on the stream bottom made footing precarious. She struggled to dredge up an added reserve of strength, but in the last horrible hours she had dredged up too many such reserves, and she simply had none left to give. Her breathing, which had slowed almost to normal during their unhurried procession through the reeds, came hard again, and her side felt on fire. She wanted to double over with the pain of it.

She had fallen a dozen paces behind when Rick swung around, his impatience clear in the tight set of his jaw. "Is there a problem?"

Julie halted right where she was in the middle of the stream, bending over so her hands rested on her knees, her hair hanging down into her face as she panted for breath.

"Yes, there's a problem!" she retorted. "I've been running for hours. I'm dead tired! My side is killing me! I can't keep going like this." Julie felt an odd nibbling where her sock had slid down into her wet sneakers and stifled a shriek as she caught sight of something black and shapeless attached there. "And I'm being eaten by leeches!"

Rick splashed back to her side. Without a word, he unsheathed his knife and reached down to flick the leech free from her ankle. Straightening up, he made a quick scan downstream, then up. "Okay, I think we've lost them. We'll take a short breather. Can you walk just a little farther? I'd prefer better cover than this."

Suppressing a groan, Julie stood up straight and splashed slowly after him onto the bank. "I can walk fine. Just don't ask me to run."

Rick kept his stride down to a sedate walk as he led Julie away from the stream. He didn't allow them to rest in the open but kept walking until they came to an odd experiment of nature. Two mahogany trees had survived the sapling stage a little too close together so that as they grew, the two trunks had grown into one.

Eventually, either the symbiotic relationship or some disease had killed the trees, for now the only green festooning their branches was of moss and a tangle of vines that made the whole thing look like a jungle gym for Tarzan. At the base of the double trunk, rot from ground moisture had eaten into the dead wood, leaving an opening that led into its interior. Producing a penlight from another pocket of his ammo vest, Rick flashed it around inside.

"It's empty. We'll take fifteen minutes."

As they stepped inside, Julie saw that the hollow was bigger than she'd expected, extending the width of both trunks and above them as well. The parasitical relationship of the mahogany twins had kept them from growing to normal height so that the fork where they branched out into their first limbs was only about twenty feet overhead. This too was rotted through so that a dim green light filtered down through the opening.

Empty pods and a pile of rotted grass and twigs indicated that some animal had once had a den here. But there was no sign of residents now, and the floor of the hollow was agreeably dry. Julie sank gratefully down onto it, slipping her knapsack from her shoulder. Beside her, Rick lowered himself to the floor as well. Julie noticed he had positioned himself directly opposite the opening where he could watch what lay outside, and she saw him glance upward as though measuring the opening overhead for an escape route.

Leaning her head against the rotting wood, Julie eyed him surreptitiously. She'd had no time since his astonishing revelation to do more than slip and slide at his heels. She made a conscious effort to reshuffle his image into this new shape that was not a guerrilla or the killer she'd presumed him to be, but a soldier of her own country. An elite soldier at that.

It wasn't so difficult once the surprise had worn off. Even Julie's inexperienced eye had caught the trained grace of his walk and the expertise of his fighting skills that far outstripped seasoned guerrillas like Victor, and were certainly nothing like the under-equipped and poorly trained Colombian soldiers Julie had known in her childhood.

He didn't even look particularly Colombian, now that Julie knew he wasn't. His hair, no longer styled ruthlessly back but a sweat-darkened tangle that had grown to shoulder length during their weeks in the jungle, and the mustache that edged the firm line of his upper lip were both somewhat lighter than her own curls. His skin was tanned rather than brown, and his eyes were lighter than her own coffee brown as well, and tinged with green in this light. She'd seen them blaze copper when he was angry.

Though there were many Colombians as light-skinned, especially around Bogotá where many Europeans had settled, like Julie he could have been one of many ethnic backgrounds, and it had been his flawless Spanish with its unmistakable Colombian lilt and the stiff accent of his English that had made him so convincing to Julie—and, it would seem, to the guerrillas as well.

"So, who are you?" she asked quietly as his glance dropped from the fork overhead to her face. "What were you doing in that camp—and on that plane? And why are you pretending to be a guerrilla?"

A puzzle piece she'd not yet had time to consider fell into place, and she added, "You're the spy they've been looking for, aren't you? The one they thought was with the UN mission."

Rick rose to peer out the opening in the trunk. "I guess there's no point in denying that now. The guerrillas were tipped off—and I'm going to find out how when we get out of here—that the Americans were sending some-one in besides the official team to investigate the deaths of our citizens. What they didn't know was that I was already in on the ground—part of an operation to find out just what the guerrillas were up to here in the DMZ. I'd spent months working my way close to the leadership of this area's FARC front when this whole environmentalist thing blew up. When Aguilera started agitating about a spy, I was afraid my cover was blown until I found out they were concentrating on the UN mission. No problem. You'd all be here and gone in a day, and I could get back to work."

His jaw tightened as he pulled his head back inside to glance over at Julie. "It was bad enough when Aguilera chose to parade me on interna-tional television where anyone in my unit or even some of the Colombians I've trained might recognize me and wonder what a Special Forces training officer is doing hobnobbing with the local FARC big wheels. I never dreamed anyone would be dumb enough to sneak out of that airport and give the guerrillas reason to believe that their reports of American spies were true. I should have known better with a plane full of reporters."

His last statement was as flat and expressionless as the others, but it flicked Julie on the raw, and she flinched. No wonder he'd been so furious with her! How much damage had her impulsive excursion—and Tim's—done to this man's carefully set-up operation?

"But then who is Tim McAdams? I was sure—I thought he was a spy."

"I don't know anything about the man," Rick said flatly, striding back across the hollow trunk to lower himself to the floor beside Julie. "For all I know, maybe there really was an intel agent on that plane. It wouldn't be the first time another agency screwed up an op by not letting us know what they had going down. I will say I wondered myself if either—or both—of you were intel. But it didn't take long to figure out that you at least were who you said you were. No real agent would have ever come up with that story!

"As for McAdams, if he's one of ours, his cover is way overdone. We checked his story—the FARC, I mean—and it's all there right out on the Internet. He's been in Colombia several times over the last couple years to cover religious stories. And he has articles in Christian publications to prove it. He's been written up in plenty of other parts of the world as well."

"Then he was telling the truth! He really is a missionary journalist. But—" Julie shook her head, bewildered. "If you knew Tim and I were who we said we were, how could you have just left us there? I mean, you weren't a prisoner like we were. There must have been something you could have done to free us. At the least you could have gotten word out to someone that we were there!"

A hot, painful pressure was building up in Julie's chest. The weeks of captivity. The sleepless nights. The humiliation and boredom. Uncle Norm. Carlos. It had all been hard enough to endure. But now to find out that it was unnecessary?

"You let them keep me a prisoner cooped up in that horrible little hut, thinking all the time I was never going to get free. You let my friends and . . . and family think I was dead. You let me believe I was about to be murdered when all that time you could have gotten us out—and didn't! Why? Why would you do that?"

Rick glanced across at her, his long lashes coming down to shade his eyes. "Sure, I could have—and blown my cover and the entire operation," he said evenly. "You weren't in any immediate danger. I'm sorry, but there was simply a whole lot more at stake here than the comfort—or the feelings—of a couple of civilians whose foolish actions got them into this situation in the first place."

Julie had seen it in many an old-fashioned movie, read it in books. But she'd never understood the impulse that could lead an otherwise mature adult to such behavior. It had always seemed so . . . so corny. But as she stared at him in disbelief, all the long weeks of fighting down fear and worry and despair, the terror and desperation of these last frantic hours of running and hiding, the horror of Carlos's death—the images of which were still stark in her mind—all this welled up in a white-hot eruption of hurt and anger. Without any seeming volition of her own, her hand flew up.

It was a hard blow, the flat plane of his cheek solid against her open palm, the smack of her slap a loud crack in the hollow interior of the tree. As suddenly as her fury had risen, it drained away to be replaced by shame. Julie stared with horror at the bright red imprint of her fingers on his face.

"I'm sorry," she said in a small voice. "I . . . I can't believe I did that."

Rick rose to his feet, his mouth a straight grim line. "I guess I deserved that. Now, if you'll excuse me, I'm going to call in your ride so I can get back to that mission."

He pulled the two-way radio from his belt. As he turned it over, Julie overcame her embarrassment to ask diffidently, "But won't that just call in the guerrillas?"

Rick opened a panel on the back of the radio. "There are a few things in this unit that aren't quite standard guerrilla issue. Chiefly, a radio signal on a very secure channel that should be bouncing these GPS coordinates right now to our communications unit over on San José. If I change this setting, the signal will upgrade to my lifeline—a last-ditch distress call I'd hoped not to use. Unless Colonel Thornton has totally fallen down on the job over there, they should have a chopper scrambled over here within the hour to lift you out."

"Me? But—what about you? You can't be thinking of going back there!" Julie demanded incredulously. "Won't the guerrillas shoot you too for helping me?"

Rick shrugged as he did something in the interior of the radio. "Not if I can talk Victor into buying why I've been out of contact this long. He'll assume I've been looking for you, and if I can get him to believe I had radio problems—anyway, that's a chance I'll have to take. I've still got a mission to do."

He shut the back of the radio. "All this dead wood may weaken the signal. I'm going to set this outside. Stay here!"

With that curt order, he ducked through the jagged hole of the opening. He had barely disappeared when Julie heard the blast of gunfire. She scrambled to her feet. "Rick!"

He was already diving back inside, landing at her feet in a slide that would have done credit to a major league base runner. As he rolled over and onto his feet, Julie saw a small bleeding slash along his cheekbone. Otherwise he seemed unhurt.

The radio in his hand was another story. A bullet had struck it square in the middle, shattering the casing. Shoving the broken radio back on his belt, Rick snatched the AK-47 from his shoulder, thrust its barrel out the opening, and let loose a spray of gunfire.

"Well, that's done it," he said grimly as he pulled his head back inside. "They now know I'm not one of theirs. And so much for calling in the cavalry. The radio's busted." He glanced upward, and Julie followed his eyes to the cool green light filtering through the cavity in the tree fork overhead. "That's our only way out. Can you get up there?"

Julie was climbing before he finished. The rotting wood had been eaten away deeply by insects, so there were plenty of holds for her groping hands. Once a chunk broke away under her fingers so that she almost lost her grip, but she caught at another hold and made it the rest of the way in an unbroken scramble fueled by new fear and desperation. Would this never end? They'd disposed of the tracking device. How had the guerrillas found them again?

Below her, Rick fired another long burst, then climbed after her. He caught up as Julie pulled herself through the jagged opening. The fork where the two trunks joined would have been the size of a small table if it weren't for the hole in its center, and it was almost as flat, giving ample room for Rick and Julie to pull themselves upright. Rick didn't pause for a moment. Setting his foot on the next branch, he snapped back to Julie, "Hurry!"

Julie scrambled upward behind him. Though the intertwined crowns of the two trees were dead, they were a hanging garden of leafy vines and gourds and moss that offered an abundance of hand holds while providing the climbers with an effective screen to hide them from the forest floor below.

Ten feet. Twenty.

Julie slipped on a patch of moss, and a steel grip on her wrist yanked her up to the next branch.

Thirty.

Resolutely, Julie set her eyes only on the next step, resisting the temptation to glance down through the tangle of vines to where the ground lay more than fifty feet below. The branches were thinning out, but the limbs were still plenty thick enough to hold their weight, and while these Siamese mahoganies were considerably stunted in growth, Rick and Julie were level with the lowest branches of the other trees. Their crowns, interwoven by connecting vines and hanging curtains of moss and orchids spilling down tree trunks and over branches, stretched away in a tangled maze as far as Julie dared lift her eyes to see.

This was the jungle canopy, the playground of monkeys and sloths, where they spent a lifetime leaping from tree to tree and vine to vine without ever touching the ground. Reaching down to pull Julie onto a branch beside him, Rick gestured down its length to where it disappeared into the broad leaves of a neighboring tree, this one dripping with bulbous brown gourds.

"Can you make it over there on your own?" he demanded tensely. When Julie hesitated, he added sharply, "If you can't, say so now!"

Julie had heard it too—harsh shouts reverberating inside the hollow trunk below them. She identified Linda's angry call: "They are not inside. They have vanished into the air."

Snatching her wrist from Rick's grip, Julie hissed, "Of course I can make it. I grew up in these jungles, remember? I've climbed these trees before. You just do what you have to. I can take care of myself."

Grabbing for a vine, she wrapped it tight around her fingers and began to inch her way forward, her knuckles growing white with her grip as she felt the branch sway under her feet. Glancing back, she saw Rick take a grenade from his belt. Her eyes widened as she realized what he had in mind, and even as he pulled the pin and tossed the grenade down toward the cavity through which they had climbed, she increased her pace, reaching for one vine after another at reckless speed.

Rick caught up with her as she pulled herself onto a branch that belonged to the next tree. He had just stepped up after her when the grenade detonated. The rotted trunk did not so much explode as implode, tumbling in on itself with a thunder that rivaled the grenade itself. Julie clung to the branch, shutting her eyes as the tree they were now on swayed under the impact of the shock wave.

"We have to go!" Rick's whisper was as harsh as the furious shouts rising from below. Clamping a hand on her wrist, he hauled her to her feet. He placed a loop of vine in her hand, barely glancing back to make sure she was holding on before stepping to the next branch. Julie swallowed down vertigo as she pulled herself up after him. Higher and higher they climbed into the canopy even as they worked their way to the other side of the gourd tree. Rick, one step ahead of her, glanced back periodically to check on Julie's progress, occasionally reaching a hand back to help her over the more hazardous spots.

"Hurry!" he snapped as she hesitated before stepping across the gap to the next tree. Fury gave her the adrenaline to make the leap.

"Did it ever occur to you I've been through a rather traumatic experience and could use some sympathy and consideration instead of . . . of . . . yelling at me all the time?" she hissed as he yanked her up to his side.

His mouth set in a straight line as he glanced down at her. "When we're on the ground, remind me to offer a shoulder to cry on. Right now I'm trying to keep us alive. And to think I was congratulating myself that you didn't scream and cry and fall to pieces like nine-tenths of the female race I know!"

*Women!* Julie could almost see the word hovering between his teeth as he swung himself to the next branch. Biting back her own retort, she scrambled after him. But he was right. They didn't have the luxury for hysterics now.

"Beast!" she said under her breath. Rick threw her a sharp glance over his shoulder, but if he'd heard, he didn't comment, and as she lifted her chin and reached doggedly for another vine, he gave her a thumbs-up and an approving nod. Julie blinked and was infuriated with herself to find tears springing again to her eyes.

The next interminable period was one more nightmare in a day full of them. Julie had been telling the truth when she'd said she'd climbed trees like these before. What she hadn't said was how much she'd hated the experience. Where the I'paa children had scampered among their branches like monkeys, collecting gourds and pods, Julie had always been afraid she would fall, afraid she would lose her grip on the vines that, unlike Tarzan movies, tore loose only too easily in her hands, or that she would slip on the mossy limbs. Just the enormity of the drops made her dizzy every time she looked down, though they never seemed to bother the I'paa. It had been a relief when her mother had found out what she'd been up to and had forbidden her to climb again.

Julie's stomach stayed permanently in her throat as she pulled herself from branch to branch and inched out on limbs to spring over to the next tree. Wind whistled through the canopy, and more than once Julie found herself clinging helplessly to a branch, waiting for a gust to subside. *Don't look down, don't look down.*

The guerrillas couldn't possibly see their mad scramble through that tangle of vegetation below, and their occasional shouts were growing more distant. At some endless point later, Rick reached up to help Julie down onto the concave platform of another tree fork. For once he didn't start immediately across but walked over to the edge. He looked down, listening. Then he swung around.

"We've lost them. But that won't last long. There's got to be another bug on you—that's the only explanation for how they've managed to follow us. And now that we've stopped moving, it won't take them long to triangulate our exact position. We've got to find that bug—and fast."

He reached for her knapsack. "Is there anything else you were given in the camp besides those clothes?"

"Just a few toilet things. But—why would they put two tracking devices on the same person? Couldn't it be coincidence that they found us? Or . . ." Julie stopped as a thought struck her. "Are you sure they couldn't have put a bug on you? Is there any way someone might have gotten suspicious that you aren't really a guerrilla?"

"Of course not!" Rick answered impatiently. "Do you think I wouldn't have known a long time ago if they'd had any suspicions I wasn't who I claimed to be?" His hands stilled suddenly where they were exploring the canvas material of the knapsack. "At least—"

He broke off to stare at her, and Julie, staring back, saw the same realization dawn in his eyes.

"Oh no!" she breathed out. "Last night when I was talking to Tim, I told him we weren't the only ones who fit the description of their spy— that there were guerrillas in the camp who'd been on the UN plane and in the airport—you and Carlos and *Comandante* Aguilera and Manuel Flores. I wasn't serious, but if someone heard me . . . I've wondered all along if *Comandante* Aguilera knows more English than he lets on—or one of those guards of Tim's."

"And I'm the latest recruit in that camp, and I speak fluent English—the obvious suspect. They couldn't be certain—I've been too careful for that. But it might have been enough for them to lay a trap." Rick already had his AK-47 off his shoulder and was running a searching hand over it, his mouth a straight grim line. "Not my clothes. I was wearing them last night. The radio never leaves my belt. But the gun. Or . . ." He shoved the assault rifle back on his shoulder with a frustrated shake of the head, and his hands went to his ammunition vest. "Or the ammo."

Rick popped the shells from one of his ammunition clips as though he were shucking peas. "Victor handed these to me when we moved out." He made a small sound of combined annoyance and satisfaction. "There it is!"

The device he held out was round, metallic, and no bigger than a battery for Julie's watch. Dropping it to the surface of the tree hollow, Rick raised his boot, then paused. "No, if the signal stops, they'll know we found it. We'll leave it here—and see how they do climbing up here after it."

Quickly, he checked over his remaining ammo clips, then retrieved the bug and tucked it into a gnarl of wood above him.

"Okay, let's shake these guys once and for all. And then it's time we worked our way down to ground level." His mouth twitched ruefully in the first admission of inadequacy Julie had ever heard from him. "I'm not much on heights."

"Yeah, well, you could have fooled me," Julie muttered, reaching reluctantly for a vine. Still, the hope that they had finally thrown off their pursuers and would soon be down on levels designed for human legs gave her new energy, and she even managed a thumbs-up of her own and a grin as she clambered onto a branch after him.

Which made the panorama that assaulted her eyes not fifteen minutes later an even greater consternation.

Rick had begun maneuvering their descent as soon as they were out of sight of where they'd left the tracking device. Behind them they heard the shouts of the converging guerrillas, and Julie contemplated with grim pleasure the thought of the slippery climb ahead of them with not so much as a twig for fifty feet or more off the ground.

They saw daylight ahead, and Rick turned their course toward it. Their difficulty was to find a tree without the tall straight trunk of the hardwoods so they could climb back down to ground level. But as they descended, they had to keep a sharper lookout for the guerrillas. They were now vulnerable to spying eyes from below.

As the daylight brightened, the huge hardwoods were becoming interspersed with shorter, less massive trees, and they were finally able to slide into the upper limbs of a wild guava tree whose branches were truncated enough to allow them to scramble quickly earthward. Sunshine streaming through a grove of the wild guavas made it clear they had reached the opening in the jungle canopy toward which Rick had headed them. Dropping the last meters to the ground, Julie hurried eagerly through the guavas until she could see what that promise of daylight held.

Then she gasped. "Oh, no!"

It wasn't a swamp this time, but a river. A murky-brown, slow-moving jungle river that in dry season would shrink to a shallow stream, but whose banks the recent rains had overflowed until it lapped at the very roots of the wild guava where she stood and stretched away the distance of at least two Olympic-sized swimming pools.

As Rick strode up beside her, Julie glanced up at him in blank dismay. "We can't cross that! What are we going to do?"

Rick was studying the river himself, his eyes narrowing as he measured its width, then scanned both banks upstream and down. "We have no choice. The best bet we have to throw those guys off our trail and keep them off is to get across there. You *can* swim, can't you?"

"Sure I can swim. But if you think we can cross that without a boat, you don't know the jungle very well. Do you know what's in that water? Piranhas, stingrays, crocodiles—oh, watch out!" Julie choked back a shriek before it got out of her throat. "There's one now! It's coming straight at us!"

Rick glanced down at the cylindrical shape floating leisurely downstream on a direct course toward his army boots, then straightened up to throw Julie a sardonic glance. "That's not a crocodile! It's a tree branch." Unslinging his AK-47, he used the butt to snag the drifting log and pull it up to the bank. "And it's just what we need to get us across. Here! Give me your pack."

He was already peeling off his ammo vest and gun belt. Laying them and the AK-47 on top of the log, he held out a hand for Julie's knapsack. Julie edged back a step, her face white. She had endured much over the last hours of flight, obeyed him without question in that mad scramble through the jungle canopy, accepted meekly his continual strictures to keep up and keep moving. But this was too much!

"I'm not going into that!" she told him flatly. "You're crazy to even think of it! We'll just have to take our chances on this side. Now that we've found their bugs, I don't see why we can't just head downriver. We've got a start."

She took another step back, but as she did so, Rick's hand shot out, grabbing not her knapsack but her wrist. His grip bit cruelly into the small bones there, but it was no less inflexible than the steel of his gaze. "You will!" he answered even more flatly. "Do you hear that?"

Julie grew still under his hold as she heard the gunfire, first just one burst, then what was unmistakably several weapons joining in.

"They've triangulated the tracker position," Rick said grimly. "They're trying to drive us down. When they realize we aren't up there anymore, Victor's going to have a good idea we've found the second bug. He'll have his unit spread out to flank us, hoping to throw a net wide enough to pull us in. I know. I taught him the tactics. And since they're on the ground and moving a whole lot faster than we've been, it won't take long before they stumble on this too, and know they've got us backed up against the river. We can keep running, but you're tired and so am I, and they've got radios and can call in reinforcements, even bring boats up that river. Sooner or later, we're going to make a mistake and they're going to have us backed into a corner. Look, I know the dangers in that river as well as you do—"

"Do you?" Julie demanded in a hot whisper, tugging at his iron grip on her wrist. "Have you ever seen anyone torn to pieces by a crocodile?"

"Maybe not," Rick retorted. "But I do know one thing. At least out there we have a chance to end this. To be safe once and for all from Victor and his band. If we stay here, we have no chance at all."

When Julie kept shaking her head, his tone grew biting. "I'm not giving you a choice here. That kid back there, Carlos—he died to get you this far. I guess he figured you were worth that sacrifice. Don't ask me why. But you're not going to throw that away. Not if I have to drag you across there myself!"

It was as much a slap as the one she had dealt him. Julie flinched at the anger blazing in his eyes. It was the same anger she'd encountered before when she'd wandered across his path and into his camp, and Julie knew now what it was—fury that she'd messed up his plans and his life and who knew how many other people's as well. And because she couldn't totally blame him, she only glared back at him in mute misery.

As suddenly as it had flared, the anger left him, and his voice gentled. "I'm sorry. I'm not doing this too well, am I? Look, Julie, don't you think I'm just as scared as you are to go out there? But you told me once you believe God runs this universe. So do I! I'm not going to say that if we trust God, He's never going to let anything bad come into our lives. We both know that isn't true. But I believe with all my heart that He knows what He's doing—for both of our lives. And that nothing can touch us unless He chooses to allow it for His own perfect reasons. Right now that includes getting us across that river—crocodiles or no crocodiles. Either way, we have no choice!"

His gentleness hit Julie harder than his anger, and she found herself blinking back tears. It was ironic. She was the daughter of missionaries. That God knew what He was doing—that He was in control of her universe—was a tenet by which she had lived her life. Yet here was this army officer taking it upon himself to explain that difficult theological concept to her with a simplicity and acceptance that were a world away from Tim McAdams's confident assurances that all would be well. Bowing her head, Julie let the resistance ease from her muscles.

Accepting her silence as capitulation, Rick hooked Julie's knapsack over a protuberance on the log that was the stump of a broken bough. Unsheathing his army knife from the belt he'd already loaded on the log, he gripped it in one hand while with the other he pushed off the log and waded out to swim alongside it.

Julie followed him into the river, grabbing at the broken-off limb that held her knapsack as she helped to push the log out into deeper water. Rick kept a sharp eye on her until he was sure she was obeying his orders, then began kicking with strong strokes toward the other shore, one arm hooked around the log to pull it after him.

Julie's legs felt horribly exposed as she kicked with all her remaining strength. She wasn't really concerned about the piranhas or stingrays. The stingrays buried themselves in the mud at the bottom of the jungle rivers and weren't really a hazard unless you were foolish enough to step on them. The piranhas too were basically a scavenger fish and wouldn't attack a healthy living creature unless there was blood or an open wound to attract them.

The crocodiles were another story. They were not true crocodiles, though they were commonly misnamed as such. The South American caiman that infested these waters belonged to the same family, but was at once both smaller and more vicious and agile. Julie had watched her father amputate the leg of a screaming Indian who had fallen from his canoe into their jaws. She'd seen a village playmate pulled down under the water when he had wandered outside the wooden stakes planted as a barricade around the communal swimming beach. He had never resurfaced, and Julie found Rick's combat knife little comfort as she tensed herself for any movement besides their own in the water.

But whether the heat of the late morning discouraged the caimans from leaving their naps along the riverbanks, or whether it really was God's hand of protection as Rick had suggested, the log bumped into the far side with no further incident than the handful of leeches Julie discovered attached to her ankles as she staggered ashore. Almost absently, she paused to pull them off before grabbing her knapsack.

She glanced back toward the river and her eyes widened. She reached out to touch Rick on the arm as he buckled his belt back around his waist. "Look!"

A long, sleek shape was moving torpedo-like through the muddy water they had just abandoned. This time it was no log. Besides the fact that it was moving upstream against the current, Julie could see the cold, unblinking eyes that were the only thing showing above water. Julie glanced up at Rick, and she saw in his face some of the same chill that was going up her spine. If they had delayed in crossing even thirty seconds longer!

Rick let out a sudden exclamation under his breath. Snatching up his ammo vest and the AK-47, he pulled Julie away from the bank and into the cover of a patch of elephant ears. They were just in time. Across the river, two figures in battle fatigues stepped out onto the flooded bank. They were at least fifty meters downstream, too far to distinguish individual features. But the big, dark one had to be Jaime and the smaller one Linda or Marcela. Julie stiffened as Jaime raised binoculars to his eyes. Rick's hand was hard on her wrist to keep her still, his long frame tense and motionless as the binoculars swiveled in a slow scan of the opposite bank.

A feminine shout rang across the water. The woman—Linda or Marcela—pointed to the caiman still making its leisurely way upriver. Lowering the binoculars, Jaime walked over to her. There was a brief, inaudible discussion. The two guerrillas turned and disappeared back into the jungle. Julie felt the tension leave Rick's body, and he released her wrist. He was smiling as he glanced down at Julie.

"Thank God!" he said quietly, and from him it sounded like a serious suggestion rather than an exclamation. "Because of Mr. Croc there, they think we can't have crossed the river. I think we just might have done it!"

# NINETEEN

JULIE'S LEGS SUDDENLY REFUSED TO hold her up, and she sank down into the patch of elephant ears that had given them cover. She was shivering in her wet clothes, even with the heat of the day, and she had to resist an absurd impulse to check over her limbs to make sure they were still intact.

Rick hunkered down in front of her, and she could feel his keen gaze on her face. "You're as white as a sheet even under all that mud," he said quietly. "You've had some kind of bad experience with those crocodiles, haven't you?"

"A couple of friends of mine," Julie said flatly.

Taking off his cap, Rick ran a hand through his hair, amazingly still dry, unlike Julie's. "I'm sorry about that. I wish there'd been some other way."

"No, you were right," Julie admitted quietly. "We didn't have any choice. Anyway, we made it. So what now?"

Rick replaced the combat cap with a frown. "I wish we could take time for you to rest up a bit. But we need to move on immediately. They're not going to give up searching. They'll keep throwing the net wider, calling in reinforcements if they haven't already, and sooner or later, when they get a boat up here or a canoe, someone will be over here to check this side. When they do, I want us far enough outside the perimeters of their search grid that they won't be stumbling over us—by accident if nothing else."

First Rick took the time to wash away the tracks they had made coming out of the water, not stepping out onto the riverbank where watchful eyes might still be searching, but using his cap to dip water from among the reeds and sluicing it out through the stems and down the bank until only dimples remained in the smooth surface of the mud.

Rick eyed with disapproval the broken elephant ear stems where they had crouched. "There's not much we can do about that. We'll just have to hope they figure it was a croc or pig in here if they find it."

As he had done earlier in the swamp, Rick led them through the shallow water of the reeds rather than up onto the bank. They were coming into a stretch of fresh-water mangroves, their exposed root system a tangled maze that ran out into the river and over and under and around each other as far back from the bank as Julie could see. After threading through the reeds for some distance downstream, Rick turned their course up into the mangroves, stepping from one root to another away from the river.

The roots were slimy with moss and from the recent floods, and they were slippery enough to make Julie thankful that this time they were only a few feet off the ground. It was an exhausting scramble to keep up with Rick's long, easy steps, and when he turned to give her a hand down onto ground that was both solid and dry, she glanced back with aversion. It would take a determined tracker to bother searching through that. Which was probably the point.

"Do they teach you that in Special Forces?" she asked Rick curiously. "Throwing off a trail like that?"

"Some of it," Rick shrugged. "Some is just common sense."

Sliding his AK-47 from his shoulder, he began to remove his ammo vest. "We're not out of range yet. But I want to make sure they have no more surprises for us before we go any farther. If you need a rest, this is the time."

Without further explanation, Rick slid the wide belt that held his knife and other items from his waist and began a careful inspection of every seam. He was clearly a man of few words, as Julie had already observed during the weeks at the guerrilla camp.

Which was fine with her, since it was also clear he held her responsible for their present predicament and wasn't exactly harboring friendly sentiments toward her. Rick Martini might have yet again saved her life, but he'd treated her as an unwelcome appendage ever since, and hadn't shown the slightest compassion for the nightmare she herself had endured that day. He had in fact been a whole lot kinder back when she'd thought him to be a guerrilla.

Until he'd found out that his precious mission was being interrupted to baby-sit her.

Letting her knapsack slide from her shoulder, Julie slumped against the mangrove root from which she'd climbed down. A wave of exhaustion threatened to carry her away until she hastily forced her eyes open. No, she couldn't let herself fall asleep or she'd never move again.

Instead, she watched as Rick meticulously checked over his ammunition vest, then upended her knapsack on the ground. He glanced up to meet her eyes. "I'm going to need to check through the clothes you've got on as well," he told her brusquely.

Julie clambered hastily to her feet. "I'll do it!"

The sardonic curve of his mouth told her he'd expected her reaction. "That won't be necessary. If you'd like to change into something clean, you can just toss those out to me."

Stepping behind a tree, Julie hastily stripped off her muddy clothing and pulled on a dry T-shirt and another pair of khaki slacks. The clean clothes felt heavenly against her damp skin. She changed her socks as well, grimacing as she tugged her wet sneakers back over them.

Rick was sliding the clips for his assault rifle back into the ammo vest when she emerged. He quickly ran a hand over her wet clothing, then rolled it up and scooped all her belongings back into her knapsack. His clothing clung to his hard, lean frame, but if they were causing him any discomfort, he didn't show it.

"We're clear," he announced shortly. "Unless they've got technology a lot more advanced than anything I've seen them with." He scooped up his AK-47. "Let's move out. I'd like to put a few more kilometers behind us before we stop."

As he swung around on his heel, Julie bent over to pick up her pack. She regretted the action immediately; a wave of dizziness and nausea swept over her, and she had to grope for the nearest tree trunk to keep from stumbling to her knees.

She could have sworn she hadn't uttered a sound, but Rick spun around. "What's the matter?" he demanded sharply. "Are you sick?"

"I'm fine!" Julie retorted, but she had to brace herself as another wave of dizziness swept over her. "Just low blood sugar. Making time for the most important meal of the day wasn't exactly on my agenda this morning!"

Ignoring her sarcasm, Rick strode back to her side. He muttered something under his breath as he studied her pale face. "Why didn't you say something?" he demanded harshly. As she opened her mouth, he added unexpectedly, "No, I'm sorry, this is my fault. I just wasn't thinking."

He sounded as though he really meant it, and Julie, raising confused eyes to his, saw that they weren't angry, but dark brown with concern. Maybe he wasn't as hard as he appeared.

His mouth curved ruefully. "Truth is, you've been doing so well, I keep forgetting you're not one of the guys back there. Here!"

From one of the pockets on his ammo vest, Rick pulled out a long oblong that Julie recognized as a popular Colombian candy bar. Tearing it open, he handed it to her. It was a sticky white nougat studded with nuts, not one of Julie's favorites. But as she sank her teeth into it, its rather cloying sweetness was like the finest nectar melting down her throat. She almost whimpered with the pleasure of it. Rick watched her closely as she swallowed, then nodded approval.

"Good, you've got some color back in those lips. Do you think you can go on? I hate to push you, but we need to get as far from this point as we can before night. I . . ." He frowned suddenly. "I'm still getting the feeling that someone might be watching us."

Julie nodded, her mouth too full to answer. The sugar racing through her veins had brought with it a new surge of energy, and though she knew it wouldn't last long, she was also determined that Rick was not going to add holding him back to the other charges he had against her.

He no longer pushed the pace. Once they stepped out of the mangroves, the trees grew high again overhead and the underbrush was scant, so they made good time. They encountered no more rivers, but several small streams crossed their paths, and Rick had them splash up the middle of each for a distance until Julie's clean clothing was again wet to the knees and her feet felt as though they were beginning to rot within her shoes. The mosquitoes too were a plague now that Julie had the leisure to notice them, the salt of her perspiration a perfume that drew them in swarms until, in desperation, Julie yanked up the leaves of an aromatic plant that grew along the bank of one of the streams and rubbed its sticky sap over her hands and face.

Rick swung around to watch this procedure. The legs of his fatigues were wet, but the heat of the jungle and his body had steam-dried the rest of his uniform except for patches of sweat where his ammo vest rubbed it. Resting his shoulders against a tree trunk in a rare gesture of relaxation, he tilted one corner of his firm mouth in amusement as Julie gave her cheeks a final rub.

"Looks like army makeup," he commented laconically. "Where did you learn that trick?"

It was the first unnecessary conversation he had ever directed her way, and Julie glanced over at him uncertainly. Was he making fun of her? "From the I'paa Indians when I was a kid."

"Hmmm! Not a bad idea." Leaning forward to pluck the bunch of

crushed leaves from her fingers, Rick sniffed its pungent odor before applying it to his face and neck. He was as mud-spattered as Julie was, and the
plant matter left green streaks intermingled with the grime. Julie had to
repress a giggle at the banditlike appearance it gave him.

Except for this diversion, Julie felt as though she were traversing the
same piece of forest over and over. At least there was no further signs of
pursuit or any human presence at all in this vast wilderness, and after an
hour or so, Rick allowed the occasional rest period. But with each stop,
Julie found it harder to push herself to her feet again when Rick announced
it was time to move. By the time the jungle gloom darkened to twilight,
she was moving in such a daze of exhaustion that an entire unit of guerrillas
could have sneaked up on her without her noticing, and she hardly heard
Rick when he glanced back to say, "You're doing good. We'll be stopping
for the night as soon as we can find a safe place."

They had just splashed across another brook—this time Rick didn't even
bother to detour upstream—when they came across a dead hardwood. This
one had been the victim of lightning, and the bulk of it had long since
broken off. All that remained was a blackened, jagged shell about twenty
feet high. Even this had crumbled away on one side, and the interior had
been hollowed out by bugs and pecking bird life to leave a reasonably flat
surface about five feet off the ground.

Swinging himself up onto the stump, Rick kicked loose a profusion of
toadstools before reaching a hand down to Julie. The lightning victim had
been a big tree, and the area afforded by the hollowed-away stump was
good sized, Julie discovered as she looked around—easily the size of her
small apartment bedroom—and the remaining shell of the burned trunk
offered an illusion of shelter.

Rick gave the stump a critical examination. "I don't like camping down
on the ground—not without a fire, which we can't risk right now. Too
many predators coming out after dark. But at least it gives us a wall to
guard our backs, and it's as good as we're going to get tonight." He glanced
over at Julie. "You want to wash up first, or shall I?"

He accompanied Julie to the stream, checking the area all around
and even the stream bed itself before striding back to the stump. Julie
hurried to perform her toiletries. At one time this would have been
because of embarrassment and the fear of being spied on. But weeks in
a guerrilla camp under a constant barrage of eyes had done much to

strip away self-consciousness and inhibitions, even if Enrique Martinez—or Rick Martini—up there had not proven his decency long before she'd known who he really was.

She hurried instead because of the lengthening shadows and because she didn't care to be alone in these woods even with Rick only a scream away. The bottom of the stream was a sludge that oozed up over her feet once she'd pulled off shoes and socks, but the water itself was clear enough that she risked drinking and deep enough for a thorough sponge bath as long as she was careful not to stir up the muck. She even washed her hair, then scrubbed the mud from both the clothes she'd been wearing and those stuffed into her knapsack, before changing into her last clean pair of khaki slacks and shirt.

She was combing her curls out as she walked back to the stump, her wet laundry in a bundle over one shoulder and her knapsack over the other. It felt glorious to be clean again, and the cool water had washed away her exhaustion along with the mud. She felt wide awake again.

Rick raised an eyebrow as he pulled her up onto the stump. He had removed his ammo vest, and on its spread-out leather back had dismantled his shattered hand radio. The pieces were laid out in a precise order that meant nothing to Julie. "I was just about to come looking for you." He looked her over critically. "Looks like you put your time to good use."

Hardly a gallant compliment, but Julie chose to take it as such and returned his scrutiny just as frankly. The mud and grass marks streaking his stubble below the sweat-darkened tangle of his hair hardly gave him the look of a prepossessing character, and now that she was clean, she could smell the sharp tang of the perspiration that darkened his shirt where the ammo vest had rubbed. She wrinkled her nose at him and retorted satirically, "Yeah, well, looks like you could stand to do the same!"

"Yeah, well," Rick mimicked sardonically, but the straight line of his mouth curved as he ran a sharp eye over her shining cleanliness. "We didn't all think to drag a week's worth of laundry along." He leaned forward to breathe in deeply. "Is that shampoo I smell?"

Without a word, Julie dug into her knapsack and brought out soap, her small bottle of shampoo, toothpaste, and even a razor. It was a woman's brand, but in these extremities, he'd better not complain. She added her towel, damp but still usable. Rick raised his eyebrows again, but took the articles with a brief, "Thanks."

He handed Julie the AK-47 before he swung himself down from the stump. "Pull that trigger and point if you have any trouble," he told her as he slipped off the safety catch. "Just don't point it in the direction of the creek. I have a fundamental objection to being shot with my own weapon."

"Very funny," Julie retorted, but he was already gone. Julie spread her laundry and wet shoes out at the edge of the stump to dry and was eyeing the scattered pieces of the radio, trying to push down thoughts of a hot meal, when he returned. The pants of his fatigue uniform clung wet to his legs, though they had been scrubbed clean of mud. He had removed the shirt to wash it and himself, and his chest was bare except for her damp towel tossed over one shoulder.

The mud and grass stains and stubble were gone from the lean planes from his face as well, and his hair was slicked back and neat. Julie realized again with a shock that Rick Martini was—or could be—a very presentable man if you went for the hard-boiled, military type. She averted her eyes from the play of muscle in his shoulders and back as he swung himself up onto the stump and walked over to spread his shirt and the towel to dry.

"Thanks! I needed that," he said briefly as he dropped the toilet articles into Julie's open knapsack. He squatted down beside his scattered hand radio, and his face grew grim as he looked over the pieces, but he said only, "There isn't much we can do with this tonight."

Scooping the pieces into the shattered casing, he dug another bar of nougat and a small bag of peanuts from the ammo vest. This time he split them evenly, passing half to Julie.

"We're going to have to take turns on watch," he told Julie as they ate. "I'm not too concerned about the guerrillas right now. They'll be bunking down for the night just as we are. But there's plenty of nasties out there that like to hunt by dark, and I'd just as soon not offer them supper on a platter." Julie could feel his eyes sharp on her in the growing gloom. "Are you up to it?"

"Of course I am," she said indignantly. "Actually, I feel really good."

Rick leaned back against the rotting shell of the stump, facing himself toward the unprotected edge of the stump, a defensive maneuver Julie was beginning to recognize. He laid the AK-47 across his lap, his long legs stretched out in front of him and crossed at the ankles.

Already, even in the short time since they had bathed, the twilight had faded to evening, and Julie could make out only the outline of his strong profile as she slid back beside him to rest her head against the crumbling wood behind them. In a few minutes it would be pitch black under the jungle canopy. Julie finished her peanuts before asking quietly, "Rick?"

"Hmmm?" His laconic grunt came from the darkness beside her.

"If . . . if I promise not to slap you again, would you tell me what you're doing here and . . . well, who you really are? How did you end up down here pretending to be a guerrilla? And what were you doing in that camp and . . . and with *Comandante* Aguilera?"

He shifted positions as she finished her question, and Julie could see the ugly shape of the assault rifle as he moved it to a more comfortable position, and could hear the faint clink of something metallic as his foot brushed against the ammo vest. It seemed with the movement that it was the guerrilla Enrique Martinez, a dangerous and complex man dedicated to a deadly cause, who sat only too close in the darkness beside her, not Rick Martini, U.S. Special Forces, whom she'd known only a few hours and, in fact, did not really know at all. That he was not her guard but her savior, that this was not another guerrilla camp but freedom, seemed suddenly unreal, as though Rafael or Jaime might abruptly materialize out of the dark to take their turn on guard duty.

"It's just . . . you seemed so real—as Enrique, I mean. Even now, thinking back, I can't believe it was all an act. All those things you said to Carlos and me—about the guerrillas and what you—they—believed. That what you're doing is the best chance Colombia has to find peace. And all that stuff back in San Ignacio about the blood of the martyrs, and that Colombia will never have freedom until its people are willing to shed their blood fighting for it. You sounded like you really meant it, not like some kind of act to fool the guerrillas—or me."

"I did mean it," Rick said flatly. "I wouldn't have volunteered for this op if I didn't believe that what I'm doing is the best chance—maybe even the only chance—to stop something really ugly from going down here. And I wouldn't support the American presence in Colombia at all if I didn't believe in our mission. The drug traffic we're fighting here is doing as much to hurt the Colombians as it is the Americans, and we have a responsibility to do more than wall ourselves behind our borders and let countries like this take the fallout for a problem that has come about through the self-indulgence of our own citizens."

The ammo vest clinked again as Rick shifted his feet, and he leaned over to tug it out of range. "But I don't believe that Americans—or any outsiders—are going to achieve any kind of lasting peace down here. I really believe, as I told you, that the only way Colombia is going to have any hope of lasting peace or freedom is for them to stand up together as a people—city-dwellers and *campesinos,* rich and poor—and fight for it! They can't keep asking the United States or anyone else to bail them out or solve their problems. This country has forty million people. The guerrillas and the paramilitaries together are just a fraction of that . . . a few tens of thousands altogether. But those few thousands are going to keep grabbing them by the throat unless they are willing to make a stand against the violence, whichever direction it comes from. That may mean some bloodshed—even some serious fighting. But freedom has never been won without a willingness to shed your own blood—and not someone else's.

"That's what the old saying means: 'The blood of the martyrs is the seed of the church.' Christianity grew because people like your parents were willing to lay down their lives for it. And those who do not care enough to bleed and die for what they hold dear will always be held hostage by those who do. Until the Colombian people learn that lesson, they will continue to lose far more people killed piecemeal than if they'd simply declared war once for all. Maybe that's a simplistic way to look at things, but it's how I feel. If there's anything I admire about these guerrillas, it's that they are willing to shed their blood for what they believe."

As might be said about him. It would seem that Rick Martini was as interesting and complex a man as Enrique Martinez, and Julie yearned for her micro-recorder. She was immediately ashamed.

*Are you really so frivolous that your career is still the first thing on your mind at a time like this?* she demanded of herself bitterly and was suddenly angry with Rick for making her feel that way. Why should she feel guilty over making the choices most others would have made in her position?

"So what were you doing on that plane?" she asked aloud. "It couldn't have been just those dead environmentalists. You would have had to be in with the guerrillas long before that happened." When he didn't answer right away, she added impatiently, "Look, I'm not planning on running to CNN with all this. But I think by now I deserve to have some answers. At least whether all this was worth these . . ."—her voice caught—"these last weeks."

For a moment, Julie thought he still wasn't going to answer. Then he stirred in the darkness beside her and said quietly, "I guess that's fair. It isn't anything that's going to be secret much longer in any case—my cover is blown beyond repair, I'm afraid."

Julie winced, but there was no hint of accusation in his words, and when he went on, it was in the flat, measured tones of an intelligence briefing.

"It all goes back several months now. I don't know how much you follow the Colombian news. You may be aware we had a U.S. surveillance plane go down in these parts a few months ago."

Julie nodded, then realized he couldn't see her in the dark and said aloud, "Yes, I knew that. It was in some of the research I did for this assignment."

"Then you know it was flying over the DMZ at the time. There was talk that the FARC had gotten lucky with a SAM—a surface-to-air missile. Only we knew better. The plane's defenses were too good for that. A month later we lost our second asset in the zone. A Black Hawk SouthCom had just delivered to an army base right on the edge of the DMZ. We lost an American technician in that one. Did your research go that far?"

Despite the dark, he evidently caught her nod. He continued right on. "Army intelligence has been kicking around for some time the idea of getting some HUMINT—human intelligence—assets into some of the bigger guerrilla groups out here. It didn't go anywhere because intel on the guerrillas was proving easy enough to get. They've invited every reporter and activist group on the planet right into the zone. And the Colombians had their own contacts on the inside. We knew what was going on in there—or thought we did. The guerrillas weren't at war with us anyway, so it didn't seem worth the potential political fallout of getting caught running a covert operation in a country that's supposed to be a democratic ally of ours. Until we started losing American assets, that is."

A grim note entered Rick's voice. "At best, we could be sure the FARC was in possession of some new and advanced weapon capacity that was a clear threat to both Colombian security and any further American assets in the zone. At worst . . . well, we had no idea what 'worst' could be. So . . ."

Julie heard the quiet rise and fall of his chest before he finished. "They sent me in. I'd been a Special Forces instructor over at San José a couple years back so I knew the area. And I could pass as a native. My mother was Colombian, and since my father, who I assume was at least part Italian with a name like Martini, took off before I was old enough to remember, I grew up speaking Spanish at home. Not just any Spanish but with a Bogotá accent. Which made me a logical choice for the mission. The only risk was that someone might recognize me from my tour at San José. But the counter-narcotics troops don't exactly associate with the guerrillas, and back then I had a regulation army butch cut."

Julie could hear the smile that crept into his voice. "Not even my own mother would recognize me right now, as I think you'll agree. Anyway, it was a risk we chose to take."

He was leaving out a lot. Just who "we" happened to be. Precisely which agency had assigned him to this mission. Julie was too experienced a journalist to press for details he probably wouldn't give. That he was an officer—a captain, he had said—with the 7th Special Operations Group out of Fort Bragg, said enough. Even a civilian like Julie had heard of the Green Berets and their reputation as one of the toughest and most highly trained units in the American military. That Rick Martini could indeed be a very dangerous man had not been her imagination. That he was also a dedicated one was becoming equally clear.

"Colonel Thornton—you met him when you were at San José—was assigned as my controlling officer. We worked out a way for me to keep in contact. That radio and a secured voice-mail drop when I could get access to phone service. A Colombian contact got me in. Andy—not his real name—is a paid informant for Colombian intelligence as well as one of the senior officers in one of the FARC fronts. He recommended me to his brigade leader as a disgruntled member of one of the smaller guerrilla factions who had received military training from the Syrians and wanted to move where the action was. The communication between these different bands is poor enough that they had no way of disproving that story.

"Besides, they wanted my military training and my English—which was easily explained by my supposed education in Bogotá. They were happy to set me to work training recruits and translating material from American military Web sites off the Internet. After a month or so, I pushed to get transferred to *Comandante* Aguilera's front in the demilitarized zone—again under the pretext of getting into the real action. Fortunately, there haven't been any major engagements since I got here, so I haven't actually had to prove my bloodthirsty inclinations."

He made it sound so matter-of-fact. What he was leaving out was the risk he was taking if his infiltration were uncovered, the unrelenting stress and terrible loneliness that had to come with being totally on your own in enemy territory. For the first time Julie began to concede that Rick's position in that camp had been no less enviable than her own, and with it came a reluctant admiration and respect that tinged her tone as she asked, "What did you find out?"

His arm brushed against hers as he shrugged. "Nothing much we didn't already know. I was able to confirm the presence of Islamic terrorist groups among the guerrillas, including the delivery of several shipments of surface-to-air missiles from Syria. But not what they wanted in Colombia, other than a straightforward exchange of consultant services and arms for American dollars, of which the FARC had plenty from drug sales. If there was anything more, it was soon clear to me that the rank-and-file guerrillas knew nothing about it. Maybe not even most of the leadership."

Julie heard frustration in his even tone. "Yet there was something I couldn't put my finger on. An unease and expectancy, as though everyone was waiting for something to happen but they just didn't know what. Parts of the demilitarized zone where it was common knowledge in the camps that even the guerrillas didn't venture into. And of course, once I'd seen the arms the FARC was getting in, I knew they had nothing that could have taken down that surveillance plane or the Black Hawk.

"Then there was San Ignacio. Planes were coming in on that airstrip with passengers and cargo that never made it into town or into the guerrilla encampment. When they came in, nobody—but *nobody*—went near them, not even Aguilera or Manuel Flores. They had their own guards and did their own off-loading onto boats that came from downriver—always after dark. Most of the guerrillas assumed it was an exercise with some other guerrilla commander. The different fronts work in competition with each other as often as they run joint operations, and the handlers were dressed as Colombian guerrillas. But I recognized one of them—a rather well-known member of the Iranian Hezbollah movement. Or at least well-known in U.S. intel files."

"So this *is* related to *Comandante* Aguilera's *musulmanes* friends. I knew it!" Julie exclaimed.

"You knew it," Rick repeated. "And just what could you know about Aguilera's Middle Eastern connections?"

Julie had forgotten that it was Tim, not Rick, to whom she had earlier related her theories. She repeated the conversation she had overheard while emerging from the truth drug at the first camp. "Back then I thought you were one of the voices I heard talking. Either way, doesn't it sound like they were planning something big—and soon?"

"Yes, it does." Rick sounded grimmer than Julie had heard him yet. "I just wish I'd had this data three weeks ago. All this time—"

He bit off what he was going to say, then went on in a more even tone. "In any case, our Iranian friend came afterward to speak—in private—to Aguilera and Flores. I had no chance to eavesdrop, but I knew I was getting close. Unfortunately, it was only a week later that we lost our next American asset in the zone."

"You mean, the three environmentalists?" Julie asked incredulously as he paused. "But—you don't think that was related to the other attacks? I thought the autopsy came out that they died of some tropical disease."

"I know it was related," Rick said flatly. "You see, I knew one of them— John, the photographer. Not personally, but I'd read his file. He was one of ours. Never mind what agency, but he was intel. He didn't know who I was—fortunately, or I wouldn't be sitting here telling you this right now. But Colonel Thornton tipped me off that he was in the zone. I was to be his backup if the guerrillas reneged on their safe passage. In any case, John was good, and he knew the jungle if the two civilians with him didn't. Besides, he was carrying a GPS. There's no way he got them lost out there for three full weeks.

"So you think the FARC *did* kill them?" Julie asked.

"No, I don't. Aguilera signed their safe passage, and he was all for what they were doing. The guerrillas are big on keeping the multinational corporations out of their territory. Besides, I was there when they brought in the bodies. He was as shocked as anyone. No, I think they died because John found what I've been looking for. And I think, too, despite his protests of innocence, that Aguilera knows this was no natural death because he tried to cancel the press conference after he'd called it. Someone further up the chain of command ordered him to go ahead with it, but to limit any serious laboratory tests."

"But . . ." Julie's forehead wrinkled in the dark. "That means whoever called Aguilera had to know what killed those guys and that a thorough autopsy would show it."

"That's right," Rick agreed. "Meaning that this mystery caller was most likely responsible in some way for their deaths. Problem was, we had no idea where John and the others ended up. We knew the location of the Indian village where John was last seen. What we don't know is what the Indians told them or where they took them, because the whole village promptly disappeared. We know they headed downstream in dugout canoes— that much came from the pilot. Coincidentally, both the village and their canoe trip were in the same general direction as those cargo shipments I'd seen going downriver. My gut feeling is that John stumbled on the destination of that cargo . . . some kind of a terrorist camp or military training base, maybe."

"And you think those Muslim terrorists or whoever is running the place killed them to cover it up," Julie concluded. "But why return the bodies? Wouldn't it make more sense to have them disappear altogether and avoid all this fuss?"

"When VIPs disappear, there are search parties and questions. No, having them turn up—and a long way from where they were last seen—was the easiest way to put an end to it. Especially if they could convince the world of their 'natural causes' theory. Which didn't work for me, of course, because I knew who John was."

Rick's arm brushed against Julie's again as he made a small shift in the position of the AK-47 on his lap. "Which is why I knew I had to retrace his steps, find out just where he'd gone and why, even if it meant waiting for the next plane and tracking its cargo upriver. When Aguilera decided instead to send me to Bogotá with Manuel Flores, I tried to talk him out of it. The last thing I needed was to have someone back at Fort Bragg or San José picking my ugly mug off the six o'clock news and asking why Rick Martini, 7th Special Operations Group, was standing on a platform translating for a guerrilla commander instead of on special assignment out West where I had ostensibly been reassigned. But I couldn't talk too loudly. I was supposed to be their interpreter, and Aguilera is no different than any commanding officer when it comes to handing down orders and expecting them to be obeyed."

"So you think maybe someone recognized you?" Julie asked. "No—that wouldn't work, or they wouldn't have been so sure I was their spy. Unless— you don't think that's why they put that tracking device in your gun clip?"

"No, I don't," Rick answered definitely. "It's been weeks. If someone had recognized me and reported back to the FARC, they would have grabbed me long ago. Especially since we know now that they have a source in counter-narcotics. Whoever tipped Aguilera off yesterday that there was still a spy in camp didn't know whether it was male or female and was still assuming it was one of the UN team. No, I think you hit the nail on the head—someone besides myself overheard you last night and figured your theory was worth checking out. With what just happened to be the worst of timing for me.

"In any case, going back to where we were, right after the autopsy, Aguilera received a phone call. He has the only sat-phone in the zone. Another plane was coming in, and they wanted the UN team out of there before arrival. I hoped this might be the break I'd been waiting for. Unfortunately . . ."

His voice turned wooden. "A half-hour later, he received another call with new orders. It seemed Aguilera's mysterious contacts—whom we can assume now were these Middle Eastern friends of his—had received a tip that there was an American spy among the UN team, and they'd just made a positive ID. A certain Julie Baker had been seen sneaking out the gate."

*Sondra Kharrazi*, Julie thought hollowly, already knowing what was coming next.

"You can fill in the blanks from there. As soon as Victor radioed that he had you and McAdams, Aguilera announced your kidnapping by the *para-militares*. That reporter woman who was with you confirmed that you'd left the grounds voluntarily. You know the rest. The next morning, the UN team took off, Bill Shidler protesting every inch of the way. And I received new orders to accompany Aguilera, not to meet that incoming cargo plane as I'd hoped, but to interrogate their newest prisoner."

Rick didn't allow even a hint of blame to creep into his brittle voice, but Julie felt tears prickle at the back of her throat and nose. No wonder he'd been so furious when he'd ridden into camp that day. And she had kept him chained to her side all these last weeks as well, when he could have been out looking for whatever it was that this John had found out there or at least at *Comandante* Aguilera's side where something useful might have surfaced to complete his mission.

*He must really hate me,* Julie thought.

But none of that anger was in his voice as his head turned toward Julie in the dark. Instead, it was quiet and even apologetic. "For what it's worth, Julie, leaving you—and McAdams—in that situation was the hardest call I've ever made. But I couldn't stop that interrogation. It would have only gotten us both killed. And afterward—well, like I said, you were in no immediate danger. Sure, I had the radio. I could have called in a rescue mission. But the guerrillas are ready for that—as you saw! An all-out assault would have just gotten people killed—maybe even you. And it would have been the end of my mission.

"Even if I'd just tried to get word out that you and Tim McAdams were alive and safe, it would have tipped the guerrillas off that they had a mole in the camp. I had to believe my primary mission was more urgent than your temporary comfort or even the men and equipment being expended to search for you."

Not to mention his life, if he were overheard communicating with some-one outside the camp. "Couldn't you at least have told me?" Julie asked. "If I'd known who you were and what you were doing, I'd have under-stood. At least I wouldn't have been worrying myself sick, thinking I might be there for the rest of my life or . . . or killed!"

"When?" Rick demanded. "We were never alone in that camp, you know that. Besides, what did I know about you? You're a reporter, and you don't exactly come across as a devious young woman, Julie Baker! How was I to know whether you could be trusted not to let slip who I really was? The smallest change of attitude on your part could have been fatal. No, I'm sorry I had to put you through all that, but I saw no other option."

*He was so inflexible and so . . . so right,* Julie thought bitterly.

"Okay, maybe you are right," she admitted aloud. "So the feelings of a couple of reporters dumb enough to get in the way don't count much compared to this . . . this mission of yours. I can accept that. But my life too? Or did you just decide to write me off, like the expendable crewman in those old *Star Trek* episodes."

There was a short silence beside her. Then Rick asked coldly, "And what, exactly, do you mean by that?"

"Last night!" Julie cried out, and the anguished words fell so loud into the silence of the night that they startled her, as well as some small animal nearby that she heard scurrying away through the brush. She dropped her voice to a hiss. "They were going to kill me! You knew it, and you were going to let them! Carlos overheard the whole thing. You were the one who suggested pretending to take me to San Ignacio and then shooting me along the way. You were willing to let them kill me—maybe even shoot me yourself for all I know—just to protect your precious cover and this mission of yours!"

"Now just hold it!" Rick's tone was suddenly icy steel, and Julie broke off at the clipped harshness of his order. "I had a feeling something like this precipitated your little escape effort this morning. Well, you can rest assured I had no plans to sacrifice you to my cover or my mission, as you put it. On the contrary, last night I was doing my level best to save your life!"

"But—"

"Let me finish!" he went on inexorably. "Carlos was right. I *was* in on the discussion to kill you, and you can be glad I was, or Aguilera would have taken you out and shot you out-of-hand right there in the camp. Believe it or not, I've been bracing myself for this ever since they captured you, and I've never had any intention of just walking away, even if it meant blowing this mission once and for all. But there was no way I could intervene in the camp—there were just too many of them. My plan was simple and with a reasonably low risk factor. I'd get you out of camp and down the trail with Jaime and Victor."

Julie listened with unwilling fascination and a growing horror as his words punched at her out of the darkness. "When the time was right, I'd take the two of them out—no, not shoot them, unless I had to," he responded to the small sound of revulsion in Julie's throat. "Just get the jump on them and take them captive. They'd have been too valuable for intel to waste anyway. Then I planned to call in Colonel Thornton to airlift you—and them—out. With any luck, I might even have wangled a story that would get me back into camp—you'd escaped, and we'd split up to go after you, Victor and Jaime dropped out of radio contact, I'd searched for a day or two but couldn't find them or you, so I headed back to camp. It might have worked—enough to save both you and my mission. But when morning came—"

"We were gone," Julie finished in a whisper. While Rick had narrated his rescue plan, she'd felt as though the very air were being pressed from her lungs, and now as the horrible realization sunk in, she felt physically sick. It hadn't been Rick's sins that had gotten Carlos killed; it had been hers!

"Then Carlos—it was all unnecessary!" Julie dropped her head onto her knees, and her voice came out as a muffled groan, her hands clenching convulsively where she was resting her forehead on them as she fought to hold back the long shudders that were running through her. "We didn't need to escape at all! I . . . I got him killed for nothing!"

A tentative touch brushed across Julie's hair, briefly rested on her shoulder before dropping away. "Don't start blaming yourself," Rick ordered harshly. "You couldn't know—anymore than I could have guessed Carlos was out there listening to our plans and that he would risk his life to warn you before I could get to you. I'm not going to be able to live with that too easily myself. But you have nothing to blame yourself for. You made your decisions based on the data you had—and so did Carlos, and so did I. What came out of it was nobody's fault—unless you want to blame the guerrillas. They're the ones who killed Carlos, not you."

Julie couldn't stop the sobs that were shaking her body, the tears pouring down her cheeks. That all of Carlos's sacrifice, his turning his back on his new life and cause and comrades to help her, his violent death, had been unnecessary just seemed so . . . so cruel an irony.

Julie didn't realize she'd spoken aloud until Rick said quietly, "Don't denigrate Carlos's sacrifice by calling it unnecessary, Julie. He knew exactly what he was doing—and it was a lot more than just helping you escape. He made a choice back there. A good one. And if it cost him his life, we don't know that it was unnecessary—not for him, not for you. Not even for me, because if Victor and Jaime really did have a suspicion I wasn't who I claimed to be, they might have gotten the jump on me out there. In which case Carlos may have saved both our lives. Only God knows that, or where Carlos might have ended up if he hadn't made that choice. On the casualty list of the next FARC raid for all we know. Or rotting in a Colombian jail cell like a lot of guerrillas. Carlos's life—and death—were as much in God's hands today as yours, and I think if you could ask him, he would say it was worth it even the way it turned out."

Yes, Carlos had felt it was worth it. Beyond belief, he had felt that *she,* Julie Baker, was worth it. That she had been sent by God to rescue him as he had rescued her. *He's with his family now—Don Ramon, Gabriela, all of them,* Julie told herself and found comfort in the thought. And if there was a future Julie had wanted for him that the boy would never see, that too was God's province, not hers.

*Okay, God, I can't even figure out the whys of my own life. I'll let You figure out Carlos.* Julie would never forget the merry little boy who had grown into the hardened teenage guerrilla and then, in a bizarre twist of fate, redeemed himself and her with his life. But she could let him go now, and with him the sharpest edge of her grief, and as Julie made that conscious decision, an overwhelming weariness pressed in on her that she didn't understand was the release of all the fear and sorrow and spent adrenaline of the past hours. With a last ragged sob, she let her eyelids droop shut, no longer fighting the waves of fatigue that swept over her, along with the soothing rise and fall of Rick's quiet voice.

"It's something we all go through when a companion gets killed in battle and we survive. You blame yourself—figure if you'd only done something different, they'd still be alive. 'Survivor's guilt,' they call it. You can't let it get to you. It'll paralyze your actions, your decision-making capabilities, if you do. Which we can't afford right now. We're not out of the danger zone yet. In fact, if you're up to it, there are several things we need to discuss."

Rick paused for a response from his companion. But the only sound in the darkness beside him was a slow, rhythmic breathing. Then he heard the girl stir and a small unhappy sigh.

"Julie?" he asked quietly.

When there was no answer, he took out his penlight and switched it on, shielding its thin beam with his hand as he turned it on his companion. The girl was still sitting up, her arms wrapped around her knees, her head turned sideways where it was resting against them. Rick could see her face where her damp curls had fallen away. But she wasn't listening to his careful advice. She was sound asleep, her breath coming softly through her parted lips and her long eyelashes lying against the one cheek he could see.

There were tears on that cheek and a scratch he hadn't noticed before that extended in a vicious red line from the edge of her eyebrow down almost to the corner of her mouth. Even as he examined the injury, that very vulnerable-looking mouth quivered, and the girl let out another small, unhappy sigh in her sleep before turning her face away from the light.

Rick switched off the flashlight. Feeling around for her knapsack, he eased the sleeping girl over so she was lying on her side, her head on the canvas bag as a pillow. She didn't even stir. Rick listened to her soft breathing for a long moment. Then he picked up the AK-47 and rose to his feet.

Walking over to the edge of the stump, he lifted his head, straining every sense of sight and smell and hearing into the night. He wasn't searching for his former companions. He knew their patterns too well. They would be bedded down now around a fire and wouldn't move out again until dawn. Still, he couldn't shake the feeling that watching eyes had been pursuing him all day. Not hostile nor benign. Just eyes.

But there was none of that ominous quiet that came with intruders into alien territory. Even their own intrusion had been inspected and dismissed as harmless by the denizens of this part of the jungle, and the night around him was alive with the normal small sounds of frogs and monkeys and sloths and birds settling down to sleep. A pair of eyes that gleamed green against the darkness before vanishing was too close together and near to the ground to be a serious predator.

Satisfied, the Special Forces officer hunkered down on his boot heels and settled himself to keep watch over the night and the sleeping girl.

# TWENTY

"Julie!"

The hushed call roused Julie from a dreamless sleep. Raising reluctant eyelids, she saw only darkness and closed them again. She was sinking back into slumber when a hand shook her shoulder, insistently. "Julie, would you wake up, please?"

Brightness penetrated her eyelids. Grudgingly Julie opened her eyes. The soft beam of the pencil flashlight outlined the stark planes of Rick's face above it. "Julie, I'm going to have to get some sleep," he said quietly. "But we need to keep someone on watch. Are you up to staying awake for a couple hours?"

"Mmmm!" Julie sat up, stiff muscles protesting the move. Sleepily, she hauled her wrist into view. Four A.M.! Straightening hastily, she took in the Special Forces officer squatted down beside her, the butt of the AK-47 resting against the wood of the stump, his eyes dark and alert above the narrow beam of light but lines of weariness etched deeply around his mouth.

"Yes, of course I can stay awake. You should have woken me hours ago!"

"You needed your rest." As Julie scrambled to her feet, Rick laid his weapon down beside him and stretched out with a tired sigh.

"Mind if I borrow this?" Reaching for her knapsack, he paused long enough for her to nod before shoving it under his head. "If you see or hear anything, call me. Anything—even if it turns out to be a false alarm. Okay?"

He held her gaze until she nodded again, feeling a sudden impulse to salute and say, "Yes, sir!" Then he turned off the flashlight and handed it to her. The night went immediately black, and he said out of the darkness, "Don't use that unless you have to. Those are the only batteries." His voice slowed, slurring with tiredness. "It'll be light in a couple hours. Wake me then."

His breathing slowed further to the deep, even rhythm of sleep. Julie switched the flashlight on briefly to find her way to the edge of the stump. Darkness restored, she thrust the light into a pocket and sat down, her legs dangling at first over the edge. With a sudden feeling of unease, she pulled her legs up and crossed them beneath her.

The action brought back wry memories of the monster that had resided for years under her brass bedstead in San Ignacio. But if there was anything lurking over the edge of the stump, it was as silent as that product of childhood imagination.

Julie relaxed. She was wide awake and would have given much for a cup of coffee. But the last weeks had taught her a capacity she'd never had before for stillness and patient waiting, and she settled herself to both. This was the quietest hour of the jungle night, when the frogs and chirping insects had ceased their serenade and all but a few nocturnal hunters lay deep in slumber. The only sound Julie heard was the quiet breathing behind her.

Dawn stole gray into the jungle, the massive columns of the trees and the feathery outline of ferns and other underbrush coming so gradually into focus that it was like watching a negative being developed. Julie waited until the grayness brightened to green before responding to an increasingly urgent call of nature. She washed up at the edge of the stream, running wet fingers through her hair to coax out all the snarls. Stepping over a shallow mound in the mud of the stream bank, she walked back to the stump and hoisted herself up onto the surface.

Rick was still sleeping. Julie walked over to look down at him. He was lying stretched out on his side, his back against the rotting wood of the eaten-out shell as though to ensure nothing could creep up on him, one arm wrapped around her knapsack that he was using as a pillow, the other stretched out to touch the AK-47. Even in sleep he looked ready to jump to his feet at the slightest intimation of danger.

He must have been very tired. The long lines of his body were relaxed as Julie had never seen them, and the grim concentration that had tightened jaw and mouth during their march the day before had eased as well. He looked younger and less forbidding than she would have thought possible.

Sitting down, Julie drew her knees up to her chin, wrapping her arms around them, and studied the sleeping man. Since she'd first seen him striding through TV cameras back in the airport in Bogotá, her view of this man had forcibly undergone so many changes that she had to ask herself again—just who was this Rick Martini?

Julie knew of the Green Berets and other such elite military units. She'd seen the movies, read the books. But she'd never thought to consider what kind of people they might be. They were taught to fight and kill with an efficiency no one else on the face of the planet possessed, that much she knew, and as a journalist in a field that traditionally held her country's massive and pollution-wracked military machine in poor esteem, this had certainly colored Julie's initial opinion of him, an impression she held even after she'd discovered Rick was not the guerrilla she'd thought him to be.

That a soldier might view the skills he'd learned in the same way a surgeon did—unpleasant and painful and to be used only when there were no other options—had never occurred to Julie before. Yet Rick had not killed yesterday even when it might have made their escape easier. Nor by his own account did he enjoy or condone violence any more than Julie herself. The discipline and commitment it had taken to exist months on end in enemy territory was—well, impressive, to say the least.

There was, in fact, an air of competence about this man, even in his sleep, that was a world away from the easy self-confidence that had so impressed her in Tim McAdams. The journalist's jovial self-assurance seemed based on the spurious assumption that everything was sure to turn out all right, that nothing really bad could possibly touch him. Rick's quiet authority was born of having faced up to only too many deadly obstacles and won through to the other side.

And if Rick Martini had been impatient and cold and angry with her, he had also on occasion been kind. And Julie recognized now that he had watched out for her well-being from that first moment when he'd snatched her out of death's way back in San José.

"You know, I think I like you, Rick Martini," Julie said softly.

Too bad the Special Forces officer didn't share that sentiment. To Rick, Julie was a meddlesome reporter who had stumbled into his life and mission with disastrous consequences, who now hung around his neck as an unwelcome appendage for whom he was responsible, and who was holding him back from more urgent duties. He would no doubt be more than happy to shake her out of his life once they got out of this mess, and would certainly feel nothing but relief if he never saw one Julie Baker again.

"So—do I have mud on my face, or are you just checking out the local wildlife?"

Julie flushed as she realized that Rick's eyes were open and fastened on her. She jumped to her feet. "No, I was just debating if I should wake you up. You looked so tired. You've only slept for maybe three hours."

Getting to his feet, Rick reached for his shirt and shrugged it on. "I've done with less." He yawned hugely as he ran a hand over his face and hair. "Oh, boy," he groaned. He glanced quizzically down at Julie. "Did I see toothpaste somewhere in that bag of yours?"

"Sure—here." Digging the tube out of her knapsack, Julie handed it to him. "But you're going to have to use your finger. I'm afraid I draw the line at my toothbrush."

His mouth curved briefly at that, but his expression was distant and preoccupied, and to Julie it seemed he hardly saw her as he picked up the AK-47 and walked over to the edge of the stump. His gaze narrowed to study the jungle around him, his head high in that listening attitude of his. Walking over to his side, Julie listened too, but she could hear only the morning cawing of parrots and a troupe of spider monkeys awakening overhead.

"What is it?" she asked anxiously. "Do you think they're still out there?"

Rick shook his head without relaxing the intensity of his survey. "No, I think we've lost the guerrillas. Without a tracker, they'll still be combing the banks of that river. But . . ."

His gaze dropped finally to Julie, but not as though he were seeing a person, she thought. More as though he were studying a problem. "When I get back, we need to talk."

"Yes, I know," Julie said quickly. Her stomach rumbled as she said it, a reminder that breakfast was long overdue, and Rick threw Julie a wry glance as the color rose to her face. "About that, among other things."

He was back in less than ten minutes, his hair damp like hers, so that despite its length he looked as neat and groomed as a soldier on parade, his fatigues holding no wrinkles from their unorthodox laundering and even his boots polished clean of mud.

A few weeks ago, the contrast with Julie's slept-in appearance and un-ruly curls would have been cause for a corresponding self-consciousness, and sent her hurrying to dig out mirror and makeup case. Her public image had long since ceased to be of importance, and if Julie had first encountered this man carefully made-up for the lens of any roving camera, he had since seen her cowering and hysterical, bruised and battered, soak-ing wet, and in every other possible situation. There was little point now in trying to maintain impressions.

Julie sat down at the edge of the stump as Rick vaulted up onto its surface, this time letting her legs dangle over the edge now that she could see the innocuous tangle of ferns and fungal growths sprouting there. Rick walked over to retrieve the casing of his hand radio before joining her. Julie could see the hole where the bullet had gone clean through and the shattered pieces of the interior, and even with her limited technical ability, it was clear to her that the radio would never transmit again. Rick poked at the contents of the casing, moving around broken pieces of circuit board and wires, before he set it beside him with a sigh.

"Julie, I'm not going to lie to you," he said harshly. "If there is any danger of Victor and his unit catching up to us now, it's small and decreasing with every hour we put between them and us. It's hard enough to find someone who wants to be found in this jungle without going after someone in hiding. But that doesn't mean we're out of trouble. This radio was our only communication, and it's done for. I'd hoped I might at least salvage the GPS transmitter so HQ could home in on our location and send someone to get us out. But if there's a hope of piecing it back together, it would take a better tech than I am. Which means that we have no way of knowing where we are, or letting anyone else know where we are. And without either sun or stars as guide . . ."

He glanced up at the swaying canopy of leaves and vines that blocked any glimpse of what had to be blue sky beyond. "The odds of getting out of here and back to base are not good. Do you understand what I'm saying?"

Julie nodded. "Yes, I understand, and I'm . . . I'm really sorry. Your whole mission is in jeopardy, and it's all my fault. I feel terrible."

"My mission!" Rick looked down at her with exasperation. "Are you not getting the seriousness of what I just said? I'm not worried about my mission right now. I'm concerned about our lives. We are lost in a jungle that's thousands—maybe tens of thousands—of square miles. We have no food at all. What we ate last night was the last I had on me. And frankly, I haven't seen a whole lot out here that's on any survival food list I ever studied. Even if we don't starve to death, there are jaguars and anacondas and who knows what else out there, besides your crocodiles. And that's if we don't stumble over some hostile Indian tribe. People who get lost out here usually don't come walking out. We might have more chance of getting out of here with our lives if we could reactivate one of those bugs and let Victor catch us."

As Julie's face whitened, he added roughly, "I'm not trying to frighten you. But you're a responsible adult, and you deserve to know the truth. We will, of course, make every effort to walk out of here. Hopefully, we will come across some game. But we need to face the reality of our situation. The odds of making it even if I was on my own—"

"And not held back by a female city-slicker reporter?" Julie finished evenly.

"That isn't what I meant."

"I know what you meant!" Julie cut in bitingly. "Okay, I don't blame you. You haven't exactly seen my best side these last weeks, have you? And yesterday, well, I . . . I just don't like crocodiles. But if you think I'm going to hold you back—where did you learn to move around in the jungle?"

Rick gave her a hard glance, then shrugged. "Fort Benning, Georgia. Special Forces training. Though the emphasis there was on sneaking through the brush without being seen, not on finding your way around. Sure, we all practiced basic survival techniques, but never where it would take more than a day or two to walk out to civilization. I've been in the jungle here plenty—both in San José and with the FARC. But never without native guides, I'm afraid."

"Yes, well, I grew up in these jungles, remember? And I can assure you that people have been finding their way around in here without a GPS for thousands of years. No one ever starved to death, either—or needed to anyway."

"You mean, the Indians," Rick said slowly.

"That's right, the Indians. And if they can do it, so can we. Maybe it'll take us a while, but there's no reason why we shouldn't get out of here in one piece." Julie stopped to find Rick's eyes intent on her face.

"Go on," he said quietly. "I'm listening."

Julie looked at him uncertainly. He was wearing that inscrutable look that had served him so well among the guerrillas, and she couldn't tell what he was thinking. But he sat there waiting as though he were genuinely interested in what she had to say, so she went on. "Well, when I was a kid, my father always told me that if I ever got lost in the jungle, there was one surefire way to find my way out. Just find water and head downstream."

Rick's eyebrow shot up. "Find water?"

"That's right. You see, if you follow water downstream long enough, it will eventually empty into a larger stream. And then into a larger one. It might not be the most direct route, but if you keep following it, sooner or later you're going to make it to a good-sized river. And rivers are where people live. Maybe just an Indian village, but Indians have canoes and access to other rivers and villages, and sooner or later you're going to find someone who can get you back to civilization. At least . . . well, I've never actually had to put it to the test. But that's what my father always said, and he should know."

Julie trailed off into his silence. Was that scorn or approbation behind those immobile features? Rick shook his head slowly. "Your father was a wise man. It just—yes, it just might work. Except—there's one major problem. Have you ever seen a map of this zone? Well, I have, and I'm afraid it isn't as easy as you make it sound."

"I didn't say it would be easy," Julie started, but Rick cut her off with a sharp gesture. "The rivers in these parts don't flow toward civilization. The entire river system of southern Colombia drains away from settled areas and down into the Amazon basin. Some of them into the Amazon River itself. Maybe if we reversed the process and followed them upstream— no, that wouldn't work, would it? They'd just peter out. But following rivers downstream is going to take us deeper and deeper into the jungle. It could take us months to walk out, even if nothing else went wrong.

"And what guarantee do we have that any Indian tribes we come across won't be headhunters—or at least harbor a grudge against invaders in their territory? And if we do by some miracle make it through to some outpost of civilization, the colonized areas south of here are major strongholds of drug trafficking as well as guerrilla and paramilitary fighting. We could be walking from one cooking pot straight into another."

"Do you have a better idea?" Julie demanded. "It beats wandering around in circles until we give up and die! As for your headhunting Indians, that's more Hollywood than anything. Even out here, there aren't many Indian groups who haven't had some contact with the outside world—indigenous rights activists and anthropologists if not missionaries. Or Spanish traders. My parents had contacts with some of the tribes in these jungles. I'm not saying they're 'civilized' the way we would term it. But most of them are pretty peaceful anymore. The guerrillas and drug dealers are a whole lot more likely than the Indians to shoot first and ask questions later. As for starving to death—here, give me your knife."

Rick raised his eyebrow again, but without further argument, he slipped the heavy combat knife from its sheath and handed it to her. Sliding down off the stump, Julie walked over to a stand of saplings that had sprung up among its roots. Few would mature much further, but the death of the parent tree had allowed a gap in the ecosystem that might allow one at least to take its place.

But not the one that came first to Julie's hand. She sliced off a length as tall as herself, discovering with approval that Rick kept his blade razor-sharp, and with a few quick strokes sharpened one end of the sapling into a point. He followed silently on her heels as she carried the makeshift spear down to the stream bed. A quick glance located the barely perceptible curve of the mound she had stepped over earlier. The smallest indentation on top of the mound was an airhole. With a sharp thrust, Julie speared the center of the mound. Reaching down to dig into the mud, she pulled out a large toad and handed the limp carcass to Rick. Two more quick thrusts into nearby mounds netted her another pair.

For the first time in weeks, she felt like laughing as she caught the expression on Rick's face. "Just don't try this if you don't know what you're doing. Some of these are poisonous. By the way, you do have matches, I hope!"

\* \* \*

A half-hour later, Rick looked at Julie across the small campfire he'd built at the base of the old stump. "Like chicken, right?" he said ironically.

Julie dropped a thigh bone to the ground beside her. It felt good to have a full stomach, however unorthodox the fare. "That's what gringos always say. Iguana, crocodile, just about anything you catch out here—it all tastes like chicken. Personally, I think it tastes like toad, but that's me!"

Tossing his own bones aside, Rick pulled the matchbook he'd used to light the fire from his shirt pocket, frowning at the scant two-dozen matches it contained. "This isn't going to last us too many days, even if we're careful."

"And I thought you Special Forces types were supposed to be prepared for everything," Julie retorted. Her glance across the campfire was challenging. However valid his excuses, she hadn't totally forgiven him for the deceit of the last weeks nor the cool impatience of his attitude toward her.

Rick's eyes were hooded as they met her challenge. "I wasn't counting on spending a month in the woods. And if we 'Special Forces types' "—he emphasized the title she'd given him—"believe in being prepared for any emergency, the guerrillas don't! Taking along the usual seventy-pound pack complete with MRE rations, first-aid kit, and a full checklist of field equipment would have been difficult to explain to the FARC. Even an extra canteen on a hunting expedition would have raised eyebrows. So we're just going to have to go with what we've got.

"However . . ."—Rick dug a Bic lighter from another vest pocket—"the guerrillas do smoke like chimneys. And since I don't, this one is still full. Even so, we're going to have to be careful. In fact, we're going to have to ration everything we've got, from soap to toothpaste to those medical supplies I noticed you're carrying in your backpack there. We don't know how long we're going to be out here."

Julie had no retort to that. She nodded soberly. Rick was right. They would have to treat every possession they had as gold. The emergency items she packed so casually for every trip and so seldom used might now make the difference in their very survival.

Julie looked up at Rick, who had gotten to his feet and was already dousing the fire, dumping the toad bones and skins on top, and burying the whole thing under dirt and brush as she'd seen the guerrillas wipe out traces of their camps before moving on. Whatever her lingering resentments against this man and whatever sentiments he might harbor against her, they had both better put them aside until they were back in civilization. She needed Rick, and he needed her, however reluctant he might be to admit it, if they were ever to walk out of this rainforest alive.

Rick had been right. However lightly Julie might have touched on the obstacles ahead, she was well aware of them. The Indian tribes might roam these woods freely. But they were a larger population group, and even with their expertise, death struck them on a regular basis. A snake bite. An unwary misstep along the caiman-infested riverbanks. A predator hungry enough to overcome its distaste for human flesh. A tropical fever. If she or Rick got sick out here, the limited supply of over-the-counter remedies she was carrying wasn't going to do much good.

Retrieving her knapsack from the stump, Julie swung it to her shoulder. Rick walked down to the stream to fill his canteen, then gave their campsite a final cursory glance. "Are you ready? Fine, let's head out. We'll try it your way—downstream."

Julie fell into step behind him. The trick was to not think beyond the present. *Just take one day at a time. One hour. The next step.* Looking further ahead only meant a quick descent into fear and madness.

They were an hour into the day's trek when the stream petered out, disappearing into a gully that must have caved in on itself at some point. Both gully and stream were swallowed up in a jumble of earth and rocks and an overgrowth of vines and ferns. Julie braced herself for some reproach from Rick. But after studying the cave-in, he simply skirted the patch of green and continued straight ahead. A quarter-hour later, they picked up the stream again, bubbling out of the ground in a trickle of wet that gradually became a full-fledged brook.

Rick was no more communicative than the day before, striding along with his AK-47 cradled in his hands, his head turning constantly to search the woods around them. He hardly seemed to notice Julie at his heels, but she had only to stumble or lag behind a few steps to find him back at her side.

Julie left their safety from either human or animal predators to Rick, keeping her eyes open for anything edible. Those toad legs, palatable though she personally found them, wouldn't carry them far, and the same factors that allowed for easy passage also made foraging difficult because any smaller fruit-bearing trees were choked out by the giant hardwoods overhead. Even the toads that had burrowed into the bank at night had hopped into the water by the time morning wore on.

By early afternoon, as she had predicted, the brook tumbled into a wider stream, not quite wide enough to classify as a river, but wide enough to allow sunlight to pierce through the jungle canopy. The result was an explosion of vegetation, and Rick had to unsheathe his machete to chop a path along the stream bank.

Julie recognized edible plants and fruit, though few would be identified as such by a North American grocer. She stopped under a branch that hung thick with brown globules no larger than a Ping-Pong ball. Picking one, she cracked the thin shell and handed it to Rick.

"Mamones. They called them 'snot balls' at boarding school."

Rick eyed the translucent flesh inside with distaste. "I can see why!"

The edible membrane was wrapped around a large seed. Each globule offered little more than a taste, and though vaguely sweet, it left a dry, puckering taste in the mouth. Still, it was food, and Rick and Julie worked their way through a dozen before piling all they could easily reach into Julie's knapsack.

Further downstream, Julie stopped to pick some foot-long pods that held a white cottony fluff wrapped around shiny black seeds. Dried out, they were used as a rattle by I'paa dancers, but the fluff was edible too. Later in the afternoon, she directed Rick in chopping down a small palm. There were countless varieties of palms in the jungle, but only a few were edible, and these had been over-harvested in colonized areas to the point where environmentalists were mounting a campaign against their continued appearance on the menu of gourmet restaurants around the world. But her colleagues' opinions on her intended diet were the last concern on Julie's mind now. This was about survival, not environmental policy. Wrapping the palm's edible core in one of its fronds, she added it to her collection.

Though supper was now assured, Julie saw none of the game she'd hoped for along the banks, not even caimans, since this stream was too shallow and swift running to offer the reptiles a comfortable habitat. She and Rick would need protein. The problem wasn't a lack of game. It was that jungle creatures had good ears and didn't hang around for the bumbling intruders in their territory to stumble over them.

Just as the narrow band of sky overhead was fading to green, the stream began to spread out and slow down. At the same time, the tumbling waters began to fall away from the bank along which they were hiking, or else the embankment began to grow. Ten minutes later, a final swing of Rick's machete brought them out onto a high promontory formed by the joining of the stream bed down which they had climbed all afternoon, with a real jungle river.

There were rivers in the Amazon Basin that were more than a mile wide. The Amazon itself was two miles across in parts, more like a great inland sea to the human eye than a river. With the difficulties of building roads through dense jungle and the prohibitive expense of air travel for most of the area's scant population, the riverways had early on become the veins of transportation and trade that connected the vast and still largely untouched rainforest banding South America's equator from southern Colombia and Venezuela through much of Brazil all the way to northern Bolivia and Peru.

This particular river was by no means a large one. Even in the growing dusk, Julie could easily make out the opposite bank. But it was several times as wide as the stream they'd swum across the day before, its muddy, placid flow amply deep for canoes and the flat-bottomed river barges. It was, in fact, precisely the sort of major tributary Julie had hoped they would eventually stumble across, and to come upon it so early into their trek was encouraging. Surely there would be Indians, if not colonists, living somewhere along its length.

Julie stepped up to the edge of the promontory and looked down. The embankment rose several times a man's height above the water level, and across the river Julie could make out a similar bluff, showing just how high the waters could rise in full flood season.

But at this season the waters had receded to leave a wide, rock-strewn beach on either side, and with a shudder Julie realized they wouldn't be fording this river, at least not without some kind of raft or boat. Long, ugly shapes stretched out along the far bank and downstream on their own side as well. Even as Julie watched, one of the caimans moved, its triangular-shaped snout swinging from side to side as it shuffled down to the water and slid smoothly under the surface.

Julie raised her head. Though she knew they were deep into the rainforest, there was an openness here that made her feel she was free from the jungle for the first time in weeks. Behind them, the sun had dropped below the tree line, and its setting rays reflecting off the river had transmuted the water's muddy surface to a deep, glorious gold.

From the far bank, a flock of fruit bats rose with a flutter of wings and wheeled out over the water, their outstretched wings black aerodynamic shapes against the fantastic color palette of the evening sky. Below them Julie spotted the first star springing out just above the ragged line of the jungle canopy.

In the midst of the ugliness of the last days and the uncertainty of the next, it was all so unexpectedly lovely that Julie gasped in delight. Rick stepped to her side, his head turning to make a careful survey of the panorama spread out beneath them.

"Pretty, isn't it? When I come across a piece of God's creation that man hasn't had a chance to screw up yet, it makes me feel there really is something still worth fighting for in this crazy world."

Julie looked up at him in surprise. "You sound like an environmentalist. I never thought I'd hear a soldier on the tree-hugger side of the fence."

Rick dropped his gaze to her, a wry twist touching the corner of his firm mouth. "Is that some kind of slam? Well, don't confuse me with any of your 'save the whales over starving street kids' pals, like that C-PAP bunch. But I figure, if God gave us a world this grand to live in, we should take care of it."

He nodded toward her knapsack. "Might as well rest that load. We won't find a better place to camp before dark."

The promontory on which they had emerged formed a small triangular-shaped peninsula, jutting out above the junction of the waterways. It was covered with the same heavy brush through which Rick had chopped a path most of the afternoon. Rick used the machete to gesture around him. "I'll clear us a campsite if you'll get a fire started."

He tossed Julie the matches, adding with distaste as she unloaded the frond-wrapped package of palm heart, "I hope you know how to cook that. If we've been reduced to eating tree trunks, I won't kick up a fuss. But I'd rather not try it raw."

"Oh, I've got more than tree trunk on the menu. Now that we've found that." Julie nodded toward the river. "It won't be pretty, but it'll be meat."

"Is that so? And what, exactly, do you have in mind?" Rick lowered the machete to watch as Julie dug into her knapsack. She'd used her one dress and slip with Carlos. It would have to be the sweatshirt.

"You'll see. May I borrow your knife?"

Rick eyed Julie suspiciously as he unsheathed his combat knife and passed it to her. "I don't know what you're planning on doing with that thing, but I'll tell you right up front that I draw the line at insects, high protein or not."

As he caught her next move, he sprang forward and grabbed her wrist. "Are you crazy? What do you think you're doing?"

Julie widened the gash on the back of her hand before Rick could wrest the combat knife away from her. "Getting us some supper," she told Rick calmly, twisting her wrist free from his strong fingers. "That palm heart isn't going to keep us on our feet, and I haven't seen any other meat all day. Trust me—unless you want to try for one of those crocodiles out there."

Picking up the sweatshirt, she wiped one sleeve over the blood tricking down the back of her hand. A finger would have bled more easily, but she didn't want to risk reducing the use of her hands. Rick, thrusting the combat knife back into its sheath, watched her grimly. *He's trying to decide whether to throw me in the loony bin or have me court-martialed for insubordination,* Julie thought, with an impulse to giggle.

Wrapping the blood-stained material around her hand, she walked over to the embankment. The caimans didn't seem to like the rushing water of the stream tumbling into the river because there were none on the beach below them—the only reason she was trying this stunt. Rick followed right on her heels as she scrambled down the steep bank, his AK-47 off his shoulder and balanced in his hands and his narrowed gaze on the caimans sleeping peacefully downstream.

His expression lightened somewhat as Julie walked down to the water's edge, unwrapping the sweatshirt from her arm as she did so. "Okay, I get what you're trying to do. Here, let me have that. If anyone's going to try a crazy stunt like this, I'll do it."

The forbidding set of his jaw didn't allow for argument, and Julie didn't even consider offering one. She watched as Rick flicked the blood-stained sleeve of the sweatshirt as far out into the water as he could reach. For a long moment, nothing happened.

Then Julie saw a bubbling under the muddy water that grew almost immediately to a rapid boil as the smooth surface of the river was broken with a roiling, churning mass of slippery, twisting forms so violent it threatened to pull the sweatshirt from Rick's grasp.

With a startled yelp, Rick yanked the sweatshirt from the water and flung it up onto the beach. Clinging to the material were half-a-dozen fish. They weren't large, no more than a foot long. At least a third of their length was head, dominated by a mouth that clung to the thick cloth with vicious-looking, razor-sharp teeth. Snatching up a rock, Julie dispatched the piranha with a blow to each head.

"Where'd you learn that trick?" Rick demanded some time later.

It was now full night. While Julie had worked on supper, Rick had chopped back the brush to make a large enough circle that neither snake nor larger animal could creep up without being seen. He had even stripped down saplings and some nearby palms to build a *caleta*, though—Julie slapped at a buzz near her ear—without the mosquito netting or mattress pad of the guerrilla camp. He'd had Julie build the campfire between the jungle and the *caleta*, which he had placed so that the steep embankment offered added protection at the back, and now he was hunkered down beside the fire, balancing easily on his heels. He had the jungle on one side of him and the *caleta* and embankment on the other, as though he never for an instant lost sight of the need to stay on guard.

"The I'paa," Julie answered Rick.

Balancing the palm frond she was using as a plate, she sandwiched a piece of piranha with a chunk of palm heart and popped them into her mouth. She had cooked both fish and palm heart wrapped in more palm fronds, cutting off the heads and splitting the rest of the piranha open into halves before burying the entire meal in the coals. Without salt or seasoning to moderate the strong flavor of the piranha, the meal would hardly make its way into the annals of high cuisine. But hunger was its own seasoning, and Julie, popping in another bite, was pleased to see Rick eating with a relish to match her own.

Swallowing, she added, "The piranha won't touch you if you don't do anything to stir them up. But if they smell blood, they'll come swarming out of nowhere. They may not be the best-tasting fish in the river, but they're the easiest to catch. I've seen the I'paa toss a dead bird carcass in the river on a string and pull out their supper hanging off the bones. If you don't have anything else, a nick of blood on a piece of cloth or even a stick will work."

"Yeah, well, just don't do it again," Rick ordered sternly. "We'll have to hope that cut doesn't end up infected—all we need out here. And next time, you tell me *before* you plan a stunt like that."

*Yes sir!* Julie retorted silently. But aloud, she said with deceptive meekness, "I won't have to. Just keep some of those fish guts for tomorrow. As long as we're on the river, at least we won't starve."

"Not while you're around, anyway." Setting down his palm frond plate, Rick gave Julie an intent look across the campfire. "Don't think I don't appreciate what you've done. You're . . . ."—he glanced down at the remains of supper set on the ground beside the campfire, the charred fronds peeled back from the remaining fish halves and half-eaten hunk of palm heart— "a rather impressive person. I guess all those weeks back at camp, I really didn't know you, did I?"

Julie blinked. Was that an actual compliment out of the Special Forces officer? "I guess neither of us really knew each other," she answered cautiously.

Rick made no response. Glancing across the fire, Julie saw that his gaze had shifted out over the river, his face thoughtful. He might have once again forgotten she was there. Julie rebelled. It was bad enough to trail in silence at his heels all day. But she wasn't going to walk clear to the Amazon being ignored.

She cleared her throat. "So, what made you decide on the army? Or the Special Forces? Aren't those units pretty difficult to get into?"

Rick brought a cool glance back from somewhere far away. "Why do you want to know? Or are we back to the nosy reporter looking for quotes?" he added sardonically.

Julie wanted to scream. Tossing aside her organic plate, she said tensely, "I am not a nosy reporter! I happen to have spent the last month sitting by myself in a guerrilla camp, ostracized from practically any human contact, with everybody scared to death to say more than two words to me. You should know! You were one of them. Well, I'm sick and tired of being ignored and treated like I don't exist. You're not Enrique Martinez anymore, forbidden to get too chummy with the prisoner. You're an American citizen just like me, and if you think I'm going to trail at your heels all the way to the Amazon without so much as some civil conversation—"

"Whoa! Hold it!" He was actually laughing, Julie saw indignantly. She'd never seen him laugh before, and it transformed his usually somber features, making him at once more approachable and disturbingly attractive. But Julie was in no mood for such distractions, and she sternly repressed an answering tilt of her own mouth.

Sobering, Rick rocked forward on his boots to focus his sharp gaze on Julie, and for the first time that day Julie felt he was seeing her as a person, not as a problem to be solved. "You're right! I've been pretty rotten company, haven't I?" he said quietly. "I'm sorry. I wasn't trying to ignore you. I guess I just haven't been in the habit of conversation. It's been so long since I haven't had to watch every word I said."

He rocked back on his heels, and an eyebrow shot up. "So—what do you want to talk about?"

"Oh, I don't know." Julie was at once mollified and discomfited by his ready agreement. She hunched her shoulders. "How about your life story? We've got all evening."

Rick reached for a stick to poke the dying fire back into flame. "There's not much to tell. I grew up in one of the tougher parts of Los Angeles. Single-parent home. Low-income projects. You get the picture. It was the kind of place you only get out of through professional sports, the rare academic scholarship, the armed forces, or a well-paying career in crime.

"I had an after-school job—no time for sports. And I wasn't focused enough for an academic scholarship. That left the armed forces or crime.

My guidance counselor told me I'd better sign up with the army recruiter because I was too poor a liar to get away with crime—I'd talk my way into jail in no time. I was good at fighting. In my neighborhood you learned to fight just to make it to school and back. In fact, I got into so many fights, I think they graduated me just to get me off the school grounds. So I guess the army seemed a natural choice. It was the best decision I ever made."

Julie eyed Rick uncertainly. Was he pulling her leg? "But you said you were an officer, a captain. Don't you need . . ."—she hesitated, not wanting to seem rude—"some kind of higher education to be an officer?"

Rising to his feet, Rick prowled around the perimeter of the campsite, peering into the blackness of the jungle and walking over to the embankment to look up and down the river before coming back to squat down on his boot heels.

"Sure! Just because I did a lot of fighting doesn't mean I never studied. I finished high school with a reasonable GPA. And after I got to boot camp—well, once I'd had some discipline pounded into me by the meanest, toughest sergeant that ever kicked a squad of raw recruits into shape— he told me I should go back to school, figured I was officer material. I finished my bachelor's degree while doing Special Forces training at Fort Bragg. Then I put in for officer's training—went on for a master's while I was on duty tour in Germany. It wasn't long after that I transferred to San José to help train the Colombian counter-narcotics battalion. The army does offer more educational opportunities than weapons training and jungle warfare," he finished dryly. "I just happened to take them."

He was making light of an impressive accomplishment for any kid from an inner-city Los Angeles barrio, and Julie knew it. Before she could comment, Rick looked across at her with a crooked half smile.

"What about you, Julie Baker? You aren't exactly a Joe-average news reporter. Some of the things you've done these last couple days would put a Special Ops to shame. It all seems a little wasted in Washington, D.C. Did you ever think of coming back to Colombia? Doing missionary work like your parents, or signing on with one of those environmental NGOs you write about? It seems like you'd be a natural for something like that."

Julie's face hardened at the question. "No, never! You forget what this place did to my family—my friends." She looked across at Rick. "You were there at that interrogation. You should know how I feel about this place. No, I have my own plans for my life, and they don't include wasting it down here in the jungle like my parents did. I wouldn't be here now if there hadn't been a story involved. And if I ever get out of here . . ."

Julie lifted her chin, defiance and challenge in its tilt. "The chances of that Pulitzer are looking better all the time. Not just a story—a whole book. Guerrilla captivity. The inner workings of a FARC front. An escape that'll make pretty exciting reading, you have to admit. And of course a guerrilla fighter who turns out to be a Special Forces operative on a covert mission. I won't have any problem finding a publisher." She eyed the tightening of Rick's jaw. "You don't mind if I put you in, I hope. You did say your cover was blown."

"Can I stop you?" Rick demanded dryly. "As you said, my cover's blown. You're a free agent, and while I may not know all the ins and outs of freedom of the press, once we're out of here I doubt there's much I can do to muzzle you, short of tying you up and throwing you in the river. Unless someone up the line decides the story constitutes a breach of national security." The look he shot her under his long lashes was cool. "Is it really that important to you—winning this Pulitzer, making it big on the news front?"

"The Pulitzer Prize just happens to be the greatest honor in journalism," Julie retorted. "And if you mean that's all I care about, of course it isn't. Do you think I like seeing people fighting and hurting and . . . and dying?" Her voice wobbled, and she tilted her chin another defiant fraction. "But I learned a long time ago there was nothing I could do to change it. So why not do what I can do and be the very best I can at it? A book like this—telling about Carlos and the situation in San Ignacio and what's happening down here in the demilitarized zone—maybe it will even raise public consciousness enough to make a difference somewhere. Is that so wrong? Or are you like the rest of the army types and just dislike reporters on general principle."

"No, there is nothing wrong with journalism," Rick said slowly. "If that's what you want to do with your life."

He added nothing further, nor did Julie. Their conversation lapsed again into silence. The campfire had burned down to red coals, but here on the riverbank there was the glimmer of moon and stars to lighten the night, as there hadn't been for so long. A complete lunar cycle had evidently gone by during the weeks that Julie had spent under the jungle canopy, because the moon above the river was again the fingernail shape it had been that night in the plaza. In a few more days it would be reduced to nothing.

Its crescent gleam was bright enough to outline Rick's face as he turned his head to peer out again toward the river, giving his strong, lean lines an austere, distant look. Julie felt the weight of his disapproval, whether real or her own imagination. Was he already reconsidering his earlier complimentary words and writing her off—Julie's mouth twisted wryly at that journalistic pun—as a hopelessly frivolous and selfish member of the press? Not that it should matter what he thought of her. But, somehow, it did.

"I . . . I really am sorry about your mission," she ventured as the silence dragged on. "No matter how kind you've been about it, I know it's my fault you had to abort it. If there was any way I could change it all, even now, I would."

Rick turned his head to face her, which had the effect of leaving his face in shadow. She could see nothing at all of his expression.

"Look, there's no point in continuing to apportion blame," he said evenly. "None of this was anyone's fault. It simply *was*. If you hadn't been there, and they were looking for a spy, they might have turned me up even earlier. Or I may never have learned anything more useful than I have so far. We'll never know, so there is no point in blaming either ourselves or each other over it. As for my mission, Colonel Thornton may already have intel from other sources as to exactly what's going down here by now. I've never fooled myself into believing that I'm indispensable. In any case, if we are going to make it out of here, we have to put the past behind us, stop second-guessing what went wrong, and concentrate on our own survival."

He was right, Julie admitted silently. *As usual.* Recriminations and dwelling on the past would simply distract both of them from the very difficult task that still lay ahead of them. And that went for the future as well. It was futile to be making plans for anything beyond this wilderness. It simply drained energy and thought needed to survive the here and now.

*Easier said than done.* Julie watched a glowing-red branch in the campfire break apart and begin to die to ash-white.

"So, what are you thinking about now?"

Julie looked up, startled both by Rick's question and the amiability of his tone. He had gotten to his feet again and was prowling around the perimeter.

"Actually, I was thinking about Tim," she said honestly. "I know there's nothing we can do about him now, and it's a waste of energy to keep worrying. And I guess in some ways he may be safer with the guerrillas than we are right now. But—well, when I thought he was you . . . or one of you—you know, a government spy—I figured he must be trained to take care of himself." She eyed Rick's lean, muscled outline. "Like you! He always seemed so—well, sure of himself. But if I was all wrong and he really is just a journalist, like he said—what if they do blame him because I've escaped? What if they decide to kill him?"

"They won't," Rick said quietly but definitely. "Look, I can understand your concern, but it isn't necessary. I know how Aguilera thinks. If they were going to kill McAdams, they'd have done it when they decided to kill you. Killing him now won't bring you back. McAdams is worth more as a hostage to them than he would be dead—especially with you out on the loose. So I wouldn't worry your head about them. As you said, he is probably safer, and certainly eating better"—Julie caught the wry tilt of his mouth in the moonlight—"than we are out here. Once we're out of here, we'll report to the authorities what has happened to him, and they can take it from there. Until then, there isn't any point in dwelling on it."

Cold but logical. And however unemotional Rick's response, Julie found it comforting. Pushing herself to her feet, she had begun to pick up the remnants of supper when she caught Rick's quick swing to study the brush behind him.

"What is it?" Julie emulated his narrowed scrutiny, but she could see nothing beyond the campfire but the black wall of the jungle. "Do you see something out there?"

Rick shook his head, but it was a long moment before he relaxed his watchful stance. "No, I don't. But I just feel—I don't know. As though there are eyes out there on us."

"I know. I've felt it too," Julie agreed. "But I haven't seen or heard anything. I'd pretty well decided it was my imagination."

"Maybe," Rick agreed, lowering the assault rifle that had come up automatically as he spun around. "Maybe there's a jaguar or puma on our trail—though they aren't usually so persistent."

He dumped an armful of dry branches he'd gathered on the fire. The coals caught at the wood, and the flames shot up. "I don't like marking our position with a fire. Anyone watching could see this clear downriver. But we're going to have to risk it. The guerrillas won't be searching for us at night, if they still are at all, and we've seen no sign of other human habitation out here. Right now I'm more concerned with warding off four-legged predators than alerting two-legged ones."

He nodded toward the *caleta*. "I'll gather some more wood, then take the first watch. Why don't you get some sleep?" The terseness of his order was ruined by a huge yawn, and as the flames leaped up from the fresh fuel, Julie saw deep lines of weariness as he rubbed a hand over his face.

"Oh, no, not this time!" she said firmly. "I had a decent sleep last night. You didn't. *You* get some sleep. I'll take first watch." As he opened his mouth, she added quickly, "I mean it. I'm not even sleepy. I'm not going to bed this early anyway, so you might as well."

It was a mark of his exhaustion that he didn't argue. Collecting another armful of broken branches and brush, he dumped it close to the campfire and said briefly, "Keep the fire going, and don't let me sleep too long. Call me if anything moves."

As he crawled into the *caleta*, he paused to add quietly, "Thanks for everything, Julie."

\* \* \*

The watchers had seen Rick and Julie searching for them. But they were not concerned. These two moved in the jungle better than most foreigners. And it was clear that the girl had not forgotten all she had learned of the ways of the rainforest. Even so, the two foreigners were loud and clumsy enough to alert all but the slowest of the jungle creatures to remove themselves from their path. All but one jaguar that had indeed been tracking their scent. Though it was probably only curious, the watchers had dispatched it earlier that day.

They watched now as the girl walked around the campsite, picking up additional pieces of wood, before settling herself between fire and shelter. Though she didn't have their preternaturally sharp night vision, if she wished to watch the dark, they judged, she would do better without the fire. Still, she couldn't know that the fire wasn't necessary to keep predators away.

The watchers withdrew from their vigil before the debate began. They had obeyed thus far in trailing the foreigners to this place. But now danger lay ahead. And the very core of the evil that infected the jungle. Should they continue or turn back?

Or choose a third path—to reveal themselves to those they watched?

They had no clear orders to govern their decision, and if the girl was known to them, the man was not. Nor were his weapons, the deadliness of which they had already witnessed. He did not act like a captor, yet he was one of those who had taken the girl captive. Perhaps they should destroy the man and take the girl with them.

But if he were not an enemy, she might be angry. And even if they took the girl, could she help them in this crisis? Would she? That had been the question all along. Children did not always follow the patterns of their parents.

Still, the matter did not have to be decided tonight. If the man and the girl continued on their present course, they would uncover the danger that filled the jungle for themselves. Then the decision would have to be made.

* * *

For once Winston Crawford the Third was not in General Brad Johnson's office when Colonel Thornton called. The SouthCom commander himself answered on the third ring of the sat-phone. Colonel Thornton waited only to hear his laconic, "Hello, Jeff. Brad here," to say emotionlessly, "He's gone."

There was a pause as the SouthCom commander processed that cryptic information. Then, "What do you mean he's gone? I thought you said you knew exactly where he was and that you were confident he was alive and well even though there hadn't been verbal communication."

"That situation has been altered," Colonel Thornton told him. "You see, when we sent Captain Martini into the DMZ, we provided him with a lifeline. A GPS tracker embedded in the walkie-talkie he carried. In a last-case scenario, it was designed to send off a distress signal to call us in for retrieval. Only last night we lost the signal. We've spent the last twenty-four hours checking all possibilities of technical failure on our end. There are none, and we haven't been able to reestablish contact."

"Meaning?" Brad Johnson demanded, though the sinking sensation in his stomach was already responding to the answer.

"It means that his radio has been compromised. So either Rick is doing just fine but his equipment has somehow been destroyed, or the guerrillas are on to him and have discovered the tracker. Or . . ."

"Or?" the SouthCom commander prompted.

"Or he's dead, sir."

There was momentary silence on the other end of the transmission. "And the mission?"

"Compromised. I'm afraid we have to assume it's a total write-off."

"And we have no other assets in place?"

"None that have produced results. Our communications surveillance hasn't picked up so much as a whisper of anything going down in the zone. Nor have any of the Colombian informants. Whatever is happening, we don't have a clue, and at the moment, I can't offer any reasonable possibility of finding out—barring a miracle, sir."

The other end of the line was silent so long, Colonel Thornton thought the connection must have been severed. When the words did come, he couldn't be sure if the SouthCom commander had voiced them or if it was his own unspoken thought. "Then God help us all!"

* * *

Taqi Nouri set the canister down to take the sat-phone an Iraqi soldier hurried over to hand to him.

"Yes?" he snapped. He listened only briefly before breaking in. "What do you mean, you lost the girl? What . . . she had help! Are your people completely incompetent?"

*Comandante* Aguilera's voice on the other end was shrill with his own fury. "You and your friends have no need to be concerned. There is nothing this Enrique Martinez—nor any of my personnel—knows that could be of use to the *americanos*. I have not been so careless, as I am sure you have assured yourself. And if we have lost them, they too are lost, and I do not think we need to concern ourselves about them again. Those who go into that jungle do not often come back out."

"Perhaps," Taqi Nouri said icily. "That does not mitigate the errors that permitted this to happen. If you wish us to continue our support of your cause, you need to do better in training your men."

He proceeded to give his Colombian ally a piece of his mind in harsh, precise terms. But when he had handed the phone back to the guard, he turned to his companion with less displeasure than he had indicated on the phone.

"At least we have at last flushed out the true spy. It seems this Enrique

Martinez was an informer for the Americans. He has escaped with the girl. One man is dead." He snorted. "Incompetent natives!"

"Should we advance our plans, then? Everything is here now—the men, the weapons, the supplies. We could move tonight if need be. The faster we finish and get out of this godforsaken country, the better for all of us."

"No!" Taqi Nouri waved the idea aside. "Aguilera is correct. Those who disappear into those jungles do not often find their way out. Not quickly, in any case. Besides, it is true they know nothing, and it is too late now for anyone to stop this."

Replacing the canister in the crate, Taqi Nouri pulled the wooden lid over it. "No, we will not be panicked into haste. The skies are not yet ripe. It is foolishness to make oneself invisible in the darkness, then risk a careless eye glancing upward in the wrong spot. We have been patient this long. Four days—five at the most, and it will be over. Our people will have their just revenge, and at last the Great Satan will be no more."

# TWENTY-ONE

JULIE MANAGED TO STAY AWAKE until the phosphorescent hands on her watch read 2:00 A.M. before she had to awaken Rick. Twice she caught a gleam of animal eyes in the woods beyond the campfire, and there had been an occasional rustle in the brush along with the usual serenade of frogs and insects. But these were all the normal sounds of a jungle night, and nothing transpired to alarm her as the slow, quiet hours passed.

The dawn coolness had already burned off by the time Rick in turn shook Julie awake. They breakfasted off the remaining fish and palm heart, a far less appetizing repast now that it was cold. Then Rick kicked the *caleta* apart and buried the campfire in a pile of brush, though nothing could disguise the clearing they had made.

They hiked along the river bank for the rest of the day. By noon, Julie was relieved to come across both wild limes and a grove of tall, spiky palms. The spikes were far too sharp to permit climbing, but at Julie's direction, Rick climbed a tree close enough to one of the palms for him to reach over with his machete and slice through what looked like hanging ropes suspended from the palm fronds.

Julie collected the palm nuts as they dropped to the ground. Like an elongated green tomato in appearance, they were hard as rocks and inedible raw. But they could be cooked up like a potato, and for supper she roasted them in the coals along with an unwary turtle she'd spotted crawling up the bank from the river and which she cooked with a squeeze of lime juice in its own shell.

That first day set a pattern for the next several. Rainy season seemed to have given its last gasp; it didn't rain, other than an occasional afternoon drizzle. Though the days were hot, they weren't unbearably so, as long as Rick and Julie kept to the shade of the jungle edge. And if the heavy vegetation there meant Rick had to keep his AK-47 in one hand while wielding the machete in the other, they made steady progress downstream nonetheless. Julie found more of the fragrant grasses that served as a natural repellent, so that the mosquitoes and gnats dancing in clouds above the river's brown surface were no longer such a pestilence.

They stopped each afternoon in time to build a *caleta* and campfire before dark. Food, as Julie had predicted, was no longer a problem. There were fruit trees and palm nuts and fruit-bearing vines in abundance along the river, and Julie gathered in turn coconuts and passion fruit, papaya and cantaloupe-sized avocados.

There was *guanábana* too, a large green fruit with a soft, lumpy shell and a custardy, seed-studded flesh inside that was as white as vanilla ice cream and more delicious than a hot-house strawberry. They didn't take the time to hunt larger, faster game, but there was never a shortage of turtles and frogs and the strong-tasting piranha if they tired of those. Once, as he chopped back the brush, Rick startled an iguana curled up around the base of a mango tree. It hissed at them like a miniature dragon as they tried to pass. Rick clubbed it with his machete, and that night Julie roasted the tail, its white meat richer than any chicken breast.

They saw no further sign of the guerrillas, and Julie gradually stopped looking back for them. Nor did they come across any evidence of other human existence. There was only the wide, placid river with the caimans drawn up on its beaches, the tall, green wall of the jungle on both sides, and arching overhead, the deep, tranquil blue of the open sky. Almost, they might have been Adam and Eve, alone in a primeval wilderness that had known no other human step.

*Well, not quite,* Julie dismissed ironically.

Though they might yet be reduced to wearing skins or less if they continued out here too long. Her own wardrobe, with its various changes of clothing, was holding up fairly well, but Rick had only the combat fatigues he was wearing. They couldn't wash in the caiman-infested river or even use its water for drinking. But they came sporadically to other, cleaner streams tumbling down into it, and as Rick and Julie forded them, they took time to fill Rick's canteen and occasionally to bathe as well.

Rick scrubbed his fatigues along with his body and put the clothing back on, wrung out but still damp. The heat was so intense that the fatigues dried on him within the hour, providing in the meantime a welcome air-conditioning that tempted Julie to follow suit. But her soap bar was now reduced to a sliver, and her small bottle of shampoo was almost gone. Soon they would be forced to look for alternatives.

Her shoes were another difficulty. A reversal of the clothing situation, Rick's army boots were tough enough to endure weeks—even months—of slogging through jungle rivers and swamps. Julie's sneakers were already rotting through, with a hole worn in the heel of her right shoe and the sides beginning to separate from the soles in several spots. They were always damp, never quite drying overnight from the previous day, so that her feet also stayed damp and grew increasingly sore from the wet leather rubbing against them.

Still, despite the inconveniences and the hardship of the trek, there were moments—the delight of two baby monkeys playing hide-and-seek overhead, the flash of jeweled wings across the trail, a perfect sunset over the river—when Julie could almost forget the urgency and danger of their situation. Though Rick had said, and she'd agreed, that they must push aside all thoughts but survival if they were to survive, Julie wouldn't have thought it possible to banish the terrors of the past weeks, as well as fears for the future, from her mind.

Yet as the hours and days slipped by, she found the world from which they had so narrowly escaped and even the world to which they fled, becoming increasingly remote until the guerrilla camp and Carlos's death, Tim McAdams's fate, and whatever crises were assaulting the rest of the planet seemed infinitely distant, like an image seen through the wrong end of a telescope. All that was real was the next lazy curve of the river ahead, the next meal to gather and campsite to find, and her companion striding one pace ahead of her along the bank.

Her companion . . .

Julie's relationship with Captain Rick Martini, 7th Special Operations Group, a.k.a. Enrique Martinez, guerrilla fighter, had hardly gotten off to a propitious start, and Julie couldn't rid herself of the lingering feeling that he considered her both frivolous and, however courteous his denial, heavily to blame for their present situation.

Yet it was perhaps inevitable—as their world closed in, holding just the two of them in that endless circle of river and sky and jungle—that a certain curious intimacy should spring up between them. To call it friendship would have been too much. The Special Forces officer could be abrupt, and he was certainly bossy. If he had stopped looking constantly over his shoulder, he continued to treat every stop like a covert stakeout, and Julie felt he still forgot at times that she wasn't some subordinate on one of his reconnaissance units.

It was more as though with the passing of days, the two of them were coming to know each other's thoughts and actions so well there was no longer a need to voice them aloud. Julie found herself anticipating Rick's next movement without even consciously having to think about it. More than once, she discovered Rick's canteen in her hand when she had just begun to realize how much she needed a drink. And when Rick handed Julie his machete so he could level the AK-47 on a bushmaster, that most deadly snake of the Amazon Basin, Julie found herself already reaching for it without even wondering that she'd known he would pass it to her.

And if Rick took it for granted that Julie would be right at his heels, no matter the pace he set, he also had an uncanny knack for knowing just when she did need a hand over a bad spot. There were even times—when they had negotiated a particularly difficult scramble across a ravine or when Julie had faced down an irate wild pig that crashed into their path—that Julie surprised what might have been a look of approval in those narrowed brown eyes.

Nor was Rick silent any longer. Not that he allowed more than the most strictly necessary conversation as they hiked along—more of his stringent field discipline. Julie hardly needed to raise her voice above a whisper for him to come down on her. But he relaxed that curt directive once camp was built each evening. And if he had indeed forgotten how to communicate during his months alone with the guerrillas, he learned again quickly, or perhaps he too felt some of Julie's own need of human companionship, because once darkness fell and they were alone around the campfire, he showed no further reluctance to talk. Julie, used to the tight-lipped Enrique of the guerrilla camp, was at once astounded and bemused at the articulate—and opinionated—man who had taken his place.

At Julie's prompting, Rick told in greater detail of growing up on the streets of inner-city LA, some of his stories so unbelievable, Julie couldn't help wondering if he was making them up. He even answered with reasonable tolerance her numerous questions about his Special Forces training, laconically recounting fifty-kilometer marches, rappelling 150 feet from a hovering Black Hawk, and night-op parachute jumps into remote wildernesses until Julie, listening with eyes grown wide in the light of the campfire, no longer wondered at the don't-sweat-it air of competence oozing out of him.

In turn, Julie found herself telling Rick far more about growing up in San Ignacio than she had any other acquaintance over the last seven years.

They discussed books and musical tastes and politics, arguing in a desultory fashion when they disagreed. By the second day, Julie had noticed that their disagreements were invariably about politics—Colombian politics.

"I don't see why we have to send all these troops and combat helicopters down here or encourage the Colombians to do it either," Julie argued one evening. "Why can't we just concentrate on making it economically feasible for the *campesinos* to grow something else so they won't feel they have to grow coca or heroin to feed their families? Just think of all the roads and clinics and schools we could have built with the money the U.S. has poured into military intervention down here. A good alternative development program would be a lot more peaceful and a whole lot less destructive of the environment."

Rick snorted audibly. "That's just the kind of thinking that has led to a lot of the mess down here. Do you think you're the first to come up with that solution? For your information, the U.S. has spent literally billions of dollars in alternative development down here in South America. Peace Corps. UNICEF. Agricultural projects. Education. Health. You name it—we've paid for it."

"But that's impossible!" Julie broke off her sharp retort, hesitating. "At least—well, sure, I remember a few Peace Corps volunteers coming through San Ignacio when I was a kid. But there's no billions of dollars in alternative development out here. Not anywhere near. In fact, there's more drug dealing than there's ever been."

"Precisely my point," Rick retorted. "You see, there's one major flaw with the idea of paying people to quit drug production. It assumes that these people are tripping over themselves to trade growing coca or heroin for legitimate crops like rice and bananas. And it assumes that the locals who end up with these funds are more eager to see the peasants get ahead than to line their own pockets—which has unfortunately been the case only too often with these programs. The wealthy get wealthier—and a few new ones rake in a fortune—while the *campesinos* stay as poor as ever.

"And even that trickle of money that does make it down to the farmers— well, too many of them have simply surrendered their coca crop or poppy field, taken those new tools, cash, seeds, whatever, and moved farther into the jungle to plant another drug crop—compounding that environmental problem of yours."

"That isn't fair!" Julie said stiffly. "You make it sound like all the

Colombian *campesinos* support the drug dealing. They aren't all like that. I knew plenty of honest farmers when we lived in San Ignacio."

"Sure, but they aren't the ones the programs are designed to help. Did you know you can't even get AD aid unless you're involved in growing drug material? Which means that if you're an honest farmer and want to get involved in the program, you actually have to plant yourself some coca in order to qualify.

"And what do you think the narcos or the guerrillas would have to say if all the *campesinos* walked away from growing their drug material? They're making billions here. They're not going to give up that kind of money without a fight. And let me tell you, their methods of dealing with *campesinos* who won't cooperate aren't pretty. Don't kid yourself. If we walked out of here tomorrow and handed the locals a blank check to switch to food crops, you wouldn't get either peace or fewer drugs. You just can't give handouts without corresponding accountability. And unfortunately, in these parts it seems that accountability doesn't come without a solid show of military force. The reality is that they will always be able to make more money drug dealing than planting legitimate crops. So why should they change unless someone actually makes them?"

Julie was silent. Rick threw her a challenging glance through his long eyelashes. "You disagree? You might as well spit out what you're thinking. I can see you're dying to!"

Julie shook her head. "It just seems like you military types always think in terms of fighting without even considering other solutions! It's like they say—violence never settles anything. So what's wrong with looking for an alternative?"

Rick's expression hardened instantly in the light of the campfire. "Now if that isn't a naive thing to say!" he retorted bitingly. "Though what I might have expected from a member of your profession. For your information, violence has settled more things than anything else in human history. Just ask all those nations steamrolled by the Babylonians or the Assyrians or the Romans later on if violence settled anything. It sure settled their futures. You civilians are all the same—especially Americans. You've got this naive idea that everybody out there really wants to be good, and that they're only fighting because they don't have their fair share of the pie. So if you give them enough money and send in some Peace Corps volunteers, you can pat everyone on the head, send all the soldiers home, and everyone will be happy."

"That's not what I meant—" Julie protested.

Rick cut in ruthlessly. "The problem is that everyone doesn't want to be good and never has. There are real bad guys out there who are corrupt and greedy and just plain evil, and they don't care who they hurt to get what they want. And some of those guys run countries. You want to talk quotes. How about 'nature abhors a vacuum'? Or bad guys do! They see a weakness, and they'll step in and exploit it. And you saying, 'Hey, we don't want to fight' isn't going to make them go home and say, 'Sure, let's not have a war today.' They'll just smile and say, 'Good, this will be over real quick!' If someone wants a war and the other side doesn't show up, like the old Vietnam slogan, the side that shows up wins and wipes out everyone else."

"But—" Julie tried again, but Rick went on inexorably. "You like to call our American military trigger-happy. Well, let me tell you this—the reason you can show up in peace and freedom at your little magazine office isn't because of our country's peace-loving nature and democratic ideals. It's because we have a military that's the best in the world and is willing to lay it on the line for our peace and democratic ideals. There are a whole lot of nasty little dictators and other people who hate America and what it stands for who would take us out in a minute if they could. But they don't because they know if they step over the line our military has drawn in the sand, we'll blow their heads off. Same goes for our allies and a whole lot of other little countries around the world that can't defend themselves. Maybe it sounds corny—and I know there are plenty of civilians who disagree—but it is the American military and our willingness to stand our ground that's keeping what little peace there is in this world."

By his glare, he was expecting Julie to argue the point.

"Okay, I'm sorry," she said meekly. And she was. She hadn't meant to insult his profession or the undoubted role of peacekeeper American armed forces had played around the world. Clearly, she had pushed some sensitive buttons.

"You're right—you can't make peace by wishing people would get along. It's just . . . I wish there was a solution where no one else would get hurt—especially here in Colombia. It's such a beautiful country."

"We all do," Rick agreed.

\* \* \*

It was the next evening—the fifth since Julie had escaped from the guerrilla camp—that their tenuous understanding blew up. It had been a good day until then. A game trail they'd stumbled into along the top of the riverbank had made for easy walking. In early afternoon, they'd come across a slow-moving armadillo crawling right down the middle of the trail.

"Tell me you don't cook that!" Rick demanded as Julie picked up a stick.

Julie shot him an impish glance. "Try me. They even serve it in restaurants down here."

Rick refused to have anything to do with dispatching the creature, but since it moved slower than a turtle, Julie had no problem dealing with that aspect herself, and though grumbling good-naturedly, Rick even slung it over his shoulder, its shell bouncing against the back of his ammo vest as they hiked along.

At midafternoon, the river made a sudden sharp curve to the left. The shift of the land left Rick and Julie on top of a high bluff down which they would have to scramble to continue following the river. The top of the bluff was grassy and open, and they couldn't see what lay ahead around the bend of the river, so Rick called for an early stop.

As had become routine, Julie started a campfire while Rick walked back a distance from the bluff to find palms and saplings for the *caleta*. As she had the turtle, Julie cooked the armadillo in its shell, basting it with coconut milk and lime juice. A large avocado split in half served as salad. Though it looked like an overgrown potato bug, the armadillo was delicious eaten directly from the shell, which Rick chopped into large chunks with his machete, the fatty richness of the meat a welcome addition to their lean diet.

For the first time, it was still light as they ate their evening meal. Perhaps because they could see for a long distance up on the bluff, Rick seemed more relaxed than Julie had yet seen him. Sprawled against a boulder he had rolled over to serve as a back rest, he dug a chunk of armadillo out of its shell with his combat knife, giving Julie a thumbs-up as he chewed and swallowed.

"I wouldn't have believed it if I hadn't seen it with my own eyes, but this is really good. I'm going to have to see it gets added to the survival list back at Fort Bragg." He shook his head, and this time Julie wasn't imagining the approval she saw in the brown eyes. "You really are something, Julie

Baker! You know, when we started on this trek, I would never have believed a woman could—"

"I know what you believed," Julie interrupted dryly.

Rick sloped her a rueful grin. "Okay, so maybe it was a little chauvinistic. In any case, I was wrong, and I don't mind admitting it. Truth is, if I could pick any man in my unit with whom I'd care to be lost in the jungle, I'd take you any day, Julie Baker." He sliced another piece of armadillo flesh from the shell and popped it into his mouth. "For one, none of them can cook worth beans."

Pleasure tinged Julie's cheeks. Maybe he was thinking only of his stomach, but she'd worked hard not to be a burden on their partnership, and his approbation warmed her. She shrugged dismissively. "Yeah, well, I guess there's one good thing that came out of growing up in San Ignacio."

She could hear the bitterness that tinged her words even as they emerged, and she regretted them instantly as his expression cooled, the approval evaporating as though it had never been there. Tossing the chunk of shell aside, he demanded harshly, "Why do you talk like that? As though San Ignacio—your whole life growing up down here—were some horrible nightmare you're trying to forget."

"I . . . I . . . ," Julie stammered, but he swept on relentlessly: "If you hated it so much, why did you come back? And don't give me all that about just coming here for a good story. I saw the way you looked when we landed and you first saw the place. The way you just couldn't help sneaking out of the airport!"

"But I didn't hate it," Julie interrupted with a wail. "You don't understand! I—well, I even loved it. But you heard what happened there. You know about my parents. It was just such a waste! For them—not just for me."

"Was it? So you keep saying," Rick retorted. "What I understand is that this isn't about your parents. It's about you. From all accounts, your father and mother were the kind of parents any kid would be happy to have. Decent, caring people who did a whole lot of good for a whole lot of people. Isn't that right? Or is there something you've left out—like maybe they were secretly beating the tar out of you or something?"

"Of course not!" Julie said indignantly. "My parents loved me—they loved everyone! That's not the point!"

"So what is the point?" Rick demanded. "Do you know what most kids—myself for example—would have given for a family like yours? I never knew my father—if I had one, which they tell me is a biological certainty, however small the evidence. My mother was a lush—and yes, she did beat the tar out of me until I got big enough that she didn't dare try anymore. Okay, maybe I deserved it. I was always getting myself into fights—trying to prove I was tough enough I didn't need a dad to fight my battles. My mom died of cirrhosis of the liver by the time I was out of high school. The best thing that ever happened to me was when the recruiting officer at our school signed me up for the army. That's where I met a chaplain who actually showed me there really were people out there in this world who were decent and kind. People who loved God and who actually took seriously things like sacrifice and service. People like your parents!"

The muscles bunched along his jawline, and under his glare, Julie felt like something that had crawled out from under a rock. "And you—you had a family I'd have given my shooting arm for! But you're all eaten up inside because they took you to live in the wilds of South America. You didn't get to have all of the advantages of American kids—toys and clothes and a nice house and all the other things you would have had as an upper-class physician's daughter back stateside. You had to go to boarding school, and okay, you had some hard times. And you resent that. Oh, don't bother to deny it—the bitterness practically oozes out of you every time you talk about it. Well, let me tell you, you weren't the only kid to have a few hard knocks in life. Growing up in a single-parent home in inner-city LA doesn't allow for a whole lot more of life's little luxuries than growing up in San Ignacio."

"But—that isn't true! You don't understand!" Julie was shaking her head frantically, wanting to shut out that relentless voice. "I never resented the things I didn't have. I never wanted an American lifestyle. And I never resented growing up in San Ignacio—at least not for myself. It was for them. I loved my parents! They were wonderful people—and brilliant and talented too. If you'd known them . . . They could have done anything with their lives. And I watched them get sick and old out here. And poor. They were practically retirement age when they died, and they didn't have a cent in the bank. They just kept giving and giving everything to other people. And never holding anything back for themselves. I . . . I just always wanted something better for them."

"Did you?" Rick countered, and there was no relenting in the expression on his face. "I don't think so. By your own admission, your parents were perfectly happy doing just what they were doing. They could have walked away any time they wanted, right? The fact is, they were happy with the life they chose. They loved San Ignacio and the people there. You say their ministry was worthless—that it didn't amount to anything in the end. Well, I don't think from the sounds of it that they would agree with you. Nor would the people whose lives they touched. Maybe they *didn't* make any earth-shattering impact that we can see, but they made more difference than you're giving them credit for—just ask Carlos, among others.

"But that isn't the point. They did what they felt God was calling them to do, and they were happy doing it. And if they sacrificed their careers and even their lives in the process, that was their choice. Only you didn't like that. But it wasn't for them you resented it. It was for yourself, because, willy-nilly, in sacrificing themselves, they sacrificed you too. And they didn't ask your permission, either. That's what's been eating at you all these years, isn't it?"

Rick broke off when he saw the stricken look on Julie's face. "I'm sorry. I had no business saying that."

But he didn't say he didn't mean it.

Julie got to her feet stiffly. "It doesn't matter. You're entitled to your own opinion of me."

Dropping the armadillo shell in her hand, she walked away from the campfire. When Rick made a move to get up, she rounded on him sharply. "No, I want to be alone, do you mind?"

She walked swiftly along the bluff until she could no longer see the smoke of their fire and the fresh green top of the sleeping shelter. Below her the river was making its sharp curve to the left so that all she could see ahead and to her right was the canopy of jungle rolling away from the bluff in a sea of green. The river was the same silty brown here as elsewhere, yet its placid surface still allowed a murky reflection of the tree-lined banks and one white cloud floating overhead.

*I hate him! How dare he? He has no right!* Julie raged silently. But though she tried to dismiss what he'd said, it was as if Rick's harsh words were as much a mirror as the water below, and she couldn't shut out the Julie Baker she saw reflected there.

Although she had deceived herself all these years, and however much she loathed admitting it, Rick was again, and uncannily, right. It hadn't been her parents' feelings, her parents' needs that had roused her bitterness and resentment all those years ago. It had been her own.

*Yes, Mom, Dad—God, don't you see? When you sacrificed yourselves, you sacrificed me! Didn't you ever think of that? Didn't you think of me? Didn't you love me?*

Tears stung Julie's eyes. She blinked them away impatiently. She was not a weeper—she had seldom cried since those early bedtimes at boarding school. She hadn't cried when the news from the Red Cross team came—there had been too much disbelief at first, then too much to do. When her whole world had dissolved with the closing of a plane door behind Norm Hutchens, she still had not cried. Not in front of strangers. In the years since, she had prided herself that she wasn't one of these weepy females who bawled on the shoulders of any teacher, friend, or available male who came along.

Yet she had found tears coming to her eyes more often in the last few weeks than in her entire life. It was as though the dam she had so carefully erected against grief and loss and pain was crumbling brick by brick, and all her efforts were doing nothing to stop it.

Spinning on her heel, Julie strode away from the bank and across the bluff, not stopping until she came to the jungle edge. She sank down under the enormous umbrella of a mango tree, its fruit still green and small overhead. Her hands clenched as she struggled to force the floodgates shut again.

"Except a grain of wheat fall into the ground and die . . ."

But, God, I never asked to be a grain of wheat. I never asked to be part of this.

"He who loses his life for my sake . . ."

I didn't ask to give my life! I didn't ask to give my parents!

The tears began to come. *Mom, Dad—didn't I matter as much as all those people you poured out your life for? Didn't it matter what you were doing to me? Oh, I know it was for a good cause. I know those people needed you. I know you were doing God's work. But I needed you too. I loved you—and I know you loved me. But you weren't there when I needed you. You weren't there when I cried myself to sleep at night in a room full of other homesick girls. You weren't there when I had a birthday and no one remembered even to sing. You weren't there to tell when the bigger girls were mean to me. And on vacation I had to be brave so you wouldn't know how much I missed you. I learned not to cry—not to let you know how I felt.*

*And then you went away! I didn't even get to say goodbye. If you had left earlier—if you had thought more about me than your patients—we would still be a family. I wouldn't be so alone. When I got on that plane, I lost my whole world. Not just you, but every person I'd ever known, everyone I'd ever cared about—even my dog! Did you think of that, Mom—Dad? Did you think of the consequences to me? I needed you too! I still need you!*

And she wept. She wept as she had not wept in all the long years when strangers had told her how well she was coping and what a brave young lady she was, wept as she had never permitted that independent, resilient young woman she had trained herself to be. Somehow, she wasn't sure how, Julie found that she was face down on the ground, her face pressed against the warm moist earth, the dirt crumbling under her hands. *O God, why?*

It was not a question to which she expected an answer. Nor did she receive one. At long last, she raised her head from the ground. She could smell the familiar warm fragrance of the grasses where she had crushed them in her clutching fingers.

Julie rolled over on her back. A tangle of lianas hung down from a branch just above her head. Orchids grew among them, and only an arm's length above her was one exquisite specimen, its heart deep purple with traces of gold that lightened by shades to a pale lilac, then paled again to cream on the petals. The creamy petals curled back from that gloriously colored heart in long, slender curves that tapered to a tendril at the end of each point like a spider plant.

The blossom was far more exquisite in that web of wild vegetation than it would have been in the refrigerated case of a florist shop, and as Julie turned her head, she glimpsed beyond the overhanging branches a piece of late afternoon sky that was so deep blue it didn't seem real. Above her, among the vines and leaves, she caught the brilliant turquoise and scarlet of a macaw that peered down at her, making an inquiring sound as though to ask what was hurting her. The first cooling breeze of dusk whispered through the branches overhead, touching Julie's hot face with its soft caress.

It was all so beautiful. And she loved it so! Julie could admit that now, give herself over to the pain of it. This lonely, wild, beautiful spot on the planet was part of her heart and soul. As Rick had said, so much of her was bound up in this place. Her independence. Her confidence—sometimes overrated—that she could tackle anything if she put her mind to it. The resilience and adaptability birthed by constant change. Kenny back at WCI in Travel & Equipment had once said that if Julie were dropped into any remote spot in the world, she would in short time have made herself understood, recruited local allies, and be busily writing up her experiences while arranging her own rescue.

Yet the constant underlying ache that no place on earth was home, the barriers that kept even close friends at arm's distance because any new change might snatch them from her life, an aversion to accepting help or leaning on anyone, an aloofness that never quite left her no matter how many people were around—these too came from this place.

That was what it came down to. How could she love a place that also held so much hurt? How could the same God who had placed such beauty into her life place such pain as well?

*Why did You give me such wonderful parents and then take them away? Not just when they died, but all those boarding school separations when I needed them so much. Maybe that's just the way missionary life was back then. Maybe it was the way it had to be to bring Christianity to the world. Why does winning the world for God have to involve breaking apart families and saying goodbye?*

Julie sat up, brushing the dirt and twigs from her clothes and arms. Her hair was undoubtedly full of debris as well, but Julie didn't bother to check. With a ragged release of breath, she lifted her head. Better get back before Rick thought a guerrilla or wild animal had her—if he would care.

That was when she saw him, sitting just a few yards away, his back resting against the trunk of the mango tree, his long legs stretched out in front of him, his AK-47 resting across his lap. He'd been watching her—for how long? Julie didn't bother to turn her face away or try to hide the evidence of her tears. They were way past that. As she lifted her chin to meet his gaze, he said quietly. "Are you okay?"

Shifting to dig into his pocket, he extricated a handkerchief, folded into a neat square, and passed it to Julie. Julie took it, bemused. All this time, and he still had a handkerchief in his pocket? It was even clean, though damp from the last time it had been used for washing, and Julie could smell on it the warm musk of his body scent.

"I'm sorry," he went on as Julie blew her nose. His mouth quirked ruefully. "I keep saying that to you, and let me tell you, I don't make a regular habit of apologies. But I didn't mean to hurt you." His mouth twisted again. "Okay, maybe shake you to your senses a bit. But I had no business shooting off like that."

Wadding the handkerchief in her lap, Julie pushed her hair back from her face with a weary hand. "Look, you don't need to apologize. You were right. It wasn't my parents I've been angry about all these years. It was me. I . . . I guess I really have been a spoiled brat."

"I didn't say that," Rick countered swiftly.

"No, but you've been thinking it." Julie rushed on past his immediate denial. "It's just—oh, I know all those years they gave weren't really all for nothing. Carlos, Doña Nina—they've showed me that much. It's just . . ."

She took a shuddering breath and dropped her eyes to the handkerchief in her hands. "I missed them!" she said, her voice quivering. "All those boarding school separations—it really wasn't the things . . . the American lifestyle. I never cared about that, and I knew they didn't either. It was them. I . . . I guess I resented that they just accepted so easily that they had to do without me most of the year. Oh, I know they were thinking of what was best for me, and I'm sure they would have liked us to be together all the time, but . . ."

Julie raised her eyes from the handkerchief, now a twisted knot. "I don't know what I wanted. For them to cry a little when I left, maybe? Oh, I know they were trying to be brave for me, and maybe they did cry when I was out of sight. Their letters always said how much they missed me. But they were so content with their work. They didn't seem to mind what it was costing them . . . costing us! Even when they died in that epidemic— you're right; they would have felt it was worth it. Whether or not they had any idea what was going to happen, they wouldn't have walked away from people who were hurting and sick and needing them anymore than they'd have robbed a bank.

"But what about me? I was their daughter! If they loved me as much as they always said they did, as much as they loved the Colombians and the I'paa, shouldn't it have mattered to them to stay alive—not to go taking risks—*for me*? Wasn't I, our being together as a family, as important as saving the world . . . or San Ignacio?"

Why she was trying to explain herself to this man, Julie didn't know. Nor had she expected an answer to that very rhetorical question. But she had hardly finished that bitter wail when Rick responded slowly, thought-fully, "I think you know how much you mattered to them. I guess maybe your parents really believed what they were doing out there was worth the sacrifices they made—including you."

Rick eased the AK-47 to the ground beside him and leaned forward to flick a wandering fire ant off his boot. "There was a Bible passage that came up in one of that chaplain's study groups back at Fort Bragg. It never really meant anything to me because I had no family. But Jesus was talking to His disciples, telling them that far from those crowns and thrones they were expecting, His message of salvation was going to turn families against each other, bring persecution to those who dared follow, bring about His own death on the cross. He told them it might even cost their lives to follow Him and that anyone who wasn't willing to put Him above father and mother and even sons and daughters wasn't worthy to be His disciples. I guess your parents—unlike most people—took that call seriously."

"I know the passage," Julie interrupted wearily. "Matthew 10. I found the last part inscribed on my parents' grave. 'Whoever loses his life for my sake will find it.' That's the whole point. Why should losing family need to be part of saving the world?"

Rick moved his shoulders in a shrug against the rough wood of the mango tree. "It would make sense to any soldier. If the enemy is coming at you, and your men start whining that they can't leave their families or risk getting hurt because their families are going to miss them, then the battle is already lost. If you're a soldier at war, you go out to fight, knowing you may never come back, because you believe that your country—and that family you're leaving behind—is worth that sacrifice."

"Yes, well, that's fine," Julie argued. "But my parents weren't in a battle."

"Weren't they?" Rick said quietly. "I don't think your parents would agree. If every missionary—or every aid worker or Peace Corps volunteer working to save people in some of the nastier corners of the world—chose to stay home because of the potential cost, where would the world be today?"

"Maybe." Julie took another deep breath and was pleased to hear her voice emerge even and steady. "Getting off the subject of me, there is something I've been wanting to ask you for a long time—or someone like you. Everything you say—it's obvious you have a real faith in God. I believe in God too, and the Bible and—well, everything. I mean, it's only natural. I grew up in church, had Christian parents, went to a missionary boarding school. I'm not saying I only believe because of my parents. I believe for myself that the God of the Bible is exactly who and what He says, that He intervened in human history by sending Jesus Christ to pay the penalty for our sins. I've checked out other religions, and I've never found anything that made better sense. But you . . ."

Julie looked Rick over consideringly. They hadn't come across a stream for bathing that day, and Rick was almost as unkempt as she herself felt, perspiration visible against the heavy material of his uniform, his hair darkened from sweat under a headband he had cut from her ripped sweatshirt, the shadow of a day's beard dark against the uncompromising line of his jaw.

He looked every bit as tough and dangerous as her first impression had been, so that right now she could believe any story of his past exploits. But there were lines of weariness at the corners of his eyes and around his mouth that had not been there a week ago, testimony that the long days of hiking and the nights of guard duty were taking their toll on him too.

"I've always wondered if I would accept it so easily if I hadn't heard it all my life. I mean, I can understand why someone hearing it all for the first time would write it off as a fairy tale—or science-fiction plot. An all-powerful God creating the universe, then coming down to live among the people He created and dying to save them from their sins. You, for instance. What made you choose the God of the Bible over, say, some Native American folktale of mankind emerging from a hole in the ground or something? Or reincarnation, or any of the other popular philosophies floating around these days?"

Rick had retrieved the AK-47, and Julie saw his narrowed gaze sweep the plateau beyond the mango tree, then flicker back into the brush before he looked over at her.

"I guess it's like you said," he said simply. "It—He—makes sense out of my universe."

He tossed aside a piece of grass he'd been chewing. "Oh, I checked out a lot of religious systems too. By the time I got into the army, I knew there was something missing in my life, and there were a lot of options on base. Everyone was trying to get you to come to their service or religious ceremony. I even toyed around with some of those eastern gurus."

Rick slanted Julie a sudden grin. "I just couldn't stomach those robes or bald heads! But when it got down to it, every belief system I saw came out to pretty much the same thing. Some great big, impersonal God, or gods, or just some Force way out there which didn't really have much to do with mankind, and mankind didn't have much to do with it either. From what I could see, people practiced their religion for two basic reasons. To placate their Supreme Being, or Beings, so they'd be left alone—you know, ward off bad luck or evil spirits or just getting struck with lightning or some other disaster. Or to offer enough bribes—whether literal sacrifices or prayer wheels or donations or burning candles and counting rosaries like my barrio back home—so your God, or gods, would do what you wanted.

"But none of it made any difference in how people lived their lives. You could kick your dog, beat on your wife, cheat the poor, whatever—and as long as you paid your dues, that was it. None of it changed people—and I knew I, at least, was in desperate need of change.

"Then I met that chaplain, and he introduced me to the God of the Bible. I must have read the whole thing in a month, and it turned my life upside down. I mean, here you have a God who created the universe with so much love and joy, it just shouts off the pages. Then, like putting a kid in a great big sandbox or inside a room just chock-full of art supplies and fun things to do, He puts human beings in the middle of that universe and says, 'Have some fun. See what you can do.'

"Now, He's an all-powerful God. It would be easy for Him to force us to fall down and worship Him and obey His laws. Human history would have sure been different if He had! But He goes and does something incomprehensible. He sets mankind free to choose. He loves us enough that He wants us to love Him back—not because He's programmed us that way, but because we choose to as free living beings. And when we use that freedom to choose our own selfish way instead of His, when we make a terrible mess of this beautiful world He's given us, He doesn't do what we deserve—just wipe us out and start over. He comes down Himself as a human being—Jesus Christ—and lives our life with us. Then He gives His own life to show us the way back to God.

"Even the laws He gives us—and the Bible's full of them, I'll say that. But God isn't asking for us to sacrifice our firstborn sons or repeat a hundred chants before He'd consider our latest interruption to His nap. He tells us to do things like love one another. Do to others what you would like done to you. Love your wife and kids. Don't steal. Don't lie. Don't murder. And all of it isn't for His benefit but for ours—because He cares enough to keep us from hurting ourselves and others. If everyone in the world followed those commands, just think what a place it would be."

Getting up, Rick walked outside the overhanging branches of the mango, making one of his swift surveys before he returned. When he did, he hunkered down on the heels of his combat boots right in front of Julie, his intent gaze disturbingly close.

"I'm a soldier. And as a soldier you've got to decide before you ever pick up a gun whether the leaders you're following into battle are the kind you're willing to risk your life for. It's like Aguilera and his band. They've got great ideals. But people who would use murder and kidnapping and extortion to reach those ideals aren't the kind of hands into which I'd want to put my future.

"But the God of the Bible—I hadn't reached the last page before I knew this was what—*who*—I'd been searching for my whole life. And you know what? Even if it was just a fairy tale like you said, even if none of it were true, that's the kind of God I'd cross the line to fight for any day. But He *is* real! I guess that's where faith comes in, but I know that as surely as I'm breathing. And because He's real, my life—and this whole sorry world—makes sense."

Julie looked at Rick in wondering silence. His long lashes were lifted to hold her eyes with his own, and their brown depths were not, as they had so often been, scornful or mocking or furious but utterly serious. Julie swallowed as she pulled her eyes away.

*Captain Rick Martini, I really like you!* If only she hadn't ruined so completely any possibility that he would ever think as well of her.

Pushing away a pang that had nothing to do with the last hour's turmoil, Julie said lightly, "I wish my life made as much sense. Maybe I really am that spoiled brat. My parents gave their lives to help others. Me—so far, all I've done with mine is chase a Pulitzer. I can't even let my parents go, much less make the kind of sacrifices they made."

"Maybe you're selling yourself short," Rick answered quietly. "You don't know what you have in you until you're called on to use it. I think you are more your parents' daughter than you give yourself credit for."

"Maybe," Julie retorted skeptically. Swiftly, she rose to her feet, and Rick stood up immediately with her, slinging the AK-47 over his shoulder. Brushing off her slacks, Julie glanced toward the tangle of jungle beyond the mango tree. The shadows were growing dark with the onslaught of dusk above the river bluff.

"Well, if we're not going to have every animal in the area rummaging through our leftovers, I guess we'd better get back to camp."

Then her hand shot out to grip Rick's forearm. Her voice came out just above a whisper. "Rick!"

Rick's head turned in the direction of hers, and Julie knew from the sudden stillness of his lean body that he had seen it too. A face. Framed in the lacy arch of a fern patch not a dozen paces into the jungle. It wavered among the shadows curiously indistinct in outline like a shadow itself. Or a ghost.

But this was no ghost. Features round as a moon and the dark bronze of mahogany under those misleading streaks of gray and white. Flat, wide nostrils. Jet black hair cut in a straight bang above an oriental slant of eyes.

Like few other North Americans, Julie knew those features. One of the rare, wandering natives of this equatorial rainforest.

But who? And from where? Hostile or peaceful?

Julie blinked in her effort not to move. And though the closing of her eyes was only the fraction of a second, when she looked again, the face had vanished.

## TWENTY-TWO

JULIE WANTED TO START DOWNRIVER IMMEDIATELY.

"If this is his hunting ground," she argued, "he must come from a village somewhere in the area. And that's bound to be on this river. He's probably heading downstream just like we are. In fact, if he's on his way home from a hunting trip at this hour of night, his village can't be very far away or he would have started home a lot earlier. It's almost dark out there, and the natives around here don't travel after dark—not if they don't have to. Besides wild animals and snakes, that's when they believe the evil spirits come out."

Rick was more cautious. "How can you be sure he isn't hostile?"

"If he were hostile," Julie said impatiently, "we'd have an arrow through us right now. Or these days, even a bullet. No, odds are he was as startled to see us as we were to see him. He's probably on his way home right now to report to the village elders about the crazy gringos he's spotted in the jungle."

She paused. "I wish I knew what tribe he's from. My parents provided medical service for several of the tribal groups in this region. If these people have heard of them—"

"Aren't you getting ahead of yourself?" Rick interrupted. "We haven't even established that there's a village yet. In any case, we're not moving from here tonight. It'll be dark before we'd get a hundred meters, and I'm no more excited about wandering around at night here than the natives are."

Despite her eagerness, Julie conceded he had a point. If they were going to stroll up to a native village, better to do so in broad daylight, when they could make it good and clear that their intentions were harmless, than after dark when strangers tended to be shot first and examined later. Especially dressed as Rick still was, in guerrilla clothing. Who knew what report that native would make of what he'd seen?

Julie didn't allow herself to doubt that they would find the village. Unless game was scarce or they were on a war raid, the Amazonic tribal groups rarely wandered farther than they could travel back before night. And at this hour, where would the native they'd seen be heading but home?

Julie had the first watch that night. Once Rick took her place, she didn't expect to be able to sleep but did so, dreamlessly.

It was earlier than usual when Rick shook her awake, the sun not yet risen into view. They were both eager to get started. She eyed Rick as she rummaged through the previous night's leftovers for their breakfast. He had already dismantled the shelter and scattered the ashes of the campfire, and he now stood at the edge of the bluff, studying the lay of the jungle and river below. His expression was remote, telling Julie nothing of his thoughts, and she wondered if it had occurred to him, as it had to her, that this might well be the last day of their curious partnership. Or if he was thinking of her at all.

Suddenly, insanely, though last night she'd been ready to start off at once, Julie felt that she did not, after all, want to take that final trek downriver. She wanted to stay right here in this strangely beautiful paradise, just the two of them, shutting out forever the world that clamored for their return.

*Are you crazy?* she demanded of herself sternly. There were people looking for them, worried about them. They had jobs to do out there, their own lives to live. *What are you thinking, Julie?*

She brought her mind firmly back to the leftovers from supper. The uneaten armadillo meat had turned rancid overnight and would have to be discarded. But there were two avocados and a dozen of the long pods, their white fluff a little dried out but still edible. Dividing the food onto two palm leaves, Julie carried Rick's portion to him and began methodically working her way through the rest. There had been a time when she had missed having salt or even the simple seasoning Linda had used at the guerrilla camp to make their meals palatable. Now she hardly noticed. Food was simply energy to fuel the day's march.

Rick split the remaining water in his canteen with Julie to wash the meal down. They would have to find more clean water before long.

The sun was just showing its upper rim above the jungle canopy as Rick and Julie made their way down the bluff. This put them for the first time on level ground with the caimans, and they had to retreat deeper into the brush to stay beyond reach of the sudden lunge of a hungry reptile. Rick unsheathed his machete again, and their going slowed. Though they kept a sharp eye out, they saw no further sign of the native they'd spotted or anyone else, for that matter. The river was wide and the bend in it a leisurely one, so that the sun was high overhead by the time Rick and Julie could again see before them an unbroken panorama of muddy water and high banks stretching away downstream.

"There it is!" Julie announced triumphantly.

It was just as she'd hoped. Half a dozen canoes drawn up on the beach not a hundred meters beyond the bend. Better yet, they were on Rick and Julie's side of the river, and even at this distance Julie could see above them on the bank the dried-leaf brown of thatched roofs among the green of leaves and palm fronds. The jungle here wasn't the huge, liana-choked hardwoods through which Rick and Julie had traveled the first day, but the single-canopy scrub jungle of the river's edge, no more than forty feet high. Above the treetops, a lazy black spiral promised human cooking fires and with them, human inhabitants.

And yet . . .

Julie had a clear view of the stretch of river downstream and studied the scene with sudden unease. A close-set row of stakes had been driven into the soft ground of the beach and riverbed to form a semicircle that ran out into the water around the beached canoes and back up to the bank again, providing the villagers a caiman-free zone for washing and bathing. Julie could see no sign of the normal daytime activities of a riverside village. No fishermen were sliding out the canoes. No women were scrubbing clothes at the river's edge or hauling water in gourds up to their cooking areas. No children splashed in the river or scampered through the tree branches.

And there were no voices. No children's shrill playing or women calling to each other. Or the rhythmic pounding of the huge wooden pestles the Indian women used to grind corn and manioc, which could sound like a drumbeat from a distance.

The beach, the village, the jungle itself was absolutely still.

Julie wrinkled her forehead. "That's odd! If that Indian was from this village, I really expected the elders would have someone out to check us over by now. Do you think we frightened them, and they've all gone into hiding?"

Rick suddenly reached out to grab her arm. "Don't move!"

The unexpected harshness of his order froze Julie instantly. Rick's narrowed gaze did not shift from the scene downriver as he gripped Julie's arm, and confused, Julie, glancing up at him, realized that his focus was not on the beach but above it. As her eyes followed his, she gasped in revulsion.

That lazy black spiral above the jungle canopy was not, as a first glance had misled her, the friendly smoke of cooking fires, but birds! Carrion birds, by their size. Hundreds of them, the swirling, dark cloud of their wings circling slowly upward above the treetops under which the village lay sheltered.

"Oh, no! What is it?" she demanded in a horrified whisper.

"I don't know," Rick said grimly.

For the first time that day, he unslung the AK-47. Cradling it in combat position, he glanced at Julie. "Follow me! Keep quiet! And do exactly as I do!"

This was not a time for objecting to that autocratic tone. Julie followed as Rick faded back into the cover of the jungle perimeter. It took almost an hour to cover those last hundred meters, as Julie stepped precisely at Rick's heels, freezing each time he stopped to study the jungle around and above them before slipping forward to the next tree or patch of elephant ears or ferns. Rick no longer used the machete. If they couldn't slip through the vegetation, they crawled under it on elbows and belly.

This was the elite commando Rick was trained to be, and try though she might, Julie couldn't match his pantherlike silence of movement. Once, when they were negotiating a fern patch, a twig snapped under her knee with a crack that was like an explosion in the silence, and Rick rounded on her with such savagery in his expression that Julie shrank back. His anger faded immediately as he took in her startled dismay. It was a sign of the tension that gripped them both.

They saw no sign of human life, nor any life at all. Not a bird call or a scampering monkey, and for once Julie didn't sense watching eyes upon them. After the first fifty meters, Rick dropped to his belly. Julie obeyed his impatient gesture to follow suit, and they covered the remainder of the distance even more cautiously, inching forward under constant cover of the underbrush. Julie could no longer see Rick's expression, only the back of his head and sometimes just his boots slithering forward ahead of her. But she knew by the stiffening of his body lines when his senses caught the same anomaly that had been tugging at hers.

It was a smell, and it had been growing almost imperceptibly for some time before Julie recognized it for what it was. A horrible, sickly sweet smell that caught at the back of Julie's nostrils and intensified with each meter until she had to breathe through her mouth to keep from gagging.

Julie had encountered that smell once before. In the ice-cold storeroom back at the San Ignacio airport. Only here it wasn't disguised with formaldehyde, and it was far stronger. Julie's heart began to race and her stomach to hurt.

It was the smell of death. Human death.

Ahead of her, Rick stopped moving forward. Through the wide leaves of a palmlike plant that sheltered his head and shoulders, Julie glimpsed the hot yellow of sunlight falling through some opening in the jungle canopy. He lay there, his head raised, watching for so long that Julie began to stir impatiently before repressing the movement.

Rick turned his head to glance over his shoulder at Julie, and her heart almost stopped at the expression she glimpsed there—so cold and hard and dangerous, she wouldn't have recognized the companion with whom she had walked and lived and talked these last days. Obeying the jerk of his head, Julie slithered forward to stretch out beside him.

At first glance, the village was as quiet and serene as the jungle behind them had been. A dozen bamboo huts nestled back under the shade of trees around a clearing that served as a common meeting and working area for the villagers. Under the nearest tree stood a large *tacu,* the concave wooden mortar in which the Indian women ground their flour. The pestles for pounding the corn or manioc lay on the ground beside it. A pile of fifty-kilo sacks of rice were heaped on a scaffolding of bamboo under an open thatched shelter just beyond.

In front of one of the huts lay a fishing net freshly woven from lianas, the machete that had chopped them down still shiny-new on the ground beside it. The sooty pit of a community campfire was cold and black in the center of the clearing without even a lingering thread of smoke rising from it.

It all looked eminently peaceful—and empty.

Then Julie saw the body. It lay facedown in the dirt between two of the huts, just far enough back under the branches of a citrus tree that she hadn't seen it at first glance. It was an adult—male by the loincloth, though the thick black braid could have belonged to either sex—and it hadn't been there long because it was still intact. Or so Julie assumed until it moved so suddenly she thought the person was still alive. Crawling out from under the chest, a small rodent scampered away.

Swallowing down bile, Julie averted her eyes. But what she saw next was even worse. A writhing, seething mass of wings and beaks and vicious claws. The birds—a few of them still rising in the spiraling cloud Julie had mistaken for the smoke of a cook fire. They swarmed over a large mound just outside the perimeter of the village green. And they were feeding silently, greedily.

The sound from Julie's throat was enough to make the birds rise with a thunder of wings, and as they fluttered upward through the tree branches, Julie saw with fresh horror and revulsion what they had hidden.

An open grave.

Bodies were piled there—lots of them. And they weren't all grown men like the one lying under the trees. Although what the birds had done to them would make identification impossible, Julie saw torn shapes that were too slight to be male—or adult. Children. Even babies.

"A massacre?"

Beside her, Rick shook his head, and the cold harshness of his expression didn't ease as he glanced down at her. "Not a massacre. There's no blood."

The birds were already spiraling down, but Julie could see that Rick was right. The bodies, piled up in the open grave like so much firewood, had been so damaged that Julie had to swallow down another rush of acid in her throat. But there were no outward signs of violence inflicted on these people. No gunshots or visible wounds. Nor was there any of the blood spilled out into the dusty, trampled earth that would have marked the San Ignacio massacre and so many others in this country.

In fact, now that she was looking more closely, Julie could see that there had been some initial attempt at burial, a pit under that mound that had been at least partially filled in with dirt before digging animals disturbed it.

Clearly, the earliest victims of whatever had attacked this community had received some semblance of funeral rites until the remaining villagers had become too weak to do more than drag the dead to the pit and toss them in. Even the dead man under the tree looked as though he had simply pitched forward in his tracks.

"Disease?" Julie asked, and her mind went instantly to the cholera epidemic that had claimed her parents and so many others. Few knew better than she how illness could rampage through one of these villages whose occupants had no natural immunities or medical attention.

Other signs around the clearing supported that theory. The dark head and sprawled torso of someone who had fallen in the doorway of a hut off to her right. Another body that had been abandoned just short of the burial pit.

She heard a rustle of movement inside the hut just beyond the *tacu*. The rustle shifted to a soft scuffling, then the clatter of a small object tipping over. Someone trying desperately, perhaps, to rise from a sleeping pallet and stagger outside for help. Maybe even a child?

"Rick!" she whispered urgently. "There's someone alive in there! There must be survivors. We've got to help them!"

Instinctively, she was rising to her feet, and it roused both shock and anger when Rick yanked her back down with a steel grip on her wrist.

"Don't go out there, Julie!" he ordered, and his command was as cold and hard and deadly as his expression. "They're all dead. Look!"

The rustle of movement inside the hut exploded through the doorway to become a gaggle of chickens that had been rooting around inside the hut. A buzzard fluttered out after them, and Julie's stomach heaved again as she realized what that hut must contain.

Then she realized that Rick wasn't referring to the hut. His grim attention was on the *tacu*, and as Julie followed the direction of his eyes, she caught the glint of metal, half-hidden behind the wooden base of the mortar.

Releasing Julie's wrist, Rick reached to break off one of the palm-like plants under which they lay. Rising to a crouch, he used the long stem to roll the metallic object into view. It was a stainless-steel flask, brightly polished, like a quart thermos, only much smaller. More the size of a mousse or hair-spray can. On the side of the flask were markings, graceful, flowing in line. Julie couldn't decipher them. In this remote Indian village, the flask was as out of place as a computer keyboard would be.

Then Julie saw what lay beside the flask. It was just a coconut, like those bunched at the top of a palm on the far side of the clearing. But this coconut had its hairy fibrous cover scraped away everywhere but the top, and on the resulting smooth surface had been carved crude eyes, a nose, and a mouth. A toy made by some Indian parents for their child. An image sprang to Julie's mind of a little girl dropping that primitive doll to reach for the shiny new toy she'd discovered.

"What is it?" she whispered.

"The answer to our questions," Rick answered, and his voice was no less bleak as he dropped the stem and rose swiftly to his feet. Reaching down a hand, he pulled Julie to hers. "Let's get out of here, now!"

Rick made no further attempt at stealth as they retreated from the village, striding so fast through the brush under which they had belly-crawled that Julie was almost running to keep up. He didn't pause until they were back at the avocado tree.

Squatting down on his heels under the overhanging branches, Rick stared out over the muddy water, his lean face grim with concentration. Julie, who had never mastered the hunkered-down crouch that seemed to be an integral part of guerrilla training, sank down cross-legged beside him. His silence dragged out unbearably, but there was something still so cold and dangerous in his tight expression that Julie didn't have the courage to interrupt his thoughts.

At last his breath left him in a sigh. Without shifting his focus from the muddy surface of the river, he said quietly, "That Indian we saw. He wasn't from that village. Not if he's still alive!"

He made the statement distantly, not as though he were speaking to Julie, but as though he were mentally putting puzzle pieces together. Julie jumped on the broken silence. "How can be you so sure? What is it, Rick?"

Rick turned his head from the river to glance at Julie, but didn't seem to see her. "Biological warfare."

The terse statement hit Julie like a blow. "But—how can you say that? How do you know it isn't plague? I've seen villages wiped out like that before. It could be yellow fever or . . . or cholera!" She broke off, and her voice dropped to a whisper. "It's that metal canister, isn't it?"

Rick nodded, and a deep weariness replaced his dangerous look. He seemed suddenly older than his years. "Yes, I recognized it. It's an aerosol spray device for releasing small amounts of fluid or spores into the atmosphere. Used in bio-warfare experiments to test airborne viruses or chemical agents."

His glance flicked to Julie again. "And the writing on the side is Arabic."

"Arabic?" Julie gasped as the significance sunk in. "The *musulmanes*. Oh, no, Rick!"

Getting up from her cross-legged position, she moved in front of him. Her eyes were wide and frightened. "Then—this is what you were looking for? This is what *Comandante* Aguilera and his people are hiding out here in the demilitarized zone? All those poor people!" Julie's breath caught in sudden realization. "The environmentalists—do you think what killed the villagers killed them?"

"I don't know," Rick said tiredly. "The medical team dismissed it as a tropical fever or flu. But there are bio-weapons that fit into those parameters. It would certainly explain Aguilera's sudden reluctance to allow any serious lab testing."

He broke off to look keenly at Julie. "How much do you know about biological warfare?"

Julie shrugged. "You can't follow the news these days without knowing something about it. Both the U.S. and the Soviet Union had biological and chemical weapons programs during the Cold War, but they've supposedly dismantled them under treaties banning such weapons. There are rumors of other nations, some of them unfriendly to the U.S., suspected of trying to develop those kinds of weapons."

"Not just suspected," Rick said. "Actually, there are at least a dozen nations we know of with bio-weapons programs. And the majority of them, unfortunately, aren't entirely friendly to U.S. interests. Nations like China, North Korea, and some of the hard-line Middle East regimes—Iran, Iraq, Sudan, Libya."

"Muslim countries," Julie recognized with dread. "Then—you think one of those countries is supplying the guerrillas with bio-weapons?"

"Not just one!" Rick's tone was grim. "I know exactly where that canister came from. I was eighteen and barely out of basic training when my unit was deployed to the Persian Gulf. We were responsible for dismantling some of Hussein's biochemical warfare stockpile after the war. I don't read Arabic, but we learned that bit really fast. 'The Lightning Bolt of Allah'! It was stenciled all over his bio-weapons program, including warheads filled with the stuff. Hussein's little joke—terror from the sky and all that. We knew then we hadn't got it all—or even most of it. Army intelligence estimated that Iraq stockpiled eighty-five thousand liters of anthrax alone— enough to wipe out every person on the planet. Then there was the smallpox. Butulinum toxin. Others."

"Anthrax?" Julie grabbed at one of his litanies of horror. "You mean, the cow disease all those people died from after the World Trade Center attacks?"

Any American would have had to be comatose to miss all the news coverage during those months. Someone—one of the al-Qaida terrorists connected to the World Trade Center attacks, a mad scientist, a disgruntled lab worker—no one had yet figured it out—had slipped small amounts of anthrax spores into envelopes and mailed them to prominent politicians and media figures. More than a dozen people had been contaminated by the disease. Five had died.

Julie mentally reviewed what she remembered from the news coverage at that time. In its natural form, anthrax was rarely fatal. It was caused by contact with contaminated cattle or their waste and resulted in skin lesions and flu-like symptoms. A strong course of antibiotics was usually enough to take care of it. But dried and milled properly, the anthrax spores could be used to induce a more deadly form of the disease—inhalation anthrax. Inhaled into the lungs, even a few spores would immediately begin multiplying in the damp environment, producing within days flu-like symptoms and shortness of breath. By the time the victims realized they had more than the flu, it was too late for antibiotics. Another day or two, and almost all of those exposed would be dead of acute respiratory failure.

"That's exactly it," Rick nodded. "Personally, I'm betting it was anthrax in that canister. I took a good look at those bodies. They weren't disfigured, so it wasn't smallpox. And butulinum toxin is food-borne—you have to ingest it. Whatever was in that aerosol can was designed to be released into the air. Anthrax matches the symptoms of flu and pneumonia the medical team identified in John and the others."

Julie's face was white with horror. "But it's been more than ten years since the Gulf War. Surely germs wouldn't stay alive that long!"

"You saw the village. Anthrax, for one, if properly stored, will keep twenty-five years or longer," Rick answered. "It wouldn't take much. There were only a few milligrams in those envelopes they found. Our own military experts estimate that as few as a hundred kilos dumped from a plane over Washington, D.C., on a windy day could kill between one and three *million* people. Taking out that village would require only a fraction of a teaspoon released into the air. In fact, if you have the guts for mass murder, it's the perfect weapon. No mess, no destruction of property. Even better—or worse, depending on what side of the equation you're on—no one would even know there had been an attack until symptoms started cropping up a week or more down the road, by which time your terrorist would be long gone."

"Then you think that cargo you saw was these Muslim allies of *Comandante* Aguilera smuggling in some of Hussein's old stockpile?" A shudder went up Julie's spine. "But—it doesn't make sense! Why would the FARC want to kill off their own people? And why would these Islamic terrorists want to help them do it? No—"

Julie stiffened suddenly. "It's not Colombians they're after. It's Americans! That's what you're thinking, isn't it? That's the big strike they've been hinting at! And that's why they were so worried about an American spy! They're planning on hitting our American forces with that stuff—San José, or maybe even the embassy. Or—do you think they could smuggle these . . . these spray things into the U.S.?"

Rick's hands tightened on his weapon. "I don't know!" he admitted harshly. "I wouldn't put it past them to try it. But San José would be an easy enough target. Or our other bases down here. And the embassy wouldn't be much harder. Whether Aguilera or the FARC are involved is another matter. Not that I think they'd blink an eye if every Colombian politician—or American either—came down with the disease. But if the guerrillas were dabbling in biological warfare, I can't believe there wouldn't have been some rumor in all these months. And don't forget, neither Aguilera nor Flores were allowed near those cargoes."

"That's right—I heard the *comandante* myself asking what was going on out here when I was under that drug. Or at least I think it was him." It seemed suddenly incredible to Julie that they were sitting here on this jungle riverbank, quietly discussing weapons of mass destruction while a village of the dead lay within eyesight and a terrorist organization was plotting to strike somewhere else with disease and devastation. "Then— you've completed your mission after all! We know what they're after. Now we just need to get it to Colonel Thornton. And the embassy."

Rick shook his head. "Not quite. There are still a lot of unanswered questions. That canister was part of the Iraqi bio-warfare program, but the agent I spotted was Iranian. Does that mean a new cooperation between those two countries, or is it some kind of pan-Islamic rogue organization, like al-Qaida? And where is this facility—or whatever it is they're hiding out here? Why are they hiding it out here to start with? If they want to smuggle bio-weapons into the U.S., why go to all this trouble? It would be just as easy to smuggle them directly into the U.S. than to haul them into the jungle and still have to get them across the border. And the attacks on the surveillance plane and our Black Hawk. That was no bio-weapon that took them out. No, we're left with almost as many questions as we started with."

Another shudder went through Julie, and she at last allowed her inwardly burning question to surface. "Yes, like—what about us? Are we contaminated too?"

"You just thought of that?" Rick said grimly. "I hope not. We didn't touch anything. If it's anthrax, it isn't transmitted from one person to another. And with the timetable on the disease, it would have had to be released at least a couple weeks ago. The sun and rains have likely eradicated any remaining spores by now."

"And if not?" Julie asked, and she congratulated herself that her voice was almost even. "How much time do we have?"

"For antibiotics to be effective, they'd have to be started within the first few days. Which is the main reason anthrax is so deadly in a bio-warfare attack. People don't know they have the disease until the symptoms are full-blown. By then it's too late for treatment. And of course, if there ever was a real epidemic, there wouldn't be enough antibiotics for the entire population."

Rick paused again, visibly hesitating. "There's something you should know, Julie. If you've followed the news, you must be aware that there's a vaccine for anthrax—has been for some thirty years."

"Of course I know," Julie answered impatiently. "It was never given to the general population—no need and too many side effects. It was given only to parts of the armed forces." She broke off to stare at Rick. "You were one of them."

It was a statement, not a question. Rick nodded. "Special Forces were among the first to be vaccinated, since they're rated as part of the front line of defense against a biological warfare attack."

"That's great! Then *you're* safe, at least!"

Rick shot Julie an odd look at the relief in her voice. Had he thought she would resent the fact that he was safe and not her? "But you aren't—at least not completely. Julie, I don't want to alarm you unnecessarily. My personal feeling is that odds are good against contagion. But we can't take any chances. We need to push downriver as fast as we can—get you on antibiotics as soon as possible. If we've found one village, we'll have to hope we find another. If we take one of those canoes, we can double or triple our speed. We'll have to forget trying to be inconspicuous. There's no time for that anymore. Right now I'd turn myself in to the first person with a radio or telephone, guerrilla or not!"

But Rick did not rise immediately from where he was hunkered down.

His tight expression did not reflect the decisiveness in his words but was bleak and harsh.

"What is it, Rick?" Julie asked quietly.

"Nothing." Shoving the AK-47 up onto his shoulder, Rick made a movement to rise, but Julie knew him too well by now to be fooled. She put out a quick hand to stop him.

"Come on, Rick. Don't shut me out! We're in this together. What is it? You've completed your mission—at least as far as possible. You've done everything you can. So tell me what's wrong!"

The irony of her question struck Julie even as Rick wryly answered, "What's *wrong*? Not a whole lot—except a village back there full of dead people. For all we know, there could be others out there dying right now who don't even know it yet."

Rick slammed his right fist into the palm of his other hand. "I just can't help feeling we're out of time. These people aren't going to be waiting around for us to make our report to the authorities and bring back an investigation team. They're going to strike! My mission is to find out where and how and when. And I haven't fulfilled that mission."

Julie stared at him. "But what else can you do? Even if that canister came from some kind of biological warfare lab out here, there's no way to find it. You said yourself, you could wander around forever out here without stumbling over the place."

"Not necessarily. Have you asked yourself why they picked that village for their little biological experiment?" Rick didn't wait for Julie to respond. "Okay, maybe they needed a test case to see if their biological agent was effective. But why this one? And those sacks of rice and that machete—where did they come from? There isn't a store for days around here—even if these people possessed money. No, outsiders have been in that village. Outsiders bringing supplies. And what other outsiders do you know of in this area? Even the guerrillas stay clear!"

Julie's breath caught as she followed his reasoning. "Then you think those villagers worked for the terrorists? That those supplies were payment? That maybe this lab, or camp, or whatever it is, is close by?"

"Not too close," Rick said. "They would never release biological agents where a change of wind could carry it into their own camp. But close enough that village hunters might have stumbled into their base and been conscripted as labor. Close enough that a boat ferrying cargo to it might have spotted the village. And I'm betting they died for the same reason as the crew of that surveillance plane, and the Black Hawk crew, and John and his party. These people aren't risking any witnesses."

Rick made an abruptly dismissive movement with his hand. "Anyway, that's irrelevant at the moment. Right now we need to get you to safety."

Julie swiftly moved closer to Rick and knelt before him. She was almost touching his knee and could feel his warmth through the camouflage material, along with the tension of his body. "Just forget about me a minute, Rick. If you were by yourself—if you didn't have to worry about me—what would you do?"

A muscle bunched along his jaw, and he turned his head from Julie to stare out over the river before admitting harshly, "I'd go look for the place. I'm estimating a twenty-kilometer radius—partly because it would be futile to cover anymore than that, and partly because I don't think the settlement would be considered a threat any farther away. Unless they're prepared to wipe out all indigenous life in the area."

"And if you did go looking? A circle with a radius of twenty kilometers is still a lot of territory," Julie said steadily. "If you found them, what would you do? You're only one man. They would kill you if they caught you."

"I don't know, but I'd have to try something." Rick turned a direct look on Julie. "This is what I do for a living, Julie. There are always risks in this business. But the risk to one operative is an acceptable price compared to the lives at stake here." He shrugged. "But that's immaterial, since I'm not on my own."

"No, you're not. So let's both go!" Jumping to her feet, Julie adjusted her knapsack over her shoulder. As Rick stared at her, she added impatiently, "Come on! Let's go look for this place."

Rick didn't move. "You don't know what you're saying, Julie. It could take days to search an area like that. And we don't have days if we're to get you to civilization before your window for medical treatment is over. Besides, there's no way I can take a civilian on a high-risk mission like this."

"You can't stop me!" Julie answered calmly. "Look, you said yourself the risk of contagion was small. Certainly a whole lot less than the risk of these people carrying out another terrorist attack. Like you said, there are people who could be dying out there. More people who could die if we don't find out what's going on and try to stop it. Do you think I want that on my conscience anymore than you do?"

Julie got right in front of Rick, squatted down, and looked deep into his eyes. "You know I'm right, Rick! If you were in my place, knowing the risks, that's the decision you'd make, isn't it?"

Rick met her gaze, his own hard and somber. Then he looked away and burst out forcefully, "Yes, I would!"

"Then let me make it!" Julie pleaded. "Don't you think I can see the urgency of this as much as you can? I've already caused you enough trouble on this mission. Now we actually have a chance to make a difference. *I* have a chance! I can't just head downriver knowing I held you back from saving people's lives. Let me do what I can to help.

"Besides . . ." She paused. "Whatever—or whoever—is hiding out here is bound to have communication, right? We might be able to get off a warning—and call for help—faster this way than by wandering downriver to who knows where."

"I'd thought of that," Rick admitted. "But it doesn't mitigate the danger." He shook his head slowly, his eyes not leaving Julie's face. "I really shouldn't let you—"

"You have no choice," Julie interrupted firmly. "This is my decision, not yours."

Rick got to his feet and reached down a hand to Julie. "Let's call it a mutual operational plan. How about a compromise? We'll give it two days. If we haven't found anything by then, we head back to the river and downstream. Okay?"

Julie nodded as he released her. "Okay!"

"Let's do it!" Unslinging the AK-47, Rick moved out toward the sunshine beyond the overhanging branches of the avocado tree. He'd taken only one stride when he stopped, turning to look down at Julie.

"You know," he said slowly, "all those months I was in the guerrilla camps, I had to keep my faith private. I couldn't pray with another person—I'd almost forgotten what it was like. But I'd like to pray with you now before we move out. Would you mind?"

Julie shook her head wordlessly. Shoving his weapon back on his shoulder, Rick held out his hands. Julie, bemused, placed her own into his. It was the first time he had touched her except in the line of duty—helping her to her feet or over a log—and his hard palms against her smaller ones were warm and callused, not trembling like hers but rock-steady.

He made a last swift scan of the river before he began to pray, and even then he didn't close his eyes or relax his watchfulness as he cleared his throat and quietly prayed. "Our Father, the forces of evil seem very strong in the world right now and our own strength very small. We can't see the path ahead. We don't know what is happening beyond this jungle right now. Not a whole lot in our universe is making sense, and what does is pretty frightening.

"But You know. You hold the threads of the universe in Your hands, and You see where every path leads, including ours. Be with us now. Guide our path and our decisions. We don't demand safety for ourselves because sometimes You have other plans for our lives. But I'm convinced You brought us to this place for a purpose, and I pray that You will use our actions today to bring an end to this evil that threatens our world."

"Amen," Julie echoed softly. She had to swallow tears at the bottom of her throat as she withdrew her hands reluctantly from his. *I don't just like you, Rick Martini!* Julie discovered with a sudden shock. At this very inconvenient time for extraneous emotions, she was terribly afraid she was beginning to fall hopelessly in love with him.

# TWENTY-THREE

THEY WOULD TAKE A CANOE AFTER ALL. Squatting down on the beach where the canoes were drawn up, Rick explained his strategy.

"I have no idea where we are. But we entered the DMZ with the guerrillas from the north." With a stick, Rick was drawing a rough map of Colombia in the damp earth. "John and his two companions flew into this area too, somewhere south of San Ignacio. And their pilot testifies that they headed downriver from there, deeper into the zone. So if my hypothesis is correct and our terrorists discovered the village while ferrying cargo to their base, odds are they'd be coming downstream past the village in the same direction we've been heading. So we'll head on downstream and keep an eye out for a likely turn-off within that twenty-kilometer radius."

There was one thing more to be done before they embarked.

"I know you don't think there are survivors," Julie said hesitantly as Rick inspected the canoes, "but we can't leave without at least checking. I . . . I just couldn't feel right! Please, Rick, even if it was too late to help them, at least they wouldn't die alone. And you said it isn't contagious from person to person."

Rick glanced down at her pleading face, and his mouth tightened. "I'll go! You stay here—no, don't argue! For me, there's no risk. It would be foolish for you to expose yourself again."

Rick was right. It would be senseless to expose both of them. So while Rick strode up the bank, Julie sank down under an overhang to watch an adolescent caiman test his snout against the stakes of the bathing area. The reptile had time to try the full length of the barrier and drift downstream before Rick returned. His face was even more forbidding than before.

He shook his head at Julie's questioning look. "Don't come near me!" he added sharply as she rose to her feet. "Not until I've scrubbed."

They had no more soap, but Rick submerged himself completely in the shallow water, shedding only his belt, weapons, and ammo vest, ducking even his head beneath the water. Removing his shirt, he scrubbed arms, face, chest, even his boots with handfuls of sandy soil from the water's edge as though he were scrubbing away the memory of what he had just seen as well as any lingering germs.

"That bad?" Julie asked quietly when he waded ashore.

"That bad," Rick answered grimly. Wringing the water from his shirt, he picked up his ammo vest and weapons and tossed them into the nearest canoe. "I don't know if that did any good, but at least the smell is off. I hid the canister in case we get a chance to come back for the evidence. Let's go!"

Julie helped Rick push the canoe off the bank. Lying inside were several hand-carved paddles and two long poles. Hoisting herself into the stern, Julie picked up one of the poles and waited for Rick to climb into the front before thrusting the pole into the riverbed. Rick's eyebrows went up as the canoe glided smoothly out into the water. But he picked up a paddle without comment, and Julie was relieved to find that he was as expert with it as she.

How the villagers normally got the canoe past the barrier of stakes, Julie couldn't tell—maybe lifted it over. But Rick had an easy solution for that. No one would be using this beach as a swim area anymore, so Rick simply leaned over and yanked out a section of stakes while Julie used her pole to maneuver the canoe through.

The sun was almost directly overhead, and out on the river it was blistering hot, heat waves reflecting from the water to burn Julie's face as she paddled. Rick had spread his shirt and boots and socks to dry on the bottom of the canoe, and Julie averted her eyes from that muscled back bent over the other paddle. This was no time to allow personal feelings to distract from the urgency of their mission, she reminded herself sternly. Certainly Rick wasn't distracted. His lean profile as he turned it to study the bank was set in that tight look of concentration he always wore when focused on the task at hand.

*Get a grip on yourself,* Julie ordered herself. A week from now, one way or another, this would all be over. If it went well, she would be back in Washington. And Rick would be—where? His next assignment, presumably. Would he ever be curious enough to look her up sometime?

*First, we've got to survive this.* Julie set herself to watching the banks. Rick was looking, she knew, for a likely turn-off for a cargo barge. A tumble of rapids to their left was an impossibility. Rick shook his head as Julie spotted another small stream. It was wide and placid, but too shallow for anything bigger than a canoe.

They had been paddling downstream for almost an hour when it appeared just around a bend—a narrow tributary flowing into the river on the same side as the village, the mouth shielded by overhanging branches and lianas. A casual glance would have missed it.

As if they could read each other's minds, they dipped their paddles simultaneously to turn the canoe in that direction even before Rick glanced back to make a gesture toward the shore. Branches closed overhead as the canoe slid through the hanging vines and boughs into the other stream. The grim satisfaction of Rick's mouth echoed Julie's sudden certainty. The narrow channel was deep and smooth, and with the leaf cover overhead, it was a perfect turn-off for anyone sophisticated enough to be concerned about aerial surveillance.

The channel lasted about a kilometer before widening out into a vast, reed-choked swamp like the one through which the guerrillas had cut off Julie and Carlos's escape. Julie looked around instinctively. She saw no one, but the open stretch of bog and sky left her feeling exposed and unprotected.

Even without that feeling of exposure, the swamp was an eerie, inhospitable place, the water thick with algae that clung like green slime to the paddle when Julie lifted it. Clouds of mosquitoes rose off the stagnant water. Rick reached for his shirt and pulled it back on.

Huge lianas and dangling strands of moss cloaked the branches that reached down from occasional knolls of solid ground. The canoe was gliding between patches of reeds when a vine wrapped around a branch overhead begin to move. Julie caught a glimpse of a diamond-shaped head sliding into the water, followed by meter after meter of sinuous length. An anaconda, more than big enough to tip the canoe if it was in the mood.

Julie shuddered. There would also be water moccasins and deadly *fer-de-lance*, the Amazon's most poisonous snake, in that stagnant water, plus other creatures that would emerge with the falling of night.

She was relieved when Rick glanced over his shoulder and said, "We're too visible out here. There could be sentries. We're going to have to find land and abandon this canoe."

He directed their paddling toward the shoreline, where a long stretch of freshwater mangroves promised solid ground somewhere beyond. Docking the canoe under a curtain of hanging moss, Rick snatched up the AK-47 and stood in the prow of the canoe, his body taut as he studied the tangle of moss and vines above them. Julie, obeying his sharp gesture to stay put, felt it too—the sensation of being under surveillance.

She lifted her head to search the bank above them but saw only an explosion of growing things—poisonous green mosses, fungal growths budding from tree trunks, bladderlike pods sprouting like floating balloons from the algae. Were they being watched by that Indian they'd seen? If so, his skills of stealth and tracking were even greater than Rick's.

She saw the tension ease from Rick's shoulders. But the tightness of his expression didn't relax as he glanced down at Julie. "From here on, we don't know what's out there—or who!" he said harshly. "That means we follow full field discipline. No talking. No breaking cover. No sounds—if possible." Julie flinched at that last. "You have a problem keeping up, you let me know immediately. If you need a break, tell me!"

He paused to search the shoreline again. "My bet is that they beached somewhere in here. If they've unloaded cargo, they're bound to have left some sign. So we'll follow the perimeter of this swamp until we see some sign that they came ashore."

Julie nodded silently. This wasn't the man who had debated leisurely with her around a campfire or who had held her hands and prayed, but the professional soldier, and she offered neither argument nor opinion as she sloshed after him through the muck that filled every available space between the mangrove roots. Within minutes, her slacks were muddy to the knees, her sneakers soaked through. Julie felt a rip as a submerged branch grabbed at one foot, the weakened material giving way so that muck oozed in around her sock. They would have to get to dry land if these shoes were to last much longer.

But they didn't reach dry ground. Though Rick and Julie clambered for hours over the exposed roots and back down into the filthy water, they never came to the end of the mangroves. The swamp itself seemed to stretch forever. If the terrorists had docked somewhere in this mire, it wasn't here.

Under the constant submerging, Julie's feet grew soft and wrinkled, then swollen and sore. She had to bite her lip to keep from begging Rick to slow down. The pestilence of insects didn't improve matters. The stagnant waters of the swamp were a breeding ground for stinging, biting things—and not just mosquitoes. There were gnats and candelillas, an almost microscopic flea that stung like fire where it bit. Julie couldn't find any of the pungent leaves she'd used for repellant, and when she tried an acrid-smelling plant she came across, it left her with a rash that itched worse than the bites.

Rick showed a scattering of mosquito bites, but the insects seemed to find his weather-toughened flesh less tasty than Julie's softer skin, and the heavy material of his fatigues offered greater protection than Julie's short sleeves.

Julie, lacking his thick boots, was deathly afraid of snakes in the mire. She kept those fears to herself, pulling off the occasional leech with tight lips as she clambered after Rick.

She was hungry, too, and she knew Rick had to be as well. But if there was anything edible in all this wild fungal growth, Julie didn't recognize it. They found no fresh water either, and by late afternoon, Rick was strictly rationing the small amount left in his canteen.

Julie voiced no discomfort nor desire for a rest stop. There was no place to rest that was out of the mire, and besides, Rick's expression had grown steadily more stern and remote as the hours wore on. There were times in his glances back that Julie felt a glimmer of anger from him. Was he again resenting that her presence held him back?

Toward dusk, Rick steered them back toward the open water of the swamp. If the going was no easier, at least there was the pale green of the evening sky to let them see their way. As dusk fell, Julie caught a glimpse of the moon through a scattering of clouds, only the faintest sliver of a crescent now.

Rather than camping, they perched for the night on one of the tree-covered knolls that rose out of the swamp to offer a patch of solid ground. The vegetation was too wet for a campfire, even if Rick had chosen to risk one, and both the penlight and Carlos's flashlight were now out of batteries. There was no light except from the sliver of moon peaking through a spreading cloud cover and an odd green phosphorescence that rippled here and there through the swamp waters.

For once, Julie didn't sleep at all, not only because of hunger and thirst and an almost unbearable itching, but out of sheer terror of what could be crawling up onto their bit of land or dropping out of the branches overhead under that cloak of darkness. She didn't even try to find a piece of dry ground to stretch out on but sat braced against a tree trunk, her knapsack clutched on her lap and her eyes straining wide open in the dark to follow every ripple of green out in the water.

Rick didn't sleep either, and if he didn't speak, his prowling around the knoll gave an illusion of protection. At some point during the night he slid his long body down beside her and, without a word, slipped an arm around her shoulder. After a long moment, Julie relaxed her stiff posture and, with the softest of sighs, let her head rest against the knobby surface of his ammo vest. She must have dozed a bit; the next thing she knew, it was growing lighter, and Julie saw at least two snakes slide from the knoll into the water when she shifted position.

As soon as she moved, Rick slid his arm from Julie's shoulder. His jaw tightened as he glanced down at her exhausted face, and he stood up abruptly and walked over to look out across the swamp, saying curtly over his shoulder, "Unless you have breakfast tucked away somewhere, we might as well get moving."

The morning went no better than the day before. Julie's sneakers were in shreds, the soles hanging to the leather uppers only in spots. Her feet inside were so swollen and raw it felt as though they were literally rotting away inside her socks. Rick had to slow his pace repeatedly for Julie to keep up, even with all her determination.

By midmorning the canteen was empty, and they hadn't come across any food, either. Julie, whose biggest concern had been that her slow pace would keep them from meeting Rick's two-day deadline, began to be afraid they wouldn't leave this swamp at all. What killed people in the jungle far more surely than wild animal attacks or snake bite was the slow debilitation from harsh conditions that left them too weak or disabled to go on. They eventually died of thirst or starvation or fell prey to one of the predators that wouldn't attack a healthy individual but hung around to prey on the weak.

It was past noon, going by her watch rather than the sun, which they had lost sight of as they detoured away from the open swamp, when Julie clambered after Rick over another root and onto dry land—real dry land, hard and firm underfoot. The tangled root system of the mangroves had ended abruptly in smooth, open ground that didn't have the swamp waters to support the mangrove's unbridled proliferation.

Were they still circling the perimeter of the swamp? If not, they were back where they had started—hopelessly lost.

Right now, Julie didn't care. From somewhere not far ahead she caught the gentle gurgle of running water. Her thirst had long since driven away any hunger pangs, and the prospects of quenching it gave her the adrenaline to scramble after Rick up a slight incline that carried them farther out of the swamp. The humid fungal growth they had been pushing through for the last twenty-four hours gave way to the cathedral-like marching columns and dim, open aisles of the tall hardwoods with their massive branches spreading out 150 feet or more overhead. The sound of trickling water came from a brook spilling over an outcropping at the top of the incline to form a clear, still pool at its base. Julie hurried eagerly toward it.

The haste of her scramble ripped the final threads holding her left shoe to her foot, and as the sole twisted away under her, and her raw flesh touched the ground, Julie could no longer keep back a gasp of pain. It was a small gasp and quickly bitten back, but Rick whirled around immediately.

"What is it?" he demanded. "What's the matter?"

"Nothing!" Julie choked out. "I just—stubbed my foot."

"Don't give me that!" Rick said harshly. "Did you think I haven't noticed the way you've been limping these last few hours? Here, let me see."

Julie was in too much pain to resist his hard hand on her shoulder. The rush of water over the outcropping and down the incline during the rainy seasons had over the years eaten away the earth around the rock face. A large overhang had been exposed, creating what was almost a shallow cave beside the pool of water. An immense cedar grew up against the rock face, and the rainwater had washed away at the roots on the pool side so that they too were exposed, one of them thrusting up out of the rocky soil right under the overhang. Swinging Julie up into his arms, Rick strode swiftly to the overhang and lowered her to a sitting position on the rock.

Yanking off the remainders of tattered shoes and socks, he dipped clean water from the pool in his canteen and sluiced it over her feet. They looked even worse without the cover of leather and muck— puffy and misshapen like bread dough, the skin cracked and bleeding on the soles as well as where the leather uppers had cut into the top and sides.

Rick muttered something, then said aloud, "You won't be going anywhere on those. Not unless someone carries you!"

Placing his AK-47 on the ground beside him, he reached to slide Julie's knapsack from her shoulder and rifled around inside. But there was little left—either of clothing or the small first-aid kit Julie had packed. The remaining antibiotic cream wouldn't cover even one of those oozing gashes. The tiny bandages were hopelessly inadequate, the hydrogen peroxide bottle empty. The sweat shirt was gone, too ripped and filthy with fish guts to keep. Rick pulled out one of Julie's khaki shirts.

As he unsheathed his knife, Julie ventured, "I . . . I'm sorry. I know I should have said something earlier, but it really wasn't so bad. I didn't want to slow you down."

Her apology withered under his glare. He was furious, Julie saw with a sinking heart, his brown eyes blazing copper with anger, his mouth in a thin straight line, his jaw clenched so tight, Julie could see the muscles bunch at the base of his ear.

"I should never have brought you!" he ground out between his teeth as he sluiced more water over her feet. "I should have stuck to my guns and put you in that canoe straight downriver and got you out of here to where you'd be safe. What was I thinking? No, I know what I was thinking. I was thinking of my mission, and who gives a rip about anything—or anyone—else!"

Julie stared at him, recognizing with astonishment that he was furious not with her, but with himself.

"You didn't bring me," she told him quietly. "It was my decision, remember?"

Rick ripped at the material of her khaki shirt with a force that didn't need the knife.

"Don't kid yourself—or me! I was in command. I made the call—a wrong one, clearly. We've found nothing. We've lost two days. Even if you were in any condition to walk, the odds of making it back to the canoe and downriver . . ."

As he broke off, Julie silently finished his thought: *In time to reach medical care if it turns out I've been exposed.*

"We haven't even managed to get a warning out!" he groaned. "If we'd headed downstream, we might have accomplished at least that much."

"We don't know that," Julie denied. "We don't know what we might have found downstream. Maybe something even worse! It's like you told me once. You have to make the best decision you can with the information you've got. And that was what we—you—did."

Rick's mouth twisted wryly as he glanced up from the smaller strips he was tearing. "If you're trying to make me feel better, okay, it's working—a little! But that doesn't do anything to improve our present situation."

He sluiced her feet one last time with the canteen before opening the remainder of the antibiotic cream. The action reminded Julie of how thirsty she was, and she ran her tongue out to moisten her dry lips. Reading her action, Rick handed her the canteen. The water was wonderfully cool on her throat, but the hard metal of the canteen made Julie's mouth throb. Julie touched the back of her hand to her lips. It came away red. Had she cut herself without realizing it?

Setting down the canteen, Julie reached for the knapsack and pulled out the makeup case she hadn't bothered with since she'd begun her captivity. The lid held a mirror about the size of a postcard. Flipping it open, Julie touched a finger to her sore mouth as she glanced at the reflection.

She stared in disbelief. That couldn't be her in the mirror! It was the face of a hideous stranger. The skin that had been a smooth, clear olive was mottled and bumpy as though attacked by some horrible disease, marred further by a bright red rash that ran across the forehead and down both cheeks. The eyes were sunk deep into circles so dark they looked bruised, and they were mottled with insect bites even across the eyelids. The cheekbones thrust sharply up under the skin, giving the cheeks a gaunt, concave look. And the mouth was dry and pale and cracked. Even as Julie bit her lip in dismay, another thin red line began to bleed.

Rick glanced up sharply from the length of material he'd begun to wrap over the antibiotic cream. "What is it?"

"I'm so ugly!" Julie choked out. With a click she snapped shut the mirror and shoved it back into her knapsack. For a person who'd always prided herself on not putting undue emphasis on her appearance—certainly not the kind of obsession she observed in women like Sondra Kharrazi—she was behaving badly. Unexpectedly, tears stung her eyes. She forced a rueful smile that stung her cracked lips. "I'm sorry. It's pretty silly to care, when . . . when we might die out here. It was just such a shock. I guess I have a lot more vanity than I like to admit."

Rick's grip tightened suddenly on the bandage. "You're *not* ugly," he said abruptly. "You're beautiful."

The forcefulness of his statement brought another rueful smile. "If you're trying to make me feel better . . ." Julie mimicked. Then the smile faded, and she looked away. "It isn't necessary. I'm adult enough to face reality. And it doesn't really matter—not now!"

"I don't try to make people feel better," Rick answered roughly. "And I never say anything I don't mean."

Giving up on the bandage, he sank back on his haunches and held Julie's eyes with a direct look. "Do you want to know what I really think of you?"

If she didn't, she was going to find out anyway. When Captain Rick Martini of the 7th Special Operations Group got that determined set to his jaw, there was little point in arguing. Rick stood and walked out from the pool for a swift look around before returning to Julie.

"The first time I saw you in that press mob in Bogotá . . ." Rick's mouth twisted at the surprise in Julie's eyes. "Oh, sure, I noticed you long before you ran in front of a plane's wing on the San José runway. And I thought you were a pretty girl, all right—a very pretty one. So what? The world's full of pretty girls, and in my line of work, we like to stay a long ways away from your profession. I had no reason to think you were any different from any of the other reporters I've run into, shoving their way onto military installations, more interested in getting their name on a byline—and that Pulitzer Prize you always talk about—than the lives of the people they affect by what they choose to write. Then Victor and his goons picked you up."

Fire smoldered again in the brown eyes, but Julie knew it wasn't she who had drawn his anger. "When Aguilera went after you that day, I could have killed him! I would have, too, if it wouldn't have made matters worse for you. I knew you were scared to death—and with reason. But you didn't whine or scream or demand your American rights like most gringos would have done. You stood there with your back straight and your chin high and answered Aguilera like a pro. Which is why I wondered awhile if maybe you weren't."

Rick shifted his hunkered-down position to where he had a better panorama of the woods beyond the pool and outcropping before he went on. "It didn't take long to figure out you were a civilian who'd wandered into the wrong place and didn't have a clue what was going on. But in all those weeks, you never complained or let them get you down—never even let them see you cry. You were more worried about those *campesino* friends of yours, and Tim McAdams and Carlos, than about yourself. I thought you were one of the most courageous, caring people I'd ever seen."

Julie, embarrassed, started to speak, but Rick stopped her with a finger to her cracked and bleeding lips. "No, don't talk! Just let me say this. These last few days, I'd never have dreamed that a civilian—and especially a woman—would have the grit to come through what we've run into without snapping. But you—again, you didn't complain even once. I don't know another woman in this world I could say that about.

"And you haven't just kept up; you've been a partner all the way. I said it before, and I'll say it again—if I ever had to pick a person to have at my side when the going got tough, it's you, Julie Baker."

Rick reached up—so unexpectedly it brought fresh tears springing to Julie's eyes—and ran the knuckles of his hand gently down her bumpy, mottled cheek. The expression in those brown eyes so close to hers was one she'd never seen before but dared not try to read.

"You were a very pretty girl when I met you, Julie Baker," he said softly. "And you will be again someday when we get out of this, and those mosquito bites go away, and you get a haircut and those new clothes. But right now, when I look at you, I don't see a pretty girl. I see the most beautiful person I've ever known."

Julie opened her eyes wide to keep the tears from brimming over. "But— I didn't think you even liked me! Everything you said—about my parents . . . and me."

Rick dug into his pocket before remembering he no longer had his hand-kerchief. Instead he ran a finger gently under her eyelashes and wiped away the drops quivering there.

"Me and my big mouth," he said ruefully. "It's just—you had so much to offer. I hated to see you holding onto the past, resenting it—especially when so much of what made you so special was this place, those parents of yours. As for not liking you . . ."

Julie could hardly breathe under the intensity of his gaze. But he never finished, and she felt the stiffening of his body, his almost physical withdrawal from her, even before his head shot up, his eyes narrowing and his face hardening. Julie wondered if she had imagined that glow in the brown eyes, those moments of tenderness.

Even as she swallowed her disappointment, she felt it too—the sensation of someone watching that had been plaguing her all day, now so strong it drove all thoughts of Rick from her mind. She turned her head, searching.

Then she saw him, peering around the base of the cedar, the gray-and-white streaks that dappled his bronze skin blending into the wood of the trunk so that Julie caught first the menacing slant of his black eyes.

If this wasn't the same Amazonic native they had spotted two days earlier, it was his twin brother.

This time the face did not waver. It disappeared but only to reappear as a stocky Indian no taller than Julie. He was naked except for a tattered pair of men's black running shorts. A surreal illusion of clothing was created by his streaks of a tarlike substance that Julie knew to be a type of pitch, plus the gray of ashes and touches of white that on closer inspection proved to be the down of bird feathers pressed into the pitch.

Not that his almost clownish attire projected an impression of harmlessness. The bow of polished ironwood in his right hand was as tall as himself, and the arrows bound by vines into a bundle and slung over one shoulder and down his back were almost as long. From a woven bag hung over the other shoulder protruded a bamboo dart gun, and Julie hadn't been so long absent from these parts to forget the deadly poison that tipped its darts.

Glancing past him, Julie saw that the woods was full of them—shadowy figures among the trees, their body paint creating an illusion of camouflage. They seemed to flicker in and out of view against the undergrowth like ghosts or a hologram.

Rick, sliding back on his heels to where his AK-47 was within easy grasp, had lowered one hand out of sight to where he could snatch up the weapon.

"Rick!" she whispered.

"Don't look at them," he muttered through his teeth. "We don't want a confrontation. If we don't show any reaction, maybe they'll just pass on through."

Julie was already shaking her head. "We'd have never seen them if they didn't want us to. They've shown themselves because they want something from us. In fact, I'm betting this is who's been following us all this time. We'll just have to hope it isn't our skins they want. I grew up with some of these people—let me try to speak with them."

Rick nodded a curt acquiescence, but his hand that was out of sight closed on the AK-47, and his tense body didn't relax as Julie stood. She winced as her weight rested on her feet, but she didn't allow herself to hobble as she took a step toward the native.

What could she say to communicate with this primeval tribal warrior? *We come in peace? We're lost and don't want any trouble? Our weapons are more powerful than yours, so don't try anything?* The man's tattered shorts indicated that the tribe had had some contact at least with the outside world. Did this man, or any of them, speak Spanish?

The native was stepping forward to met her, a broad smile crinkling the black eyes and banishing the menacing look.

"Señorita Julia?"

# TWENTY-FOUR

IF JULIE'S MOUTH DIDN'T DROP OPEN, it was only because she'd snapped it shut as she bit back her prepared greeting. That there were those in San Ignacio who had remembered the little *gringa* they had helped raise wasn't so surprising. But a primitive native in the depths of the densest rainforest left on the planet?

As the Indian stepped into the open, Julie marked more details about him. He was younger than she'd first thought—about her own age, if she could still judge the passing years on these natives—with a bone structure that was broad and barrel-chested for his height compared to the more lanky build of the average Caucasian.

The expression on his round face seemed less intimidating now and more anxious as his initial smile faded. His black eyes darted in that side-to-side flicker that indicated worry or fear in these natives, as rapid blinking might indicate for Julie's people.

Try as she might, Julie could see nothing familiar in this adult tribal warrior that he should call her by her name, or in any of the others who were drifting closer in around them. Too close! At the edge of her vision, Julie saw Rick rise soundlessly to his feet behind her, the AK-47 hanging loosely from his hand but needing only a split second to bring into play.

There were pleasantries to be followed in establishing contact with a potentially hostile jungle tribe. But right now Julie couldn't think what they were. Even after opening her mouth and snapping it shut again, all that emerged in stammering Spanish was, "How . . . how do you know my name?"

The Indian stepped closer, and with him came the strong musk of his body odor, a smell that combined a lack of soap and antiperspirants with the smoky overtones of campfires, compounded by the blood scent of a fresh-caught opossum that was tucked somehow into the waist of those tattered shorts.

It was a scent that attracted far less attention from the denizens of the jungle than the deodorants and colognes that clung to "civilized" intruders into their territory, and in Julie's childhood it had seemed as natural as the perfume of a flower or the smell of wet dog, and unique enough to each individual that she, like the natives, could pick out the scent of those she knew well even in the dark of a jungle night. But after long years in a more sanitized environment, Julie had to consciously restrain the flare of her nostrils as the native approached.

"You do not remember me, Señorita Julia?" His own Spanish was halting and slow, as though it hadn't been used for a long time, and he switched with his next words to what sounded at first to Julie like gibberish. Then, as her brain began separating long unused patterns, the meaningless sounds converged into speech.

"I am Bernabé. I taught you to use one of these when we were children." He patted the blow gun protruding from his shoulder bag. "You shot at the opossum I was hunting and missed. Your father gave my family rice instead for our supper. Can you truly have forgotten me and my people?"

Julie shook her head, too stunned to speak. Yes, she remembered Bernabé—though she would never have recognized the child she'd known by that name in this adult warrior. The son of the *curandero*—shaman—in the Indian village where her parents had frequently ministered. While they had tended the sick and discussed theology with the village elders, Julie had played with their children. The boys' activities had seemed far more interesting than the weaving and pounding corn and washing clothes that were the chores of even the smaller Indian girls, and Julie had climbed trees with the boys to pick mangos or guava and let them teach her to use their blowguns, child-sized but still deadly.

Those days hadn't lasted long. By age ten, both boys and girls in the tribe were taking on what to North Americans would be considered adult responsibilities, and by age twelve, Julie had been considered marriageable and was no longer allowed to associate freely with the males of the tribe.

Bernabé had not been the boy's birth name, though it was the only one Julie had known. His father had been one of the village's first converts to Christianity and, like many other native Christians, had chosen biblical names for his children in addition to the Indian names outsiders found unpronounceable. In his case, the name chosen was the Spanish equivalent of Barnabas, the apostle Paul's first traveling companion.

Julie couldn't have been more than eight or nine when Bernabé had yielded to her pleading to take her with him into the jungle, but she still remembered her poorly aimed dart that had deprived him of the supper he'd been sent out to bring home. Elizabeth Baker had been frantic by the time the two children finally reappeared out of the jungle. Her father had simply given the family some of their own food supplies to make up for the lost meal, and his quietly delivered lecture on the flight home had been effective enough to keep Julie from ever wandering off again.

Rick spoke up, in low English. "What is it, Julie? Do you know these people?"

Julie swung around, hope lighting up her tired face. "Oh, Rick, I think we're saved! These people are I'paa. The Indian tribe my parents used to work with. I used to play with Bernabé when I was a child."

A sudden realization struck her. "Rick, the press releases said the I'paa were the tribe those environmentalists were visiting! It could even be Bernabé's own village. They were in that part of the jungle when they disappeared. Maybe these Indians know what happened to them."

Julie turned eagerly back to Bernabé, shifting into Spanish rather than I'paa, not only because she wasn't sure her tongue could twist itself around the long-unused phrases, but so that Rick could understand.

"Yes, Bernabé, of course I remember you and your people! But what are you doing here? Have you been following us? And the rest of your village—where are they?"

Shooting a swift glance at Rick, Bernabé switched with clear reluctance into his halting Spanish. "I do not know where the others are, only where they were when we saw them last and where they are to be. There was great trouble in the village—evil and death brought by the *riowa* from the outside. We were afraid, so we left."

Julie threw Rick an eager look over her shoulder. "Then the three foreigners who died—the *riowa*—they did come to your village! Do you know what happened to them, then? How they disappeared?"

There was no mistaking the sideways flicker in the black eyes. "Yes, the three *riowa* came to our village. They wished to know about the white ghosts who dwell in the jungle."

"White ghosts?" Rick murmured into Julie's ear. "Sounds as though these guys might have had contact with the people we're looking for. Your average Arab would be considered white by these guys—as would a fair share of Colombians."

Rick said aloud in Spanish, "White ghosts—or white men?"

Bernabé favored him with only a brief glance. "That is what the other *riowa* asked too. They wished us to help them fight these ghosts. We told them that there was only evil and death in that part of the jungle. But they insisted that they see for themselves. When the ghosts took them, we knew there would be more trouble. So we left the village. But then the evil and death began to spread in the jungle, and we did not know where to go to be safe. We did not know who we should tell."

He looked directly at Julie. "In the past when trouble came from the outside, the elders spoke to your father. He helped us. But he is gone, and we did not know what to do. Then the word came that the daughter of Don Ricardo had returned to the land of the I'paa. We did not know if you were like your parents or if you had changed in the long years away. But we hoped you might listen to our fears as others would not, and speak to the authorities outside."

Julie could feel exhaustion settling over her again because everything the I'paa native was saying seemed only to confuse her more. His halting Spanish didn't help. "I don't understand. How could you possibly know out here in the jungle that I was coming back to San Ignacio?"

"Yes, how?" Rick demanded softly behind her. "Julie, you didn't know you were coming yourself until the day before. I don't like this! If these guys aren't telling the truth, they may be involved with the very bunch we're looking for."

But the I'paa warrior was already answering. "You were seen. When you came in on the . . ."—Bernabé groped for the Spanish word, failing to remember it—"on the bird of metal on the great field where the *riowa* train their warriors. Word was sent to our people. When the . . ."—he groped again and triumphantly came up with the Spanish term—"the *avion* arrived in San Ignacio, there were eyes to see you. I was among them. We sent word to the elders that the daughter of Ricardo and Elizabet Baker had returned to the jungle."

"Yeah, right!" Rick muttered again. "He's saying they saw us fly into San José. That's an hour's flight from San Ignacio—a good 150 kilometers. And they sent word to their people to be waiting when we landed in San Ignacio? How—some kind of jungle telegraph?"

Rick's skeptical remarks had been in English, but something in their tone must have conveyed itself to Bernabé. The native's glance toward Rick was far from friendly as he said, "It was on the *teléfono* that we heard. Does he believe that the I'paa know nothing of *riowa* machines?"

Bernabé switched into I'paa, and the impatient gesture with which he made the shift only emphasized the razor-sharp tip on the spear he held in that hand. "Señorita Julia, you we know and your father. But this man we do not! He is dressed like those who held you prisoner, and he was one of them. Now he walks with you and acts like one who is not a stranger or your enemy." Bernabé threw Rick another darkling look. "Is he an *amigo?*"—he used the Spanish term for friend. "Or shall we kill him for you?"

"No, of course not!" Julie said, horrified. "I mean, yes, he is an *amigo*. He saved my life from those who held me prisoner."

The angle of the spear eased back perceptibly. "That is well. But it is taking too long to explain in the language of the outside. Besides, it is best that the others understand what is being said, and they do not speak the Spanish. It will be easier if I speak to you of all that has happened and you tell it to the *riowa* in his language."

Julie nodded respectfully. This was no longer the young boy with whom she had played so many years ago, but a leader among the tribal warriors, and as a woman, she was clearly expected to acquiesce, not argue. Turning to Rick, who was watching the I'paa with a look as dark as the one Bernabé had given him, she left out Bernabé's first comments as she explained. "Rick, Bernabé isn't comfortable speaking Spanish, and the others don't speak much, if any. He says it will be faster to explain to me in I'paa, then let me pass it on to you. Do you mind?"

Rick's jawline tightened, but he made no argument. "Just don't make this too long," he said shortly. "I don't like hanging around here with so many people around. We're too exposed. If these 'white ghosts' of theirs are anywhere out here . . ."

He caught a grimace of pain on Julie's face as she shifted her feet and added sharply, almost pushing her back down onto the root where she had been resting when the I'paa appeared, "And for goodness' sake, sit down before you fall down!"

In Spanish, he added to Bernabé, "The woman is injured. She must rest."

Bernabé didn't bother acknowledging Rick's suggestion. As he began to speak in his own language, the other Indians drifted in closer. Rick watched for a few moments, then strode a few paces away where he could keep an eye on both the I'paa and the surrounding jungle.

It was no more than ten minutes later before the lift of Julie's head drew

Rick back over to her. Bernabé stalked away as Rick approached, melting into the trees as swiftly and invisibly as he had appeared.

"He'll be right back," Julie said in answer to Rick's upraised eyebrow. She was chewing on what looked like a piece of dried-out rawhide, and as Rick squatted down on his heels in front of her, Julie handed him a similar length. "Here! Bernabé had some charky on him. It's made from—"

"I know what it is," Rick interrupted, cramming an end of the strip into his mouth. Julie smothered a grin at the grimace that crossed his face. The sun-cured jerky was a jungle traveling staple, but "tasty" wasn't an adjective often applied to it, and with the added flavoring of the I'paa's personal scent and a tinge of what must be the unskinned opossum, only their hunger made it palatable.

Rick chewed off another piece and washed it down with a swig from his canteen. "Okay, what's going on?"

Julie tried to swallow her own bite without tasting and failed before answering in the same low English. "We were right. It *was* Bernabé's village where the C-PAP group ended up. Bernabé was actually one of the paddlers who took them downriver. But it seems the story started a long time before that. It's funny, but outsiders don't seem to think of the Indians when they try to sneak around out here. It's like they think of them as just part of the wildlife. But these people don't miss much of what's going on in their lands, and Bernabé says it's been a couple years now that they've been seeing strange boats coming into their territory."

"The cargo boats from San Ignacio," Rick confirmed with satisfaction.

"Yes, it sounds like it," Julie agreed. "The I'paa weren't too happy about it. The colonists have been eating away at their territory for years. But the boats moved farther south, and when they didn't bother them any or touch their hunting grounds, the I'paa let it go. That is, until a few months back when Bernabé and a few of the other hunters went on a—well, the closest translation in English would be a 'long trek.' An expedition, I guess you could call it, out of their usual hunting range. It's a tradition for the younger men of the tribe—to add to the tribal knowledge of the area. Or more than anything, just to see what's over the next hill, as they say."

Julie shifted position and winced as one foot brushed against the root on which she was sitting. "Anyway, they were out in this area where we are now when they came across what Bernabé calls a 'big path'—some kind of road, in other words. They'd never seen colonists that far into the jungle, so they moved in closer to check it out. Bernabé isn't very clear about what they saw—there just aren't the words in I'paa. But it sounds like some kind of an installation. He was very clear that they saw white men there—not Colombian. Whatever they were speaking wasn't Spanish or any Indian dialect. He says they were dressed like you—in other words, in combat fatigues.

"While they were checking it out, two of his party disappeared. Bernabé insists ghosts took them. He kept talking about a 'ghost cloud' and something about a giant bug too. I can understand the cloud. Ground fog isn't unknown out here, and I can see it would spook them even more. But the bug . . ."

Julie gave her head a perplexed shake. "When I asked him if it was an airplane or helicopter like he's seen at San Ignacio, he said no. And he insists it was impossible for human beings to have taken his men. They didn't go too close or allow themselves to be seen. You've seen the way these guys move—like ghosts themselves."

"Surveillance cameras," Rick said. As Julie looked at him questioningly, he threw a measuring glance at the circle of I'paa who stood patiently and silently watching the two Americans. Then with some impatience he said to Julie, "Don't you see? This explains their whole ghost story. These guys may move like ninjas, but they don't know beans about technology. If surveillance cameras were there—maybe even motion sensors—those guys would be picked up."

Julie nodded. "Anyway," she continued, "when the other two didn't turn up, the hunting party headed home. They'd hardly made their report to the village elders when the C-PAP bunch showed up. You know what happened from there. The chief sent some of the hunters, including Bernabé, to show Dr. Renken where they'd seen the white ghosts—or men. It seems the chief was as skeptical of their story as you were. To give the I'paa credit, they didn't just run off when Dr. Renken and the others disappeared. They waited until the next morning, then sent three of the hunters after them while the rest waited with the canoes. But after two days, when no one came back—not even the last three they sent—they panicked and got out of there.

"By the time they reached the village, the pilot had taken off, looking for his passengers. The village elders decided that was it. They'd had unhappy experiences with outsiders before, and they figured somehow they were going to get blamed for their visitors' disappearances. So they just up and abandoned the village, leaving behind Dr. Renken's computer that had been left in the canoe, so they wouldn't be accused of stealing it. After a couple of weeks they drifted back, figuring anyone looking for them would have come and gone by then."

Julie paused, and her expression revealed that what was coming next wouldn't be pleasant. "Rick, those environmentalists—they weren't the only ones to die."

"What do you mean?" Rick demanded.

"Bernabé says that when they got back to the village after those weeks away, the bodies of the three missing paddlers were there, plus those of the two men who disappeared on the first hunting trip. He would hardly talk about it—just said that evil ghosts killed them and brought them there. There were no visible wounds, just like the C-PAP party and those villagers. But if they were killed by our 'ghosts,' why haul the bodies clear back to that village?"

"A warning!" Rick answered grimly. "We've already seen these guys' pattern with leaving witnesses. I'll bet if that village hadn't been abandoned, they'd all be dead by now. As it was, the bodies did the trick—drove the villagers out of the area."

Julie nodded agreement. "The I'paa—well, any native tribe—has a horror of infectious disease. They've had enough experience at seeing whole tribes wiped out. They burned the whole place to the ground right down over the dead bodies. Then they left. But there was still the problem of the rains. Besides, the village elders were beginning to think this 'evil,' as Bernabé calls it, was too big for them. I think they figured one bunch of white men would know what to do with another, so they headed north toward San Ignacio. That's the closest outsider town, and they've had contact there since my parents' day. Only they didn't know who was responsible for bringing these 'ghosts' into the jungle—the paramilitaries or the guerrillas or even the multinationals, who haven't always been innocent themselves in their treatment of the native tribes. Anyone they talked to could be an enemy. Especially once they found out that Dr. Renken's party had turned up dead! Then they found out that I was back."

"That still doesn't hold water!" Rick interrupted. "You want to tell me how a bunch of Stone Age natives are supposed to have gained access to a restricted military base like San José?"

Julie shrugged. "That's easy. As maids or gardeners or any general labor. Like I said, people treat the native Indians as though they were invisible or part of the local animal life. But there are those who leave the jungle and even learn Spanish. Bernabé, for one. Problem is, they get outside, and they have no education or usable skills, so they end up as servants. Bernabé says there's a couple of I'paa at San José now, serving as jungle trackers for the counter-narcotics troops."

"Come to think of it, he's right," Rick admitted. "I've been out with them myself when I was over there on TDY—though no one ever said what tribe they belonged to. Okay, so that's where they learned how to use a phone. You're telling me they have tribal members with phone service in San Ignacio?"

"That's the incredible part. It was my own father who first suggested to the village chief that it would be good for the tribe if some of the children had a chance to study. The chief's youngest grandson was one of the first who came into San Ignacio not long before I left. He's still there, even with the guerrilla takeover, working for the family my father arranged to take him in—basically as a gardener and all-around laborer, from the sounds of it. But he's going to school and is due to graduate this year—the first in his village. I guess San Ignacio has gotten phone service since my day, because when they saw me in San José, the trackers telephoned the place he works. He passed the message on to the tribe, who were temporarily living on the outskirts of town.

"To give the guerrillas credit, they usually leave the tribal groups alone unless they stir up some kind of trouble. So by the time we landed in San Ignacio, the I'paa had staked out the airport, and like everyone else, they recognized me right away. I guess I haven't changed as much as I thought since my teen years. They were deliberating whether they should approach me and ask for help"—Julie grimaced—"when I was dumb enough to get myself kidnapped."

Rick made no comment, and Julie hastily went on. "To make a long story short, the chief has had these guys trailing me ever since. They were watching the whole time I was with the guerrillas, but they've had enough experience with modern weapons, they didn't dare try any kind of a rescue operation. Then after we got away—well, they weren't sure about you. They'd seen you with the guerrillas, but I wasn't acting like a prisoner. So they played it safe and just kept obeying their orders to keep a watch. Besides, we were heading in the right direction."

Julie broke off to glance around at the listening Indians, and though she knew they couldn't understand a word she was saying, she lowered her voice instinctively. "Rick, they seem to have the idea that we're deliberately heading for this 'ghost' place, that it's been our destination all along. That village—they found it two days before we did. They didn't go inside the village, but they saw enough to decide it was the same great 'evil' that had killed their hunters and Dr. Renken's party. When they saw us heading right into the village, they panicked and almost turned back, they were so sure we were going to die too.

"The only reason they stuck around at all was because they weren't going to go back and tell the chief they'd abandoned Don Ricardo's daughter out here. But they stayed well back on our trail until they saw by our tracks that we'd made it out of the village and through a whole day and night alive. Since they assumed we knew where we were going, they couldn't figure out why we'd head into the swamp. But when they finally closed in our trail and saw that we were going around in circles and that I was"— Julie's color rose under the mosquito bites—"uh, not keeping up, they . . . well, Bernabé didn't quite put it this way, but basically that's when they realized we *didn't* have a clue where we were going, that we were lost and likely to kill ourselves out here like some of the other dumb gringos they've seen over the years. So they decided to show themselves."

She paused, her forehead wrinkling. "What doesn't make sense is why they didn't realize we were lost earlier, why they would think we were deliberately heading into this 'ghost' territory they spoke of."

Rick got abruptly to his feet, the swift movement triggering a soft murmur among the watching Indians. "Don't you get it, Julie? Remember, they think your family—and you too—are some kind of miracle workers. They think we came here to do something about this great evil."

The clipped harshness of his tone quickly raised Julie's eyes to him. He was looking out toward the jungle with his cold, forbidding profile. There was nothing of the man who a short time earlier had expressed such tenderness to her. Julie was silent for a moment before she answered quietly, "And can we do something about it?"

Rick didn't turn his head. "I don't know." The murmur of the Indians rose suddenly in decibel, and he added sharply, "Julie, ask them to be a little quieter. We don't know what, or who, is out there, and I'd just as soon we didn't draw any more attention our way than we have already."

He broke off as Bernabé stepped into view around the base of the cedar, reappearing as silently as he had disappeared. He uttered a swift phrase, and the rest of the I'paa fell silent. Throwing Rick a swift, hard glance, he muttered to Julie. As she translated, it became clear that if he hadn't understood their English, he'd once again read Rick's expression.

"He says there is no reason to be concerned. There are no strangers but ourselves in this part of the jungle. The white ghosts are too far away to hear or see. And I can tell you," Julie added, "if he says there's no one out there, you can be sure there isn't."

Rick didn't question Bernabé's veracity but swung around instead to demand sharply in Spanish, "Are you saying you know where we can find these white ghosts? Where are they? How soon could we be there?"

Bernabé ignored Rick as he propped his spear and bow and bundle of arrows against the trunk of the cedar. Lifting his carry bag from over his shoulder, he dug out a handful of small, freshly picked leaves. He dipped the leaves into the pool to rinse them, shook off the water, and crammed the bunch into his mouth much as though it were a wad of chewing tobacco. Then, around the wad, he muttered his answer.

Julie translated. "He says yes, he knows where to find the white ghosts. As for how long it takes—that depends on how quickly a man walks and how many times a man stops."

From the tightening of Rick's lips, she suspected he thought the Indian was being sarcastic. Julie might have thought so as well if she hadn't known the I'paa thinking.

Bernabé spat the wad of leaves, now a pulpy green mush, onto a palm frond he removed from his carry bag. "If you do not stop to hunt . . ."—he paused to thrust another handful of leaves into his mouth, and Julie could see him struggling to put into terms these foreigners would understand a distance that meant nothing to a people without measurements of miles or kilometers—"perhaps the time to watch *Betty La Fea* twice on the *tele*." He used the Spanish abbreviation for TV as the I'paa language contained no words for such technology.

Rick nodded as Julie translated. *Betty La Fea* was a popular Colombian half-hour soap opera. "About an hour, then," Rick said. This time he didn't try to speak directly to the I'paa warrior. "Maybe he can show us where it is. Tell him I need to see this place for myself."

Julie relayed the request and caught surprise in Bernabé's black eyes as he spat the second wad into the leaf. "Of course! That is why you are here, is it not?"

*Rick's right,* she thought in dismay. *They really do think we're some kind of miracle workers here to take care of this evil for them. But just what do they think two people can do?*

At least by going to this place, they could see for themselves what lay hidden out there. With the I'paa as guides, there was every chance they could then return downstream and to the proper authorities before anyone else got hurt. At the least, they were miles ahead of the desperate situation that had faced them only a half-hour earlier.

"They'll take us." Julie pushed up her sleeve to read her watch. "We've still got most of the afternoon. If we leave right away, we could be there and gone again well before dark."

"Not *we!*"

Rick's uncompromising statement drew Julie's gaze upward in surprise. Rick wasn't even looking in her direction, but was busily checking over his equipment, counting his remaining banana clips, removing a grenade from his vest pocket for inspection before returning it, though Julie was sure he must know every bullet in his ammo vest by now.

"What do you mean?"

The slide of the AK-47 made a click as Rick pulled it back. "I mean," he said flatly, "that it was one thing to drag you into this when there was no other alternative—or anyone to leave you with. Now that your friends have shown up, there's no point in risking the two of us. I'll take a party with me, and the rest can stay here until you're back on your feet, then get you out of here and to safety."

The soft sound as he released the slide was as much a dismissal as the uncompromising set of his jaw. *In other words, time to clear civilians out of the way and let the professionals get to work,* Julie interpreted.

"No!"

Her flat rejection drew Rick's attention. Shoving the AK-47 back on his shoulder, he squatted down on his heels in front of her. "Come on, Julie, be sensible!" he said harshly. "Can't you see I'm trying to do what's best here—for you and this mission? Just look at you! Right now you wouldn't get ten meters on those feet."

Julie met his hard gaze levelly. "I am being sensible, Rick. These people don't know you. Do you really think they're going to take you anywhere without me? And how are you going to talk to them? Bernabé won't speak to you as it is, and from what I've seen, the others don't know any Spanish at all. You need me!"

*Besides, I'm afraid! Afraid to have you go out there without me. Afraid of seeing the man I love*—there, she'd said it—*walk away from me and never come back . . . just like my parents.*

"No, I'm sorry, Rick. I'm not trying to be uncooperative, but if you're going, I have to go too."

Rick's eyes were narrowed and somber. He nodded abruptly, his jaw tightening to a grim line. "You're right—unfortunately. Which leaves us right back at square one, because there's still no way you're going to walk on those feet."

"Well, actually, there is," Julie interrupted with a half-apologetic gesture. "Bernabé is taking care of that."

She nodded toward the I'paa warrior, who had been stolidly masticating one mouthful after another of the leaves he'd brought back until he now had two palm fronds spread with the green mush. He knelt down to place one of the fronds carefully, pulp-side up, under Julie's nearest foot. Julie's mouth tilted wryly as she caught Rick's upraised eyebrows.

"Bernabé is the son of the *curandero,* the village witchdoctor. He hasn't practiced any of the curses and charms since his family became Christians, but the *curandero* is also responsible for the healing arts. Even if some of it is hocus-pocus, they do know a lot about medicinal herbs and plants."

Whatever plant it was that Bernabé had chosen as poultice, it was an effective one. Julie could already feel the stuff drawing the pain from her swollen and broken flesh as though it had some kind of natural anesthetic in it. Wrapping the leaf around Julie's foot, Bernabé picked up the pieces of Julie's khaki shirt that Rick had endeavored in vain to fashion into a bandage and used his knife to slice them into long, thin strips. In seemingly no time, he had them plaited rather than tied around Julie's foot to form a covering that tied off with a neat knot around the ankle. Swiftly, he wrapped the second leaf around her other foot and repeated the process.

Standing up, Julie found that the bottom was woven flat enough to walk on, yet thick enough to offer protection for feet not as toughened to walking barefoot as those of the Amazonic natives. Despite her lingering soreness, it was surprisingly comfortable and supple under her first tentative steps.

She looked up to find Rick's eyes on her as he demanded, "Can you make it?"

Julie nodded, and reached down to shove the remnants of her shoes and socks into her backpack.

"Good." Swinging around to Bernabé, Rick said in slow, clear Spanish, "We are ready. Will you allow us to follow in your footsteps as we do not know the jungle as well as you and your people do? And could you please tell your men to stop when we reach within an arrow's flight of this place? The white ghosts may have eyes in the forest, and we'll need to hide ourselves."

Rick had phrased it well, Julie approved, acknowledging Bernabé's authority and the I'paa's tracking skills while diplomatically conveying the necessary warning. Bernabé grunted agreement and turned to relay Rick's statement to the others without waiting for Julie to translate. When a murmur of agreement swept across the I'paa party, Bernabé lifted his spear, and the other I'paa began melting into the woods. Rick looked down at Julie.

"You stay with me," he said curtly. "And for goodness' sake, if you're having problems, this time tell me!" He held her gaze. "And Julie—there'll be no time for committee meetings or explanations out there. I need to know that whatever I say, I can count on you to do it immediately—no questions asked. Do you understand?"

"I understand," Julie said levelly, but she swallowed miserably at the sternness of his tone. Did he really think she would jeopardize their mission by challenging his authority? She reached down for her knapsack, but as she slung it over her shoulder, Rick caught her wrist in his hand.

"I would give anything if I'd never gotten you into this!" he said urgently. "You know that, don't you?"

The look in his eyes dissolved a cold, hard knot in Julie's chest. She stood still under the grasp of his fingers. "We already went through this, remember?" she answered with quiet firmness. "You didn't decide—I did!"

Rick's grip tightened almost painfully around her wrist. "If anything happens to you—"

"It won't!" Freeing her wrist gently, Julie managed a brief smile as she nodded toward Bernabé, who stood waiting for them at the far end of the outcropping. "Let's go!"

# TWENTY-FIVE

Julie's renewed hope that there was something positive they could do and every likelihood of reaching freedom and safety afterward, was more energizing than Bernabé's jerky. In fact, if it hadn't been for the urgency of the situation, the writer in Julie would have exulted at the incredible picture of which she was a part. The Indians flitting through the trees around her as shadowy and intangible as the ghosts they feared. The tips of Bernabé's weapons a few paces ahead unhesitatingly setting their zigzag course through the tall hardwoods. The larger-built Special Forces officer, who was almost as noiseless and lithe in his movements as the I'paa.

Even Julie herself was moving more silently and easily than she'd ever been able to do before, the thin material of her foot-coverings enabling her to feel the jungle floor beneath her feet in a way her sneakers hadn't allowed. She avoided twigs almost instinctively, feeling out bare spots of ground. In time, the anesthetic effect of Bernabé's poultice began to wear off, but the pain wasn't unbearable, and without the rubbing of her sneakers against cuts and bruises, she could ignore the dull ache.

Still, it was clear that the I'paa could have moved even faster without the Americans along. It was well over an hour when Bernabé waved his spear to signal a halt. A fresh plague of mosquitoes had already alerted Julie even before she caught sight of open sky through the trees and an explosion of ferns and elephant ears ahead.

It still astonished Julie how quickly the I'paa melted into cover. She spotted one warrior flat on his belly under a low-hanging elephant ear but only because she'd seen him standing there an instant earlier. Only Bernabé remained in sight. Stepping into the undergrowth, he motioned for Rick and Julie to follow. The vegetation closed in above them, tall enough to hide even the tip of Bernabé's spear, and a moment later, they were peering out from beneath a thick cover of fronds onto an open body of water.

"This is as far as my people and I will go," the I'paa warrior said flatly.

The water was as stagnant and algae-choked as the swamp through which they had wandered the last two days and might even have been an extension of the same system. If so, some geological upheaval in the past had spilled it into this part of the jungle, because here the majestic columns of the hardwoods marched right down to the water's edge. Out in the open water, Julie could see the rotting stumps of what had once been dense forest. Bernabé indicated the far side of the slough, where the rainforest rose again from the drowned jungle floor.

"It was through there that we saw the boats come. But not to this place. To the place where the great path begins. That is where we saw the white ghosts." He gestured with his spear toward the right. "It lies an arrow's flight that way."

As Julie translated, Rick withdrew his narrow-eyed scrutiny from the swamp to look down at the I'paa warrior. "Thank you, Bernabé," he said quietly in Spanish. "You've done exactly what I needed."

The I'paa hunter only shot him an oblique look. Rick let out a small sigh. "Why do I get the impression your friend here doesn't trust me?" he demanded of Julie in low English.

Julie hunched her shoulders under the knapsack. "Can you blame him? These people haven't had much reason to trust outsiders."

"Yeah, well, just so he doesn't take off on us. He looks tight enough to spook if I said boo! Tell him I'm going to check things out. I want you to stay here. I shouldn't be long." His tone brooked no discussion, and Julie offered none. "Whatever you do, don't come after me. If I'm not back within the hour, you take Bernabé and his men and go downriver to the nearest authorities."

Julie nodded. Then he was gone. She watched but could see no sign of his progress through the brush. She shifted her position under a patch of ferns to where she could look both across the swamp and back into the forest. Mosquitoes settled around her, and the need for silence made it more difficult to swat them away. A long-legged specimen landed on Bernabé's exposed ribs, but the I'paa hunter didn't seem to notice. Rick was right. The I'paa hunter looked jumpy enough to stampede into flight at any moment, his eyes darting nervously in all directions. What was she to do if Bernabé and his companions vanished before Rick ever returned?

But Rick was back far sooner than Julie expected—less than ten minutes by her watch. "It's there," he informed Julie grimly. "And way too close for safety, no more than twenty meters from here. Some 'arrow flight'! If this is an example of your friend's distance perception, we've got problems."

Julie's eyebrows rose. "But he *was* accurate. How far do you think an arrow goes in the jungle?"

"He—" As her question sank in, Rick broke off to glance above him where a sloth hung sleepily from a nearby tree branch.

"You've got a point," he admitted. "I should have been a little more specific. In any case, I didn't see any guards, but there were surveillance cameras, all right. I've taken care of them for now, and I want you to come with me. Bernabé too. I know he said they wouldn't go any farther, but I'd like him to see for himself that there's nothing supernatural about the place. The others too, if they'll stay out of sight. You seem to connect well with these people. Can you explain it to him in a way he'll understand? Tell him there's no danger, at least not for now."

There were no terms in I'paa for "surveillance" or "camera." "The American *riowa* has found the 'eyes' of the white ghosts," was as close as Julie could come. Even before she finished explaining, she read their refusal behind their streaks of camouflage.

"Please, Bernabé," she pleaded. "The *riowa* is telling the truth. I swear it to you. He doesn't lie." *Unless you count pretending to be someone you're not!* "It is important that you come. He wishes to show you how the eyes of the ghosts can be made harmless."

Bernabé gave Rick a hard look, then nodded reluctantly. "If this is so, then it would be a great thing to learn. But it is not the word of this man I believe. It is yours. If you are so sure he tells the truth, we will go with you."

He hadn't spoken above a murmur, but the other I'paa were suddenly with them, rising up through the underbrush or slipping forward between the tree trunks. Julie caught the upthrusted movement of Bernabé's spear and thought she'd discovered something about their communication methods.

Rick took the lead with Julie on his heels and Bernabé right behind. Because of the swamp, the belt of vegetation was wide, extending well into the first line of trees. Julie, glancing back, knew the other I'paa had to be there, but she could never see more than one or two spread out beyond Bernabé's stocky figure.

They had covered fewer than two dozen paces when Rick's warning hand stopped Julie. Dropping to his belly, Rick wriggled forward around the base of a tall mahogany that was growing close enough to the water's edge that the swamp had eaten at the earth in which it stood, leaving the roots on the outer side exposed and thrusting out into the water. Julie followed suit, and behind her the I'paa dropped to the ground, Bernabé so close on her heels that when Julie paused to loosen her backpack from a briar, the sharp head of his spear narrowly missed her leg.

Then Rick stopped crawling and released a hand from his AK-47 to motion Julie up beside him. Already, she could see an opening through the broad fronds cloaking his head and shoulder, but as she squirmed up to peer out, she stifled a gasp.

Julie had expected some form of road from Bernabé's mention of a "great path." But this? This was a highway! Concrete rather than asphalt, but as wide as any six-lane highway and as smooth as any of the better secondary roads in this country. Was it possible they'd somehow mistaken their position and wandered back into a settled area?

Bernabé crawled up beside her, his naked ribs quivering. Behind her she heard quickened breathing from two other I'paa who had crawled close enough to peer out.

Why were they so afraid? Julie couldn't see where the road led, only the panorama between the mahogany around which they had crawled and another huge tree trunk that cut off her view to the right. But that section looked harmless enough—an empty stretch of concrete running between two shallow banks that were bordered on either side by a straight line of the massive hardwoods.

The vegetation ended abruptly before them, and along both banks the brush had been cleared as far as they could see. The crowns of the hardwoods arching overhead had to be enormous; there was no open sunlight on the wide road, only dappled shadows. Julie was inching forward for a better look when Rick's arm blocked her passage.

"Watch it!" he hissed. He hooked his thumb upward. "Take a look up there. No, higher—about ten feet up."

She saw it—a piece of camouflage netting decorated with very realistic artificial leaves and stretched across a wire cage, so that Julie would never have noticed the surveillance camera inside if Rick hadn't pointed it out. The camera was bolted to a tree trunk since there were no branches at this low level. Only the fish-eye lens of the camera thrust out beyond the camouflage netting, and just as Julie spotted it, she heard a faint whir as the camera swiveled to a new position.

"That one's okay. I adjusted it. But there's plenty of others out there."

Following the jerk of Rick's head, Julie saw what he meant. Straight across the road, shadowed by the branches above it so that she had to look hard to spot it, another piece of camouflage netting marred the smooth trunk of a cedar. With horror, Julie watched as the lens below the netting shifted position to angle in on the bank where she'd been about to emerge.

"Just keep your head down, and you'll be okay." Glancing across Julie to Bernabé, Rick switched to Spanish. "These are the eyes that detected your men. As you can see, they are but machines built by men, not ghosts." He added in low English to Julie, "Does he understand what a camera is?"

"It is like the *tele*," Julie explained to the I'paa warrior. "What that eye sees"—she indicated the convex glass of the camera lens above them—"can be seen on the TV screen a great distance away." Seeing that she wasn't getting through, she added, "Like *Betty La Fea*."

Light dawned on Bernabé's face, and he turned his head to speak in swift I'paa to the two men bellied down behind them. A faint murmur carried the phrases "Betty La Fea" and *"tele"* back down the line.

"I think he got it," Julie whispered wryly to Rick. "He's just told them that the eye on the box—the camera—captures their image like the *tele* captures the image of Betty La Fea. I guess he isn't the only one who's been introduced to TV. I'm afraid he still thinks it's magic. Television too, for that matter. But he's told them they must not let the movement of the eye fall on them, or the white ghosts will see them and carry them away."

"That'll do as long as they know to stay away from the cameras." Rick began to slither back the way they had come. "Let's go! We're done here." There was a rustle as the I'paa behind them shifted out of his way. Julie was only too glad to wriggle back away from that probing eye across the road.

As soon as Rick had rounded the base of the mahogany, he stood up and strode out of the undergrowth into the open. Julie felt horribly exposed as she obeyed his gesture to follow, but Rick showed no worry, and as he reached the trunk of the tree beneath the surveillance camera, he glanced back at Bernabé, who was still hesitating under the broad leaves of the vegetation. "You can come out. It's safe."

Reluctantly, Bernabé joined them under the surveillance camera, though once again the other I'paa vanished. At this range, Julie could see what Rick had done to neutralize the camera. A broken-off twig was thrust into the wire mesh. The camera still rotated, but its angle was now directed out over their heads rather than down toward the ground.

Rick nodded toward the camera. "There's another one on this side farther down. The pattern's repeated about every twenty meters as far as I was able to check. I'm assuming they have the same on the other side of the road. But whoever set up the system is used to thinking in terms of wide-open spaces."

*Like a Middle Eastern desert?*

"They've got the road out there fairly well covered. But on this side they haven't taken into account that these cameras aren't going to pick up a thing beyond that next line of trees—or they don't care. There are no motion sensors either, which makes sense with the amount of wildlife coming through here. That means they're counting on their isolation for defense, not their surveillance system. These . . ."—Rick gestured toward the camera—"are designed basically to keep a lookout for any natives wandering into the wrong place, not a trained covert insertion. Which is good news for us. It shouldn't be hard to bypass their perimeter simply by circling around out of camera range."

He shook his head disbelievingly as he studied the line of hardwoods that formed the outer perimeter of the road. "If John got caught by this, then he was being pretty careless. Or his companions, more likely!"

Bernabé had been growing more relaxed as the minutes passed and nothing happened. Now he prodded at the wire cage with his spear, examining the camera above his head with as much concentration as though it were an animal he were hunting. Julie, who had been translating Rick's Spanish into I'paa, though she was sure Bernabé understood quite well, listened to his muttered question, then turned to Rick.

"He wants to know if his spear will destroy the eyes so the white ghosts will no longer see us. I guess he's been on the outside enough to see that machines can break."

Rick looked down at Bernabé. "Yes, your spear will destroy this machine. But then those who placed it here will come to see why it isn't working. They'll know we've been here. It's better to leave it this way."

Bernabé nodded even before Julie finished translating. "But what about that?" she added, gesturing to the branch that was jamming the camera base. "Won't they check on that when they notice the angle is wrong?"

Rick shrugged. "If they check it out, it will just look like a piece of dead wood has fallen in there—or a monkey trying to get at the camera. From that cage, I'd say they've had problems with that in the past."

*They!* Here she and Rick were, talking as if they'd already identified the mysterious "they" who built roads and set up surveillance cameras in the middle of the jungle. "But who are these people?" Julie demanded. "And why would they build a road out here? Or any of this?"

"That's what we're going to find out," Rick said grimly. "Ask your friend just how far this road goes. Where are the buildings he mentioned?" His mouth tightened as Julie translated Bernabé's answer. "What do you mean, two arrow flights? I can see that far from here! What is he trying to pull?"

Julie choked down a grin at his expression. "You forget—you can shoot a lot farther down an open road."

Rick made an exasperated gesture, then stopped himself. "Fine. Just ask him if he'll take us there. That's all we need. I'd like to circle around to come out in back of these buildings he's talking about. And it would be good if he'd have his men spread out again to keep watch. Just because we've seen no patrols so far doesn't mean there aren't any. Can you make sure he's got all that?"

From the dark look the I'paa hunter slanted at Rick, it was clear that he did get "all that." Lowering his spear, he drew himself up to meet the taller American's narrowed eyes with a hard gaze that carried not a hint of deference, and before Julie could translate, he addressed Rick directly and in Spanish for the first time since their initial meeting. "You do not need to fear. We will take you to where you may see the *riowa* without being seen. My people do not know these machines of the white ghosts. But they do know how to watch for men."

Julie saw Rick smother a grin of his own as he acknowledged the rebuke. "Thank you, Bernabé. I know your men know what they are doing. If you will take us, then . . ."

They kept to the belt of vegetation along the swamp edge until Rick indicated they were too far for the surveillance cameras to spot them through the trees. Then Bernabé led them at a right angle from the swamp directly back into the rainforest. The other I'paa faded from sight into the trees, vanishing so completely, Julie couldn't help wondering if they had chosen to disappear permanently rather than continue this foolhardy venture into the territory of their "white ghosts."

But when Bernabé stopped, they were suddenly there again. This time it was Bernabé's sharp eyes that spotted a surveillance camera bolted to a trunk three feet off to the right. He seemed to have chosen to lay aside his distrust of the Special Forces officer because once again he addressed Rick directly instead of through Julie. "The *riowa* you seek are just beyond the ghost eye."

Rick grunted his approval. "Can you show us?"

Bernabé shook his head emphatically. "No, we have already seen what lies there. We do not wish to see again. But we will wait here—at least until the night begins to fall. Not even for the daughter of Don Ricardo will my people agree to remain in these woods past the coming of night."

Rick nodded acceptance, then clapped a hand on the smaller man's shoulder. "You have been a real friend to the daughter of Don Ricardo and to myself," he told the I'paa hunter gravely. "We will not forget this."

Bernabé looked both surprised and pleased at the gesture. He made no answer but raised his spear in an unmistakable gesture of salute as Rick glided away from him through the trees. Julie saw him emerge noiselessly below the surveillance camera. Inserting another branch into the wire cage to disable it, he stepped to one side to disappear around the tree trunk. She was sure he meant to leave her behind and equally determined he wouldn't, but a moment later he stepped back into view and motioned for her to join him.

He didn't glance at Julie as she slipped up behind him, his intense gaze occupied in studying their surroundings. But there were no other surveillance cameras in sight, and just beyond the next line of trees, the rampant ground growth that marked an opening in the jungle gave them further direction as well as cover. At Rick's gesture, Julie dropped again to the ground and crawled forward behind him. Suddenly, both the ground and the vegetation dropped off in front of them, and this time Julie's intake of breath was so audible that Rick turned a furious glance on her.

Julie didn't need his warning. The sudden drop revealed a military camp. Soldiers in battle fatigues were patrolling the perimeter, and others stood guard outside a huge metal Quonset hut the size of an airplane hangar. Their faces were white—by Indian standards at least.

From their position above the embankment, Rick and Julie had a clear view of the camp's layout. The Quonset hut sat at the edge of the road, which ended abruptly to their right. On one side of it was a smaller brick building. Julie spotted a satellite dish attached to its roof. On the other side was a trio of smaller aluminum sheds. Structures with thatched roofs and plastic walls were tucked back into the trees. *Cambuches*. Through the open end of the nearest, Julie could see hammocks slung. Another held stacks of boxes and burlap sacks. Supplies. The sacks looked identical to those they'd seen in the village the day before.

There were other people too. More soldiers, lying at ease in the hammocks. A handful of what looked like native Indians wielding machetes to chop back the weeds growing between the buildings.

As Rick and Julie watched, the door of the brick buildings opened, and a man in a white lab coat walked down the concrete steps and onto the road. He was followed by a second man who wore the same battle fatigues as the guards, but with a black turban instead of a cap. His untrimmed beard was almost as dark as the turban. Julie felt Rick stiffen with the same recognition that had struck her. Their Middle Eastern connection.

Around the edge of the perimeter were knee-high posts like those seen on a cattle farm as an electrified trip wire to keep animals in the pasture. But here there was no wire, only some sort of electronic device attached. "Motion sensors," Rick mouthed.

One of the Indian laborers drifted toward the perimeter edge beyond the sheds. The closest guard immediately raised his weapon and shouted at him. The words were not Spanish nor any other language Julie recognized, but the Indian understood his intentions, because he scuttled back toward the others.

As a military base, the place wasn't large. Julie counted no more than two dozen occupants, including the indigenous workers, though there might be more inside the buildings. Still, it was a mind-staggering construction project to have gone up undetected in the middle of this triple-canopy jungle, where every scrap of material would have to be brought in by boat through jungle rivers and across that fetid swamp out there. How was it possible that it had remained undetected by the surveillance flights and satellites that regularly scanned the Amazon Basin for drug activity?

As Julie's scrutiny traveled upward, she saw how it was possible. Her eyes opened wide in stunned disbelief. The construction crew had been careful to remove only as many of the huge trees as was necessary to make room for the buildings, leaving the others as pillars between the *cambuches* and sheds and on either side of the Quonset hut, just as the guerrillas did in their jungle camps. Over any remaining holes torn in the jungle canopy, enormous camouflage nets had been strung on steel cables stretched between branches as big around as the average tree trunk.

The entire mesh between the cables was overgrown with lianas and the other broad-leafed vines and parasitical plants that knit together so much of the jungle canopy. The stretches of mesh had been placed on different levels, fifty, seventy, even a hundred feet off the ground. Over time—and perhaps with some human intervention—the vines had spilled from one level to the other, creating a living canopy that from above could have been distinguished from the real thing by only the closest examination.

The process had been repeated above the road, an even more incredible feat across that wide stretch of concrete. But here the very height of the hardwoods came into play because the spreading umbrella of their branches spanned more than half the gap, and again, the heights of the netting below them had been staggered to create a realistic rise and fall in the canopy.

The whole effect was that of a long, green tunnel, and from where she lay, Julie could see the full straight length of it, ending at a wall of vegetation that had to be more camouflage, since she knew the roadbed ended in the swamp. The road itself seemed a particularly senseless effort. It wasn't long—perhaps five times its width—and something about that very width nagged at Julie. Altogether, the very amount of effort and time involved staggered her.

"I can't believe it!" Julie whispered, appalled. "It's all so much work!"

"So much hate!" Rick replied softly against her ear. "Look!"

Rick had been less impressed than Julie by the technical details of the encampment. While unique in its scope, it was a fairly standard application of military camouflage techniques. His gaze was concentrated instead on the human contingent of the base. Julie followed the jerk of his head toward a flurry of activity that had erupted at the first aluminum shed, just past the Quonset hut. This had been the destination of the turbaned soldier and the man in the white coat with him, and while Julie had been looking at the canopy, the door of the shed had slid upward. In the open doorway, a pair of soldiers were lifting a large wooden crate onto a trolley. Behind them, Julie could see that the shed was full of similar crates.

She could see something else too. A white mist drifted out of the shed to disperse around the legs of the soldiers. The "ghost cloud" of the I'paa!

Julie had no problem recognizing what it was—air-conditioning hitting the warm, humid air of the jungle. Which meant that those crates contained no mere supplies such as she'd seen in the *cambuches*. Not if they warranted costly ferried-in fuel for an air-conditioner and a generator to keep it running.

The turbaned soldier was evidently some sort of officer. As he snapped his fingers, the other two soldiers backed hastily away, allowing Julie a clear view of what Rick must have already seen. Though she couldn't read Arabic, Julie had a trained journalistic eye and an almost photographic memory that had served her in good stead in school days, and she recognized immediately the graceful flow of lines on the side of the crate. They were the same that Rick had deciphered for her on that deadly metal canister back in the carnage of the Indian village. *The Lightning Bolt of Allah*. Saddam Hussein's pseudonym for his biological warfare program!

The man in the lab coat lifted the lid off the crate. With a kick, the turbaned officer knocked down the nearest crate wall, then followed with the other three. Styrofoam filler spilled out onto the ground, leaving a metallic object that even in the dappled shadows managed to glint silver. It was many times the size of the canister Julie had seen in the village, and shaped like a cross between some sort of bomb and the gas cylinders the Bakers had used for their cookstove back in San Ignacio days. Even without the Arabic characters swirled across the smooth metal, Julie, like Rick, had no doubt what it contained—and the sheer hatred it represented.

A cold chill gripped Julie's stomach. That tiny canister had annihilated a whole village. There had to be enough in that shed to wipe out half the world! What had Rick said—that fifty kilos could wipe out Washington, D.C.? Then that *thing* alone could annihilate all of Bogotá!

One thing was for sure: this was far too extensive an undertaking to be aimed at the small American contingents scattered across the country. Then what? Did the FARC's unholy alliance with these terrorists include genocide of their opponents? And how? Could these people possibly have a way to haul that huge metal object down these rivers and roads and into some city without being seen?

Again that absurdly wide tunnel of a road nagged at Julie. No, not a road! An airstrip. Julie's stomach chilled further as she studied the road. It was the same concrete surface that served many a rural airport across Colombia. She would have recognized it earlier were it not for the tangled ceiling of the jungle canopy overhead. But that canopy was high enough to permit a small plane to lift into the air. With the camouflage net removed from the far end, a plane need only get airborne by the time the concrete gave way to the swamp. Then it would have all the open water of the swamp to gain altitude and clear the trees.

But no. The chill in her stomach eased a fraction. Not even Dr. Baker's Cessna could clear a runway as short as this. Certainly not with the weight of the metal object she was seeing down there.

And if it was a pontoon?

No, that wouldn't explain the airstrip, road, whatever! And with the stumps of that drowned forest Julie had glimpsed out there, a pontoon plane could barely maneuver, much less pick up enough speed to lift off. Besides, Bernabé knew well enough what a plane was—he'd grown up with the Bakers' Cessna—and he had categorically stated there was none here.

Just a big bug!

That wry thought died in Julie's mind as a new commotion drew her attention. The huge front entrance panel to the Quonset hut was rising. A billow of white vapor rolled out from under the door as it rose. More costly air-conditioning.

Then slowly, like a black phantom materializing from the mist, it emerged, and Julie's hopes withered with it. She knew now the meaning of that too-short runway—and why Bernabé had insisted there was no plane. This was like no aircraft the I'paa hunter would have ever glimpsed.

Julie herself wouldn't have likened it to an insect, but she could see how the hard black carapace, the sharp-edged nose with its sword-shaped protrusions like questing feelers, and the butterfly-wing double tail like two antenna above the body would suggest to a jungle native a beetle or black-shelled cockroach. To Julie, it looked more like a bat, its slitted eyes the dark, rectangular vents on either side of its dorsal spine. Or with those back-slanted wings, something out of Star Wars—something flown by the evil Empire.

She, like Bernabé, had never seen such an aircraft before, but it wasn't unfamiliar. She had seen its likeness on countless news programs and war documentaries. Horribly and clearly, she recognized its implications even as her mind fought to reject the impossibility of what she was seeing.

"But that's one of ours!" she whispered blankly. "Only it can't be!"

"It's ours all right!" Rick's grim reply grated against her ear. "The F-117A Nighthawk. A U.S. Air Force stealth fighter!"

# TWENTY-SIX

THE DOOR OF THE QUONSET HANGAR clanged down as soon as the F-117 had taxied out onto the runway, abruptly cutting off the billows of fog. It braked to a stop lengthwise across the airstrip, and soldiers ran forward to swarm around it, allowing Julie to grasp for the first time its full dimensions.

It was huge. The length alone covered more than half the width of the runway, and the top of the cockpit canopy was twice the height of the running soldiers. The pilot, if he had a mind to, could look straight across to the top of the embankment where Julie and Rick were lying. Julie froze as the flight helmet inside the cockpit swiveled in their direction. Could he see through these weeds?

But as a soldier heaved a portable ladder against the side of the stealth fighter, the pilot turned his head away. Another pair of soldiers ran forward with a fuel line. The turbaned officer snapped his fingers, and the two soldiers with the trolley began to trundle the crate's contents over to the plane. As though this were a signal, two panels below the belly of the aircraft popped open. Bomb doors.

*We have to stop them! We have to do something!* Julie looked blankly at Rick as he tugged sharply at her sleeve and began to wriggle back. How could he think of retreating when people were going to die?

She saw the F-117's canopy pop open, and the pilot clamber out and down the ladder to the ground. The aircraft wasn't going anywhere right away. Sliding carefully back from the embankment, Julie worked her way after Rick until he rose to his feet and pulled her up beside him.

Rick didn't release Julie's hand as they threaded back through the hardwoods. She waited only until they were beyond range of the surveillance cameras to tug her hand loose and swing around on him.

"We can't leave here," she told him. "There's no time to warn anyone. That plane! When it takes off—" The horror of the thought choked her.

"I'm well aware of that!" Rick answered tightly. "We'll have to stop it, somehow! If it gets across our borders—"

"Then, I'm right! That stealth fighter—it isn't anyone in this country they're after." Julie swallowed hard. "It's the United States! They're going to try to cross the border with that thing!"

The cold, dangerous look was back on Rick's face. "Not if I have anything to do with it! We've spent all this time wondering what Islamic terrorists wanted down here in Colombia. I guess now we know. Their goal is the same as it's always been—the destruction of the U.S., their Great Satan. They've just modified their launching point."

Julie glanced around, suddenly aware that the I'paa were still not in sight. Had their Indian guides abandoned them? Just then Bernabé slipped into the open, and Julie saw shadows coalesce into painted bodies as other I'paa began to drift out of the trees.

Bernabé stalked up to the two Americans. "So, you found the great evil you were seeking?"

Julie took a deep breath to calm herself before swinging around to face the I'paa warrior. "Yes. Yes we did."

The sideways flicker was back in the black eyes as Bernabé looked from one American's face to the other, and Julie could only guess what he was reading in their tense expressions. "Then you will now destroy this evil?" he asked doubtfully.

He looked poised to vanish at the snap of a twig, and Julie did her best to infuse confidence into her voice. "We're working on it, Bernabé. Would you please have your people keep watch? The *riowa* and I need to consult now on what we have seen."

At the barest movement of his spear, the other I'paa faded back into the trees. Bernabé moved off a few meters, though his eyes didn't leave the two Americans. Julie swung back to Rick.

"But—I don't understand, How could these people have one of our stealth fighters? And just who are they?"

Rick shook his head. "I don't know, but I can make a few guesses. The F-117s were the backbone of the war effort back in the Gulf War. They got in and took out the Iraqi command centers ahead of the rest of our forces, making it possible for us to go up against the fourth most powerful war machine in the world and take them out with just a handful of casualties. They won us the war.

"They told us we never lost a bird. Other planes, yes—but not the F-117s. I guess they weren't telling us everything, because those crates came from Iraq, and I'm betting the stealth fighter did too. It must have been sitting over there since the war. There's no other explanation for its presence here."

"Then the Iraqis have been plotting ever since the Gulf War to use that stealth fighter against the U.S.?" Julie asked incredulously. "But why wait until now?"

"It wouldn't have been so easy. The F-117 couldn't fly to the U.S. from Iraq. Not without refueling tankers and support craft and other things we'd have spotted in a minute if they'd tried. Not to mention that Iraq has to be the closest-watched spot on the planet—and has been since the war. We have surveillance planes and radar everywhere. Which is probably why he had to find an ally."

Julie didn't ask who *he* was. "What do you mean? There's more than just the Iraqis?"

"I'm afraid so. Those crates are Iraqi, no doubt about it, and I was in the Persian Gulf long enough to recognize what that guard was shouting— Arabic. But don't forget that Hezbollah agent I saw in San Ignacio. He was Iranian. And so is the man we saw down there in the black turban."

"But . . . how can you be so sure?" Julie demanded, bewildered.

"I recognize him," Rick said flatly. "I served in a counter-terrorism unit after the Gulf War—the reason I ended up down here. Part of what we did was to memorize the faces of every terrorist leader on file. That's how I knew our Hezbollah friend. And that man in the turban is Taqi Nouri, head of the Iranian intelligence service. Which, by the way, is known to be a front for half the Islamic terrorist groups out there, including the Islamic Jihad and Hezbollah. He also happens to be the personal sidekick to the Ayatollah Khalkhali, the real power behind everything going on in Iran today."

"But . . ." Julie said blankly. "I thought Iraq and Iran were enemies. Didn't they fight a war?"

"They hate each other's guts," Rick agreed. "But they hate us Americans even more. Somewhere way up at the top, someone has made an unholy alliance to take out a common enemy. Iraq supplies the weapon. Iran supplies the means to deliver it. And I'm betting they've spent the last ten years or so figuring out how to do it. It's no coincidence that the Islamic terrorist groups started showing up on Colombian soil just around the time Pastrana established the demilitarized zone. The DMZ has given them just what they were lacking—a protected and secret striking base within flight range of American soil."

"But . . ." Julie's mind cast around frantically for a thread of hope. "Even if the plane takes off, surely our military can stop it! Don't we have radar and . . . and military bases to keep unfriendly planes from crossing our borders?"

Rick's expression drained her hope even before he answered. "If it were a regular aircraft, yes. Though even at that, drug planes slip through our radar shield with depressing regularity. But the F-117 was made to be invisible—to our own radar as well as everyone else's. And if it comes in over the water, and at night . . . That's why they're waiting to take off. They won't risk some stray surveillance plane or satellite pointed in the wrong direction spotting a UFO emerging from the jungle."

Julie drew in a sharp breath. "The surveillance plane that went down!"

"It's a good possibility, though we may never know. Either way, you saw the moon last night. Tonight's a new moon—the darkest night of the month. I'm betting that's what they've been waiting for. That thing they were loading—it wasn't a bomb. It was some sort of spray mechanism. They slip across the border with that, head to the nearest city, and . . ."

He didn't finish, but he didn't need to. The images his words had conjured up were furnishing the rest in nightmare technicolor in Julie's mind. A black batlike shape gliding silently in over a dreaming coastline, its passing shadow barely troubling the pale glimmer of starlight above. Slowing to release its toxic cargo into the cool night. A rain of microscopic spores drifting down over the twinkling lights of the city below. Millions of warm, moist lungs breathing them in, unconscious that they have just given root to death. And as the spores sprang to their frantic and lethal activity, that black shadow moving on to repeat its mission again, and again, and again.

Julie's mind reeled at the contemplation of what would come next. She had seen the carnage of one small village. Her brain could not compute the destruction represented by the aircraft she'd seen. She ran a hand over her face. Even with the steam-bath temperature of the jungle, her skin was clammy and cold. She'd been afraid so often since returning to this country. Afraid of the guerrillas. Of the dizzying heights of the treetops. Of the black jungle night and the dangers she knew only too well lurked there. Of her own emotions that had betrayed the sensible, ordered life she had created at such pains for herself.

And always the fear of death had confronted her at every turn, only to be time and again and beyond belief snatched away, until—because even the strongest emotions cannot be sustained forever—she had passed beyond fear to a dull acceptance of whatever might come.

But now she was afraid again—so afraid, she thought she was going to throw up, and only the knowledge of Bernabé's black eyes on her face kept her from giving in to that weakness.

But this time Julie wasn't afraid for herself. She feared for a world of unsuspecting people who did not know—could not imagine—the devastation about to be unleashed on them. The horror of it burned into a blaze of terror and helpless rage.

Julie didn't even notice Rick's steadying hand at her elbow. "What are we going to do?" she whispered. Then, catching the wary gaze of the I'paa leader on her, she steadied her voice. "How can we possibly stop them?"

"I don't know—yet. I need to think." Rick glanced down at his watch. "We have an hour still before twilight. Just give me time to think."

The harshness of his voice drew Julie's head up to look at him. Unlike herself, Rick had seemed little shaken by what they'd found. His movements showed the same quick and measured action as always; his face was set in the hard concentration to which Julie had grown accustomed when problems arose. But now, with the eyes of love and familiarity, Julie saw a paleness around his pinched nostrils and the grim line of his mouth, and the bunching and unbunching of muscles along his jaw that told of emotions held under iron control. Beneath the cool mask that was the Special Forces officer, could he be as afraid and uncertain and helplessly angry as she herself felt?

Julie watched that taut profile as Rick paced back and forth between one tree trunk and another. She knew the instant he'd made his decision, even before he spun around and strode over to her.

"I have a plan," he said abruptly. "Maybe not much of a plan—it has a million holes in it, and I won't pretend it will be easy. But with the help of your Indian friends, I think it's doable." His broad shoulders lifted under the ammo vest. "And right now it's all we've got!"

"So what is it?"

Rick was already removing items from his ammo vest. First, two rectangles of what looked to be oversized bars of the nougat he'd fed Julie the first day. But Julie knew the difference. Semtex, a military explosive. She'd watched Victor instruct the newer guerrillas in its many possibilities. Then a fuse and detonator cap. With a roll of electrical tape, Rick began taping explosive and detonator together.

"We're going to take out the F-117," he told Julie coolly.

"What—but how?" Julie looked warily from the homemade explosive device that was taking shape in Rick's hands to the primitive weapons Bernabé and the other I'paa were carrying. They didn't look like much to take out a well-armed security force and a state-of-the-art military plane that undoubtedly had defenses of its own.

"That's what I want you to explain to your friends. We'll hit at dusk. That gives us enough light to see what we're doing without giving them any better a look at us than we have to. And to let them see this uniform but not the face above it. What I need from your Indian friends is a diversion. They don't have to set foot on the base. A few arrow shots will distract the guards—better yet, those blow guns of theirs. Hopefully, that will draw the bulk of Nouri's men out into the woods after them."

Rick held up the explosive device. "Then, in all the confusion, I'll simply walk up to the plane, slap this on somewhere, and set it off. If that doesn't go down"—he pulled his remaining grenade from his vest pocket—"I toss this into the cockpit. It goes off, and there won't be an instrument left in that plane that's usable. Either way, the plane won't be taking off."

Rick glanced briefly at Julie as he stowed the grenade again. "You, by the way, will not be in this at all. I'll have Bernabé leave a couple of his people with you. Your part will be to head downstream just as soon as we get everything ironed out here and make contact with the outside world. Get hold of Colonel Thornton over at San José and get him out here on the double. Whatever happens, I want to ensure that warning gets through."

*Whatever happens.* "And you? How are you planning on getting away afterward?"

Rick didn't look up from the finishing touches he was putting on his makeshift bomb. "Simple. If we time it right, it'll be dark by then. One uniform looks like another. The instant that plane goes up, I walk out into the dark. They'll come after us, but they'll be at a disadvantage at night. Once it's light, I regroup with Bernabé and his men, and we head downstream and catch up to the rest of you."

It didn't sound simple at all, rather suicidally dangerous, and Julie could see a dozen things that could go wrong. What if the other side had night vision goggles? This wasn't like giving the slip to Victor's poorly trained guerrilla band. But as Rick had said, it was doable. Besides, what other option was there? Except to walk away—and that was no option at all.

Julie motioned to Bernabé. As the I'paa warrior stalked over, the rest of his party began to drift in again. Rick addressed Bernabé in Spanish but signaled to Julie to translate so the others could follow as well. "We have discovered a way to defeat the great evil that has been brought to this place. But we need your help to fight and destroy it."

The effect of his request was electrifying. Julie saw the murmur of dismay ripple across the party of Indians even before she finished translating. By the time she had spelled out his plan, the rest of the I'paa had melted back into cover, leaving only Bernabé to stand his ground.

"Now what?" Rick demanded irritably. "Where did they go? Bernabé, please tell them to come back. This is very important."

"They are afraid of the ghosts." Bernabé spoke directly to Rick. "You ask them to go to where the ghosts snatched their companions. They will not go. They do not wish to be lost to the evil spirits like the others."

"But there are no ghosts!" Rick clamped his jaw to contain his exasperation. "Haven't we already shown that to you? Evil men, yes. But there are no ghosts, I promise."

"Evil men. Evil ghosts. It does not matter. They still bring death." Turning back to Julie, Bernabé switched to I'paa. "Daughter of the friends of our people, you must explain to him. It is not for me to decide. I speak the *español* from my years working for the *riowa*. But I am not senior of the warriors. They will not do what I say but what they choose. We are far from our families—farther than we have ever come. We would not have come this far if we had not been ordered to watch over the daughter of the friends of our people. But now these others have seen the death in the village, like the death of those taken by the ghosts. They know that this death lies over there. They are afraid, and they wish to turn back. Some say that this is an evil the *riowa* have brought to the jungle, and that it should be for the *riowa*—you—to deal with it."

Though Bernabé spoke of the "others," Julie was accustomed enough to the dappled mask of his face to see the fear behind the ash and pitch and in the darting black eyes that would not meet hers. She knew it was only the bond of that childhood acquaintance that held the I'paa warrior here at all. Nor could she blame him. She could feel the fear clenching at her own stomach, drawing her face into taut lines.

Bernabé glanced at the other I'paa, a few pairs of dark eyes peering out from cover. Then his chest rose under the camouflage streaks. Julie could see him gathering courage. "Perhaps they will think differently if you give them your promise that they will be safe. Your father, when he came to our village, told us of the great God who created the universe—that He was a God of great strength and the friend of your family and of all who worshiped Him. He said that you spoke to this God and that He spoke to you. That is why it was thought that you could defeat the ghosts when others could not. If you can swear to us that you will not let the ghosts—or evil men, if so you wish to call them—harm us, if you can swear that the God who protects your family will protect the I'paa too, then perhaps they will agree to go."

Julie sighed. What garbled theology had been passed down among the tribe since her parents' departure! "I can't promise that, Bernabé. It is true that the God who created the universe is powerful and that He can protect those who follow Him. And yes, it is true that I pray to Him and that He is my friend, as He is the friend of all who will worship and obey Him. But God is not a man that we can tell Him what to do. His ways are not always our ways, and He does not promise that all will go well if we obey Him. Have you forgotten that my own father and mother died here obeying their God?"

Julie added gently, "I too am afraid, Bernabé. And so is my companion Enrique." She glanced up at Rick, but his lean face was expressionless, the downward curve of his mouth impatient at Bernabé's switch into I'paa. Only the bunching of muscles at his jawline gave any sign that he felt the same fear that had caused the knot in her own stomach.

"I too wish that I could turn back and run away," Julie said. "But if we do not fight this evil—if we do not stop it in this place this very night—then many more villages will die like the one you saw. Perhaps not your own people. But many others. More than all the stars that shine in the night sky above the jungle."

The I'paa warrior was listening, Julie could see, and she added pleadingly, "Please, Bernabé. I could lie to you and promise you that no one will get hurt if you come with us. I will not! But I will tell you that I believe, as surely as God sent my parents to this place and to your people, that He has brought us—myself and Enrique and the I'paa—to this place for this time. And I can promise you that if we fight this evil, the God who created the universe will go with us and bring His purpose from this night. But we cannot fight alone. We need your help."

Bernabé was silent as she finished. Then he said abruptly, "I must speak with my people. I will see if they will fight." He faded into the trees, and as Julie explained to Rick what had happened, she saw the other I'paa gather around her childhood friend. She watched anxiously as he spoke, his spear gesturing along with his words. Surely her persuasiveness had won!

But when Bernabé stepped back into the open, Julie knew the instant she caught sight of his face that they had lost.

"We have made the decision—to leave!" The I'paa warrior spoke harshly in Spanish that included Rick as well. "This fight is not ours. It belongs to the *riowa*. We will take the news of this to the outside, and we will guide you there if you wish to come. But we will not go to that place."

His eyes shifted away from the two Americans as he uttered his ultimatum, and Julie knew he was feeling shame because he had been unable to talk the others into staying. But in the I'paa way, he had presented the group position as a unanimous one, and she knew too that it would be useless to argue that decision. Her shoulders slumped in defeat.

"No," she answered him, "we cannot leave with you. But if you will take the news, then please contact the American commander at San José—the one your hunters saw me speaking with—and tell him all that has happened. Tell him about the plane like a bug and the metal bottle that brought death to the village. He will know what to do. And Bernabé . . ." It took all her fortitude to summon a smile. "Thank you for what you have done."

Bernabé gave a brief nod. Then with two strides, he disappeared behind a tree, and though Julie hastily stepped around the base of the tree after him, she saw no further sign of her childhood friend or any of the I'paa.

They were alone.

Rick looked after the vanished Indians, his mouth a thin, straight line. "So, I take it they bailed out on us."

"I'm afraid so." Julie had to choke down her disappointment before she could say resolutely, "I guess this means we go to Plan B."

"Not we!" Rick said in a hard voice. "I!"

As Julie started to speak, he raised his hand. "We already had this argument, Julie. You won—I needed you to get here. But not now! You think I don't know why you let Bernabé go before I could speak with him? But it isn't going to work! Your part in this hasn't changed. All I want from you is to get to Colonel Thornton and get him out here. So you go after those Indians before they get any farther away than they are. No—don't give me that look! You know as well as I do that they'll find you if you don't find them."

"I know that," Julie said steadily. "And you're right—I did let Bernabé go. Did you think I would leave you here alone? How do you think you're going to get in there by yourself? You'd never get past the motion sensors. And do you think they're going to let you just walk up to the plane with two sticks of Semtex in your hand? You'd just be throwing your life away!"

"I'll figure something out." Rick's expression was unrelenting. "And just how do you think you would make a difference? You don't know how to fight! You would just be in the way, and I can't afford any distractions right now."

"No, that's just what you *do* need!" Julie answered. "That's what you wanted from the I'paa, wasn't it—a distraction? Maybe I can't fight, but at least I can give you that! I set off the motion sensors. Get the attention of the guards. I'll just tell them I'm lost. That'll give you a chance to slip onto the base while they're thinking it's me who set off the alarm. As for getting out a warning, Bernabé is going to contact Colonel Thornton. He might not have been able to talk his people into staying, but if he says he'll get a message through, he will."

The line of Rick's jaw did not relent. "Do you know what would happen to you if those guards got hold of you? You'd be right back where you started. Worse! Remember what happened to the last foreigners who wandered onto that base?"

"Rick, do you think I don't *know* the consequences? I . . . I don't want to go in there! I know I don't have Special Forces training like you. If I really thought you could do better without me, I'd go after Bernabé right now. But we have no choice. Can you honestly say you wouldn't have a better chance with me to distract the guards?" Julie read the unwilling answer in his face. "Then you . . . I . . . *we* don't have the right not to take that chance!"

Rick ran a hand through his hair so roughly, his camouflage cap fell off. "Julie, I'm aware of those factors, but you don't understand!" His voice grated raw, and for a brief moment, Julie saw his iron control slip and anguish break through. "Don't you get it, Julie? This is no well-planned operation with support and a backup plan. I don't know if I'll be coming back. And I can't guarantee that you will either! You won't even have my odds of getting away in the uproar. I can't allow you to put yourself in that position!"

He cleared his throat as he ran his hand through his hair again. "Julie, I . . . we don't have time for this, and I swore I wouldn't say anything until we were safe and could afford that kind of distraction. But in these weeks we've been together, I've come to care for you a great deal. I just—if I'm going to go in there, I want to be able to know you'll be safe. Can't you understand that? I don't want you to get hurt!"

As a declaration of love, it was a far cry from the one Julie had dreamed of, and the Special Forces officer looked more angry than anything at his admission. Julie had to suppress a hysterical impulse to laugh.

"So you'll sacrifice yourself instead of me!" Her voice wobbled. "Oh, Rick, don't you see? I . . . I care about you too—so much that I feel sick at the thought of you going in there! I don't want anything to happen to you. I'd give anything if the two of us could walk away right now and forget all this. But this isn't about us anymore! It's about millions of people who are going to die if we don't stop this thing. And if it takes risking our two lives—even if we care about each other—then I don't see that we have any choice."

There was an obdurate set to his jaw, but he was listening. Julie went on steadily. "You told me once that God made sense out of your universe. I said I wished He would make sense out of mine. But now, all this . . ." She made a gesture that encompassed not just the woods around her but the whole of her life experiences. "Growing up here in the jungle with the I'paa. Coming back here right now after all these years. Getting kidnapped like that. Even Carlos! It's as though for the first time I can see a reason for it all. I mean, think of it! If I hadn't been kidnapped and you hadn't come after me when I escaped, we'd have never found that village. We'd have never found out what these people were planning in time to stop it. It's as though God put every one of those steps into my life to bring me here to this place for this time."

She covered a fresh wobble in her voice with a wry twist of her mouth. "If I were running the universe, I sure wouldn't have picked me for this job. And for sure, I know I'd never have volunteered. But we're here now, and I don't see anyone else, so I guess . . . I guess it's up to the two of us to do what needs to be done—whatever happens to us."

Julie kept her eyes steady on Rick's face to keep from wavering, and as she did so, she saw his expression change, the anger softening to tenderness, even wonder, and as he'd done once before, he raised his hand to her face, the callused hardness of his palm so inexpressibly gentle against her cheek that moisture once again stung her eyelids. "You really are a chip off the old block, aren't you, Julie Baker? Just like your parents—you see someone in trouble, and you don't stop to count the cost before throwing your own life over the line to help."

Julie swallowed back the tears in her throat. "Look who's talking," she said shakily. "Oh, Rick, you've got me all wrong! I'm no hero. I'm the girl who can't think of anything but her career and that Pulitzer Prize. And right now I'm so scared I want to throw up. It's just—there's some things in this world worth dying for, that's all—and a few million people is one of them!"

*Some things worth dying for.* The words struck Julie with a force that took her breath away even as she said them. *Oh, Dad! Mom! I get it! It was never a question of how much you loved me, of choosing Colombia over me. It's just that some things really* are *worth dying for. And living for too. And even if we'd like to keep the people we love safe and make things pretty and easy for them, sometimes we just have to follow the path God puts in front of our feet and believe that if He knows what He's doing with our lives, then He also knows what He's doing with the people we love. You knew that, if I didn't! You never abandoned me—you just gave me to God.*

"Like I said," Rick's voice came softly. "A chip off the old block."

He let out his breath. Though the grim line still tightened his mouth, it was as if a weight had suddenly fallen from his shoulders. "Okay, you win, Julie Baker! Let's go save the world."

\* \* \*

There was something about abandoning all hope that thrust out fear as well. Julie felt curiously alert as they slipped through the woods toward the encampment, every sense intensified to catch the minutest detail around her. The gathering shadows alive with hidden life. The musty, ancient scent of the rainforest. The chitter of a monkey hushing its offspring as the two Americans passed beneath its home. The moist pulsation of a tree frog under Julie's groping fingers. The barest whisper of her feet against the forest floor. Was this how soldiers felt when they went into combat?

Rick had chosen another spot from which to make their entrance. It was closer to the F-117, and there was no embankment except the cleared border that sloped down to the airstrip. In the final glimmer of twilight, it was hardly necessary to avoid the surveillance cameras. The designers of the base were evidently counting on the motion sensors and the locals' fear of the dark for nighttime security measures.

Bellying down in the underbrush, Julie saw the stealth fighter, not far to their left, the Quonset hut behind it. The cockpit canopy was still standing open, the ladder ready for the pilot to mount. But the weapon doors under the belly were closed, and the trolley that had carried the spray mechanism was pushed back against the shed and empty—an ominous sign.

Two sentries stood at attention on either side of the plane, and two others patrolled the runway, one pacing along the perimeter edge where Rick and Julie were bellied down, the other on the far side in front of the buildings. The rest of the base lay surprisingly quiet and empty until Julie caught the sound of raised voices and a clatter of tin plates from the *cambuches* beyond the hangar. *A hearty meal before committing mass murder.*

Though not everyone was at supper.

Julie saw them just as Rick stiffened beside her. Four men emerging from the *cambuches* to walk around the side of the storage shed and toward the brick building with the satellite dish on its roof. It was too far in the growing gloom to make out features, but the white coat of one and the black turban of another identified the technician who had supervised the loading of the deadly anthrax spores and the head of Iranian intelligence, Taqi Nouri. Behind them walked a man dressed in standard-issue camouflage. Julie guessed him to be a guard, because he carried a weapon ready for instant use and constantly swiveled his head as though surveying the perimeter for danger.

But it was not those three who drew Julie's astonished gasp. It was the tall, broad form marching directly in front of the guard and between the terrorist leaders. He stood a head above the others, his hair not dark but so blond it looked silver in the light, and Julie would have recognized that confident stride anywhere.

Tim McAdams!

So this was where they had brought him! And he was alive and well and no more cowed, it would seem, by his prolonged captivity and the men flanking him than he had been the last time Julie had seen him.

Julie had half-risen when she caught the warning shake of Rick's head. She subsided into the brush as the three men climbed the steps of the brick building. Rick was right. Their only thought now had to be that plane, not rescuing a hostage.

She watched instead as the door opened, letting out a slit of fluorescent lighting that glimmered on something metallic under Taqi Nouri's armpit. The butt of a weapon in the largest shoulder holster Julie had ever seen. Still, even as the door shut behind them, Julie felt her heart lighten. Tim might be a prisoner, but it made a difference to know they had one more ally in the camp.

Rick didn't give the signal to move out immediately but waited until the gloom under the huge camouflage nets had darkened. By then, Julie and Rick's faces were just a pale blur to each other. Out on the runway, the lighting was perfect, not yet dark enough for lanterns to have been brought out, though Julie could see a yellow glow back among the *cambuches*, but dark enough that the sentries were just shadowy outlines.

Julie's stomach tightened—with anticipation, not fear, she assured herself— as Rick rose to a half crouch beside her. There was no need for more discussion. Everything had already been covered back in the woods. His voice was almost inaudible against Julie's ear: "Once this goes down, I'll be back for you, okay? You just hang in there!" She felt a quick brush of his hand across her hair and down her face, and then he was gone.

Julie counted to fifty before slithering back to where she could stand up without being seen. The near perimeter guard had passed the F-117 and was strolling back. A few more paces would bring him past her. Drawing in a steadying breath, Julie got to her feet. *O God, don't let me mess this up for Rick!* Then she stepped out through the underbrush and walked down the bank.

The shrill whine of the alarm as Julie crossed the line of the motion sensors provoked the reaction they had counted on. The near guard, a few paces past her to the right, spun around, raising his weapon as he spotted Julie stepping onto the runway. As his finger tightened on the trigger, Julie called out hastily in Spanish, "Please, I'm lost! Can you help me?"

The guard's grip on his weapon eased, but he didn't lower it as he sprinted toward Julie. The other guard who had been patrolling the opposite side of the runway was now running toward her as well. Down the runway, the sentry stationed on the closer side of the F-117 took a step away from the wing. In the *cambuches,* the clatter of supper did not miss a beat, but the door of the brick building slammed open and black silhouettes erupted down the steps. Julie didn't dare glance sideways, but at the edge of her peripheral vision, she caught the shadow that was Rick, his own breach of the perimeter timed to the alarm she had set off. He was striding rapidly toward the F-117, his dark head and camouflage fatigues indistinguishable even to her from those hurrying toward her.

She raised her hands above her head to indicate she was unarmed. "Please, I'm lost! Can you tell me where I am?"

Only someone watching for it would have noticed the noiseless movement under the belly of the stealth fighter, the sudden slump that could have been a shadow or a body. The two perimeter guards were pounding up to Julie, and the sentry by the plane had swung around to watch. Julie must have been as dark a figure to them as they were to her. First one, then the other of the guards switched on a flashlight, blinding her as the glare of their beams caught her in the eyes.

And wiping out their own night vision as well.

Julie quickly swung around, her movement seemingly aimless, but leaving the two guards as they followed her movement with their backs to the plane and their search beams away from it. Loudly, she repeated, not only for them but for the running steps she could hear across the airstrip, "Please, I've been lost in the jungle for days! Can you help me?"

The two guards' swift exchange was gibberish to Julie, and whether they had understood her, she couldn't tell. But something in her tattered appearance and thin, travel-worn face must have conveyed her meaning; they lowered their search beams from her face and eased their hold on their weapons. A flashlight played over her makeshift foot-coverings. Then one of the guards snatched a hand radio from his belt and spoke rapidly into it. The shrill sound of the alarm was abruptly cut off.

Behind the guards, Julie saw a shadow detach itself from under the swept-back wing of the F-117 and glide up behind the remaining sentry, whose eyes were still on her. The sentry slumped, and his body disappeared under the belly of the plane. The shadow began climbing the ladder. It was working! If Julie could keep attention on herself only a few seconds longer.

Already in these last minutes, the tropics' quick transition from twilight to night had taken place, and even knowing he was there, Julie could hardly make out Rick's crouched shape clambering past the open canopy onto the black shell of the F-117. He had explained earlier what he planned to do. The difficulty with their limited arsenal was to inflict enough damage to the stealth fighter to keep it from taking off, preferably disabling it permanently. Slapping the Semtex against the RAM (radar absorbent material) shell that encased the plane's aluminum skeleton might do it—or it might only make a dent. Only its engineers could tell them that.

Rick had opted for the fuel opening on the dorsal spine of the plane behind the canopy, where under normal flight conditions a U.S. Air Force tanker plane would insert the long tube of its fuel probe for in-flight refueling. With this "gas cap" pried open and the Semtex thrust inside, the fuel itself would make a blazing fireball of the plane.

*O God, I think we're going to do it!* Julie swung around as footsteps approached across the concrete, no longer running, since the alarm had shut off, but at a brisk walk. She braced herself as the search beams shifted to the oncoming men. Another party had been added to the group she'd seen enter the brick building—the pilot, still in his flight suit with his helmet under one arm. Beside him strode the Iranian intelligence agent, Taqi Nouri, with his weapon now out of his shoulder holster—an Uzi automatic pistol like the one Victor had carried.

But it wasn't the long, deadly shape of that weapon that widened Julie's eyes with dismay. It was the man tagging along behind him, the white-coated technician at his own heels, his blond head a glitter of gold under the play of the search beams. Julie had hoped to see Tim McAdams again. But not now—not like this!

*Please don't say anything! Don't let them know you recognize me! Don't—*

But it was too late. Tim's eyes were already widening in startled recognition, and a moment later, his vigorous preacher's voice boomed out, "Julie! What are you doing here? Where—?"

Before Julie's frantic signal could stop him, he had swung around, instinctively searching. His action had the effect Julie had feared. The flashlight beams swung toward the F-117.

The pilot was the first to spot Rick. With a shout of rage, he dropped his flight helmet and sprinted toward the ladder. Julie found herself suddenly forgotten as the two guards broke into a run behind the pilot. One paused to drop to one knee and raise his machine gun.

Rick had to have heard the pilot's shout, but he didn't move from his crouch. Julie, glimpsing a rectangular object in his hands and the combat knife with which he'd been prying open the fuel cap, knew he was working frantically to place the Semtex charge before they reached him. Then she saw the machine gun lifted to the guard's shoulder and his finger tightening on the trigger.

"No!" The scream ripped from Julie's throat as she launched herself at the guard. The impact knocked him sideways, and the machine gun flew upward, the burst of gunfire spraying harmlessly into the air.

A heartbeat later, the butt of the gun struck Julie across the face so hard, she was thrown backward onto the concrete. By the time she scrambled frantically to her feet, the guard was raising his gun again. Only now the pilot was up the ladder and launching himself at Rick so that it was impossible to fire at one without hitting the other. Lowering the gun, the guard broke back into a run toward the plane.

Julie started after him, but she had taken only a step when a steel grip snatched her back. Struggling, she glanced up to catch sight of the black turban. Below it, Taqi Nouri's teeth glinted white against the black beard, but not in a smile, and even in this darkness his eyes glittered with fury and hate. Julie fought against his hold, but he held her easily. The muzzle of the Uzi pistol grinding painfully against her cheekbone froze her into immobility.

On top of the plane, the pilot and Rick were fighting. Rick was unable to bring his AK-47 to bear but was using it to block the pilot's attack. As Julie watched helplessly, the force of the pilot's assault knocked both men from their feet, their grappling bodies rolling over the edge of the dorsal spine and landing with a thud on the wing. The AK-47 flew through the air to clatter at the feet of the guard below. Over and over the two men rolled along the length of the wing. Briefly, Rick managed to separate himself from the pilot and scrambled to his feet. Nouri's Uzi left Julie's cheek to level on the Special Forces officer. Then the pilot launched himself at Rick, knocking his legs out from under him and sending him over the edge, and the barrel of the Uzi dropped.

Rick hit the concrete at a roll, then was back on his feet and diving for the AK-47. But the second guard had now reached them as well, and he kicked the assault rifle under the belly of the plane while his companion threw himself at Rick. Rick's vicious kick swept his attacker's legs out from under him. Then, in a series of movements too swift for Julie to follow, one guard went down with a heavy grunt. Rick slammed into the concrete with the other on top of him. As he hit the ground, he kept rolling, throwing the guard over his head. The guard's machine gun skittered across the concrete to land just a few feet from Julie.

But these men, too, were trained soldiers, and even as Rick rolled back to his feet, the pilot launched himself from the wing onto Rick's back. One of the guards was up again, his weapon in hand. He brought it up, again hesitating only because the pilot was in the way. *Why didn't Rick duck under the cover of the plane?* Julie wondered desperately. *And why did he have one arm down to his side instead of using it to defend himself.*

With shock, Julie realized Rick wasn't trying to escape his attackers but to complete his mission, maneuvering himself close enough to toss the grenade hidden in his hand into the canopy that still stood open above him.

It was obvious by now that the pilot had less combat training than the other two guards, and as Rick slammed into him with his body, he went flying backward under the wing.

Against Julie's ear, Nouri screamed out a harsh phrase. It was clear he was ordering the guard who still held a weapon to shoot. The soldier instantly sighted his machine gun on Rick and tightened his finger on the trigger. But before he could shoot, the other guard had thrown himself again at the Special Forces officer, blocking his line of fire.

Rick went down hard, and to Julie's horror as he hit, she saw a small dark object roll away from his out-flung hand and settle against the wheel of the plane. Then Rick's forearm took the soldier across the throat. As the man's head snapped back, Rick grabbed him around the neck. Using the man's body as a shield, he rolled back to his feet, and only Julie knew that his glance around was for the grenade he had dropped.

In the face of his companion's plight, the other guard lowered his weapon. At his hesitation, Nouri screamed again against Julie's ear. Then, with what even Julie's ignorance of his language could guess to be a curse, he raised the Uzi and fired.

Julie's heart stopped beating.

It was like one of those slow-motion moments in an action movie, as though time itself had decelerated. The exaggerated jerk of the guard as the burst struck him in the chest. Rick's forearm slowly dropping away from the man's neck. The limp body sliding down to the concrete, leaving a rapidly expanding stain on Rick's fatigues. As though he were simply sitting down to take a rest, Rick slid down beside the sprawled body, and in that instant Julie knew he was dead and wished she were dead too.

Then Rick groaned, and as one hand came up slowly to clutch at the side of his chest, Julie's heart took its next beat. A moment later, his hand still clutching at his ribs, he rolled over to his knees and raised his head. He was still alive! By some miracle—or maybe the ammo vest he wore—he didn't seem seriously hurt.

Though that wouldn't be for long.

The remaining guard once more had his weapon up, and beside Julie's ear the Uzi was rising again. Though in real time scarcely sixty seconds had passed since Tim McAdams's bumbling recognition and the pilot's warning shout, Julie could already hear the running feet of reinforcements erupting from the *cambuches*. Julie cast around frantically for—anything! *Please, God, we can't have lost! This can't be it!*

And there it was just a short distance away—the machine gun that had flown out of the grasp of the now-dead guard. Julie could not reach for it; Nouri's iron grip still held her fast. But only two strides from the gun, unattended now by anyone except an unarmed technician, stood Tim McAdams.

He hadn't moved since the pandemonium evoked by his incautious action had broken out, his handsome profile unreadable in the dark as he watched, his tall, broad outline looming over the white-coated figure beside him, and if in reality there had been little time to react, it seemed to a resentful Julie that he could have done something!

"Tim!" she screamed in English. "The gun! Pick up the gun!"

"No!"

Julie heard Rick's hoarse denial with astonishment. Then at last, Tim was moving, striding forward to snatch up the machine gun in two quick steps. To her relief, the ease with which he raised it showed that he was no stranger to weapons. But that relief turned to cold horror as Tim brought the weapon to bear, not on Taqi Nouri or on the guard who was closing in on Rick, but directly at the center of Rick's ammo vest.

"Why don't we do this the easy way, Enrique—or whoever you are," he said pleasantly. "Unlike my colleagues, I would rather not test the effect of a high-speed bullet on the skin of that plane. But then, I don't need to, do I?"

He made a very un-American hand gesture. "Perhaps your little friend here can talk you into being a little more cooperative."

Julie cried out with pain as the barrel of the Uzi dug viciously against her cheekbone. Slowly, Rick's hands rose in surrender.

"That's better!" Tim said affably. He directed a low phrase to the white-coated technician beside him. Julie's confusion and horror deepened as the man opened a work pouch around his waist and took out what the glimmer of a dropped flashlight revealed to be a syringe. As he strode over to Rick, who was still on his knees, she stared in disbelief.

"Tim—are you crazy? What—what are you doing?"

"Oh, he knows exactly what he's doing!" Rick interjected bitterly. He didn't flinch as the technician slapped the syringe against his neck. "Though I doubt very much his name is Tim McAdams. Is it?" he asked bitingly. "Or that's he's even an American—missionary or otherwise."

"Then . . ." Julie stared at Tim, but he wasn't trying to deny Rick's incredible charges. Julie hardly felt the sting against her own neck as the horrible implications sank in.

"That's right!" Rick's speech was already thick with the drug. "He's one of the bad guys! An Iranian intelligence agent is my guess!"

## TWENTY-SEVEN

"How did you know that he was an Iranian agent?" The question must have followed Julie into unconsciousness because it was the first to rise to her lips as she became aware of her surroundings.

She was seated in a gray box of a room, the walls unpainted cinder blocks. A lone fluorescent tube was suspended from the ceiling; under her feet, the floor was rough cement.

The room's only other occupant, Julie had already discovered, was Rick, bound as she was to a hard-backed wooden chair placed in the center of the room.

Julie guessed they were in the building with the satellite dish. On hand-built tables around the room she saw electronic equipment—an enormous two-way radio, a sat-phone setup, computer monitors, and two television screens shifting through images of trees and an airstrip that at the moment were no more than flickering shadows. So it was still night outside.

She eyed the communications equipment longingly. If they could just reach that phone! Only it wasn't just the ropes that held the two prisoners to their seats but the lingering paralysis of whatever drug they had been given. Even that small turn of her head to survey the room had left Julie with the deep lassitude she remembered from the injection she'd received at the guerrilla camp, and she didn't have the strength to strain against the ropes. The reason, no doubt, their captors had risked leaving them alone in this place.

"It wasn't hard." Rick's answer came with an effort. "Once you'd tipped me off that the guy wasn't a missionary. That last night in the camp, I saw the expression on his face when you came out with that. You had him! Only you figured he might be part of some covert operation. I knew he wasn't. At least not on our side."

"But—why?" Julie demanded, bewildered. "How could you be so sure— that he wasn't on our side, I mean? Undercover, like you. I mean, he seemed so . . . so American!"

"Simple." Rick tried to shrug and discovered that he couldn't. "U.S. intelligence will use just about any cover in the book. But there are two that have been off-limits for decades—by Congressional law, not any ethical considerations on the part of the intelligence community. Journalists and missionaries. The reason being easy. If they're caught or even come under suspicion, they place every legitimate charitable organization or member of the press who works in these remote areas in jeopardy."

Julie could appreciate that. How many times had her parents and even she herself been routinely accused of being American spies during her childhood years in San Ignacio?

"And whatever tales people like to tell of the CIA and the rest of the intelligence community, I can assure you that is one injunction that is taken seriously."

The rise of Rick's chest as he took a breath tightened his bonds, and Julie saw a grimace of pain crossing his face.

"Are you sure you're okay?" she asked anxiously.

At least they'd had the decency not to let him bleed to death. At some point while Rick and Julie had been unconscious, Rick's ammo vest and shirt had been cut away, and though the rusty brown of dried blood still streaked the tan of his bare skin, a wide bandage had been slapped across his side. Julie realized suddenly that the stiffness of her own speech wasn't totally due to the drug but to the soreness of her face and jaw where the butt of the machine gun had struck her.

"I'm fine!" Rick answered shortly, not with irritation, but because another breath had tightened the ropes across his bandage. "It just creased my ribs. Anyway, the other side doesn't share that ethic. So if this Tim McAdams wasn't who he said he was—a journalist *or* a missionary—then he not only wasn't one of ours, odds were he was the mole who fingered you to Aguilera."

Julie gave her head a disbelieving shake that she immediately regretted as it sent the gray walls swirling around her. "And all this time I had pretty well decided it had to be Sondra Kharrazi. Just because she was originally from somewhere in the Middle East—or her parents at any rate. And she was always asking questions, and *Comandante* Aguilera admitted she was the one who told him we'd gone out the gate. Tim—it still doesn't seem possible. He's so blond, for one thing!"

"Iranians are Caucasian too," Rick reminded her. "And not all brunette. Or he may be Iraqi. But even if that plane out there spells Saddam Hussein, it's pretty clear that Taqi Nouri is running this show. And they have an intelligence network the CIA would give its teeth for. There are a lot of Iranians who come to study—and live—in the U.S. It would be easy enough to feed in someone loyal to the ayatollah's regime. No, I'm betting McAdams is Nouri's man."

"So why didn't you tell me?" Julie demanded, unable to keep the hurt out of her voice. "I thought we were done with keeping secrets! If . . . if you've known since that night in the camp, how could you keep letting me think he was a hostage—worrying about him?"

"I had no proof." Rick winced again as another attempt at a shrug tightened the ropes across his bandage. "Not until I saw him here. And any suspicions I had were irrelevant at the time. I didn't expect we'd come across him again. Besides, the guy seemed to be a friend of yours—how close I didn't know. Maybe it was a bad call. I seem to be making plenty of those lately. But I didn't think you needed anything else to worry about."

"He *was* a friend," Julie whispered. That was what hurt. All the times Tim McAdams had comforted her and cheered her up, even told her to trust God. "He was so good. Pretending he was a prisoner with those guards at his heels. Getting me to talk about my family and my job and even my feelings about the guerrillas. Offering to help. And all the time he was just trying to get me to admit that I'd lied to *Comandante* Aguilera, that I really was CIA or something. And when I thought I gave him away that night—it was really the other way around." Julie remembered with a shudder that ice-cold sensation of death she had felt as the two men's eyes had locked. "That's when he realized it was you and not me who was the spy."

"Yes," Rick said, "I figured that as soon as I found the second tracking device. You thought maybe someone else who spoke English—Aguilera or one of the guards—had overhead you. I knew no one else in the camp beside myself understood English, and so did McAdams, evidently. Once you suggested he take a look at the guerrillas and not the press team . . ."

Rick was charitable enough not to finish, but Julie had already moved on to a horrible realization.

"Oh, no!" she whispered, appalled. "I remember now—those voices I heard talking when I was coming out of the drug that first time back at camp. The ones that mentioned the *musulmanes*. I was so out of it, I couldn't recognize their voices—just that they were familiar. Afterward I thought it had to be *Comandante* Aguilera and Manuel Flores or even you. But one of them was Tim! Only he was speaking in Spanish, not English. I guess that's why it didn't click. He was the one who said it was none of their business what the *musulmanes* were up to. And when they saw I was awake, Tim pretended he was unconscious. And I bought it! If I'd just been thinking straight, maybe . . ."

Julie blinked hard at the single window opposite her. Its glass pane framed a patch of the same unrelenting darkness that the surveillance images revealed, proof that less time had passed than Julie would have thought from the stiffness of her muscles.

Unless more than one day and night had gone by. Not that it mattered now. The despair and pain Julie had been holding off since she'd opened her eyes on these walls broke over her in a flood that was carrying her down into that blackness out there. She closed her eyes convulsively. All that effort . . . their own sacrifice . . .

"No—don't even think it!" Rick said quietly from beside her.

The urgency of his order opened Julie's eyes. "What—?"

"You're thinking you should somehow have been able to stop this if you'd just put the pieces together earlier. And that all of this, your sacrifice, your life—that it's all been for nothing, just as it was for your parents."

"How . . . how did you know?"

"Because I've thought it myself. If I'd put the pieces together earlier. If I'd broken radio silence and gotten something off to Colonel Thornton. If I hadn't been careless enough to let that radio get broken. If I hadn't brought you with me here tonight . . ." The pain that crossed Rick's face wasn't from his wound. "But we made our choices based on what we knew—you said that back there in the woods. And the choice we made—no matter how this turns out, it *was* the right thing to do, you know that! Don't be sorry you made that choice."

Julie was silent for a moment. "No, I'm not sorry. I won't fall back into that again. My parents' lives—and their deaths—were not meaningless, however little I could see God's reasons for it at the time. And all of this—even if it hasn't turned out as we hoped, it wasn't in vain. It never is when you give yourself for another person. And if none of this makes sense to me—why God would let it end this way, why He would let us fail and let all those people die . . ."

Julie took a deep breath. It was easier to do so this time. "I choose to believe that it does make sense to Him. And if I had to make the same choice all over again to come here tonight, I would."

*Slam!* Her resolution was tested immediately as the door to the room banged open and two guards burst in.

"Well, well! Look who's awake!" Tim ducked his blond head through the door frame, the white-coated technician at his heels. Smiling, he crossed the room to stop in front of Julie's chair, giving Julie only a view of his belt buckle until he took her chin between his large thumb and forefinger and tilted her face up to meet his twinkling gaze. "Hello, Julie. What a surprise! I certainly never expected to run into you again."

Still under the effects of the paralysis, Julie couldn't even twist her face away from his grip, so she glared up at him helplessly. Tim chuckled at her mutinous expression, his blue eyes bright and merry. "Hmm, you don't look quite as happy to see me as the last time we met."

Releasing her chin, Tim perched his large frame on the corner of the nearest table. "Truth is, I'm rather sorry to see you too, Julie Baker," he said cheerfully. "Believe it or not, when I heard you'd escaped from Aguilera, I was kind of rooting for you to make it back to civilization. Who would have ever dreamed you'd make your way here instead!"

Tim shook his head disbelievingly. "I warned these guys their security needed beefing up. Those surveillance cameras are just about worthless, as you've shown us, and the local wildlife have set off the motion sensors so often, it would take an earthquake to get the guards to budge now. But the hardware came from our Iraqi allies, and they don't like taking advice. No wonder they lost the Gulf War! Granted, they do have a point. In two years, we hadn't had a soul through here except a few wandering natives until your tree-hugger buddies showed up. Brought here, of course, by those same wandering natives who later brought you."

He wagged his head in mock commiseration. "And let down by the same! I could have told you, Julie, not to count on your little native friends. They're an ignorant, superstitious lot who will bolt at the drop of a hat if you don't keep them under lock and key. Though we did obtain one useful asset from them while they were helping us build this place."

He nodded toward the white-coated technician, who had been removing a collection of rubber-stopped vials from the front pouch he wore and laying them out on a table. "Raman here is one of Iran's finest biochemists, trained in one of your U.S. universities. He's been having some fun with the poison they use on their blow gun darts. As you've found out, it produces a paralysis of the body—very much like a black widow spider uses on her prey. My colleague here has managed to modify it with a touch of scopolamine and a few other ingredients that are beyond my vocabulary, and he's produced a very effective combination truth serum/prisoner restraint."

As Tim talked, the biochemist took out a syringe and plunged the needle through the rubber stopper of one of the vials. Julie shrank back against her bonds as he drew its contents up into the syringe. *Oh, please, God, not again!*

Seeing her flinch, Tim let out his booming chuckle again. "Hey, not to worry! He won't knock you out again. On the contrary, this will put you back on your feet."

He nodded to the white-coated Raman, and as Julie felt the sting of the needle against her neck, he went on cheerfully, "See? What you just got there was the antidote. You've run into it once before, though you were out at the time."

As Raman stepped over to Rick, Tim added, "No, we have what we want out of you two. And quite a tale that was! Stumbling over that village. Running into a bunch of natives you knew when you were a kid. And they just happened to know the way to this base! Almost too much coincidence if we didn't know you had to be telling the truth. I have to tell you, my boss, Taqi Nouri, is madder than a lake of brimstone, if you know what I mean, at how close you two came to blowing this operation."

He glanced over at Rick. The biochemist had finished with him and was putting away his syringe. "Oh, yes, you ID'd him correctly, Captain Rick Martini of the . . . let me see, what was it? Oh, yes, the 7th Special Operations Group, am I right? In fact, your entire assessment was remarkably accurate considering the scant information you had in your possession. Your analysis of our chances of success, for instance, agrees a hundred percent with our own."

Julie didn't ask how Tim had found all that out. Though she had no conscious memory between that injection out on the airstrip until awakening in this room, she retained a vague impression of her own voice babbling on and on. At least he'd told the truth about whatever new drug the white-coated Raman had pumped into them. Already Julie could feel the paralysis ebbing from her limbs.

Rick, too, was sitting straighter in his bonds. His battered face showed no response as he looked coolly at the Iranian agent. "Well," Rick told him, "my analysis was wrong. You won't get away with this—not unless you're planning on making this a suicide run. I know the specs on that plane out there. Your fuel will barely get you to the U.S. border. Unless you're planning on flying home on fumes—or you have another target in mind."

Julie glanced at Rick, surprised at the uncharacteristic adversarial tone of his remarks. Then she caught the intentness with which he was watching Tim, the quick, unobtrusive survey of the communications equipment now that he could move his head freely. He wasn't trying to needle Tim, Julie realized incredulously. He was still trying to provoke information out of him.

Tim chuckled. "Sorry, but I'm not going to fall for that one. You're just going to have to get by without the traditional last-chapter explanations of the bad guys' plans," he said mockingly. "Suffice it to say we've had ten years to plan for every eventuality. Two weeks from now, when Washington, D.C., finally wakes up to the fact that they've got an epidemic on their hands, we'll have hit every major city in the U.S., starting with the capital itself, and be well on our way through the smaller ones. Our pilot is a volunteer and perfectly willing to be a martyr to the cause. He'll keep flying until he's shot down, which if the U.S. military lives up to its normal efficiency, will come sooner or later. But by that time—well, to put it bluntly, the U.S. will no longer exist as a nation."

Julie stared at Tim unbelievingly. Even now, knowing what she knew, it didn't seem possible that this good-looking, personable extrovert of a man was capable of conspiring mass murder. He just seemed so . . . normal."

"Tim—or whatever your name is—why are you doing all this?" she burst out. "It's clear you've lived in America before, your act is so . . . so perfect! All your talk about God and serving Him, you were so good at it. You even helped me! So how can you just stand there and talk about murdering millions of people? What have we done to you that you should hate Americans that much?"

The Iranian agent's eyebrows shot up in good-natured surprise. "You can call me Tim. I've been using it long enough. And yes, I did think I did the missionary bit pretty well. I still don't see where I went wrong. I spent a lot of time studying your TV evangelists."

*That explains it,* Julie thought sourly.

"But, hey, I don't hate America. My own mother was American—my father married her during his college years in America. She made sure I was well indoctrinated with Disney and baseball and apple pie before the ayatollah came along and abolished degenerate American culture from Iranian soil. That was the last I saw of her, because she didn't care for the ayatollah's plans for women—or for the fourth wife my father had just taken. Fortunately for me, Khalkhali—the present ayatollah—was an old family friend of my father's, and he decided it would be useful to have someone who could pass for an infidel in his intelligence network. He arranged for tutors so I wouldn't forget my English, then a boarding school in New York—under another name, of course—and college. With Islamic studies on the side, so I wouldn't forget my duty to Allah and country."

Glancing at his companions, whose uncomprehending expressions showed they didn't understand the English he was speaking, Tim added confidentially, "Though, if you'll promise not to spill the beans, I'll admit they never did manage to instill in me my countrymen's religious zeal. You wouldn't catch me wasting my life on martyrdom! No, I'm afraid I'm in this for that oldest of American values. Sheer capitalism. This job lets me live in a way I never could back in Iran. Truth is, I like the United States— at least the conveniences and freedoms of living there. It's a lot more fun than under the ayatollah's regime. I even tried to talk Nouri out of this madness when I found out about it. A few smaller epidemics would make their point, but knocking off the most prosperous nation on the planet— it's crazy! Khalkhali has no concept of what it will do to the world—including his own nation."

"If you feel that way, why are you helping them?" Julie cried out. "You could have stopped this with a phone call!"

Tim's eyebrows went up again. "And who's going to come up with my next paycheck—a sizable one, I might add? Besides, maybe Khalkhali's right. After all, he's the one with the direct line to God—Allah, I mean. No, I've already transferred my bank account overseas. I'll miss America, but Rio or the south of France will offer a tolerable alternative for entertainment."

Julie felt sick with disgust. Tim had never looked more handsome, his mouth curved with that warm, confident smile of his, the blue eyes twinkling down into hers. The contrast to Rick's battered, grim features and blood-streaked torso was that of a joyous golden Apollo to a battle-worn gladiator.

But behind Tim's twinkling eyes and handsome face there was—nothing.

No humanity or concern—not even for his own side. No spark of moral conscience. None of the caring—for the people of this country, for the world, for herself—that Rick managed to keep hidden most of the time under a brusque exterior and his almost implacable commitment to duty. Not even the fanatic dedication the guerrillas and perhaps these Iranians and Iraqis too, gave to their cause.

Just shallow self-interest and a facile tongue enclosed in a well-decorated facade.

"So—what are you going to do with us now?" she demanded bitingly. "Infect us with anthrax like you did with those poor villagers and Dr. Renken and her party? I presume that's what happened to them."

"Their arrival did prove rather opportune." Something in Julie's expression finally pierced Tim's self-complacency because the white-teethed smile thinned into a sneer. "We had just received the first shipment, and we weren't too eager to sacrifice any of our workers—at least not then. Your friends and those bumbling Indian guides of theirs were—convenient. But, no, we aren't in need of any more test subjects. We've already proved that Saddam Hussein's bio-weapons are still thoroughly effective. For you we have other plans!"

"Julie, don't try to argue with him," Rick cut in tiredly. "He isn't worth it."

Tim was unruffled by his comment. Lifting his heavy frame from the edge of the table, he got to his feet. "You're right, we're wasting time with this discussion. And you two have cost us enough time tonight already. Raman!" At Tim's gesture, the biochemist sprang forward to cut at Julie's bonds with a surgical knife, then moved over to repeat the process on Rick. "You should find yourself able to walk now. Let's move! Any more delays, and it'll be daylight before the F-117 is back home and under cover."

At his signal, the guards prodded Julie and Rick to their feet with their machine guns. But even with the sharp jab to her ribs, Julie stopped dead in her tracks. "Delays? You mean, the plane hasn't taken off yet? I . . . I thought it was all over!"

Tim's eyebrow shot up again. "We couldn't exactly take off until we found out what you two were up to, could we? Or whether you had alerted a reception committee to be waiting for us. And since we now know you've failed miserably at your attempt to sabotage this operation"—his sneer deepened—"it's time to get this show on the road. Unlike myself, Taqi

Nouri hates Americans with a passion. He wants to see the expression on your faces when his cargo of death lifts off to rain destruction and damnation over your homeland. His words, not mine!" Tim added sardonically. "Then . . ." Tim made a dismissive gesture that was oddly un-American. "He plans to have the personal pleasure of shooting you."

The threat was intended to strike terror into the two prisoners, but instead it brought a jolt of excitement to Julie. Hope was not entirely dead! She managed a surreptitious glance at her watch as the guard prodded her out the door. Incredibly, if her watch was still accurate, only two hours had passed since their capture on the runway.

Stumbling down the steps, she made a swift search for the F-117. Even if this were not the darkest night of the lunar calendar, the huge camouflage mats overhead blocked out any glimmer of stars or moon, but there was actually more illumination than when Rick and Julie had made their futile assault. Glow sticks had been placed at intervals to mark both sides of the runway clear out to the swamp, and out in the middle of the airstrip, two fluorescent lanterns created overlapping circles of light.

Above the lanterns loomed the F-117 like the crouching shadow of some prehistoric beast. It hadn't moved, as far as Julie could tell, not even to taxi into position for takeoff, and the ladder still led up to an open canopy. Was it possible that Rick's dropped grenade still lay somewhere in the blackness beneath those swept-back wings?

But there was no way she or Rick could approach the stealth fighter for another attempt, even a suicidal one. Every living being in the encampment had to be out there on that airstrip waiting for them. A ring of soldiers circled the plane. Others were fanned out in a V-shape from the foot of the ladder, and as the two prisoners stumbled onto the runway, Julie heard the sharp click of slides being shot back. Any false step, and they would be gunned down in an instant.

Even the Indian laborers were gathered for the show, huddled together under the watchful eye of one of the guards, and Julie saw women among them. The kitchen help? Did they have any idea what these intruders in their territory were up to? What they had done to their own people?

Taqi Nouri himself was watching their approach from the foot of the ladder. At his left side stood the pilot, his recovered helmet in hand. As the guards prodded Rick and Julie to a stop, the Iranian intelligence agent began to speak.

It was a ceremony, Julie realized. The occasion was far too momentous for a simple takeoff. And whatever language he was speaking—Persian or Arabic—he was doing a good job of stirring up emotions. An angry rumble rose among the soldiers, with dark looks toward the two prisoners.

With the briefest of pauses, Taqi Nouri switched to precise, cultured English, and as the fury of his speech blasted over them, Julie understood why she and Rick had been brought here. They were to be the stand-ins for all those sleeping Americans who weren't present to hear the outpouring of hate with which this mission of death was being launched. More than just mass annihilation, Taqi Nouri and his colleagues wanted to see with their own eyes the horror and agony on the faces of their victims as they realized what had been done to them. Since that wasn't possible, Rick and Julie were to be their representatives.

"You have chosen to wage war against the followers of Allah!" Nouri shouted across the runway. "You have wantonly invaded our territory and given aid to our enemies, the infidel Jews. You have visited death and destruction on Muslim cities and countrysides and brought disease and starvation to our children. Your imperialistic ambitions and the decadence of your culture with its godless immorality have spread like a cankerous sore across the entire world. But tonight that will stop. Tonight death will rain down on your cities as you have rained death on ours. Tonight your children will fall to disease and destruction. Tonight by the will of Allah, justice will at last be visited upon the infidels, and the cleansing fire of righteousness will obliterate the spawn of the Great Satan."

Abruptly, the Iranian cleric switched into his earlier language, his voice rising in one last fervent outpouring before he suddenly broke off. Whatever that last passionate speech had been—a blessing? a prayer?—the ceremony was over. Climbing the ladder, the pilot clambered into the cockpit and pulled the canopy down over him. Two soldiers pulled the ladder out of the way. The powerful turbo-fan engines rumbled to life, and the nose of the F-117 began slowly to turn, not nose-forward, but in a leisurely circle that would back it up against the embankment at the end of the runway.

The soldiers scattered out of its path, two pausing to snatch up the fluorescent lanterns. At Tim McAdams's gesture, Rick and Julie's guards shoved them over to the side of the runway, and a unit of soldiers closed in around them. As the stealth fighter continued its slow taxi, Taqi Nouri strode over toward the prisoners. Already, the Iranian intelligence agent was unholstering his Uzi machine pistol, and with shock, Julie saw that Tim McAdams had somehow acquired an Uzi as well and was holding it on the prisoners with the ease of long experience. His cool expression showed little more than academic interest in the two Americans, but the smile on his superior's face was gloating. The burning hatred in Nouri's eyes was reflected in the faces of the other guards.

*This is it.* Closing her eyes against their hateful glares, Julie braced herself against the bullets that had to be imminent. *O God, I know this is just a step from here to You. But I'm so afraid!* She had always heard that when death was at hand, her whole life was supposed to flash before her eyes. But all she felt was an enormous weariness.

Opening her eyes, she looked to the rugged profile of the Special Forces officer beside her. Incredibly, his own narrowed gaze was still focused on the slow taxi of the plane as though even now some opportunity for action might present itself. Julie watched him, imprinting desperately on her mind every curve of the firm mouth that could be grim and sardonic and angry and yet tender too, the strong planes of his face, the sweep of those long lashes dropped concealingly now over his cool gaze. And if her heart was only too clearly revealed in her own eyes, it didn't matter anymore. Of all the hopes and dreams Julie had relinquished that night, this was the hardest to let go.

Suddenly, Julie felt the tautness leave Rick's lean frame. As though drawn by her eyes on him, he looked down at Julie, and as their eyes met, he smiled. It was a surprisingly carefree smile, as though he too had at last recognized the futility of struggle and had thrown in the towel, relaxing the grim, weary line of his mouth and crinkling the corners of his eyes with a wry tenderness that was as intimate as an embrace. Reaching over in the darkness, he slid his hand over Julie's, his long fingers folding around hers. The warmth of his hard palm against hers was like a current of strength pulsing between them, and Julie read in his steadfast gaze what he couldn't say aloud. *It'll be okay. Just hang in there. I love—*

The butt of a machine gun struck their hands apart. A guard shoved Rick back, the muzzle of his weapon against Rick's bare chest. Taqi Nouri raised his Uzi to zero in on Julie's forehead. She closed her eyes again, exhaustion drawing her into a black cloud. *O God, just let it be over!*

Smack! The blow across her face was almost more of a shock than a bullet would have been. Cruel fingers bit into Julie's chin, and another cruel hand yanked her hair back.

"Oh, no, you will not spare yourself!" a gloating voice hissed in her ear, the cultured English a direct contrast to the malice of its tone. "You will watch until it is done."

As the merciless grip bit deeper into her face and hair, Julie opened her eyes to the black-bearded features of Taqi Nouri, distorted with mingled hate and satisfaction. Viciously, he twisted his hand in Julie's hair to force her gaze to the F-117, the Uzi grinding against her cheekbone. Julie watched helplessly as the stealth fighter began the final rotation that would turn its tail to the bank and its nose outward, ready for takeoff.

But in the next heartbeat, as abruptly and unexpectedly as he had grabbed her, Taqi Nouri's vicious grip loosened, the Uzi dropped away from her cheek. Julie stumbled under the heavy weight as the Iranian agent sagged against her. Recovering herself, she stared with bewildered amazement as his body slid to the ground. Had his very spite and hate brought on a heart attack?

Then she saw Tim McAdams slap at his neck. His hands flew into the air, his Uzi flying out of his hand as he hit the ground. The muzzle against Rick's chest fell away as the guard slumped down. Then another.

Suddenly, incredibly, Julie and Rick were standing alone and free.

Stunned, Julie saw a feathered dart protruding from Nouri's neck. With sudden realization, she whirled around. Yes, there it was—a flicker of movement at the jungle edge beyond the motion sensors. Down the runway a few meters, a shadow moved across the firefly glimmer of the glow sticks. An instant later, one of the soldiers holding a fluorescent lantern went down. The huddle of natives, who had already retreated from the taxiing aircraft back toward the *cambuches*, scattered screaming.

"Rick!" Julie whispered in dazed incredulity. "The I'paa—they came back!"

It wasn't quite that easy. As one of the guards went down, the soldier beside him raised his machine gun. A rat-tat-tat of gunfire stitched a trail of light across a tree trunk, and a scream of agony rose from the shadows beyond.

"Get down!" Rick dove at Julie, carrying her to the ground with him. As they hit the ground, more gunfire erupted. With another choking scream, a body tumbled forward down the bank to lie spread-eagled on the concrete.

From the jungle, a cry of rage arose, and an arrow shot out of the trees to catch the gunman in the chest with such force that he was thrown back through the air before landing with a crunch in the middle of the runway.

A shower of arrows followed. Rick covered Julie's body with his own, pressing her head down to the ground as they whistled overhead, some so close Julie could hear the hiss of their passage and the thud of arrowheads striking concrete.

And that quickly, it was over. There was a moment of silence, broken only by the idling rumble of the F-117. Then a yell of triumph arose from the edge of the jungle. As Rick rolled away from her, Julie raised her head cautiously. Everywhere, it seemed, bodies littered the ground, most fallen where the security forces had retreated to the edge of the runway. Several dark shapes were spread-eagled against the lighter concrete of the airstrip, casualties of a futile dash for cover. At least four bore the long arrows of the I'paa thrusting upward from their bodies.

Julie scrambled shakily to her feet, ignoring the sting of scraped flesh on her knees and hands. This was no dream! Incredibly, miraculously, they were alive. And their enemies—

"Rick! The plane!"

It was moving again. The pilot had to have seen his companions going down, and it was enough to make him pause in his final taxiing maneuver. Clearly something had gone terribly wrong, but the pilot was carrying on his mission. He no doubt had been chosen for it because of his fanatic commitment to the cause; if what he saw outside his canopy denoted a serious setback, he still had a bellyful of death to deliver to the infidel.

But in the pilot's haste to finish his turn, the F-117 nudged into the embankment. There was a scream of accelerating RPMs in the twin turbofans. Julie looked about frantically. If only they still had the Semtex or . . . or something!

Rick was one step ahead of her. Grabbing a pair of grenades from a guard's belt, he snatched up the Uzi from where it had fallen beyond Taqi Nouri's outstretched hand and sprinted toward the F-117.

He shouldn't have made it, but the force of the pilot's hasty reversal had thrust the twin butterfly-wing tails of the stealth fighter right up over the embankment. An avalanche of dirt spilled onto the airstrip as the twin tails gouged deeply into the bank. The engine RPMs dropped abruptly as the pilot realized his error and stood on his brakes. As the pilot eased the plane's rear out of the dirt, Rick caught at the edge of the wing and vaulted aboard. By the time the tail was clear of the bank, he was on the roof behind the canopy. In the dim glimmer of the glow sticks and one fluorescent lantern still alight beside the runway, he was hardly more than a moving shadow, but Julie heard a blast of gunfire above the accelerating whine of the engines and knew that he was attempting to blow off the hatch that covered the refueling drogue.

By now the pilot realized he had company. A stamp on the brakes jerked the plane, throwing Rick forward and knocking him off his feet. Only a quick grab at a protuberance on the roof kept him from sliding over the edge. Julie watched with held breath and clenched fists as he pulled himself back to a crouch. *Please! Oh, please!*

But the whine of the engine had now risen to its necessary acceleration for takeoff. Rick threw himself forward, grabbing for the edge of the refueling drogue as the F-117 began to move. Julie saw one hand release its hold to go to a pocket. The grenades.

The stealth fighter picked up speed. It rolled by, the nearest wheel passing so close to the sprawled shapes on the runway that an arrow protruding from one back scraped at the underside of the wing. Julie's stomach caught in her throat to see Rick's form clinging to that black shell. How could any human possibly hold on?

He couldn't. Even as Julie broke into a run after the accelerating plane, the dark shape on the F-117 dropped away. Rolling off the roof, the body struck the wing, and with horror, Julie saw it literally bounce before falling clear to hit the ground.

Finally unimpeded, the F-117 raced down the runway, still gathering speed, its black shape aimed unerringly between the two dotted lines of light. Julie hardly noticed or even cared anymore. Sobbing, she sprinted toward that ominously still form.

*One thousand one. One thousand two. One thousand three.*

The F-117 didn't lift its nose until it reached the last set of glow sticks. Then the wheels left the ground. Julie reached Rick's side at the same moment. He wasn't moving, and blood seemed to be everywhere. With a cry of anguish, Julie fell to her knees beside him, but even as she felt for a pulse, her head went up instinctively to watch the stealth fighter climb steeply toward the canopy, the black shadow of a bat leaving its cave.

Rick's final heroic act had not succeeded. They had failed.

But even as Julie bowed her head in grief, a thunderous explosion rocked the night. The burst of light that accompanied it was so bright, it penetrated even the camouflage nets, dazzling Julie's eyes. As she sprang to her feet, she could see only a haze of fire beyond the jungle where the F-117 had disappeared. As the thunder died away, Julie saw a shower of flaming meteorites raining down into the swamp. The wreckage of the F-117.

Behind her, Julie was only vaguely aware of the shouts of triumph and running feet, of Bernabé racing toward her with one of the fluorescent lanterns held high in one hand, his spear still waving in the other. Her eyes were held with incredulous wonder by that raining curtain of fire. Beyond all hope, beyond all despair, as night itself had turned to day, defeat had turned to victory.

*God, we did it! I don't believe it! We really did it!*

*No, not we—You!*

From behind her, as the last of the flaming debris extinguished itself in the swamp, she heard a groan. Julie whirled around in time to see Rick roll over. As he raised a bloodied hand to his head, she fell again to her knees beside him with a cry of joy.

"Boy, that really hurt!" He groaned again. "What did I miss?"

# EPILOGUE

JULIE WALKED OUT TO THE END of the runway. Without the camouflage nets that had previously concealed the entrance, the opening created where the airstrip dead-ended in the swamp gave the impression of an enormous portal onto the outside world, the two massive mahoganies on either side suggesting the doorjambs, while the camouflage mat stretched between the umbrellas of their branches overhead formed the lintel.

Julie stepped out onto what would have been the threshold—the concrete edge where the runway dropped off into the water. Dawn was just laying the first streaks of color above the jungle canopy on the far side of the swamp, staining the algae-choked water with rose and gold so that its placid surface was for the moment a vision of splendor. It was going to be a cloudless day.

Stopping at the water's edge, Julie noted where the wheel tracks of the F-117 still showed just how closely calculated that takeoff had been. She breathed in the perfume of a night-blooming jasmine crawling up the tree trunk to her left, its petals just beginning to fold up for the day. Other exotic blooms less sweet-smelling but more colorful, were spreading their own petals to greet the morning.

Above the swamp, a flock of fruit bats wheeled against the growing light, heading home to roost. Out in the water, a fish leaped, a streak of silver. With a screech, a heron dove down to snatch the fish up. The bird rose, the beating of its long, white wings a symphony of sound and grace, the fish flapping and struggling in its powerful beak.

There was so much beauty here, Julie reflected, as the bird gobbled its breakfast—and so much pain as well. Just as both beauty and pain had intertwined in her own life, even when she had chosen to see only the pain. What she hadn't recognized—had refused to recognize for so long—was that both could come into her life by the same hand of a loving God; both were part of anyone's life in one way or another.

Steps signaled someone's approach. Julie turned to see Rick striding toward her. He was fully dressed, wearing a clean set of fatigues he had scrounged out of one of the *cambuches*. He moved a little stiffly, but looked alert and wide awake. She would never have guessed how many bandages he carried under his clothing if she hadn't applied some of them herself. Miraculously, he had broken no bones in that final fall, though Julie suspected at least one cracked rib either from the fall or the earlier bullet crease. Despite the blood that had frightened her so, his injuries had proved to be only scrapes and bruises—though a good many of them.

Julie pushed away the memory of that unmoving, blood-stained form. It held too many horrors.

"How are you feeling?" she asked him.

"Hyped up on painkillers at the moment. Ask me when they wear off." Rick grinned down at her. Despite a nasty scrape down one cheek and deep lines of tiredness at the corners of his mouth, he was looking more relaxed than Julie had ever seen him, the restlessness and iron control, the constant air of vigilance that had been there as long as she had known him, laid aside, at least for the moment. This mission had cost him so many months and nearly his life, and Julie could only imagine his sense of release at seeing it over—and successful.

"And how about you?" he asked.

Julie had almost forgotten about the machine gun butt across her face, though now that he had reminded her, she realized just how sore her cheek and jaw still were. "Oh, I'm fine." A smile touched her eyes as she glanced pointedly at the jacket of his fatigues. "It would be a little hard to complain after seeing what you've got under there." She stifled a yawn. "Though I could sleep for a week now that the adrenaline is wearing off!"

"Well, it won't be much longer. That's what I came to tell you. I just got off the phone with Colonel Thornton. They're on their way."

Once events had slowed down the night before, Rick had gotten though to San José on the base's communication equipment. The colonel had in turn been delighted to hear that Rick and Julie were still alive, incredulous at their story, then coldly furious. With the base already secured, there had been little point in risking a night drop, so he ordered them to stay put until first light, when he would be there with a full team. Their first order of business would be the arrest of a certain counter-narcotics sentry assigned to the American operations team, Jaime Ramirez.

"They're bringing a team of our guys—Special Ops from San José. And a Colombian unit as well from Colonel Serano's troops. Once they've secured the site, they'll airlift us and the prisoners back to San José. Oh, and they've got a medic team with them too."

"Good!" Julie said with relief. "Because Raman doesn't think one of the Iraqis is going to make it if we don't get him to a real medical facility fairly soon. Yacu—the I'paa with the leg wound—is doing better. But Raman figures he's going to need major surgery."

Raman, the Iranian biochemist, had been the only one of the base contingent to be spared by the I'paa attack—because he wasn't armed or in uniform, Bernabé explained afterward. Rick had found the scientist cowering behind the crates in one of the *cambuches* and had pressed him into service as a medic. There had been little that could be done for one of the I'paa, who had caught a burst of gunfire full in the chest. But the other— Yacu—had a shattered femur. Of the six Iraqis caught in that deadly volley of arrows, only two had survived long enough to receive medical attention. One of them had suffered an abdominal wound that looked to have missed any vital organs, but the arrowhead had punctured the other through his right lung.

"I'm afraid it's too late for surgery for him." Rick shook his head. "I just came from there. He didn't make it through the night. Those who got the poison darts are the lucky ones. Raman's antidote seems to do just about as well on them as it did on us. Though they may not find a charge of murder and attempted genocide much of an improvement."

"At least they're alive," Julie said dryly. "Bernabé asked me with all seriousness if we wanted them to dispose of the prisoners. He figures it's a great waste of time and energy to be guarding them when we could have finished them off and all had a good night's sleep. They're lucky the I'paa aren't still cutting off their enemies' heads and shrinking them."

She glanced back along the runway to where a dozen I'paa had the survivors corralled on the concrete in front of the hangar. The Amazonic natives had flatly refused to place them under guard indoors. Not enough open space to watch for enemies, Bernabé had said. Only the wounded and Raman were under the thatched cover of one of the *cambuches,* where two of the I'paa warriors monitored their every move. Compared to the well-equipped soldiers who had patrolled that perimeter the night before, the semi-naked bodies and primitive spears and bows of the I'paa seemed almost ludicrous. But neither Julie nor Rick doubted their capacity to keep the prisoners under control.

Nor, from the furious expressions Julie had seen as she walked down the airstrip, did the prisoners. Though Julie thought of herself as a mature, forgiving adult, she had to admit it afforded her no small pleasure to note a certain blond head and black turban among them. *I hope you rot in jail for the rest of your lives!*

"I still can't believe they came back," she said aloud. "Do you know what Bernabé told me when I asked him why? He said that they'd always gone to the *riowa* when they had trouble—to my parents, to me. The other villages of their tribe had turned to the environmentalist groups and the aid organizations. They believed that we knew everything and could do anything. But now they saw that we were only men like themselves who could fear and bleed and die just as they did. And if we could give ourselves for those who were not our family without any promise that we wouldn't suffer harm, then how could they continue to call themselves men if they weren't willing to do the same? He said that it was time that they gave instead of only taking—to you and me, their friends, to the people who were dying, to the God who had created them."

Julie swallowed down the emotion that tightened her throat. "What he didn't say—but I know—is that he spent all those hours convincing them to come back!"

Julie had made another phone call once Colonel Thornton had finished his debriefing and allowed them off the air. It had taken some time to track Norm Hutchens to a U.S. embassy VIP guest apartment in Bogotá, into which only his vast influence could have gotten him. The emotion that had wavered through the old newspaperman's voice as he came on the air had laid to rest any lingering doubts Julie might have had as to her place in his life, even followed as it was by a scathing indictment of his young reporter's carelessness in getting herself kidnapped on the job.

Julie smiled as she recalled some of those remarks. By tonight he would be demanding his story. Her world was returning to normal.

Rick had insisted on one other thing once his own scrapes and ugly leg gash had finally been attended and security arranged for the prisoners—a nasal swab to test for anthrax exposure, not just for Julie but for the I'paa who had approached the village. For a biochemist like Raman, it had been a routine task, and he had been eagerly cooperative. *Hoping we'll put in a good word for him,* Julie concluded.

It had been a shock for Julie to find out that she had indeed tested positive for anthrax, along with four of the I'paa who had gone closest to the village, including Bernabé. Fortunately, the Iranian biochemist had also had the foresight—or misgivings—not to settle himself in a stockpile of the deadly disease without an ample supply of the appropriate antibiotics. Already that night, Julie and the I'paa had started on the long course of treatment, though it had taken some persuading and intervention from Bernabé as village healer to convince the Indian warriors that these white pills would kill the evil that was growing in their bodies.

Julie shuddered to think what might have happened if they'd gone on downriver just a few more days. What a quirk of fate—or another evidence of God's hand on this whole venture—that Julie's decision, and the I'paa's, to make a stand against evil had saved her life and theirs.

A silence fell between the two at the water's edge. Out over the swamp the sky was brightening, its reflection below beginning to fade from rose and gold to just gold. Dawn would soon be lifting its face over the horizon.

In the growing light, Julie could see that the drowned forest in front of her wasn't as dead as she'd thought. Not far out into the swamp, a tall specimen of hardwood had broken off under its dying weight, its remaining stump thrusting only a short way out of the murky water. But rising from the center of the stump was a hint of green—tender new shoots springing up from the nourishment of that rotting corpse.

Unless a kernel of wheat falls to the ground and dies . . .

*Whoever loses his life for my sake will find it . . .*

Beside her, Rick was watching another fish leap out of the water, the silver of the concentric rings that rippled out from it cutting a perfect jeweled pattern through the gold. A deep breath of appreciation escaped him before he said quietly. "It's going to be one beautiful day."

He glanced over at Julie. "I still can't quite believe I'm standing here. I can honestly say I never expected to see another sunrise!"

"I know, I was just thinking of that," Julie said. She shook her head wonderingly as she turned her gaze back to the serene panorama of water and jungle and sky. "You know, I fought so hard against ever coming back here, and when I came, it was with only one thing in mind. Getting that Pulitzer and putting my career on the fast track. Not in a million years would I have ever dreamed I'd end up helping to save the world instead. Or that I even had it in me!"

"I knew you had it in you—and so did those I'paa," Rick said quietly. "Your parents would be very proud of their daughter right now."

"I know they are," Julie answered softly.

Rick cleared his throat. "As for that Pulitzer Prize, I'm afraid I may have some unwelcome news. That was something else Colonel Thornton had to say on the phone right now. Already, the powers that be are dropping a news whiteout over this whole thing—national security threat, classified information, the whole bit. They say if the American people knew how close they came to total destruction last night, they'd never sleep easy again. And they don't want to give other terrorists ideas. Oh, they'll have to give some explanation as to what's happened out here, but it'll be given out as another not-to-be-taken-seriously terrorist attempt, and the real story will be labeled top-secret and stuffed in a drawer—or computer file—for the next hundred years."

Julie grimaced. "And the public's right to know?" But there was no real indignation in her query.

"Hey, it won't be my call. But I *am* sorry. You may just have saved the world and lost yourself that Pulitzer."

Julie smiled ruefully. "You know, somehow that just doesn't seem like the end of the world anymore!"

"Good!" Rick said absently. "I was hoping you'd feel that way."

Silence fell between them, but this time it wasn't comfortable. Julie glanced up to find Rick's eyes on her face, and something in them made her heart begin to race. She rushed to fill the vacuum. "What about Tim McAdams and Taqi Nouri? What's going to happen to them?"

"Julie!"

Rick's simple statement of her name cut through her babbling speech. She swung around to face him. "Yes?"

"I was just wondering." He was smiling, but Julie saw an uncertainty that was very un-Ricklike under the long lashes, along with that something else that was making her heart pound so hard, it seemed he had to see it. "If that Pulitzer isn't on the immediate horizon, is there any chance you might settle instead for one slightly worn Special Forces officer who doesn't always know where he's going to be from one end of the week to the next?"

Though his words had been lingering, unspoken, for an eternity, they caught Julie off guard. Speechless, she stared up at him. Then a slow smile rose to her eyes, lighting her thin, bruised face with a radiance that made Rick blink. "Just what are you trying to say, Captain Rick Martini?"

What he read in that smile banished the uncertainty from his eyes. One step closed the gap between them, and the upward quirk of his mouth once again held its customary cool assurance as Rick took her hands in his.

"What I'm trying to say, Julie Baker," he said softly, "is that I love you, and I'd like to ask you to marry me, and I'm tired of waiting around for the world to stop falling apart before I let you know how I feel!"

Julie had been wanting to do it for such a long time. Now, stepping within the circle of their clasped hands, she yielded to the impulse and stood on tiptoes to kiss the unshaven shadow of his chin. An impishness that Rick hadn't seen in long weeks curved her lips as she answered just as softly, "So what are you waiting for?"

Across the swamp, a burning circle raised its blazing rim over the jungle canopy, a reflection of the copper flames that leaped into Rick's eyes. Out on the water, another fish leaped high. The watching heron shot down after it, but this time the bird came up empty-beaked. Dawn had at last arrived.

* * *

The pilot of the MH53J "Pave Low" helicopter was the first to spot open water ahead.

"There it is—the swamp Captain Martini told us about," he shouted above the powerful throp-throp of the six-bladed rotor.

The Pave Low, used for combat search-and-rescue as well as transport for SouthCom's Special Ops units, was the biggest helicopter the American forces had in Colombia, big enough to hold close to fifty crew and passengers. At the moment it was running almost empty, but that wouldn't be for long.

"Not Captain—Major," Colonel Thornton corrected. "Or will be soon enough, though Martini doesn't know it yet. That's one exceptional job he's done down there. Now to find that airstrip he mentioned. He said there would be two of them—he and the girl—standing at the entrance to wave us in."

The Pave Low flew down over the swamp, remaining just high enough to avoid the broken spars of the drowned hardwoods. The pilot checked his instrument panel. "Colonel, we've got something wrong here. By the co-ordinates that Captain—uh, Major Martini gave us, that should be it right over there off to the right between those two trees. But I'm not seeing anyone out in the open. I am picking up a heat signature on the infrared, but just one. Either we've got the wrong place—and a suspect life sign down there—or one of them's gone missing."

Already, members of the Special Forces team were moving to the rotary mini-guns mounted in each doorway of the helicopter. Colonel Thornton spoke into the radio, addressing the two Black Hawks closing in behind them. "Proceed with caution. We may have a situation here."

As the Pave Low hovered down over the murky waters, the Joint Task Force commander peered through the windshield, his sharp eyes searching the tangle of jungle that bordered the swamp. Then, spotting the concrete airstrip under the overhanging camouflage of vegetation, he suddenly chuckled. "No, those are the right coordinates. I see them! And there may be only one heat signature, but there's two people there, all right."

Two heads very close together shot up as the Pave Low swooped in through the opening in the trees. Colonel Thornton raised the radio to his mouth. "Belay that last! We've got Martini and the girl. And they're doing just fine . . . really fine, I'd say!"

\* \* \*

James Whitfield switched to mute the flat-screen TV that occupied one wall of the conference room at Southern Command headquarters in Miami. The NBC news channel played on in silence, its beautiful brunette anchorwoman, Sondra Kharrazi, gracefully gesturing against a background of Amazonic jungle that was only a projected image behind her. She had already informed her audience that the kidnapped journalist, whose recent rescue by Colombian counter-narcotics troops had exposed a terrorist plot to smuggle bio-weapons into the United States, was a personal friend. The NBC anchorwoman believed what she was saying to be the unadulterated truth. The four men in the conference room knew otherwise.

"So that's what we have to take to the president?" the National Security Advisor demanded incredulously. "No great technology involved. One of our own planes. Out-of-date bio-weapons. Nothing we wouldn't consider war surplus. And yet they came that close to taking out the most powerful nation on earth?"

"The whole thing was fiendishly clever," CIA Director Martin Sawatsky said quickly. "The Iranian minister of intelligence, Taqi Nouri, has been less than forthcoming—unfortunately, our oversight laws won't allow us to use the kind of persuasion on him that he would use if roles were reversed. But Tim McAdams, their sleeper agent, is made of weaker stuff. He's spilling everything he knows—in return for a plea bargain and the chance he might get to use those overseas bank accounts of his again someday. They had every detail worked out, including fuel stops in Mexico and the Bahamas—thanks to their FARC buddies, they have access to every narco airstrip in the hemisphere. We've already picked up the personnel they had manning those sites.

"The spray unit doesn't weigh much compared to the F-117's usual bomb load, and the difference in weight allowed them to rig up an additional fuel tank as well. There were three Iranians and a dozen Iraqis at the Colombia base, and forty or fifty more between the fueling sites and operations in Iran and Iraq—and only a handful knew what was really going down. And every one of them was a handpicked Islamic fundamentalist—the reason we never got so much as a whiff of this."

"What we never got a whiff of is how they managed to come up with one of our own stealth fighters!" James Whitfield retorted. "I understood the Iraqis had never so much as come close to tracking our F-117s during the Persian Gulf War."

The SouthCom commander Brad Johnson stirred uncomfortably. "Well, that wasn't exactly the case."

"Not exactly the case—or just flat out a lie?" Whitfield demanded bluntly.

"Okay, the truth is we did have a stealth fighter go down, though we'd assumed it was destroyed. It was toward the end of the Gulf conflict. We'd sent in two F-117s after a suspected bio-warfare plant north of Baghdad. It was a fluke thing as far as we know, just some stray anti-aircraft fire. The one Nighthawk got clean away, but he saw the other take a hit before he cleared out. When the pilot never showed up as a prisoner of war, we assumed he didn't make it out of the plane . . . at least alive.

"Frankly, it never entered our thinking that the pilot might have tried to land the plane. I guess we'll never know all the circumstances, but from what this Tim McAdams admitted, the plane was still flight-worthy, though its instruments were knocked out—including radio and locator beam—or he would have signaled his location. The pilot hoped he could coax the plane back into allied territory, but somehow he got turned around, because instead of flying back into Saudi territory, he ended up over northern

Iraq. He managed to set it down in the desert before he ran out of fuel and ran up a rescue flare. Only it was the Iraqis who showed up in response. We can assume they didn't parade the pilot as they did our other prisoners of war because they wanted to keep their possession of the plane a secret."

The SouthCom commander didn't elaborate. Every man in that room had been involved in the Persian Gulf War, and they had no desire to dwell on the kind of long, drawn-out death that young pilot must have undergone.

"And the fact that we'd lost a plane?" Whitfield asked dryly.

"Well, when the Iraqis didn't announce it, neither did we. For all we knew, it could have crashed into the mountains and never been found. In fact we were banking on something like that, as we figured the Iraqis would have been bragging all over the place if they'd managed to down one of our stealth planes. They'd been trying long enough. It didn't seem" —the general paused, searching for words—"politically expedient to announce that we'd spoiled our perfect record."

"Our perfect record?" Whitfield echoed. "When maybe if we'd gone after that plane instead of hushing it up, we just might have had some warning here? Instead, Khalkhali and our friend in Iraq have had more than ten years in which to put together a plan to wipe out the United States of America."

"Do you really think these attacks would have been enough to take our entire country down?" Unlike the others, the country's drug czar, Charles Wilson, no longer had any official standing here now that the terrorist operation had proved unrelated to either drugs or the Colombian guerrillas' running of them. "Surely we could have stopped them before they got that far."

"Don't kid yourself!" the CIA director answered bluntly. "Running at night without lights—sure, we might have picked him up eventually—almost certainly, in fact. There are ways of detecting even a stealth plane."

The drug czar didn't ask for details. He knew he wouldn't get any.

"But odds are," Sawatsky continued, "we'd think it was one of our friendlies. After all, this was clearly one of our own planes. The reality is, they could have hit an indefinite number of targets by the time we got around to checking our own training patterns."

Martin Sawatsky shook his head, and his narrow features were uncharacteristically pale even for his desk-bound complexion. "Deaths would be in the tens of millions—certainly most of our center of government. The panic and dissolving of any public security could take out millions more. If they'd had two weeks, up to ninety percent of our population could have gone. A lot of the military would have survived, but not all, as we haven't yet finished our vaccination program. But the rest of the country would have been gone.

"What never entered their minds is the domino effect it would have had on the rest of the world. Total crash of the stock market. Collapse of a world economy that's based on ours. Even greater collapse of governments as the deterrent of our forces is removed from the picture. China invading Iran. Certainly the Arab countries invading Israel. India full tilt against Pakistan and Sri Lanka. You're talking World War III!"

"Well, it didn't happen," Charles Wilson said after a moment. "Though when I think that all our technology, all our safeguards, didn't do a thing to stop this, that if it wasn't for a bunch of Stone Age natives and a rookie reporter and one measly intelligence asset—"

He broke off, and a collective restless stirring that might have been a shudder went over the group. Running a massive hand over his face, James Whitfield shook his head ponderously. "I'm not sure I can take this anymore. Every time we foil one plot aimed at bringing this country to its knees, it seems another one comes along. And what happens when one slips through? It's bound to happen—by the laws of probability, if nothing else!"

"What I can't believe is that it hasn't yet," Martin Sawatsky said quickly. "We always seem to slide though—if only by the skin of our teeth. If half the crises we've stopped in this country came to light, people would swear it was a Hollywood scenario—and a pretty improbable one at that. Or be so terrified they wouldn't be able to function."

"It *is* rather astonishing with the kind of enemies we have that no one has succeeded until now," Whitfield said thoughtfully. "You know, if my mother were still on this earth, she'd say there had to be a bigger hand than ours guiding events in this country."

"So would mine," Brad Johnson put in. "But then, she was quite a God-fearing woman."

"Yeah, well, let's just hope," James Whitfield added somberly, "that the God they feared doesn't choose some day to lift His hand of protection off our nation."

There was a silence for all of five seconds before the next item on the agenda was picked up.

\* \* \*

The Ayatollah Khalkhali paced angrily across the mosaic floor, his long robes flopping with furious lack of grace around his legs. Where was Taqi Nouri? Why had he not yet received a report of their mission's success? Why had he heard nothing at all in almost twenty-four hours? His minister of intelligence had assured him that the new Western communication equipment was infallible, even in those jungle regions.

A loud pounding on the heavy wooden doors at the end of the reception salon intruded on his angry reflections. He swung impatiently around as the doors burst open. How dare anyone interrupt him in such a manner!

He stood stiff with outrage as a squad of soldiers marched into the large salon, not the Revolutionary Council forces of his own judiciary branch, but regular military. Khalkhali recognized the general heading up the party, one of the main proponents of the new Iranian president's weak-kneed reforms and one of the main reasons the ayatollah had not been able to trust the military with this mission. Where were his own guards who should be taking care of this intrusion?

"What is the meaning of this?" he demanded coldly.

The general waved his soldiers to a halt in front of Khalkhali, and there was in his bearing none of the deference and even fear to which the spiritual leader of Iran was accustomed from his inferiors. "You are under arrest for crimes of high treason committed against the state."

"I?" The ayatollah drew himself up to the full height of his formidable presence. "You forget who I am! I will have you executed for this. And what have you done with my own men?"

The general showed no signs of wilting under his glare. "Taqi Nouri and his capitalistic lackey spy have been arrested by the Americans."

So—somehow they had failed! And now, it would seem, their enemies had communicated with the Iranian leadership, and the reform-minded weaklings who believed they were running this country had chosen to capitulate to the infidels' pressure. The ayatollah did not allow his fury to touch the impassive mask of his face. "You will not get away with this!"

"Perhaps not," the general shrugged. "But at least this time the people of Iran will know what manner of man their spiritual leader has proven himself to be!"

With a snap of his fingers, he ordered his men to surround Khalkhali. "Take him!"